South Riding by Winifred Holtby

An English Landscape

Winifred Holtby was born on 23rd June 1898 to [illegible] Rudston in Yorkshire.

A governess provided her early education and then she went to Queen Margaret's School in Scarborough. After passing the entrance exam for Somerville College, Oxford in 1917, she decided to join the Women's Army Auxiliary Corps (WAAC) in early 1918. However soon after her arrival in France, the War ended.

The following year she returned to study at Oxford where she met Vera Brittain, a fellow student, and they became lifelong friends.

After graduating from Oxford, in 1921, Winifred and Vera moved to London, hoping to establish themselves as authors.

Winifred's early novels; 'Anderby Wold' (1923), 'The Crowded Street' (1924) and 'The Land of Green Ginger' (1927), met with only moderate success.

As a journalist though she was both prolific and well-known. Articles appeared in more than 20 newspapers and magazines, including the feminist journal Time and Tide and the Manchester Guardian newspaper. To this she added a weekly column for the trade union magazine The Schoolmistress.

She still found time to write novels and published both 'Poor Caroline' (1931), Mandoa! Mandoa!' (1933), as well as a study of Virginia Woolf (1932) and a short story volume, 'Truth is Not Sober' (1934).

Winnifred was a committed feminist, socialist and pacifist. She gave many lectures for the League of Nations Union and was a member of the feminist Six Point Group. She was active in the Independent Labour Party and was a campaigner for the unionisation of black workers in South Africa.

After Brittain's marriage in 1925 to George Catlin, Winifred shared their home, although Catlin was not best pleased by either the arrangement or his wife's close friendship with her.

In 1931 the symptoms of high blood pressure, recurrent headaches and bouts of lassitude brought forth a diagnosis of Bright's disease. She was given two years to live. Winifred now put all her efforts into what was to become her crowning achievement: South Riding.

Winifred Holtby died on 29th September 1935, aged 37. South Riding was published a few months later in March, 1936. It received voluminous praise and won the James Tait Black Memorial Prize for 1936.

In her will she left funds and her own collection of books to a library in Soweto which opened its door as the Winifred Holtby Memorial Library in December 1940. It was the first library to be built in Africa specifically for Africans.

Index of Contents

"I tell the things I know, the things I knew
Before I knew them, immemorially;
And as the fieldsman with unhurrying tread
Trudges with steady and unchanging pace,
Being born to clays that in the winter hold,
So my pedestrian measure gravely plods
Telling a loutish life."

V. SACKVILLE WEST
The Land.

PREFACTORY LETTER TO ALDERMAN MRS HOLTBY

MY DEAR MOTHER,

Because you are a county alderman and because this book concerns a county council, I feel that I owe you a certain explanation and apology.

I admit that it was through listening to your descriptions of your work that the drama of English local government first captured my imagination. What fascinated me was the discovery that apparently academic and impersonal resolutions passed in a county council were daily revolutionising the lives of those men and women whom they affected. The complex tangle of motives prompting public decisions, the unforeseen consequences of their enactment on private lives, appeared to me as part of the unseen pattern of the English landscape.

What I have tried to do in South Riding is to trace that pattern. I have laid my scene in the South East part of Yorkshire, because that is the district which I happen to know best; but the South Riding is not the East Riding; Snaith, Astell and Carne are not your colleagues; the incidents of the schools, housing estates and committees are not described from your experience. I have drawn my material from sources unknown to you. You had no idea that this was the novel I was writing. Alderman Mrs. Beddows is not Alderman Mrs. Holtby. Though I confess I have borrowed a few sayings for her from your racy tongue, and when I described Sarah's vision of her in the final paragraph, it was you upon whom, in that moment, my thoughts were resting.

It may seem to you that in my pattern I have laid greater emphasis upon human affliction than you might consider typical or necessary. But when I came to consider local government, I began to see how it was in essence the first-line defence thrown up by the community against our common enemies—poverty, sickness, ignorance, isolation, mental derangement and social maladjustment. The battle is not faultlessly conducted, nor are the motives of those who take part in it all righteous or disinterested. But the war is, I believe, worth fighting, and this corporate action is at least based upon recognition of one fundamental truth about human nature—we are not only single individuals, each face to face with eternity and our separate spirits; we are members one of another.

Therefore I dedicate this story, such as it is, to you, who have fought so valiant a fight for human happiness. I am conscious of the defects, the clumsiness and limitations of my novel. At least let me record one perfect thing: the proud delight which it has meant to me to be the daughter of Alice Holtby.

"Take what you want," said God. "Take it—and pay for it."

OLD SPANISH PROVERB
Quoted in This Was My World
by Viscountess Rhondda.

Characters in their order of appearance
LOVELL BROWN, a young reporter on the Kingsport Chronicle.
SYD MAIL, his senior.
COUNCILLOR ROBERT CARNE of Maythorpe Hall, a sporting farmer.
ALDERMAN FARROW, a memory.
ALDERMAN ANTHONY SNAITH, a rich business man.
A FAT REPORTER, from the Yorkshire Record.
ALDERMAN MRS. BEDDOWS, née Emma Tuke.
COUNCILLOR SAXON, a local celebrity.
ALDERMAN GENERAL THE HONOURABLE SIR RONALD TARKINGTON, K.C.M.G., D.S.O., of Lissell Grange, Chairman of the South Riding County Council.
LEET OF KYLE HILLOCK, a farmer.
COUNCILLOR CAPTAIN GRYSON, a retired regular army officer.
LORD KNARESBOROUGH, a pre-war beau of Muriel Carne.
COUNCILLOR PEACOCK, member for Cold Harbour Division.
COUNCILLOR (afterwards Alderman) ASTELL, a Socialist.
MISS L. P. HOLMES, retiring Head Mistress of Kiplington High School for Girls.
MISS SARAH BURTON, M.A. (Leeds), B.Litt. (Oxon), the new head mistress.
MIDGE CARNE, Carne's fourteen-year-old daughter.
ELSIE, Carne's maid.
APPLETON, labourer on Carne's farm.
TOPPER BEACHALL, labourer on roads at Maythorpe.
MISS MALT, once governess to Midge.
WILLIAM CARNE, Robert's younger brother, architect at Harrogate.
BARON SEDGMIRE, Carne's father-in-law.
CASTLE, Carne's foreman.
MRS. CASTLE, his wife.
DOLLY CASTLE, his daughter.
MURIEL CARNE, née Sedgmire, Carne's wife, in a mental home.
GEORGE HICKS, Carne's groom.

ELI DICKSON, a dairy-farmer, tenant of Carne.
MR. BANNER, killed in the hunting field.
POLLY, Mr. Dickson's pony.
MR. AND MRS. TADMAN, grocers of Kiplington.
COUNCILLOR TUBBS, member of County Council.
MISS TORRENCE }
MISS SLAKER } rejected candidates for
MISS HAMMOND } head mistress-ship.
MISS DRY }
THE REV. MILWARD PECKOVER, Rector of Kiplington.
CHLOE BEDDOWS, Ph.D., daughter of Mrs. Beddows, Lecturer in English at the Sorbonne.
DR. DALE, D.D., Congregationalist minister at Kiplington.
COLONEL COLLIER, Chairman of Governors of the High School.
MR. DREW, Estate Agent, Governor of High School.
BURTON, Blacksmith at Lipton Hunter } parents of Miss
MRS. BURTON, a midwife—married to Burton } Sarah Burton.
MR. BRIGGS, a Lawyer, Governor of High School.
CISSIE TADMAN, daughter of the Tadmans, pupil at High School.
MR. FRETTON, Manager of Midland Bank, Kiplington.
WENDY BEDDOWS, granddaughter of Alderman Mrs. Beddows.
JIM BEDDOWS, Auctioneer, Mrs. Beddows' husband.
MR. FRED MITCHELL, Insurance Agent.
NANCY MITCHELL, his wife.
PEGGY MITCHELL, his baby daughter.
BARNABAS HOLLY, builder's labourer.
ANNIE HOLLY, his wife.
BERT HOLLY, his son, aged 16.
LYDIA HOLLY, his daughter, aged 14.
DAISY HOLLY, his daughter, aged 12.
ALICE HOLLY, his daughter, aged 8.
GERTIE HOLLY, his daughter, aged 7.
KITTY HOLLY, his daughter, aged 4.
LEN HOLLY, his son, aged 10 months.
MADAME HUBBARD, a draper's wife, runs dancing classes.
MR. HUBBARD, her husband.
GLADYS HUBBARD, their daughter.
MISS TUDLING, head mistress of elementary school, Maythorpe.
PAT AND JERRY, campers at the Shacks.
GRANDPA SELLARS, father-in-law to Topper Beachall.
WILLY BEDDOWS, Mrs. Beddows' son, a widower.
MR. CROSS, a member of the Rescue and Preventive Committee at York.
SYBIL BEDDOWS, Mrs. Beddows' spinster daughter.
COUNCILLOR ALFRED EZEKIEL HUGGINS, of Pidsea Buttock, haulage contractor and lay preacher.
MRS. HARROD, friend of Mrs. Beddows.
MISS TATTERSALL, Head Mistress of the South London United School for Girls.
PATTIE, Sarah Burton's married sister.
DERRICK }
TONY } London friends of Sarah Burton.
NICK }
JERRY BRYON, a singer.
NELL HUGGINS, wife of Councillor Huggins.

FREDA ARMSTRONG, her married daughter.
MRS. RANSOM, worshipper at the Methodist Church, Kiplington.
MISS DOLORES JAMESON, Classics Mistress at the High School.
PHILIP (PIP) PARKHURST, Miss Jameson's fiancé.
BILL HEYER, an ex-serviceman smallholder.
AGNES SIGGLESTHWAITE, B.Sc., Science Mistress at the High School.
JEAN MARSH, pupil to Madame Hubbard.
MRS. MARSH, her mother.
GRACIE PINKER, another pupil.
MRS. PINKER, her mother.
ROY CARBERY, friend of Sarah Burton, killed in war.
OLD MR. COSTER, an old sportsman.
MR. LAIDLOW, a farmer near Garfield.
MR. STATHERS, smallholder, tenant of Snaith.
COUNCILLOR BEALE, member of South Riding Council.
MRS. BARKER, a Methodist at Spunlington.
BESSY WARBUCKLE, a girl at Spunlington.
REG AYTHORNE, marries Bessy Warbuckle.
POLICE SERGEANT BURT OF LEEDS, friend of Sawdon.
TOM SAWDON, landlord of the Nag's Head, Maythorpe.
LILY SAWDON, his wife.
MRS. DEANE, Christian Scientist in Leeds.
CHRISSIE BEACHALL, married to Topper.
ELSIE AND DORIS WATERS, broadcast entertainers.
MRS. CORNER, landlady to Astell.
ELLEN WILKINSON, Socialist M.P.
MISS PARSONS, Matron at the High School.
BEN LATTER, Socialist M.P., once engaged to Sarah Burton.
JAN VAN RAALT, South African farmer, once engaged to Sarah Burton.
MISS MASTERS, English Mistress at the High School.
ILL JACKSON, pupil at the High School.
MISS BECKER, Games Mistress at the High School.
MISS RITCHIE, Junior Mistress.
MR. TURNBULL, a farmer near Maythorpe.
BLACK HUSSAR, Carne's heavyweight hunter.
SIR RUPERT CALDERDYKE, founder of Cold Harbour Colony.
MRS. BRIMSLEY, smallholder at Cold Harbour.
GEORGE AND NAT, her sons.
MR. AND MRS. CHRISTIE, servants to Snaith.
CHADWICK, a warehouse builder.
SIR JOHN SIMON, a Tom Cat owned by Alderman Snaith.
BERYL BRYSON, pupil at High School.
EDIE SIGGLESTHWAITE, sister of Science Mistress.
PROFESSOR GELDER, scientist at Cambridge.
URSULA CROSSFIELD, Jim Beddows' sister.
MR. CROSSFIELD, her husband.
ROSE CROSSFIELD, their daughter.
COLONEL WHITELAW, Alderman, Chairman of Public Assistance Committee.
GWYNETH ROGERS }
NANCY GREY }
LESLEY TUCKER } Midge's friends at the High School.

JUDY PEACOCK }
JENNIFER HOWE }
MRS. GREY, Nancy's mother.
MR. STILLMAN, an undertaker.
REX, an Alsatian, bought by Tom Sawdon.
ADDIE }
MAIMIE } married daughters, of Mr. and Mrs. Sawdon.
DR. STRETTON, Specialist at Kingsport.
SIR WILSON HEMINGWAY, Specialist at Leeds.
PRATT, a commercial traveller.
AN EX-OFFICER, camping at the Shacks.
LADY COLLIER, aunt of Colonel Collier.
ERNST, German Communist friend of Sarah Burton.
MATRON AT THE LAURELS, Harrogate.
DR. MCCLEMMAN, psychiatrist at Harrogate.
MR. THOMPSON, a Relieving Officer.
MILLIE ROPER, a dressmaker.
MRS. BRASS, a jeweller's wife.
MRS. SNAGG, landlady to Millie Roper.
RICKY BARNES, a carrier.
DAVID SHIRLEY, a coal merchant.
MRS. POLLIN, a drug taker.
MRS. FORD, an inmate of the County Mental Hospital.
DR. FLINT, Medical Officer at the County Mental Hospital.
MOTHER MAISIE, inmate at County Mental Hospital.
KATE THERESA, a kitten at the Mental Hospital.
MISS TREMAINE, a deaconess.
SPURLING, an employee of Huggins.
BERTIE BEDDOWS, son of Jim and Emma, gassed in France.
STANLEY DOLLAN, retired solicitor, afterwards Councillor.
MISS EMILY TEASDALE, Board of Education Inspector.
MISS VANE, succeeds Miss Sigglesthwaite as Science Mistress.
DR. WYTTON, Medical Officer of Health for South Riding.
MR. EDWIN SMITHERS, Clerk to the County Council.
MR. PRIZETHORPE, County Librarian.
COMMANDER STEPHEN KING-HALL, Broadcasts a description of the Silver Jubilee Procession.

PROLOGUE IN A PRESS GALLERY

"The quarterly session of the South Riding County Council was held yesterday in Flintonbridge County Hall. Alderman General the Honourable Sir Ronald Tarkington, K.C.M.G., D.S.O., took the chair. The meeting adjourned for one minute's silence in respectful memory of the late Alderman Farrow; then the Cold Harbour Division proceeded to the election of his successor. . . ."

Extract from the Kingsport Chronicle.
June, 1932.

PROLOGUE IN A PRESS GALLERY

Young Lovell Brown, taking his place for the first time in the Press Gallery of the South Riding County Hall at Flintonbridge, was prepared to be impressed by everything. A romantic and inexperienced young man, he yet knew that local government has considerable importance in its effect on human life. He peered down into the greenish gloom and saw a sombre octagonal room, lit from three lofty leaded windows, beyond which tall chestnut trees screened the dim wet June day. He saw below him bald heads, grey heads, brown heads, black heads, above oddly foreshortened bodies, moving like fish in an aquarium tank. He saw the semi-circle of desks facing the chairman's panoplied throne; he saw the stuffed horsehair seats, the blotting paper, the quill pens, the bundles of printed documents on the clerk's table, the polished fire dogs in the empty grates, the frosted glass tulips shading the unignited gas jets, the gleaming inkwells.

His heart beat, and his eyes dilated. Here, he told himself, was the source of reputations, of sanatoria, bridges, feuds, scandals, of remedies for broken ambitions or foot and mouth disease, of bans on sex novels in public libraries, of educational scholarships, blighted hopes and drainage systems. Local government was an epitome of national government. Here was World Tragedy in embryo. Here gallant Labour, with nothing to lose but its chains, would fight entrenched and armoured Capital. Here the progressive, greedy and immoral towns would exploit the pure, honest, elemental and unprogressive country. Here Corruption could be studied and exposed, oppression denounced, and lethargy indicted.

Lovell Brown knew himself to be on the eve of an initiation. To-day would open a new chapter in British journalism. "Do you remember when Brown started those articles of his on Local Government?" people would say fifty years hence. "By jove! That was an eye-opener. That was something new."

Syd Mail, Lovell's predecessor on the Kingsport Chronicle, had come with him to put him wise during his first visit to the Council. Mail had been promoted to the Combine's Sheffield paper. Mail was a man of the world. He sprawled sideways on the hard bench running through the little enclosed Reporter's Gallery, known as the Horse Box, and muttered information to his colleague and pupil with the inaudible fluency of an experienced convict.

"That's Carne of Maythorpe—big chap in tweeds just come in. He'll be next Alderman, they say, instead of Farrow, but don't you believe it. That's Snaith—grey suit, horn-rimmed spectacles, by the chairman's desk. He'll have had something to say about Carne."

Lovell saw Carne, a big heavy handsome unhappy-looking man. Under a thatch of thick black hair his white face was not unlike that on photographs of Mussolini, except for its fine-drawn sensitive mouth with down-turned corners. He bore little resemblance to Lovell's notion of a sporting farmer, which was what, by a county-wide reputation, Carne was known to be.

Alderman Snaith, supposed to be the richest member of the Council, a dapper grey little mouse of a man, was more like the secret subtle capitalist of tradition.

"There's Alderman East just come in," muttered Syd Mail. "Vice-chairman. Eighty-four. Deaf as a post."

Snaith detached himself from a gossiping group and made for the vice-chairman.

"Are they friends—East and Snaith?" asked Lovell.

"Friends? I wouldn't go so far as to say that Snaith's any man's friend, except when it suits him. He's clever. Sharp as a sack of monkeys and knows how to make himself indispensable to authority. A dark horse. Ah! There's Mrs. Beddows."

"Oh, I know her!" cried Lovell with enthusiasm, then blushed to realise that he had been overheard.

Alderman Mrs. Beddows halted, looked up at the gallery, recognised him and gave a smiling gesture of salutation. She was a plump sturdy little woman, whose rounded features looked as though they had been battered blunt by wear and weather in sixty years or more of hard experience. But so cheerful, so lively, so frank was the intelligence which beamed benevolently from her bright spaniel-coloured eyes, that sometimes she looked as young as the girl she still, in her secret dreams, felt herself to be. Her clothes were a compromise between her spiritual and chronological ages. She wore to-day a dignified and beautifully designed black gown of heavy dull material; but she had crowned this by a velvet toque plastered with purple pansies. She carried a large bag embroidered with raffia work and had pinned on to her rounded bosom the first crimson rose out of her husband's garden. Actually, she was seventy-two years old, a farmer's daughter, and had lived in the South Riding all her life.

She was talking about clothes now, in a clear carrying Yorkshire voice, unaffectedly accented.

"Now there's the nice young man I saw at the Lord Mayor's reception!" she cried, waving to the embarrassed Lovell. "I told him that if he wrote in his paper again: 'Alderman Mrs. Beddows looked well in her usual navy,' I'd have him sacked. It's not navy anyway. It's black crêpe. Chloe brought it from Paris. Lovely material, isn't it? But he said he didn't do the dresses, so I had to chase all over the building hunting for Gloriana or whatever that young woman calls herself, to see she got it right. I always send Chloe the bits out of the papers with my dresses in them. Then she can't say I never wear anything but my old red velvet, not that I really fancy all these blacks she buys me. I like a bit of colour myself, I must say. At my time of life, if you wear nothing but black, people might think you were too mean to change frocks between funerals."

"I see you've got off with Mrs. B. already," said the fat man from the Yorkshire Record, wriggling his massive thighs over the narrow plank of the bench. "Good for you, Brown."

"Heard her latest?" asked Mail. "The travelling secretary of a birth control society called to ask for her support as Alderman. Mrs. B. replied 'I've had five children already, and I was seventy-two last birthday. Aren't you a bit late in the day for me? Try Councillor Saxon.'"

Smothered guffaws shook the bench, for Councillor Saxon, after fifty-two years of childless married life, had suddenly lost heart and virtue to a blonde in a tobacconist's kiosk on Kingsport Station and found himself at seventy-four the proud but embarrassed father of a son. The whole South Riding, apart from Mrs. Saxon, appeared aware of his achievement. Most of the South Riding, whatever its outward disapproval, was delighted. It enjoyed all unusual feats of procreation.

Lovell did not yet know that more than half the anecdotes repeated about Mrs. Beddows were apocryphal. She was a portent; she was a mascot; she was the first woman alderman in the South Riding and therefore she must be a character. If she did not utter witticisms, they must be invented for her. Her naturally racy tongue was credited with malice and ribaldry quite foreign to a nature fundamentally decorous, comfortable and kind. She enjoyed her popularity, however, and appreciated its power, and though she was frequently shocked by the repartee accredited to her, did little to contradict it, and, half-consciously, played up to its inventors.

Lovell had not made up his mind whether he should become a worshipper or iconoclast. This was a day of momentous decisions. He stared and blushed. He was determined to accept nothing, not even Mrs. Beddows' popularity, without question.

But his speculations were cut short by the entry of the Chairman. Alderman General the Honourable Sir Ronald Tarkington, K.C.M.G., D.S.O., of Lissell Grange was a fine figure of a man and a fine man for any figure. His chairmanship of the South Riding County Council was the most successful in its history. The fact that his speeches were almost wholly inaudible in no way detracted from their popularity, for never in his life had he uttered an unexpected sentiment, and what he said could be noted down before he spoke it almost as easily as afterwards. A soldier, a Yorkshireman, a sportsman and a gentleman, believing quite sincerely in the divine right of landowners to govern their own county, his diligence, honesty and knowledge of the intricacies of procedure made him a trusted and invaluable administrator. His unfeigned pleasure in killing the correct animals at their orthodox seasons made him an affectionately respected neighbour. Few doubted that he was the right person to guide the deliberations of those whose business it was to decide whether necessitous children should be provided with meals at school, whether the county librarian should be paid mileage allowance for his car, or whether ex-gratia payments should be made to Leet of Kyle Hillock in compensation for damage done by flooding.

Lovell Brown had made up his mind about him all right. Landowners were wicked, selfish and retrogressive. Their political influence was a remnant of Feudalism. Russia knew how to deal with them.

But the chairman's entry imposed some order upon the Councillors. Their groups dispersed and filled the semi-circle of seats.

Sir Ronald rose and mumbled. He drew the councillors to their feet.

"Prayers?" breathed Lovell.

"Farrow," muttered Mail sideways. "Dead."

They stood.

Perhaps, thought Lovell, the ghost of the dead alderman hovered above the virgin fields of rose-pink blotting-paper, the quill pens, the horsehair, the sporting tweeds, the gents' light-weight suitings, the bored, amused, restless or sorrowful thoughts of the mourners. Farrow had been a quiet little man, his public interest largely confined to the disposal of rural refuse, but he must, thought Lovell, have had some private life. Generously his imagination bestowed upon Farrow a gipsy mistress, three illegitimate children, a conscience racked by knowledge of secret pilfering from the parish funds, and a blighted ambition as an amateur actor. After all, people don't just live and die as elementary school children, rate-payers and aldermen, he reasoned. Even he, at twenty-two, had had Experiences . . .

The silence was over. The Councillors sat down. The ghost of Alderman Farrow passed, officially, out of the Hall for ever. The Cold Harbour Division proceeded to consider the nomination of his successor. The alderman is dead; long live the alderman.

"It's a foregone conclusion surely," said the Yorkshire Record man, as seven or eight Councillors pushed their way out against their colleagues' knees and made for a door.

"That so? Who?" asked Mail, the cynic. Too clever by half, thought Lovell.

"Carne, of course."

"Carne?" If there had been a spittoon, Mail would have spat.

"Gryson told me."

"Oh, Gryson! Army and county stick together."

"Carne's not county."

"Lord Sedgmire's son-in-law?"

"Runaway match. And she's in an asylum."

"Private mental home, you mean. At Harrogate. He pays ten guineas a week, they say—not counting extras."

"It would have been cheaper to divorce her when she was carrying on with young Lord Knaresborough."

"They say there was nothing in that. The kid's supposed to be his anyway, and queer."

"Mental?"

"Tenpence halfpenny in the shilling. Midge's never gone to school."

"They're taking a darn long time."

"Division. You'll see. Peacock will nominate Astell."

"Astell? The socialist chap? But he's T.B. isn't he?"

"A corpse would be good enough to beat Carne if Snaith's got his knife into him. They say he loves him like a weasel loves a rabbit. Besides, Carne's failing, and they don't like to county-court an alderman."

"Failing?"

"Have you seen Maythorpe? Crumbling to pieces over their heads. He lent the garden and drawing-room for that Conservative Fête last year. Always sucking up to the gentry, is Carne. Big drawing-room with painted ceiling, gilt and plaster flaking down on every one's best hats. Huge candelabra, no candles. Stables full, though. He can't resist a good horse."

"Well, he deals in 'em, doesn't he?"

"Deals? Aye. But you can't make on horses what you lose on sheep these days. Look at wool—six shillings a stone, and prime fat Leicesters going for a pound a piece."

"What should wool be?" asked Lovell, suspicious of all tales of agricultural difficulty. He believed farmers to be unfairly pampered by a sentimental government.

"Why, before the War you got eight to eighteen shillings. I've known it thirty-four once. Maythorpe's a big place, but Carne can't lose on farm, and pay all that for his wife and keep going."

There was a stir in the hall.

"They're coming back."

A door opened under the gallery, and the Councillors filed back to their places. One man looked at Mrs. Beddows and slowly shook his head. The big handsome Carne clumped down again in the seat beside her. Another man handed a paper to the chairman. He rose and read something, and this time even Lovell could catch the words:

". . . Councillor Astell 5, Councillor Carne 4."

"That's torn it. . . ."

"Dirty work somewhere. . . ."

"One up to Snaith."

Papers were being handed round. All the Councillors present were now voting. There was no excitement, no apparent concern. Snaith's grey, precise, well-cut features wore no look of triumph when Astell was declared the new alderman for the Cold Harbour Division. No applause followed. If dirty work had been done, it left no trace on the ordered monotony of the proceedings.

The chairman of the Education Committee moved that the resolutions on his minutes should be approved and confirmed. The newly appointed alderman rose and complained about the cutting down of maintenance allowances to scholarship and free place holders. He was a tall thin man with curling ruddy hair and a girlish pretty complexion. When he spoke, his voice was singularly harsh and unattractive. Lovell, prepared to find in the one socialist alderman a hero and a martyr, was disappointed. Shelley, he told himself, had a high shrill voice. But Councillor Astell did not look like Shelley. There was about him something ungainly yet impressive, a queer chap, Lovell thought.

The Mental Hospital business appropriately followed that of the Education Committee. Again Alderman Astell was dissatisfied. Again Lovell Brown felt the chill of disillusionment creeping across his heart.

Without emotion, without haste, without even, so far as Lovell could discern, any noticeable interest, the South Riding County Council ploughed through its agenda. The General mumbled; the clerks shuffled papers, the chairman of committees answered desultory questions.

Lovell had come expectant of drama, indignation, combat, amusement, shock. He found boredom and monotony.

Disillusion chastened him.

BOOK I

EDUCATION

"3. KIPLINGTON HIGH SCHOOL FOR GIRLS.

APPOINTMENT OF HEAD MISTRESS.

The Sub-Committee have received a communication from the Governors of the Kiplington High School with reference to the appointment of a Head Mistress in place of Miss L. P. Holmes, who will retire at the end of the Summer Term, 1932. The Governors have appointed Miss Sarah Burton, M.A. (Leeds), B.Litt: (Oxon) as Head Mistress, the appointment to take effect as from the beginning of the Michaelmas Term. . . . The Sub-Committee recommend that the appointment of Miss Burton be approved. . . ."

Extract from the Minutes of the Higher Education Sub-Committee of the Education Committee established by the County Council for the South Riding of Yorkshire. June, 1932.

CHAPTER I

LORD SEDGMIRE'S GRANDDAUGHTER AWAITS AN ALDERMAN

The June day spread itself round Maythorpe Hall, endless, amorphous, ominous. It had no shape—not even a dinner hour, for Elsie was baking and had given Midge ham cake and apples to eat whenever she felt like it, and those had disappeared hours and hours ago.

If only it would stop raining, she could go out into the horse pasture and try that game of throwing a tennis ball over her shoulder and then turning back to find where it had fallen; or she could burrow deeper into the tunnel she was making in the thrashed oat stack, or she could climb the medlar tree in the low orchard—dull occupations, but better than sitting here with her nose against the pane of her bedroom window, watching the dun grey cup of the sky pressed down over the mottled green of the landscape.

Acre beyond acre from her bedroom window, Midge could see the broad swelling sea of rain-rinsed green, the wet bluish green of wheat in blade, the dry tawny green of unploughed stubble, the ruffled billowing green of uncut meadow grasses, the dark clumps of trees, elm and ash and sycamore. There was not a hill, not a church, not a village. From Maythorpe southward to Lincolnshire lay only fields and dykes and scattered farms and the unseen barrier of the Leame Estuary, the plain rising and dimpling in gentle undulations as though a giant potter had pressed his thumb now more lightly, now more heavily, on the yet malleable clay of the spinning globe.

A dull landscape, thought Midge Carne. Nothing happens in it.

If only she had brothers and sisters to play with.

If only the books in the house were not so dull—sporting novels, stable compendiums, Debrett, the complete works of Sir Walter Scott, bound volumes of the Ladies' Realm—

If only she liked reading—

If only Daddy had not told her that she was too old now to play with the little Beachalls and Appleton children—

If only Miss Malt had not gone home to look after a sick father. Miss Malt had grumbled at the house and scolded Elsie. She didn't like cold joints for lunch and called Midge backward. She was always praising her former pupils, who must have been hateful little prigs, thought Midge. But even so, lessons and ex-governesses were preferable to this loneliness and monotony of leisure.

If only Midge had not been afraid of horses, ever since that time Black Beauty fell on to her, and she woke up at night screaming and shuddering, and Dr. Campbell said she was never to ride again. Midge was immeasurably relieved. People had told her that riding and hunting were superb, unrivalled pleasures. She believed them. But they were pleasures which she, herself, could do without.

But Daddy had been disappointed. She was always disappointing him. He had wanted his daughter to be beautiful and proud and fearless like her mother, and Midge was ugly and thin and delicate and afraid and wore spectacles and a gold bar across her teeth. And she flew into horrible passions that made her lie on the floor and kick and scream. A fiend entered into her. She knew all about the man in the Bible who had an evil spirit. One moment she would feel nothing but good and gentle and polite and then these storms would seize her for no purpose, lashing her into fury. And afterwards she would feel ill and sick all over. It was no fun having an evil spirit.

If only Daddy would come home and be pleased and talk to her, and tell her what it was like to be an alderman.

The afternoon had lasted for ever and ever already.

It seemed to Midge that more than half her life had been spent shut up in the house with rain on the window waiting for some one to come home and talk to her. Yet often enough when Daddy came, he would sit silent drinking whisky and soda, companioned only by the dark oil paintings of ancestors in the dining-room and by Mother's lovely terrifying portrait; or he would work, bent over his desk adding columns of figures that never came out right, because there was a slump, because the Labour Bill was double what it used to be and because men worked for half the time and prices stayed the same. Midge knew all about the agricultural crisis.

The Carnes, she knew, were not Poor People. Poor people lived in cottages; the Carnes lived in a Hall, which was the biggest house for miles round, with a smoking-room and a breakfast-room and three sets of staircases and a top floor nobody ever used now, and a drive nearly half a mile long. Uncle William, Father's youngest brother, was an architect and lived near Harrogate and had two motor-cars; and Grandfather, Lord Sedgmire, whom she had never seen, was a Baron on the Welsh Border and lived in a castle. These splendours were part of Midge's heritage. No matter how torn her frocks, how broad her accent, how wild her conduct, screaming and laughing through barns and cowsheds with the village children, she remained conscious of this foundation of grandeur sustaining her. When a tramp saw her perched on the wall spitting cherry stones into the water-butt with the Beachall children, and asked, "What would the lady of the house say if she could see you, little girls?" Midge had replied, "I am the lady of the house."

She was too. Her father was a squire even if also a farmer. The house was a hall even if the silver cups on the dining-room sideboard grew tarnished, and of the former servants only Elsie was left to answer the door and roast the mutton and scrub the kitchen floor.

Grandeur remained; but the need for money overshadowed it. Daddy was lord of his estate, but beyond Daddy was the Bank. This, that and the other could not be done because the Bank said so. Carnes could not buy motor-cars, rebuild stables, play polo, train racehorses, visit London or plant new coverts because of the Bank, the Bank, the Bank.

Nor was money the only trouble. Mr. Castle was ill, and Mrs. Castle nursed him, and Dolly Castle, brought home from smart service in Kingsport, sulked and grumbled, and the lads groused, and Hinds' House was not at all what it used to be, and Daddy was lost without Foreman Castle.

And if Daddy was not worried about the Bank and Castle and money and Midge, there was always Mother—Mother, the brilliant and gay and regal, for whom the whole house lay waiting. But she was ill, and away in a nursing home, and did not return. If only Daddy would come home quickly and be happy because he was an alderman.

If only all grown-ups could be less unhappy.

From a window at the top of the house, there was a northward view along the road from Kiplington. Perhaps, thought Midge, if she went there she would be able to see Father driving with Hicks in the dog-cart, and wave to him, and run downstairs and wait for him in the stable yard, and greet him.

She wandered slowly along the first floor passage, delaying mistrustfully to give fate a chance.

If she wanted anything very much, she would count to fifty and then another fifty before she let herself think that it might happen.

She paused at the door of the Big Spare Bedroom and counted fifty. The furniture there was shrouded with holland dust cloths. One brass ball from the foot of the bed was missing. Midge had once unscrewed it too far, playing there last year, dropped it, and let it lie.

She went on to the Bachelor's Room and counted fifty. It smelled of dust and boot polish and tobacco. A man's smell. Yet no man had slept there for years.

She dawdled up the stairs to the second landing that ran from end to end of the long old house. Now she was far away from Elsie singing in the kitchen. Ivy overgrew the windows. Chestnut branches darkened them. Yet in Cook's Room the pink wallpaper had faded to dingy cream, except on the squares where pictures once had hung. The black iron bedsteads were bare; a pair of discarded shoes, bulging to fit cook's bunions, lay against the wall, exposing their battered soles, a home for spiders. In the open drawers of the dressing-table, Midge had already found two big black hairpins, a twist of tape fluffy with dust, and an artificial daisy. But when she had picked up the daisy, last summer, an earwig had run out of it, and she had dropped it in disgust, to lie on the floor with the shoes, an old box lid and a coil of grey hair combings.

The window was hard to open, but Midge knew its tricks, thrusting up the warped frame, showering down white petals of flaking paint. She knelt and looked on to the tops of lilac bushes, the stable roofs, and the red moss-grown bricks of the back yard. Beyond the roofs lay the Kiplington Road, twisting away among the wet green fields.

If I shut my eyes and count to a hundred, thought Midge, I shall see him coming.

She shut her eyes. She counted. But time stood still. Endless, amorphous, ominous, time enfolded the crumbling house.

It can't be That. They can't want That of me, thought Midge with rising terror. She clutched the window-sill on to which rain was dripping.

She shut her eyes and counted, praying silently that no further devoir should be exacted from her. If she prayed, if she counted, surely that was enough to propitiate Them and bring her father home, an alderman.

It must be so. Surely now she could hear the clop of horse-hooves, the sound of wheels splashing through the puddles?

She screwed her eyes tight. Ninety-seven, ninety-eight; he was coming nearer, her darling, her God, her father; ninety-nine. Oh, she would give them due measure; she would not cheat.

"A hundred!"

She shouted it aloud and opened her eyes and saw Mr. Dickson's milk float turning into the stable-yard.

Her prayers had failed her.

Then, with a shock like a blow, she thought, "He's had an accident. They're bringing the body home in the milk float like Mr. Banner from the hunting field." She was almost sick with terror.

But Mr. Dickson had climbed stiffly from the back of the float, let Dolly go loose, and clumped to the back door where Elsie had greeted him.

"Is Maister in?"

Then he had not found the body.

"He's at Flintonbridge, getting hisself made alderman."

Like most of her generation and locality, Elsie was trilingual. She talked B.B.C. English to her employer, Cinema American to her companions, and Yorkshire dialect to old milkmen like Eli Dickson.

"He's not, then. Astell's alderman."

"Go on."

"I've just heard from Mrs. Tadman who's been to Kingsport by bus, and got it from a chap in Flintonbridge."

"Get away with you. Our Maggie saw Mr. Tubbs in Kingsport, Wednesday week, and he said it was sure as death. An' he's a councillor."

"I tell you, Astell's alderman. Socialist chap. They put it about that Carne's failing, and no one likes to county-court an alderman."

"Failing? Mr. Carne? You're crazy."

"Then why don't he do up my cow-house? That's what I say. He promised to do it a twelve-month back and now muck from yard's running right through to dairy. I'll be having government chaps on me. . . ."

They went into the house. The back door clapped to.

It didn't mean anything. Nasty old man, with his little fringe of beard and greasy hat. He smelled.

Midge crumbled flakes of paint between thin, dirty fingers.

What right had people to prevent her father, father, father from getting what he wanted? What did it mean—to county-court an alderman?

Oh, she had failed him. She had not prayed enough, not thought enough. If she counted to a million, that would be inadequate to propitiate destiny.

The stern inimicable force of fate brooded over the house.

Daddy was not an alderman.

Midge, Lord Sedgmire's granddaughter, knew what she must do.

With lips compressed and fire burning in her sallow cheeks, she went out of cook's bedroom and set off downstairs, leaving the window open so that the rains blew in and seeped through the crack in the oilcloth and moistened the rotting boards until a brown patch spread across the North Room ceiling.

She went, like a victim to the sacrifice, into her Mother's Room.

It was a big southward facing bedroom on the first floor, overlooking the lawn and the rose garden, and the willows and the duck pond. Ever since Mrs. Carne had been carried out, dazed and unresisting, her rebellion quenched, the room had lain ready awaiting her return. The curtains were drawn; their green taffeta, faded and rotting at the folds, left only a whispering light, shifting in the great mirror the reflections of silver and glass and walnut wood. On the dressing-table, the creams cracked in their jars, and the nail polish crumbled to powder, the scents evaporated from cut-glass bottles among the rusting files and pins and scissors. In the wardrobes hung Mrs. Carne's deserted dresses, her thirty pairs of shoes on their wooden trees, her three riding habits, her cloak of mink and velvet.

When Midge had nothing better to do, she came up here, exploring. No one had ever told her not to, nor scolded her for it as they scolded her when she was found reading Elsie's love letters from the blue biscuit box on the maids' dressing-table. No one had ever found her at it. She opened drawers filled with embroidered cambric, smelling of lavender and camphor moth balls. She tried on gloves and scarves and evening dresses, stuffing the bodices with tissue paper or rolled silk stockings. She paraded up and down in front of the swinging mirror. She was her mother. She was Lord Sedgmire's daughter. She fell in love with Father, Carne of Maythorpe, in the hunting field. He carried her off and her relations cursed her. They hung out of castle windows, shaking fists, cutting her off with a shilling. Their curses doomed her. She was ill, imprisoned. Midge could never see her.

Curses could be lifted by spells. Midge was always trying them, inventing her own runes and incantations.

From time to time the obligation came to her, challenging her to perform terrific devoirs. It might be to catch at a bough as the trap span under it, to lean far out from a window to touch a sprig of ivy, to climb across the central rafter in the high barn, dizzily straddling far above the stone-paved floor. But for three years now a central challenge confronted her—reserved for some crisis when all other resources failed.

She had had a dream.

In her dream she was playing with her mother's things, dressed up in a black velvet coat and a great plumed hat, parading, when suddenly terror had come upon her.

Her terrors, like her tempers, descended without warning out of calm and safety, sending her screaming, frenzied, towards the kitchen, the dining-room, wherever were lights and fires and grown-up people. But from this dream terror, she had not fled. Instead she had turned to God, kneeling down, dressed as she was in velvet and lace and feathers, beside the ottoman where the furs were kept at the foot of her mother's bed, and she had prayed while dusk fell and the room grew darker until through her latticed fingers she saw the door from her father's dressing-room open slowly, slowly, revealing—what?

She never knew. The scream with which she awoke dispelled that knowledge.

But she had been aware, ever since, with relentless certainty, that one day she would have to put herself to the test.

This was the way out. This was what They demanded. Thus alone could she serve her father, restore her mother, and bring back to Maythorpe its legendary happiness, when the silver polo cups on the sideboard winked and glittered, and men drank deep after a long day's hunting, toasting her mother the bride, the brave, the beautiful, lifting their glasses, tossing them, emptied, to splinter on the wainscot, when the lawns were clipped like velvet below the feet of sauntering silk-shod ladies, and the bedrooms were lit by firelight, and there was hot water in all the muffled cans, and scented soap upon the washstands.

Oh, Midge knew, from Cook and Hicks and Castle, what Maythorpe Hall had been in its glory.

Trembling, her pulses thumping, her eyes brilliant with fear and resolution, she opened the wardrobe, starting at every creak of the door.

There hung the velvet jacket, its swaggering skirts spread like a highwayman's, its collar high, its cuffs and lacy jabot. She wrapped the skirt around her; she buttoned the jacket above her cotton overall; she arranged the yellowing lace, the braid, the pockets. From its tissue paper she took the immense black picture hat and set it sideways on her tumbled elf-locks. Her mouse-coloured hair hung each side of her pointed, resolute face.

She must do this thing. She must face her destiny. To this hour had pointed the nods, the nudges, the sentences broken off, the stories curtailed at her appearance. All the fragmentary enlightenment about doom and flight and darkness, her "poor," "ill-fated" or "unfortunate" mother, the Maythorpe tragedy, her father's "trouble," led to this awful, inevitable moment.

Her stumbling figure passed the wardrobe mirror. She started from her own grotesque reflection. She fell on her knees beside the ottoman, facing the dressing-room door. Her hat lurched sideways, heavy, weighted with feathers. She pressed her hands against her staring eyeballs.

"Our Father, which art in Heaven . . ."

She began slowly and firmly.

Through her fingers she watched the green unearthly twilight, the bed, the mirror. Her mounting panic urged her on, louder and louder, till at a gallop she took the "Power and the Glory, for Ever and Ever, Amen" and plunged straight into, "Please God bless Father and Mother and make Mother well and bring her back again. . . ."

Her eyes were still open, yet she saw no longer anything but the slanting mirror. Her voice rang out, shrill and frantic, drowning all other noises. She was no longer conscious of what she said, "and bring her back again, for Christ's sake, for Christ's sake, for Christ's sake."

The door was opening. Like doom it swung towards her. In the mirror she saw what in her dreams she had not seen—the tall black figure, the blazing ball of a face.

"For Christ's sake! For Christ's sake! For Christ's sake!" she screamed, on her feet, beating away from her in maniacal horror her father who stood, seeing his wife, in 1918, frenzied, in her gallant highwayman's costume, beating him off in the outburst of hysteria with which she accompanied her announcement that she was going to bear his child.

CHAPTER II

KIPLINGTON GOVERNORS APPOINT A NEW HEAD MISTRESS

The Governors of Kiplington Girls' High School had already interviewed Miss Torrence, Miss Slaker, Miss Hammond and Miss Dry, from out of five short-listed applicants for the post of head mistress; and they liked none of them.

It was true that the appointment was not much to offer. The school owed its independent existence to masculine pride rather than to educational necessity. Thirty years earlier the County Council decided that a daily train journey to Kingsport, suitable enough to Grammar School boys, was unsafe for girls. Girls were delicate. Life imperilled them. So four grim tall apartment houses were bought cheap on Kiplington North Cliff, facing the Pidsea Buttock road; walls were knocked down; dining-rooms became classrooms; a separate building housed the thirteen boarders, and there for a quarter of a century the High School mouldered gently into unregretted inefficiency under the lethargic rule of the retiring Miss Holmes. Miss Holmes had done well enough. Miss Holmes was amiable. It was a pity that age and health persuaded her to go now and share a semi-detached villa in Bournemouth with her widowed sister. Another Miss Holmes was what the chairman hoped for.

The Reverend Milward Peckover, however, was financially compelled to send his own daughters to the High School. Three nice, good, clever girls they were; and he cherished ambitions for their future. They might even do what he had never done—win scholarships to Oxford and the Sorbonne, like Chloe Beddows, the one star pupil whom the High School had quite failed to discourage. He had good reason for desiring a more effective successor to Miss Holmes, and, until he saw her, he had canvassed his fellow governors avidly in favour of the highly qualified but personally unprepossessing Miss Dry. But, having seen her, he was out of love with her, and his second choice had been given to the still uninterviewed Miss Sarah Burton, whose testimonials both public and private were almost suspiciously favourable.

He sat back restlessly listening to Mr. Tadman's idiotic remarks about a little more accommodation for the Buttocks.

There were Pidsea Buttock and Ledsea Buttock, and Mr. Peckover recognised the ancient and honourable nomenclature of the villages. He particularly detested the puerile vulgarity of persons who would make jokes about them, suspecting Mr. Tadman of a wish to shock the clergy when, being a Nonconformist, he rolled the words round his tongue and proclaimed with a sort of sensuous relish, "the Buttocks this," "the Buttocks that," "with regard, Mr. Chairman, to that bit of unpleasantness about the Buttocks." And the worst of it was that, whenever Mr. Tadman started, some nervous affection contracted the muscles of Mr. Peckover's nose and throat; his eyes pricked; before he could collect his defences, he began to giggle.

He turned to the chairman, driven to action.

"Mr. Chairman, I see we have another candidate, Sarah Burton. A good plain name. Let's hope,"—(snigger, snigger, snigger; but the explosion was now respectably justified)—"let us hope a good plain woman."

Dr. Dale, the Congregationalist Minister, pulled forward the typed papers containing Miss Burton's particulars.

"Yes, she is an Oxford woman," he said, preparing to be impressive. He was a Cambridge man and a Doctor of Divinity—two qualifications which made him a thorn in the side of Mr. Peckover, who was a Manchester B.A. and Lichfield.

"Only a post graduate course. B.Litt, after graduating at Leeds," corrected Mr. Peckover. "Then she had—ah—Empire experience—South Africa. Well, well. That should broaden the mind a little. Broaden the mind."

Mr. Peckover had himself spent a year with the Railway Mission in Canada, and was a great believer in the psychological influence of the great open spaces—especially those within the British Empire.

The chairman, a vague though ferocious little man, grunted that, whatever she was, Miss Burton must be seen.

The clerk summoned her.

Miss Sarah Burton, M.A., B.Litt., entered the unwelcoming ugly room.

She was much too small. Though her close fitting hat was blamelessly discreet, her hair was red—not mildly ginger but vivid, springing, wiry, glowing, almost crimson, red. Astonishing hair. Nothing could have been more sober and business-like than her dark brown clothes; but from her sensible walking shoes rose ankles which were superfluously pretty. Head mistresses, ran the unformed thought in the mind of more than one governor, should not possess ankles as slender as a gazelle's and flexible arched insteps.

On the other hand, her face was not pretty at all, the nose too large, the mouth too wide; the small, quick, intelligent eyes were light and green.

"But she looks healthy," thought Alderman Mrs. Beddows. "Good skin. Good teeth. And she wasn't born yesterday."

Miss Burton had been born, according to her official papers, thirty-nine years ago.

"Er—er—Miss Burton." The chairman frowned and stuttered, wrinkling his face. "Won't you sit down?"

She sat, as she moved and spoke, with deliberation. She placed her formidable leather bag on the table before her. Then she looked round at the governors and she smiled.

Her smile was not in the least like those of the other candidates, nervous, ingratiating, chilling or complacent. It was a smile friendly yet challenging. Well, gentlemen, here I am. What next?

"Well, Miss—er—Burton," began the chairman. "You've been teaching in—er—London."

He pronounced "London" as though it were an obscure village of whose name he was uncertain.

"At the South London United Secondary School for Girls," replied Miss Burton. There was hardly a trace of North Country inflection in her pleasant, unexpectedly contralto voice. "I have been there for eight years, the last three of which I was second mistress."

The chairman had never heard of the South London United. Dr. Dale had. "That's a very famous centre of education," he said. "A large school, I believe."

"Too large. We have seven hundred and forty pupils now."

"I wonder why you should want to leave it and come to our little town?" smiled the Congregationalist minister.

"Soapy Sam! Our little town indeed!" snorted Mr. Peckover to himself.

"I wanted to come back to Yorkshire."

"Indeed. Indeed," sniffed the chairman. "A Yorkshire woman, ha?"

Mrs. Beddows lent forward.

"May I ask Miss Burton a question, Mr. Chairman? Miss Burton, we had a much better appointment in the South Riding last winter at Flintonbridge. You didn't apply for that, I think?"

The candidate faced the alderman with a smile that was not wholly ingenuous.

"I didn't think I should get it," she replied.

"Indeed?"

The chairman removed, polished, and replaced his pince-nez; the Rev. Mr. Dale, Mr. Drew and Mr. Tadman stared at her. Mr. Peckover beamed benignly upon this candidate for headmistress-ship who actually answered questions frankly. The only person, Sarah Burton noted, who appeared entirely indifferent to her, was a large dark sullen man sunk into his chair next Mrs. Beddows. She gathered all eyes but his and held them.

"You see," she said, with the engaging gesture of one who puts all her cards on the table, "I am very small, and not by birth a lady. My hair is red and I do not look like the sort of person whom most governors want to see reading reports at Speech Day. At the same time . . ."

It was the alderman who saw how, by pleading her smallness, her femininity, she had evoked some masculine sentiment of protective chivalry in the breasts of the other governors. Mrs. Beddows was moved differently.

"Yes, I see," she said—kindly but with the air of one who stands no nonsense. "Your head mistress at South London gives you quite remarkable testimonials."

"She was far too generous," admitted Miss Burton, as well aware as Mrs. Beddows that head mistresses sometimes give glowing references to subordinates whom they desire to see elsewhere. "She's taught me almost everything I know; but she understands why I want to come north again, and she sympathises with my wish to have a school of my own."

"Of your own?"

Miss Burton accepted the challenge. "Of which I was the head," she replied.

"I see." Mr. Peckover had been waiting with his question. The governors knew that the only thing to be done with their chairman was to take all initiative out of his hands. "I see that you have had overseas experience."

"Yes. I taught for a little while in a Transvaal High School, and then in a native mission college in the Cape. I meant to go on to Australia, but family reasons brought me back to England."

"Has—er—any other—governor any questions?" asked the chairman.

Mrs. Beddows had.

"Now then, Miss Burton, you've had a very interesting life and met very interesting people. I wonder if you know just what you'll be in for, in a little out-of-the-way town like this? Some people call Kiplington the last town in England, though of course we don't think so. But it's no use pretending it's the hub of the universe. The children here are mostly daughters of small tradesmen and lodging-house keepers, with just a few professional people and clergy. The buildings are not up to much, and I don't see, with the country in the way it is, that they'll soon be put right. Now, the point is, can you throw yourself into the kind of work you'll have to face here? Because if you can't, it's not much use your coming. Do you realise, I wonder, how very different it'll be from what you're used to?"

Miss Burton shook her head, smiling.

"Less different perhaps than you think. I come from these parts." As she said, "these parts," her voice thickened, as though the thought of Kiplington recalled a forgotten dialect.

"Indeed, indeed," barked the chairman, "and where was that, pray?"

Again it was to Mrs. Beddows that Miss Burton turned.

"Do you remember the blacksmith's shop at Lipton-Hunter?" she asked.

"Why—yes."

"Do you remember a red-haired blacksmith there, about forty years ago, who married the district nurse?"

"Why—yes—of course, yes. Let me see. . . . Didn't the husband . . .?"

Then she remembered.

Coming home more drunk than usual one Saturday night, the blacksmith had fallen face downwards into the shallow water-butt in his yard used for cooling irons. His wife, accustomed to his straying from more paths than those of strict sobriety, had not even sought him until the Monday morning. Soon after the inquest, the wife had left the district, taking her children with her.

"They were my parents," said Miss Burton quietly. "My mother went into the West Riding. She got work there through the kindness of the schoolmaster in Lipton-Hunter. He was splendid to us. It was through him really that I got scholarships later on to Barnsley High School, and then to Leeds and Oxford. I came back from South Africa when my mother's health failed. She died five years ago."

"She was a very fine woman," said Mrs. Beddows. "I remember."

The governors livened up after that. They asked Miss Burton questions about Yorkshire and teaching methods and social theories; but nothing really interested them half so much as the fact that she had lived at Lipton-Hunter.

Mr. Dale nodded and smiled. She has worked her way up, he thought, even as I did. A good girl.

Mr. Peckover thought of Miss Burton's scholarships and his daughters' future. What she had done, they might do.

The chairman, fumbling with his tongue for a bit of gristle caught in a hollow tooth, thought, "Let them get on with it. A blacksmith's daughter. Good enough for Kiplington."

Tadman thought, "Like Mrs. Beddows' darn cheek to talk about small tradesmen's daughters. What else is she herself but a pig-killing smallholder's daughter? All the same, this Miss Burton looks a bit of all right. Got some go in her. She's seen a thing or two outside the four walls of a school. Let's have her. She may knock a bit of sense into Cissie."

Mr. Briggs, the solicitor, thought, "She looks like a business woman. If she's a business woman, we shall get on all right. Miss Holmes never answered her letters. By Jove, Carne looks hard hit. Did he mind not being alderman as much as all that? Or can he be ill?" That unexpected possibility led him to make a quick memo on the paper generously provided for other purposes by the Higher Education Committee. "Carne. Will? See Fretton. Overdraft."

Mr. Drew felt suspicious. Everything about Miss Burton appeared quite proper, quite decent. Propriety and decency were the virtues which he primarily demanded in all women. Yet. Yet—

He watched Tadman. Tadman was a grocer, a business man, and, in a small cheerful way, a speculator in real estate. Drew, as an estate agent, needed Tadman's friendship. Kiplington was not such a prosperous place that an estate agent could ignore personal influence. He had decided to vote for Tadman's candidate.

Alderman Mrs. Beddows had made up her mind. Sarah Burton's brilliant testimonials and neat business-like appearance represented, she considered, a tribute to her own perspicacity. Thirty years ago she had declared the widowed district nurse of Lipton-Hunter to be a fine woman, and here was her daughter who had developed against all odds into a candidate for headmistress-ship. Didn't that just show she had good breeding in her somewhere?

Emma Beddows' face was blithe with satisfaction. This was her choice, her candidate. Not only would Miss Burton be appointed; she would be a success. Emma Beddows would see to it that she was one.

Slumped heavily into his chair beside his friend and ally, Mrs. Beddows, Carne of Maythorpe relinquished yet another hope.

He had accepted the governorship of the High School, not because he was specially interested in problems of female education, but because Kiplington was in the South Riding, and the Carnes of Maythorpe were the South Riding, and aristocracy dictated a rule of life, and nobility must oblige.

Since he was governor, since periodically he must leave coverts undrawn or men uninterviewed to sit at that inkstained green baize tablecloth and discuss such matters as gas-lighting, lavatories and the place of domestic science in a girls' curriculum, he might at least find in return some small advantage.

After Midge's last outburst and that horrible episode in Muriel's bedroom, Dr. Campbell had advised him: "Get her to school. Get her with other children. Why don't you send her to the High School? It's the only thing."

Carne was not one for definition. During his happy childhood among the places and people and things he loved and trusted, before first his mother died and then his father and he met his lovely Muriel and inherited Maythorpe, he had known little need for words. In his unhappy and bewildered manhood, with wave after wave of misfortune breaking over him, he had found small comfort in articulation. Words lacked reality; words were nothing. But Dr. Campbell's phrase, "It's the only thing," chimed like doom in his heart.

Whatever had befallen Muriel, Midge must be spared. He had failed as a husband; as a father he must not fail. That fragile chalice of blue blood in his keeping must be treasured wisely. He must do his best for Midge, who was small and frail and plain and short-sighted and subject to terrifying outbursts of hysteria. He had engaged nurses for her and governesses; he had tried to preserve her from contact with rough boys and epidemics. Now Campbell urged that she should be sent to school—to "make her more like other children—to keep her normal."

The High School, Carne considered, was definitely low. Tradesmen's daughters, even one or two labourers', went there. It was not the school for Lord Sedgmire's granddaughter.

On the other hand, it was near. Hicks could drive Midge there daily. Wendy Beddows went there and could keep an eye on her. And boarding schools, of the superior type, cost money. He had inquired.

Besides, a new fear haunted Carne now. On that recent evening when, returning from the council meeting at Flintonbridge, disgusted by dirty work about the aldermanship, he had found Midge, a grotesque and terrible image of her mother, screaming and shrinking from him in Muriel's bedroom, he had been seized, even as he held in his arms her struggling figure, by physical pain so violent, by breathlessness so crippling, that for a few moments he had been completely helpless.

Midge had recovered; but Carne, remembering how his father had died from heart failure, faced a new menace to his beleaguered peace. Supposing that he were to die himself suddenly, in debt as he was, hard pressed as he was, and left the care of poor Muriel and his little Midge to the tender mercies of his brother William? He thought of young William, his architect brother, building houses for West Riding business men near Harrogate; William was clever, had always been the brighter brother; but Carne did not trust him to deal generously with Muriel and could not see him coping successfully with Midge.

If a nice motherly woman could be appointed to the High School, some one gentle and kind, or shrewd and capable like Mrs. Beddows—only a lady—then perhaps she might help him to solve his domestic problem. But none of the candidates had been kind and motherly. Miss Torrence was aggressive, Miss Slaker ineffective, Miss Hammond was cranky, Miss Dry had a hard mouth. As for this blacksmith's daughter, there was absolutely nothing to be said for her. Clever she might be; but Carne wanted affection, he wanted experience and sympathy and a big motherly bosom on which a little girl could cry comfortably. Midge, he knew all too well, cried a great deal. Miss Burton was neither gentle nor a lady, and her bosom was flat and bony as a boy's.

Besides, Carne could remember now why he felt he had a grudge against something at Lipton-Hunter.

He looked back into his youth and remembered a grey mare, a pretty creature with dark dappled flanks and a paler belly—a beautiful leaper. Hounds ran once from Minton Riggs to Lipton Bottom and lost their fox in Lipton Sticks. The mare cast a shoe and Carne led her round to the blacksmith's shop at Lipton-Hunter before riding the twenty odd miles home to Maythorpe. He remembered a red head and grimy face bent over the mare's foreleg, a smell of beer and a hand fuddled by drink that slipped and drove the hammer home hard on to delicate flesh. The mare reared, the blacksmith fell, Carne cursed and finished the shoeing himself; but the mare's shin-bone was bruised. She never carried him again quite so easily, and fell breaking her back in the Haynes Point to Point eighteen months later. Carne had never forgiven the drunken blacksmith.

No, by God. If this was Burton's daughter he'd see her further before he'd trust Midge to her.

In the discussion following Miss Burton's withdrawal from the room, Carne was the only governor who opposed her appointment.

CHAPTER III

MR. HOLLY BLOWS OUT A CANDLE

Two miles south of Kiplington between the cliffs and the road to Maythorpe stood a group of dwellings known locally as The Shacks. They consisted of two railway coaches, three caravans, one converted omnibus, and five huts of varying sizes and designs. Around these human habitations leaned, drooped and squatted other minor structures, pig-sties, hen-runs, a goat-house, and, near the hedge, half a dozen tall narrow cupboards like up-ended coffins, cause of unending indignation to the sanitary inspectors. A war raged between Kiplington Urban District Council and the South Riding County Council over the tolerated existence of The Shacks.

In winter the adjacent ground was trampled mud, crossed by cinder paths trodden into accidental mosaic with broken pottery and abandoned sardine tins. In summer the worn and shabby turf was littered with paper, stale bread, orange skins, chicken food, empty bottles, and the droppings of three goats, four dogs, one donkey, three motor-bicycles, thirty-six hens and two babies. In summer The Shacks hummed with exuberant human life. Young men rattled down at week-ends on motor-bicycles from Kingsport. Young women tumbled, laughing and giggling and clutching parcels, from the buses. Urban youths with pimpled faces and curvature of the spine exposed their blotches and blisters to the sun, turning limp somersaults over the creaking gate, hoping thus to cultivate within the brief summer months the athleticism which they associated with football teams, the M.C.C. and the Olympic Games. Gramophones blared, loud-speakers uttered extracts of disquieting information about world politics or unemployment in cultured voices, children screamed, mothers scolded, schoolboys fought, revellers returned late from Kiplington bars; the lighted tents glowed like luminous convolvulus flowers in the dark humid nights.

But from October to April only two families remained in residence—the Mitchells and the Hollies.

The Mitchells, a young couple from Kingsport, had married on hope and found small substance for it. Mr. Mitchell had been a clerk in a coal-exporter's office. Owing to the contraction of the European markets, he found himself one day without a job, without a shilling saved, his wife pregnant, and the instalments on his furniture and house in North Park Avenue still incompletely paid. From the shameful fear of creditors, from the yet more shameful patronage of relatives, from the apprehensive benevolence of friends and the ruin of their romantic love, the Mitchells fled to the simple life in the form of a tarred wood and corrugated iron hut in this rural slum. From thence Mr. Mitchell, still natty, urban, conscientious, haggard, sallied daily on his bicycle armed with an insurance "book" bought as a final ransom from responsibility by his uncle, eager to persuade Cold Harbour colonists and South Riding tradespeople to buy from the Diamond Assurance Company that security which he had failed himself to find.

He wrote laborious letters in careful clerical script on paper headed "Bella Vista, Maythorpe Road, Kiplington," and preserved thus his sense of still belonging to the middle classes.

The Hollies had no such pretensions. Mr. Holly was, when in work, a builder's labourer; when out of work he drew unemployment insurance benefit for himself, his wife and six dependent children. When unemployed he was actually two shillings a week better off than when employed, because he could walk or cycle to the Kiplington Labour Exchange; but to reach the housing estates near Kingsport he must travel by bus or train. The rent of his railway coach amounted to five pounds a year, and his wife, a competent stout impatient woman of forty-three, cooked on a small oil stove with a box oven, washed, baked, ate, slept, scolded and loved in one of the two compartments, and in the other brought up seven children in the fear of the Lord, the sanitary inspector and the Poor Law Authorities. Mr. Holly himself took life more easily. He liked his glass of beer when he could get it, and would play darts for hours in local pubs contentedly on the strength of a half-pint or a packet of woodbines.

One July afternoon Lydia Holly sat on the roof of the untenanted railway coach and tasted rapture.

From her sun-warmed seat she could see, if she lifted her eyes, beyond the squalor of huts, hen-runs and garbage, the long green undulating land, netted with dykes like glittering silver wires, and cut short on her left by the serrated cliff. The fields changed colour from week to week, springing or ripening, but the sea altered from hour to hour and Lydia loved it. The wide serenity of the South Riding plain, the huge march of the clouds, the tides that ran nearly a mile out over the ruddy sand, had become part of her nature. But when she dropped her eyes on to the page before her she became sharply conscious of a very different beauty:

"That very time I saw (but thou could'st not) Flying between the cold moon and the earth, Cupid all arm'd: a certain aim he took At a fair vestal thronéd by the west, And loos'd his love-shaft smartly from his bow, As it should pierce a hundred thousand hearts: But I might see young Cupid's fiery shaft Quenched in the chaste beams of the wat'ry moon, And the imperial votaress passed on, In maiden meditation, fancy-free."

She did not know what it meant, but it was glorious. She forgot the angry sawing cry of a very young baby, lamenting life from the pram near Bella Vista. She forgot her mother's weary voice, scolding Gertie for letting Lennie, the latest baby, cut his lip on a discarded salmon tin. She only heard, as a gentle and appropriate accompaniment to Shakespeare's words, the Light Orchestral Concert played on the wireless belonging to two young men living in "Coachways."

"Yet marked I where the bolt of Cupid fell: It fell upon a little western flower, Before milk white, now purple with love's wound, And maidens call it love-in-idleness."

Mr. Mitchell had lent her the complete Works of Shakespeare. In Bella Vista stood a splendid bureau, with desk below and glass fronted bookcase above, legacy of better days, certificate of respectability, pledge that one day Nancy Mitchell might return to dining-room, drawing-room, alabaster light bowl, pastry forks, walnut suite and a "girl" to push the pram. What meant social resurrection to her, meant Self Improvement to Fred her husband. When the news of Lydia's scholarship reached the Shacks, he said, "Better try to improve your mind. Read something worth while. Culture—not just this trash. Read Shakespeare." He lent her a book. She, bewildered, enchanted, intimidated, read:

"I am your spaniel; and, Demetrius, The more you beat me, I will fawn on you: Use me but as your spaniel, spurn me, strike me, Neglect me, lose me; only give me leave, Unworthy as I am, to follow you."

A fond way to carry on, thought fourteen-year-old Lydia Holly. She'd see a man further before she'd feel like that about him. Yet she had known her mother, a proud, scolding, impatient woman, give way almost as softly to her father, and it was her mother whom she loved and could admire. Her mother was brave; her mother was a fighter; her mother had insisted that she should take the second chance of a scholarship to Kiplington High School. When she was eleven she had won a place at Kiplington, but her parents had needed her to escort her small sisters to the village school, so she had missed her chance. Now Daisy was old enough to take her place there, the transfer could be arranged, and she might go to the High School.

Below the magic of Shakespeare's uncomprehended words, the wood near Athens, the silvery sweetness of Mendelssohn from the wireless, the benign warmth of afternoon sun on her arms and shoulders, below all these present pleasures lay the lovely glowing assurance of future joy.

Bert was working at Tadman's. Daisy was getting real handy about the house. Lennie was ten months old. Mother thought that he was the last, thank God, and Dr. Campbell told her he must be, anyway.

So Lydia Holly was going to the High School. She had, her teacher said, exceptional ability, a big brown strong girl born before her mother's vitality had been exhausted. She could climb and run like a boy, do splits and cart-wheels at Madame Hubbard's dancing class—(Madame took her free—a tribute to her agility.) She could add up sums faster than Mr. Mitchell, and write sprawling untidy blotted essays about "Heroes" or "Why I like History Lessons," which Miss Tudling read, with difficulty, but with approval, aloud to the class at the Maythorpe Village School.

So bliss awaited her. She was to wear a brown tunic and white shirt blouses, a brown felt hat with a green crest on the ribbon. She was to ride to Kiplington daily on Mrs. Mitchell's cycle, to eat her dinners at school, to learn French and Science, to play hockey, to have a desk and locker, and to read books and books and books, unreprimanded, because it was her business. Only she must work, read and learn and lay hold fast upon her knowledge.

She bent her head.

". . . I pray thee give it me. I know a bank where the wild thyme blows, Where oxslips and the nodding violet grows; Quite overcanopied with luscious woodbine, With sweet musk roses and with eglantine. . . ."

That rich Warwickshire woodland flowered across the bare blossomless landscape. Lydia Holly had never been inside a proper wood. Violets she knew; with wild thyme she had academic acquaintance. There was a song played by the caravaners' gramophone:

"When we find wild thyme I'll have a wild time with you."

Lydia thought it pretty. But woods, musk roses and eglantine were beyond her experience.

Happiness encircled her. Glory enfolded her. The words, the sun, the brilliant summer day, the salt wind fanning her cheek, the music seducing her heart, all these flowered into a symphony of rapture—Oh, lovely world. Oh, certainty of splendour. Oh, glowing illimitable royal summer. Her brown chin on her fists, her bare toes beating the roof of the railway carriage, Lydia lay loving her life, her future.

"Lydi—ar! Lydi—ar! Come down. Your mother wants you!"

Down scrambled Lydia from glory—an untidy fat loutish girl in a torn overall.

She entered the railway coach that was her home and stood blinking, dazzled. It smelled of lamp oil and unwashed clothes and beds and onions and of something else—not unfamiliar.

"Our Gertie's been sick again," said Mrs. Holly. "Wash her and put her to bed while I clear up, will you? And keep an eye on Lennie. Where've you been hiding yourself all afternoon? Can't trust one of you out of my sight a minute. They've been eating raw turnips again, if you ask me."

"It was only a teeny weeny bit," sobbed Gertie. "We were playing at ladies—at a whist drive."

"And the imperial votaress passed on, In maiden meditation fancy free," sang Lydia's heart.

She fetched water in a dipper from the rain tub; she poured it into a cracked enamel basin.

"There's a dead fly in it. I won't be washed with a fly," protested Gertie, and was very sick again.

"Now, do you think you've finished?" asked Lydia patiently.

"No," the child gulped. "Oh Lyddie, I do feel bad. I've got such a pain."

"Well, you shouldn't eat things. You know what happened before."

". . . Fetch me that flower; the herb I show'd thee once . . ."

Lydia's mind jerked free from the dark stifling bedroom of the railway coach. She was a robust child, uncritical of her surroundings and well fitted by nature to ignore them. Attending to Gertie, her mind ranged free through moonlit Athenian forests.

Eventually she got her sister to bed, but Gertie's pain continued; her sickness persisted; she grew hotter and more querulous. The summer afternoon became a hurried nightmare. Bert, home hungry and clamorous for tea, was sent straight back for Dr. Campbell. He was out, but his young assistant came, diagnosed appendicitis, wrapped the child in a blanket and took her, with Mrs. Holly, in his car, to Kiplington Cottage Hospital.

Mr. Holly returned soon after they had gone. Even he was hushed by the catastrophe. Lydia prepared the "tea"—kippers for Dad and Bert, jam for the children. They ate doggedly, silently oppressed by apprehension.

After tea Mr. Holly could bear it no longer. He was soft-hearted and pain distressed him; he was volatile and trouble bored him. Gertie, after Lydia, was his favourite child. Poor little lass. Poor Gertie. He felt helpless and clumsy, as during his wife's confinements. He borrowed a shilling from Pat and Jerry and went off to the Nag's head at Maythorpe where he had good luck with the darts, won an extra florin, drank it, remembered his sick child, told Grandad Sellers all about it, had another half pint offered from sympathy, and set off home tearful with beer and remorse to find Mrs. Holly, footsore and weary, climbing out of the Kiplington bus at the field corner.

"I came to meet you."

"Who's been treating you?"

"I met a man . . ."

"Good thing it wasn't a woman."

"Have they . . .? Did they . . .?"

"They didn't operate, if that's what you mean. Small thanks to you. It's colic and a chill. They're keeping her in hospital under observation. Why couldn't you have been about to fetch doctor? You take good care never to be where there's work going . . ."

Lydia, having put the children to bed, sat on the step of the coach awaiting her parents.

She had read till it was too dark to see, even by straining her eyes. The evening drained the fields of all their colour, leaving hedges and skyline, the broken edge of the cliff, the faint horizon of the quiet sea still visible, warm lead-colour against the liquid silver of the sky. The moon had risen, but in the north hung tattered streamers of a fading sunset. Bats flitted.

"Flying between the cold moon and the earth," thought Lydia.

The loud speaker still crooned lazily—a dance tune.

"Set your heart at rest: The fairy land buys not the child of me."

Lydia's heart was at rest. Beyond the squalor and fear lay loveliness and order.

She felt good and kind and loving.

She saw her father and mother, two dark clumsy figures stumbling along the path. She ran to meet them.

Mrs. Holly told her that Gertie wasn't going to die.

It was all right then. The promise of the afternoon was crowned with relief.

"You ought not to be up. It's past ten," scolded Mrs. Holly.

"I got the kettle boiling. I thought you could do with a cup of tea."

"Aye, I could then."

It was dark in the coach. Lydia lit a candle, shading it with a propped newspaper from the sleeping Lennie. She cut bread and brewed tea while her mother drew her shoes from her burning feet and loosened her corsets.

"Eh, I'm tired," she groaned, but smiled up at her daughter.

Lydia would have died for her.

Mr. Holly, swinging from the depths of remorse to the heights of jubilation, washed away the soporific effects of beer with Lydia's strong sweet tea. Gertie was all right. He was all right. The day had been all right. He was a fine fellow. He shared his daughter's rapture.

Looking round for some means of expressing the energy and delight surging within him, his eye fell on his wife seated in candle light on the side of their bunk, bare footed, the cup in her hand, her heavy body relaxed, her brown hair round her shoulders.

"Go to bed, Lydia," said Mr. Holly.

Lydia crept quietly through to her younger sisters in the other room.

Mr. Holly blew out the candle.

CHAPTER IV

ALDERMAN MRS. BEDDOWS CONSIDERS HEREDITY

The following evening the light waned quickly; a chill rain blew across the South Riding, and Alderman Mrs. Beddows sat warming her knees over her drawing-room fire. Her skirt was pulled high, exposing her taut rounded calves and well-turned ankles. She was proud of her legs. For a woman of over seventy they did her credit; but it was to save her skirt from scorching that she lifted it. Chloe might send her dress-lengths of brocade and marocain and dark luscious velvets from Paris, and Mrs. Beddows had by nature a taste for lavish generosity, but she had learned parsimony and forethought in a hard school.

Carne, drinking whisky and soda in the big arm-chair, sat enjoying both warmth and Mrs. Beddows.

She was his friend. To her alone had he ever been able to speak freely about his wife and daughter. She had stood by him during the terrible days when he returned from France to find Muriel unable to recognise him. It was to her hospitable house that he sent Midge whenever her absence from Maythorpe seemed desirable. It was because of Midge that he was here now. The child had been spending the afternoon with Willy Beddows' children, and Willy, a widower, lived with his father and mother. Carne had come to fetch his daughter on his way from Kingsport market. He found Mrs. Beddows by the fire.

"I've been at York at a Rescue and Preventive Meeting," she said, explaining the fire. "After wrestling all day with fallen girls and upstanding bishops I feel I need my bit of comfort."

"How did you get on?"

"Not so long-winded as usual, but I feel I've soiled my ticket. I said to the secretary, 'I want to catch the four o'clock train if I can, and I'd give a pound note to the collection if only they'd cut it short a bit.' And would you believe it, that wretch of a man went and told the bishop, and after he'd been speaking about ten minutes, he said: 'Well, there is much more that I could tell you of this good work, but one lady member of our committee has said that she will give a pound note to the collection if I would cut my eloquence short, so in this case, though speech is silver, silence is certainly golden.' And down he sat."

"Good for you."

"But that's not the worst of it. When they came round with the collection, there they stood in front of me chuckling—waiting for the pound note. And I hadn't got one. I don't know when I felt worse; I don't really. I said to Mr. Cross who was sitting next to me, 'For Heaven's sake lend me a pound,' and he said 'So you're the lady!' and roared with laughter and told every one. So now it's all round the county and I've had to borrow a pound from Willy, and what my husband will say when he hears of it, I don't know."

"He probably has heard," comforted Carne, "and decided to say nothing."

"Well . . . now don't stand about like a lad on hiring day. Sit down and make yourself comfortable. Yes, of course smoke your pipe, and help yourself to a drink. I wanted to see you."

Meekly, Carne sat.

"What's all this nonsense about Midge being too delicate to go to school?"

Carne bit on his pipe, smiling quietly. Mrs. Beddows could not offend him. In her ugly, cheerful house, life seemed sane and simple. All problems could be solved by courage, humour and plain common sense. Madness and doom and passion faded like wraiths.

"Good schools cost money," he told her.

"Bad schools cost more. What's wrong with the High School? It did well enough for Chloe and Sybil, and it's doing well enough for Wendy."

"Midge is a bit difficult."

Mrs. Beddows studied him. She was never sure how far he recognised the extent of his daughter's evil heritage. She sympathised with his reverence for the aristocracy. She herself set great store by breeding. She was far from thinking Jack as good as his master and explained failure in plebeian upstarts by saying with suave contempt: "Well, what can you expect? Wasn't bred to power." On the other hand, the Sedgmires were by all accounts a queer lot, and Midge had inherited more than blue blood from her maternal ancestors. Maythorpe could not afford two patients in private mental homes. Mrs. Beddows had talked to Dr. Campbell, who said it was touch and go with the child and recommended the High School.

Accustomed to take the bad with the good in this world and having wide experience of both commodities, Mrs. Beddows wasted no undue sympathy. Some people, she would say, are so full of the milk of human kindness that it slops over and messes everything. If Midge can't stand up to normal life, she reasoned, she might as well quit it early as later. Coddling and sentiment help no one.

"There's one thing about the school as it stands to-day," she said cleverly. "Under Miss Holmes the numbers fell off so that it's small enough for every girl to get individual attention. Fifty-seven day girls and fourteen boarders, isn't it?"

"Fifty-three and thirteen," corrected Carne, who could remember figures.

"I know it's not easy for you to send Muriel's daughter to school with the children of fish-and-chip-shop men and common labourers. But times are changing, and we've got to change with them. Why should you be afraid of other girls influencing Midge? She's as likely to influence them."

That was not true. As she said it, she thought that Midge, poor scrap, would influence no one.

She must try a different appeal.

She was enjoying herself. Assured of her own common sense and the wholesome wisdom of her arguments, she proceeded to the fuller education of Robert Carne, who was, like most men, a child, she considered, in practical affairs.

"It's not the past, it's the future you've got to think of. It's your girl you're educating, not Lord Sedgmire's. If he'd lend a hand, that would be a different matter. But he doesn't. He left his daughter and his granddaughter for you to deal with and we've got to work with the tools that providence sends us. It's not your fault that Muriel's where she is, poor soul. If her people had been more reasonable about her marriage, all this might have been different. And if you hadn't insisted that only the best was good enough for Muriel, there'd have been more now to spend on Midge, and I'm not sure that would have been any better for her in the long run. Midge is a dear child, but she needs knocking into shape, and company of her own age. It's not good for her to be so much alone."

"I know that."

The fear haunting Carne looked for a moment through his eyes. He drained and set down his glass.

He's tired, thought Mrs. Beddows. So was she. But hers was the pleasant fatigue that comes of work well done. When at night in bed she went over the events of the day, it was with a modest yet certain satisfaction at this misunderstanding disentangled, that problem solved, some other help given in time of need. Her good deeds smoothed her pillow.

But Carne looked like a man whom peace had deserted. Some central spring of hope had failed within him. Wherever his mind dwelt, on his farm, his public work, his wife, his daughter, his financial prospects, his health, his house crumbling to ruin, he found no cause for comfort.

Mrs. Beddows saw in this no reason to stop urging him.

She crossed her legs, remembered her blue petticoat, silk, but with a patch in it, pulled down her skirt and pushed her chair farther back from the fire.

"I suppose you knew how they worked the election," she snapped abruptly.

Carne's slower mind followed her dully. "Yes," he said.

"I told them you were as sound as the Bank of England, and that this rumour about failing was a lie and a damned lie," said the alderman. "How true is it?"

"I shall get through. I'm selling some horses to pay harvest wages."

"Is that wise?"

She knew the effect upon credit when a farmer sells horses before harvest.

"I'm dealing through a chap in the West Riding. I shall lose a bit."

"Of course you know it was Snaith who worked the whole business."

"I don't need telling."

"It's largely your own fault. You will go at him. I told you he was a queer friend but a worse enemy. There's not a thing going on in the South Riding he doesn't know and not a thing he doesn't know he can't make use of."

"He's straight as a corkscrew."

"There you're wrong. He's slim, but he's not crooked. He'll never break the law. He'll only work in the dark for the causes he thinks righteous. He sees you as an obstructionist. You are, too; I always told you you overdo your economy cry. It's one thing to champion the rate-payer; it's another to block all action. The difference between you and Snaith is that he thinks the end justifies the means and you think the means justify the end. You'd never play a dirty card; but when you do win—what is it? Just putting full stop to everything."

She loved him so much that to scold him was a sensuous pleasure to her. When a small child she had regarded Maythorpe Hall as a superb and inaccessible palace. To have Robert, old Mr. Carne's elder son, there at her mercy, sitting in her arm-chair, smiling at her, accepting her reproof, submitting to her advice, gave her satisfaction too profound for words. He was so handsome, so big, so masculine. He bought such admirable clothes and wore them splendidly. A natural dandy, Muriel Sedgmire had taught him how to dress, how to order wines, how to help a woman into her coat. His official education had been completed at St. Peter's, York, but his social education in the hunting field, at shooting parties with the "county" and in his wife's company, had given him an air found irresistible by Mrs. Beddows. Whether he was thundering round the ring at agricultural shows on his huge heavyweights, or strolling, sullen and apathetic, into the County Hall, or sitting here in her drawing-room, melancholy and gentle, she gloried in his presence.

Mrs. Beddows had, in her time, endured humiliation, disappointment, and the sharp twisting pangs of fear and jealousy. But the tragedy of Carne's marriage had placed him at her mercy, in need of reassurance and of comfort. She gave both, open-handed, and was unconsciously grateful to Muriel Sedgmire for afflicting Robert with that desolation which drove him to her side. In her hard, rich, varied, unconquered life, his friendship for her was one of her most treasured experiences.

She smiled at him now.

"We'll get you in next time. Astell's a sick man. That's what I said to Captain Gryson. He was mad, I can tell you. He came raging to me. 'It's dirty work, Mrs. Beddows, dirty work,' he kept on saying. 'Snaith's using Huggins and his gang to keep Carne out because Carne's a straight man and a pukka sahib.' 'Have you heard Astell cough?' I asked him. 'What's that to do with it?' he said. I said, 'There's perhaps six months good work in that poor fellow and then we shall have to elect another alderman. And if you can't work for your candidate as Snaith worked for his, you're not the man I thought you.' I sent him away with a flea in his ear, I can tell you. But you mustn't go out of your way offending Snaith, and you mustn't give cause to the heathen to blaspheme. Can you afford another two hundred or so a year to send Midge to a good boarding school?"

"No—But—I thought . . ."

"You thought you could do it cheaper. You thought you could put off deciding. You can't. Face up to it. Be a man. Send her to the High School with Wendy."

Then she remembered his solitary vote at the governors' meeting.

"Don't you like our Miss Burton?"

"No."

Mrs. Beddows cocked her head on one side—as though by this physical effort teaching herself to see Sarah Burton as Carne would see her.

"I remember her mother. She had breeding in her. Touch of the bar-sinister in that family somewhere, I shouldn't be surprised."

"I knew her father," said Carne grimly, and told the tale of the drunken blacksmith.

Mrs. Beddow twinkled: "I can't say I saw signs of our lady lifting her elbow."

"Oh, no." He was shocked at the suggestion.

"You don't know what you mean. But I do," she teased him. "You mean she has red hair and a snip-snap manner and isn't frightened of all your pompous governors, eh? Well—I'll tell you something. I remembered Jess Harrod's girl went to that South London United and I wrote to Jess and got glowing reports back. You mark my words. That girl will wear well. I'll see to her."

Carne's smile warmed her heart's core.

She flung out her plump, work-roughened hand.

"Don't take things so hard," she said. "When you're over seventy you'll have learned that we have to make the best of the world that God has given us, and not expect too much of any one, even of ourselves."

The door opened. Gas-light from the hall streamed into the twilit room.

"Ah—ah—You've got a fire on. Very hot, isn't it? Who's that there? You, Carne? Glad to see you. That your kid playing in the coach house?"

Mr. Beddows, auctioneer and corn dealer, ten years his wife's junior, looked round the room, noticing the fire, the whisky decanter, his wife's abandoned attitude of luxurious enjoyment. His quick little eyes discerned all evidences of extravagance and totted them up against his wife's account. But he was none the less genial in his jerky fashion.

"So they didn't make you alderman, eh Carne? Won't let you join my wife, eh? A long suffering husband, I am. Never know who I'll find my wife with when I come home from market."

He sat down and began to unbutton his leather leggings. His daughter Sybil had followed him into the room, and Carne watched the quiet dignity with which she waited upon him, removing his boots and leggings, handing him his slippers, curbing the spirits of the noisy children who came rioting along the passage.

Sybil, he remembered, had attended Kiplington High School.

The children entered the room and Carne saw Midge, her face too radiant, her eyes too bright, her voice too shrill in its excitement.

Muriel had been like that.

It was too late now to save Muriel.

"Midge, d'you want to go to school next term with Wendy?"

"Yes, yes, yes. Please, please, darling Daddy!"

"Will you look after her, Wendy?"

"Oh, rather, Granny."

Wendy Beddows had no special love for Midge, whom she regarded as a spoiled cry-baby; but the Beddows family had been implacably trained in public spirit.

"That seems to be settled, then."

Mrs. Beddows sighed. She had conquered. Carne was hers. She could twist him round her little finger.

On the drive home, with Midge tucked in the trap beside him, Carne could see his wife's pale scornful profile outlined against the sombre hedges. He could hear her clear voice.

"The Kiplington High School? Are you out of your senses? We talked of Cheltenham or Heathfield, Ascot—then Paris—or perhaps that new place at Lausanne. I suppose that you want Midge to revert to type—now that I'm safely out of the way? Oh, very well! I cannot stop you. Do as you like with your own daughter, Robert, since you are so sure that she is your daughter."

Her high thin scorn lashed him.

He had loved her so much. He had always failed her. He had muddled the interview with her parents. Muddled his war leave. Muddled that child business. His slower mind could not keep pace with her swift reactions; his emotions, not easily aroused, were still less easily subdued. Always he felt himself left far behind her, dull, clumsy, insensitive, too fond, too gross, too awkward. But now that she was gone he could invent for her invective more violent than any she had used; scorn, anger, criticism, mockery sprang to his hurt and groping mind. All the abuse she might have left unuttered, all the distaste she might never have felt for his uninstructed bucolic habits; all the resentment she might not have known, all the nostalgia for her former status, for the great house in Shropshire, for the London season, for the house parties, the family foregatherings which she had renounced for his sake, all the pain of her bitter quarrel with her parents—all this he imagined, made articulate, and repeated to torment his unhappy spirit. While she was with him he was so far seduced by the charm of her presence that he often forgot how much that presence cost her. Now that she was shut off from him, a wild shrinking tragic creature, wearing her life away in angers as inhuman as the moods of the sea, now when he could not touch her, smooth her brown hair, coax her to the tranquillity of exhaustion, call her his own, his dear, his little love, hold her fierce panicking body till it was quiet—now that neither love nor remorse could comfort her, he was comfortless.

He must not fail Midge now. She was all he had now. Well, she should go to the High School. Mrs. Beddows chose it. Mrs. Beddows might choose wisely. At least she had managed her own life better than he had.

CHAPTER V

MISS BURTON SURVEYS A BATTLEFIELD

A few days afterwards Miss Sarah Burton, emerging from the huge glass-covered arch of Kingsport Terminus, learned that the Kiplington bus was about to depart from the other side of the square.

With a leap, she was after it, her slim legs springing lightly, head up, chest out, small suitcase slapping her hip. She ran like a deer, dodging in and out of Kingsport citizens, nearly boarding the Dollstall bus by mistake, and finally sprinting the last fifty yards, clutching a rail, and swinging on to the Kiplington bus as it rounded Duke Street corner.

"Now, now, now!" cried the conductor. "Hold tight. What d'you think you're doing? Hundred yards championship?"

Sarah grinned amiably and sank on to the nearest seat, which she discovered to be the knee of a portly gentleman. She sprang up, apologetic. "So sorry."

"Not at all."

"He likes it," winked the avuncular conductor.

Sarah was about to wink back when she remembered that she was nearly forty and a head mistress.

She set down her case demurely and, climbing to the top of the bus, disposed of herself in a corner.

Well, well, well, she admonished. You've got to behave now. No more running after buses. No more little sleeveless cotton dresses. No more sitting on the knees of strange fat gentlemen. Dignity; solidity; stability. You've got to impress these people.

I'll have to buy a car. So long as I have to catch buses I shall run. I know it. I wonder if Derrick would sell me his for thirty pounds. He said he would once.

She pressed her bare strong hands together.

I must make a success of this, she told herself. I must justify it all. "All" meant the wrenching of herself away from South London, parting from Miss Tattersall, leaving her friends, her flat, her security—the delightful groove that she had hollowed for herself out of the great complicated mass of London—the Promenade Concerts, the political meetings, the breakfasts with Derrick, or Mick, or Tony, in summer dawns at the Ship, Greenwich. Once they had taken Tatters there for supper. On the top of the bus Sarah smiled again to remember Tatters watching the great ships gliding up London river, her round face flushed with excitement, a sausage speared on her fork, repeating firmly: "No more beer. Impossible, my boy, impossible. I'm a head mistress."

Tatters was a great woman and a darling.

But it had been time to get away. It was all too pleasant. It had been now or never. Another year or two and she could not have broken free. She would have stayed until Tatters retired, slipped into her place, and never never struck out for herself, nor built for herself till death.

She counted her slender assets: brains, will-power, organising ability, a hot temper, real enjoyment of teaching, a Yorkshire childhood. She counted her defects—her size, her flaming hair, her sense of humour, her tactlessness, her arrogance, her lack of dignity.

(All the same, Tatters had called her the best second mistress that she had ever known.) She must write and tell Tatters about her day's adventures. She began to frame in her mind a letter to her friend—one of those intimate descriptive letters which so rarely reach the paper. She would describe the Kingsport streets through which she rode, swaying and jolting.

Five minutes after leaving the station, her bus crossed a bridge and the walls opened for a second on to flashing water and masts and funnels where a canal from the Leame cut right into the city. Then the blank cliffs of warehouses, stores and offices closed in upon her. The docks would be beyond them. She must visit the docks. Ships, journeys, adventures were glorious to Sarah. The walls of this street were powdered from the fine white dust of flour mills and cement works. Tall cranes swung towering to Heaven. It's better than an inland industrial town, thought Sarah, and wished that the bus were roofless so that she might sniff the salty tarry fishy smell of docks instead of the petrol-soaked stuffiness of her glass and metal cage.

A bold-faced girl with a black fringe and blue ear-rings stood, arms on hips, at the mouth of an alley, a pink cotton overall taut across her great body, near her time, yet unafraid, gay, insolent.

Suddenly Sarah loved her, loved Kingsport, loved the sailor or fish porter or whatever man had left upon her the proof of his virility.

After the London life she had dreaded return to the North lest she should grow slack and stagnant; but there could be no stagnation near these rough outlandish alleys.

The high walls of the warehouses diminished. She came to a street of little shops selling oilskins and dungarees and men's drill overalls, groceries piled with cheap tinned foods, grim crumbling façades announcing Beds for Men on placards foul and forbidding as gallow signs. On left and right of the thoroughfare ran mean monotonous streets of two-storied houses, bay-windowed and unvarying—not slums, but dreary respectable horrors, seething with life which was neither dreary nor respectable. Fat women lugged babies smothered in woollies; toddlers still sucking dummies tottered on bowed legs along littered pavements. Pretty little painted sluts minced on high tilted heels off to the pictures or dogs or dirt-track race-course.

I must go to the dogs again some time, Sarah promised herself. She had the gift of being pleased by any form of pleasure. It never surprised her when her Sixth Form girls deserted their home-work for dancing, speed tracks or the films. She sympathised with them.

The road curved near to the estuary again. A group of huts and railway carriages were hung with strings of red and gold and green electric lights like garlands. The bus halted beside it. Sarah could read a notice "Amicable Jack Brown's Open Air Café. Known in every Port in the World. Open all Night."

She was enchanted. Oh, I must come here. I'll bring the staff. It'll do us all good.

She saw herself drinking beer with a domestic science teacher among the sailors at two o'clock in the morning. The proper technique of headmistress-ship was to break all rules of decorum and justify the breach.

"Oh, lovely world," thought Sarah, in love with life and all its varied richness.

The bus stopped in a village for parcels and passengers, then emerged suddenly into the open country.

It was enormous.

So flat was the plain, so clear the August evening, so shallow the outspread canopy of sky, that Sarah, high on the upper deck of her bus, could see for miles the patterned country, the corn ripening to gold, the arsenic green of turnip tops, the tawny dun-colour of the sun-baked grass. From point to point on the horizon her eye could pick out the clustering trees and dark spire or tower marking a village. Away on her right gleamed intermittently the River Leame.

She drew a deep breath.

Now she knew where she was. This was her battlefield. Like a commander inspecting a territory before planning a campaign, she surveyed the bare level plain of the South Riding.

Sarah believed in action. She believed in fighting. She had unlimited confidence in the power of the human intelligence and will to achieve order, happiness, health and wisdom. It was her business to equip the young women entrusted to her by a still inadequately enlightened state for their part in that achievement. She wished to prepare their minds, to train their bodies, and to inoculate their spirits with some of her own courage, optimism and unstaled delight. She knew how to teach; she knew how to awaken interest. At the South London School she had initiated debates, clubs, visits, excursions to the Houses of Parliament, the London County Council, the National Portrait Gallery, the Tower of London, the Becontree Estate; she had organised amateur housing surveys and open-air performances of Euripides (in translation), she had supervised parents' conversaziones, "cabinet meetings," essay competitions, inquiries into public morals or imperial finance. Her official "subjects" were History and Civics, but all roads led to her Rome—an inexhaustible curiosity about the contemporary world and its inhabitants.

Her theories were, she felt, founded upon experience. She had known poverty; she had known hardship; she had watched her mother struggle triumphantly under the double burden of wage-earning and maternity; she had seen her sister, Pattie, crippled by a fall from her drunken father's arms in childhood, wring from life beauty and love and assurance and the marriage which she had always declared to be an essential condition of her happiness. She had herself abandoned a joyous expedition to Australia to make a home in England for her mother whose health had finally broken down. She had thought then her adventures over; she disapproved on principle of sacrifice; but she loved her mother, and had found at the South London School work which satisfied her and abundant friendships. Courage conquered circumstance. She thought that it could conquer everything.

Her turbulent strenuous vivid life had not been without vicissitudes. She had a habit, inconvenient in head mistresses, of falling in love misguidedly and often. She had been engaged to marry three different men. The first, a college friend, was killed on the Somme in 1916; the second, a South African farmer, irritated her with his political dogmatism until they quarrelled furiously and irreparably; the third, an English Socialist member of Parliament, withdrew in alarm when he found her feminism to be not merely academic but insistent. That affair had shaken her badly, for she loved him. When he demanded that she should abandon, in his political interests, her profession gained at such considerable public cost and private effort, she offered to be his mistress instead of his wife and found that he was even more shocked by this suggestion than by her previous one that she should continue her teaching after marriage. She parted from him with an anguish which amazed her, for she still thought of herself as a cold woman. Yet nothing that had happened to her had broken her self-confidence. She knew herself to be desirable and desired, withheld only from marriage by the bars of death or of principle. She had never loved without first receiving courtship; her person and her pride remained, she considered, under her own suzerainty. She had even the successful woman's slight and half-conscious contempt for those less attractive than herself, only she felt that on her heart were tender places like bruises on an apple, which could not bear rough handling.

Well, I've done with all that, she thought, as the red and grey huddle of Kiplington spread itself into a fair-sized watering-place. No chance of a love-affair here in the South Riding and a good thing too. I was born to be a spinster, and by God, I'm going to spin.

I shall enjoy this. I shall build up a great school here. No one yet knows it except myself. I know it. I'll make the South Riding famous.

Four wretched houses. A sticky board of governors. A moribund local authority. A dead end of nowhere. That's my material. I shall do it.

The bus turned a corner into the square containing the Municipal Gardens and Bowling Green—an oblong of weary turf surrounded by asphalt paths and iron railings.

"All change!" shouted the conductor.

Sarah climbed down and retrieved her suitcase.

"Can you tell me my way to the Cliff Hotel?" she asked.

"It's a good walk."

"I'm a good walker."

"You'll find that case heavy."

"That's my business."

"If I were a single man and out of a job, I'd carry it for you."

"I'll take the will for the deed," Sarah twinkled, still, in spite of her heroic resolutions, pleased by opportunities for flirtatious back-chat.

She extracted directions from the man and set off walking briskly through her new domain.

Kiplington was taking its evening pleasures.

Along the esplanade strolled couples chewing spearmint, smoking gaspers, sucking oranges. All forms of absorption, mastication and inhalation augmented the beneficent effect of sea air, slanting sun and holiday leisure. Mothers with laden paper carriers and aching varicose veins pushed prams back to hot crowded lodgings; elderly gentlemen in nautical blue jackets leaned on iron railings and turned telescopes intended for less personal objects upon the charms of Kingsport nymphs emerging from their final bathe. The tide was coming in, a lid of opaque grey glass sliding quietly over littered shingle. Sarah felt suddenly aware of the heat and grime of her long journey.

She ran down the steps and hired a bathing tent.

Five minutes later she was wading out into the agreeable salty chill of the North Sea.

It did not worry her that her fellow bathers were spotted youths from Kingsport back streets and little girls with rat-tailed hair from the Catholic Holiday Home. It did not worry her that the narrowing sands were dense with sweating, jostling, sucking, shouting humanity, that the sea-wall was scrawled with ugly chalk-marks, that the town beyond the wall was frankly hideous. This was her own place. These were her own people.

She swam with blissful leisurely strokes out to sea, then turned and floated, looking back with satisfaction at the flat ugly face of the town, the apartment houses, the dust-blown unfinished car-park, the pretentious desolation of the barn-like Floral Hall.

Away to her right she could see the red crumbling road of the higher North Cliff, and the group of houses among which was her new school—"Until I get something better," she promised herself, lying back and kicking the water happily.

Then she remembered that she wore no bathing cap, cursed the tangled profusion of her springing hair which took so long to dry, and swam reluctantly, slowly, back to shore.

A breakwater of soft satiny wood polished by a thousand tides ran down to the sea. Taking the hired towel, Sarah perched herself on one of its weed-grown stumps and sat in her brief green bathing dress, one foot in the water, drying her hair and whistling, not quite unaware that Mr. Councillor Alfred Ezekiel Huggins, haulage contractor, Wesleyan Methodist lay preacher, found in her pretty figure a matter for contemplation. He propped his plump stomach against the sun-warmed paling, and remained there, enjoying the pose of her slim muscular body, her lifted arms, her hair like a flaming cresset. From that distance he could not see her physical defects, her hands and head too big, her nose too aggressive, her eyes too light, her mouth too obstinate. Nor did he dream that here was the head mistress whose appointment he, as a member of the Higher Education Sub-Committee, had recently sanctioned.

Sarah, her hair dry enough, the tide within ten yards of her tent, slid off the breakwater and went in to dress. Aware of approving eyes upon her, she increased, unconsciously and almost imperceptibly, the slight swagger of her walk. She was her father's daughter.

CHAPTER VI

ALDERMAN SNAITH CONTEMPLATES A WILDERNESS

"The Wilderness and the solitary place shall be glad for them," read Mr. Huggins. "The desert shall rejoice and blossom as the rose."

Looking down from the desk of Kiplington Wesleyan Methodist Chapel he devoutly wished that Alderman Snaith had not chosen to attend that service. The consciousness of Snaith's urbane attention put him off his form. Councillor Alfred Ezekiel Huggins, lay preacher and haulage contractor from Pidsea Buttock, was accustomed to success. He loved the cosy evening services, the pitch pine pews and scarlet cushions, the congregation rising and bending forward so decorously, the hymns, the lamplight. He knew how to deepen his fine emotional North country voice till it reverberated through their hearts and drew tears to his own eyes. He felt familiar with the Mind of God, and reasoned with Him as with a friend.

But that dapper grey little man was of unknown quality.

"Strengthen ye the weak hands and confirm the feeble knees. Say to them that are of a fearful heart, 'Be strong, fear not.'"

That's me. My knees are weak. I've got the wind up proper. His humour rescued him.

"Then the eyes of the blind shall be opened, and the ears of the deaf shall be unstopped."

No doubt of it, Isaiah made grand reading. Even the half-moon of choir girls behind him must feel some splendour from that resonant poetry. Sixteen of them, there were—all plain as cod-fish, and thirteen out of the sixteen wearing spectacles. Adenoids, curvature of the spine, anæmia and acne afflicted them—no, they were not afflicted; they simpered like beauty queens and patted soiled puffs against their pinched pink noses, quite complacent; it was Mr. Huggins whom their physical defects afflicted.

"And the parched ground shall become a pool, and the thirsty land springs of water; in the habitation of dragons, where each lay, shall be grass with reeds and rushes. . . . No lion shall be there, nor any ravenous beast shall go up thereon, it shall not be found there."

Be damned to his supercilious high and mightiness in the pew below, with his Benevolent Society and his name upon foundation stones and his Daimler saloon and his invitations to supper. No lion nor any ravenous beast. . . . Councillor Huggins would not be intimidated.

Opening his lungs, breathing deeply from his great diaphragm, stretching the silver watch chain across his stomach, with its seals and mascots and badges and orders tinkling, Mr. Huggins let his big voice triumph above the heads of clerks and coal merchants and shop assistants.

"And the ransomed of the Lord shall return, and come to Zion with songs and everlasting joy upon their heads: they shall obtain joy and gladness, and sorrow and sighing shall flee away."

The congregation was not unduly impressed. It was accustomed to Mr. Huggins' histrionics. He was a popular but not greatly respected preacher, and to-night Gladys Hubbard, the child vocalist who had won two gold medals though she was still only in form IV lower at the High School, was to sing the solo in the second anthem. Anticipation eagerly awaited her performance.

But the reading had fortified the reader. His weak hands had been strengthened. His feeble knees had been confirmed.

Why, after all, should Snaith not ask him out to supper? They were colleagues on the County Council, weren't they? Snaith was a democrat on principle, wasn't he? And even if he was a Power now, President of the Kingsport Housing, Self-Help and Mutual Improvement Association, on the Committee of the Kingsport Hospital, certain to be next Vice-Chairman of the Council, director of half a dozen companies with interests in trawling, cod liver oil, local railways, and artificial manures, reputed to be worth five hundred thousand, he had been nothing when he started, hadn't he? And there was still something a little queer about him, wasn't there?

Mr. Huggins, who was rarely worth more than his two lorries and the clothes he stood in, took heart of grace.

For it was surely odd that Snaith had never married, nor anything else either, so they said. A bachelor life—now Huggins could understand that. And there were some who happened to be queer and couldn't help it, like that poor parson fellow who got himself into trouble up Norton Witral way with choir boys. Nothing like that about Snaith, or you'd have heard it. Just—odd. And in more ways than one, for, taking it by and large, it was not quite natural that he should keep himself so closely to the South Riding. Never stood for Parliament, for instance. Now there was scope for a man of initiative. Huggins who, as an ardent Liberal, had campaigned through many elections, never quite abandoned his dream that one day he himself would be the candidate, to stride up the room through the applauding audience, to fling hat and top coat on the chair behind him, to crush his hecklers by unanswerable retorts before dashing away by car to another meeting, and perhaps even to stand on the floodlit balcony of the Town Hall acknowledging the cheers that greeted him as elected member for the Kiplington and Cold Harbour Division of Yorkshire. . . . If only business had not gone so badly; if only he had not married; if only Nell were other than what she was . . .

Parliament was a life for a man. There was triumph worth winning. Queer that Snaith never tried for it—unless, poor chap, there was something a bit wrong with him.

The choir shrilled through the Gloria and sank with relief to its seats.

Mr. Huggins sprang forward, nimbly for one so large, and announced the second lesson:

"The fifth chapter of the Epistle of Saint Paul to the Hebrews. First verse. For every high priest taken from among men is ordained for men in things pertaining to God."

He never enjoyed reading the New Testament like the Old. Less body in it . . . "Who can have compassion on the ignorant, and on them that are out of the way; for that he himself is also compassed with infirmity."

Ah, if that were the only qualification for priesthood, thought Mr. Huggins—being himself all too often compassed with infirmity.

If he hadn't messed up the insurance policy on that second lorry; if he hadn't missed the Dollstall U.D.C. contracts; if Freda hadn't quarrelled with her husband; if Bessy Warbuckle. . . . Now, a man like Snaith would never understand anything like that. Huggins considered himself to be a good-living man; but flesh and blood has limits. And his infirmities made him able to help other People. They were, you might almost call them, a gift from God. It was perhaps because Snaith couldn't show natural human feelings that he went no further.

Reading mechanically, Huggins ended the second lesson, sat through Gladys Hubbard's solo and knelt to pray.

For he had reached a solution of his problem. Snaith was not quite all that he ought to be. A good enough chap, but not a proper man. Therefore he could go no further. Some timidity, some limitation of spirit held him. While Huggins, why—if only he could escape from his entanglement of debts and children and responsibility—from Nelly and her querulous hypochondria, from Freda and her matrimonial troubles—there was no knowing what he might not do, where he might not end, a man with his talents . . .

He rose from prayer feeling strengthened and encouraged. His was a devout nature, and the god whom he worshipped rarely left him comfortless.

He found himself able to look Snaith straight in the eye, and, bending over the desk, preached him a sermon as eloquent, rich and full of "body" as even he, with his high standard, could desire.

He took as his text the words: "In the place of dragons . . .", romantic and suggestive.

"Isaiah's call," he boomed, "comes to us to rebuild the wilderness. We can fight the dragons misery, squalor, overcrowding. Do you know these little alleys of East Kingsport? Filthy, verminous, crawling with sin—sin! The prophet talked about the solitary place, but it's the overcrowded place we think of to-day. Five or six adults in a bedroom. What purity can you expect there? Boys and girls, yes, and men and women together . . ."

Huggins knew a thing or two about the Kingsport slums. He had been born in one. He was on the Public Health Committee of the South Riding County Council. He was a compassionate man. He really hated misery. Had he created the world not a woman should ever be over-burdened, not a child forlorn, not a man discouraged. Youth should endure for ever; strength should never fail; and love and gaiety, song and feasting, should reign on earth as they surely did in Heaven.

For Huggins wholeheartedly believed in Heaven and entirely hoped that he would go there one day.

The dissimilarity of East Kingsport from Heaven was a cause of real distress to him, and he cursed the proud and cruel men who made money by grinding the faces of the poor and by driving girls into vice and men into drunken squalor. He praised the public-spirited and noble who made the wilderness break forth into joy and singing. He drew vivid pictures of the touts and procurers who, like ravenous beasts, walked through the evil dripping yards and stinking alleys, and he prophesied their flight when the ransomed of the Lord should return to the Zion of Christian decency, with songs and everlasting joy upon their heads.

He did it all the better because he had only now fought his fight against depression and lack of confidence. The reaction drove him high into exaltation. The glow of his triumph endured through the singing of the final hymn, the last verse repeated softly, the congregation kneeling, the caretaker waiting in his seat to pounce upon the lights; it endured as the people rose to their feet, and Madame Hubbard at the organ swayed into the valedictory sweetness of Gounod's Ave Maria, and Mr. Huggins plunged across the chapel to shake hands with the retreating worshippers.

"Good-evening, Mr. Hubbard. How well your little girl sang. A real gift from God. Good-evening, Mrs. Ransom. Good-evening. I hope you enjoyed the service?" "I've known worse." "Good-evening."

He did it well—much better than the minister, he thought, a little bitterly, aware that he lacked the prestige of a "Reverend."

"Good-evening. Good-evening."

A small sedate youngish woman in brown slipped unobtrusively past him.

He caught her hand. "Why now, I'm welcoming a stranger, surely? I hope you enjoyed our service?"

Now where had he seen before those pale greenish eyes that glanced so coolly over his puzzled face?

"Very much, thank you," replied the woman, and made for the door.

"Ah, I see you've already met our new head mistress," said Alderman Snaith's precise quiet voice.

"Head mistress?"

"Of the High School. Miss Sarah Burton. I understand that she's Church of England, but your fame has obviously seduced her."

"I hope not—I hope not," began Huggins, realised that this was not quite what he meant to say, and coloured. Snaith stood examining his polished finger-nails, an irritating trick, but characteristic. The chapel was almost empty. Huggins felt his courage dwindling with the congregation. It was as though they carried away with them something that was his—that was—in its way—himself, and left him, with Snaith there beside him, helpless and empty, a big, brown-bearded, coarse-featured, powerful yokel dominated by the little neat grey dapper alderman.

"You are coming round to supper with me, aren't you? I've got Astell too. Just the three of us."

"Thanks very much. Yes. I'm looking forward to it."

But he wasn't. Uneasiness shook him. He was aware of fatigue. He wanted to go with the Tadmans or Hubbards to a homely meal of bacon pie and cocoa, or beef and pickles, strong rich foods that satisfied his big body, pious gossiping easy talk that relaxed his mind.

But he had to follow the alderman into his waiting car and summon his resources for ordeal at the Red House.

Huggins had visited the Red House for purely business interviews already. He had never been there for supper. He was prepared for discomfort, formality and the stiff finicking queerness of a bachelor establishment.

He found himself, to his disarmed surprise, seated before a small but well-spread table, eating enormously of cold sirloin cut in paper-thin slices, cooked to a turn, potatoes baked in their jackets swimming with butter, a perfect apple pie, its fruit sweet, tart, invigorating, under the sliding yellow cream, its pastry short enough to melt in his mouth, and Stilton cheese that was ripe and mellow as wine. A teetotaller on principle, Huggins could find in food some quality of elation for which others, less temperate, required alcohol. Well-being like the Grace of God crept warmly through his body. Perhaps, thought Huggins, they are not so far different. Food is one of God's gifts. So is well-being. The peace of the body which is beyond all understanding filled his heart with love for God and man.

He could listen, without irritation, to Astell's harsh solemn voice, criticising an article by Mr. J. L. Garvin in the Observer.

By the time supper was over and the men withdrew with coffee, liqueurs and cigars to the library upstairs, Huggins knew that life was good and that God was on his side.

Except that envy now lay dead in his heart, Huggins could have envied Snaith his library. The alderman had built the Red House for himself just after the War, on the only eminence that could be called a hill between Kingsport and Kiplington. At night from the big uncurtained window of the first floor library, Snaith could watch as he worked the formless glow in the sky westward over Kingsport, the shivering spangling lights from the docks across the Leame in Lincolnshire, and eastward the long rotating beam of the Leame Hook lighthouse. Huggins, an imaginative man, found that view superb, and wondered whether Snaith realised entirely what he had done when he designed his window. But to-night he was content to lie back in a large arm-chair, inhaling deeply the smoke from a half-crown cigar, and watching without contempt the dry small figure of his host outlined against that gold-splashed panorama.

"You missed something to-night, Astell," Snaith was telling his other guest. "Pity you don't come to Chapel. Huggins surpassed himself."

Astell read Kant in translation, spoke at meetings of the Rationalist Press and was an agnostic. Snaith upheld the proud intellectual traditions of nonconformity with a theological precision far above Huggins' head.

But it was Huggins whom he praised.

"He took as his text 'The habitation of dragons . . .' and turned it against East Kingsport housing conditions. D'you know Gladstone Passage? Ah—I thought you had it in mind—You too, Astell. As magistrate in the Junior Court I had a case up from there last Wednesday. Girl. Thirteen. Soliciting. Eight people at home sleeping in one room. Elder sister pregnant by the father, procured an abortion. This child told us. Mother in mental hospital. Pretty, eh?" Snaith delicately clipped the end of his cigar. "Eh, Astell?"

"You know what I think. You know too that Gladstone Passage is Kingsport's responsibility. But we've got some pretty warrens ourselves in Dollstall and Spunlington and Flintonbridge."

"I know. I know. I'm quite ready to pluck the beam out of our own eye—and if I wasn't, you'd soon prompt me to it, Astell. As a matter of fact . . . it was queer you preaching that sermon to-night, Huggins. Because I'd asked you two up here with a special purpose. You're both men who have specialised in housing one way or another. You know, I think, that Kingsport feels it can't go much further by itself. It's got to that point when it needs our co-operation."

"More land for housing estates, you mean?"

"Precisely. Ever thought about Leame Ferry Wastes, Astell?"

"No drainage, is there?"

"But supposing the Ministry sanctions the new road from Skerrow to Kiplington. It would pass right across the wastes. We should have to drain to some extent any way. And it would make the place exceedingly accessible."

On the table in the great bow of the window lay piles of papers. Snaith switched on a lamp. Light flooded them. "I should like you, if you will, to come here for a moment and look at these. I've been having some plans made out—partly for my own amusement. But I want you to help me to decide if there might not be something more than amusement in it. Now here's the Waste—two and a half square miles of absolutely useless property—at present. Belongs to the Rammington Panel Company. Going for a song. But it's no further from Kingsport than Clixton Garden Village—in fact it's much nearer for men working in Skerrow and Fleetmire. And, if the Ministry of Health would let us drain it as part of a big town planning scheme—and co-operate with Kingsport to move out the families from Skerrow yards and Gladstone passage way—It's a dream, of course, and Westminster may turn us down, but . . ."

His two guests, bending over the papers, were aware that Snaith's dreams had a habit of coming true. That house itself, that library, that admirable supper which they had just eaten, must have seemed an impossible dream to the undersized raw out-of-elbows boy once running errands in a back street insurance office.

Snaith talked well and he talked eagerly. When he became enthusiastic he became likeable. It appeared that he had gone further into facts and figures than he had at first suggested. He had foreseen possibilities and met difficulties.

A new market would be opened up for that part of the South Riding. The figures for tuberculosis, rickets and other infantile scourges in East Kingsport would be reduced. The children could have an elementary school of their own; but secondary school pupils could be divided between Dollstall, Kiplington and Kingsport. Fresh air, space and freedom could work wonders for them. Perhaps far-sighted industrialists could be persuaded to move their factories out of the grime and congestion of the city.

"We've got to plan. We've got to build for the future," said Snaith. "We've got to justify our power."

Huggins could feel a slight nervous hand gripping his arm. "Here's your desert all right, Huggins. The question is—can we make it blossom?"

Not a word was said of how the opening out of this estate might affect local incomes, increase Huggins' opportunities for haulage contracts or rescue a moribund railway line in which Snaith was interested from ruin. It was Astell, the Socialist, who had no possible financial stake in the matter, who was first converted. Afterwards Huggins could have sworn that though it was Snaith who conceived the Leame Ferry Waste idea, it was Astell's dogged persistence that carried it forward.

Snaith's car drove Huggins and Astell home.

Before he got out at Pidsea Buttock, Huggins remarked, "Clever chap, Snaith. Knows what he's talking about."

"Does he?" asked Astell.

"Eh, eh? Don't you think so?"

"I hope it may be so."

A trifle deflated, Huggins fell back upon consoling platitudes. "Well, well," he yawned, agreeably fatigued, "God moves in a mysterious way."

"God?" Huggins was too sleepy to catch the precise meaning of that inflection. "We have to . . . very mysteriously sometimes. But we move all right. We move . . ."

"Well, I get out here, I'm afraid. Good-night," said Huggins.

CHAPTER VII

MADAME HUBBARD HAS HIGHLY TALENTED PUPILS

Miss Dolores Jameson looked at Sarah Burton's red hair bent over her time-tables, and smiled indulgently.

"These spinster school-marms," she thought. "No wonder they stick to their job."

As for Dolores, she had something better to do than to conjugate Latin verbs for ever. Amo, amas, amat. To hell with it. Ten more minutes and she'd be due to meet Pip.

If it had not been for Pip, of course, she'd be in Miss Burton's place this very moment. Pip was Philip Parkhurst, a bank clerk who lived as paying guest with the Jameson family at Hardrascliffe. He was going to marry Dolores the moment he got his promotion, so she had not even put in for the headmistress-ship. Miss Burton was welcome to it. Plain, red-headed, managing. A typical school-marm. It made Dolores smile to think what Pip would say of her. Dear Pip. He thought Dolores wonderful with her temperament and her flashing eyes and her Spanish ancestry.

She lit one cigarette from another, pressing out the stub with slender brown-stained fingers, on which Philip's moonstone glowed romantically.

"I see that Miss Sigglesthwaite had five periods with III.a and seven with V. Upper, but none at all with the Lower Fourth last term," observed Sarah.

The two women sat together preparing time-tables in a bare distempered office as attractive as the average station waiting-room. It was a fortnight before the opening day of term.

"She can't manage the Fourths," said Dolores. "She's quite hopeless. The usual Jonah. Not bad enough to be given the boot, and she'll never resign because she's at the top of the scale and no other place would take her."

"I see. She can't manage the Fourths, so these children only start science in the Fifths and their matriculation results are deplorable." Sarah, who was tired and disliked her second mistress, sounded particularly brisk. "What's your solution of the problem, Miss Jameson?"

"Well, I don't know that you can exactly do anything," said Dolores, who under Miss Holmes had proposed one identical solution for all problems during the past ten years. "What I always say is—the really important thing is to equip these girls for life. And most of them will go into shops, or become nursemaids, or help their mothers run lodging houses till they marry. So really, as long as they've been to the High School and can count as High School girls, I don't see it matters so much what they do here. Speaking honestly as a woman, if you know what I mean."

Sarah knew what she meant. She looked with disfavour at the sallow, elegant, lackadaisical classics mistress and wished heartily for the promotion of Philip Parkhurst. Poor Philip. Ten years if a day younger than his intended bride, and a poor little pip-squeak at best; but anything was good enough to relieve the High School of those Spanish combs stuck into greasy hair, those trodden-down pin-point heels, that complexion with blackheads blocking neglected pores. Whatever Miss Sigglesthwaite is like, thought Sarah, she can't be much worse than our Dolores.

"Sixty if she's a day. Calls herself forty-seven, of course. They're all forty-seven when they get past fifty," the classics mistress continued. "She knits her own jumpers, and dances into form with a great band of cotton camisole showing above her skirt, chirruping, 'Girls, Girls. Would you believe it? The little chiff-chaff's back again!'"

Miss Jameson was a cruel and clever mimic. She made Sarah see Miss Sigglesthwaite's absurdity and guileless ineffectiveness. She did not know that she also made Sarah see her second mistress's own vapid heartlessness.

Sarah changed the subject coldly. Whatever she wished to know about Miss Sigglesthwaite she preferred to learn without Miss Jameson's intervention.

She doesn't wash enough, thought Sarah cattily. Perhaps that's her Spanish ancestry.

She turned her attention to the problem of the appalling buildings and showed Miss Jameson a letter that she had written to the Chairman of Governors.

"I don't really mind a hall the size of a cupboard, a pitch dark cellar-gymnasium and laboratories housed in a broken-down conservatory; but these beetle-haunted cloakrooms I will not have. They're enough to constipate any child for months. I will have those altered."

"What a hope you've got. You don't know Colonel Collier."

"Why is he Chairman of Governors if he's not interested in education?"

"Oh, he is interested. He's interested in seeing that the children of the working classes aren't educated above their station."

"I see."

"Oh, and by the way, Mrs. Beddows called while you were at Kingsport this morning to talk about the Carne child."

"What about her, and why should Mrs. Beddows come?"

It was exasperating to be dependent on Miss Jameson's ten years' knowledge of the town. Once term had started, Sarah vowed that she would be free of her.

Dolores lit another cigarette and leaned back to enjoy herself. She explained Carne—a local farmer who had ruined himself by running away with the daughter of a West Country nobleman.

"A born snob. These gentlemen farmers are. He went for blue blood and found it tainted. Serve him right, I say. They say the kid's probably not his, but the mother's in an asylum and the child's mental as anything. We shall have to have her, of course. He's a governor. So's Mrs. Beddows. Deputy-God, we call her. General undertaker. Divorces arranged, relatives buried, invalids nursed, municipalities run free, gratis and for nothing. All for the love of interference. You must have seen them both when you came up to be interviewed."

"I remember Mrs. Beddows."

Miss Jameson noted the omission. Wishes to suggest she didn't see Carne. Probably a man-hater, she concluded. Her thoughts veered.

"Look here, I must rush now. The boy friend said he would call for me at seven pip emma, and it's half-past now."

To be martyred would be beyond Miss Jameson's dignity, but she could be breezily self-righteous.

Sarah hailed her departure.

If she's a specimen of my staff, she thought, Heaven help me. Yet she was not depressed by the prospect before her. The greater her isolation, the greater her glory of achievement.

She had already achieved something. By bullying the porter, slave-driving cleaners, snubbing Dolores, importuning the governors, she had reduced to some state approaching cleanliness the wretched buildings under her control. She had rented a cottage for herself on the Central Promenade, between the plebeian North and superior South sides. She had bought a second-hand car, explored the neighbourhood, and taken measure of her own position.

It was not strong, but it had, she felt, possibilities.

She rose, tidied her desk to its habitual order, and cast critical eyes round the unprepossessing office. She would alter that, if she paid for it herself. Her imagination introduced a carpet, Medici prints, hand woven curtains.

She yawned. She powdered her nose. She combed, with vigour, the crackling electric tangle of her hair. She put on her hat. She reached her coat from the cupboard.

She was tired, but her day's work was not yet over. There lay on her desk a sheet of brimstone-coloured paper, cheaply printed.

"Grand Gala Evening"

it proclaimed.

A CONCERT in the Floral Hall to be given by MADAME HUBBARD and her very Highly Talented Pupils. Première Danseuse—Madame Gordon. Solos by the Renowned Child Vocalist, Miss Gladys Hubbard (Gold Medalist at Leeds, Blackpool, London, Manchester and York.) The Kiplington Memorial Subscription Band. At the Piano, Madame Hubbard. Lovely Scenic Effects. Gorgeous Costumes. A Feast of Fun and Beauty. In Aid of the Kiplington Kiddies Holiday Home. Tickets 1s., 6d. and 3d. Book Early.

J. Astell, Printer.

Sarah had booked early. She was not interested in the Kiddies Holiday Home, but she was very much interested in Madame Hubbard. She expected the worst of the Fun and Beauty; but she had not been a week in Kiplington before she realised that Madame Hubbard was a power. Gladys, her daughter, was a High School girl; half her contemporaries were among Madame Hubbard's highly talented pupils. Whatever happened at those dancing and singing classes, which appeared to be the chief centre of Kiplington social life during the long winters when no visitors came and the bleak winds swept the Esplanade Gardens, Sarah would have to reckon with it.

She found her car and drove to the Floral Hall.

The long barn-like auditorium was not more than half full. A handful of visitors augmented the local audience, which was, Sarah observed, almost identical with the congregation in the chapel. Here were the same shapeless middle-aged women with bodies like sacks and broken discoloured teeth, the same limp spectacled girls, the same elderly men propping pendulous stomachs uncomfortably on the narrow wooden benches. But here also were a few local Bloods sprinkled among their sober elders, and three rows of giggling, tittering, sweet-munching adolescent girls, the raw material, Sarah presumed, from which she must build her great public school.

It would not be easy.

She had just taken her place when the Kiplington Memorial Subscription Band broke into the first brays of its Classical Overture.

Eleven honest citizens, sweating like bullocks in tight scarlet uniforms, blew brassy triumphant noises through their instruments. Their leader, seated in the middle, raised with one hand a cornet to his lips, and in the other waved an ivory knitting needle.

Two ladies behind Sarah were discussing precisely why he should have left his baton at Spunlington after the Cricket Dance. So clear were their tones, so scurrilous their insinuations, that it was a few moments before Sarah realised fully the obstacles against which the band were scrambling. For the conductor obeyed all too literally the proverbial mandate. His right hand rarely knew what his left hand did, so that as the Classical Overture proceeded, his knitting needle might be beckoning the bandsmen on to the Toreador's Song from Carmen before his cornet blew the last notes of the Pilgrims' Hymn from Tannhäuser. When, after a fantastically warbled variation of "La donna é mobile," the whole band burst simultaneously into the Soldiers' Chorus from Faust, Sarah could hardly forbear to cheer this triumph of co-operation over individualism. Before the overture ended, her sporting instincts had overcome fatigue and disapproval and she wanted to rise in her seat and applaud the wild chase of trumpet, trombone, flute and bugle after the fugitive cornet. Even while she clapped the hysterical Coda, choking with excitement as the trombone tripped, stumbled, recovered and wound up with a superb flourish only half a tone flat, the tinned-salmon coloured curtains parted, a fat little lady in green lace sidled round them to the piano in the right-hand corner above the footlights, and the massed tableau of Madame Hubbard's pupils confronted her.

She drew a long breath, clasped her hands in her lap, and prepared to endure.

For there they stood, those vulgar, nasty, tiresome young women, exposing knock knees, bow legs, skinny or opulent thighs, beneath brief frills of coloured gauze, pink, white and yellow. Their arms and necks were bare, their faces painted, their hair waved or frizzed or cork-screwed into ringlets. The row nearest the footlights consisted of small children, but beyond them, rising in tiers till they reached the Première Danseuse and her adult assistants, posed and ogled forty to fifty girls of all ages and complexions.

The lady in green lace struck a chord on the piano.

Madame Hubbard's pupils burst into song.

"Hurraye! Hurraye! Hurraye!"

shrilled their piercing, tuneless but mercilessly clear articulation.

"We welcome you to-day! Oh, we are so glad to meet you, See how cheerfully we greet you! We shall do our best to please you, Soothe you, cheer you, love you, tease you. Some of us are rather haughty—"

A row of older girls stepped forward and turned sideways, hands on hips, lips curled in a pantomime of hauteur.

"Some of us are rather naughty!"

Their place was taken by a line of minxes, lifting abbreviated skirts, winking sophisticated eyes with so vivid an imitation of music-hall naughtiness that Sarah gasped.

"Never mind old Mrs. Grundy! We have jokes for all and sundry. And we hope before you go, You'll have found you like—our—Show!"

The word Show was squealed on a wavering approximation to High A, and held there by the perspiring chorus till it melted into the pure sweet treble of Miss Gladys Hubbard.

She walked from the wings, her jetty ringlets bound with scarlet poppies, her poppy-coloured frill of a skirt revealing naked dimpled thighs, her dark eyes rolling, her ringed fingers gesticulating with refined affectation. Behind her trotted a troup of poppy-clad babies in scarlet crinkled paper, who clustered round her as she halted in the centre of the stage, to sing with immense self-confidence the second verse of the Song of Welcome.

"Fling away your cares and troubles, All life's worries are but bubbles, There's no sense in looking blue! See what wrinkles do for you! Dance like us, your griefs beguiling. Soon you too will be a'smiling. We've a cure for every ill. You can learn it If—You—Will."

The babies were too young to have learned the tricks displayed by Madame Hubbard's older pupils. With solemn eyes they stared into the footlights or waved at friends and neighbours in the audience. With lovely rounded limbs they conscientiously followed their leader's gestures, pointing when she pointed, stamping when she stamped, bowing when she bowed. Sometimes they got into each other's way and sensibly changed their positions. They're too good for this: it's a shame! Sarah protested to herself, angry and indignant that this vulgarity was the best that Kiplington could offer to such delicious youth, such bold innocence.

Gladys Hubbard's voice was an exquisite natural instrument. Every artifice of vulgarity failed to ruin it. The girl shrugged and tossed her ringlets, squirmed and warbled, but the notes of her odious song glittered like a cascade of jewels, a fountain of pellucid music, sparkling, perfect.

Her successors shared her affectations without her talent. They sang songs about spooning, moonlight, triplets, ripe cheese, honeymoons and inebriation. Sarah watched in a turmoil of emotion. She did not know whether most to loathe or to admire the draper's indefatigable wife, who had obviously taken such pains to teach the children these tricks far better unlearned.

For the children were disciplined; they were word-perfect; they pronounced in flat Yorkshire voices with shrill precision the fatuous words of song and dialogue; they performed their tricks and pirouettes without an error. Whatever Madame Hubbard's pupils might be, thought Sarah, it was evident that they had a highly talented teacher.

She moaned in spirit.

If she could have employed Madame Hubbard instead of—say—Miss Sigglesthwaite. . . .

The final turn before the interval was announced:

"A Humorous Duet—By Jeanette and Lydia."

On to the stage waltzed two big well-grown girls, one dressed as a man in a morning-suit and topper, the other a "lady" in blue satin and tulle, bare to the waist behind, split to the thigh, revealing a jewelled garter between tulle frills. They began to shout and mime, for neither had any pretensions to tunefulness, a song of which the refrain ran thus:

"I've had my eye on you A long, long time. I've sighed my sigh for you A long, long time. You know I'd die for you, I dunno why I do, But 'less I die I'll soon have my— More than my eye On you—a long, long time."

The words were idiotic, but seemed innocent enough, the gestures accompanying them were not. The dance was as frankly indecent as anything that Sarah had seen on an English stage. The girl taking the female part "shimmied" her well-formed breasts and stomach, leered and kicked, evoking whistles, shouts and cat-calls from the delighted young men in the audience. Her partner, after a robust and rabelaisian mimicry of courtship, ended her performance with a series of cart-wheels across the stage, culminating in the splits, from which uncomfortable attitude she raised her hat and kissed her hand as the curtain fell.

Sarah felt sick.

She had had enough. She had seen Madame Hubbard's pupils. She would go home. She was preparing to rise when she saw the band return and stuff itself into the inadequate accommodation provided for it. The fat lady in the torn red cardigan beside her sighed, a long explosive sigh of satisfaction.

"Don't they do it lovely?" she asked complacently.

"They're very well trained."

Sarah groped for her glove.

"That was our Jennie in the last bit."

"Oh: which?"

"The one in the blue dress. She's been two years with Mrs. Hubbard. Sings and dances lovely. She wants to go on the films. She was on the short list in the Kingsport Beauty Competition last year. They say she might have been queen if she was a bit stouter. The gentlemen were judging and I always say—never mind the fashions. A gentleman likes something to get hold of. She won't eat potatoes, but I tell her all skin and grief never got anywhere. Her pa's dead set against the pictures. But I say, a girl might do worse. They say it's a hard life for a girl, but I used to get eight shillings a week as help to Mrs. Biggs—up and down them big houses on the front with the lodgers sleeping three in a bed, and sand in the basin and early morning teas and babies. Then since I married I've took visitors myself, and nine kiddies—six living—and him out of work as often as not, and my leg bad. I'd as soon be kicking in the chorus as standing all day at the wash tub, leave alone the life of sin they talk about. You're not married yourself, are you?"

"No," said Sarah.

"Not yet, eh? Oh, well, Mr. Right'll come along some day. You're not all that old, are you? Jennie's partner's Lyd Holly. Madame Hubbard takes her free because she's a natural acrobat. She's going to High School next term. A real clever girl. Ought to have been three years back, but her poor ma was always expecting and Holly's not all that. D'you like aniseed?"

Sarah found a sticky bag thrust upon her.

"Go on. Good for the digestion. I always get two penn'orth every Friday, qualifying for the Christmas Club at Bosworth's. Good-evening, Mrs. Pinker. Eeh, your little Gracie, she's a born dancer." She turned back to Sarah. "Got a floating kidney and her Gracie's a bit feeble, but Madame Hubbard's brought her on wonderful with the dancing. Any amount of patience. Have an aniseed ball, love. A.1 for flatulence."

"But I haven't got flatulence," cried Sarah into a horrid silence caused by the parting of the curtains, revealing a flower-tableau woefully marred by the presence of a small dusty gentleman who clutched tenaciously at the gilded chair on which the Première Danseuse, dressed as a butterfly, precariously balanced.

"That'll be Mr. Hubbard again," observed Sarah's neighbour happily. "Last concert he wanted to come on and play the triangle. Wouldn't be shifted, so she just had to let him. He sat in the front and held his triangle all through. Gentle as a babe once he has his way. But she doesn't really like it."

"I suppose not," agreed Sarah, fascinated by the spectacle of the entire company endeavouring heroically to ignore the wrestling match taking place between Madame Hubbard and her stage-struck husband.

It occurred to Sarah that the songs about drunken home-comers and bullying wives which she had found so gross dealt after all with commonplaces in the lives of these young singers. Was it not perhaps more wholesome to be taught to laugh at them by the Hubbard method than to turn them into such a tragedy as her father's habits had seemed to her mother's ambitious, anxious, serious mind? Jokes about ripe cheese and personal hygiene—("Take your feet off the table, Father, and give the cheese a chance!"), about childbirth and deformity and deafness—were not these perhaps necessary armaments for defence in a world besieged by poverty, ugliness, squalor and misfortune?

But Madame Hubbard was winning. Suddenly retreating to the wings she called in a deep stentorian voice, "Time, Gentlemen, Time!" and Mr. Hubbard, slowly detaching himself from the ballet, lurched off grumbling quietly into the wings.

Madame Hubbard hurled herself at the piano. The chorus, stimulated to even greater efforts by this alluring interlude, embarked upon the plaintive query:

"Have you heard the tale of Love-in-a-Mist? (Love in a mist might lie!) Have you heard of the fairy who'd never been kissed? (Love in a mist knows why.)"

Sarah had passed beyond judgment and beyond criticism.

She watched a Gipsy Ballet, a Fairy Ballet. She heard Gladys Hubbard sing "Lily of Laguna." She watched Lydia Holly romp with noisy and cheerful athleticism through a Dutch Doll Dance.

She endured until the end.

But the end surprised her.

The curtains were down. The conductor, cornet in hand, rallied his men. "Grand Patriotic Finale," announced the programme.

The Kiplington Memorial Subscription Band crashed into the smashing affirmation of "Land of Hope and Glory" as only a local brass band well plied with beer and enthusiasm in a too small room can play it. The curtains parted. On to the stage marched the Highly Talented Pupils dressed in costumes intended to represent the Army, Navy, Air Force, and Nursing Services. As the tune changed, Gladys Hubbard, a flirtatious and unorthodox V.A.D., tripped forward to sing:

"On Sunday, I walk out with a soldier."

while the obedient babies trotted round her to take their places as soldier, sailor, boy scout and other escorts. Again their serenity and beauty affected Sarah irrationally, but this time another emotion also was besieging her.

Like many women of her generation, she could not listen unmoved to the familiar tunes which circumstance had associated with intolerable memory.

"If you were the only girl in the world," sang Madame Gordon, and Sarah bit her lip remembering a last leave and a matinée of The Bing Boys.

"Keep the Home Fires Burning," sang Jeanette Marsh, and the inappropriate tears pricked Sarah's hot eyes.

"There's a long, long trail," wailed the chorus, and Sarah wanted to run away.

For though, apart from the death of young Roy Carbery, she had suffered less from the war than many women, seen less of it, remained less keenly conscious of its long-drawn catastrophe, the further it receded into the past, the less bearable its memory became. With increasing awareness every year she realised what it had meant of horror, desperation, anxiety, and loss to her generation. She knew that the dead are most needed, not when they are mourned, but in a world robbed of their stabilising presence. Ten million men, she told herself, who should now have been between forty and fifty-five—our scientists, our rulers, our philosophers, the foremen in our workshops, the head masters in our schools, were mud and dust, and the world did ill without them.

She was haunted by the menace of another war. Constantly, when she least expected it, that spectre threatened her, undermining her confidence in her work, her faith, her future. A joke, a picture, a tune, could trap her into a blinding waste of misery and helplessness.

She gazed through burning eyes at the medley of khaki, blue and scarlet. The first notes of "Tipperary" shook her into sick despair. She no longer disliked the precocious unpleasant children. She no longer resented the perverse efficiency of Madame Hubbard. She only felt it intolerable that the greed and arrogance and intellectual lethargy, the departmental pride and wanton folly of an adult world, should endanger those unsuspecting children.

The helpless tender charm of the smallest singers wrung her heart. She longed to save and to redeem them, no longer from the nauseating inadequacy of the well-intentioned Hubbards, but from the splintering shrapnel, the fog of poison gas.

The passion of all crusaders, missionaries and saviours tore her soul.

For to hear them singing, as jolly dancing tunes, the songs so pregnant with association; to see them marching, drilling, obeying the barked commands, "Form Fours! Sa-lute!" as though these motions, these melodies meant no more to them than the gipsy ballet and the flower chorus; to watch their youth and silly innocence aping that which had meant anguish of apprehension and pain and panic—all this was too much for her. She could not bear it. She could not bear it for them. What she herself had been through, what still confronted her, were matters between her and her own conscience. But for them, these silly children . . .

In the darkened, stifling, stamping, shouting audience, Sarah dropped her head into her hands and wept shamelessly.

She became aware of some one patting her knee, of a motherly voice saying below the din:

"There, there. It's all right, love."

"I know." She fumbled for her handkerchief. "It's nothing. I've no right . . ."

"It takes you like that sometimes. I know. I lost my man."

The first notes of God Save the King swept them to their feet. Sarah and Mrs. Marsh stood up together. Mrs. Marsh knew that Sarah suffered from unaccountable weaknesses. Sarah knew that Mrs. Marsh's "man" was not her present husband.

They had shared an experience.

BOOK II

HIGHWAYS AND BRIDGES

"3. The Ministry of Transport have intimated that they will make a grant of 60 per cent. of the cost of constructing the new road from Skerrow to Kiplington, and instructions have therefore been given for the work to proceed."

Extract from the Minutes of the Proceedings of the Highways and Bridges Committee of the South Riding County Council. County Hall, Flintonbridge, November, 1932.

CHAPTER I

COUNCILLOR CARNE MISSES A SUB-COMMITTEE

One November morning, hounds were to meet at Garfield Cross and the day promised good sport. As Hicks trotted to the meet on the little bay mare he was schooling for sale next spring, behind Carne's heavyweight Black Hussar, he sniffed with satisfaction. The morning was moist and warm yet fogless, the air fragrant with burning wicks, damp earth and horses. An untidy litter of rooks, like smuts from a giant chimney, blew across the grey sky. On Turnbull's land the wheat already stood three inches high. Robins and tits sang in the rusty tangle of brambles. The mare danced merrily.

"Bucking a bit?" asked Carne.

"Wick as a kitten," grinned the groom. "She'll be all right when we've taken the tickle out of her feet. Easy, my lass."

Carne eyed her affectionately. "I could get a hundred and fifty for her if she does anything like she should in the Rimsey Point to Point."

Hicks frowned. This preoccupation with money jarred on him. He was a sportsman. Horses were bred for pleasure. It was alien to Carne's nature to regard them as so many potential pounds, shillings and pence. Hicks had never considered his own wages inadequate, but he hated to feel his employer short of money.

"Shouldn't be surprised if we draw the wastes first," he ran on, trying to banish from his mind the thought that times had changed, that Carne, who made so handsome and proper a figure in his pink on the well-groomed horse, was no longer a gentleman out to enjoy himself, but a salesman exhibiting merchandise. "Leckton told me last month they threw in sixteen and a half couple of hounds and couldn't see a dog. Lost in thistles and willow herb—but lousy with foxes."

Carne did not answer.

It's that damned letter from Harrogate, thought Hicks.

He met the postman, read postmarks and postcards, and kept an anxious, paternal eye on his master's business. He knew all too well the discreet blue typewritten envelopes from the nursing home, or the sprawling uneven hand, tilted towards the top right-hand corner, which was his mistress's. They let her write once a month, poor devil, but lately her letters had not appeared.

Hicks wondered if she had changed much. He could see her now as she was when she first came to the South Riding—a slim pale girl with wild brown eyes on a raking chestnut. She had been staying with the Lawrences. Mrs. Lawrence was laid up with a broken collar-bone and Mr. Rupert hunting his own hounds that day. "Miss Sedgmire comes from the West Country," Hicks had heard him saying to Carne. "I want you to look after her for me. Give her a lead. She's not used to our drains yet."

After that, thought Hicks, it was she who'd led Carne. And what a dance she'd led him, not only across country but across Europe. Baden-Baden, Cannes, San Remo—seeking cures for her "nerves." She never had nerves in the hunting season. It was the War that finished her. Not getting abroad and not able to hunt when her child was coming. Aye. That was it. If she'd been able to ride in the winter of '17 and '18, she wouldn't be put away where she was now, poor lady—costing all that money and forcing Carne to sell his horses.

Hicks could remember how she walked up and down the dripping avenues at Maythorpe, fretting her heart out. "They won't let me ride any more, Hicks," she used to complain, her eyes puzzled and bright as a startled hare's. Then she'd order the horse and trap and drive to the station and be off away to York or Doncaster or Newmarket—looking for race meetings that had never been billed.

Aye. It was a queer job for Carne. Pity the old man was gone. He might have helped him. Mr. William was no manner of use except to find the Home when she had to be put away.

Carne had had to go back to France before the baby arrived. He'd come out one day and stood in the stable-yard, a big fine chap in his uniform, but awkward and unhappy—and no wonder. "If Mrs. Carne orders you to get the trap ready, Hicks, don't do it. Make some excuse. Say the mare's lame or the shaft's cracked. Lame the mare—crack the shaft if necessary. But don't let her go. Doctor's orders. Understand, eh?"

He knew she was queer then, and he had to go off and leave her alone to the care of grooms and servants.

It wasn't right, thought Hicks. And it wasn't right for her own folk to have cast her off like that. As if the Carnes of Maythorpe weren't good enough even for a baron's daughter. Leaving Carne to pay all that money for her too. They must have known she was a bit queer from the beginning. The wild Sedgmires. But she could ride. By God, she could ride. A clinker across country. Pity Midge never took to it.

The village street was crowded. Every one was making for the Cross—the butcher's boy in his blue coat on a bicycle, the clergyman's daughters trotting in their governess car, old Mr. Coster, nearly blind, on a white Pony, pedestrians with walking-sticks, motorists, cyclists, hurrying between the raw red cottages, where women with babies in their arms leaned from the doorways.

"Hounds arrived yet?" Carne asked an old labourer, grinning through his whiskers and clutching a thorn stick in knotted hands.

"Aye. Yessir. Just gone through."

There they were—moving and whimpering round the white war memorial.

The Master spoke to Carne.

"Thought it was going to be a frost. Said so last night on the damned wireless."

"Never listen to the things," said Carne. "Don't believe in 'em."

"You're right. You're dead right. Been to the Wastes this season?"

"No, but my groom says it's lousy with foxes."

"Good man."

Carne and the Master both grinned at Hicks. Hicks grinned back. Now he was happy. Here even Carne was happy. This was the life—this was the life undoubtedly. Farmers, county, villagers, yes, and even townsfolk, all drawn together by one common interest. And then some fools said fox-hunting was immoral.

Hicks reined the little mare aside. Aye, she was bonny. He didn't approve of this salesmanship-in-the-field business, but she was a beauty—a rare little bloodstick. By Romeo II out of Galway Girl. Hicks liked a touch of Irish in a horse.

There was Alderman Mrs. Beddows driven up in her shabby car by Miss Sybil. A nice girl. Hicks approved of Sybil Beddows.

"Coming to Highways and Bridges this afternoon?" Mrs. Beddows asked Carne. He often hunted all morning, left his horse with Hicks, and caught a train from the nearest station to a committee at Flintonbridge. He had gone there once with two broken ribs and a bang on the head fit to knock out three other men.

"I'm coming if we land up anywhere within reason."

"Anything I can do for you if you don't get?" she twinkled.

"We-ell." His horse moved impatiently beside the car. "They won't get to that new Skerrow road business, I don't suppose."

"Can't tell. Any orders?"

"Stamp on it. Nonsense. Waste of money. We've got the whole place splintered with motor roads now.—Can't keep a horse on its feet. Hopeless for farmers."

"I can't say I feel all that about it. The new road might benefit us a good deal at Kiplington."

"More trippers. Come up!"

The big horse pulled at the curb.

"Have you been to see Miss Burton yet?"

Carne shook his head.

"Well—you really are—! First you make all that fuss about the High School not being good enough for Midge. Then you can't even bother to go and call on her head mistress."

Mrs. Beddows teased, but her heart melted towards him. She loved to see him thus, superb in his pink, on his great black horse, standing beside her shabby car, talking to her, though half the county was present and ready to greet him. Flattered and charmed, she rallied him.

But hounds began to move off along the chalk road to Leame Ferry Waste, and Carne, waving good-bye to the Beddows, joined the jolting, tittirruping, creaking, plunging field. His eye was on the little bay mare, his mind absorbed by her. To him she meant both gracefully perfect horseflesh and the hundred and fifty pounds which would pay nearly four months of Muriel's expenses. The ten guineas a week charged by the Laurels nagged at his mind, haunted his dreams, sat, like indigestion, upon his chest all day. Even the joy of riding towards a covert on a moist November morning was robbed of flavour.

He was losing now steadily on the farm—had been losing since 1929—not much at first, but each year increasingly. He was cutting into capital; he had a heavy overdraft and a mortgage on the estate. Another year like last and he would be ruined.

He liked the matron at the Laurels Nursing Home; but he knew the charges, fixed by her employers, to be inordinately high. Yet he dared not refuse one of the extras they demanded. He carried too vividly in his mind the memory of Muriel, crying, as she had cried that time he found her in

Doncaster, standing wide-eyed and tense in the hotel bedroom. "Don't let me down, Robin, promise! Promise! They've all failed me. Promise me you'll stand by me, always, always!"

He had promised, and he had kept his promise. He had mortgaged Maythorpe, stinted Midge's education, strained his overdraft, jeopardised the living, the sane, the active, in order that Muriel might be kept in comfort. A phantom rode with him to hounds, sat with him at table, shared with him his bed, a voice accused him, "You ride. You hunt. You take your pleasures, while I am for ever cut off from life and freedom. I am here, trapped in a living grave. Because I violated my own instincts and traditions; I married you; I bore your daughter; I am doomed and damned eternally."

North of Garfield the South Riding no longer lies dead flat and striped with ditches. Tall hedges cut the round contours of undulating hills. The fields lie eighty and sixty acres broad, winter wheat, ploughed land, beautiful hunting country. If the fox got away North-East of the Wastes, he might give them a clinking run clear to the sea.

A familiar and lovely noise broke the tension of waiting. It had happened.

Away North-East of the tangled marsh and undergrowth of the Waste rang the Gone Away.

Black Hussar wheeled abruptly, and if Carne had not been so experienced a horseman, lost as he was in melancholy thought, he might have been unseated. They were off down the side of the covert, crashing over the broken bank, plunging through thickets of thorn and hazel, and out, down, away across the open stubble.

The little mare shot past Carne like a bullet from a gun. His spirit saluted her. She could go and Hicks could ride her.

The big black brute that Carne rode was built for weight and staying power. He could keep going all day, pounding doggedly.

The little mare, rising to the fence ahead, took it like a bird. Hicks turned back to grin at Carne. She's a natural jumper, thought Carne. But can she stay?

They were on heavy ploughed land now. The black horse thumped with regular powerful strides across the furrows; but the little bay danced ahead as though her light hoofs hardly broke the layers of earth.

Beyond the ploughed field came Laidlow's farm, then the Minston allotments. Allotments made queer going. It was better to cut up sharp to the north, even if that meant making a detour. Here lay three parallel fields with highish fences. Further up still was a gate. Hicks, racing ahead, waved to Carne his decision. Carne nodded. He wanted to see the mare at work over banks and fences. Her Irish blood should help her there. Reining back a little, he watched Hicks put the mare straight at the first thorn hedge.

She rose lightly, beautifully. Carne, holding his breath, lost no line of that proud and lovely movement. Then, as though checked in mid-air, she seemed to falter. Hicks screamed, "Wire, wire!" Carne saw a flurry of tossing hoofs, a somersaulting belly, and knew that the mare was down on the other side.

The field swerved to the gate. Dragging the black horse's mouth Carne checked him ruthlessly and followed them, sweating with agony as he waited his turn in the jostling stampeding crowd. The seconds seemed hours.

Then he was through, jerking Black Hussar out of the stream of horsemen, and making for the tumbled tossing huddle below the fence.

Hicks was extricating himself.

"You all right?" Carne slid to the ground and helped to pull him clear.

Captain Gryson, on a stiff, panting pony, pulled back to help them.

"Any damage done?"

The groom, white-faced, clutched his right elbow, staring at the threshing hoofs of the plunging, struggling mare. Carne flung the rein of Black Hussar to Gryson and approached the fallen beast.

"Look out, sir!" called Hicks. But Carne knew his business. Speaking quietly, he stooped down beside the mare, got one knee on her neck, and loosened her girth, pulled aside the saddle, and ran his big hand down her spine.

Her plunging quieted.

He looked up, shaking his head.

"I'm afraid it's no use. Her back's broken. Can you get me a gun from somewhere, Gryson? One at that house perhaps—" he chuckled grimly. "Why, it's our colleague, Snaith's."

Gryson galloped off.

Hicks coughed apologetically.

"I'm sorry, sir."

"Not your fault. But if ever I learn what blank, blanketty blank of a fool put up that wire without marking it, I'll . . ."

The flow of language comforted even Hicks, nursing his broken shoulder, sick and giddy.

"It's new, too. I've come across here a dozen times last year." His voice faltered. He was faint with pain and nearly in tears. Carne realised for the first time that the mare was not the only casualty.

"Better sit down. You've had a nasty toss."

But he still knelt by the twitching, kicking animal, cursing softly, gentling her head.

They were still thus when Snaith, walking hatless across the paddock, approached them.

"Is there anything I can do?"

Carne looked up and saw him standing, neat, grey, urban, a figure from another world.

"Where's Gryson?"

"I suggested that he should ride on to the village. It happens that I possess no lethal weapons in my house. I have never been—er—a great taker of life."

The thoughts boiling in Carne's head could assume no articulate expression. He paused a moment to recapture control of his feelings, then asked, "Do you know who put up that wire?"

"Certainly," said the little alderman. "Stathers, my tenant. He did so on my suggestion."

"At your suggestion," repeated Carne, breathing hard, his hand still automatically fondling the ears of the dying mare. "I see. Good of you to acknowledge it."

"Not at all. Why not? I am sorry you have had an accident, but I always said that hunting was a risky game, even for others beside the fox."

"It's not marked."

"No? Any compulsion? You weren't asked, you know, to come galloping over my land."

Snaith was still in the best of tempers, mild, superior.

"My God," half whispered Carne. "Don't you see your bloody carelessness has cost the life of a beautiful mare and hurt a man, and you haven't even got a gun so that I can put her out of her suffering?"

"I realise that this is hardly an appropriate moment to discuss the ethics of fox-hunting. But if fifty grown-up men will amuse themselves by riding after one little animal to watch it torn to pieces by dogs, on other people's property, they must accept the consequences."

Hicks said afterwards that he couldn't tell what might not have happened if Gryson had not then come cantering up with an old service revolver borrowed from an ex-soldier in the village.

"It's loaded all right. Shall I do it?"

"No. Give it to me."

Carne put the muzzle against the mare's head and pulled the trigger.

The body plunged once and was still.

"Was she insured?" asked the practical Gryson.

"No."

Then, what with a broken shoulder and, he declared later, a broken heart, life became too much for George Hicks. He fainted.

They refused Snaith's offers of help, revived the groom with brandy from Carne's flask, and Gryson fetched a car.

The alderman stood by, polite, sardonic, co-operative and ignored.

Carne took his injured employee back to Maythorpe, arranging for the disposal of his poor mare's carcass. He missed the afternoon meeting of the Highways and Bridges Sub-Committee.

CHAPTER II

COUNCILLOR HUGGINS INCURS AN OBLIGATION

"Oh, God," prayed Councillor Huggins, "Thou knowest that I am a sinner. But I know it, too. I never pretended to be better than other men, or to be able to get on without Thee. Oh, God, to Whom the hearts of all men be open, Thou knowest that if once I get out of this mess, I'll never sin this way again, so long as I live."

The bus swayed and rattled along the Dollstall road. Councillor Huggins was on his way to take the mid-week evening Sisterhood Service at Spunlington. Until that morning he had forgotten this engagement. He was a careless man, jotting down appointments, business details and notes for sermons on the backs of envelopes, and stuffing them into his pockets. It was in the pocket of his mechanic's overalls only worn on the rare occasions when he himself repaired his lorries, that he had found the note about this evening's service scribbled on an old invoice.

It had turned him sick.

He sat down on the bench in his tool-shed staring at it, running over in his mind a dozen different evasions. He could send a wire pleading illness. He could pretend to forget. He could . . .

He had never meant to enter Spunlington again.

It had seemed such a simple resolution. The village was off the beaten track. His lorries rarely visited it on business. In any case, he could always send a driver. It did not belong to the Kiplington or Cold Harbour divisions of the council. . . .

He had forgotten the chapel and his ministry; yet here he was, swinging down the dark country road in the lighted steaming chariot of the bus, on his way to fulfil the engagement so light-heartedly made three months ago.

At least, in the end, he had not tried to run away. Surely God would count that to him for righteousness? He was on the Lord's business. If this involved, not only fatigue and effort, but the grave imperilling of his reputation, surely that only increased his merit? After all, we are but little children weak. All men are sinners. What if, in a careless moment (three careless moments, to be precise,) he had sinned with Bessy Warbuckle? He had seduced no virgin; and he had not been unfaithful to his wife, for Nell was no wife to him these days, and he was tolerably certain that the child which Bessy was trying to father on to him was another man's.

But proof would be awkward. The whole business was awkward.

He bowed his head on his hands. His beard was wet with sweat. He wrestled with God.

After all, life had not been easy for him. Since the birth of his third daughter his wife had lived with him as though she were his sister. That was hard on a man of normal instincts, a kind man, who would not force himself where he was not wanted, a God-fearing man, who preferred to take his pleasure within the law.

For eight years now he had enjoyed, as you might say, no home comforts, and Bessy Warbuckle was notoriously anybody's girl for half a crown or an evening's fun in Kingsport.

"I can't face it. Oh, God, I can't face it."

Supposing she turned up there in the chapel, her eyes black as boot buttons, her smile bold as brass? Her tilted nose, blue hat and bright cheeks floated towards him in a vision. How could he preach the Lord's word with sin staring at him?

They had oil lamps at Spunlington which stank; the harmonium wheezed and creaked. Bessy might stand up and denounce him in the chapel.

Yet he was going. Every rotation of the wheels brought him a little nearer. Because to have run away would mean permanent, irreparable defeat.

"Unto Thee will I cry, O Lord, my strength! Think no scorn of me. O pluck me not away, neither destroy me with the ungodly and wicked doers. I will wash my hands in innocency, O Lord. And so will I go to Thy altar. . . ."

Supposing she had not seen the notice?

7.30 Sisterhood Meeting. Address by Councillor Alfred Ezekiel Huggins of Pidsea Buttock.

Supposing she never came at all? That letter might have been a try-out. How did he know she had not sent a dozen others to her more vulnerable clients?

He would dismiss all thought of her. He would remember happier things, the meeting, for instance of the Highways and Bridges Sub-Committee last Monday. Snaith was a card. Snaith was a wonder. What really had happened about the Ministry of Transport? Beale swore he had never known that the Ministry had been approached directly. How much had Snaith done on his own responsibility?

It was there, certainly. All straightforward and above board. Astell was dead keen. It was Astell who said, "If we get the road, we shall get the Leame Ferry Waste housing estate. One leads to the other." Queer chap, Astell. A crank. But he had guts.

If the road ran direct from Skerrow up to Kiplington, it must cross the Wastes, and if it crossed the Wastes. . . .

The wilderness and the solitary place should be glad for them. They would triumph. They would bring such happiness to Kingsport that future generations should call them blessed.

Unless—

Like a tormenting fly, buzzing round the desk in a hot chapel, fear returned to him. If Bessy denounced him, if she named him as father of her child, it was not only that he would be exploited, pillaged, mocked. All that was nothing. But he would lose his chances of the Lord's own service—the addresses he delivered, the visits he paid, the work on the council, the slum clearance, the houses built, the roads made.

And a highway shall be there and a way, and it shall be called the way of holiness. The wayfaring men, though fools, shall not err therein.

Oh, God, if I stand by you, stand by me in my peril—in my hour of bitter need. Cut me not off from the congregation of the righteous.

The bus came to a halt in Dollstall market place. The first stage of Huggins' journey was achieved. He descended, looking down almost in wonder at the curved cloth of his black preaching coat thrust out before him.

Fear is a fire which burns without consuming. Mr. Huggins had passed through it, but remained visibly unaltered. His too, too solid flesh did not melt, though his pulses pounded, his skin perspired, and the boiled egg he had eaten with his tea lay like a leaden weight across his chest. His mind leapt from triviality to triviality.

Carne wouldn't like the Kiplington Road scheme, but Carne hadn't bothered to turn up at the meeting. A day's pleasure was more to him than the county's business. Fox-hunting. What papish monks had been called the Hounds of God? These were hounds of the devil. Huggins had once preached a first-rate sermon against fox-hunting.

The Dollstall market-place harboured peace. The shopkeepers were putting up their shutters, quenching the streams of golden light that rolled across the shadowed pavements.

Oh, God, how easy and pleasant it must be to live as little shopkeepers, to close one's shutters for the night, to retreat into the cosy firelit kitchen, to drink cocoa for supper with one's family, to be untouched by sins and dreams and missions, unafraid of conscience, undriven by desire. Deliver me, deliver me, O God, from the evil doers of whom I am chief.

Then it seemed to Mr. Huggins as though God laid His calming hand upon him and told him to be a man and go and have a drink.

There was a quarter of an hour to wait for the Spunlington bus. The windows of the Tanner's Arms glowed like rubies behind their crimson blinds.

God tempered the wind to the shorn lamb, and, though it was not always easy to recognise His commandments, Huggins was an experienced disciple. Before peculiarly exacting spiritual ordeals, he would permit himself little harmless relaxations—a tin of salmon for tea, an extra pipe of tobacco, a squint through the closet window at Mrs. Riley washing herself at the sink next door. God knew that a warrior in His service must have his rum ration before he went over the top.

Mr. Huggins entered the Tanner's Arms and found young Lovell Brown, the cub-reporter, there before him.

Lovell did not look in the least like an angel with a flaming sword at the gate of paradise. He stood sipping cheap sherry and trying to warm his feet after three hours spent at an autumn ploughing match on the wolds and a long cold bus ride; but he recalled Huggins to his sense of responsibility.

"Ginger ale," the councillor ordered sullenly. Beastly stuff, popping about in your guts. But he had told this youth that he was a teetotaller, and he had a public reputation to maintain.

Lovell grinned cheerfully.

"Good-evening, councillor. Cold, isn't it?"

"Nice nip in the air."

"Off anywhere?"

"Preaching—at Spunlington. Sisterhood."

If it was the Lord's will, it was the Lord's will, and at least he was accounting truly and openly for his movements. "We ought to see more of you young people nowadays at chapel."

"You don't give us time," grinned Lovell. "Work us too hard. They told me I shouldn't have anything to do in the South Riding. But look at it. Concerts, football, ploughing matches, hunting accidents. . ."

"None of those lately, are there?"

"On Monday. A fellow called Hicks, groom to Carne of Maythorpe. Broke a shoulder and killed a horse near Minston Allotments."

"Was Carne with him?"

"Yes. Valuable horse, I understand. He took the groom home."

So that was why Carne had not come to the meeting. Truly a sign from heaven. This is the Lord's doing, and it is marvellous in our eyes.

No withdrawal now. God meant the salvation of the South Riding to go forward. Huggins was a humble instrument in His hands.

He lurched out, to see the Spunlington bus lumber up from Flintonbridge. "Nothing's ever as bad as you think it's going to be." He repeated to himself this tag that had been his consolation in former times of trouble. It had never failed. It would not fail him now.

And, sure enough, when he arrived at Spunlington, there was Mrs. Barker, her face like a rising sun beyond the misted glass of the bus window. There was his name printed large on the chapel notice-board. There was the congregation nicely filled out for a week-day meeting. And there was no Bessy Warbuckle.

Councillor Huggins rose on the tide of his elation. He announced the psalm, "The Lord is my shepherd"; he prayed with deep, tender understanding for those in trouble; he preached an address so kind, so intimate, so human, that Mrs. Barker pressed his hand afterwards—an unprecedented demonstration—and besought him to come to her house for supper until bus time. Instead of lurking cold, wretched, hunted in the dark lanes with Bessy Warbuckle, he sat in Mrs. Barker's cosy parlour, a citadel of safety, drinking cocoa, eating apple pasties, welcomed with respect and gratitude, assured that his words had brought help and comfort to many.

Oh, it was better to be good than to do evil. Whoso dwelleth under the shadow of the Most High shall never stumble. Never again, no never, would Alfred Huggins stray from the paths of righteousness.

"There are times," said Mrs. Barker, handing cocoa-nut buns frilled with a freshly netted d'oyly, "when a word in season is a real gift from God."

"I was moved to-night," said Mr. Huggins humbly. His spoon stirred the thick rich cocoa and melting sugar. "I was moved. Not unto us . . ."

He meant it. Tears moistened his eyelids. He felt good and weak and simple. The Lord had been his shepherd. He had wanted nothing.

It was 9.45 and bus time.

"Now don't come out. You've been good enough. I'm set up with that hot drink."

The door opened into the darkness of the road and closed again. He groped in thick mud towards the bus stop.

"Alfred," said Bessy Warbuckle's hoarse unhappy voice. "I've been waiting for you all evening."

Now, steady, steady. At any moment the bus might turn the corner and carry him off to safety. O God, Thou has been my refuge. . . .

"Good-evening, Bessy. Well. I saw you weren't in chapel."

"You've been preaching up there in chapel. You've been sucking up to Widow Barker. God's good man, you are. But I know what you are. I know what you've made me."

"Come now. Come now, Bessy. Run away now. I shall miss my bus."

"It's you who run away." She clung to his arm, her heavy body against his. "But you won't run far. I'll write to your wife. I'll tell Mrs. Barker. I'll go to Alderman Snaith. He's a magistrate and chairman of that home for poor girls in trouble. He'll see right done by me. A dirty old man like you, and me not eighteen till Martinmas."

"That's a lie."

"Is it? Wait till you've seen my birth certificate."

"It's not my responsibility."

"Oh, yes, it is. And I can prove it. Reg Aythorne says he saw us coming together out of Back End Plantin' night of harvest festival."

"What do you want me to do?"

Nothing's ever so bad—dear God—sweet Christ—nothing's ever so bad. Don't take away my chance of serving You. . . .

"Reg says he'll marry me and father it if you'll make it worth his while—Five hundred pounds down—It'll buy that shop in Station Road we wanted."

"You're mad. I haven't got it."

"I was mad. I'm not now. I've learned a thing or two. Treated like a slut and you canoodling with fat widows! Beloved minister for you and the best chair by the fire—workhouse infirmary for me and a charge of soliciting. I don't think! But I'm not having any. Five hundred to Reg and me and you'll hear no more about it."

"Bessy—I can't—"

"Before new year—or I'll tell Mr. Snaith. . . ."

The last bus came rattling round the corner—a lighted chariot. But it carried no safety to Councillor Huggins. No safety on earth, no rest, no peace, no hope. Oh, God! Oh, God! he cried as he jumped aboard.

But this time there was no sign from heaven. The worst had happened.

CHAPTER III

TOM SAWDON DECIDES TO BUY A DOG

When Tom Sawdon bought the Nag's Head on the road between Maythorpe and Cold Harbour, he did not know that it would kill his wife. For several months Lily had seemed tired and out of sorts, but Police-Sergeant Burt, who knew all about these things, told him that middle-aged women were often like that. Look at his missus! Hadn't enjoyed a bite of solids for three years back before he took her to Cleethorpes. Sea air and time. That was what women in their difficult age all wanted. Sea air and time.

After twenty-six years of marriage, Tom Sawdon was still in love with his wife. Burt used to say he'd never seen enough of her to find it too much. Well, there might be something in that. He'd never been long at home. Before the war he'd driven a motor van for the North Eastern Railway. Then he'd driven an R.T.O. Colonel's car in France until he and his officer had got to know each other and after demobilisation the colonel asked him if he'd like to keep on at the job. You bet. Who wouldn't? So he'd driven in Turkey and Tangiers and Mexico for the colonel, who had a stiff arm and needed attention. He'd seen a bit of the world, had Tom, while Lily lived on quietly in the house at Weetwood. Then in 1932 the colonel got 'flu, and the lung that had been touched with gas went back on him, and he died, leaving to his chauffeur, a still young, handy, experienced, athletic fellow, with grown-up married daughters, a legacy of £750 and the big Sunbeam saloon.

It was only then that Tom noticed the change in Lily's health, and learned that its cure lay in sea air. With him, to think was to act, a virtue in a chauffeur. He saw the advertisement of the Nag's Head for sale in the Yorkshire Record, took his cap from the peg, told Lily to expect him when she saw him, and drove off in the Sunbeam to the South Riding.

Visited on a warm August day, the inn attracted him. The heavy wagons creaked past in the slanting sunlight; on the stacks beyond the chestnut trees, labourers were forking. "That'll put a thirst on a man," observed Mr. Drew, who was acting for the late publican's executors. There was only one pub at Maythorpe, a squalid little alehouse kept by a quarrelsome widow, ripe to lose her licence at any moment. Cold Harbour had none at all. It was obvious to Tom that the Nag's Head stood in a grand position. Between a rural village and a colony of ex-servicemen smallholders, with cyclists swooping down like a flock of starlings and all the seaside traffic south of Kiplington, what more could he want? As for sea air, you had only to lift your nose—about a mile from the coast, said Drew—well, a mile and a half, then.

Tom was no fool, but he believed the evidence of his own eyes. Having seen so much of the world at large he did not realise how little he knew of the South Riding. He bought the inn on the nail, dashed back to Lily and was prepared to see her a strong woman and himself a rich man before a twelve month. He knew that he could make himself popular. He knew that Lily could cook and manage a house. He saw the Nag's Head becoming as famous as the Catterick Bridge Hotel, or the Bell, Hendon.

It just happened that there were a few vital matters which he had not foreseen.

He did not know that the late licensee had drunk himself to death from loneliness and disappointment, that the Cold Harbour colonists could hardly make a living and had no extra cash for Bass and Guinness, that for nine months of the year the Maythorpe Road was practically deserted. Nor did he know that his wife was dying of cancer.

She knew.

When Tom went on his voyage of exploration to the South Riding, she visited a specialist in Leeds and received confirmation of her panel doctor's diagnosis. The trouble, they said, was too deep-seated to be operable; but it might be arrested by treatment, if she visited the hospital twice a week as an out-patient. Otherwise . . . a year, they said, or two at the most, would finish her.

She was lying on the sofa, drinking a cup of tea, and wondering how she should tell Tom without disturbing him, when he burst in, pleased as a schoolboy with his purchase, and laid the Nag's Head at her feet, his gift to her, a reward for her fidelity, a pledge that he had come home to settle down and confide his volatile person to her keeping.

Lily Sawdon had certain kinds of courage, but not the kind which would enable her to shatter that happy confidence. She said nothing.

Competent, except when crippled by pain, quiet and smiling, she packed her furniture, sent it ahead on a van, and followed with Tom to her new home in the Sunbeam.

Perhaps Tom was right. Perhaps sea air would cure her. Miracles sometimes happened. Mrs. Deane, their neighbour, was a Christian Scientist and said that illness was only error, mind conquered matter and everything was God. All the way to the Nag's Head Lily Sawdon prayed that God would justify Mrs. Deane.

But when she saw her new home, God and her courage both momentarily failed her.

The weather had broken. The strong October rain beat down into the tawny stubble. The wagon wheels had churned the yard to treacly clay. The inn was lost in dirt, the tap-room filthy, the yard a morass, the storehouse a den of broken bottles, the bedrooms damp, the earth closets unspeakable.

For half an hour Lily sat among the packing-cases and wept—not so much for her present pain and her coming death, for Tom and his reckless, hot-headed, stubborn ways, for her lost strength and hopeless situation, as for the damage done to her rosewood cabinet on the lorry. But after a good cup of tea she pulled herself together. By the end of the month they had both worked miracles. The kitchen behind the tap-room shone with bright chocolate-coloured paint and polished brasses. Tom chose a sensible wallpaper, patterned with nice brown cherries. There was a green cloth on the table, there were plants in the window, the wireless on the chest of drawers, and arm-chairs by the fire. It was a kitchen in which you could offer teas to any one. ("Tenpence a head. Tea. Bread and butter and jam, as much as they like. Then they'll tip twopence and we shall get a shilling," said Tom.) The tap-room itself was lovely, painted bright green, with oilcloth on the floor and three spitoons and Tom's Jerry shell-cases on the mantelpiece. There were petrol pumps in the yard, and a garage made out of the old stable, and a woman for an hour every morning to give Lily a hand.

Nothing was lacking now except the clients.

"Give us a month or two to work it up and it'll be a little gold mine," Tom promised Lily, as they lay awake in the room above the kitchen. And she would clutch to her side the hot water bottle which was now her only relief from dragging pain, and be grateful for the darkness which prevented the necessity for her careful smiles.

The weather grew worse and worse, the roads more desolate; but Mr. Drew, interviewed angrily in Kingsport, declared that it was only a matter of patience. "Wait till the spring. You'll never know the place. Anglers, motorists, cyclists. . . ."

They were prepared to wait until the spring.

Meanwhile the little tap-room was not empty.

Every morning Chrissie Beachall turned up to earn her tenpence, scrubbing floors, washing clothes, cleaning bedrooms. Every evening her husband came, as regularly, to spend it.

Mr. Topper Beachall was a roadman, employed by the county council, and earning £1 7s. 8d. a week. He had living with him his wife Chrissie, his five children, and his wife's father, an old-age pensioner, a very clean, gentle and kind old man who asked for nothing better than to be able to work in his garden all day, and to drink his half-pint in peace at the pub in the evenings. What with the washing and baking, the babies' nappies and Chrissie's nagging, the cottage, two up, two down, held little peace for him. By November he had adopted the Nag's Head as his second home.

Tom and Lily were worried about the Beachalls. When they knew how hard Chrissie worked, and what a pinch she had to make both ends meet, it did not seem right that Topper and Grandpa Sellars should come every night to the inn, spending their money. Tom didn't quite know what they ought to do about it. He wished the colonel were still alive. He'd have known all right. Lily had to listen to Tom for hours going on about the ethical justification of selling drinks to a chap, when you know his kiddies are hungering. She soothed their conscience by giving broken scraps and half-worn clothes to Chrissie.

But Chrissie's earnings were not the only ones that found their way through the till—though they might be put in at night and taken out in the morning. Tom had dreamed of his pub becoming a general club-house for the ex-servicemen of Cold Harbour Colony where they could count upon congenial company, and he was right there. The only difference was that, though they had plenty to say, they had little to spend. Half a pint of pale ale, some ginger beer or a packet of five Woodbines had to serve as excuse to sit through a long wet evening in front of the tap-room fire. There were darts; there were dominoes; there was talk about old times and new troubles, and best of all, there were the host and hostess, Tom so sanguine and talkative, Lily so quiet, but always bonny to look at, always a lady.

The Nag's Head was a very pleasant place.

Thus one November evening Grandpa Sellars sat smoking by the fire and watching his son-in-law playing dominoes with George Hicks, whose arm was still in a sling from his broken collar-bone. It was not a profitable company, though Hicks paid for his drinks and was a good fellow. But the place looked like an inn. Tom felt like a landlord. He leaned against the bar, polishing glasses, and considered that a stranger entering could not fail to observe that the place at least seemed cosy and comfortable—a proper village pub. It satisfied Tom's æsthetic sense.

The latch clinked and a new comer entered—a commercial traveller, post-war vintage, with sleeked hair, pretentious accent, noisy motor-cycle, and the expectation of impressing his companions. He dropped his case of art silk stockings and jumpers in the corner and asked for a pint of Bass and some bread and cheese.

His arrival, and his demands, seemed to bring a new atmosphere into the place, though until he had satisfied hunger and thirst he did not talk. The others kept quiet. Tom was the only person who appeared to have noticed him. Perhaps this piqued him, for, after draining his glass and flicking the crumbs from his plus-fours with a stylish if dirty purple handkerchief, he sat up and took patronising notice of the company.

"Cosy little spot, you've got here," he observed to Tom. "Have a gasper?"

"Thanks." Tom accepted one from the ostentatious gilt case.

"A bit dead-and-alive, isn't it? Other end of nowhere, eh? But I suppose if you've never seen anything different, you don't know what you miss."

"No," said Tom.

"Been here long?"

"So-so."

"I suppose when they run the new road through Minston out to Kiplington, you'll get even less traffic this way."

Roads were Topper's speciality. He looked up from his dominoes.

"Roads?" he asked. "Who's talking of a new road?"

"I am." The stranger flicked cigarette ash with a finicking finger. "Haven't you heard? They're going to open up South Riding north of the railway line—run a big road straight to Kiplington from Skerrow and Minston."

"I've heard nowt about it," repeated Topper, "and if any one knows owt about roads, it's me."

"Indeed? Well—it appears that the county councillors know better. They must have forgotten to consult you."

"I'm so to speak a civil servant," grunted Topper. "I work on roads and I know."

The stranger ignored him. "About time, I suppose, that the other side of the railway line had a chance. After all, the council's been pouring money like water into the colony. These farmers. They think they own the world, and little wonder. Look at the way the government spoils them." He was fairly launched into his hobby now—the old cry of the town against the country. The authorities wasted money on subsidising an industry that could not possibly pay, drained marshes, gave grants for sugarbeet, built fold yards, and their money's worth vanished as soon as it was spent.

"Now a bit spent on Kiplington and you would see it back. There's not a decent health resort, as you might say, in the South Riding. Not a bad site perhaps, but needs developing."

"Over-developed," growled Topper. "When you say development you mean bathing-belles. I've gotta family and I'm a good chapel man. Ask any one."

"Bathing belles? Well, I won't say a few mightn't improve it. But what about a skating rink, a good dance palace, and dog tracks? There's a deal of money to be made nowadays at the dogs."

"Made and lost," said Grandpa Sellars, removing his pipe and spitting with great sagacity. "Made and lost."

"Some one has to lose," said the stranger. "That's economics. The question is—who loses? That's progress. And I say the farmers have lost enough for us already. But perhaps you've never seen dog-racing in these parts?"

The question was meant to be offensive. The stranger was offensive.

Tom winked at George Hicks. He was enjoying himself. It was part of his role as popular landlord to keep offensive strangers at their distance. He picked up a glass, already polished to perfection, and squinted at it critically.

"That's right," he said quietly. "I've never seen dog-racing in these parts. But I remember a little place in Florida—two years ago it would be—eight dogs, quarter-mile track, I was there when Blue Velvet beat the world's record for the quarter on a quarter-mile track at 24.38 seconds. Twenty-five thousand people in the grandstand. No. I've not seen any dog-racing in these parts."

The traveller stared—trying not to appear deflated.

"Ah. So you've been in the States?"

"Haven't you?"

"Well—not exactly—I mean, not yet," said the commercial traveller.

The latch clicked again and Bill Heyer, the big one-armed colonist from Cold Harbour, entered.

Tom winked again.

"'Evening, Bill. I owe you a pint, don't I?"

He didn't, but he guessed that Bill had dropped in for a packet of Woodbines and would fade out again with equal abruptness unless tempted to stay, and Tom needed him.

"This gennelman here," continued Tom, pouring beer with an expert hand, "says we ought to start the dogs at Kiplington."

"Go on."

"Why not roulette? Why not baccarat? Remember Le Touquet, Bill?"

"Ah."

"Those frog places—They're not so hot. Remember that chink place at Deauville, George?"

Hicks had made one excursion abroad, taking horses to Deauville. Tom made the most of it. Then, having established the sophistication of Hicks and Heyer, he proceeded to enlarge upon his own experience. The commercial traveller, who had prepared to put it across a group of country yokels in a dreary pub at the other end of nowhere, found himself listening to casual mention of New York and Aden, Port Said, Constantinople and Vienna. He was the bumpkin, he who had never journeyed farther than Wembley Stadium for a cup-tie final. These veterans just ran rings round him, and he was not experienced enough to realise that they did it for his benefit.

He picked himself up and pulled himself together, a sadder if not a wiser citizen.

"Well, so long, folks." He tossed a shilling as though it were a sovereign on to the table. "Got to make Kingsport to-night."

"Mind you make it strong then," tittered Grandpa Sellars.

"With the cheese, that's one and two," observed Tom coldly.

The traveller flung down two coppers and left, slamming the door. Tom grinned.

"Who's the little bed-bug?" asked Heyer.

"Blew in on the draught. Look here, Heyer, have you heard anything about this road from Kingsport to Kiplington?"

Heyer shook his head.

"There may be nothing in it. What I don't like is—where did he pick up this gossip?"

"If it had been owt about roads, I'd have known it," Topper reaffirmed.

"The point is—we know they're sore and jealous about the colony."

Heyer laughed.

"They'd better come and see us. There's not one of us with a pound in the bank or a well-stocked fold yard. Does Carne know owt?"

"Well," said Hicks cautiously. "I don't take much heed of council doings, and he's no talker. But there was something I know a bit back upset him, because they had a meeting the day I caught that wire," he indicated his shoulder. "I know he missed a committee, and I know he was fair put out. I heard him telling Captain Gryson. He said, 'It's that damned Snaith again. A man that'ud put up wire and never mark it is capable of anything.'"

"That'll be it. Snaith's dead set on developing Kiplington and yon parts north of the railway. He's said before that we've had too much of our own way down here. Our own way—By God! I'd like him to see my books."

They jeered, but there was anxiety in their laughter. Tom knew enough already to realise that a big new road and the consequent development of Kiplington would shift regular traffic and, still more, summer visitors, northwards. Heyer knew that he and his fellows in Cold Harbour Colony were singularly at the mercy of the Council. Both men were gamblers. Both had pluck. But they were realists enough to appreciate the precariousness of fortune.

Tom didn't like it.

His vanity was imperilled. He had seen himself carrying Lily off, making their fortune, proving that it takes a man who has seen the world to be a man of the world. But sometimes, for a second, there opened before him a dark pool of doubt in which he saw reflected not the virile, successful, dashing, volatile ex-soldier, but a reckless fool gulled into investing all his capital in a moribund business in a dying area.

He knew one certain way of reassurance.

He strolled off to seek Lily in the kitchen.

At least to his wife he was still a hero and adventurer. She saw him most satisfactorily, as he wished to see himself. In her calm presence he knew he was Tom Sawdon, the Colonel's trusted friend, the conquering lover, the popular host of a successful inn.

It happened that Lily had had a good day. She was thinking: Perhaps it's all nonsense; perhaps I shall grow out of it.

She sat darning stockings and listening to the radio.

"Oh, Tom, do stop and listen a bit," she pleaded, her charming head on one side, her lips parted. "It's Elsie and Doris Waters. They are a scream."

This was how he liked to think of her—enthroned by the fire that he had lit, in the chair he bought her, her cheeks flushed with pleasure, her fair hair only a trifle faded, a blue ribbon round her still pretty throat.

It was not possible that their venture could fail. He had never failed. The external intervention of contrary political interests simply did not enter into a world which had preserved Tom Sawdon through war and peace and brought him safely to haven at Cold Harbour.

Yet he felt the need of action. He was anxious, and all anxiety, all sorrow and disappointment bored him. He must transform circumstances until they gave him cause for pleasure. He must prove the little scut wrong. He would go to Kingsport. He would listen to gossip.

He would know for certain.

"I may have to go to Kingsport to-morrow, Lil. Think you can manage?"

"Why not? Haven't I managed all those years when you went rattling away to the ends of the earth?"

Ah, that was it. He had left her too often. He had wasted long years of her beauty and serenity.

"Are you afraid Grandpa Sellars will run off with me?"

That gave him an idea.

I know—by God—I'll buy her a dog. That'll be company for her.

He was restless, and knew that he must go somewhere, do something, put an end to the doubts teasing him. But he must also buy her something and prove his love for her. He must buy her a dog, for dogs went with the picture of successful inn-keeping which he had formed in his mind—a happy twilight—Darby and Joan, the firelit parlour and the dog. Something handsome and exotic—a Great Dane, an Alsatian. Something that would give character to the Inn and pay tribute to Lily's quality—a watch dog, a present, a love token—because he was disturbed by the rumour of a road north of the railway line, because he had played that evening the high-handed host of the Nag's Head, because he loved his wife, and because he liked dogs.

His mind was made up. He would buy a dog to-morrow.

CHAPTER IV

SARAH ACQUIRES AN ALLY, AND CARNE AN ENEMY

"I wouldn't go, Mr. Astell, I wouldn't really. It's not as if you held with them voluntary hospitals."

Mrs. Corner, Alderman Astell's landlady, paid spasmodic tribute to Socialist theory as she understood it, whenever it coincided with Astell's interests. This was not often. The conviction which had driven him through desperate poverty to a hardly-earned schoolmastership, out of school into a conscientious objector's prison, from prison to a semi-amateur printing press on the Clyde, from Scotland to Dublin, Dublin to South Africa, and from South Africa back, a physical wreck, to England, had done, she considered, damage enough already. She held no brief for it. Her late husband had voted first Radical, then Labour, but now here was Mr. Astell turning out on a cold November night, with a sea roke blowing, to sit up till all hours in a stuffy hall just because the Mayor, who was a friend of his, had asked him, as the new alderman, to present the prizes at the Hospital Fancy Ball.

"I've no patience," said Mrs. Corner, who had nursed one man till his death through pneumonia and pulmonary tuberculosis, and had no desire to bury another for the same reason. "Go out and sit talking there till midnight and wake up to-morrow with one of your coughing fits, but don't say I didn't warn you. You'll go and kill yourself one of these days and then may be you will be satisfied."

Astell was not afraid of death. He was afraid of a hæmorrhage, of a sanitorium, of the survival of his restless mind imprisoned within a helpless body. When he returned a doomed man from the Transvaal, he had been told that any further political campaign or emotional excitement might finish him off quickly. Only by a quiet light routine in the open air, and preferably by the sea, could he hope to preserve some kind of utility during the crippled remnant of his life.

"Live like a cabbage," said the doctors. Astell, coughing, sick, exhausted by fever and emaciated by hæmorrhage, submitted to their orders. Once he had known himself. He had been a fighter, driven by faith, shrinking from no hardship. In his Glasgow days nothing had been too much for him. He knew well that he was distinguished by no special talent; but to possess energy beyond the common run seemed simply a matter of individual choice. Others could speak better, write better, negotiate better. Joe Astell worked. He would do anything, go anywhere. Even when he married, he chose a little Jewess, gay, dark, equally ardent, selfless, who followed him from Glasgow to Dublin, where he went to report on Black and Tan outrages, from Dublin to Lanarkshire again, then died from influenza in 1924, before he left to work as a trade union organiser among the native miners in the Transvaal. He had thought himself inexhaustible, if ever he thought of himself at all, until the week when he had collapsed, after a speaking tour, with what at first was thought to be pneumonia, and which developed into tuberculosis. He had spent three months in South African Hospitals, then he had come to England for an operation at the Fulham Hospital for Tuberculosis. From that time he had been a stranger to himself, constantly ailing, unable to be sure that he could keep an appointment or fulfil a promise, horrified by his own unreliability, ashamed of impotence.

His colleagues had been kind to him. In Yorkshire there had been a little printing press kept by the deceased John Henry Corner. He had turned out pamphlets, leaflets and a small local monthly paper cheaply for the trade unions and co-operative societies. It was suggested that Astell should inherit his work—a light job, run as an excuse for pensioning invalids. So he came to Yorkshire, lodged with Mrs. Corner, and slept in the garden hut built for her late husband.

There were days when he could not work at all, nights when he lay in terror waiting for the cough which tore his body, dawns when he woke with racing pulses, hunted down corridors of dreams by hounds of fancy. Yet, month by month, confidence returned to him, his attacks of fever recurred less frequently, he dared to stand for election to the County Council, and find himself a councillor, then alderman, the pampered lodger of good Mrs. Corner, the guest of the Mayor of Kiplington at a dance for the Cottage Hospital.

The hot air from the Floral Hall puffed out as the door opened and hit him like a blow. The powdered chalk from the dance-floor made him cough. But he handed his coat to a boy scout and went forward doggedly, when necessary he smiled at an acquaintance, shook hands with the Mayor, and permitted himself to be led up to a row of basket-work arm-chairs on the platform. There he sat, under palms and paper festoons, a silent, lean, lonely man, with a flushed pretty face, as incongruous as a mask. Before him whirled pierrots and Dutchmen, Quakers and Oriental Ladies. Beside him sat clergy and doctors and councillors. At his feet the Jazz Octette crooned soulfully.

Joe watched the Carnival and thought of death. "If you killed yourself at it, you might be satisfied," Mrs. Corner had said. Perhaps she was right. For what tormented Joe was not his career cut short nor his threatened life, but that he was living while better men were dead. He thought of them—of O'Leary shot in a Dublin yard in '21, of Mullard worn out in the strike of '23, of Cook, Grimshaw, Vender, of his wife, Rebecca. These had been warriors. The movement could ill spare them. Yet they were gone and he remained, a semi-invalid, nursing himself, coddled and comforted, presenting prizes, if you please, instead of giving 'em hell at a street corner.

There had been a time when he had railed against his treacherous body. It had seemed then that his disease alone was enemy enough for him. He had sweated and agonised and panicked. He had woken at dawn to wonder if he would live to see the noon. He had feared to sleep, lest he should be awakened by a hæmorrhage.

But now that was over. The disease was temporarily checked, and he had time to turn his attention to a battle in which he had allowed himself to be put upon permanent light duty. Surely other men had fought to the end and died in harness? What was he waiting for? In what future event would his existence be of such importance that he must treasure it now while his betters went into the fighting line and died?

"Glad to see you, Astell. Good of you to come."

"I say, ought you to be here? On such a night? Why, that is good of you."

They crowded round him. They were pleased to see him. Their friendliness embarrassed him, and made him cough; his coughing increased their sense of obligation. He was in a trap of humbug. He loathed his popularity. If he had done his duty, they would have hated him. Their cordiality was the measure of his defeat.

"Hope you're keeping as well as possible," said Mr. Peckover. "Don't think I've seen you since you achieved your new honour. Allow me to congratulate you."

"The first Socialist, surely, to be made an alderman in the South Riding? I don't agree with your politics, you know, Astell; but we know we can trust you to keep them in the background, eh? No politics where the South Riding's concerned, eh?"

Oh damn them, damn them! Every word insulted him. There was not a soul here, not a soul, who could understand what he felt about it all. Why had he come? Why had he thought it his duty?

Fool, fool, fool!

The waltz ceased. The Jazz Octette departed. The Ladies' Committee ran out with little tables, and set on them plates of queen cakes and tarts and sandwiches—ham, salmon and potted beef—trifle and jellies. Four people, not in fancy dress, made for the table immediately below Astell's seat—a big fine one-armed man, a plump talkative middle-aged woman, a handsome, smiling, merry man with a smart moustache, and his faded pretty wife. Astell recognised the one-armed fellow as Heyer, the ex-service man from Cold Harbour Colony. He did not know the others, but he saw the care with which both men attended the fragile pretty woman, heard her called "Lily," and also "Mrs. Sawdon," and realised that these might be the new host and hostess of the Nag's Head at Maythorpe. He liked the look of Sawdon, a pleasant fellow, and found himself listening to their conversation.

"Well, we had only the girls, but if I'd six sons," Sawdon was saying, "I'd put 'em all into the Army or the Police Force. Army for choice. The King's uniform—you can't beat it. It's a grand life if you know how to behave yourself."

"That's right," Heyer handed the widow a cup of coffee with his one hand. "You do know where you are in the Army."

"And look at trade now! Look at farming."

"That's right," agreed the widow.

Here, thought Joe Astell, is the raw material of canon fodder in capitalist quarrels. You know where you are in the Army—do you? He looked at Heyer's mutilated body; he thought of the millions dead in the Great War. He tried to confirm his certainty of conviction. His apt mind responded with a score of arguments. Not for a moment did he retract the opinions which had earned him imprisonment and contempt.

But the easy comradeship of these men wounded him. He liked them. They were comely and courageous, honest and gay and decent. In a big town he too would have had comrades. But here in Kiplington he was isolated. Here he lacked men of his own kidney, and these Colonists were his political opponents. He had fought against their interests on the council. He thought them over-favoured, the spoiled children of an outrageously unbusiness-like and sentimental administration. Their ideas were pernicious, their memories alien. Yet seated there between Mr. Peckover and a potted palm, his bowels yearned towards them.

He had become a Socialist through love of his fellow men, not through dislike of them, and now he felt an emotional barrier between himself and his neighbours which no logic could remove. He saw himself, an awkward priggish man, with a harsh voice and tactless manner, tolerated simply because illness had reduced his fighting powers, weakened his quality.

It was all wrong.

"I don't know if you've met our socialist alderman—Alderman Astell, Miss Burton, our new head mistress at the High School." Mr. Peckover beamed appropriately. Joe Astell found himself shaking hands with a small red-headed woman who reminded him so much of somebody that he stood staring at her.

Miss Burton smiled.

"He says 'Socialist Alderman' rather as if it were Prize Freak," she said unexpectedly. "Are socialists such rare birds here? Aldermen seem to be three a penny. May I sit down here?"

"Excuse me," said Joe in the solemn rasping voice which so much offended him. "Are you any relation to Miss Ellen Wilkinson?"

"Oh, the hair? No, I'm not. I wish I were. I think she's a grand girl. But hers is soft and beautiful with a natural wave. Mine's a vulgar frizz. It's very sad for me. Do you know her?"

"I've met her. There's some think she takes too much upon herself. But I liked her. I think she's got guts."

Guts.

He thought of the ex-service man and public house keeper below him. They had guts, but the wrong ideas. He had the right ideas but—would a man with guts have given way so easily? Would a chap like Heyer be sitting on that platform because he had only half a lung? Wouldn't he rather be carrying on somewhere, somehow?

The red-haired school mistress was talking. Her voice was attractive, deep, clear and amused. Joe thought of his own harsh solemn tones and hated them.

"I once took some of my girls to hear her speak in London. I thought it would do them good."

"Did it?"

"We-ell. I'm not sure. They liked her hair and her green frock, and her way of speaking. But I'm not sure how many took in any of her ideas."

"Did you want them to do that?"

"Well, I think any ideas are better than none for sixth form girls. They've got to go through their political adolescence, and I'd rather they fell for Ellen Wilkinson than—say—Oswald Mosley."

"You're a socialist then?"

"I'm a school-marm. I take no part in politics."

"That's evasion. You're either a socialist or not. There's no half-way house."

"Isn't there? I should have thought there were a dozen. If you mean—do I vote Labour? Yes, I do. I'm a blacksmith's daughter, you know. I come from the working-class and I feel with it. There are certain things I hate—muddle, poverty, war and so on—the things most intelligent people hate nowadays, whatever their party. And I hate indifferentism, and lethargy, and the sort of selfishness that shuts itself up into its own shell of personal preoccupations."

"That's all right as an emotional background, but emotion isn't enough."

"I know that. But it's the beginning. It prompts our first subconscious recoil from or attraction to new ideas. The emotions bred by our circumstances and nature decide where we shall get off, as they say. Or whether we get off at all. I'm a teacher and it's my job to watch young things. Some girls only react spontaneously to one group of ideas—say 'husband,' 'love,' 'babies,' and off they go quite clear of their direction—moved by a Life Force or instinct or whatever you choose to call it. Others, while they are still at school, are simply immature play-boys—mention games, colours, matches, sport, prizes and they're wide awake. With others the words exploitation, injustice, slavery, and so on start the wheels going round."

"You don't think it matters?"

"I don't think you can change the first and third groups much. You can educate their minds—give them a certain amount of knowledge to direct their energies. The middle group you might alter a bit—but many women, like many men, never grow up. They prefer games all their life. They like to attach their instincts for competition, achievement and the rest of it to something immediate, concrete and artificial—golf, bridge—even money making."

Joe watched her. He liked her eager ugly face, her quick confident speech. She was a woman of his own kind. He could imagine quarrelling with her to be great fun. His spirits rose. The sense of isolation sloughed from him.

"You're not really such a philosopher, I bet," he smiled at her. "I don't believe you naturally let ill alone."

"Good Lord, no. But after you've been teaching for nearly twenty years, you learn to accept some of nature's limitations."

The party at the lower table was enjoying itself. Mrs. Brimsley, the widow, had not had an evening in Kiplington for years. They were teasing her now about Bill Heyer. Joe saw Miss Burton listening with interest, her red head cocked, her face quizzical. She observed his attention.

"Who are they?"

He told her.

"I've driven round the colony. Three or four of our girls come from there. A grim place."

"Yes—a socialist experiment carried out by people who don't believe in socialism."

"Poor devils. Look here—are you on the Higher Education Committee?"

Joe shook his head.

"A pity. I'd like to do a bit of lobbying. Have you seen my buildings? How would you like to run a school with a basement full of black beetles?"

He laughed.

"It's all very well to laugh; but they get into our shoes. I have to pretend I don't mind and that the girls are idiots to be scared, but I'm simply terrified. I dream of them at nights. Can't you do anything? You're an alderman."

"Have you seen our council?"

"It seems to me that you hardly need to see it. Tell me—is there really any hope from any of them? They can't all be as reactionary as they seem."

"They're not. We have a few fellows with imagination."

He was thinking of Snaith and the clever work he had done with the new motor road to Kiplington. Get that through, and the Waste Housing Scheme was as good as adopted.

He began to explain to Miss Burton just why it was so important.

"It should affect you and your school too. At present this place is a dead end—the waste-paper basket of the South Riding, people have called it. They come here after they've failed in Kingsport or Hardrascliffe because the rates are low and the air's good and nobody keeps up an appearance. But—you wait . . . I'm not really an enthusiast about local government, but you do at least get solid concrete results—swimming baths, sewage farms." He smiled bitterly. "You begin by thinking in terms of world-revolution and end by learning to be pleased with a sewage farm."

The voices from the table below rose clearly.

"We'll get Carne down to the Club. We'll ask him for a lead. If Snaith thinks he can twist the Council round his finger, we'll teach him there's some one still works for our interests."

"It'll have to be after Christmas then," said Mrs. Brimsley. "There's the Children's Concert, and then the W.I. play, and then the Christmas parties."

"Will that be time enough? We don't want to wake up one morning and find the road laid and the Wastes drained and all our traffic lost, while we dance round Christmas trees."

"Nay—they won't start work till after Christmas. Scheme's got to be approved by Ministry of Transport," said the more easy-going Heyer.

The interval was over. The tables were being swept away again, the Jazz Octette returned. The four colonists moved their chairs against the wall. They were not dancers.

"What has Carne to do with this?" asked Sarah Burton.

"Oh, he'll fight the new road, I expect."

"Why should he?"

"Because he's a gentleman farmer—survival of the feudal system. Because he hates Snaith and does everything he can to block his programmes. Because whenever we propose anything for Kiplington and Kingsport, he drags up his fifty or so colonists. They're all ex-service men. Old Comrades of the Great War."

Sarah's sharp green eyes read his. She nodded.

Another black mark against Carne of Maythorpe. She knew now—through Mr. Tadman who told Mrs. Tadman who told Cissy who told Miss Parsons who had told Sarah, that Carne alone among the governors had opposed her appointment to the High School. He had done well. She was against him.

I know his type, she thought—aristocrats, conservatives, vindicators of tradition against experiment, of instinct against reason, of piety against progress. They were pleasant people, kind, gracious, attractive. They cultivated a warm human relationship between master and servant. They meant well. And they did evil.

She said as much to Astell.

"You know the story of the difference between the North and South Americans and their attitude towards the negroes? The Southerner says: 'You're a slave, God bless you;' the Northerner: 'You're a free man, damn you!' I remember how a man I used to know in South Africa said he loved the natives. He was an Afrikaans farmer who believed in flogging blacks for breach of the Masters and Servants Act."

"Of course—you were in Africa too."

"I hate this feudal love in which there's no give and take. 'I love the ladies.' 'I love my labourers.' Love needs the stiffening of respect, the give and take of equality."

She flushed. She was thinking of Ben and his attitude towards women, of Van Raalt and a hot night in Cape Province, when she stood among the orange and lemon blossom with violets at her feet, a night made for love and beauty and kisses, and she had wasted it arguing passionately about the colour question. She had broken with Van Raalt and determined to take a new post in Australia. Her South African dreams had exploded in a burst of anger. Her mother's illness had intervened; she had forgiven her puzzled lover long ago. But she still resented the sacrifice of so sweet a night.

She looked at the scene below her.

It seemed to her that the evening had melted into a triple fugue. There was the carnival—pierrots and butterflies, gypsies and Quaker girls flowed out again across the floor. The saxophone wailed its dirge—the closing song of 1932.

"No more money in the bank; No cute baby here to spank. What's to do about it? Let's turn out the lights an' go to bed."

Dancing, weaving the mazes of their formless unpatterned pattern, they forgot the empty boarding houses along the esplanade, the stagnant shops, the hunger of uncertainty. They were no longer typists and accountants and engineers and market gardeners. They belonged to a pageant without design; they moved to a rhythm without reason—"What's to do about it?"—dancing their way towards 1933.

A little above them sat the four older people from Cold Harbour, more experienced, wary, conscious, planning what it was that they would do about it. They would persuade Carne to oppose the Skerrow-Kiplington Road Scheme. They would obstruct progress. Their movements had a pattern—drawn according to what they thought was their local interest and others' civic duty.

And higher still among the palms and dignatories sat Authority. Astell, Sarah—planning a new order of government, planning dignity, planning beauty, planning enlightenment.

She turned to Astell, a little amused at the conceit and solemnity of her vision.

"You'll have to help me. I'm lost in the quicksands of local politics. And Carne's one of my governors. What's to do about it?"

She hummed her tune.

"In the long run," said Astell solemnly, "he can't stop us. But the undertone of reaction is always strong."

He had almost forgotten how to talk to a woman, but he was so grateful for her vitality, so glad of her congenial indiscretions, that his face, stiffened by pain and loneliness, learned new expressions of mobility with which to smile at her. Sarah, thinking that in Carne she had acquired a new enemy, felt confident that in Alderman Astell she had found a friend.

CHAPTER V

LYDIA HOLLY GOES HOME

"Jill Jackson, six out of ten. Neat, careful work, but you don't seem able to use your own mind much, do you, Jill?"

Miss Masters was handing back English Literature essays to Form IV. Upper and found in most of its members a lamentable lack of enthusiasm for Shakespeare's descriptive powers. They were "doing" A Midsummer Night's Dream. "Gladys Hubbard—careless and dull and much too short. I don't believe you try, Gladys. If you don't do better next time I shall make you take it home and copy it out on Saturday as a Refused Lesson."

Gladys Hubbard, secure in her fame and confidence, marched up to the staff desk, her ringlets tossing unrepentently. She was singing at Leeds in the Christmas holidays. She had put away childish things.

"Lydia Holly."

Lydia stood up, a humpish stocky schoolgirl, her brown hair hanging in a neglected bob round her high-coloured, good-humoured face. There was a great hole in her stocking. Her tunic, acquired second-hand by Mrs. Holly, strained to bursting point across her mature young breasts.

Miss Masters contemplated her and sighed.

No flicker on Lydia's stolid face revealed the tumult of her emotion. It never occurred to the English mistress that the criticism of Lydia's essays marked the summit of a mounting excitement almost too high to be endured.

"Lydia, when I look at your exercise books, I groan in spirit. I can't think what you do with them. Look at this." She held up a stained and blotted page. She sniffed at it. "Did you eat fish and chips all over it? I thought so. Oh, it was only chips, was it? Well, then they must have been quite near the fish and caught a fishy flavour. It's a terrible looking book. I can't think how you ever got a Scholarship. Twenty-six spelling mistakes. No punctuation. Five blots, and seventeen crossings out. I can't possibly accept such work. Of course it's refused."

The blank horror invading Lydia's soul failed to reflect itself in the wooden face. Lydia was trained to meet catastrophe; but this blow to her vanity was appalling. Perhaps Miss Masters realised something of this, or perhaps, being a nice, fresh, eager girl, she simply preferred pleasant to unpleasant words. Her blonde, pretty face changed. She smiled at Lydia.

"At the same time, it's much the most interesting piece of work I've had sent in from this form—this term—indeed, it's really one of the most interesting school essays I've read. Lydia chose as her subject—'The landscape round Athens as Shakespeare imagined it, compared with any other rural landscape with which you are familiar,' and she knows her South Riding. She has observed and she can describe. And she's studied Shakespeare. So that when you've overcome the terrible appearance of this work, it's a joy to read. You've got imagination, Lydia, of course, but you've got sense too. So, although it's refused as an exercise—because we can't do with such slovenly, dirty work—when you've copied it out—without a single blot or spelling mistake—I shall send it up to the head mistress as a possible entry for the essay prize. Do you understand?"

"Ooh. Yes, Miss. Thank you, Miss."

"Miss Masters. Not plain Miss. And for goodness sake, during break, ask Miss Parsons for some wool and mend that stocking. How can I think about A Midsummer Night's Dream when every time I look up I'm confronted by that terrible potato!"

All the girls laughed. Lydia laughed. She was in Heaven.

For she was clever. It had not been a lie then, that ecstasy which visited her when she read A Midsummer Night's Dream on top of the railway coach last summer. It had meant something. She had understood something. She was drunk with an intoxicating wine of gladness.

Oh, she would copy her essay, perfectly, perfectly . . . Miss Burton was to see it—Miss Burton, the deity who ruled this Olympus. Miss Becker, the games mistress, was jolly, even if she discouraged Lydia from doing the splits and called her dancing vulgar; Miss Parsons, the matron, who presided over school dinners, wasn't a bad old bitch; Miss Masters was grand and ever so clever and pretty; even old Siggs made a good butt to tease, so had her uses. But Miss Burton, red-haired, imperious, unexpected, adorable, with her swift ferocity and her sudden kindness, to her Lydia's heart paid its deepest allegiance.

"I am your spaniel; and, Miss Sarah Burton, The more you beat me, I will fawn on you."

Miss Burton punished her for swearing, derided her singing, despised Madame Hubbard's choice of entertainment, scolded her for untidiness, lashed her careless work with ridicule, but she filled to the brim Lydia's cup of bliss.

"Use me but as your spaniel, spurn me, strike me, Neglect me, lose me; only give me leave, Unworthy as I am, to follow you."

Once when Sarah was asked—"How do you deal with Schwërmerei in your school?" she had replied serenely, "I control them all by monopoly and then absorb them. It's quite simple. We needs must love the highest when we see it. I take good care to be the highest in my school." She knew well enough what had befallen Lydia Holly; but she reckoned that it would do the girl little harm.

Lydia delighted her. The girl's roughness, her ability, her exuberance, were qualities desired by Sarah for her children. You could make something out of a girl like that. She had power. It was for such as her that the Kiplington High School of Sarah's dreams should be constructed. The conversation with Alderman Astell had confirmed her ambition. The projected road from Kingsport, the subsequent development of the town, were steps towards the education of Lydia Holly.

Lydia, during break, plunged to the dark underground cloakroom three steps at a time. What she saw there stirred her to action without impinging upon her deep-seated satisfaction.

"Hi! Midge Carne. What are you doing in my pigeon hole? Get out. Them's my gym shoes. Cheek!"

"Cheek yourself. D'you think I want your filthy gym shoes?"

"Who says they're filthy? Sneak thief. Get off and drink your milk—milk-baby!"

To Lydia such brief exchanges of courtesy meant no more than brushing a fly off her breakfast margarine. At the Shacks, controversy was voluble and unrestrained. But Midge Carne, Lord Sedgmire's granddaughter, took it far more seriously.

She had been poking about the cloakroom out of curiosity. In her lonely life she had seen so little of other people that all their ways fascinated and puzzled her. To be caught exploring was horror enough, flooding her with shame, for the habit was as dark and unsurmountable as secret drinking. But to be caught by Lydia Holly, a fat vulgar girl from the Shacks, lowest of the low; to be accused of stealing; to be scolded by a village child—it was unthinkable.

"How dare you? How dare you?" she screamed, inarticulate with rage, dancing up and down.

"Midge! Be quiet. Lydia, what does this mean?"

Miss Burton stood in the cloakroom doorway.

"She said I was a sneak thief! A milk-baby!" sobbed Midge, white and shaken.

"I don't want to hear what she said. Neither of you had any business to be talking in the cloakroom at all. You know there's a rule of silence here—and the rule is made precisely because, as you see, you apparently can't be trusted to behave like civilised human beings. Midge, go and wash your face. Lydia, hadn't you better darn that hole in your stocking?"

"But she said . . ."

"Be quiet, Midge. What she said is of no interest to me. Put your things tidy, both of you. Midge, don't be such a cry-baby. Run to Miss Parsons. Oughtn't you to be having milk and biscuits? You must learn to take life more calmly."

Miss Burton waited until Midge had darted away to hide her shame and tears in the Battle-haunted lavatory—a safe and private refuge in time of trouble. Then she turned to Lydia.

"Lydia, you must be careful. Don't take advantage of your quick tongue. Midge is a delicate proud little creature, and rather hysterical. She hasn't had your luck to be brought up rough, in a big family. She'll have to learn but you might let her down gently. You've got imagination. Use it to discriminate between people."

Ah, that was like Miss Burton, thought Lydia, worshipping dumbly, to take the sting out of a scolding with a compliment.

Miss Burton went on.

"And now, for goodness' sake, try to tidy yourself. Go to that mirror and look at your hands, your hair, your stocking. To be so untidy isn't clever. It's just undisciplined. And if you're going to get that university scholarship you'll need every ounce of discipline you can manufacture for yourself."

Now, how did she know I mean to go to college? Lydia asked herself, scrubbing her cheeks with harsh carbolic soap, staring at her ragged brown hair in the small square mirror.

She knows. She thinks I can do it. She means me to go. Oh, there is none like her, none. She's glorious. She's perfect. Even her scolding was a delight.

"I pray thee, gentle mortal, sing again: Mine ear is much enamoured of thy note."

Pale and still shuddering with sobs, Midge emerged from her retreat. Lydia's heart was filled with love and compassion towards the whole world. Cheerfully she ignored the rule of silence.

"It's all right, Midge. Come on. Use my soap if you like. I was only teasing. I didn't mean really that you were stealing."

"I should hope not," said Miss Carne of Maythorpe, haughtily. "And I wouldn't touch your filthy soap."

Lydia laughed.

She wanted to laugh all day. All the other classes went well. For dinner there was jam roll. At hockey Miss Becker told her that she would make a very useful half-back. She started to cycle home along a road crackling with frost.

Icicles. Bicycles. That was a lovely rhyme. Who would have thought that there would have been a rhyme for bicycles? She rode balancing along the knife-edged ridge above a wheel track, carolling extemporised verses as she wobbled skilfully:

"Cracking the icicles All on our bicycles— We'll get to college one day."

She cared for nothing, was afraid of nothing. Neither squalling babies, nor a scolding mother, neither the crowded van nor jam smeared over her school books, could separate her from the glory which was hers now and which was yet to come.

"I've had my eye on you, A long, long time!"

her happy tuneless voice shouted into the frosty buffeting wind.

She forgot Miss Burton's detestation of Madame Hubbard's songs. The words had meant nothing to her. It was of her newly discovered power of writing that she sang, of beauty, of method and order and power and learning, of the divine Sarah who ruled enthroned above these splendours.

"I've sighed a sigh for you, You know I'd die for you I don't know why I do . . ."

She flung her leg backwards, like a boy, and stood on one pedal, as the bicycle bumped down the cinder-path to the Shacks.

The door of her home was closed. Bert's cycle was not there yet. Lydia knew better than to dash up the steps to her mother, crying out her great good news that her essay had been recommended for a prize—and in her first term. But she hoped, perhaps after tea, to be able to convey something of this wonder.

From the inner compartment came the sound of children playing and squabbling. But when she opened the door into the kitchen-living-room-parents' bedroom, she stopped dead.

Tea was not ready. The table was not laid. But there, sprawled across the untidy bunk, her mother lay. And not only lay—marvel enough, on an afternoon. She lay weeping.

"Mother!" cried Lydia.

Mrs. Holly raised her ravaged face.

"Aye. It's you. Back from school, eh?"

She propped herself on her elbow, and looked at her daughter blocking the doorway. Resentment, pride, love, compunction and envy dwelt in that long, steadfast glance.

"What is it?" asked Lydia, hushed.

"You might as well know sooner as later. I'm done for, Lyd. I'm in for it. I'm going to have another. I've taken stuff to stop it and half killed myself, but it's no good."

"Mother!"

"It's no good looking at me like that. You'll be a woman yourself one day and know all about it. Maybe I shouldn't be talking to you like this; but you'll have to see the end of it, so you might as well know the beginning."

"But—the doctor . . ."

"Aye. He said I wasn't to. Well—it isn't doctor what has last word. Maybe it will finish me. Then that'll finish you too. You'll have to quit your grand school and come home to look after the kids."

It was as though she took a grim pleasure in breaking her daughter's dreams. Yet even then Lydia knew, by the understanding which ran between them, that if by dying her mother could have saved her, she would have died. It was her own failure which she was lashing—jeering at the fate which was forcing her to fail her beloved daughter.

Lydia came forward into the bleak, cluttered, comfortless room and closed the door behind her. She understood.

"You lie there. I'll get tea," she said.

"Aye. I could do with a cup. I've been fairly off my head with pain all day."

She lay watching Lydia, her eyes glittering with fever. She was perhaps not quite in her right senses.

"Aye," she muttered. "Get tea again. It was that cup you got us the other night what did it. When Gert was sick. He'd fairly gone off with sleep till you gave him that tea. That roused him up. That did us both in." Her head fell back on the soiled pillow. "I've done no baking. Ask Nancy Mitchell to lend us half a loaf, Lyd, will you?"

CHAPTER VI

TWO ANTAGONISTS MEET

It was February when the great snow-storm came. For a day and a night snow smothered the South Riding. Drifts blew across the bleak stretches of Cold Harbour Colony, burying by the dozen the huddled sheep. The Council Library van, blinded by the blizzard, was abandoned in a blocked ditch outside North Wirral, the driver barely escaping with his life. Business men, snow-bound on trains, arrived at their Kingsport offices after the lunch hour. From Yarmouth to the Tyne harbours were crowded with shipping sheltering from gigantic seas.

A fierce quarrel broke out between Maythorpe farmers and the Kiplington Urban District Council. For that body had established a public incinerator on the cliffs between the Shacks and Kiplington, and on the first night of the storm the wind had entered the open enclosure and torn papers and posters and strips of rag and cardboard, and whirled them out into the nearby hedges, so that when next day the shepherds and small holders staggered after their sheep in the blinding storm, they saw patches of white along the hedges and struggled to them, to find only rags and rubbish from the refuse pile. It was enough to madden a community of saints.

All Wednesday and Thursday, the storm raged and blustered. By Friday its fury had subsided; a sullen sun gleamed from the ashen sky on to a transfigured landscape.

Sarah sent for Miss Jameson and told her that such dramatic weather was too rare to waste in classrooms.

"The girls may never see anything like it again. I'm told that it's forty years since snow lay thick on the shore. We won't have any afternoon classes. Scrap everything. Those girls who are fit will take part in a tracking game—day girls and boarders. Ask Miss Becker to come and see me, will you?"

Miss Jameson disapproved of Miss Burton's sudden decision to turn an afternoon's time-table upside down. Not thus had Miss Holmes acted. But since the arrangement meant more leisure for herself, she made no protest. It was Miss Sigglesthwaite the science mistress who appeared, flushed and palpitating, to explain that she had taken special trouble to prepare a demonstration class on snow crystals for the Fifth form, and to ask whether Miss Burton thought it quite fair to upset the girls like this in the middle of term.

"I shouldn't think it fair not to," smiled Sarah, sitting back in her chair and contemplating her science mistress.

She wished that Miss Sigglesthwaite would take offence and resign from the staff. One day she might have to drive her to do this, for she feared that the science mistress would never give her adequate cause for dismissal. Academically, she was the most distinguished member of Kiplington Staff. Her degree was excellent. She wrote papers for Botany and twice her letters, over a column long, had been published in Nature. One on "Variations in chromosome numbers in sexual and asexual individuals among Phoeophyccæ" had involved her in a learned correspondence with a young reader in botany at Cambridge. But an aptitude for the study of seaweeds has little relationship to a gift for teaching. Tall, faded, nervous, with a nose perpetually polished by dyspepsia, and dust-coloured hair that dripped from a dreary bun, Miss Sigglesthwaite justified all too well the libels spread by their detractors about school teachers. Sarah considered her influence, her appearance, her ineffectiveness, bad for the school. She guessed that children not only terrified but bored her. She was both too good and too bad for her position. Sooner or later—in spite of Phoeophyccæ, Miss Sigglesthwaite must go.

Sarah smiled blandly at her and explained: "You see, nothing like this may ever happen again. It will be an experience for the girls to remember long after, perhaps, they've forgotten all that we can teach them—oh, and talking of teaching, by the way, Miss Sigglesthwaite, we must do something about Form IV. Upper. We really can't have another mass refusal."

"Miss Holmes realised that it was useless to start science before the Fifths."

Poor devil, thought Miss Sarah. This is desperate for her. There's an invalid mother, isn't there?

"But you see," she pressed, patiently, "some of these girls will take science for their matric. I don't want them to scramble all their work into the last few terms. I want them to learn to think along scientific lines."

She smiled to herself at the farce of Jill Jackson and Gladys Hubbard learning to think along scientific lines, but she knew what she meant. Almost anything could be done in teaching by enthusiasm and self-confidence. At South London she herself had worked miracles with lumpish adolescents. Miss Sigglesthwaite must learn to work miracles, or go.

She repeated her point with gentle ruthlessness. Agnes Sigglesthwaite, aware of the hidden menace in that bland manner, trailed off, despairing. She was all too conscious of her own shortcomings, of her fanatical responsibilities, and of the weakness of her position. The delight planned by Miss Burton that day for her school children did not include the science mistress—and she knew it; but in a clash of interest between girls and staff, Sarah never hesitated in her choice.

It was nearly three o'clock when Sarah joined the tracking party. The plan was that Miss Becker and two of the senior girls should set off on a route known to themselves and Sarah alone. Ten minutes later the others with Miss Masters and Miss Ritchie should follow their trail, wherever it might lead.

Sarah, having answered twenty-two letters, interviewed a mother whose girl had septic tonsils, inspected a burst pipe, discussed with Miss Parsons the comparative merits of brown and wholemeal bread, and accepted an invitation from Jerry Bryan to hear him sing the bass solos in a performance of the Messiah at Kingsport on Easter Sunday, set off in her car to an appointed rendezvous with the runners on Maythorpe Cliffs.

The car was open, but, muffled in furs to the nose, she did not feel cold. The road through the town was polished like white porcelain. A wild wind blew the tossing seagulls about the esplanade, wheeling and shrieking.

How right I was. They'll never forget this, she congratulated herself. The day might have been a present which she had made to please and amuse her girls.

The road led south through the outskirts of the town, passing small, neat bungalows and urban villas. She thought of the lives of women in little houses—adding accounts and writing grocery lists, carrying trays to invalids, washing babies, nursing the very young, the very old, the sick, the helpless, waiting for letters, reading school reports, mourning beside the bodies of the dead.

Life could be very drab and very bitter, she thought. She wondered a little about poor Miss Sigglesthwaite.

But her hands tightened on the wheel as she swung her car cleverly past a lumbering bus and off the main road south to Maythorpe village. There was all the more reason why she must fortify her children, equip them with knowledge and confidence and ambition, arm them with weapons to fight the deadening monotony of life, arm them with joy, with memories, with passion. She would challenge them to make something better of their lives than their parents had done. She would inoculate their minds with her own gospel of resolution and intelligence. "Go therefore, and do that which is within you to do. Take no heed of gestures that beckon you aside. Ask of no man permission to perform"—that was the motto she gave to the girls who left her care to become housewives, typists, children's nurses, shop assistants. She laughed at her extravagance of vision. Oh, but that wasn't what she meant. It was something unexpected and spontaneous—an afternoon snatched from the fixed routine of time-tables, a chance of joy, a burst of music, an insistence upon beauty or pleasure or daring. Something positive and wild and lovely—like driving out before the dawn to Greenwich and watching the ships sail up the silver Thames.

A gate to a field road towards the cliff was open. The farmer had been carting turnips from an opened pie. Fragments of rotting root lay on the frozen road. It would be hard going, but possible. She turned in, enjoying the difficulty of driving along the slippery, pitted track between shining drifts.

Scuttering and slithering over the rutted snow, she passed through three open gateways, and found herself right on the edge of the cliff where, sure enough, according to plan, she saw the track of the "hares" leading down a slope where the earth had fallen on to the snow-covered shore.

Then she waited, hanging, it seemed, suspended between the white frozen earth and black tumbling sea.

An extraordinary scene, she found it, a reversal of natural colour. The foam blown back from the fringe of the waves was white; the gulls were white; white snow shrouded the sands and piled against the cliff; but the retreating tide stained its shining surface with huge black semicircles; the water was black; the sombre sky was ashen; away to the north lay Kiplington, a litter of black walls under white roofs scattered along the shore. The sheltering ships rode huge and dark above the angry water. The sun hung like a painted circle in a child's landscape giving no obvious illumination. All light came from the white, transforming snow.

Sarah stood up in her car, its engine still softly throbbing, and saw, even as she rose, the first of the "hounds" come laughing and panting and calling across the field. They were shepherded by golden-haired Miss Masters, pretty as a picture in her scarlet beret. The girls were happy. Their cheeks shone bright as apples, their eyes sparkled, their breath steamed as though they were little engines puffing and churning through the snow.

When they saw Sarah, they crowded round her car, grinning and merry.

"Have you seen the hares, Miss Burton?"

"If I had, I shouldn't tell you."

"Miss Ritchie's behind with the other lot, Miss Burton."

"Oh, we're the first! We are the first, aren't we?"

"I'll wait for Miss Ritchie. Off with you!"

They cheered her as they plunged off down the slope. It pleased her. Self-confident as she was, her popularity reassured her. She watched the brown, tumbling bodies of the girls as they raced down the slope, falling into drifts, scrambling out again, shaking themselves like puppies, lean, fat, stolid, swift, galloping away far below her, over snow-covered sand. Their voices were carried back to her on the strong north wind.

"Do you know that you are trespassing?"

She spun round at the question, to face a big dark man on a big dark horse, towering above her from a bank of snow.

So startled was she that for a moment she could say nothing, aware only of the tossing black neck of the horse, flecked by white foam, its white, rolling eyeballs, its black, gleaming, powerful flanks, and the dark eyes challenging her from the white face of the rider. It was as though some romantic sinister aspect of the snow-scene had taken heroic shape.

She gasped and stared. Then her temperamental resilience reasserted itself.

"Am I trespassing? The gates were open, and I thought that this was the usual road to the cliffs."

"It's not you so much," he admitted. "It's those girls—breaking down fences, scaring what ewes are left alive."

Into Sarah's irreverent and well-educated mind flashed the memory of Jane Eyre and Mr. Rochester. She watched the impatient movement of the great horse.

"I'm sorry you feel upset," she said demurely. "But we can't have done much damage, have we?"

"I don't know what you call damage. There's a gate left open in the forty acre." He pointed.

"But we didn't come that way."

"My neighbour, Turnbull, has lost close on forty sheep, and he can't afford it. My tenant on this farm has lost a cow in calf. God knows what this has done to the winter wheat. There's a shepherd been lost two days at Ledsea Buttock. I suppose we shall turn him up somewhere after the thaw sets in. He's a married man with three children. They're skinning sheep as they dig them out along Cold Harbour—squashed flat some of them are with the weight that's been on them and the force of the driven snow. The place is like a shambles. And this is the time you choose to let your young women career over the farms. As though it was fun, this snow."

Fun was just what she had thought it. What she did think it. She was furious with him for spoiling her lovely carnival and furious with herself for her failure of imagination. She should have understood what this must mean to farmers.

Self-accusation did not come easily to her.

"I take all responsibility," she said proudly. "If any damage has been done, we will of course pay compensation."

But the stragglers were approaching, shepherded by Miss Ritchie. They trotted more solemnly, sparing their breath. Among them Midge, light and elvish in her brown tunic, ran nimbly.

She saw the horseman before she recognised her head mistress.

"Why, Daddy!" she shrilled, and came panting and waving to him across the snow.

Sarah saw the harsh face above her illumined by the smile which had won his wife, chained Mrs. Beddows, and given Carne of Maythorpe a reputation for popularity. It was, she decided afterwards, only a physical accident, a trick of bone and muscle, a flash of white teeth, a widening of long-lashed eyes; but it had its effect.

"Why, it's Miss Burton!" cried Midge, pulling up short. "Oh, Daddy. You know Miss Burton, don't you? This is my father, Mr. Carne, Miss Burton," she added in her grown-up Miss Carne-of-Maythorpe manner.

"How do you do, Mr. Carne?" said Sarah politely. "We met once before, I think—at a Governor's Meeting."

BOOK III

AGRICULTURE AND SMALL HOLDINGS

"WORKS ORDERED BY THE COUNTY LAND AGENT.

"The sub-committee have approved and confirmed action of the County Land Agent in ordering the following works to be carried out at the Small Holdings named below, which works had not been previously authorised:—

COLD HARBOUR ESTATE (Mrs. Brimsley, tenant) Repairs to stable roof - - - £3 : 2 : 4."

Extract from Report of Small Holdings and Allotments Sub-Committee of Agricultural Committee. March, 1933.

CHAPTER I

THE COLD HARBOUR COLONISTS STATE A CASE

Mrs. Beddows equipped herself for action, moving about the ugly square bedroom that was overcrowded with mahogany furniture. Solid comfort, she thought, turning from the double bed canopied with rosy chintz to the wardrobe that was large as a coach and smelled of cedarwood. Solid comfort, that was what she had given Jim.

She wore her brown cloth dress, because it was short and the roads at Cold Harbour would be muddy. She put on her fur coat because it was warm and the weather was fearful. Although the thaw had set in snow still smothered the hedges and lined the drains. She found her best brown hat, velvet, with a feather curled around it, and chose newish gloves and sprinkled the silk "front" of her gown with scent. Carne was taking her to the meeting in the Sunbeam car hired from Tom Sawdon.

The Cold Harbour colonists had invited him to be guest of honour at their Club this evening, and asked Mrs. Beddows—an honorary member since its foundation—to take the chair for him.

She consented, for she had business of her own there—the inclusion of the Colony in a subscription scheme for supplying nurses to South Riding cottagers. Also any expedition with Carne was a delight.

She had scorned his dog-cart.

"I may have as neat an ankle as any in the South Riding," she had told him. "But when you get to my time of life you'll think twice before scrambling into that trap of yours like a monkey up a puzzle tree."

But she was proud to have him hire a car for her. He could afford this small extravagance, though commonly she grudged every payment that he must make as though his depleted resources were her own.

She was contented and gay and eager. This was her night out; she would enjoy herself.

She paused to look at her reflection in the long mirror before she turned the gas down, and recognised with a shock the woman of seventy-two. When she tossed the scent on to her brown frock she had felt not a day older than thirty-five. She sighed, restored to the sad realism of common sense, and went downstairs to find Carne already in her dining-room, straddled before the fire, his overcoat thrown on to the table.

Deflated as she was by the knowledge of time's victory, she could not quite control the lift of her heart as he came forward to greet her, to ask if she would be warm enough, if she had everything—gloves, scarves, notes, rugs enough. She knew that such solicitude was not born in him. Muriel had taught him. His whole life and nature had been reshaped by his marriage. He moved through the world now, the ghost of Muriel's lover. "If I were a younger woman, I should hate her," thought Emma Beddows.

They went out to the car together, and she let him tuck the rug round her and put a cushion behind her back. She greeted Tom Sawdon approvingly. He was smart in his chauffeur's uniform, a fine fellow, a great acquisition to the district. They swung together through the cold February night, mainly silent, and when they talked, only discussed affairs of the Colony and the Council.

Cold Harbour Colony owed its existence to a nineteenth century philanthropist, Sir Rupert Calderdyke, who believed in making two acres grow where one had been before. He had set thorn fences in the mud of the Leame Estuary, against which receding tides piled clay and drift-wood that slowly from week to week grew from piles to banks, from banks to shallow islands, from islands to outworks of the coast itself, then, mile by mile, into level arable land, lightish towards the river where the tides drained off the clay, and heavy as pudding farther in. Sir Rupert raised dykes, dug drains, built heavy double cottages in pseudo-gothic style marked with their varying dates, 1845 to 1889, then died full of plans and debts, leaving to his heirs his many problems.

Those problems increased. The land was isolated and uneven, the buildings too elaborate, the drains and dykes expensive to maintain; but in 1919 an adventurous county council took over the whole estate as part of an abortive scheme of reconstruction, bought the dark, gabled cottages as homes for heroes, and the reclaimed acres as holdings for ex-service men.

But it was one thing to beat swords into ploughshares, another to provide the three horses required to pull them through the heavy clay. Few colonists had had previous agricultural experience. The agents sent to supervise their efforts were unpopular with the local farmers, and by the spring of 1933 poverty and despair had weeded out all except the bravest, the most sanguine or the most efficient. A source of financial loss to the Ministry of Agriculture, of controversy to the Council, of ridicule to their neighbours and bewilderment to themselves, the survivors hung on tenaciously, some of them even learning to love the wide Dutch landscape, haunted by larks and seabirds, roofed by immense pavilions of windy cloud; the miles of brownish-purple shining mud, pocked and hummocked by water and fringed by heath-like herbs; the indented banks where the high tides sucked and gurgled; the great ships gliding up to Kingsport, seen from low-lying windows as though they moved across the fields; the brave infrequent flowers, the reluctant springs, the loneliness, the silence, the slow inevitable rhythm of the tides.

"Was it Heyer who wrote to you?" asked Mrs. Beddows after a longish silence.

"Yes."

"He's a fine fellow. That Recreation Club was really his idea. Shouldn't wonder if there's a bit of breeding somewhere about there."

"Butcher's son near Ripon," said the practical Carne.

"Ah," Mrs. Beddows was romantic. "You never know. He's got initiative. Queer that he never married."

"He lives next door to Widow Brimsley. Says she does him very well."

"Still—a good-looking man like that. Not that there's any reason why he should marry." Mrs. Beddows laughed at herself. "I always want to pair them all off—two by two—like the animals in Noah's Ark. I remember Heyer once said, 'They say I'm good company to myself.'"

"He wants us to go and have a cup of tea with him after the meeting. Do you mind?"

Mind? Prolonging her evening with Carne? She even preferred visiting with him Bill Heyer's cheerful cottage to the gloomy haunted stateliness of Maythorpe Hall.

"I've been there before," she said. "He keeps it perfectly. I believe he takes his disablement as a game. He enjoys finding out just what he can do—and showing it off."

They were in perfect harmony. If Carne was grave, she knew him to feel as much at peace as his tormented spirit could ever let him be. He liked the colonists; he was glad to serve them. "And he's at ease with me. He trusts me. He's glad I'm here," Mrs. Beddows told herself. She glowed with the satisfaction of that knowledge.

The car stopped outside the recreation hut. Bill Heyer came forward to greet them. Inside the rough wooden building a score or so of men and women huddled on benches round a black smoking stove. Oil lamps hung from the rafters. A Union Jack spread across the platform table, and paper festoons, wilted relics of Christmas festivities, slung from wall to wall, made the only colour. The women wore shapeless cloth coats with rabbit fur collars and deflated hats. The men wore their workaday clothes. But they clumped with heavy boots on the floor as Heyer escorted the visitors up the room.

They all liked Carne—a sportsman, a gentleman and a practical farmer, but it was Mrs. Beddows who lit the candles on the Christmas tree. She tripped up the room, throwing open her fur coat, scattering the luxury of expensive perfume (sent by Chloe, who knew her mother's tastes), distributing smiles like prizes. She recognised everyone. She had greetings; she had jokes. She refused to mount the platform.

"Now," she said, "I'm going to suggest that instead of moving forward, like Mr. Heyer here says you ought to do, you all go and get as close to the stove as possible, and Mr. Carne and I will come and join you. It's not as though this was a formal meeting. Anything Mr. Carne and I have to say, can be said as well sitting as standing, can't it?"

They clapped her.

Her presence had the effect of turning a formal meeting into a party. Carne was an indifferent speaker; slow and awkward. "The wind has time to change between every sentence," they said of him; but he could answer questions and give advice which they respected. Before five minutes had passed he knew that the real object of the colonists was to secure his support over two matters: the more rapid repairing of buildings for which the council was responsible, and opposition to the proposed new road from Skerrow to Kiplington.

"It stands to reason," George Brimsley explained heavily, "if they make road there, they won't make it here. Now we need a better road to Yarrold. We'd like railway an' all."

"Hear, hear."

"But if they spend north, they won't spend south. Why should they? Stands to reason."

"We know that there's jealousy. We know what they call us, but what we say is . . ."

"Who wants more motor roads to Kiplington, anyway?"

The smallholders drew towards him, warming to their grievance. The women collected round Mrs. Beddows. She did not wait for Carne to finish. She never had any use for forms or ceremonies. In a few minutes there were two meetings—a masculine one to plead for the transference of the new road from north to south of the railway line, so that it could benefit Cold Harbour Colony, and a feminine one to consider the establishment of a district nurse.

The two discussions formed a blended symphony of rural experience—strophe and antistrophe, arguing, reaffirming—transport from farm to market, transport from death to life.

Men.—Mind you, apples ain't worth the packing. What the missus don't make into pies, we give to pigs.

Women.—Nay, now, Mrs. Beddows, I said: If Jack's got quinseys he'll get better, and if he's got diphtheria, likely he'll die. But if he goes into fever hospital, there's no telling what'll happen, so I'll just keep him at home.

Men.—They used to pay 4s. an acre for binding sheaves, but now reapers does it all so we get no tack-work even if we tried to go out and earn a bit. . . .

Women.—Mrs. Beachall's a nice little woman and has obliged for many of the ladies round here, for all Doctor says she's dirty and uncertified; but I was three days and three nights in trouble with our Percy and if the devil hisself could have helped me, I'd have took him.

Men.—So his fowls never got no prizes; no more would the Angel Gabriel himself if he'd been moulting.

Women.—We thought the air out here would do Lucy good, so we brought her straight home and she never went to no "after-care." Maybe if there'd been a nurse to tell her she was going wrong way we'd not have lost her.

Men.—It's the going on year after year with no prospect for the lads that vexes me. What you grow, you eat, and what you can't grow, you do without.

Women.—But what should we have to pay her, Mrs. Beddows? Dad and me's putting weekly into the Christmas club and boot fund, and burial, and if we had to put down 6d. or so for a nurse as well, we'd have to drop one of 'em, and burial would go. And I know what that means. We've been owing ever since we lost our Benny, because we'd no insurance and had to pay money down. You may say it's like sacrificing the living to the dead, but what I say is—you never need get ill, but you're bound to die some day. . . .

Men.—Government put us here. Government should help us. If we could get our stuff straight to Kingsport market we might sometimes make a little profit. . . .

Mrs. Beddows sat back and let the talk ripple round her. She could watch Carne's face under the swinging lamp, and learn by heart the concerned kindliness of his expression. To see him listening, nodding, frowning, answering, so good, so patient, so serious in his desire for understanding, was to be confident of his ripeness for giving comfort, because only by giving could he receive it.

They ought to have made him alderman, she thought. He must never give up his public work. It's his salvation.

She did not care much whether the road ran from east to west or from north to south, but she cared urgently that Carne should have a case worth fighting for. The championship of the colonists would involve him in a quarrel with Snaith, but, since the chestnut mare was killed, that enmity seemed past mending anyhow. She was too old to hope for romantic reconciliation. Well then, let Carne fight; warfare would distract him.

One day, of course, his hurts would heal; he would be able to stand outside his grief and look all round it, take its full measure and accept it as Bill Heyer accepted his crippled body, as she had accepted her disappointing marriage.

He's too sore now, she thought. His wounds were still open and agonising. She could remember well when she had been in the same case. For she had gone to Jim Beddows in love with his brisk efficient geniality, expecting him to prove a gallant lover and stalwart companion. She had found him a man of straw, mean, ungenerous, jealous, hugging his little grievances and grudges, rejoicing when other men could lose a fortune, but lacking the enterprise himself to make one. Emma's first two babies had died at seven weeks, and in both cases she was sure they could have been saved if her husband's economics had not included the prohibition of medical advice. For years she had thought her hatred and unhappiness irremediable.

But one comes through, she reflected. One comes through it all. She had learned to manage Jim; she had her living children; she had built up a new life on other people's needs. The regret, the anguish, the humiliation faded as one grew older. If only she could persuade Carne that this was so indeed, that his loneliness would fade; that his pain was mortal, but that the love and tenderness which he had expended upon his wife and daughter, the kindness which he showed to his neighbours, were bread cast on the waters and would return to enrich his later years.

Only he must be brave; he must endure; he must learn that even remorse can be used as a weapon to conquer wisdom. It was the man of sorrows acquainted with grief whom the world needed.

The business was over; the meeting had drifted into desultory discussion of the storm.

"I've seen nothing to turn my stomach like them sheep since I was at Passchendale," said Heyer. "You coming to have a cup of tea with me now, alderman? And you, Mr. Carne?"

Alderman and councillor went off together with him, to his clean lamplit cottage.

No dwelling place in the colony was neater. The coarse white tablecloth shone like damask; the red tiled floor was spotless; hyacinths in pots lent their faint melting sweetness to the smell of tobacco, harness and scrubbed linoleum. Tom Sawdon, no longer the chauffeur but the innkeeper, rate-payer, and neighbour, came in to add his word to that of the colonists.

Mrs. Beddows smiled happily and helped herself to a third slice of saucer cheese cake.

"I shall have indigestion to-night and blame you, Bill."

"Mrs. Brimsley's cook," he defended himself.

"Why do you never come and patronise the Nag's Head, Mrs. Beddows?" asked Sawdon. "I'd get Lily to make you pastry West Riding way."

"I'm afraid of your big dog."

"The Alsatian? That's my wife's. Gentle as a kitten."

"Not in sheep folds. You'll have to watch out, Sawdon," Carne warned him. "Folks round here don't like Alsatians about lambing time." But he spoke casually. There was no threat in his warning.

The whole evening was splendid—an unqualified success. It was not until they were shut away again together in the car that Mrs. Beddows remembered something.

"Look here—Have you called yet on Miss Burton?"

"No."

His convivial humour was suddenly clouded over by the old sullen darkness. "No. But I've met her," he added.

"Well?"

No answer.

"You didn't like her?"

Oh, he could be difficult. He must have driven Muriel crazy sometimes. That was, of course, just what he thought he had done. Poor boy. Poor boy.

"I didn't think much about her at all."

"You did. I'm sure you did. Or you wouldn't sound so cross."

"Did I?"

"Oh, it's all right. But you can't come the strong silent man over me, you know. I'm too old. And I know you too well."

He paused at that, then confessed ungraciously, "Midge thinks she's the world's wonder."

"And you're jealous," concluded Mrs. Beddows. She pressed on. "Aren't you?"

"Oh, she's harmless, I suppose."

"Well. I think you're both wrong myself," said Mrs. Beddows.

CHAPTER II

ALDERMAN SNAITH IS VERY FOND OF CATS

Alderman Anthony Snaith entered his beautiful bathroom to wash his hands.

He never set eyes on that bathroom without pleasure. Through his mind floated the memory of a shallow enamel basin half full of cooling grey suds, a dank flannel, a cracked slab of red carbolic soap, and a moist thread-bare towel dropped on to the worn brown oilcloth. There had been no bathroom in his aunt's house at Kingsport; he had been a fastidious and self-conscious little boy.

Now he could make a delightful entertainment even of washing his hands before afternoon tea.

He removed his coat and hung it on a special padded hanger. He slid the links through the cuffs of his delicate lavender grey poplin shirt and rolled up his sleeves, baring his slender blue-veined forearms. He turned a hot tap and a cold tap and watched the rising steam bedew his stainless fittings. The water was artificially softened. It gushed out into the pale green porcelain basin. The soap was of a deeper green, with a faint herbal fragrance.

The towel was bordered with green, and hung, warm and smothering-soft, on the shining water pipes.

Alderman Snaith regarded his fine toothbrushes, his loofahs, shaving tackle, disinfectants and mouth washes. Everything was in order—neat, expensive, the thoughtfully designed equipment of a man of sensitive taste.

Washed, brushed, provided with a clean linen handkerchief, he went along the corridor to the library, where, before a leaping cheerful fire, the tea-table waited, silver kettle bubbling and shining teapot already warmed, caddy of Earl Grey mixture, a covered hot-plate of buttered anchovy toast, an angel cake like a sugar snowdrift.

He surveyed the table critically, but his inquiring eye found no imperfection, no finger mark on the silver, no crease in the cloth. He sat down with satisfaction to make the tea, to nibble the toast and cut the powdery cake, from time to time pausing to stroke with affectionate foot the immense tom-cat that lay trustfully on its back along the hearthrug.

The cats were the only incongruous occupants of that precise impersonal room. Critics said that it was impossible to imagine anybody actually working and living there. No trace of ink stained the virgin whiteness of the blotting paper on the desk, where clips, pins, elastic bands, covers and files were put to their proper uses. The books lining the walls were arranged according to height as well as subject—not a page dog-eared, not a corner loose, not a title upside down. The papers and magazines on the table behind the door lay drilled like guardsmen, as though challenging idlers to disturb their intimidating order.

Yet the Times and Economist were closely studied; the books were read; letters were answered; even meals were eaten in the library, and once a cat, mother of the present tabby tom and his six brethren, had given birth to kittens in front of that very fire.

The incident had been a complete surprise to Snaith. He was unfamiliar with scenes of birth and death, his imagination shrinking with horror from their crudities. But when he realised what was happening on his hearthrug, before he had time to interfere with nature and the whims of his elderly and decorous lady-cat, Selena, he was surprised and charmed by the neatness and economy of the business. Stooping down from his arm-chair he watched the kittens exploding like silent cannon balls, one after the other, five in all, from their mother's interior; he watched her lick them clean and repair all visible disorder caused by that cataclysm of creation, then settle herself into so lovely a limber half-moon to suckle her children, that his heart melted with gratitude and affection. This, then, was nature—this amusing, tidy and rather charming process. This was maternity—the busy motion of the tawny-shaded blunt-nosed tabby's tongue over the wet sealskin jackets of her progeny. Snaith drew a handkerchief across his forehead. He was exhausted. Within that brief period of time a thousand half-formed images had been destroyed, a hundred nightmares broken. A serenity of liberation began to dissolve the horror surrounding all thoughts of mating and procreation haunting him since that one hideous initiation, when, a little pink and white boy, brought up by a maiden aunt, too soft and pretty and innocent for safety in Kingsport streets, he had fallen into the hands of evil men and fled from them too late, a psychological cripple for life.

Selena was dead; but before she died she blessed her grateful owner with three more successive families. Remnants of these, undisposed of to farmers, orphanages and mental homes (the institutions of the South Riding were supplied free with guaranteed mousers by Alderman Snaith), lay about the library. A smaller and finer brother of the massive tom on the hearthrug lay stretched along the back of an arm-chair; his sister gazed soulfully at the alderman with enormous amber eyes in the intervals of performing an extensive and voluptuous toilet on the coal scuttle.

One of the few disagreements that Snaith had had with his housekeeper arose over his treatment of the toms when they reached years of indiscretion. "You let me take 'em away and have 'em seen to. You can't let 'em multiply for ever, let alone the smell, and we can make up to 'em other ways." At first he refused; but after three necessary drownings, he let her have her way with the younger generation, treating his gelded toms with specially tender indulgence.

Snaith was permitting Sir John Simon—the tom on the hearthrug—to curl a luxurious tongue round his fingers, removing the last flavour of buttery anchovy paste, when his manservant Christie (husband and appendage of his housekeeper) appeared and announced the arrival of Mr. Huggins.

"I've put him in the dining-room, sir."

"Oh, better ask him up. Give me a second to wash. I'm all over cat. And bring fresh tea—Indian—strong. And more toast. Don't waste gin or cocktails. He's a teetotaller."

When Snaith returned, he found Councillor Huggins in the library. The big man seemed unhappy and excited. He had cycled from Pidsea Buttock, and his dark preaching trousers were mud-flecked, his thick fingers purple with cold.

Snaith made much of him, poked the fire to a brighter blaze, poured out strong sweet tea, pressed on him slices of hot savoury toast dripping with butter, and watched physical comfort, warmth and satisfaction slowly work their expected effect upon him. Meanwhile he talked easily of this and that, of the recent storm, of a celebrated preacher visiting Kingsport, of a local motor accident. He would let Huggins take his own time and make his own approach to whatever subject had inspired this visit.

Meanwhile he gently rolled in the hearthrug, with his pointed patent leather shoe, the vast billowing body of Sir John Simon.

At length his visitor pushed back his empty cup and wiped his beard.

"Aye. That's good. That's just what I wanted. Beer drinkers don't know what they miss."

"They say we don't. However, on a cold February afternoon I agree with you. Tea's the thing."

Huggins made further business with his great white handkerchief.

"What d'you think of Carne's new move?"

"Oh—that—" Snaith smiled indulgently.

"Think he'll be able to do anything? There's more than one or two on the 'Roads and Bridges' think anything he says is gospel if it's about farmers."

"It's a pity," murmured Snaith, "that, as a spokesman of smallholders, he has made such a mess of his own farming."

"Mess?"

"Well?—He's failing, isn't he? Of course, I don't know. Not my business. But I understand he'll have to borrow heavily if he's to see this year out."

"But that hardly affects his position on the council. If he gets all the men south of the railway line organised to oppose our Kiplington Road, and does a bit of lobbying among the farmers too—you know how they feel when it comes to motorists and holiday resorts."

"I see your point. I see your point, of course. If he could do it, then, I admit, it would be awkward. But—"

"And if he stopped the road, what about the Leame Ferry Waste Housing Scheme?"

"Precisely. But he won't—at least—I should be very much surprised. Oh, he'll get busy. Hold meetings perhaps. Lobby a bit. Spend more than he can afford, too, I shouldn't wonder. Afraid the new developments north will detract from Maythorpe land values. But—I don't think you need be frightened."

Snaith rolled the big cat over and lifted his foot. It clung, all four paws clasped round the shoe, until it was perhaps fifteen inches off the ground, then dropped, turning nimbly in the air—a perfect mechanism, supple as silk for all its heaviness. Snaith watched with undisguised and eager admiration, his light eyes shining. Huggins stared, amazed that a sane man should show so much interest in a cat, uneasy, awkward.

Snaith spoke again.

"Have you gone any further in your Ferry Waste housing scheme?"

"Mine?" gasped Huggins.

"Well—ours," conceded the smiling alderman handsomely.

"Well—I. I thought. . . ."

"Waiting to be certain about the road first? You're wise. But it will be all right. Astell, for one, is dead keen. He and Rushbottom have been going into figures. Of course, I suppose they're right—keeping it quiet still, until they're certain about the road. Myself—I'd thought of taking my coat off and stumping the country on it. But—they're experienced men."

Huggins still gasped. Surely the scheme was Snaith's; the plans were Snaith's; the secrecy was Snaith's? Had his ears deceived him? He watched the delicate finger trace the long vertebræ of the outstretched cat from head to tip of tail.

And, under his long pale eyelashes, Snaith was watching Huggins, measuring his bewilderment and credulity, wondering when he would come to the point and reveal the object of his visit. A big hulking fellow, Snaith decided. But not unlikeable. There was something rather childish and appealing about appetites so naïve and powerful, even something heroic. The man had eloquence too. That fervour often went with a rich sensuality. Probably scattered bastards in the trail of his prayer meetings. There was, indeed, a new tale about a girl from—now—which village? Yet he's not without sensitiveness, nervous but dogged. I bet he's in low water. Snaith's thin lips twitched with their secret smile. For when men were in low water, they came to him, Snaith, and he helped them; and when he had helped them, he had power over them, and, he told himself sardonically, he had taken to secret power as another man will take to secret drink. There are prettier pursuits. He had no illusions about himself; but he set certain credit marks against the ugliness. He did not bully; he did not use the power necessarily for his own profit. He was, in a queer kind of way, disinterested.

All that he asked was relief from the sense of impotence in this very certain and concrete exercise of his will.

A man like Huggins would have no such temptation. In his preaching, in his wenching, he would experience swift and immediate response. It was a shame that so healthy and fine an animal should be thwarted in the satisfaction of his natural appetites by financial pressure. Civilisation was all wrong.

"You don't look too well, Huggins. Been over-doing things?"

"I'm worried. That's top and bottom of it, Mr. Snaith."

"I'm sorry. Family all right?"

The big man gulped with relief as though a rope had been thrown to him when he was drowning.

"My daughter Freda—her that married young Armstrong of Redcar—a tobacconist—nice young fellow.—She's left him, Mr. Snaith. She's left him. Come home to us bringing her nipper with her, saying she wants a legal separation. I don't know what to do. I don't like it, you know. For better, for worse, I say. But you can't force a woman." He sighed gustily. Almost in that comfortable room, he believed in Freda's broken marriage.

"I'm sorry—that sort of thing." Snaith's gesture indicated distaste and condolence.

"I don't want it all in the paper. Not with me in my position. Of course, money's at the bottom of it. They've got into debt. . . ."

"Ah-h?"

The grey face was sympathetic and inquiring. The foot and hand caressing the cat were still.

"You see, it's like this." Huggins leaned forward confidentially. In his mind was the picture of Freda and her noisy, ill-disciplined boy filling the house with tumult and upsetting Nellie. Bessy Warbuckle hardly existed for him. "I haven't told any one. I keep my own troubles to myself—and your own daughter—that's different. That cuts deep. But you're a good living man and a Wesleyan. You know my position."

Snaith nodded gravely, really anxious to hear the big man's story, and prepared to believe quite half of it.

"Here's my girl. Been married five years. Nice young fellow. One boy. Tobacconist's shop on front at Redcar. But you know how things are. Seaside places quiet as the tomb. He's been losing steadily and while he loses, his nerves go to pieces. Shouldn't wonder if he doesn't lift his elbow a bit. She says so. No women, mind you. 'Mental cruelty,' she says. Mental my eye, I say. I know Armstrong. It's fear of the future. He's been gambling a bit too. And now they're building a cinema next his shop and it'll double the value of the business, so the bank's threatening to foreclose. Five hundred pounds he owes—for they could make a good profit on it and then he'll lose everything—everything."

Tea, emotion and fire had pimpled Huggins' brow with sweat. He wiped it, glancing anxiously at the alderman.

"Five hundred pounds," nodded Snaith thoughtfully. "Five hundred pounds."

"Three years ago, I'd have had it. Two years ago I could have raised it. If I could see my way to paying back I'd borrow it this minute. I'm fond of my girl. Maybe I've spoiled her a bit. I don't want this to go bad on her. Love and money—they do get mixed like this. But—you know how it's been. Business is bad—bad. I can't see my way. . . ."

His voice broke.

He's really crying, thought Snaith, working at the memory of that gossip about the girl as a tongue might work at a seed in a hollow tooth.

"I dare say—it's possible—I might be able to help you."

He hesitated deliberately. The man's ravaged face, wavering between hope and fear, both interested and repelled him.

"I'd have asked you for a loan. I'd have come straight to you," said Huggins with desperate candour. "But I tell you—I see no chance of repayment. I've been racking my brains. My business only just keeps going. I don't make a hundred a year net profit. I've got an overdraft—and we've got to live."

"Yes?" Snaith lifted the great cat and held it thoughtfully at arm's length, as though assessing its weight.

"You've never gone in for real estate much, have you?"

Huggins gasped, then, thinking that the alderman was changing the subject before he could be touched for a loan, shook his head sadly.

"No. I've stuck to my own business. No side shows."

"You've never thought of undeveloped property—even as part of your business? Those old warehouses that Chadwick put up, for instance, during the War? They might be useful in your business as storing-sheds, mightn't they? A storehouse between Kingsport and Pidsea Buttock. Do a bit of depository trade in them—save haulage."

Huggins frowned, unable to follow the reasoning of a shrewd business man who responded to his tale of debt with suggestions of further expenditure.

"They're going for a song, I understand. Being so near my own property, of course, I was interested. You know them, of course—between Garfield and the Wastes—in fact, practically on the Wastes."

"I dare say."

"If the new road comes—they'd still be off it a bit. So the price hasn't gone up yet. But if the Ferry Waste housing scheme went through—such property might become—quite an investment."

"Why don't you buy 'em, then?" asked Huggins, a little bitter to think that other men only had to put their hands in their pockets and could pay.

"No—no. That would hardly do. If I'm to steer this scheme through the council, I must have no personal profit to make by it—no private interest. That, of course, would be your difficulty too. But you're not on the Town Planning Committee, are you? We might arrange something. If, of course, another fellow bought them. Some one you could trust—and you could have the loan of them for a time—"

"But how could that help me?"

"I don't say it could. I only say that they're a nice proposition. If I should consider making you a loan, to reduce your daughter's overdraft, say, it wouldn't be my fault if those were the only security you could offer me. I don't say they'd be yours. But if they belonged to some one you could trust—your son-in-law, say, or, better still, perhaps, a friend of his. . . . If the property did happen to rise in value—he could of course sell out at a profit and pay me back, I've no doubt, say, in five years. Of course—you've probably got twenty better ideas of what to do with the money. . . ."

"I'm sure . . . I don't know," gasped Huggins, flushed dark red in the firelight.

He was thinking of the sheds; he could hand them over to Reg Aythorne, keep Bessy quiet, pay her off, five hundred. . . .

"There's a chap at Spunlington might consider it."

Spunlington! That was the place, Snaith remembered. That was where the girl was.

"I should have to talk to him. I don't know, I'm sure."

"Naturally," smiled Snaith.

Of course. That was it. Huggins was in trouble with a girl at Spunlington. Probably he needed this money for her. Even if he lost the whole sum, the fun was worth it. Snaith watched the preacher's clumsy advances and withdrawals. He was certain now that he would accept his offer.

He watched him depart, half an hour later, with deep satisfaction, then returned to his arm-chair.

"It's a shame, puss," he remarked to the big cat on the hearthrug. "It's a shame that a gentleman should be deprived of his natural pleasures."

CHAPTER III

MR. CASTLE COUNSELS CAUTION

Mrs. Castle, believing that the sick require special protection from chills, colds, temperatures and perspirations, had not opened the low oblong windows of her husband's bedroom since the previous November. Along the sill lay a sausage of red cotton stuffed with sand; a red plush curtain (a Hall cast-off) had been tacked across the door. A fire, banked high against the chimney, was never permitted, night or day, to die.

So the atmosphere which greeted Carne, when he appeared each day to visit his sick foreman, almost knocked him over. High on the feather mattress of the broad brass bed reclined Mr. Castle, propped by a pile of pillows. His thick twill sheets were sun-bleached and soft as wool; his calico shirt was spotless; his round pink face was closely shaven, save for the frill of grey hair outlining his jaw from ear to ear. His hands, knotted with rheumatism but now unnaturally white, plucked the canvas into which he was laboriously poking two-inch strips of coloured rag. He was making a mat for the kitchen fireside. His stroke the previous March had deprived him of all power in his left arm and leg. His left eye was sightless. He was sixty-nine, a fat powerful man, a great meat-eater, and a shrewd experienced farmer. Carne had relied upon his practical judgment ever since, as a schoolboy, they had gone ferreting together.

Three days after the Cold Harbour meeting, when he entered Castle's room, stooping under the lintel of the low door, he found his shepherd Naylor seated beside the fire. Lambing was in full swing; the hot room reeked of tar and sheep-folds.

"Well, Naylor, how are you getting on?" he asked, lowering his bulk cautiously into an inadequate chair. "Are they giving you much trouble?"

"Not more than they can help, poor things," the shepherd replied with his usual grave courtesy for the ewes that he attended.

"How many to-day?"

"Twelve couples of twins, seven singletons, four lots of triplets down here, and seventeen couples of twins and nine singletons out at Minton Riggs."

"Any casualties?"

"Not so far. But yon little blackie I've got in my hut—he's not doing too well. Foursome's don't. Stands to reason. It's unnatural, I say. If the Lord meant ewes to have foursomes He'd have given 'em another pair of dugs to feed 'em. Not that this 'un isn't a brisk little jockey. If we can rear him, we'll give him to Miss Midge for a pet."

"That's an idea," smiled Carne.

"How's she framing at school?" asked Castle from the bed.

"It's early days to say yet."

"She's not been to see my nursery this year," grumbled Naylor.

"It's all this home-work."

Carne defended Midge, but he sympathised with the shepherd. He too felt neglected. The child was far too much absorbed in her new environment. It was "Miss Burton" this—"Miss Burton" that—all day. Carne wished Miss Burton was in Jericho. He would not admit that he was jealous of her. He had to acknowledge that Midge seemed well and happy, but he would have been better pleased by an excuse to withdraw her from the High School. He compromised with all these feelings by saying, "School isn't what it was in our day, Shep."

"Nay," chuckled the old man. "For I didn't have none."

"It was A B C and the birch rod for me," said Castle, "and I doubt if we was any worse off. We learned a bit beyond school books those days. I mind when I was a little lad in Norfolk, working for a rat-catcher by I was eight year old. He'd give us so much a dozen for rat-tails—tied up in twenty-fours, they were; but if ever we came across an extra long 'un, we'd cut it in half and make two. That's how I learned arithmetic."

"Did you ever tell Maister how you saw rattens changing their spot?" the shepherd prompted. It was a well-worn tale, but Castle loved to tell it. Since his illness the memory of his youth had grown increasingly clear and radiant. The human figures of those days assumed heroic proportions. The sun shone; the land was bright with flowers. The men and women towered above the puny present as superb creatures of formidable eccentricity, uncurbed in energy and passion.

"I remember," said Castle, "how I used in those days to be out at horse-rake in harvest time till eleven o'clock or later, working with an old fellow, nigh on eighty years. It was a dry summer. Not a drop in t'ponds for miles round, and water twopence a bucket. I was walking home by moonlight, bright as day it was, and dry as a bone. Old fellow walked dot and carry one, leaning on a stick. Aye, cloppety-clop, he went. I can hear him now. We weren't saying owt, too tired to talk, when I heard a sound behind us like rain pattering on a window. Old man stops in't middle of road, leaning with both hands on stick. 'D'ye hear owt, lad?' he asks. 'Aye,' I says, 'a sound like watter running.' Old man shakes his head. 'There ain't no watter,' and turns hisself about in road and listens. Then he says, 'D'you see yon gate, lad?' 'Course I sees it. I've got eyes,' says I, pert as sixpence. 'Then, if you've got legs too,' says the old man, 'get on it—them's rattens,' and he makes for the gate, cloppety-clop, dot-an-carry one, quicker than a two-year-old. 'Rattens?' says I, ready to argue the point, but I sees him clambering on to the gate, so I clambers too, and there we were, each sitting on a post, like them monuments outside Lissell Grange. And then I sees 'em, coming along the road. Rattens. Like a black stream they were, pouring along the white road in the moonlight, pattering like rain, eyes glistening like water. It was the queerest thing I ever saw in all my born days, and if we hadn't got out a't way on to them gate posts, they'd have got us. For when rattens is on the move like yon, from one drinking place to another, there's small chance for any flesh and blood they find in their way. I've heard on 'em going straight through a horse yoked to a cart and leaving the skellington picked clean, upright still in t'shafts. But you don't see 'em like that now. We've killed off ower many."

"Rattens aren't what they were, eh?" teased Carne.

"Nothin' isn't what it was. Why, look at lads now. When I was eight, I tell you, I was scrattin' my own pickings. Now it's school till fourteen and pension at sixty-five, and in between an eight hour day and Saturdays off and overtime. After a week of rain, with half all out, first fine day a lad will come an' say, 'It's fine now, Mr. Castle—Can I have a day off to take my young lady out to Hardrascliffe?' Aye, an' then all this dole. It ain't reached the farms yet, thank God, but it will. It will. Road work too. That's what they fancy now. Twenty-six week's work to qualify, and then sit back on benefit—like gentlemen."

Queer, thought Carne. Socialist chaps like Astell think it's us employers who grudge the unemployed their dole; but it's the old workers like Castle who are far harder on them.

Castle was running on—the price of labour, the price of wheat, the vogue of mechanisation. He was enjoying himself, while Naylor dozed, head on chest, beside the guttering fire. He had been up and down intermittently with the sheep for seven nights now, and had sacrificed one of his precious hours of rest to visit Castle.

The old foreman had reached the vexed question of Cold Harbour colony.

"They say you're all for 'em, Maister—in council and such."

"They're having a rough time. We're all in the same boat."

"Boat—aye. Boat's a good word for some o' them spots. Luxury liners. Ever seen the stable Government put up for Brimsley's horses? Stalls all along side, door at one end, corn bin at t'other, and lad had to squeeze his way past tail ends to get to bin. He didn't like it—an' nor would you, and Brimsley complained to Government agent. He came down—all Oxford an' Cambridge an' haw-haw—'You've made stable too narrow, sir,' says Brimsley. 'Narrow be damned,' says he. 'Stable's all right. It's your blessed horses are too long.'"

Carne laughed as he was trusted to do. Indeed, in the company of this brave cheerful grumbling stricken old man, he found laughter easier than elsewhere. He respected Castle and Naylor. He recognised their prejudices and he shared them. He saw their limitations, but he loved them. Here he felt at home with men whose integrity and affection he never doubted. They were men of peace and men of character. They met fortune and misfortune with equal courage. He had tested their quality and felt himself honoured by their confidence.

Had he remained comfortably in the South Riding, he might have taken that confidence for granted. But the circumstances of his marriage had driven him forth into a wider and less easily comprehensible world. His war service had increased his fund of exotic memory. He returned with intensified awareness to the comradeship of these men who served not him so much as Maythorpe. He was Robert, elder son of Thomas Carne, steward for one generation of two thousand acres. He felt humble because he knew himself to be an unworthy steward.

He had endangered the farm for his wife's sake. The shadow of her thin imperious beauty crossed that hot firelit room where rested the two old men who had served Maythorpe better than its owner. Naylor nodded in his chair; Castle drowsed in the bed. Carne sat upright and communed in his shocked and sorrowful soul with the woman he loved.

He thought of the last visit that he had paid her, when she had leapt at him, wild and screaming, then, subdued and weary, turned to him with recognition, repeating over and over, "Poor Robbie. I do treat you badly. Poor Robbie. I do treat you badly."

He thought of Naylor's answer to his question: "Are they giving you much trouble?" "Not more than they can help, poor things." Not more than she could help.

Oh, he never should have married her. It had been irreparable folly. From the beginning, after their accidental encounter in the hunting field, followed by his unique determination to go to the Hunt Ball—(that night—oh, that night, with snow powdering the ramparts of Lissell Grange, and the stars so brilliant and Muriel in her scarlet cloak)—from the beginning William had sneered and his father had opposed. "It's no good, Rob. A Carne of Maythorpe can hold up his head in any company, but she's of the nobility, and there's queer blood there. Let her go, boy. Let her go. You'll bring worse on her if you take her now." But he had not listened to reason. She wrote and he followed her; he faced it out with her parents; he waited for her at a Shropshire inn until she came to him. He would not listen to reason. He carried her off to Paris on the proceeds of his two young hunters, and returned to his father's funeral after a ten days' honeymoon, lacerated, enchanted, bewildered, deeply afraid.

Oh, it had been wrong from the beginning. But these men had stood by him—when he went abroad with Muriel, seeking cures for her nerves in strange places which he hated and remembered only as backgrounds to their quarrels and reconciliations. They had stood by him and run the farm for him, while he had drained its resources to meet his wife's desires.

He had never known, for one hour, peace of mind with her. She had been able to torment and to enrapture him. She had led him into a thousand unforgivable follies—he had spent nearly a thousand pounds renovating Maythorpe only to let it fall again to shabby ruin; he had drawn on capital to supply her wardrobe; he had travelled with her all over the continent; if it hadn't been for the War, when a farmer could not help making money—and he had been specially favoured—they would have been bankrupt long ago.

And it had been all useless—all quite useless, because in one hour of jealous and exasperated passion he had forced her to conceive his child, and that had destroyed her. All his tenderness, his disastrous acquiescence, had gone to nothing, because he was a passionate man, and he had forced her to do that which was beyond her fragile power.

He was aware of Castle interrogating him from the bed. About Cold Harbour. The old man seemed weary.

"Don't go wasting pity on them as doesn't need it. Wait till mortgage is paid off Maythorpe, Maister."

"But the new road would not help us either," Carne said, and explained just why.

Castle was unappeased.

"It's all right. But you'll have a powerful lot to fight and your hands are full already. You're a bit given to biting off more than you can chew. Give Shep a thump for me, will you? He said he must set out at half-past seven, and he's gone off, sweet as a baby."

"I must go with him. I promised to look round with him to-night."

He woke Naylor, and followed his clumping boots down the steep stairs.

In the brick entry a stable lad, stripped to the waist, after working late with horses, was washing himself in a tub of lathered water. He looked up as the farmer and shepherd passed, squeezing the soap out of his hair, and grinning without embarrassment. Naylor stopped to light his lantern, and Carne spoke to the lad as he wriggled into his shirt—a fine boy, healthy, muscular.

Dolly Castle appeared at the kitchen door, pretty as paint and sour as a crabapple.

"Well, Dolly, I hope you're looking after these young men," smiled Carne shyly.

"They need a regiment of soldiers to look after them, Mr. Carne." She tossed her pretty head. "Buck up now," she ordered the young man. "Do you want to keep me waiting here all night while your tea gets dried to cinders in the oven—making the water as thick with muck as a dog's dinner?"

The boy flushed deeply crimson. Dolly had neither manners nor mercy. Carne sighed. He did not know how to reprove a pretty girl. But he felt unhappy about the whole affair—Castle's illness, Dolly's presence, his own shortcomings.

"That girl gives them the rough edge of her tongue," he remarked to Naylor as they crossed the slackyard to the buildings, the swinging lantern tossing rings of light on to trampled straw and muddy puddles.

"They don't like it, Mr. Carne. She's been spoiled by town life. I've never minded a bit of sauce from lasses, but that one's over keen. I wish we were all back in our proper places."

"I wish that too," sighed Carne.

He thrust up the heavy wooden bolt of the door to the fold yard. The soft ba-aing of sheep and high tremulous bleating of young lambs came from within. Under the sheds round the yard, pens had been built with hurdles and netting for the newly-born. In the deep straw of the yard itself, ewes near their time stirred restlessly. Naylor passed with his lantern from one to the other, speaking to them, feeling them. One family of twins had just arrived. He picked up the two little creatures by their forelegs; their fleeces glowed golden yellow, moist, tightly curled, in the light of the lantern Carne had taken from him; the ewe followed, stumbling and bleating into the shed. Naylor settled her down with her lambs, and went through the building from pen to pen, the lantern casting fantastic shadows on straw, wool, hurdles, the velvet darkness, and the warm rustling scent and movement of breathing sheep.

"It's a cold night. Come up and have a nip in my place?" invited Naylor.

"Thanks," said Carne.

He followed the shepherd to the little room opening off the fold yard which was Naylor's office, bedroom, surgery and storehouse during lambing time. A black lamb slept in a box of rags by the damped-down fire. A collie dog cringed forward whining softly to welcome his master. Naylor poked the congealed cinders, and the flames leapt revealing a clumsy bed piled with coats and sacking on an old straw-stuffed mattress, a windsor chair, polished by use, and ropes, sticks, bottles of disinfectant, harness and netting bundles against the wall.

From a cupboard beside the chimney Naylor produced a bottle of whisky, a box of cheap cigars, and two pint mugs.

The whisky and cigars were Carne's annual gift. His father and grandfather had supplied them during lambing time before him. The shepherd measured two drinks with careful impartiality.

"The little Jersey cow's in calf again, I see," he remarked conversationally.

"Yes," said Carne.

The spring season of mating and birth emphasised his personal tragedy. His spirit was bruised by reiterated disappointment and anxiety.

Muriel would never recover again.

If only he were sure of Midge.

If only the slump were over and farming would look up again.

If only he knew that on the council he would defeat Snaith and carry his point about the road.

He was certain of nothing except the recurrent cycle of the seasons.

"You'll miss Castle when she's calving."

"Aye. He has a grand way with beasts."

"If I'm through with this, I'll give you a hand."

Neither of them mentioned their knowledge that the beastman drank and was unreliable, but Carne was aware of Naylor's unspoken warning and support.

"Thank you," he said.

The shepherd raised his mug ceremoniously.

"Well, here's to us."

At least, thought Carne, one can be certain of some things. Birth comes at its appointed time. These men are honest. Summer and winter, seed time and harvest, ploughing and lambing—these at least do not change.

With grave ritual, they drank.

CHAPTER IV

MR. BARNABAS HOLLY TOASTS HEREDITY

One result of Carne's Cold Harbour meeting was that ten days later Mr. Barnabas Holly found himself, a temporary employee of the council, seated on the lee side of a bean stack near the Brimsleys' buildings, sharing lunch with his fellow "civil servant," Topper Beachall. Topper contributed two bottles of beer, Mr. Holly a couple of bacon cakes, some stale bread and a hunk of cheese.

"If Widow Brimsley was a lady," observed Topper Beachall weightily, "she'd ask us in and give us a good hot dinner."

"What's she having?"

"Steak and kidney pie."

"How do you know?"

"Smell."

Topper opened his clasp knife and hacked off a second slice of bread.

"Hum. Bill Heyer's a lucky fellow."

"Aye." Topper munched his cheese.

"Unlucky 'uns weds, and lucky 'uns lives next widows. Here's to widows, Topper!" said Mr. Holly. He raised his bottle. Any excuse served Mr. Holly for celebration—the maiden of bashful fifteen and the widow of fifty were equally welcome. But widows reminded him of widowers and widowers of an event foretold for April.

He wondered how much doctors really knew. Annie had always been all right before. Now if she'd been a nagger like Chrissie Beachall, there'd have been some consolation in the prospect of danger for her; but Mr. Holly was fond of his wife and anxious about the future of his children.

"How many kids have you had, Topper?" he asked suddenly.

"Four goals, two tries and a miss. This cheese tastes of paraffin."

"Must ha' been near the lamp."

"Your missus cutting you short of rations?"

"She's not too well. Fact is, she's expecting again, and it doesn't suit her."

"Never does. But they get over it."

"Aye. My eldest girl's at High School."

"Go on."

"Frames to be a real scholard. Takes after her dad."

"Go on."

"Aye. A real scholard. Going to college one day. Latin and Greek and all that."

"Go on."

Mr. Holly took another pull at the beer bottle.

He was beginning to feel himself again.

"End up as a teacher, I shouldn't wonder. You ought to hear her saying poetry. Makes it too. Can't sing, though. Not like her father. Always was one for singing and reciting myself. Got a prize once, at anniversary concert."

"Go on."

Mr. Holly went on.

"It was the Schooner Hesperus That sailed the wintry sea. The skipper had taken his little daughter To bear him companee. Blue were her eyes as the fairy flax Her hair like the dawn of day. . . ."

Aye. Once I get started, you can't fairly stop me. Poetry's in our family. Heredity. Funny thing that. Always popping out. You can't beat it. Now, look at our Bert. Temper! Like his Grandad Hazel to the image. When I was courting Annie we used to meet in chapel and walk home together and her ma would put a lamp in t'window, and if blind was up, I'd come right in for a cuddle in t'parlour. But if blind was down it meant old man was in and I'd have to make do with a bit of a squeeze behind the tool shed. Bert's just like him. Bit through a pudding basin when he was a nipper," boasted the proud father. But he was really thinking about Lydia—thinking of her with pride and understanding and compunction. For if anything happened to Annie, then Lyd would have to leave school and come home to look after things. Annie had said so, and there seemed no way out of it. They had talked things over one night when Lennie kept them awake—teething. Aye. Bachelors had the best of it. It was no joke to be a father. As soon as kids stopped teething they were wearing out shoe leather, with appetites like elephants. Of course when a girl was clever like Lydia, it was worth while. Just like her old dad, she was, if only he'd had half a chance.

"You ought to see her dance—like a music-hall.

'I've had my eye on you A long, long time!'

That's heredity. Wonderful thing, science, Topper. Ever thought of what they can do nowadays! Wireless. Incubators. Ether. Maybe hatch us out of eggs one day. My girl's learning all about science. Maybe a lady doctor herself one day. Give her old father the rightabout, eh?" He chuckled with complacent incredulity. "Heredity."

Topper roused himself from his after-dinner doze to catch the last word. He stared solemnly at his bottle, perceiving half an inch of beer at the bottom. He raised it. "Heredity!" he muttered. "That was a good horse. Here's to it."

"Here's to it," echoed Barnabas, and threw back his head.

He felt cheered and reassured. Everything was all right. He had a job with the council. He'd go on doing work for them. Annie would come through all right, as she had done before.

He returned to the task of repairing Mrs. Brimsley's stable with added gusto. Topper, poor fool, with his slightly defective brats, knew nothing about the joys of fatherhood. Carne of Maythorpe himself, with his funny little Midge, why, she was in a lower form than Lydia, although she was three months older. That just showed you.

One day Lydia would go to college and Mr. Holly would come to visit her and she would introduce him to all the professors and 'varsity men in caps and gowns and they would say, "Ah, Mr. Holly, many a poet lives only to pass on poetry to his children."

Poor Annie. She'd never understand his pride in Lydia. A good woman, but low-spirited. No poetry in her. Never was. Always scraping and saving and thinking about domestic things. Still, a good woman.

Mr. Holly had not been to the movies for nothing. He knew the value of a good woman's love. At the same time, he knew how affection can be lost by over-devotion to domesticity.

He settled himself straddling across the beam on the roof of Mrs. Brimsley's stable and began to clear away broken lathes, singing as he worked.

"Oh, I'm a donkey driver, The best upon the line. There isn't a donkey on the road That can come up to mine."

He had a fine resonant baritone.

Mrs. Brimsley appeared at her back door with a plate of scraps from dinner. Bill Heyer and her boys had returned to the fields.

She emptied her plate into the swill tub, then turned, hearing the song.

"Her coat it is a beauty, Her colour's fair an' pale. Her ears are long, and she's graceful, she Has a beautiful curled tail."

"Now what do you think you're doing?" she called.

Mr. Holly poked his head up through a hole in the roof and grinned at her.

"Serenading you, sweetheart."

"Get away with you—and don't go scattering your nasty plaster into the corn-bin, poisoning my horses."

She slammed the stable door, sending down a shower of plaster over the singing labourer; but he shouted to her irrepressibly, "Thank you for the confetti. Don't you wish it was for our wedding?"

She turned to annihilate him; but he had another happy thought.

"Oh, and thank you for the nice steak and kidney pie you didn't give us for lunch."

"You!" she cried witheringly, and disappeared indoors, whence emerged at length the appetising smell of hot jam and baking pastry.

Cheered by beer and badinage, Mr. Holly scraped and hammered and sang, his head full of dreams for Lydia which found their way into his shouted ballads.

"She shall wear a cap an' gown, cap an' gown, cap an' gown— She shall wear a cap an' gown— My fair laidee!"

The immediate future, his precarious livelihood, the long tiring cycle-rides against the wind, his ailing wife, the feverish fretful noisy children, the squalor, the monotony, the tedium—all these sank like sediment to the bottom of his mind. On the surface frothed the heady foam of his dreams, and the impish pleasure of a new and fine idea.

The sight of Topper, piling his tools into a council wheelbarrow, reminded him that "civil servants" keep statutory hours, and he swung his leg over a beam and dropped lightly down into the stable straw. Chuckling to himself he walked across the yard, and knocked at the back door of the widow's house.

She came, her comely face flushed with heat from the oven, her sleeves rolled up, her arms floury.

"Sorry to trouble you," began Mr. Holly, mild as milk. "But could you oblige with a drink? Water would do—but my mouth's that full of dust and plaster, and it's a long pull home with the wind against me."

"Why—" She hesitated, half amused by this shameless little man and half indignant, yet glad of any break in the dullness of her days, when Heyer and her sons were out working and the next cottage empty. Mrs. Brimsley was a sociable woman. She had never liked Cold Harbour. "I was just making a cup of tea for myself," she said. "You get thirsty, baking."

"And so you do building," grinned Mr. Holly, entering the neat, glowing kitchen. "I'll bet your pastry tastes better than your plaster. Thanks for the invitation—I will try a cup of tea—just for company, like." He sat down in the windsor chair beside the fire. "Not that I often drink tea."

"You don't, don't you? And who said you were going to drink it now?"

"You did—at least—if you were a lady, you would."

"Well, I'm—"

"A fine handsome figure of a woman."

"You—!"

"And a grand cook."

"How do you know?"

"I don't. I'm going to find out."

"I'm sure I don't know what you came in here for."

"A slice of your cake and a cup of tea."

"Well, I'm sure it won't hurt you. It's quite plain cake."

"And none the better for that. I like a taste of butter and eggs myself."

"I like your sauce!"

"Your cake's not so bad." He cut himself another generous helping. "Try a bit. Your tongue could do with a bit of sweetening."

Mrs. Brimsley boxed his ears.

"Now, now. Don't you take liberties. I might get a bit of my own back, and then where would you be? I'm the father of a college girl, I am, and must be treated proper. Going to be a lady barrister. Takes after her dad's family. Brains!"

"Go on."

"I'm going to." Mr. Holly helped himself to a great slab of saucer cheese cake, well laced with rum. He nodded over it with satisfaction. Poor Topper, he thought, a father of fools, cycling drearily back to his scolding Chrissie, while he, Holly, a man of brains, ate rum-flavoured cheese cake and drank tea with a widow. "Ah. Have you ever thought about heredity, Mrs. Brimsley? It's a wonderful power. Never lets you down. You'd know Lydia was my daughter anywhere. Handsome. Now I'll tell you something. A girl like that could go anywhere."

An hour later, when Nat Brimsley came in for his tea, Mr. Holly was still sitting there discoursing. He went soon, but only after making himself most affable to the scowling lad.

"Why did you have yon good-for-nothing in here, Ma?" asked Nat, who had a sense of a smallholder's dignity. "What were you thinking of?"

Mrs. Brimsley, with a sharp intaking of breath and glow of excitement, was thinking that she had not boxed a man's ears since she was courting.

CHAPTER V

MISS SIGGLESTHWAITE SEES THE LAMBS OF GOD

The High School term ended on the Wednesday before Easter. On Good Friday Miss Sigglesthwaite attended the Three Hours' Service, listened, during the afternoon, to Bach's St. Matthew's Passion broadcast from York Minster, then went to tea with Miss Burton in her office at the school.

After tea she wandered out along the cliffs south of Kiplington, wondering what she really ought to do.

I ought to resign. She's quite right. She's a good girl.

Agnes Sigglesthwaite had been trained in justice and charity. She recognised the quality of her new head mistress. The school was a different place since she had been there.

She's intelligent—modern, enterprising; the children like her; she stands up to the governors, yet they don't quarrel with her. She's clever enough to give way about the things that don't matter; but she stands firm as a rock for those that do.

She's quite right that the staff should be sacrificed to the girls. "I'm thinking about the girls, Miss Sigglesthwaite." She meant that. There was no malice in her. She said that she respected my mind. She told Miss Jameson that the school was lucky to have such a distinguished scientist on its staff. But that sigh when she said, "I'm thinking of the examination results." That told everything.

It's true. It's true. I shall never get IV. Upper through their Lower Certificate. They're devils. They're devils. They go out of their way to humiliate me. Callous. Cruel. Jill Jackson, Lydia Holly, Gladys Hubbard, Jean Marsh, Beryl Gryson . . . big strong girls. Miss Masters and Miss Burton thought a lot of Lydia Holly; but Miss Sigglesthwaite feared her. Those slum-girls. They knew too much. Their minds had been corrupted.

Oh, they were cruel to her. They left their home-work unprepared; they wrote flippant and even improper remarks in their nature notebooks. They answered out of turn. They threw notes at one another. Gladys Hubbard came into class one day with her ringlets screwed up on top of her head and her blouse poking out behind. It was too obvious—too cruel.

How did other women manage their hair and blouses? My hair's thin because of worry. Father used to say, "Agnes mayn't be a striking beauty, but she always looks intelligent and a lady." I'd buy a frock coat. They keep tidy better than blouses. But Edie must have her new teeth and there's the bill for the boiler.

"I'm thinking of the discipline," Miss Burton had said. Miss Sigglesthwaite walked without sense of direction, beyond the houses, across the flat, worn field-path.

It's true. I know I can't keep order. I've lost confidence. I can't trust myself to keep my temper. It's being always so tired. Those dreadful nights, when you can't sleep, waiting for dawn; and then the dawn comes and you dread it, because in an hour you must get up, in two hours you must face that dreadful staff-room. The young mistresses. It's so easy to be unafraid when you're strong and pretty. Girls get crushes on Belinda Masters. She pretends it's a nuisance, yet it gives her power. Power. Confidence. That's what I'm needing.

Oh, if only Father hadn't died quite so early.

He believed in me. Even Christ needed some one to believe in Him. Thou art Peter. On this rock will I build my church. Father was proud of me. On the Sunday after the news of my finals came through he preached from the text, "The works of the Lord are great, sought out of them that have pleasure therein." Sought out. That searching was what we meant by science. He meant me to be a great scientist—like Madame Curie. And I can't even keep order in a class of tradesmen's adolescent daughters.

That's a Smew. Margellus Albellus. Pretty thing. Hasn't got a pretty voice, though. Kaak! Kaak! I wonder if he minds. Perhaps his wife thinks it's lovely when she hears him coming home. Kaak! Kaak! There, children. That's your father. Who talked of nightingales?

I'm probably the only woman in the South Riding who would know for certain it was Margellus Albellus. I owe that to Father too. He loved birds. If botany's going to be your subject, he said, why not make birds your hobby? Be broad-minded. And I did. I hardly ever make a mistake either, except when I thought the female Cirl Bunting was a yellow-hammer. And that's pardonable when they're so rare here.

They laugh at my bird-lore. "Girls! Girls! The little chiff-chaff's come back again!" Dolores Jameson did that. She's behind it all. The staff-room's hell. It's Gethsemane. Oh, Father, Father—why can't you comfort me? If I could get away—never see them again—never see myself again. "Father, if thou be willing, remove this cup from me."

It wasn't Father's fault that he died so much in debt. The Church of England pays its clergymen so badly, and he never pretended to be a business man. It wasn't his fault. He never meant to leave me to keep Mother and Edie; it wasn't his fault that Mother got rheumatoid arthritis.

To begin every year with that financial load on one's shoulders. Never to dare to rest. Never to dare to be ill. Never, for a moment, to dare to dream of the sort of work one would really have liked to do. Professor Gelder wanted me to go on doing research—"seeking out"—but there's no money in it.

Mother and Edie were always suggesting that I should get a job in the South of England, since the north was too cold for Mother. I've tried hard enough. Over and over, I've copied out those qualifications. But no one even sends for me to be interviewed. I'm too old—too old.

If I leave Kiplington, I shall never find anywhere else—and then what shall we do for Mother?

Mechanically she climbed a stile and crossed a bridge over a sluggish stream winding down to the sea. She remembered the morning's lesson.

"He went forth with His disciples over the brook Cedron, where was a garden."

You could understand Him trying to seek consolation in a garden; but when one is really troubled, scenery isn't much help. It's beautiful here, I suppose. It's a beautiful evening.

She stood still, staring at the indented line of the low red broken cliff, the pale sea sliding out, drawing arcs of deeper fawn on the sloping sand.

Behind a group of buildings, the sun was setting. She saw the outlines of tiled roof and chimney softened by a touch of the light as though cut out of velvet. The loose straws from the old threshed stack stuck this way and that, like silver needles, dazzling and brilliant, alive with light. Around and before her stretched the open country, melting into the quiet grey of distance where trees like smoke-wraiths blurred the horizon. Behind her the quiet sea swung softly, without breaking, against the sand.

From one of the cottages an old man pottered out into his garden. It was Grandpa Sellars. He was going to shut up his hens for the night, moving cautiously, each gesture prolonged, as though, towards its end, life retarded like a slow-motion film. She heard him calling, speaking to the hens as though they were his children, coaxing, scolding, making the most of every little humour or awkwardness in their behaviour. She felt sure that he was a very kind, patient, gentle-hearted old man.

If Father had lived, he would be very old now, guarding the fragile flame of life, perhaps, with just such careful piety.

Mother is very old too, she thought; but she guards nothing. She cannot even walk in the garden talking to her hens.

If she closed her eyes, Agnes Sigglesthwaite could see the bedroom at Tunbridge Wells where Edie sat, watching their mother, the speechless, motionless twisted husk of a woman who hardly raised a bulge under the bright blue eiderdown. The gas fire hissed. Edie snipped a thread. The five-thirty bus went rattling down the hill. Time stood still.

I can't! cried Agnes Sigglesthwaite. I can't go back and face them. I can't say I've lost my job. And I can't—oh, I can't—stay at Kiplington.

Oh God, oh Lamb of God, who takest away the sins of the world, canst Thou not also take away my burden? Not sin, not sin, oh Lord, but time and life and weariness.

Here, on this cliff now, in the mellow sunset, to step backwards, so easily, into the peace of death.

They would say the cliff had crumbled.

They would say that I was gathering grasses.

So easy, so kind; oh, why should it not be done?

Suddenly at the end of the field a gate was opened, and Miss Sigglesthwaite saw all the little lambs of God come leaping over the hill. They danced on spindly legs, they twirled, they bleated. Tail up, nose down, they sprang and waltzed and circled. Behind them trotted the woolly ewes, their mothers, calling, panting, stumbling across the field, their breath like smoke on the cold clear evening air.

The ears of the lambs were rosy as apple blossom where one saw them against the light. Their long tails waggled in ecstasy as they hurled themselves upon their mother's dugs. They were lovely and innocent. They were gay and unfrightened. The slanting sun behind the ewes transformed their long wool to haloes of light.

Like doom on her heart chimed that morning's service—"Oh Lamb of God, who is it that betrayeth Thee?"

Not sin, but time.

Time, that betrays the little leaping lambs, rosy-eared, smutty-nosed, long-tailed, button-eyed, turning them into feeble, slow, blindly bleating sheep.

Time, which betrayed the eager questing girl, Agnes, her father's darling, who sought out the works of the Lord, and found them great, and took fierce pleasure therein. Time transformed her into the dreary eldritch creature, seeking suicide on a Yorkshire cliff because she could no longer keep order in the classroom.

Oh, time betrays us. Time is the great enemy, cried Agnes Sigglesthwaite. Time crowns us with thorns, exposes us to mockery, crucifies our bodies, defeats our laborious endeavours. The old prey upon the young—Mother upon me, and I upon the children. Is it true that I only have them? "I'm thinking of the children," said Miss Burton. For their sake I'd be better away; I'd be better dead. Must the young, the free, the hopeful always be sacrificed to the old, the bound, the helpless? Is this the final treachery of time, that the old become a burden upon the young? We ought to step aside, to let the young go free. But how can I do it?

She moved away, a few faltering steps from the edge of the cliff.

"He died to save us all," she muttered, and thought with sorrowful envy of the Christ from whom love had demanded only the easier sacrifice of death.

He died; but I must live; I must go on living; I must go on working; I must go on laying my burden of fear and inefficiency upon the young.

Father forgive them . . .

But she could not forgive herself; for she knew now quite well what she did.

And in that realisation came a kind of bitter triumph. She knew what she did. She knew what she must do.

She turned and walked with shambling graceless haste towards Kiplington station. She bought a monthly return ticket to Tunbridge Wells. She asked her landlady to bring her box up from the cellar. She would pack immediately. She would take her books with her. She had classes to prepare for the coming term. Miss Burton had not actually dismissed her. She would stay and fight for her rights and her position. She would fight for Mother and Edie.

The young must look after themselves. Their turn was coming. Soon they too would prey upon their betters. Time would betray them also.

With a new energy of defiance she ordered early breakfast; she made arrangements to catch the 9.10 train.

Oh Agnus Dei! Oh Lamb of God, that takest away the sins of the world, have mercy upon us. Oh Lamb of God: that takest away the sins of the world: grant us thy peace.

CHAPTER VI

TWO ANTAGONISTS MEET AGAIN

Half an hour before midnight on Easter Saturday Sarah drove back to Kiplington from Kingsport, when she had attended the Philharmonic Society's performance of The Messiah.

She had gone at Terry Bryan's invitation, and after the concert had returned with him and two musician friends to the Station Hotel where they had sat by an enormous fire, drinking coffee and cherry brandy, smoking and talking.

Sarah smiled now as she drove, for she was happy. Her senses still rang with the superb tumult and affirmation of the music, her nerves were stimulated by its frivolous aftermath. This was one of the occasions when she felt that nothing was impossible.

She had not met Terry for three years—not since the time when she had broken her engagement with Ben, and, to distract her mind from personal unhappiness, he had carried her off for a week-end to Paris—a week-end of indiscreet but completely platonic comradeship, in which they had visited restaurants, listened to operas, and bumped about queasily and excitedly in cross-channel aeroplanes together. Terry had teased her then and he teased her now, telling her that she was absurd to be a school-marm. But she cried: "You don't know how I love it. I tell you, I'm happy."

"Yes. That is true," said the bearded 'cellist gravely. "You can see that."

"But you could do anything. You could go anywhere, and you choose to bury yourself in a God-forsaken sandpit."

"Do I look buried? Do I look half-dead? I tell you I'm alive and I'm happy and I love my work. I love being alive. I love turning giggling little creatures into self-respecting women. I love bullying parents and flirting with fat governors," she added with a hushed and brooding rapture. "You ought to see the plans for my new lavatories."

They roared with laughter, but they accepted her. They were vital and generous people who could understand that one might grow drunk with triumph at the pleasure of wresting new sinks or cloakrooms from reluctant committees. They themselves had wrestled with boards and subscribers to musical societies.

They toasted her; they teased her. She was a little drunk with flattery and music, so that the cherry brandy seemed a negligible intoxicant. They came out to see her off in her little car, and Terry pressed upon her a box of American cigarettes, advertised as the "Motorist's Perfect Companion," which had been given him by an admirer in Chicago.

"You're the plutocrat; you're the motorist, Sarah, you need the perfect companion."

She laughed; she thanked them; she drove away through the silent city, below the towering elevators, the large cliff-like walls of factories, out into the dark clear night and the level country.

As she drove the gaiety of that re-encounter faded and the more profound and solemn memory of the music possessed her mind.

Sarah had been brought up as an Anglican; her shrewd and ambitious mother believed that members of the Church of England had greater social opportunities than nonconformists. But Mrs. Burton remained at heart a Methodist, and her imagination was dominated by a confidence in salvation which Sarah found smugly complacent, a doctrine of atonement which Sarah thought barbaric, and a dream of Heaven which Sarah thought materialistic and uncivilised. So the girl, clever, irreverent, inquiring, grew up with a critical and detached scepticism towards both her mother's religion, and that into which she herself had been initiated for reasons which she found inadequate. To be washed in the Blood of the Lamb appeared to her a nauseating exercise. Confession and absolution she thought to be an evasion of personal responsibility; redemption she considered to be a task for the individual will. Life was what each man made it.

She had suggested to the senior girls for their holiday reading that Easter, Lady Rhondda's autobiography This Was My World, commending especially to them an old Spanish proverb quoted there: "Take what you want," said God, "Take it—and pay for it." To choose, to take, with clear judgment and open eyes; to count the cost and pay it; to regret nothing; to go forward, cutting losses, refusing to complain, accepting complete responsibility for their own decisions—this was the code which she attempted to impress upon the children who came under her influence—the code on which she set herself to act. If only we could train children, she would say, not to fear, not to hate, not to desire those things which are ugly or futile, then indeed we might have some hope for society. Resignation, acceptance of avoidable suffering, timidity and indecision, she found contemptible. The world is what we make it, she would preach; take what you want. Take it—and pay for it. The earth belonged to those who were prepared to pay most for their dominion.

Yet even so fierce an individualist, so sceptical an agnostic, was shaken by the power and beauty of the music to which she had been listening. The words rang in her mind. "He was despised and rejected of men, a man of sorrows and acquainted with grief. . . . Surely, surely He hath borne our griefs and carried our sorrows. He was wounded for our transgressions. He was bruised for our iniquities, the chastisement of our peace was upon Him, and with His stripes we are healed." Her senses were swayed by the image, but her mind could not accept its implication.

We must do it ourselves, she thought; we are our own redeemers. Accept nothing; be resigned to nothing; refuse to make the best of a bad bargain.

The dark clear night closed round her. She slowed down the car. It is Easter morning, she thought, the day of resurrection.

She stopped, her elbows on the wheel, her chin in her hands. She lit one of Terry's cigarettes. She sat there alone in the darkness, thinking of death and resurrection and of a world redeemed from fear and cruelty by human effort.

Then she heard something.

At first her senses denied it.

It came again, a low moan of anguish rising to a wailing scream of terror.

No, she told herself; no, it's an illusion.

The black coppice of Minton Riggs rose to the right of the road, a yard or two behind the car. In its shadow squatted the old brick shed that she had passed many times, a hundred yards back from the road, facing away to the fields. Some one was in there now. A faint light came from the square window which, open towards the road, was veiled with sacking. Somebody was in there, and was in desperate pain.

Sarah heard the wild cry repeated, this time accompanied by a rattle of chains and a dull repeated thud. She sat still, listening, and now she was afraid. The knowledge came to her that she must go and investigate, for if she drove on, she might learn later of an agonising death, a hideous murder, a man gored to death by a bull, a tragedy which she, who had heard, might have prevented. It would be on her conscience for ever.

She climbed out of her car and fumbled in her tool box for her electric torch. She feared bulls and felt small and defenceless. The lights of her little car shone with homely reassurance. To leave them, to push her way through the hedge, to cross the deep wet ditch, to face whatever horror should await her, seemed almost beyond her courage; yet holding her torch, trying to negotiate thorns and mud with the least detriment to her thin patent leather shoes and new spring suit, she went. Even if she were going to her death, she felt acutely aware of the damage done to her pretty and not inexpensive clothes.

The rattling, wailing and plunging sounds grew louder. She thought that she could hear a man's deep voice. She told herself: "Well, in a minute I shall know what it is, anyhow. Oh, why didn't I go home earlier? Then I shouldn't have heard anything and it would not be my responsibility."

A corner of the little square window was uncovered by the rough sacking pinned across it. By standing on tiptoe and pulling herself up against the wall, Sarah was just tall enough to peer inside. She took a deep breath; she pulled the sacking aside; she looked.

What she saw, in the feeble light of a hanging lantern, was a man in shirt sleeves acting midwife to a plunging, moaning, terrified calving cow. As he turned so that she saw his profile, she recognised Robert Carne of Maythorpe.

Her surprise and relief, as she dropped back to the ground, almost overcame her, so that she leaned weakly against the wall, inclined to giggle at her own vanished fears. But as she recovered her composure, the image of what she had just seen reconstructed itself detail by detail in her observant and retentive mind.

She was the daughter of a midwife and a blacksmith. Years of urban life had prevented her from recognising the sounds that had so much alarmed her, but now both her own experience and inherited instinct told her just what was taking place on the other side of the wall; she knew that it was not as it should be. It happened that coincidence, which is often a result of character, had led her once before into a similar situation. When a young teacher her curiosity, her self-confidence and her mother's training had led her to offer help to the smallholders with whom she was lodging, when they were in trouble with precisely the same kind of abnormal case of animal obstetrics.

Cows were valuable animals. Birth and death were matters of common interest. Sarah remembered that without assistance on that previous evening, her landlady swore that she would have lost both cow and calf.

Sarah owed a grudge against Carne of Maythorpe. She was wearing her new spring clothes and did not want to spoil them. This was none of her business, and if she drove home no one would know anything about it.

But she could not do it. She peered once more below the sacking; she took a deep breath, then marched round the shed, in at the open door and announced quickly and firmly: "You're needing help, aren't you? Let me give you a hand, Mr. Carne."

He swung round, and his face which had been crimson with effort went grey with shock.

"Good God."

"I'm sorry if I startled you." She was pulling off her fur coat. "Last time we met, you startled me."

"You can't stay here. It's no place for a woman."

"You mean it's no place for a man. The cow and I are both females. You know, I was brought up with animals."

"Look here—it's awfully good of you—but really, if you want to be so kind—if you'd take a message to Maythorpe . . .?"

"There's not time, is there? You want help now."

As she spoke another spasm of pain convulsed the cow. It was indeed too late to fetch help.

"Quick. Tell me what to do," she said.

He surrendered.

"Hold these," he commanded. "And when I say pull, pull hard."

She obeyed. On the trampled straw in the lantern light they fought together. She was small, but wiry, and once he had accepted her help he gave his directions clearly, trying to spare her as far as possible, yet twice unable to prevent her being knocked down into the filthy straw.

Once, in a pause, he said: "The vet's away and my beastman's dead drunk. These things always would happen on Saturday night."

Otherwise they spoke little; their task was too grim and urgent. She recognised that he had great physical strength and an unexpectedly sensitive skill. He knew how to be kind and the tortured animal trusted him.

Sarah found a strange satisfaction in obeying his commands, accepting his domination, working with him in silent co-operation. They were bound together by a shared intention, throwing the whole of their united strength into the business of saving life. When at length their task was accomplished, and the thin, long-legged calf lay on the straw, they stared down at it with the unique satisfaction which comes only to those who have together accomplished a difficult and exacting task. Their task was not quite finished. Carne still feared that the cow might have a hæmorrhage. He suggested that Sarah should go now, but she found that by holding her electric torch she still could help him.

At last, filthy, reeking, aching in every muscle, they faced each other across the animals they had saved. Languidly the exhausted Jersey licked her calf. Carne brushed the sweat off his face with a lifted sleeve.

"What now?" asked Sarah.

"Now you go home to bed," he said, leaning rather limply against the wall.

"Will she be all right?"

"I'll knock up my shepherd and get him to come to her."

"Where does he live? Have you got a car here?"

"No. He's in Maythorpe village. I can walk it in half an hour."

"You'll do nothing of the kind. I'll run you there in my car. How long had you been here before I came?"

"Since about half-past eight. I'd just come round to have a look at her and found this." His speech was blurred with fatigue.

The engine of the little car was still throbbing softly as they climbed out through the broken hedge together.

"Your fence isn't any too good," observed Sarah.

"No. I'll have to get it seen to," he yawned.

"Still, it's better than my cloakrooms."

He looked sideways at her and chuckled.

They drove almost in silence to Maythorpe village. She suspected that Carne was more than half asleep; but as they passed the first cottage he said, "The second block on the left." They stopped. Carne climbed out and threw stones at a window. After two or three efforts, the narrow panes were shoved aside and a head poked out.

"Who's that?"

"Me. Carne. Look here, Shep, sorry to knock you up, but the Jersey's calved—Pudsey was drunk last night. Can you get up there?"

"Were you with her? Is she all right?"

"Not too good. What we feared. But she'll do, I think." He gave brief, clear directions.

"Right you are."

Naylor withdrew his head. The window slid back, and a light glowed softly behind its little pane.

Carne turned back to Sarah.

"That'll be all right now."

"Get in. I'll drop you at your house."

"It's not necessary."

"Don't argue. I pass your gate anyway."

He got in. She swung the car round.

It occurred to her that he had never thanked her.

"Was it a valuable cow?" she hinted.

"Prize Jersey."

She turned to her left and drove up the dark avenue to his front door. He did not speak. He was huddled in the little car, motionless with the heavy sleep of exhaustion. She smiled. He was in her power this time and no mistake.

She flashed on the inside light and he started.

"It's nearly five," she said.

He fumbled for his watch, an old-fashioned gold hunter. "Exactly six minutes past," he corrected her and unfolded himself out on to his own door step.

"Well; thank you for the pleasant Saturday evening," she said caustically, and pressed the clutch meaning to sail away, unthanked, triumphant.

But the car did not spring forward. Instead the throbbing died. The grand exit was ruined.

"Damnation," she whispered softly. Aloud: "It's the petrol."

"What?"

"Petrol used up."

"Won't it go?"

"No."

"That's the worst of cars."

He turned and climbed the steps and opened his wide front door.

That'll be like his arrogance, thought Sarah, never to lock his doors. Expects no one would ever dare burgle Maythorpe Hall. Is he going to bed leaving me stuck here?

But he had lit a candle and stood in the black entrance, shielding its flame. Grey dawn lay on the garden.

"If you'll come in for a few minutes, I'll get the trap ready and drive you home," he said.

She thought, he's triumphant because cars prove less reliable than his horses.

The hall was dark; she could see little, but felt its draughty spaciousness. She followed Carne, stumbling after his candle. He opened a door to their right and revealed a long room, lit, to her surprise with the red glow of a banked fire.

"Oh, lovely," she cried, suddenly aware that she was chilled, stiff and bruised all over.

He lit the tall silver candles on the mantelpiece; he poked the fire to a roaring blaze; the lights picked out the gold of brass, the deep ruddy warmth of old mahogany, the crimson carpet. A tray stood on the table holding a heavy cut-glass decanter and covered dishes. A kettle stood warm upon the hearth.

Without consulting her he poured out a stiff peg of whisky, added hot water, sugar, lemon, and handed the glass to her.

"You'd better drink this."

"Thank you."

She felt better for it; living heat ran through her; she crouched close to the fire. He looked down at her.

"You're frozen."

"Frozen, soaked and dead," she grinned up at him.

"Wait a minute."

He stumbled out of the room and she heard him clumping over stone flags; a door closed. She thought; he is the oddest, rudest man I ever met. She remembered, with queer rapture, the harmony of that shared effort. She thought of his fey difficult child and wondered what the wife and mother had been like. Miss Sedgmire. A hunting beauty. Shut away, insane.

She looked around her curiously. In its warm half-light of fire and candle flame, she could see the faded dignity of the big room, the array of glass and silver on the sideboard, the table where twenty might sit down together, the bases of gilded frames.

Above the mantelpiece hung a big oil painting veiled in shadow.

I wonder, she murmured.

She took the candles from the mantelpiece, holding them high in their tall silver sticks above her head; she stepped backwards from the fireplace and looked up.

The portrait of a girl in a dark riding habit leapt into light. She was holding her hat and crop, and her auburn hair framed softly her narrow pointed face that was like Midge's and yet was beautiful. The curve from high cheek-bone to chin was flawless; the pose of the perfectly set head on the slender neck a design for arrogance; the eyes, wide, brown and startled, gazed with imperious wonder at the intruding stranger.

"Oh!" cried Sarah softly. "Oh!"

For she knew who this must be, and looking at that wild unstable loveliness, she no longer found it amusing that a farmer who had married this baron's daughter should be striving to maintain against ruin and failure the dignity he thought suitable to his wife's position, though she was shut away in a mental hospital.

She had thought of Carne's story as an entertaining and rather cruel fable of snobbery punished by its own achievement. She realised now that it was something more.

Oh, poor things, poor things, she thought. Perhaps she even spoke the words aloud.

"I think it might be a good idea, Miss Burton," said a deep voice behind her, "if you had a hot bath. There is one ready."

She spun round, tossing candle grease.

Carne stepped forward and took the candles from her.

Shame silenced her.

"If I drive you back as you are, you will probably take a chill. I have only an open dog-cart."

"If—if it's no trouble," she muttered meekly.

She followed him up a wide staircase along a corridor, where draughts shook the candle flame and uneven boards creaked at their footsteps. In the bathroom clouds of steam rose from a running tap.

He shut her in. She heard his heavy tread along the passage. She saw the towels set out, the soap, the loofahs. On a chair lay a neat little pile of dry clothes—childish garments, wool, serge, and long brown cashmere stockings.

There was no more spirit left in her. His thought for her comfort and the efficiency with which he had produced its requisites, together with his disdainful silence, humbled her. She was tired, she was amazed, she was beyond question.

Without further ado Sarah bathed and changed her clothes. When she re-emerged, the house was stirring. Along the hall walked Midge, carrying carefully two silver covered dishes on an old cracked japanned tray. She set these on the dining-room table and danced forward.

"Oh, Miss Burton, isn't this lovely? Didn't Elsie and I keep up good fires? We knew Daddy might be back late, but it being you to help him! And don't my things fit you marvellously? Elsie's going to dry your own clothes while we have breakfast."

Sarah looked up and saw Carne standing in the doorway re-clad and shaven looking down proudly at his daughter. She was as tall as her head mistress and flushed with excitement.

The maid brought in the coffee and hot milk.

"Won't you sit down, Miss Burton?" Midge invited.

Carne went to the windows and drew aside the curtains. The cold morning light washed the bare garden. The room faced east and north. Daffodils waved on the neglected grass. From Maythorpe Church a single bell rang for the six o'clock Easter Sunday service.

"Sugar, Miss Burton? Half and half, Miss Burton?"

Midge, at the over-large, half-empty table, busied herself, hostess-like, with the heavy silver.

Lifting her eyes to Carne's, expecting him to share her amusement, her admiration for his daughter's precocious dignity, it was with a shock that Sarah recognised, unveiled, the bleak repulsion of his sombre enmity.

BOOK IV

PUBLIC HEALTH

"AGENDA"

"3. To consider a proposal from the Sub-Committee on Maternal Mortality for the building of a new maternity hospital.

"4. To consider an application for a grant towards the £30,000 Rebuilding Fund of the Kingsport County Hospital.

"5. To receive the report of the County Medical Officer of Health with regard to infectious diseases. . . ."

Extract from Agenda of Public Health Special Committee. County Hall, Flintonbridge. May, 1933.

CHAPTER I

MRS. HOLLY FAILS HER FAMILY

From the hour when Lydia, cycling home joyfully through the frost, found her mother in tears on the tumbled bed, life changed for her. An evil spell might have been cast upon her. She was no longer good-humoured and self-confident, assured that, in spite of present difficulty and discomfort, the future was hers and the future was good. She was afraid, and fear tormented her.

At school she was arrogant and wilful. She scribbled obscenities in her nature note-book, driving Miss Sigglesthwaite to unguessed despair. She was impertinent to Miss Parsons, noisy and undisciplined on the playing field, rough and unkind to smaller children, taking a special pleasure in tormenting Midge Carne. During the Easter term her work steadily deteriorated. She no longer wrestled with her natural faults of carelessness and disorder. Though her quick wits and retentive memory prevented her from falling to the bottom of her class, her answers lost all interest and distinction.

"You see," smiled Miss Jameson, "the girl's reverting to type. You can't make a silk purse out of a sow's ear. These slum children, they're quick enough till adolescence, but then the trouble begins. They can't keep it up."

Miss Jameson spoke bitterly. The bank management still delayed Pip's promotion. She did not know how long she would be tied to a routine which bored her and to an authority which she found irksome. She might as well have applied for the headmistress-ship. It would have meant harder work, but Miss Burton was a slave-driver anyway. She had no sense of proportion.

Sarah was deeply concerned about Lydia. It's not natural, it's not right, she told herself. I don't believe the girl is either spoiled or satiated. There's something definitely wrong. A boy? She remembered the precocity of Lydia's performance at Madame Hubbard's concert. The girl undoubtedly knew everything that was to be known about certain adult experiences. "But she's not the boy-crazy type," thought Sarah, "and she's not more homosexual than any other romantic adolescent." Lydia's sturdiness, her clumsy hoydenish strength, her humour, her intelligence, prevented her from seeming a neurotic child. Sarah pondered and watched, disturbed yet patient, with the patience that was hers only when she dealt with young, confused, imperfect creatures.

The Easter holidays approached, and on Easter morning Sarah's consciousness of Lydia Holly was obliterated by her encounter with the Carnes of Maythorpe. It was not of Lydia but of Midge and her father that she talked to her sister Pattie, to whose house she had gone immediately after Easter for a week's change of air. Her brother-in-law went out one evening to a Masonic dinner, the children were in bed, and Sarah and Pattie sat, as they had often done, over the fire, exchanging their diverse experiences. As usual, Sarah monopolised most of the conversation.

She described Carne—a sporting farmer, pseudo-county, with a big pale face rather like Mussolini's—only his nose hooks a bit.

"Handsome?"

"Yes. Certainly. And knows it. Lord, how he knows it!"

Sarah lay on the fur hearth rug, plaiting its soft strands idly. Pattie, as usual, was mending socks for her family. She listened quietly to Sarah's narrative of the adventure on Easter eve.

". . . So he sent a groom to fetch petrol from an inn down the village, and when we'd finished breakfast, there was my car ready, my clothes dried, everything splendid. Only—not a word of apology or thanks, Pattie. Well, he did send a stiff little note hoping I was no worse, but . . . taking everything for granted like that. . . . The arrogance of it! And I shall have to spend fortunes at the cleaners, and even so that new two-piece will never be the same again. What do you think, Pattie?"

"That you're inclined to be more than half in love with him, my dear."

"In—love?" gasped Sarah.

She stared at her sister, then remarked mildly. "Marriage has had its usual deplorable effect on your intelligence, my poor one. Only one single idea nowadays."

She went on to describe Mrs. Beddows, Alderman Astell, whom she liked increasingly, and her far-off plans for a re-built school.

I shall have to give up discussing personalities with Pattie, she told herself. Really she is too absurd. Yet all that night when she slept she dreamed of the governor's dark figure towering above her in the snow, and somehow incongruously intermingled with the music of Terry Bryan's solo from the Messiah, "I will shake the heavens and the earth, the sea and the dry land;" and when she woke she could see Carne's profile outlined against the lantern light as he bent over the struggling terrified cow.

I dislike, I oppose everything he stands for, she told herself—feudalism, patronage, chivalry, exploitation. . . . We are natural and inevitable enemies.

She returned to Kiplington before term started. She had to deal with correspondence, time-tables, workmen, repairs and contracts. Colonel Collier, Mr. Tadman, and a clerk closeted themselves with Miss Parsons, going over the food contracts for the year, ordering meat for the boarders from two local butchers, lump sugar from one grocer, soft sugar from another, soap straight from the Kingsport manufacturers at a rebate, jam from a London factory, "and I know what Tadman gets out of that," Joe Astell said darkly. Miss Parsons was helpless before governors and contractors. Sarah ached to take her place and send the squabbling incompetents about their proper business. "The local people pay the rates; they should get our contracts," she protested. "And as for ordering raisins from one shop and ground rice from another—it's ridiculous. Nothing but little finicking accounts with every tradesman. Why not get them all from one grocer and then take them in rotation?" But Miss Parsons was no fighter, and Sarah believed in delegation. She had to possess her soul in patience, with occasional explosions to Joe Astell.

But she had her own troubles. The grant for her boarding-house was hideously inadequate. The place looked desolate, and she had no money to spend on decorations. She pillaged her cottage for vases, books and woodcuts. She designed cupboards, bullied local carpenters, hung pictures and curtains, pestered governors. Far into the night she sat writing letters, drafting memoranda. She dragged any member of the Higher Education Committee whom she could lure into her buildings from cellar to garret, exposing their enormities. Her energy was unremitting. If the South Riding was not prepared to build a new school for her, she would make this old one a perpetual torment. And always as she planned and wrote and argued, she saw Councillor Carne in her mind's eye as the apostle and ringleader of reaction, the author of false economies, the culprit really responsible for leaking taps in the science room and blackbeetles in the basement. Because of this, it was a little difficult to banish the thought of him completely from her consciousness; but at least she never forgot to remember him with resentment.

In spite of her preoccupations she found time to visit Lydia Holly. One day she drove along the Maythorpe road, stopped at the Shacks, and found Lydia, in a torn overall, feeding hens with some dank smelling mash. She called, and the girl came towards her, slouching and reluctant. Sarah spoke crisply, asked how she was getting on, praised the plump hens, mentioned Lydia's school work, asked how her mother was, and observed the girl's awkward diffident answers.

She felt snubbed by the lack of response, but would not force a confidence. She ended by asking Lydia to tea on Sunday, and determined to collect a group of girls to serve as an excuse for the party. She drove away, depressed and quite uncomforted; but as she turned her car she thought she saw in the doorway of the coach a woman's drooping figure, heavily pregnant.

Is that it? She wondered. Is that what's worrying Lydia? Still—Sarah could not see it as a tragedy.

She could not know that the moment she had driven away, Lydia rushed to the unoccupied railway coach used by her as a study. There, wrapped in old coats and sacking, she had found privacy throughout the winter. There she could read and write and copy out her home-work. Candles had spilled grease from the bottles in which she stuck them on to the table-flap of pot-ringed deal. Scraps of torn paper, dog-eared books and well-chewed pencils bore witness to her efforts. This was her own place.

But there was no longer joy in its seclusion. Its promise was betrayed, its treasure rifled. Her mother was going to die. Lydia must leave school. She must come home and look after her small brother and sisters and the new baby too. There was no choice. Her mother's sisters were both busy harassed married women with families of their own. Her father, characteristically feckless, had no kin. She would have to do it.

She was not a religious child, and did not pray about it; she was not a self-deceiving child, and did not try to tell herself that it would be all right, that her mother would get better, and she would return to school; she was not an irresponsible child and did not dream of escaping from her obligations.

But she saw all too clearly what must happen. "These slum children know too much," Miss Jameson said. Lydia knew too much. Her lively imagination ran ahead and lived through the days which very soon would face her.

Quarter to five, wake father. Put on the kettle, get his breakfast, the cocoa, the margarine, the bread. Tidy the living-room; go and wake the children; get their breakfast. (Why isn't there no bacon? Lyddie, can't we have treacle?) See them off to school; look after Lennie and baby; tidy the bedroom, peel the potatoes, get the dinner ready, feed the hens, the pig—if they could keep one; give the children their dinner when they came home from school, noisy and ravenous. Lennie still needed his food shovelling in with a spoon; he was a slow eater; the baby would want a bottle. Wash up the dinner things; then do the shopping, pushing the pram along the dull road into Maythorpe; get the tea ready, the children are coming shouting across the fields; Daisy has fallen and cut her knee; Gertie is sick again. Bert back. Lyd, what's for tea, old girl? Bacon cake? I'm sick of bacon cake. Can't we have sausages? Washing the children. The heavy shallow tubs, the tepid water. Where's the flannel gone? Don't let Lennie eat the soap now! The tap stood up two feet from the ground on a twisted pipe twenty yards from the door. The slops were thrown out on to the ground behind the caravans and railway coaches. Rough weeds grew there; damel and dock and nettle soaked up the dingy water, drinking grossly. Broken pots splashed in it. Rimlets of mud seeped down from it. The rusting tubs were heavy. Lydia's strong arms ached from lifting, carrying, coping with the clamorous, wriggling children.

And throughout this day of servitude, there would be no mother to applaud or scold, no draggled lumpish woman whose sharp tongue cut across tedium, whose rare rough caress lit sudden radiance. Only her father's maudlin misery or facile optimism would punctuate the days.

And all the time the High School would be there, the morning prayers in the hall, the girls in rows, white blouses and brown tunics, neat heads bowed and lifted together; there would be the hymns, the lesson, the word of command, the note struck on the piano, then the march out to a brave tune, Pomp and Circumstance, or The Entry of the Gladiators. There would be the classes, scripture, history. This term they were going to "do" Nehemiah, the book about the gallant young prophet, the King's Cup Bearer, who roved by night among the ruins of Jerusalem. They were to "do" the Civil Wars. Miss Burton had told them to read Browning's Strafford, "Night hath its first supreme forsaken star." There would be botany, physics, glorious smells and explosions in the stink room. Teasing Siggles. Good old Siggles with her fading wisps of hair. There would be tennis. Cricket. Prize-giving. Essay prize, Lydia Holly. Maths. prize, Lydia Holly. Form prize. High average for the year, Lydia Holly. Sports junior championship, Lydia Holly. Oh, no, no, no, no, no! Other girls, others who cared nothing for all these things, could have them. Jill Jackson, who only thought of hockey, Gladys Hubbard, who was going to be a singer, Doris Peckover, who has as much imagination as a clothes-horse—these would gain the marks, win the prizes, take the scholarships, be clapped at prize-givings, go on to college.

It isn't fair. None of them care like I do. None of them could do what I could do. I hate them.

I hate Sarah Burton. What did she want to come here for? "Are these your hens? Is this your little brother?" As if that was all I should ever be good for again—the hens, the little brother!

Why did they ever let me go to school? What's never seen is never missed. "Your work is really interesting. You have imagination." For what? For what? "It takes an intelligent person to be kind," Red Sally told her. And Lydia had been kind. She had sat up for her mother when Gert was taken bad; she had got her dad his tea.

And that did for her. Kindness had done for her. Using her imagination had done for her.

"Oh God, oh God, how am I to live?" cried Lydia.

But she saw no respite in rebellion. With slow unchildish deliberation she dried her swollen tear-stained face on her torn overall, and made her way to the railway coach across the littered turf.

It was the dead end of the afternoon—three o'clock, and the Mitchells were both out. Mr. Mitchell on his bicycle, Mrs. Mitchell shopping with her baby.

Lennie, crouched in his pen, chewed a dirty rag-book. The older children had gone off birds-nesting.

Unwillingly Lydia opened the door and entered. Her mother had not finished the ironing. She had left the irons on the oil stove, the shirts and drawers rolled in the broken basket. She was not standing at the table. She was not in the bedroom.

Lydia, surprised but not perturbed, went across to the Mitchells. Mrs. Holly was not there. She was not speaking to a tradesman at his van on the road.

"Mother! Mother!" called Lydia.

No one answered.

"Mother! Mother!"

Then Lennie, in his pen, affected by the inevitable melancholy of the human voice calling unresponsive emptiness, began to whimper: "Mum! Mum! Mummie! Mummie!" beating with his pebble on the bar of the pen.

"Mother! Mother!" called Lydia.

There was no one. She turned from the grey unwelcoming camp to the grey unwelcoming field.

"Mother! Mother!"

In a sudden panic she ran to the edge of the cliff.

"Mother! Mother!"

An ashen sea swung silently against the crumbling clay.

"Mother, where are you?"

Round the field ran Lydia, terrified of horrors beyond her imagination.

"Mum! Mum! Mum!" cried Lennie, shuffling round and round his pen.

Near the hedge, behind the caravan, Lydia found her. She lay in the tangled clump of docks and nettles. In falling she had cut her head against a broken jam-jar. The cut bled. She moaned a little, her distorted body shaken by intermittent paroxysms of pain.

"Mother!" cried Lydia.

She knelt beside her, not even feeling the nettles that stung her arms and legs. With a child's panicking fear she shook her mother. "Mother!" But it was with an adult's acceptance of inexorable anguish that she saw the woman's eyes open slowly, fix themselves on her face, and reveal the effort towards consciousness.

Mrs. Holly fought for self-mastery and won.

"It's all right. I only tumbled. It's come. Get some one," she gasped.

Strong as she might be, Lydia could not lift her mother. She left her and ran through the empty camp to the Maythorpe Road and stood there looking up and down it for help.

The dead chill windless afternoon received her cries and muffled them in distance. Sea birds flew squawking and wheeling above her head; they mocked her impotence, then swung with effortless grace towards the town.

Should she run up the road for help? Back to her mother? Or should she wait there, risking the chance of a stray motor-car?

"Oh, come! Come! Some one. Some one must come and help me!" she sobbed, beating her hands on the gate. "Oh, help me!"

And then she heard far away the sound of a motor approaching from the south.

It was Mr. Huggins, driving one of his own lorries, who nearly ran down her gesticulating body.

"Hi, now. What's this? What's this, my girl?"

"My mother. She's fallen. You must come."

There was no mistaking this genuine distress for mischief. Huggins followed Lydia across the field and saw enough. He was a family man.

"Pity you can't drive a car. No. We can't move her. You run in and put on kettles to boil, and get some clean sheets on the bed. Had your mother made any preparations, think you? I'll send a woman. Yes, an' I'll get doctor."

He was gone again, but Lydia felt no longer isolated. She flew between the coach and the moaning woman; she filled kettles, she sought sheets. She hardly noticed when a neighbour sent by Huggins sprang from her cycle, when cars arrived, the lorryman, the doctor. The camp, which a few seconds ago contained only her fear, her anguish and her mother, seemed now overful of hurrying people.

They kept her out of the coach, minding Lennie, getting tea for the children in Bella Vista; she became conscious of other things, of her father's worried face, rather cold and injured because it wasn't his fault that he was at work when Annie was taken bad; of the Mitchells' chickens, scratching in disappointment at an empty enamel basin, fouling its side with scrabbled claw-marks; of the kindly Mitchells, trying to keep the younger children quiet, of Bert, rushing off on his cycle to the chemist.

They called her at last.

"You'd better come. She wants you."

"Is there a baby?"

"Yes. A little boy."

She did not ask of her mother, "Will she get better?"

She knew already. She had always known.

The interior of the coach was very hot. It smelled odd. Mrs. Holly's grey drained face lay on the pillow case that Mrs. Mitchell had provided.

She turned with fretful effort.

"A boy."

"I know. Don't worry, Mum."

"You'll have to look after him."

"Yes, yes—don't you talk now."

"You'll have to let the parish bury me."

There was no hope and no reprieve. Lydia and her mother waited for the death that delayed nearly another hour, held off by the woman's stubborn spirit.

Before she died, Mrs. Holly spoke once again, now fully conscious and recognising the full measure of her defeat, aware of the wreckage her death must cause, accepting it as something beyond remedy.

She opened her heavy eyes and looked straight at Lydia, and said quite clearly: "I'm sorry, Lyd," and died.

It was the first and only apology that she had ever made.

CHAPTER II

TEACHER AND ALDERMAN DO NOT SEE EYE TO EYE

Mrs. Holly's death may have seemed to her friends and family a private matter, but it had public repercussions which she could not have foreseen. Whatever misfortunes, weaknesses, passions and infirmities may have caused it, it set in motion a sequence of events which were ultimately to change the history of the South Riding.

The first was an odd little encounter between Sarah Burton and Alderman Mrs. Beddows.

On the Sunday before the summer term opened, Mrs. Beddows was dozing after lunch on the drawing-room sofa, a bull's-eye bulging in each cheek and a wild west story open face downwards on her stomach, when Sybil came in to say that Miss Burton was on the telephone.

"Ask her to tea," mumbled Mrs. Beddows, sucking peppermint.

"Aunt Ursula's coming."

"She won't bite her. Go on, dear. I want forty winks now, or I can't face the family."

Thus Sarah, who wanted a quiet interview, found herself at a Beddows family tea-party.

She joined in the stern procession to the dining-room. Tea was tea at Willow Lodge, a meal served at a solemn well-spread table, below photogravure pictures portraying those scenes of carnage so popular in Edwardian dining-rooms. Horses lashed about in agony, soldiers fell face downwards in the snow unable to answer roll call, cavalry charged across the trampled corn. It was a fashion which Sarah found unsuitable and barbarous, but the Beddows family ate with excellent appetite, quite undisturbed by hate and slaughter.

The meal itself represented the shifting compromise between Emma Beddows' lavish taste and her husband's vigilant economy. The plates were piled high with bread and butter, currant loaf and queen cakes; the cheese cakes and lemon tarts lay on frilled netted d'oylies; the spice-bread was rich as buttered cold plum pudding; but there was milk, not cream, in the silver plated jug and Mrs. Beddows did not dare to ask Sybil for the caddy once the teapot had been filled.

Sarah had not learned these subtleties of Beddows housekeeping. She was only aware that Mr. and Mrs. Crossfield dominated the conversation, had every intention of continuing to dominate it, and considered her an inferior intruder.

I can do nothing here, thought Sarah. I was a fool to come.

The talk was fixed on family affairs, on James this and Ernest that, on illnesses and incomes. Sarah crumbled her cake and stirred her tea, and found no word to say about whether a certain Beddows cousin had done well to leave her house at Buxton to live in Boston Spa, or whether a niece called Rose was justified in breaking off her engagement to a veterinary surgeon. Once or twice she tried to engage big shy Willie Beddows in conversation, but at Willow Lodge when either host or hostess talked, the lesser breeds kept silence. One monologue at a time alone was tolerated, and just then Mrs. Beddows was laying down the law about Elizabeth's cottage—she had paid too much for it; it was money wasted; one big sitting-room and a good kitchen was quite enough for a farmer's widow. What does she want with dining-room and drawing-room? Always did she put on airs and play at being her betters, did Elizabeth. Then she'll get into debt and we shall all have to help her out of it.

The voice was the voice of Alderman Mrs. Beddows, but the words were the words of Jim her husband.

You can't live under the thumb of a mean-minded little auctioneer, Sarah thought, for thirty and more years without being infected by him. And at this moment Mrs. Beddows was not the alderman at all; she was Jim's wife and Ursula Crossfield's sister-in-law. No generous impulse, no splendid defiance of common sense and caution, could survive in that atmosphere. Sarah had come to ask Mrs. Beddows not to be sensible. She had come to ask her to use her imagination and take a chance; but this was not the time nor place for persuasion, and she knew it.

She thought of the women of Mrs. Beddows' generation and of how even when they gave one quarter of their energy to public service they spent the remaining three-quarters on quite unnecessary domestic ritual and propitiation. The little plump woman with the wise lined face might have gone anywhere, done anything; but she would always set limits upon her powers through her desire not to upset her husband's family.

Listening to the conversation, Sarah became increasingly critical, and as her critical spirit waxed, her tact and caution waned. Mrs. Crossfield had arrived, via spring-cleaning and servants, at the perennial topic of the modern girl, and the modern girl led, inevitably, to lipstick. Mrs. Crossfield expressed her horror of cosmetics. Mrs. Beddows, who in other company might have shared other views, brought out a suitable anecdote, which had two merits; it was true and it flattered the judgment of her sister-in-law.

A new inspector had been appointed for elementary schools. The alderman had talked to him. In the course of conversation somebody had asked him: "'If you had two candidates for a teaching post before you, with equal qualifications in every way, but one used lipstick and one did not, which would you appoint?' and he replied: 'The girl who didn't plaster with paint the face God gave her, Mrs. Beddows.'" The alderman beamed benevolently at Sarah. "So you see, even you modern educationists sometimes see eye to eye with us old-fashioned people."

By that time Sarah was tired of keeping silence. She was, after all, a head mistress and unaccustomed to nibbling buns and accepting without controversy the opinions of her elders.

"I don't know if you call me a modern educationist," she said rashly, "but I certainly don't agree with the inspector."

"Oh, really? Indeed? Indeed?" asked Mrs. Crossfield, looking at Sarah rather as though one of the buns had spoken.

"My trouble," said Sarah, thinking of Miss Sigglesthwaite, but also by this time feeling irritably perverse, "my trouble is to persuade my girls that membership of my profession need not imply complete indifference to all other sides of life."

"Your profession?" asked Mrs. Crossfield.

"I teach," said Sarah proudly.

"Miss Burton is the head mistress of the Girls' High School at Kiplington," Mrs. Beddows interpolated—belatedly, thought Sarah, by this time thoroughly roused.

"I regard lipstick as a symbol of self-respect, of interest in one's appearance, of a hopeful and self-assured attitude towards life," continued Sarah. "If I had two candidates before me, and they had equal qualifications, but one looked as though she washed her face in sunlight soap and dried it on the hockey field, and the other looked as though she could hold down the post of head mannequin at Molyneux's, but had chosen to teach instead, I should take the mannequin every time. I should be sure that her influence on the girls would be far wider, more exhilarating and more healthy."

"Really?" said Mrs. Crossfield. "Oh, Jim, have you heard from Florence Ritchie lately? I had a letter from her in Harrogate two days ago."

"Don't you think I should be right, Wendy?" said Sarah combatively, refusing to be snubbed.

But this appeal was too much for Wendy Beddows, caught in the conflict between personalities as formidable as her head mistress and her grandmother. She choked into her tea-cup, and had to be slapped on the back and fly gulping from the room, thus causing a perhaps tactful interruption.

"Shall we go into the drawing-room?" asked Mrs. Beddows.

Sarah realised that she had made a blunder. But her blood was up. She knew far more about modern youth than Mrs. Crossfield. She had more right to speak about schools than Mrs. Beddows. She had come to Willow Lodge on important business. The future of far more than Lydia Holly depended upon her action. Mrs. Beddows had said that she could see her; see her she should.

Sarah sat in a corner of the drawing-room sofa and lit a cigarette defiantly. She was behaving badly and she knew it.

But she was still shaken by the shock of hearing about the Hollies' tragedy. The thought of Lydia's ordeal had disturbed her deeply. The sight of the girl when she had gone to visit her, of her dull despair, her animal acceptance of fatality, had roused in Sarah the most profound instincts of her nature. She would not accept; she would not be resigned. She would not display a cheerful stoicism towards the misfortunes of other people.

She sat in the ugly cheerful room listening to the ceaseless flow of trivialities, determined to outstay the Crossfield couple.

But it seemed as though they would stay for ever. She thought of the piled-up papers on her desk, the work awaiting her, her engagement she had that evening after supper with Joe Astell. The calendars pinned to the cretonne curtains marked interminable days; the marble clock on the plush-draped overmantel ticked endless hours. At half-past six Sarah realised that she must make her own opportunity.

"Mrs. Beddows," she said, "I shall have to go, I'm afraid, in a few minutes; but I wonder if you could spare me just a moment or two? To ask you something."

The alderman looked really surprised, as though no one could possibly want to consult her on public business when her husband's relatives were in her house; but she said: "Why yes, certainly. What is it?"

"It's a matter for the governors. I wanted to consult you first before term started. I'm terribly sorry; but this seemed the only opportunity."

"Oh, very well. Yes. Well, Ursula, can you excuse us for a minute?"

They made their apologies. Mrs. Beddows led Sarah back to the deserted dining-room where now the table lay spread for cold supper, the mutton and salad and blancmange and rhubarb all netted down under cages of blue wire. They sat, Sarah in the shabby leather-covered arm-chair, the alderman at her big untidy desk, strewn with unfiled papers. "And how she ever gets through all her work at such a desk," thought Sarah, "Heaven knows." But the fact remained that she got through more than five ordinary people and hardly ever confused her facts or lost her documents. Even this irritated Sarah a little, accustomed as she was to training children in habits of order which she declared to be indispensable. Mrs. Beddows constantly disturbed her theories.

"Well? What can I do? What is it?" asked Mrs. Beddows.

You can stop treating those ugly, ignorant, silly, unimportant relations-in-law of yours as though they were God's step-brothers, snarled Sarah's disgruntled mind; but aloud she said only: "You know the Hollies?"

"The Hollies—let me see? The Hollies of Cattleholme?"

"No, the Shacks, Kiplington. He's a builder's labourer out of work at the moment. The girl comes to the High School on a scholarship. Lydia Holly. She's the brightest thing we've got."

"Yes—I remember. You told me about her."

"I think, taking her all round, she's the most promising child I've ever taught. Certainly the only outstanding one in the school at present. And unless we can do something at once, she's leaving."

"Oh. Why?"

"She's the eldest of seven children, now eight with the baby. There's one elder brother working for Tadman the grocer. They live in a converted railway coach at the Shacks—you know—on the Maythorpe cliff. I'd noticed that the girl had been a bit awkward all this term. Now it appears that she knew her mother was going to have another baby, and she knew too that she'd been warned that it might kill her. She was right. The mother had a fall and died last week. The baby unfortunately lives. Lydia was quite alone in that camp for some time with her mother and the little boy, a toddler. She's only just fifteen. And now she has to give up her scholarship and go home and look after the children."

"Poor child. Are there no aunts or any one?"

"No one. I've asked. The father's a hopeless little creature. Good-natured, but drinks on and off and always in and out of work. The aunts are married women with families. Lydia and her father both take it quite for granted."

"Yes, I suppose she must."

"But she can't, Mrs. Beddows. It would be monstrous. It's been bad enough for the girl having that dread hanging over her ever since before Christmas. That's enough to affect her for life. But then to find that what she dreaded happened—that's what's so bad for her—for any one. Children shouldn't see their worst fears realised. We've got to save her."

Mrs. Beddows sighed. She thought that Sarah looked very young and inexperienced, for all her forty years.

"That's all very well, but I don't see we can stop it."

"We've got to. It's intolerable. Think of the waste."

"Waste?"

"A girl like that—all that talent—when there's so little in the world—to come to nothing."

"She's got those children to look after."

"Any one could do that. Listen, Mrs. Beddows. If you can persuade the governors to give her a boarding scholarship, I'll undertake to see that there's a woman to look after the children. We might get the baby into a home. Lydia's too young any way—at fifteen."

"You'll undertake it? Oh, I'm sorry, Miss Burton. But you can't begin to do this kind of thing, you know."

"It's for my own sake. You don't get a girl like that in a school like mine—not once in twenty years."

"Maybe. But if it wasn't once in fifty you couldn't do it. It's not common sense. Hundreds of other women die. Hundreds of other girls have to give up their scholarships. You have to begin as you mean to go on. You can't take upon yourself the management of the universe. How d'you know Holly would let you do this?"

"He would. He's the kind of little man who'd take whatever came his way."

"But you can't make exceptions—I don't think for a moment the governors would agree to it. Why a boarder, anyway?"

"Because otherwise she'd be spending all the time she should be doing home-work bathing babies."

"I wonder how many others of your girls bath babies and help their mothers to run boarding houses?"

"That doesn't make it right. The world needs the sort of woman Lydia Holly could be."

"If she's as fine as you say, she'll be fine anyway. This may make a woman of her."

"A drudge."

"My dear, you know, there are other things in life besides book-learning. What if she does give up her scholarship and doesn't go to college? There'll be one school teacher less, and perhaps one fine woman and wife the more. Is that such a tragedy?"

"Yes, yes. All waste is tragedy. To waste deliberately a rare, a unique capacity, that's downright wicked. It's treason to the human stock. We need trained intelligence."

"What about trained character?"

"Oh, that too, yes. I believe in discipline—but not frustration."

"You believe very much in having your own way, don't you?"

Sarah looked up in surprise. The room was twilit. The alderman's face was turned away from the window.

"I believe," said Sarah gravely, "in being used to the farthest limit of one's capacity."

"And you expect people to choose their own ways of fulfilment?"

"Yes. To a large extent."

"You don't believe then in a higher providence?"

"Not if it means just knuckling under as soon as things grow difficult, and calling that God's will. I think we have to play our own providence—for ourselves and for future generations. If the growth of civilisation means anything, it means the gradual reduction of the areas ruled by chance—providence, if you like."

"Chance?" The grey spring twilight seemed to reflect the melancholy of the older woman's sigh. All her habitual gaiety was subdued. "Life isn't as easy as all that. There's so much hardship, so little means of helping. If you give too much here, another must go without there. If you strain the law here, you'll break it there. We do what we can, but that's so little. We need patience."

"Oh, patience!" flashed Sarah. "Surely we need courage even more," and through her mind passed a procession of generations submitting patiently to all the old evils of the world—to wars, poverty, disease, ugliness and disappointment, and calling their surrender submission to Providence.

"We need courage, not so much to endure as to act. All this resignation stunts us. We're so busy resigning ourselves to the inevitable, that we don't even ask if it is inevitable. We spend so much time accommodating ourselves to other people's standards, we don't even ask if our own might not be better. We're so much occupied in letting live that we haven't begun to live." She drew a deep breath as though she had received a revelation. "That's it. That's it. We haven't even begun to learn yet how to live. We're still a blind and stumbling race of savages, crawling up out of the primeval slime, trailing behind us fears and superstitions and prejudices like jungle weeds, and not daring to get rid of them because patience and resignation are still accounted virtues. We've got to have courage, to take our future into our hands. If the law is oppressive, we must change the law. If tradition is obstructive, we must break tradition. If the system is unjust, we must reform the system. 'Take what you want,' says God. 'Take it and pay for it.'"

"Ah," said Mrs. Beddows quietly, "But who pays?"

Before Emma Beddows there passed another picture—not Sarah's panorama of abstractions, but the concrete memory of life as she had found it: of the neat little self-assured man whom she had married, and had found to be as empty of human kindness as a withered hazel nut; of her son, so strong, so gay, so full of promise, choking out his life in the army hospital, dying from pneumonia after gas poisoning in a war which had come upon them all like an upheaval of the earth; of her daughter-in-law, Willie's Jean, dead beside her still-born baby; of Muriel Carne, crouched on the sunlit floor, her beauty marred and raddled, her wild senseless cries lamenting incurable woe. She saw the wreckage of the mental hospitals, which she had to visit, the derelicts in the county institutions, the painful optimism of the coughing, bright-eyed patients in the sanatoria, the bleak defeat of hope and independence which brought applicants before the public assistance committees. She saw Carne of Maythorpe, betrayed in love, in fatherhood, in prestige, in prosperity, by circumstances which neither courage nor intelligence could have altered. She had seen compassion impotent and effort wasted. She was an old woman.

She felt sorry for the wilful unbroken girl before her. "It isn't as easy as all that."

"Then you won't help me?" Sarah might have known, she told herself, that she would get nothing out of Mrs. Beddows that evening.

"I didn't say that. We can keep the scholarship open in case she's able to return later. Boarding's a different matter. She's too near. We can't exceed our powers."

The door opened. Mr. Beddows slid in, a grey, ghost-like figure. He did not see the women in the alcove by his wife's desk. Cautiously he stole forward and lifted, first one cover from the supper table, and then another. Not red currant jelly and mint sauce, he decided. Not boiled eggs in the salad. Not jam and custard with the blancmange. Quietly, silently, he crept back to the larder carrying those dishes which he considered to betoken unwarrantable extravagance. He replaced the blue tin cages. He retreated.

Mrs. Beddows, looking through the mirror which, above her desk, reflected in miniature the dim green evening, never saw him. Sarah, staring, fascinated, found no word to say. She felt that she had accidentally spied upon the skeleton in the alderman's cupboard. She could be angry no longer.

"I'll go and see the Hollies. If I can do anything," repeated Mrs. Beddows.

She rose. It was all unsatisfactory. She was not quite sure that Sarah Burton had the common sense, the sober stability of temperament that she had hoped.

The interview was at an end. She switched on the light. The ugly crowded room leapt into full view, the supper table, the mantelpiece, the Death of Nelson. By the clock stood an Easter card drawn by Midge. Three rather nebulous but soulful angels, with immense eyes, adorned it, and a chime of golden bells tied with pale blue ribbon.

"Is this the sort of thing you teach at Kiplington?"

"I hope not," laughed Sarah. "Who did it? Oh—Midge Carne."

"How's she getting on?"

"Not so badly. Poor little Midge."

"She likes school."

"Who wouldn't? After that great, gloomy, isolated house."

"You've seen it?"

"Yes." Sarah outlined the circumstances of her visit. She was amusing. She could tell a good story. She did not describe the moment when she had stepped back from the shadowed portrait, the candles in her hand.

"I didn't know," said Mrs. Beddows. "He didn't tell me."

A less honest woman might have pretended. Mrs. Beddows was hurt. A chill invaded her heart. He might have told me.

"I don't suppose it ever entered his head again," smiled Sarah. "He obviously dislikes me."

"Oh, no—I'm sure he doesn't," said Mrs. Beddows falsely.

"Why shouldn't he? We're natural antagonists. We dislike everything each other stands for." The implication of antagonism established a bond between the teacher and the councillor which Mrs. Beddows found herself resenting.

"Still you did save his cow," she smiled with generous effort.

"I don't think he was grateful," laughed Sarah.

"Men never are," said Mrs. Beddows. "After all, why should they be?"

Sarah, on her way to the door, turned as Mrs. Beddows switched off the light again, and felt that they had shut up into that room more than Midge's card and the cluttered desk and the cold Sunday supper; she felt that a question remained there curled on the still air like a smoke ring.

"Take what you want," said Sarah, "take it and pay for it."

"But who pays?" asked Mrs. Beddows.

CHAPTER III

COUNCILLOR HUGGINS SECURES THE FLOODLIGHTING OF THE HOSPITAL

Sarah was not the only person to be troubled by the problem of the Hollies. Councillor Huggins was almost equally concerned. His fortuitous presence at the Shacks had affected him profoundly.

For when Lydia sprang from the gateway calling for help to the man who drove the lorry, Huggins had been in that vulnerable state of super-sensitiveness which accompanies spiritual convalescence. The grey April afternoon which had terrified Lydia by its chill indifference calmed Huggins' soul to humble gratitude.

For Snaith had saved him. Bessy was safely married to Reg Aythorne. The money had been quietly handed over. With it Reg had bought the sheds on Leame Ferry Waste and the uneven marshy ground immediately surrounding them. On these he had raised a mortgage from a Kiplington undertaker, Mr. Stillman, to whom Huggins had hinted that land values on the Wastes were likely to go up a bit now that the new Skerrow road was to be built. With Stillman's loan, Reg and Bessy had acquired the coveted general shop at Dollstall, and there they were, all settled down as easily as though no financial earthquake had recently threatened the whole fortress of Huggins' reputation.

Of course he would one day have to pay off Snaith; but that would be quite easy. Within six months, as soon as the housing scheme went through, the old warehouses would be trebled or quadrupled in value. Reg would pay off the mortgage, repay Huggins' loan, still hold the Dollstall business, and nobody would be a penny halfpenny the worse for it.

That was what came of trusting in the Lord. God could work miracles—God and a God-fearing man like Snaith worth half a million.

Since his appeal to the alderman, Huggins had lost all fear of Snaith. They now were allies, confederates in a complex but meritorious plan to make the wilderness rejoice and the desert blossom like the rose. They were doing God's work. They were both His servants.

Though Councillor Huggins' financial transactions might be complicated, his mind was simple enough. When he was disturbed by the tragedy of Mrs. Holly's death his immediate reaction was a desire to do something about it. Because Snaith had helped him once, he would help him again. Because the Leame Ferry Waste Housing Scheme was to be the salvation of Mr. Huggins, it must also become the salvation of threatened mothers.

Why had Mrs. Holly died? Because she had given birth to a child under impossible conditions. The Shacks were insanitary and unfit for human habitation. The Shacks must go. Where should their present residents find refuge? In the Leame Ferry Garden Village, of course.

There was no proper maternity hospital nearer than Kingsport. And that was overcrowded; there had been complaints about it. A new annex for mothers had been suggested as part of the General Hospital, but the money had not yet been raised nor the site chosen. Where should such a site be found if not on the cheapest and most convenient land available—Leame Ferry Waste? Why not? Why not indeed?

That the incidents of Bessy's blackmail and Mrs. Holly's death should find identical remedy, appeared to Huggins wholly as an act of guidance. He was being led to do the Lord's work. He saw all his tribulation as a pointing finger.

He rang up Snaith to say that he must see him before the next meeting of the Public Health Committee. Snaith was just off to Manchester on business, and only returning the same day as the committee. Was it urgent? Yes, yes! All Huggins' ideas, as they occurred to him, were urgent. Was it private? No, not at all. Mrs. Holly's death had upset him. It had given him an idea about the new Maternity Annexe. He wanted to discuss it before the committee met.

He thought he heard a sigh at the other end of the telephone. Relief, fatigue, impatience? But Snaith's clear even voice reached him across the buzzing wire.

"Well, my train gets in to Flintonbridge at 12.30. Could you meet me for lunch at the Golden Ball? Quarter to one? Good."

It happened that the Public Health Special Committee met in May. It was market day in Flintonbridge and the little town was astir with life.

Huggins arrived early at the Golden Ball—an old-fashioned inn, famous for its cooking and popular with sportsmen. He was told that Mr. Snaith had reserved a table and followed the waiter to one laid for two people in the bow window of the coffee-room. Impressed as ever by this evidence of Snaith's power and foresight, he sat down to await his host and watched the busy coloured scene before him. The stalls were piled high with scarlet tomatoes, clear green lettuces, tufted bundles of white-whiskered crimson radishes. Sacks of new potatoes squatted low on the cobbles. Fowls, plucked and dressed, dangled limp skinny necks; cottage women offered for sale long sticks of bright pink rhubarb and bunches of forget-me-nots or wallflowers. Enterprising young farmers' wives in white drill overalls sold their own butter, eggs and cheese, calling to husbands and friends who rattled round the square in their dusty Fords. The scene appeared so pleasant and animated that it gave the lie to tales of the slump, the agricultural depression.

They're well enough, thought Huggins. They don't need derating. Their wives don't die in childbed in wretched hovels for want of proper attention. Look at this pub! Full of 'em. Look at these girls, dolled up, going to the cinema this afternoon, tea at the cafe, hunt balls and point-to-points, I shouldn't wonder. They ought to be made to pay. What if the rates do go up?

He worked himself into a fine state of moral indignation before Snaith crossed the square towards the Golden Ball.

He walked quickly, lightly, daintily, moving like a wraith among the noisy people. Nobody greeted him; he spoke to nobody. This was not his kingdom. But when he entered the dining-room of the hotel and made for the window table, Huggins felt a warmth of admiration and championship stir his heart.

Snaith gave an order to the lethargic waiter.

Huggins launched forth into a denunciation of the wealthy and idle farmers. Snaith listened quietly, his subtle face showing not even amusement.

After a pause, he said, "What is this case of a Mrs. Holly?"

Huggins told him and began to enlarge upon the enormity of the Shacks as a place of residence. Snaith noted down one or two facts in a slim leather-covered book. Huggins watched with fascination the gold pencil moving so neatly and evenly over the lined paper. By such neatnesses were millions acquired.

The waiter was slow.

Snaith touched the bell again.

"They're half asleep here."

"They're not accustomed to busy men," laughed Huggins. "Only farmers."

Down the market-place strode a familiar figure. Snaith and Huggins could both see him. At his approach labourers touched their forelocks, stallholders called out greetings, women held up dressed guinea-fowls, prodding flexible breasts, challenging purchase. In his market clothes, breeches, tweed coat and soft hat, Carne of Maythorpe was a farmer among farmers. And he was popular. Huggins felt as though this widespread recognition were a deliberate insult to the little grey alderman, whom no acquaintances had welcomed, and who now sat, demure, non-committal, quizzical, watching the approach of his political opponent.

Outside the hotel Bill Heyer, the one-armed ex-service man, presided over the Cold Harbour provision stall. Carne stopped to speak to him. The window was open in the bright May sunshine, but the clatter of wheels on the cobbles, the clangour of voices, the cackling of fowls, barking of dogs and explosions of a motor-cycle back-firing in the square, drowned all but a few sentences.

Carne and Heyer were discussing a dog. Heyer said:

"I told him we couldn't have it running after sheep. Once they start, there's no stopping them. Pup or dog, they're damned. But Sawdon said, 'That's my missus's affair.'"

Carne said, "I agree with you it's bad luck, but there's no cure for it."

"So Carne will be at the committee," Snaith observed.

"Aye. Hunting season's over," laughed Huggins, pleased when a swift flicker of amusement crossed his host's pale face.

Both men had been annoyed by the appearance of Carne, mud splashed, in his pink coat, at committee meetings. "Damned bad form. The man's a bounder," Colonel Whitelaw once had said. Whitelaw had taken the Sedgmire's side in that ancient quarrel. Huggins treasured his words with rapture.

Heyer was laughing now, and Carne was laughing, his saturnine face lit up by the glitter of dark eyes, the flash of white teeth. The man's a bounder, Huggins repeated to himself, thinking that Carne might be the present hero of the Cold Harbour colonists, because he was prepared to combat Snaith's good work on the council; but obstruction was a poor basis for hero worship. "One day they'll learn the truth," Huggins swore to himself.

He leaned forward, "I wanted to ask you. You know this circular about maternal mortality from the Ministry?"

Carne entered the dining-room.

A group of farmers at a corner table hailed him. They had kept a place for him and he went to them, handsome, commanding, popular, his melancholy dissipated by that genial greeting.

It's not right, thought Huggins, his indignation at Mrs. Holly's death mingling with his indignation at Carne's popularity and the comparative obscurity of Snaith. Just now too, Snaith had asked for a jug of water, and the waiter delayed while he went for Carne's whisky; Snaith ordered apple-pie for two, but the waiter was bringing Carne's roast ribs of beef.

"This Cottage Nursing Association Mrs. Beddows is so keen on—it's not adequate," spluttered Huggins. "Never there when you want it. We need a proper maternity service for the South Riding and a hospital not so far away as Kingsport. Why not Leame Ferry? What's wrong with building the new annexe for mothers at Leame Ferry?"

"Nothing's wrong—except that we haven't yet raised the money or drained the Wastes."

"Look here now—Look here now. This is my idea."

Huggins shovelled pie and custard into his deep red mouth. He thumped his blunt fingers on the tablecloth. Under his eager vision the garden village rose with neat labour-saving houses. Lime and sycamore trees lined the avenues. Shops, in one comely block, faced the main road; and back from the road, equipped with all the latest appliances and comforts, lay the women's hospital.

"There!" he cried in triumph, leaning back in his chair, his coarse hairy hands outspread on the white tablecloth. There it was. Built already. A boon and a blessing to men—and women. He smiled across the emptied plates at Snaith.

"Well—of course—it certainly might be done. But I hardly think that this committee is the time to make the suggestion. The housing scheme comes up under Housing and Town Planning. Astell's handling it there. He thinks they'll elect a special joint committee with Kingsport Corporation to inquire into the estimates at the next sub-committee. I should think we can safely leave it to Astell. As a matter of fact—did you get hold of those Warehouses?"

"Aythorne did. He's got a mortgage on 'em with a chap called Stillman."

"The undertaker?"

"That's right."

"Queer about undertakers. I suppose they have their private lives like any one else. Odd though, to be a professional mourner."

Huggins glanced up, puzzled. He was unaccustomed to whimsicality.

"Your daughter getting along all right?"

"My—er? Oh, Freda! Yes. She's all right."

"Back at Redcar?"

"Quite so—quite so. Thanks to you, Mr. Snaith. I've not forgotten."

"Oh—that's all right. Purely a business transaction. Now look here. As I see it, the whole council is in a fever just now about economy. Very silly, a great deal of it, but they're made like that. Perhaps next year's elections will get us some new blood in. Lord knows we need it."

"Surely, surely."

"Now there's this thirty thousand needed for rebuilding Kingsport Hospital."

A guffaw of laughter came from the farmers' table. They had reached the stage of exchanging doubtful anecdotes.

"They can afford it," said Huggins, with a jerk of his head.

"Maybe. But we've got to see they do. I imagine that the council will give pound for pound on the money raised by voluntary contribution. What we've got to do is to make people realise that this health business is important. Publicity. That's the idea. I want you to back me."

"Anything I can do."

"You can do a lot. You can get the Methodists roused. You can work up the Kiplington area. You'll come on my committee? Good. I'll tell you another idea I've got. We'll have the old building floodlit. There it is, right in the centre of the town. Yet people hardly know it exists."

"Yes, but look here. What about the site for the new building?"

"Oh, we'll see to that all in good time."

Huggins was content. Somehow, by the miraculous subtleties of intrigue, the plan for floodlighting the hospital was going to raise the values of the Leame Ferry Waste sheds. Never mind how. Huggins was Snaith's man. He believed implicitly in his leader's power. Somehow all things worked together for good to those that love God.

CHAPTER IV

MIDGE ENJOYS THE MEASLES

To Midge Carne Mrs. Holly's death meant that when she returned to school for the summer term of 1933, Lydia was not there. Lydia, hurrah, hurrah, hurrah! Fat, rough, vulgar, slummy Lydia had gone home to look after her horrid little snotty-nosed brothers and sisters and a wretched little baby. Good riddance of bad rubbish.

But Lydia's absence was not the only treat awaiting her. Midge had a tale to tell. A marvellous tale. Miss Burton, Scarlet Sally, had—no, no, no, you'd never possibly guess it. Miss Burton has worn my combinations. Imagine it! Midge whispered to Gwynneth Rogers and Nancy Grey and Leslie Tucker—Imagine Miss Burton in your combinations!

Then, when incredulity gave way to ecstatic giggles, Midge would tell the whole story—of the calving cow, the night's vigil, of her father's return with Scarlet Sally, and of the hot bath, the borrowed clothes, the breakfast. No one else in the school had such a story. It gave Midge a prestige which she had never even dreamed of during her first two unhappy terms. It was an answer to prayer.

For at her first Communion on Easter morning, as at the most potent, sacred and magic moment of her life, Midge had prayed first that her mother might recover, then that her father might be happy, then that she might be popular at school and receive admission to the glorious company known as Them.

"They" were a small group of girls who for some indefinable quality had acquired popularity at the High School. There was nothing special about them. Gwynneth was a farmer's daughter, a pert vivacious unintimidated member of IV. Lower; Nancy Grey, Molly Gryson, Judy Peacock—all these and perhaps half a dozen others congregated in one privileged corner of the bicycle shed, cycled to games and ate their eleven o'clock biscuits together. They were exclusive. Outsiders were sternly warned away. Midge, unaccustomed to exclusion, had suffered hideously from their repeated snubs. They did not want her, and she took nearly two months to learn that even Midge Carne of Maythorpe, even Lord Sedgmire's granddaughter, found no welcome where she was not wanted. The very inaccessibility of Them made them seem more desirable. When Midge returned for the summer term, and found that her story could win eager listeners, her delight was unbounded. Even They might want her.

They did. They shared her admiration of Miss Burton and her awe at the amazing intimacies of her wardrobe. They were ready to listen with avid attention to her details. "Her own things were pale green silk. Yes, fancy, and a sort of belt with net frilling instead of stays; but she wore my brown tights, and sent back all the clothes washed and ironed in a box from Marshall & Snelgrove."

There were other pleasant features of that summer term—crisp white cotton blouses instead of cream flannel, eleven o'clock break out of doors, tennis instead of hockey.

Midge hated hockey. To her it meant hours of chill uncomfortable boredom punctuated by moments of anxiety and disappointment. Always before a game she thought: This time I shall play better. Always she found herself unable to keep in line with the forwards, fumbling her passes, missing tackles. She was no good at all. She shed tears behind the pavilion, but these did not help her. Fatigue and humiliation exhausted her.

But tennis was different. She had played before; there was a court at Maythorpe—when any one bothered to put the net up. The Beddows family sometimes played tennis. Midge liked to watch the new white balls springing on the green turf; she loved the smell of cut grass, the hum of bees in the border of narcissus and wallflowers and forget-me-not, the drowsy murmur of the mowing machine through open form-room windows. She loved the summer term.

It was not spoiled for her when during the second week Gwynneth Rogers suddenly disappeared and the school was put into quarantine for measles. The others were furious. Measles in summer! It simply was unthinkable. The Easter term was the proper term for measles. No tennis matches, no sports competition against Kingsport South. Midge did not care. She had become one of Them. She sat in the bicycle shed with Molly and Judy and pretended to mourn the absence of Gwynneth. She mourned nothing.

It was just as well that she found school so pleasant, for Maythorpe Hall was drearier than ever. No visitors came now; only men on business drove up to the back door and sat closeted with her father in the gun-room. Mr. Castle was worse. Pudsey was drinking. Daddy sat night after night at his account books. He was trying to sell the pictures from the dining-room, but nobody seemed anxious to buy the portraits of Carne forefathers in blue satin waistcoats, Carnes in hunting pink, Carnes with sidewhiskers. We can't afford it, we can't afford it, that was the rhythm chanted across the day. After the cheerful order and variety of the school routine, the time-table that changed at the bidding of a bell every forty-five minutes, the jokes, the companionship of Them, Maythorpe life stretched out in a dull monotony of inaction.

Then one morning Midge woke up with a sore throat and a slight headache. She said nothing, terrified lest Elsie should tell her she had a cold and must stay at home. She choked down egg and bacon, collected her satchel and gym shoes, and was ready, with unaccustomed punctuality, when her father came out into the stable-yard. He was driving to Kiplington to catch a train for Flintonbridge. She could go with him. On the way he told her that he must shortly go to Ireland again, about some horses. She made little comment. Her throat felt so sore that all she wanted was to keep her mouth shut. She was aware of the sombre, disappointed glance he gave her, but did not know that he was deeply jealous of her delight in the school, her preoccupation with all its affairs.

She loved him dearly. When he drove away, leaving her at the school gate, she looked at the flashing wheels of the cart, the spanking chestnut, the glittering buckles of the polished harness, and thought that there was no one like her father. Even his refusal to buy a car had distinction in it. The chestnut was one of the horses to be sold in Ireland.

Midge went in to school, but her head was heavy. She could not give her attention to her lessons. She could not eat her dinner.

Miss Parsons saw her drooping figure and flushed cheeks and called her into matron's room and took her temperature. When she removed the thermometer from Midge's mouth, she became at once pink-faced and fluttering.

"Yes, yes. You'd better lie down, dear. Here on the sofa. I'll keep the others out. Yes, Jean, what is it? Oh, your cod-liver-oil. Well, no—yes. I'll bring it out to you." She took a card marked "Engaged" and hung it on the door.

Midge was delighted. If she was to feel ill, she preferred that her maladies should evoke consternation. Miss Parsons seemed most suitably impressed.

Midge lay down. She felt hot and drowsy. She could hear the clatter of feet outside in the stone corridor, the ripple of arpeggios from the practising-room, the hollow knock of cricket balls against bats down at the nets.

She must have fallen asleep, because she opened her eyes to see Dr. Campbell's familiar red face staring into hers.

"Well, young woman," Dr. Campbell's manner was invariably facetious. Midge detested it. "Let's look at your chest. Ah, a very nice crop. Rich, fine fruity measles. Well, now, what are we going to do with her, matron? Better wrap her up and I'll take her home in my car. Where's your father, Miss Fishywigs?"

"He's at Flintonbridge on the council. I can't go home. It's all empty," said Midge with dignity and emphasis.

"Where's Elsie?"

"Out visiting her mother."

Dr. Campbell knew all about the Maythorpe household.

"Well, I suppose we shall have to wait till we can get hold of your father. I suppose one can catch him at the County Hall."

"He doesn't like being disturbed there. And I can't go home. He's got to go to Ireland. I can't stay there with Elsie if I'm ill. She's rough and her hands smell of onions, and she's not nice to me." Midge's large eyes filled with tears. Already she could see Elsie, a great rough hulking bully, herself, a forlorn deserted invalid, twilight enveloping the echoing house, her father in Ireland. "I shall die! I shall die!" sobbed Midge. "I can't be left all alone there ill. I can't! I can't!"

"Now then, now then, we're not going to desert you. Pull yourself together. How old are you? Fifteen? God bless my soul! I thought you were only five," Dr. Campbell teased her. But Midge wept and moaned, and eventually Miss Burton appeared beside Miss Parsons, and laid a cool firm hand on the girl's tossing head.

"Midge, be quiet. Because you happen to have measles, that's no reason for behaving like a baby. You're not the only one. I've telephoned to your father and he'll come here and discuss things. Of course you won't be sent home to an empty house. Do use your common sense."

Her quiet voice, her assumption that Midge was really a reasonable being, had their accustomed effect. Midge controlled herself, and dozed off again, waking at intervals to drink orange juice or to let Miss Parsons turn her fiery pillows.

Aeons passed before Miss Burton reappeared with Carne behind her. This time Midge was steeled to play the heroic invalid. She smiled up wanly at her father, swallowing painfully, and he stared down at her, gruff and worried.

It was Miss Burton who took charge of the situation.

"Well, Midge. Your father's here, and he's come to take you home if you'd like to go with him. You would have a nurse, so you wouldn't be left alone. And though you may feel rather rotten for two or three days, in a week you'll be almost yourself again. But if you prefer it, you can stay here because Nancy has measles now as well as Gwynneth, and I'm turning my house into a sanatorium. I've discussed it with your father and you are to do just whichever you prefer."

Midge turned her great feverish eyes from one adult to the other. Daddy, poor Daddy, so big and white and worried, all by himself alone in Maythorpe Hall. Sitting at night over his figures in the gun-room. Eating solitary suppers in the candlelit dining-room. Pathos choked her.

"Oh, Daddy, darling! I don't want to be a nuisance."

"Nobody's going to let you be a nuisance," said Miss Burton crisply. She looked cool and young in her green linen dress.

"You're going to Ireland," wailed Midge.

"Not if you don't want me to," mumbled her father.

"It doesn't matter whether you are at Maythorpe or here," Miss Burton said. "Stop crying and help us, please, Midge. In both cases you will be looked after. You like Gwynneth and Nancy, don't you?"

"Oh, yes, Miss Burton."

"I thought they were rather special friends of yours." The blessed compliment sang in Midge's head. "Very well, then. If you like to share their room we'll take you round right away now in my car."

"Oh, thank you, Miss Burton."

Only be good, thought Midge, only be unselfish, and all else shall be added unto you. She lay in her father's arms as he carried her, rolled in a blanket, out to the car, and sat with her, pressed against his tweed coat, while Miss Burton drove them both to her little house. He held her so tightly that Midge could feel the irregular scurrying beat of his heart, a queer motion. He carried her up to a room where a nurse in a starched apron was already laying sheets on a narrow bed between two others.

"Hallo, Midge!" called Gwynneth, boisterous and convalescent.

"Why, it's Midge!" cried Nancy, languid but friendly.

Their welcome flattered her, and perhaps cheered her father. She drew herself up in her wrappings of blanket, and said proudly, "This is my father. These are my friends, Gwynneth and Nancy."

Gwynneth and Nancy said, "How do you do?" But Daddy appeared unconversational, and soon left with Miss Burton, and Midge felt so queer that she was glad to let the nurse undress her and settle her down between cool shivery sheets.

Then began a curious time, both nice and nasty. There were interminable nights, hot, restless, aching, and pleasant days, with visits from Miss Burton, and conversations with Gwynneth and Nancy, and orange juice and custard, and delicious tangerines. There were dreams of Maythorpe restored, as one day it surely should be; her mother would come home, electric light would be installed; lovely dignified happy people would tread the emerald lawns; the dining-room would be set for twenty people, with smilax trailing between the Crown Derby dessert dishes, and carnations in the finger bowls; the stables would be full of riding horses; there would be lots of money and shooting parties every autumn.

Soaring through space and time Midge dwelt in bliss. Boastful to the girls, she was pathetic to the nurses, rapturously pleased with her own imagined visions.

Then a time came when sitting up to eat her jelly, a pain shot through her side, and she cried out, gasping. For two days and two nights she was really ill with pleurisy. She was carried to Sally's own room and lay there by herself staring at a painting on the wall of a big cactus. The nights meant a shaded lamp, and her father's big figure just beyond it. "What's that picture on the wall?" asked Midge, hoping that this odd dreaminess meant delirium. Delirium was impressive. Perhaps she was going to die.

"It's a picture of scarlet aloes in South Africa," came Sally's voice, cool and patient from the shadows.

"Are you both there? Daddy, are you there?" asked Midge.

"Yes. I'm here."

"And Miss Burton?"

"At the moment. We're just going down to have some supper."

"Why are you here so late? Am I very ill? Am I going to die?"

"No, of course not, you little goose. But your father's a very busy man and has other things to look after as well as you. He comes when he can."

They stood beside her bed, Carne large, silent, his face a mask under his thick black hair, Sarah small, smiling. They seemed to fit together very nicely, and Midge's thoughts, a rolling confusion of pain and dreams, found it quite natural that they should both be with her.

Long after, she awoke to see Sarah Burton sitting in the window, her red hair outlined against the green, deep, silent bar of the sea at dawn.

"Is father still here?" asked Midge.

"Hush, go to sleep, child."

"Is he here? I want him. I think I'm dying."

"Nonsense. You're much better. As a matter of fact, he is here, but he's downstairs resting."

"What time is it?"

"Nearly five."

"In the morning? Has he been here all night?"

"Yes."

Midge giggled happily.

"You and he seem to like to spend nights up together."

"Well—he wanted to see if you were better before he decided to go off to Ireland."

"Am I better?"

"Yes, I think so."

And so she was, and next day he went off, and Midge's convalescence proceeded slowly. Her eyes hurt a lot and she once had earache, and she often felt extremely cross and wretched. But while her father was away, he wrote her letters, and even when he returned to Yorkshire, he sent them on every day that he could not visit her.

Midge was proud of these letters. They were, she considered, far more sensible and adult than those sent by Nancy's or Gwynneth's parents. She wanted every one to know what a wonderful correspondence she conducted with her father, and one day when Miss Burton was making her usual visit, she handed her a letter, saying, "Please won't you read it to me? My eyes hurt so."

"They were well enough to finish Beau Geste last night," said Miss Burton; but all the same she lifted the heavy, expensive paper and read with suitable gravity the words she found there, written in Carne's large, childish, laboured writing:

"DEAR MIDGE,—I went to Nutholme sale yesterday. A poor lot of stuff and moderate prices. 700 head of poultry sold poorly at about two and six apiece. The ewes made up to fifty shillings but looked light. The hogs were little things, dearly sold at 10½ lb. The cattle nothing much and showed want of attention. The horses were a mixed lot—some made up to 35 guineas but £20 average and not worth that. Furniture at fire stick prices. Altogether the cheque would be a small one. The farm is not let. I fear poor Bly will have about 2,000 acres on hand.

"I may get over Saturday. Hope you are getting fit.

"Your affec. father, "ROBERT GEORGE CARNE."

Miss Burton handed the letter back to Midge.

"Don't you think," challenged the girl, "that my father writes beautiful letters?"

"Well—this is a—very friendly one."

"Poor Daddy. I expect he's worrying about the Nutholme sale because he's always selling things and they make so little money."

She sighed expansively and caught Miss Burton's quick green eyes glancing at her under their long light lashes.

"What do you mean about always selling things?" asked Nancy.

"Well, he sells horses. But he's very particular where they go to," said Midge. "I'll tell you something. One day two men drove up to our house in a motor-car. Daddy and I had just come in and were talking to Hicks—our groom—in the stable-yard, when these men arrive and come straight up to Daddy. 'Are you Mr. Robert Carne?' they say, and my father says, 'Yes, I am.' 'Thank God,' said the man. 'We've been hunting for you for days. We want to buy some of your horses.' 'Oh, do you?' says Daddy. 'Then you've come to the wrong place.' 'Indeed? Why?' 'Because you're not the sort of customers I care to deal with,' says my father. 'And why not, pray?' 'Well, if I tell you I shall only vex you,' says Daddy. 'No. Go on. It takes a deal to vex me,' says the man, 'and I want a good horse.' 'Well, then, were you at Ripon Agricultural Show in 1923 judging horses?' 'Well,' says the man, surprised like anything. 'What of it?' 'Well,' says my father, 'you gave first prize to a horse that was never heard of again, second prize to a creature that hardly was a horse, and only honourable mention to that bay gelding of Miss Grey's that swept the county later. Now, a chap that'll do that is either a knave or a fool, and I sell my animals to neither.' That's the sort of man my father is. He said, 'Good-evening,' and 'Come in, Midge,' and we both went indoors and have never seen those men from that day to this."

Midge told the tale well because she was showing off before Miss Burton. The anecdote impressed her. She thought that it displayed her father as a quite remarkable person. She was sorry that the head mistress did not stay for further discussion. Sarah threw a light word to the girls, a glance at the temperature charts, and was gone, leaving a fragrance of lavender and a sense of cool critical detachment on the air behind her.

"Oh, Midge Carne," cried Jennifer, "I'm sick and tired of your father. If he's so wonderful, why is he going bankrupt?"

"He's not. How dare you?"

"Well, my dad said . . ."

"Your father's only a common vet. . . ."

"He's not common . . ."

"And a liar."

"Oh, shut up, both of you!"

"Girls, girls, what is all this?" Miss Parsons fluttered in, fussy and ineffective but endowed, after all, with statutory powers, able to impose silence upon controversy and to report contention.

Midge Carne exposed such flushed cheeks and bright eyes to her anxious investigations that she took her temperature and found that it was 100.6 degrees again. It was too bad. Girls like Midge needed watching every moment. Miss Parsons wished that the child was safely back at Maythorpe.

CHAPTER V

LILY SAWDON PROPITIATES A GOD

I've got rid of him, thought Lily Sawdon, riding from Fleetmire in the Kingsport bus. He's gone. I'll never have to deal with him again.

A shudder convulsed her body; her triumph shocked her. Was this really herself rejoicing because Rex, the beautiful silvery-brown Alsatian, Rex, the gay, the boisterous, the uncontrollable, had been led off by Lee the vet. down the muddy path to execution? He had marched off, stepping daintily, feathery tail in air, proud as a prince, unconscious of her treachery, and it was Tom's eyes that were wet as they watched him go. Was it really true that any one could change so? Eh, I wouldn't know myself, thought Lily.

I never knew it would be like this, thought Lily. When she came to the Nag's Head, it had all seemed so simple. She had only to hold out, to conceal her secret, till Tom got his business well on its feet. Even if he did notice that she wasn't too well, it wouldn't matter. He would put it all down to her age. He had often told her that middle-aged women always felt under the weather.

I never knew pain could do this to you, thought Lily. For she had changed. It was true, she hardly knew herself. There had been hours when she had hated Tom; she wanted to hit his lean, red, friendly, handsome face; she had wanted to scream out at him her secret, telling him that she had let herself be crucified upon his simple vanity, that if she had stayed in Leeds she could have been spared this agony. It maddened her that he should be so blind, so childish, so complacent of his masculine strength and patience. He thought that he was being so very good to her.

Oh, and he was, he was. Lily's heart rebuked her. She thought of how he rolled out of bed each morning, a well drilled soldier, the moment his alarm clock jarred the early silence. He pulled on his trousers and went downstairs to light the fire. Always he brought a cup of tea up to her. His service with the colonel had made him handy. He could fill hot-water bottles, lay trays ever so nicely, wait on her with intelligent attention. He relieved her of all the hard work of the inn. He scrubbed floors, shifted cases, lighted fires, black-leaded grates, washed glasses. He got in Chrissie Beachall every morning. He attended to the garage and the bar and all the customers; she could sit for hours in the arm-chair by the fire. No husband could possibly have been more good to her. He even bought her the dog to keep her company.

How could she blame him because he did not realise? She blamed herself. Oh, no, then, she blamed no one. She crouched over herself in the jolting bus, and stared out at the flat unfriendly landscape.

How could Tom know that even on her good days their life at the Nag's Head put too much upon her? She knew by heart the burden of that house—two steps up from the kitchen to the tap-room, six along the passage, three across the scullery, twenty from the back door to the garage. Then upstairs to the bedroom were seven steps, a turn in the wall, and then another five. "They'll never get my coffin down them," thought Lily, dragging herself round the turning by the banister rail.

Oh, how could Tom know that on her bad days every demand on her drove her to voiceless fury? Then the pain uncurbed itself and seized her, and she crouched, sick and dumb in her fireside chair, clutching to herself the blistering hot rubber bottle which, while it brought no relief, was a sort of counter-irritant. Then the door-bell tinkled, and a party of hikers wanted some bars of chocolate, a thirsty cyclist wanted some ginger beer, and if Tom was not there she must pull herself together, she must hobble out to the bar, and she must serve them.

So she dreaded Tom's absences, and he guessed it because he loved her, and bought her a dog that she should not be lonely.

A dog. And Lily had never liked dogs. She, perhaps, had never said so, because it was not her way to express displeasure. But their animal smell disturbed her queasy stomach; their bounding energy rasped her taut nerves; they upset vases, trampled on cushions, printed footmarks on carpets, lifted their legs against the scullery table, disturbed the niceties of domestic order. She couldn't do with dogs.

Never would she forget Rex's arrival. Tom brought him back one night from Kingsport. It had been a bad day, and Lily had not known how to endure the evening. Up and down from the kitchen to the bar she had stumbled, drawing corks, measuring whiskies, counting change. A busy night, for once, a profitable night. The smoke blinded her, the smell of ale had sickened her. In the scullery she had wept moaning and protesting, alone for a moment with her pain, counting the seconds till Tom could come and lift the burden of petty obligation from her.

Then he had come—creeping through the kitchen door with his bright eyes and roguish little-boy air, his tongue curling round his red lips as it always did in moments of excitement, pleased as punch with himself, secret, eager. "I've got something for you, Lil. A surprise. A surprise!"

As though anything could surprise her save the end of pain.

Then, held back for a moment and now released, Rex sprang forward, a silvery-brown bounding lithe Alsatian puppy. He nearly knocked Lily over. He sprang from the door to the sofa, from the sofa on to the hearthrug, then round and round the table, swinging his great tail, leaping, slavering, wild, restless, beautiful, ebullient dog.

From that moment he claimed Lily's attention. He would scratch at doors, demanding liberation. He would fling himself into the air, race along roads, leap over hedges, whirl himself round and round in circles, wallow in ditches. Then back he would come, dripping and panting, fawning round Lily, pleading for affection.

She did not want him. She had wanted nothing, only the freedom to retire to that dim no-man's-land where she and her pain lived now in isolation. Nothing else could touch her. Once she had had a lover; she thought of Tom's eager, buoyant, dominating ways. Come on, let's take a chance, Lil. Oh, Lil, I love you. Oh, Lil, the softness of your hair and the way it curls in the back of your neck. I can't get it out of my mind.

She had a husband, and he was very good to her. No other woman she knew had such a husband. She had her girls, sweet they had been as children. Fat roguish Addie, tumbling across the floor. Maimie holding on to her knees with both short arms, crying, Oh, lovely Mummie. I love you. Dear Mummie. And now Addie had her own babies and Maimie would soon become a mummie herself.

Lily did not want to be bothered with babies. She had only one companion, the insistent comrade of her waking hours, the uninvited bridegroom of her bed. She could invest her pain with a personality. On waking every morning she lay waiting to see what sort of mood it would be in to-day. If she felt only the slight nausea and exhaustion, which were her alternatives to vivid, exacting pain, she would lie still and tranquil, humbly blessing the hour. She wanted, then and always, nothing except to be left alone.

The bus stopped near the flour mill. The inspector came to look at the tickets. Lily produced hers and held it between her neat gloved fingers. Tom had given her a pound to spend in Kingsport. "Buy a new hat; go to the pictures. Have a good tea. Sorry I can't come with you." He was kind, oh, he was kind because he was sorry for her, because they had taken Rex to the vet.'s to be put to sleep.

What would he have said if he could know the truth, that she had betrayed Rex, that she had deliberately set him on to chase those sheep? Oh, God, have pity on me. Forgive me, she prayed, horrified by this change that had overtaken her. How could she have known that pain would change her into a different person?

She had done her best for a time, taking Rex on his lead down to the village, though he almost pulled her to pieces with his energy. If she let him go, he frisked and gambolled round her, flapping his huge tail through the Maythorpe shops, panting and slavering, showing his white teeth in a wide free grin until the children screamed and ran away. Neighbours said, cautious, yet knowing a fine thing when they saw one, "You've got a grand dog now, Mrs. Sawdon. You'll have to take care he don't go after sheep." And she said, "Yes, he's a beauty," knowing that he was a beauty, a superb irrational dynamo of fur and bone and muscle. She took care of him and gave him liver and biscuit; but she led him out into the fields where the young lambs played, and when no one was looking she set him on to them—Go on, Rex. Catch 'em. Chase 'em. The silly sheep. The silly graceful dog, signing his own death warrant.

So Dickson went to the Nag's Head to complain, and Heyer was sympathetic and spoke to Carne, and Rex was put on probation for a fortnight, and beaten, and followed Lily about with puzzled meekness that did not suit her at all. She could not do with him.

His habits gave the men something to talk about. Alsatians and sheep-chasing, cures for sheep-chasing, cases of inveterate sheep-chasing, were discussed with passionate enthusiasm in the bar-room.

Rarely was the conversation interrupted, though Lily entered once to hear Tom asking, "What's this about young Brimsley wanting to court Peg Pudsey?"

"It's time enough," said Heyer. "He wants his mother out and the girl in, but I say he's a fool. Mrs. Brimsley's a rare good cook. I wouldn't change her myself for a daughter of that soaking fool, Pudsey."

"There's more in marriage than good cooking," said Tom with a wink at Lily, a loyal wink, because, during recent months, there had been little more in his, and latterly not much cooking.

But talk could not postpone the crisis. Rex one day killed a sheep. The Cold Harbour Colonists were friendly tolerant men, and all liked Lily, but this was something serious.

The dog must be put down or sold out of the district.

It was then that Lily had known just what she wanted.

"I won't have him sold into a town. It isn't fair."

She was sitting idle beside the fire, the tea unprepared, when Tom came in to her. In spite of the bright May afternoon, she was shivering.

"What shall I do then? We can't keep him."

"Best have him put down, mercifully. It's kindest. Once they get after sheep, it's a disease. Like drink. You can't stop." Her pain was so bad that her voice sounded harsh and desperate.

"I'm sorry, Lil." Tom was troubled and puzzled. "If I'd thought, I'd never have bought the dog."

"Thought? You never think. Thought's the last thing you'd be guilty of," she snapped so unexpectedly that Tom grieved all the more, assured that Lil had loved the dog even more than he had guessed.

Rex uncurled himself from his basket and strode across the room, his beautiful dignified gait appropriate to the sombre moment. He dropped his pointed muzzle on to Lily's knee. Then some spring of control broke in her, because she could not bear to behave so badly, and she rose and flung the dog aside, and snapped at Tom, "I've cooked nothing for tea. You'll have to eat boiled bacon."

But when he replied patiently, "Oh, that's all right. Don't you worry. I'll fry myself a rasher and a couple of eggs. Would you like one?" she could bear it no longer. She fled upstairs to the bedroom and cried and cried and cried, because she was dying a changed and hateful creature, because she no longer had any patience left for any one, for Tom's brave optimistic plans, for the dog's vitality, for Chrissie Beachall's complaints about her varicose veins; for the woes and joys of the visitors to the inn. They were nothing to her. She was withdrawn from them into a world of sharper pain and ultimate estrangement. She was no use—to herself, to them, to Tom.

But to-day, when they had taken Rex to the vet.'s, it was Lily who had been brave and competent. Tom had driven them both there in the Sunbeam, but he had to get back to look after the inn, and she had decided to go on by bus to Kingsport.

He had been upset to see the dog led off. Poor Tom. She knew that he had bought Rex really for his own satisfaction. But he would find comfort. Even as he climbed into the car and started the engine and swung the Sunbeam round back into the line of traffic, she knew that already his own expert competence as a driver was consoling him. He took comfort too from his wife's trim figure, standing on the curb in a grey spring costume, a lilac scarf at her throat. He would take comfort that night in the sympathy of Hicks and Heyer. Oh, he was building up his life soundly and quietly. She soon could leave him. Let once the Nag's Head get well started and he would not need her any more. He might even marry again.

To her surprise she found a sharp pang of resentment stab her at the thought of his remarriage.

Not that it mattered. How much do the dead care?

But then, suppose she didn't die!

The bus stopped again. She had reached her destination. She climbed cautiously down and made, not for the shops, but for a grey forbidding street where flat-faced houses displayed small brass plates upon the railings outside their front doors.

This was Willoughby Place, the Harley Street of Kingsport, and Lily had arranged an appointment here with Dr. Stretton, the specialist to whom the Leeds doctors had given her an introduction so many months ago, telling her to call upon him at once.

She was going now, though she had not meant to go. She had deceived Tom and stolen this day at Kingsport because the time had come when she needed reassurance. She could bear no longer this invasion by a stranger who curdled her sweetness, turned her charity to morose vindictiveness, and even led her to tempt to its death a harmless dog. What she feared now was that this might not be cancer, but some malignant spiritual change. She must know. She must confess her terror.

She saw the brass plate, climbed the clean steps and rang the bell. A maid showed her in to the bare, dark polished waiting-room. She told herself: Rex will be dead by this time. She had outlived that grace, that strength, that ebullient vitality. The expedition to the vet. at Fleetmire had given her an excuse to visit Kingsport. Her life and the dog's death were bound together.

Her pain was quiet. She could observe the bare mahogany table, the fern in the copper pot, the limp lace curtains, the obscure brownish oil paintings on the wall. Not a homely room. She could make better than that of it. She'd always been one for making a home.

A lean nervous-looking clergyman came in, chewing at his false teeth. She wondered if he had cancer, and hoped he hadn't, not from any good will, but from a sort of proprietary pride. She wanted her fate to be unique. If it must be terrible, let it not at least be commonplace.

The starched maid with pimples said, "Mrs. Sawdon, please."

Lily followed her into a small square consulting-room.

Dr. Stretton disappointed her.

He was a small pale man in the early fifties with a long cold dyspeptic-looking nose gripped by pince-nez; a ragged moustache frilled his damp restless mouth, and scurf powdered the collar of his greenish morning coat.

An unimpressive little man, thought Lily, and his breath was bad. Yet she knew him to be an authority on his subject. At Leeds they spoke highly of him. He had written books.

A file of letters lay on his desk, including that which she had sent on from Sir Wilson Hemingway.

"What I can't understand, Mrs. Sawdon, is why you didn't come to me before."

Lily smiled, a proud withdrawn little smile. Of course he wouldn't understand. How could he? What did he know of the secret pacts made by wives to guard their husband's pride? She disliked and despised him. She despised his fussy ineffective manner; yet she realised that his examination was most thorough and his questions showed her that he knew all that there was to be known about her body.

She paid her fee with a sense of quiet triumph. She did not know that out of the pity and anger which hopeless cases seen too late always evoked in him, he had charged her less than a fifth of his usual demand.

She had her reassurance. Her pain, her pride, the transformation of her gentle spirit, had not been caused by an illusion of the mind. An operation, he said, would not help her. She could eat what she liked, do what she liked, as long as she liked. He had ordered her a prescription to take if the pain grew very bad. He warned her to be careful. Well, that was all right. She had good reason to be careful.

Walking up Willoughby Place she realised that she was very tired. At the end of the road she found a super-cinema. It blazed with lights and rippled with palms; a commissionaire in a gold and scarlet uniform paraded the entrance. Up on the first floor Lily could see ladies in green arm-chairs eating muffins behind great sheets of plate glass. The thought of tea and toast suddenly tempted her. She went in and dragged herself up the shallow carpeted staircase.

The tea-room was palatial. Marble pillars swelled into branching archways. Painted cupids billowed across the ceiling. Waitresses in green taffeta tripped between the tables; from some hidden source a fountain of music throbbed and quivered, "Tum tum tum tum, ter-um, ter-um, Tum tum tum tum, ter-um, ter-um." The beautiful Blue Danube. She used to waltz to that with Tom when he was courting. A lovely waltz. Their bodies melted together. One will, one impulse, moved them.

She lay back in her chair. It was richly padded. The tea was good. The toast was hot, dripping with butter. Three months, the doctor told her. She would never have to face another winter in the country. She could let herself acknowledge now how much she had hated it, the puddled yard, the mud, the men's mucked boots upon the fresh scrubbed floor, the primitive sanitation of the rural inn. When Maimie's child was born she need not go there. She need not drag herself across the country. She need not pretend that there never were such babies as her grandchildren. She need not pretend that the Nag's Head was her ideal environment. She need not pretend about anything, any longer. After three months.

The waitress looked sulky and tired. A love affair, I expect, thought Lily. She'll get over it. Pride upheld her, because what threatened her would never be got over. She tipped a cautious threepence and walked down the corridor.

She took a one-and-threepenny ticket, sat in comfort, and watched a Mickey Mouse film, a slapstick comedy, and the tragedy of Greta Garbo acting Mata Hari.

Mata too was condemned to death, thought Lily. And what a lot of fuss they made about it.

Her pride rose and enfolded her. It wrapped her away from contact with the other watchers of the screen, the shoppers in the street.

She sat through the film and left the cinema. She walked down the crowded pavement to the bus stop. She had carried out her intention, had fulfilled herself. The long day was done, and now she could go home.

Then, crossing the road, she saw a fairy palace. It glowed before her, in softly flowering illumination, its turrets outlined in milky radiance against the pallid sky. Wondering, she stared, then saw the enormous notice, its black lettering illuminated by the floodlight: "Kingsport Hospital. Support your own Charities. £30,000 wanted."

Well, thought Lily, that's what we all come to at last. That is our final home. That is the end of all our hope and effort. Men could defeat darkness, but not death—yet.

This was the goal to which all flesh must come. She felt the evening traffic, surging round her, hurrying home to the long final rest.

But the beauty, the radiance of the floodlights pleased her. At last she had seen death and disease illuminated, honoured like health and life with brilliance and with dignity. It was right, she felt, that these should be given glory. She was tired of the discomforts and humiliations and squalor of her illness. Her weary body had weighed upon her pride.

But now she had done with the unequal contest. She had surrendered. Henceforward she was beyond all fear and sorrow. The floodlit hospital was lovelier to her than the bright gorgeousness of the new cinema. She had served those whom she loved, Tom, Maimie, and Adela. Now she had done with them. She need honour only one companion, the growth within her leading her on to death.

She had only one care now, to propitiate it, as one propitiates a jealous god. To-day she had offered Rex, an unwilling sacrifice, in all his silly mindless physical perfection. She had confirmed her faith in the consulting-room. She had seen the illuminated temple of her worship. She had refreshed and rededicated herself. Henceforward till death she was a votaress of the dread, the doom, the power which men call cancer. She was an initiate. Where others guessed in panic, she knew, and knowing, feared no longer, and being redeemed from fear, she was invincible.

Nothing could touch her now. She was as far removed from the world as a consecrated nun, locked in her convent.

She mounted the bus and rode home, bent over herself, soothing her pain as though it were a sleeping child.

Tom opened the door for her.

"Well, did you buy up Kingsport?"

"No, but I had a lovely tea, and I went to the pictures. I saw Greta Garbo in Mata Hari. Ooh, she's lovely. In the big super-cinema. But it's not so good as the Regal at Leeds, Tom."

"Didn't you get a hat?"

"No. Couldn't find one grand enough." She laughed, shaking her head.

Tom, noticing her pale face and drooping figure, drew her in gently.

"Come in. You're tired. I'll make you a cup of tea. Come in, old lady."

CHAPTER VI

THE HUBBARDS' ONLY OBJECT IS PHILANTHROPY

In the dark congested living-room behind their shop, Madame Hubbard and her husband sat making paper flowers. Above their heads six pupils were practising steps before their dancing lesson. One, two, three, thump! One, two, three, thump! Their pirouettes banged the bare boarded floor. If Madame Hubbard thought them out of time, she lifted a stick propped against her chair and tapped on the ceiling, beating out a tune hummed between closed lips that bristled with pins.

At intervals the bell of the shop door tinkled and Mr. Hubbard rose, shedding from his tremulous knees circles of green and cerise and pink crinkled paper, wool and twigs, and shambled across the room and through the door to the space behind the counter, from whence he could serve customers with tape, dress preservers, buttons and cards of press-hooks. But if they loitered and hesitated, asking for Mrs. Hubbard, sure prelude to more intimately feminine demands, he would poke round the door his head on its long stingy neck like a tortoise's, and shout, "Ma! You're wanted!" and yield precedence to his wife's desired authority.

After one absence Mr. Hubbard returned, slumped gloomily into his chair, rose abruptly to extract a pin from his grease-stained trousers, and observed, "That was Pratt."

"Well?"

"He won't."

"Won't?"

"No."

"I'll settle him!"

"He's gone."

"You—!"

What Mrs. Hubbard could have called her husband remained unsaid. He quailed before her bright boot-button eyes and tossed mane of grizzled hair.

"Well, we're not the only ones who can't get credit," he grumbled. "It's these buses. Since they've had day tickets, every one goes to Kingsport. How can we compete, when we've got to risk choosing the stock and having it brought out here?" He seized a branch of imitation almond blossom, and began to twist green wool round it with shaking fingers. "Well, we've got the lessons, haven't we?"

Above their heads the thumping pirouettes changed to the patt-patt-patter-tap of a step-dance.

"We've got the lessons! We. I like your we," cried Madame Hubbard. She flounced across the room, collected an armful of paper tulips, cleared the table and slapped a kettle on to the stove all in one effort. "We! These modern husbands. Live on my sweat and blood! Take all the credit. Where's manhood? Where's chivalry?"

Her passionate eyes asked heaven, her gesticulations challenged the whole race of man. But even her anger rippled into rhythm and her courage surging up through seas of worry about wholesale travellers, credit, bad debts, the falling custom and her husband's habits, found instinctive expression in the song that she had been teaching an hour ago to her dramatic choir.

"I hate you, I loathe you, I despise and detest you! Oh, why don't you kiss me again?"

Wiping her hands, blackened by the kettle, on her apron, and untying the strings before mounting to her pupils, she found her arms imprisoned by her husband and her lips smothered in his beer-flavoured kisses.

"Oh, get away!" she cried, smacking his face, but her anger was no longer cold and bitter.

"You asked for it," he grinned.

She capitulated.

The truth was that though he infuriated her, endangering her prestige, squandering her money, he shared enough of her ruling passion to respond effectively to her changeful moods. He capped her quotations, he whistled her songs; when he could hardly stand upright could waltz amazingly. Even when she gave him a black eye—which was not seldom—or he threatened to lay her head open with the coal-shovel, they were somehow in harmony. He was her fool, but he was still her lover. Though she responded to his caresses with a cuff, she went upstairs with raised spirits and heightened colour.

The walls dividing the first floor of the house into separate rooms had been knocked down, leaving one bleak but useful apartment, unfurnished except for a piano, a row of chairs, and a dozen or so pegs stuck into the wall to accommodate the hats, coats and handbags of the talented pupils. In the middle of the floor, polished by countless glides, pirouettes and patters, five girls, in odd varieties of undress, now stamped and twirled. The sixth, a plump, precociously developed adolescent blonde, drooped limply against the wall on a wooden chair.

Madame Hubbard's snapping eyes observed her flushed face and listless languor.

"Well, Jeanette? Resting? Word perfect and step perfect, I presume! Come and show us."

Stung to action by that merciless vigour, the girl rose and took her place. A bar of sunlight, slanting through the back window, gilded her tousled mop of hair, her rounded limbs and her young body, partially covered by pink brassière, trunks, slippers and white ankle-socks.

Madame Hubbard sat down at the piano and beat out, with metallic accuracy, the tune:

"I hate you, I loathe you, I despise and detest you!"

conscious of her husband listening in the dark room below, yet alert for imperfections in Jeanette's performance.

"Lift your feet! Lift them. Swing the legs. Looser! Looser! Bend, girl. You're not a clothes-horse. You're a woman, in love and furious. I detest and despise you! Go on. Detest him. Now melt, melt. Smile backwards. Think of your lover's arms. 'Oh, why don't you kiss me again?' No, no, no, no! You're not asking for a yard of calico! Show her—Prue! You girls have got no temperament. What I have to endure from you! Who's going to act the boy friend? Come on, Vi. You try then. No, no. Not like that. Come forward boldly. Remember you're a young fellow in love. Catch hold of her. Don't be afraid. I hate you. I loathe you. This isn't a whist drive at the Y.M.C.A. It's a scene of passion. Have none of you seen passion on the films?"

The girl called Violet, self-conscious and feminine, repeated again and again the prescribed gestures. Jeanette drooped sullenly. The other four watched with intent concentration, crouched against the wall, their coats huddled round their young rosy bodies. With complete seriousness they set themselves to study this mime of amorous hostility as the short, stout noisy woman at the piano directed it. In the soul of each pupil glowed a dream that one day she might thus pose and beckon in a real studio, under the barked directions of a great producer.

"Why don't you practice loosening your muscles? Here! Here!" Madame Hubbard darted forward, caught at Violet's lean thigh, and jerked it ruthlessly. "Stiff as a poker. Not one of you girls except Lydia Holly ever learned how to lift a leg. Stand up, Jeanette! This isn't the Dying Swan."

Jeanette's glance under her long fair lashes was sulky and self-pitying, but she did not complain of the headache knocking like hammers at her forehead, nor the rasping throat that made each answer painful. Madame Hubbard's dancing class was not the High School. No Miss Parsons fussed here shaking a thermometer at the first hint of indisposition. Jeanette pulled herself together. She lifted her heavy head, she arched her pretty foot, she submitted to the only discipline which she was willing to acknowledge, driving her weary muscles and aching bones at the dictation of her unflinching will.

Madame Hubbard pounded the piano, Vi and Jean repeated over and over again their lovers' quarrel, and the bell on the shop door tinkled and was silent. Mr. Hubbard had to lurch four times from his chair and across the kitchen to explain that he had no eleven and a half inch woollen stockings, to repulse a traveller who wanted to unload on him twelve cards of hair-slides, and to measure a yard of tape. The fourth time the bell rang he entered the shop, his hands full of artificial apple blossom, to find Lydia Holly, with Lennie and the baby in a pram and Kitty and Gertie dragging at her coat.

She had come into town to do her weekly shopping and had left till the last, like a tit-bit on her plate, this visit to the Hubbards. She needed buttons for her father's shirts and some more sewing thread; there were other and nearer shops where she might have found these; but she hungered for just what she heard as her little cavalcade trundled across the street—the pounded piano, Madame Hubbard's voice raised in shrill admonition, and the tap-tapetty-tap of the dancing pupils.

Already, within a few weeks, she had changed from the bright schoolgirl, who dreamed of scholarships to college, into an undisciplined careworn household drudge. Under her tumbled brown school tunic she wore a torn green bodice, relic of somebody else's party frock, bought at a jumble sale. Her neglected hair had been pushed under a crocheted cap rather like a sponge bag; her legs were bare; on her feet were soiled white gym shoes. She scolded Lennie, whose face was mottled with chocolate from a biscuit given him by Tadman's assistant when Lydia paid three shillings on account of her weekly bill. She snapped at Gertie, who did not see why Lennie alone should be favoured in this matter of chocolate biscuits. She wrenched her messed tunic out of Kitty's sticky fingers. She looked hot, cross, unhappy, and did not need the black band round her sleeve to mark her mourning.

"Why, it's Lyd! Well, how goes it?" asked Mr. Hubbard amiably.

"All right. I want some of them metal buttons with soft middles for Dad's shirt."

From upstairs came the slither and glide of waltzing feet. Piano and voice supplied the time and words:

"Love is the sweetest thing What else on earth can bring . . ."

Lydia had little use for the waltz—a sloppy dance offering small scope for her favourite acrobatics. She was disappointed in love. It was a bitter thing, bitter, not sweet. She had loved her mother, and a fat lot of use that had been to any one. She had loved Sarah Burton, and Sarah had forsaken her. Oh, she'd been kind enough at the beginning of term, promising to find some way out for her, running her over to supper at her own home once in her little motor-car, after the children were in bed. But since the measles started, she said she was in quarantine, and Lydia, with her brothers and sisters, must keep away from a house used as an isolation hospital.

So Lydia's heart was sore and her manner ungracious and she faced Mr. Hubbard with the stolid defiance of unhappy youth. But Mr. Hubbard happened to be one of those wastrels who remained charming to women and to children. He touched the baby's cheek with a friendly finger. He consoled Gertie with a faded cardboard lady, once used to display Saucy Slumber Caps. He gave Kitty a strip of shop-soiled lace, and to Lydia he said: "They're rehearsing upstairs. Why don't you go and see 'em? The missus has been missing you for the ballet, I bet."

"Can't," said Lydia. "Kids."

"Oh, that's O.K. I'll look after the family. Won't I, sweetie?"

He took his lip between thumb and forefinger and stretched it out for Lennie's delectation. He lifted Gertie on to the counter and pretended to sell her.

"Go on up. You know the way. We shall be happy down here."

The tune changed to a rollicking gallop. It was too much for Lydia. Off she ran, springing up the shaking stairs two steps at a time.

"Hullo! Madame!"

"Why, Lydia! You are a stranger. The very girl I wanted. Take off your cap. Find her some slippers, some one. Can you still turn a cart-wheel?"

"Can I?" laughed Lydia, and before she knew what she was doing, she was back into the old storm and glory of the ballet. Cart-wheels, pirouettes, high kicks—her disappointment, her bereavement, the burdens of her responsibilities forgotten.

When Councillor Huggins arrived collecting for the Thirty Thousand Kingsport Infirmary Fund, he found Mr. Hubbard playing shops with the three small Hollies, the baby asleep beside him in its pram.

Councillor Huggins' enthusiasm was quite simply explained. Snaith said that the Thirty Thousand Fund must be settled first. When that was done all Kingsport as well as the South Riding could be drawn into the Leame Ferry Waste scheme for a new maternity home. Therefore the sooner the thirty thousand pounds was raised, the better. He had come to consult the Hubbards about an entertainment to raise money, and the first people whom he saw were the motherless Hollies. Clearly here was an indication of providence. He had been right to come. The thirty thousand pounds were a matter of urgency, not only because Mrs. Holly must not go unavenged, but because, while the Leame Ferry Waste scheme hung fire, the warehouses deteriorated and did not rise in value, Reg Aythorne clamoured for money, Snaith's loan remained unpaid, the wilderness did not blossom. Clearly Huggins had every incentive to help the hospital.

He followed Mr. Hubbard, who still carried Lennie, up the stairs, the little girls behind him. He found himself engulfed in a flood of femininity. Brown, blonde and red heads tossed, bare arms were waved, sturdy naked legs, grey at the knees, thrashed the hot air. A scent of warm active bodies and cheap talcum powder assaulted his nostrils. The girls he saw, except for their brassières, were naked from the waist upwards.

Urgently he told himself that he was there for the glory of God. He watched with envy Mr. Hubbard's casual ease, as he threaded his way between the panting torsos and buxom rumps. He observed the flash of understanding between husband and wife, and realised that Mr. Hubbard was saved by his wife's bright eyes and rounded bosom. Now, if Nell had been different. . . . Oh, Lord, he prayed. I am Thy humble servant. Since the escape from Bessy Warbuckle, he had been doomed to strict celibacy.

"Here's Mr. Huggins come to see if we can't do our bit for the hospital," announced Mr. Hubbard. The pianist turned and saw the councillor standing fore-square, black-coated and solid, twiddling his watch chain among the giggling nymphs.

Public performances were good advertisement. The lower the shop sunk, the higher it was essential for the dancing class to rise.

"Well, girls," Madame Hubbard surveyed her talented pupils. "Do you think we could put up a show in August? Something out of doors, perhaps, to catch the visitors?"

"Oooh, yes. Yes, madam, yes."

Kiplington was not so dull in summer as during the winter months, but an open air ballet, in the Esplanade Gardens, with floodlights and photographs and fancy costumes and a band, would lend excitement to the entire season.

"We always like to do our bit for charity," Mr. Hubbard said demurely.

Madame Hubbard was reckoning expenses against assets. It would be worth it.

"You'll join us, Lydia?"

"How can I?"

"Like you did to-day. Bring the nursery. Maybe we can use the kids. Tinies are popular."

Miss Burton had not liked the Hubbards, but Miss Burton had failed her.

"Jeanette, take out—which is this?"

"Gertie."

"Gertie—swing her round a bit. Let's see how she frames. Now then, ducky."

Jeanette swung Gertie, Violet held Kitty, Lennie toddled among the other dancers.

The Holly family should perform in the cause of charity, Councillor Huggins should have his gala evening. Lydia saw the desolate monotony of her life relieved.

"I'll come if you want me. Bert and Dad must get their own teas."

The streaming eyes and flushed cheeks of Jeanette went unregarded. Nobody realised that the girl had measles. The contacts which Miss Burton had avoided had now been all too thoroughly established. But Lydia Holly went home singing, hope in her heart.

BOOK V

PUBLIC ASSISTANCE

Resolved—That rates for the several amounts required for the first six months of the current financial year be levied as undermentioned:— viz.:—

General County Purposes:—

	Rate in the £	*Estimated to Produce*
Public Assistance,	*1s. 7½d.*	*£60,411 0s. 0d.*

Resolved—That the Common Seal of the Council be affixed to the following documents, viz.:—Agreement as to the submission to the Ministry of Health of a question affecting chargeability under the Poor Law Act, the Council and the Kingsport Corporation.

Resolutions of the County Council of the South Riding County of York. May, 1933.

CHAPTER I

NANCY MITCHELL KEEPS HER DIGNITY

Since Whitsun the Shacks had been filling up with summer visitors. Five tents had been pitched beyond the Mitchells' chicken run. The railway coach which had been Lydia's "study" was now occupied each week-end by youths from Kingsport. The Turners had let their place to three school teachers who came by train every Friday night. A bronze-skinned giant whose hair was bleached flax-white by sun and weather lay all day under the cliffs and slept by night in the smallest of the huts. Rumour credited him with being an unemployed ex-officer, weary of canvassing for vacuum cleaners, who now lived on a pound a week from reluctant relatives.

The Hollies fraternised with this care-free community. Now that Mrs. Holly no longer summoned her family from her railway coach, like a hen clucking over a brood of ducklings, the girls ran wild among the visitors. The smaller children played in the dust among goats and fowls, scattering crusts and fish bones to the seagulls.

To Nancy Mitchell, keeping herself to herself in Bella Vista, this halcyon life added insult to life's injury. The girls in bathing suits, the boys sunning themselves naked to the waist, the braying of jazz from portable wireless sets and the frizzling of sausages over primus stoves jarred her strained nerves and pinched with acid disapproval her once pretty face.

She had done her best with Bella Vista, cut flower beds on the turf outside that the hens scratched to pieces, repainted the name of her house on its little gate, tied her curtains with pale blue ribbons, and washed and rewashed the blankets for Peggy's pram. But the vagabond company of the Shacks destroyed her edifice of respectability.

There was nothing, no hope, no comfort, no alleviation. Even when she cycled into Kiplington she saw nothing but poverty. Summer had come, but the visitors, the money-spenders, on whom the little town lived, were not arriving. The sands might be crowded with day trippers but they carried their own picnic parcels with them and bought nothing except the jugs of tea, 2d., 4d., 6d., sold from the wooden booths. All the shops offered cakes for sale, even the drapers and stationers, displaying buns and rice loaves among their other wares—as though a population could live by taking in each other's baking. No one wanted to be insured. Premiums lapsed. Fresh clients did not appear. The Kingsport office reprimanded Fred.

Long ago the Mitchells had abandoned their small luxuries—Fred's cigarettes, Nancy's toilet soap, bus fares and newspapers. The grim hand of poverty lay upon them, and now one final economy had undone them. For Nancy knew that she was pregnant again. It was an accident, an ironic catastrophe of over-prudence. Cheap substitutes in which she and Fred had trusted had betrayed them.

The sting of the failure lay in their unstaled love, their passion, their desire for another child. As soon as "things" grew better, Peggy was to have had a baby brother. As soon as the South Riding could afford again the luxuries of forethought and insurance. But not like this. Not now.

Nancy dared not tell Fred. She dared not follow Mrs. Holly's example and "take things for it." There were women in Kingsport who "did things," but Nancy did not know where to find them. And if she knew, where could she get the money? And if she had the money, how could she face the furtive secrecy, the doubt, the danger? Nancy knew of such things only through police court cases reported in the papers. Her fastidiousness was not superficial. She could not bear that she, Nancy Mitchell, who had been Nancy Whitfield, should come to that. She could imagine the report of the inquest, the shameful questions, the publicity.

No, she could not do it. But what shall I do? What shall I do? she asked of the dull grey sky, the trampled field.

It was Thursday afternoon and the camp was nearly full, yet Nancy felt her loneliness intolerable. Fred was away as usual, peddling through the mild July rain on fruitless errands. Hikers in mackintoshes strolled along the Maythorpe Road; bathers climbed down the muddy path to the beach. But Nancy had not a soul in whom she could confide. The aching humiliation and despair of her secret ate her heart.

It was to escape from herself that she walked across the camp to the Hollies' coach. Peggy slept in her hooded pram outside the house. The campers gathered in their tents and huts, singing or playing cards. The hatless ex-officer strolled up from the tap, a bucket of water in each hand. He greeted Nancy with his friendly grin.

"Weather to make you grow."

She stared at him, the damp air uncurling her careful waves. He exasperated her because he was a gentleman yet lived like a tramp.

"Perhaps it'll stop the drought," she suggested politely, hiding her contempt.

"Not enough for that."

"My husband says that if the tap dries up we shall have to close the camp."

"There are other places."

She could have hit his scarred amiable face. Men who had no responsibilities, men who had no children to provide for, they could be casual and philosophical. She hated them. She hated all care-free and unburdened people.

She picked her way across the hen-scratched turf, holding her mackintosh above her head like a hood, her lips compressed in a thin line of disdainful indignation. She climbed the three steps to the Hollies' coach and knocked commandingly.

Daisy opened the door—a stolid twelve-year-old with round red cheeks and greedy small grey eyes. Of all the Hollies, Nancy disliked her most, but dislike gave her self-confidence. The Hollies were so certainly her inferiors that their poverty and squalor and fecklessness soothed Nancy's pride. Here at least she could patronise and snub; here she could feel sure of her superiority.

"Is Lydia here?"

"No. In Kiplington, rehearsing."

"Rehearsing?"

"Carnival ballet."

"Carnival!"

To Nancy it seemed as though the whole world were bent on pleasure except herself. A bitter pride stiffened her.

She looked round the neglected room, the tumbled bunk, the clutter of cooking materials, the baby staring wide-eyed at the rusty stove.

"Where's your father?" she asked.

"Out."

"Oh. Got a job yet?"

"I don't know. I expect he's down at the Nag's Head helping Mr. Sawdon build a garage."

"Oh, I see."

Holly drew unemployment benefit. Fred Mitchell was a black-coated worker on his own and drew nothing. He pedalled through the rain after non-existent premiums, while Barney Holly both worked at the Nag's Head and drew his dole. Nancy had the vaguest notions about the economics of unemployment insurance. She was only sure that the lower classes were impossible.

"Who's in charge here, then?"

"I am."

Daisy moved a little so that her body screened the table with its tell-tale mounds of pink shredded cocoa-nut and bags of sugar.

"I see. Then I'll be obliged if you'll keep Kitty and Allie from teasing my hens."

"Who's that, Daisy?"

A child's voice called from the inner room.

"Only Mrs. Mitchell, Gert."

"'Only' indeed! I'll give her only."

"Is that Gertie in there? I thought she was in the ballet too."

"She'd a bit of a headache to-day and didn't want to go."

"Oh, didn't she? I'm not surprised. You children run wild half the night playing about with the camp boys, disturbing decent people, and then you expect to feel all right next morning. That baby needs changing."

Nancy was beginning to feel better, feeding on scorn; yet beneath her patronage lay the hurtful knowledge that the Hollies were dirty, careless, frivolous, yet it was she, not they, who paid the penalty of pleasure. That great lump of a Lydia, rolling about, screaming with laughter, exposing her thick brown thighs under her ragged tunic to all those camping boys, while she, Nancy, a faithful wife, lay sleepless with fear—it wasn't fair. Well, perhaps Lydia might do it once too often. Aha, my lady! We'll see who's caught out next. Like father, like daughter.

Viciously, standing on the half-rotten steps of the dark evil-smelling coach, Nancy wished Lydia ill.

"Hallo, Mrs. Mitchell! Tea ready, Daise?"

Bert Holly, grinning through the rain, swung off his bicycle.

"I came to tell your sister that if she can't keep those two young madams from poking at my chickens I'll deal with them myself."

"Go ahead, Ma."

He called her "Ma." She felt the insult to her wasted youth, her faded prettiness. Well—she was a Ma, wasn't she?

"Go on, Daise. Get busy. I'm in a hurry."

Bert squeezed in past Nancy and poured water from the bucket into a cracked enamel basin. He flung off his jacket, preparing for his evening toilet. Nancy knew that she should go, but an instinct of self-preservation held her in the doorway.

The boy sluiced water from cupped hands over his damp red face, but Daisy did not move. She stood between the oil stove and the table.

"Get a move on. I gotta date," her brother urged, groping for the towel.

The child turned slowly. She was twelve years old, and had been kept from school by Lydia to look after the baby and get the tea while she and Lennie went to a rehearsal. She had been given a shilling to buy bread when the baker's cart came round, and, instead, she had fallen victim to a bright temptation.

Moving as in a dream, she crossed to the oven and pulled out a baking dish filled with brown, sickly-smelling stuff.

"What the hell's that?" asked Bert.

The child stood dumbly, the hot dish held in a soiled oven-rag.

"It looks to me," sniffed Nancy, "like cocoa-nut ice—burned."

"Blast you, bloody bitch!" screamed Daisy, hurling her tin down on the table where it slid across the sheets of spread newspaper and fell clattering to the floor. In a burst of tearful rage she made for the door, head down, face distorted. It was only by swinging violently half off the step that Nancy avoided being thrown also to the ground. She was left to face Bert across the scattered ruins of cocoa-nut ice.

"Gosh! The little besom! Hi, Kitty, Al! Here's summat for you!"

Bert went down on his knees, collecting the charred coagulating lumps. The little girls approached nervously, their pinafores torn, their sandshoes stiff with mud. Nancy felt their fear of her. They edged round the table. The boy was unperturbed.

"Come on. Only top's burned. Give us a knife. Have a bit, Mrs. Mitchell? Where's Daisy gone? Go and fetch her, Al. Tell her it's not half bad."

His good humour shamed Nancy. Because of it, she started to scold again.

"Lydia has no business to go off like this. If your father had any sense . . ."

But the scorn ran off the imperturbable Bert. He had begun to root about for the tea, bread, jam, as Lydia came up along the cinder path, wheeling Lennie in a push chair.

"Hallo, every one. Kettle boiling? Just off, Bert? Good Lord! Where's Daisy? Why isn't tea ready?"

Nancy stood and watched her, as she flung herself upon the business of spreading margarine and cutting bread. Lydia had her mother's strong impatient movements, her brother's hot temper and quick smile; but she frowned with anxiety when Bert told her of Daisy's escapade. That frown pleased Nancy. The girl had begun to learn the lesson of the poor—to dread any unexpected action, to know that any deviation from routine meant loss.

"Where's Dad?"

"Nag's Head—or Brimsleys."

"They say," observed Nancy conversationally, "that Nat Brimsley is courting the Pudsey girl at Maythorpe."

"Nat Brimsley? Courting?" Bert gave a great gulp of laughter. Lydia looked up from carefully measuring tea into the pot.

"Why not?" mocked Lydia. "You're a bit of a lad yourself, aren't you? What price Vi Alcock?"

Beneath her momentary anxieties she was happy, elated by music and exercise. It did not occur to her to be intimidated by Nancy Mitchell, who stood like a glowering witch upon their doorstep.

"Vi? What about her?"

"She was at rehearsal doing Jeanette's part. Jean's poorly. Cissie Tadman brought her a message."

"What's that to do with me?"

"I don't know. Do I, Mrs. Mitchell? Have a cup of tea, won't you?"

"No, thanks. I must be going."

But she did not go, for Gertie appeared then at the door between the two compartments.

"Come on an' have tea, Gert. How's the head?"

In her flannelette petticoat, bare-footed, the child drooped miserably.

"It's bad. I don't want any tea. I thought you was never coming home, Lyd."

"Well, here I am. Come on. A cup'll do you good."

"If you ask me," said Nancy, "I should say that child had a temperature."

"It's only a bit of cold," Lydia began, but Gertie persisted: "I feel right poorly."

Lydia pushed her own cup and plate aside and drew the child towards her.

"Come here, pet. Come here to Lyd."

Her conscience smote her. She should not have gone to Kiplington. She should not have left the children.

"She does seem hot," she said tentatively, glancing up at the only adult person. That appeal touched Nancy. It was the recognition of authority that she needed. She said: "I've got a thermometer. I'll get it."

She hurried across to Bella Vista, suddenly compassionate. Those lost untidy children. That dreadful room.

Baby Peggy lay under the tarpaulin hood, awake but happy, playing with a rubber ring from which bells hung. It was right that she should glow with health while the Hollies suffered. Justice soothed Nancy. She chirruped at the pram, clicking her fingers, then went indoors for the thermometer.

As a girl she had attended first-aid classes organised by the Red Cross and she now kept a medicine chest with bandages and iodine. She enjoyed binding cut fingers and treating insect bites. Her skill gave her a sort of professional superiority over the campers.

She took the thermometer and hurried back to the Hollies. Gertie lay limply on Lydia's knee. Bert was just taking his departure. Alice was returning with the reluctant Daisy.

"Wait, please," Nancy said to Bert. "If this child's really sick, you may have to take a message."

"I'm not sick, only poorly," whimpered Gertie.

"I've got a date," Bert protested, but he waited. They all hung round the invalid, shuffling, staring. Nancy kept the thermometer in a little longer than was necessary, just to show her power. But when she withdrew it, genuine anxiety gripped her, like a hand on her spine.

"Has she got a temperature?" asked Lydia.

"A bit."

"It's that cold."

"Did you say some one at that dancing class had measles?"

"Jeanette."

Nancy unbuttoned the child's petticoat and pulled down the crumpled flannel. Her chest was mottled red with rash.

"It's measles all right. Put her to bed. It's too late to keep the others away. You'd better call at Dr. Campbell's, Bert. Tell him your sister's got a rash and a temperature of a hundred and three point two."

She spoke with bright efficiency, but the words "too late" fell like doom upon her heart. Gertie had been near Peggy. Her child's glowing face, those curls, her smile, her lovely rounded neck, swam before her vision. Already she tasted the horror of suspense.

"Isn't that high?" breathed Lydia.

"Not for a child. Every child has to get measles some day. Of course, you would go to that dancing class." It was Lydia to whom she spoke, but the reassurance was for her own sick heart.

She hurried back to her own home. In a frenzy of panic, she flung off the dress that she had worn in the Hollies' coach and in spite of the damp hung it outside on the line to air. It had stopped raining.

She washed her hands with carbolic soap.

But it was too late. She knew that it was too late. She was certain that the Holly children had given Peggy measles.

She went to the pram and lifted her baby and carried her indoors. She sat down by the window and began to examine with fearful attention that small beloved body—every crease in the dimpled flesh, the rings round the back of the fat little neck, the faint down on the spine. The child was perfect.

"Ga, ga, ga, ga!" chuckled Peggy. Her mother's frantic clutches were moves in a game. She laughed and gurgled, blowing ecstatic bubbles.

Nancy's lips went down to the soft rosy skin. She smelled it, she kissed it, burying her face in warm fragrant flesh, adoring the child with passion quickened by fear.

It's only measles, she told herself. Measles is nothing. But her reasonable words brought her no comfort. She snatched the child to her breast and paced the room, her tears falling on to the damp fair curls, the wild-rose face. She did not even know that she was crying.

We must go away. It's not safe here. I'll write to mother.

But Fred had quarrelled with Mrs. Whitfield and Nancy knew her mother. If she went home it would mean a breach with Fred. She did not care. At that moment there was room in her heart for Peggy alone.

"Don't get it. Darling, darling, mother's little darling. I'll save you. It's all right. It's all right."

It might have been the baby who was frightened.

Fred, limping stiffly after his long fruitless battle against the wind, against indifference, against the apathy of a suspicious world, found her thus when he came home to tea.

"Peggy?" he cried, his face blanching, if indeed it were possible to grow paler.

"Gert Holly's got measles."

"Oh, is that all?"

After his moment of piercing terror, it seemed a little thing.

Nancy's strained nerves snapped.

"Is that all? Is that all? When Peggy's bound to get it, and maybe she'll die and just as well for her. We never should have had a child. Now we'll get rid of it. She'd be better dead. And I'd be better dead too. I'm going to have another, d'you hear? I'm going to have another child! And how are we going to live? Oh, God! How are we going to live?"

CHAPTER II

MRS. BEDDOWS HAS THREE MEN TO THINK OF

Jim Beddows drove his wife to Flintonbridge Agricultural Show, and Emma Beddows wished he wouldn't do it. His driving terrified her. He knew nothing about the internal mechanism of motor-cars and lacked patience and road sense. He treated his rattling 1929 Ford with the same irascible impatience which his horses had endured from him for the past half-century. Emma had an idea that motor-cars were not so meek as horses.

But when Mr. Beddows was in a car, he drove it, just as when he had paid for a joint, he carved it. That his daughter could do the first and his wife the second far better than he, affected the issue not at all. Mrs. Beddows made no protest. When Sybil once suggested: "You know, darling, Daddy does hack the sirloin about frightfully; I do wish you'd carve," she replied: "Well, it's his sirloin, isn't it? He paid for it. He has a right to carve it if he wants to." To those who expected a county alderman and local celebrity to dominate her own household, Mrs. Beddows replied: "I prefer to see a cock crow on his own dunghill."

Jim Beddows did the crowing at Willow Lodge.

So the Beddows family, husband and wife in front, Sybil and Wendy behind, honked, pounced and jerked their way along the crowded roads to Flintonbridge. It was by good luck rather than good management that they avoided accidents, but they suffered all the minor inconveniences of bad driving. They lingered in dust from other vehicles, they cut in when that was least advisable, they scorned sneers and shouts and cursings. Twice their engine stopped dead after halts by crossroads.

But it was a fine day, and that was something. The warm summer had bleached the hedgerows early. Where they were not white with dust they were smothered in Old Man's Beard. White bedstraw sprinkled the grass like fallen powder. A field of rye grass brushed lightly by the wind wore the bloom of half-ripe peach.

"Road's plaguey dusty," grumbled Mr. Beddows. He enjoyed complaining to his wife about her public business. "Why don't you sprinkle 'em?"

"What with? There's a drought on, isn't there? Do you want us to waste water, or must we spit on them?"

Jim roared and tried to slap his thigh with pleasure. He made good capital at markets out of his wife's quick tongue. But it is not easy to slap your thigh while driving on to a fair-ground.

Converging traffic puzzled the local policemen. They puffed and sweated in their tight uniforms, as Fords, Daimlers, pony traps, milk floats, wagons, bicycles and carriers' carts all sought simultaneous entry through one narrow gate. Jim Beddows had succumbed unwillingly to the notion of a car-park. To pay two shillings simply to stand one's car in a crowded field exasperated him. But previous attempts to find his own accommodation had involved him in insuperable difficulties. With bad grace, he submitted.

Willie had gone earlier. He was judging poultry. Jim Beddows set off to inspect the exhibits. He enjoyed shows, sales, races and markets. The one commodity with which he was prepared to be completely generous was his unasked opinion. He shouldered his way through the crowds, small, wiry, self-sufficient, his large white false teeth gleaming amicably below his grey moustache. They contradicted the pessimism of his opinions which were, too often for his neighbours' comfort, insufferably right.

Emma Beddows watched him march off, saw him pause to criticise a new type of self-binding reaper adapted for horse or tractor. His remarks were loud and coldly genial, in his auctioneer's trained carrying voice.

She hoped that he was not cadging for a meal or a commission. Each time she saw him practising his technique of economy, her heart sickened. She had never grown accustomed to his habits of reading other men's papers over their shoulders in the train, and smoking other men's cigarettes, and leaving hotels before his turn came to pay for a round of drinks.

His parsimony represented her failure. She had thought before she married him that he was what he superficially appeared—gay, genial, courageous—a sturdy and reliable little Yorkshireman. Later, she blamed herself for her failure to change him. She believed that successful wives could transform their husbands into whatever pattern they chose for them. Now she had learned to accept him as he was, and in the privacy of her own house could serve his whims with humour and devotion. But she had never reconciled herself to his public behaviour. Her own generosity was, more than she realised, a gesture of repentance. She would pay back to the county what he had taken as by right.

She could hear him now.

"Wheat's not looking so bad," said a young farmer—wistfully, hoping for confirmation from this experienced dealer.

"Don't like the look of it," Jim Beddows snubbed him. "It'll make a rare-looking crop and then weigh light. Corn's not well filled."

Turnbull of Maythorpe had joined them.

"Well, Beddows," he said. "I'm going to put my boy into the butchering. Farming's a mug's game. Wheat's nowhere and middleman makes all profits. But folks will always eat beef and mutton. I knew a chap who started with a couple of hides and a chopper, and died worth over thirty thousand pounds."

"Don't be too sure," Jim Beddows answered. "It doesn't always work out like that. Butchers used to get six pounds a hide or thereabouts. They're lucky if they get six shillings now."

"I'm thinking of killing my own meat," said the young farmer. "And running a country produce shop like that in Yarrold. They seem to be doing all right."

"Aye. For the first year."

Must he never allow any one a hope? fretted Emma Beddows, knowing too well the answer.

"But you wait till you get on the markets. The butchers'll freeze you out. The private households won't want you. Mark my words—ladies don't like to see the farmer who shoots all winter with their husbands driving up to the back door in a white coat with a pair o' meat scales. These stunts do well enough for a time. Then they fall off and you're worse than you were."

There was no room in Jim's world for enterprise or originality.

I've got Chloe, thought Mrs. Beddows. I've got Sybil.

The hot sun beat down upon the trodden field. Human and animal smells mingled. If only, thought Mrs. Beddows. But it was no use. She caught sight of Dr. Campbell's red familiar face. He bred prize hogs himself, and never missed a show in the South Riding. She waved to him and summoned him to her. Again and again when her own affairs became intolerable, she could stifle all thoughts of them by public business. Her heart ached with affection and pity and regret for the dapper little man with his core of jealous bitterness who was her husband, so she turned to Dr. Campbell and began to discuss with him the problem of Holly measles at the Shacks.

Sybil interrupted them. She and Wendy had been looking round for Willie and came to report his whereabouts.

"Tell him we'll pick him up after the jumping's over," Mrs. Beddows said, then turned to see the tall bowed figure of her colleague on the council, Alderman Astell. He was leaning over a pen containing two white shiny creatures, washed and groomed to snowy radiance, and a red ticket of first prize tied to the hurdle.

"Hallo! What are you doing here?" she called, lively and welcoming.

"Admiring these," Astell indicated the goats. "I've never seen anything like them. They remind me of something."

"Your Bible. The sheep and the goats," she said promptly. "But these goats are trying to get past St. Peter into Heaven by disguising themselves in white robes."

He laughed. "No. That's not it. Something I learned at school—about the time when lilies blow."

"It was the time when lilies blow
And clouds are highest up in air,
Lord Ronald brought a lily-white doe
To give to his cousin, Lady Clare."

recited Mrs. Beddows. She heaved her plump little body up on to the hurdle and balanced there, resting her feet that ached already in tight patent leather shoes. Her flower-decked hat slid to the back of her head; her face was fiery crimson; her patterned foulard dress worked up to her knees, displaying her shapely calves and green silk petticoat. She smiled at Joe Astell, liking him, proud of her memory for verses learned sixty years ago.

"That's it. That's it," he cried.

"I trow they did not part in scorn:
Lovers long-betroth'd were they:
They two will wed the morrow morn:
God's blessing on the day!

'He does not love me for my birth,
Nor for my lands so broad and fair;
He loves me for my own true worth,
And that is well,' said Lady Clare.

In there came old Alice the nurse,
Said, 'Who was this that went from thee?'
'It was my cousin,' said Lady Clare,
'To-morrow he weds with me.'

'O God be thank'd,' said Alice the nurse,
'That all comes round so just and fair,
Lord Ronald is heir of all your lands,
And you are not the Lady Clare.'

'Are ye out of your mind, my nurse, my nurse?'
Said Lady Clare, 'that ye speak so wild?'
'As God's above,' said Alice the nurse,
'I speak the truth: you are my child.'

'The old Earl's daughter died at my breast;
I speak the truth, as I live by bread!
I buried her like my own sweet child,
And put my child in her stead!'

'Falsely, falsely have ye done,
O Mother,' she said, 'if this be true,
To keep the best man under the sun
So many years from his due.'

'Nay now, my child,' said Alice the nurse,
'But keep the secret for your life,
And all you have will be Lord Ronald's
When you are man and wife.'

'If I'm a beggar born,' she said,
'I will speak out, for I dare not lie.
Pull off, pull off the brooch of gold,
And fling the diamond necklace by.'

'Nay now, my child,' said Alice the nurse,
'But keep the secret all ye can,'
She said, 'No so: but I will know
If there be any faith in man.'

'Nay now, what faith?' said Alice the nurse,
'The man will cleave unto his right,'
'And he shall have it,' the lady replied,
'Tho' I should die to-night.'

'Yet give one kiss to your mother dear!
Alas, my child, I sinned for thee.'
'O mother, mother, mother,' she said,
'So strange it seems to me.'

'Yet here's a kiss for my mother dear,
My mother dear, if this be so,
And lay your hand upon my head,
And bless me, mother, ere I go.'

She clad herself in a russet gown,
She was no longer Lady Clare;
She went by dale, and she went by down,
With a single rose in her hair!"

"What d'you think of that—for seventy-two? I don't suppose I've seen it since I was at school."

"Marvellous," he praised her, unable to resist her goodness, her simplicity.

"The lily-white doe Lord Ronald had brought
Leapt up from where she lay,
Dropt her head in the maiden's hand,
And followed her all the way."

"Are you going to the champagne luncheon?"

She indicated the striped marquee where the committee entertained.

His thin face clouded. The bright spots of colour burned in his cheeks.

"You know they've put me on Public Assistance?" he said. "Do you know how I spent yesterday from half-past ten in the morning till four in the afternoon?"

She saw the relevance of his apparently nonsensical reply. She said: "But this is their day. You can't blame the farmers. They put a brave face on it. But many are having hard times. They make sacrifices for a show day."

She was thinking of Carne.

"Sacrifices? Champagne lunch? Two shillings for car park, half a crown for the grand stand? Don't talk to me of sacrifices. Do you know what we did yesterday? Cut down one chap's benefit from thirty-three and threepence—for man, wife and five children, mark you—to ten shillings—because he had a disability pension of two pounds a week. He lost his leg in the war. He's had eight operations. He suffers perpetually from neuritis. He says he can feel the kids laughing at him when he can go dot-and-carry-one in the street. He's terrified of going out on a slippery morning. He's fallen twice on the stump and it hurts like hell. I tried to make the committee see that his two pounds were a wretched little attempt at compensation for what he suffered when these farmers were taking good care of their skins."

She sighed. She had more sympathy with his impatience than with the complacency which surrounded her at Willow Lodge. All effort, all urgency appealed to her, but she had learned acquiescence in a hard school, and Astell, though she respected him, was a firebrand, a troubler of the peace.

She said doggedly: "We must have some kind of a check on public spending. The rates are too high already."

"The rates? Who complains? Carne, Gryson, Whitlaw—the very men who made fortunes out of the war and who now demand wheat quotas and beet bonuses and what all—and get them. They draw their own dole all right under polite names—but it's the ten shillings a week they call pauperism!"

Life was never simple. The people you most respected scorned each other. Astell's voice pronouncing "Carne" was a lash of contempt. Jim despised Carne. Sarah Burton disliked him. . . . Why were men and women so blind to real virtue? Emma Beddows changed the subject.

"You know the Shacks, between Kiplington and Maythorpe?"

"I do indeed. A public eyesore and a scandal."

"I was out there yesterday. Dr. Campbell's sent one of the Holly children into the fever hospital with measles. I'm getting the Medical Officer of Health to put the camp in quarantine. Those children are all certain to get it. Since their mother died there's no one but Lydia to look after them, and she's only fifteen. They run wild. There's no chance of isolation."

"That's the scholarship child."

"Yes."

"Miss Burton told me about her. She never should have left school."

"But that baby? Her father's so feckless. If they had neighbours who could help—as a matter of fact—there are the Mitchells."

"The Mitchells?"

Mrs. Beddows explained the Mitchells—their struggle for respectability, their failure, their adored baby, their terror of infection, Mrs. Mitchell's pregnancy.

"We've got to do something for that poor fellow Mitchell. He came to see me when I was leaving the Hollies' place. 'She's half out of her mind,' he said. 'And I'm sure I am. We've nothing in the house and only fifteen shillings in the post office. My book's not bringing in ten shillings a week now. I've no dole to draw. I was above insurance level. What are we going to do? What shall I do?' I said, 'You must do what every one else would do in the same circumstances, Mr. Mitchell. You must apply to the relieving officer.' 'That means the poor law,' he said. 'That makes us paupers.' 'Nothing of the kind,' I said. 'It's public assistance.' And I urged him to apply for immediate relief. I said I'd speak to Mr. Thompson, the relieving officer. He's a friend of mine. I'll see he helps them until the next committee. You see, if we close the camp, they can't even sell their eggs or bits of lettuce. But when the case comes before the committee, I want you to make things easy for him—a man like that—a five-hundred-a-year-man—it's hard on him."

"Isn't that largely sentiment? Is it really harder than for the others, the skilled artisans, the—? No. All right, I won't argue. I'll see what I can do. But it's the economists you'd better tackle. Carne's on our committee."

"Oh, I'll speak to him. He's a friend of mine too."

When she said, "He's a friend of mine," she felt the colour deepening in her face, and peace embraced her. For he was her friend. She was going, in a few minutes, to take her seat on the grand stand to watch him jumping. For five years running he had won the Hunter's Cup with Black Hussar. She loved his triumphs. She might turn the show ground into a lobby where she could canvass help for the Hollies and the Mitchells, but her high moments of the day would be Carne's jumping.

Gryson called her, waving his stick, and Mrs. Gryson, elegant in pale grey linen. They were on their way to the stand. Wouldn't she join them? She turned to Astell.

"That's settled, then?"

"Oh, I'll do what I can."

"I know you will."

She went off towards the stand with the Grysons.

A group of judges with blue rosettes in their buttonholes, flushed and talkative with champagne, left the luncheon tent. Willie and Jim were with them. Emma Beddows realised that somehow Jim had got himself invited in there. His cleverness never failed to astonish her, yet humiliation clouded her pleasure.

She tried not to see him. There were happier sights—the people pressing forward to the grand stand, the county in well-cut tweeds and linens, the farmers' wives in vivid silks and printed chiffons. The girls that year were wearing organdie muslin—pink and blue and primrose—unserviceable but pretty. There were children licking toffee-apples, and young red calves on their way to the judging ring. The competitors were mounting their horses, grooms leading out thoroughbreds, children on ponies, young hunting women on ladies' hacks. The hawkers, the stall holders, gipsies, farmers, labourers, the animals, the competitors all boiled and bubbled together like stew in a cauldron, shouting, excited, happy.

A groom was holding the reins of a great black horse as Emma Beddows followed the amiable Grysons. Three men emerged from the marquee and one went forward to the horse, felt the girths, examined the bridle, clapped a hand on the round ebony rump, then put a foot in the stirrup and was up. Emma saw him towering above the people. It was Carne.

She waved, but he did not see her. He was riding slowly away from her through the crowd. Her heart melted with joy and pride in him. He was her friend.

Two men just behind her were discussing him.

"Grand-looking beast."

"Was."

"Carne can ride him."

"Could."

"Fine chap."

"Has been."

The dry laconic damnation of the North.

Emma would have moved away, but the crowd blocked her. They were paying their half-crowns for the grand stand seats. The merciless dialogue continued.

"He's nowt but a has-been altogether. You can't keep cup by riding same horse year after year. You can't keep solvent by never paying your debts. You can't keep in with county by a marriage twenty-five years ago—especially when wife's in an asylum. You can't starve a farm for ten years an' have it."

"That he hasn't done. Maythorpe's stocked well enough. House may be in ruins, but farm's well enough."

"Aye—with a monkey in the chimney. If Carne's not careful, bank'll sell over his head. They say council wants land for smallholdings."

"I've got the tickets, come along. Can you manage?" asked the polite Captain Gryson.

They climbed on to the stand.

Oh, God, prayed Mrs. Beddows. Let him win. He needs success. Give him this small unimportant victory to cheer him.

She knew that credit in the country depends upon such unsubstantial things. Carne's stock was down, but a silver cup, a ribbon in his buttonhole, such minor triumphs could restore it. They would give him confidence when he most needed it. Lord, let him win.

The Hunter's Class did not come early in the programme. She had to watch the Children's Jumping, the smartest turn-out for tradesmen, the sheep-dog contest, the four-horse wagons, a superb event, the wagoners driving at a hand gallop down the track and between the stakes that left only an inch or two on each side of the thundering wheels. It was impossible not to catch one's breath as they swept rattling past the stand.

At last came the class for hunters, hunted that year with the South Riding hounds.

The first competitor was the young land-agent from Lissell, riding one of Sir Ronald Tarkington's thoroughbreds—a good performance; but he lost a couple of points at the turf-covered wall.

"Spoiled by the riding. First-rate mount," said Gryson. He too was a friend of Carne's; he too was anxious.

The second was old Lady Collier, aunt to the chairman of the governors of the High School. She was so stiff with rheumatism that her groom had to lift her to the saddle. She weighed under eight stones, "and a half of that is corsets and cosmetics," said her enemies. She had a seat like a circus monkey; but her high silk hat, flowing habit and white gloves gave her dignity, and once up, she was a holy terror. Any man in the South Riding was scared of her. She would cut across any one, go anywhere. Deaf as a post and very nearly blind, she rode the best horses in the county with such ripe experience, such tried and instinctive knowledge of the district, such complete selfishness and unfailing courage, that she could not be beaten.

"She says she'll die in the hunting field, and no doubt she will," observed Captain Gryson. "But, by God, she'll send a score of good men to Heaven first."

Yet not even he could withhold his admiration when she rode straight at her fences, not hurrying but with an easy lolloping canter, leaving the judgment to her mount, and, now that she rode alone, without the temptation to cut in, making an almost perfect circuit.

"Eighty-three if she's a day, and tough as wire. She's game, anyhow."

She was gone. She trotted out of the ring cheered uproariously. A local legend, she had lived up to her reputation.

The third was an ex-cavalry man, who dashed at the hurdles, the thorn-hedges, the in-and-out and water jump as though he were riding in the Grand National. But his horse refused at the five-barred gate, bucked and threw him ignominiously.

Then Carne came. He rode out gravely, slowly, as well aware as his critics that Black Hussar was not the horse he had been. Nor was he the man. Mrs. Beddows leaned forward, twisting her cotton gloves on her knee, and praying. Oh, God! Let him win. She felt her love for him, her desire for his success, flow out towards him as though it were a ray from a lighthouse. She was seventy-two and had lived through disappointments, but she still prayed the wild prayers of desire.

Black Hussar knew his business. Slowly, sedately he started on his round. The crowd, the band, the artificial fences were familiar to him. Nothing would shake his nerve. The water-jump and in-and-out were stiffish, especially to a big heavyweight carrying fourteen stone; but timing, action and judgment all were faultless, and Carne could control his big body to reduce its load to a minimum at any given moment. He never looked behind between jumps; he knew that he was over.

As he came down the central track, his pace was quicker. There was a broad dyke to jump, but that was tolerable. A nasty bank and rails depended more upon experience than power, and he and the black horse both had experience in plenty; yet as he cantered round for the ride home, for the wall and the fence and ditch and the five-barred gate, Black Hussar was already breathing heavily. He was game enough; but this was no longer fun.

The crowd in the grand stand was silent. This was serious riding. Carne had won the cup for five years. There was money on it. A good deal of private betting went on his chances to hold it. They had seen that the farmer was nursing his mount round two-thirds of the course, but now he changed his tactics. Coming up to the wall, he raised his crop and gave the black flank a light cut. The horse started, quickened, and went all out, paused, steadied, then they were over.

"Beautiful," breathed Gryson. "Beautiful."

Black Hussar was crashing up to the fence and ditch. His hoofs thundered on the turf; Carne's face was white and set; his hand with the crop was raised. He was riding right forward on his horse's neck till he eased off as the mighty haunches crouched back for the spring; the body stretched itself; a great liberation of muscular force convulsed both horse and rider, and they were up and away, over the fence, over the ditch triumphantly.

But the effort had been too much for Black Hussar. As he gathered himself together for the gallop to take the gate, he faltered. He limped. Carne reined up gently, started again, felt the limp, halted, and quietly slid to the ground. With the rein over his arm, he lifted his crop in a salute to the stand, and led the horse away, plodding as easily as though he were crossing his own grass field, out of the ring.

"What was it?" gasped Mrs. Beddows.

"Strained muscle, I think."

"Too heavy."

"Tendon slipped."

"He's done for now. He'll never compete again," said a man behind them.

But the crowd roared its sympathy with bad luck, its admiration of a fine performance.

Mrs. Beddows felt hot tears of disappointment pricking her eyeballs.

He might have had just that success, she thought. He might have been allowed just that.

From his lower privileged seat among the big wigs Jim saw and waved to her—his gesture a communication of victory. He had won a free champagne lunch, a ringside seat, and a conversation with three titled landowners, all because he was Jim Beddows, best judge of corn in the South Riding. He was in his glory.

Emma waved back. She could not disappoint him. But at that moment she would have liked to box his ears.

CHAPTER III

SARAH LOOKS OUT OF A WINDOW

For the thirty-fourth time that afternoon, there was a knock at Sarah's door.

"Come in."

She pulled herself together. She was tired. The last week of the summer term was always wearing, but this year, what with the measles, the quarantine, the trouble about the school fund and the perpetual guerilla warfare against the governors which must be disguised by flattery and appeal, it had been worse than ever.

Yet I like responsibility, she told herself, almost as though she needed reassurance.

Miss Jameson entered.

Deceptively, Sarah smiled at her.

"Well, how are things going, Miss Jameson?"

She need not have asked. The thundercloud on Miss Jameson's face spoke for her.

"I have to speak to you, Miss Burton. You know I never complain unless I must. But some things even I cannot tolerate."

"What is it?"

"Miss Parsons. It's insufferable. Apparently when she was sorting letters two days ago there was one addressed to me which got separated. Into her lot, or so she says. She may have her own reasons for holding up my letters. It's an old trick, I believe, with these embittered middle-aged spinsters."

"Yes, I know you have odd theories about middle-age and virginity, Miss Jameson. They don't convince me. But I suppose we must all speak from our own experience."

Don't be a cat, she warned herself. It's no use. Dolores Jameson flushed. Actually she was Miss Parsons' junior by only five years, but Pip's devotion gave her, she considered, a complete alibi in all charges of frustration and virginity. Sarah watched her, realising this.

Miss Jameson continued: "And when she had discovered it—twenty-four hours late, if you please—instead of bringing it to me and apologising, or at least putting it in the hall with the other letters, she gave it to the serving maid to put on the staff table and there it got covered with newspapers, so that I only found it now—too late. It was making an appointment, and I've missed it."

"I'm sorry. That was exasperating. Can you telephone—or wire?"

"What's the use now? It's too late."

Often before Sarah had infuriated her colleagues by suggesting remedies instead of grievances. She had not yet recognised the human preference for complaint.

"I'm sure no one will be sorrier than Miss Parsons. Of course it was an accident. She's probably rather flurried and exhausted. I think we shall have to make allowances for her. She's had an awful term."

"That doesn't excuse her. And it doesn't give me back my lost appointment. It's all very well for you to be tolerant, but you know she's a born muddler. Oh, I shall be glad to get out of this teaching profession. It's all very well for you. You don't have to spend day after day in the staff room, with the Sigglesthwaite groaning on one side of you, and the Parson chirruping on the other."

"Neither do you. You have your own rooms, you know. What did you want me to do?"

"Talk to Miss Parsons. Impress upon her about the letters. Or take them out of her hands. This isn't the first time that there have been muddles."

"I'll see her."

When Dolores Jameson had flounced away, Sarah scolded herself.

I manage her badly because I despise her. I let her be familiar and impertinent because I dislike her so much that I don't even trouble to keep her in her place. Heaven send that Pip never tires of his engagement! If only he'd marry her this summer.

Sarah sighed.

She sent for Miss Parsons, expecting fluttering repentance. But far from displaying contrition for her negligence the matron broke in quivering with a grievance of her own.

"It's no use, Miss Burton. I've tried and I've tried! An archangel himself couldn't manage all I have to do with an untrained housemaid for the serving. What do you think that girl's done now? I told her to put round the clean linen in the boarders' cubicles, with the towels folded inside the sheets and pillow-case, so that there'd be no question of them blowing away as Gwynneth said hers did, earlier this term, and would you believe it? When I went my rounds there was the linen put on the beds with the towels wrapped round outside each bundle!"

"And what did you do?" asked Sarah, genuinely eager to learn why Miss Parsons appeared perennially overworked.

"Of course I went round with her and made her refold all the bundles with the towels inside. But she was very sulky, and most impertinent, and if I have to spend my whole time redoing her work for her, I might as well have no help at all!"

Sarah looked at Miss Parsons. She was a woman ten years older than herself, who might have been any age over fifty—gentle, loyal, devoted, but a born muddler, with a muddler's irrational spurts of vindictive anger.

She said quietly, "Of course, it's your own department. You must run it your own way, Miss Parsons. But don't you think next time it might be a good idea just to tell the girl what's wrong and how you want things done, but to spare yourself the exhausting business of doing it all over again?"

But the muddler's obstinacy shone in Miss Parsons' eye. She was sure that she was right, and she spent ten minutes explaining to Sarah just why no other methods except her own were practicable.

Sarah was patient. She knew that the matron was near the end of her tether after a gruelling term, and that her fussy incompetence with domestic routine was a negligible disadvantage weighed against her real devotion to the school, the girls, even to the dilapidated buildings, and her unselfishness in times of illness and of crisis. Quarter of an hour spent in ventilating grievances was not time wasted.

When the storm was momentarily checked, she observed amicably:

"There's just one other thing I wanted to ask. Exactly what is the procedure with the staff letters, Miss Parsons? You take the whole bag from the postman, don't you? You sort them—and then—just what happens?"

The matron flushed.

"I suppose Miss Jameson's been here. Well. She's second mistress, and no doubt she has a certain right to report misconduct among her inferiors. But even I have my dignity, Miss Burton. I may not have a university degree and all that, but I have my dignity. I am not an office boy to carry messages."

"No, of course not. I was only going to suggest that when a letter has been accidentally delayed, it would be better perhaps to send it immediately to its owner."

"Accidentally. So she admitted to you it was an accident, did she? She wouldn't to me, Miss Burton. She seemed to think I did it on purpose. Really, she's insufferable. She was bad enough before she became engaged, but ever since she's been impossible." The facile tears swam in the matron's eyes. Her round indeterminate face crumpled. "Now I suppose I'm talking exactly as she thinks I talk. She's always sneering at unmarried women. She seems to think that either we all envy her her wretched little fiancé, or that we're frozen and inhuman and all riddled with complexes. It's not kind and it's not nice and it's not good for the girls."

"I agree with you," said Sarah. "I agree entirely. There's too much fuss about virginity and its opposite altogether. And I think Miss Jameson may have been reading too many of those rather silly books that profess to serve up potted psychology. It's very silly. But you know,"—her voice grew soft and persuasive—"I'm rather sorry for Miss Jameson. I feel that we shall have to be a little tolerant with her. She's not a young girl, you know, and this engagement seems to have gone to her head a bit. I understand that she's waited two years now for this young man's promotion and there's still no word of it. It must be very trying for her—tiresome for us too, perhaps. But what I feel is—there's probably a very real fear of loneliness and old age behind all this pose of superiority. You see, she's not naturally a very lovable person, is she? If she doesn't marry, I'm afraid she may one day feel terribly isolated."

"Oh," said Miss Parsons, sitting down and looking across the desk at Sarah. "Oh—I—I hadn't thought of that."

"You see," Sarah smiled, subtle, honey-sweet. "I expect it's rather difficult for affectionate and motherly natures like your own, Miss Parsons, which find it perfectly natural to love and be loved, to realise how desperately and fiercely possessive a lonely egotist feels about any symbol of attractiveness she may acquire. Miss Jameson's engagement ring is a tremendous thing to her. A sign that some one really loves her and wants to live with her, and that she returns that love. I shouldn't be surprised if this young man were the only creature whom she has ever loved. So it's not wonderful that she clings to him and all he stands for, with a rather pathetic vehemence. It's very real and terrible—to fear an unloved old age. A woman like you, perhaps, can hardly realise. I don't suppose you've ever bothered, have you, about loneliness?"

"No," muttered the matron. "No. I don't believe I have."

Lord, what a prig I sound! thought Sarah ruefully. But it's the only way. I can't have that harridan ruining my staff. And it's true. God knows it's true.

"You see—I know better than you do because I'm an egotist myself," she confessed disarmingly. "I like people to do what I want and they generally do it. So that being with others doesn't mean constant sacrifice for me. I expect that for unselfish people, it's rather a pleasant change to be alone, isn't it? I mean, then you can indulge in all your own little likes and dislikes—have the windows open or shut as you please, and choose the biggest strawberries, and all that?"

"Why—yes," said Miss Parsons in mild surprise, seeing herself now, not as Miss Jameson saw her, an envious, embittered and frustrated spinster, but as Miss Burton saw her, a woman of warm heart, naturally lovable and loving, the generous friend of those dear naughty girls.

The Parson, they called her. Good old Reverend. She smiled at the thought of them. She had been their slave for twenty years, but the fingers that she had bandaged, the tears that she had dried, the cough lozenges and cod-liver oil that she had bought with her own money to give to day-girls—since she was too scrupulous to dose them with boarders' medicines—all became part of an unconscious insurance by which she had bought freedom from the fear of loneliness.

For of course she had never dreaded retirement; the thought of being alone held no terrors for her; it was a luxury. All her life she had loved and served and given, so that her own company meant not deprivation, but a little relaxation in which she might pander to her own neglected preferences. She knew exactly how she would live when she left the High School. She would have her pension. She would have her memories. All her human appetites for love and self-sacrifice would have been amply satisfied. She would take a little cottage, or rooms with some nice woman; she would have a wireless set, a dog, a subscription to Boots' Library. Old girls would come to tea, and she would give them iced cakes and strawberries in summer time. Sometimes they would invite her to attend speech days and school concerts. They would bring their babies or young men to see her. When she was alone, she could muddle along happily in her own way. She could eat bread and treacle for supper when she fancied, wear bedroom slippers all day if she felt like it, and rest, after her long and faithful service.

Miss Jameson was wrong. She had not been frustrated. She had loved and served and feared and hoped and given. She had enriched herself immeasurably by the renunciation of possessions. All over Yorkshire, in farm-houses and shops and villas, lingered the memory of her unstinted service. Miss Parsons knew that in a hundred homes women thought of her, and would think, with affection—a little amused, a little critical perhaps, but they were grateful to her. Good old Reverend. She had her reward. She wondered that she had never thought much of these things before. She smiled radiantly into the light intelligent eyes of her head mistress.

"Well, my dear," she said. "Forgive me—Miss Burton, I mean. But, of course, I am older than you, and, as you say, a bit motherly, perhaps, if not always very clever and I dare say you're right. You often are, you know. And it's been a very tiring term. I'll try to remember about poor Miss Jameson. I ought to have thought of all that for myself. You've done me good, you know."

Smiling and pacified, Miss Parsons then withdrew.

But Sarah sat staring at her inkstained fingers. "You've done me good," she repeated—the satisfaction of the dominating, who draw nourishment from other people's troubles. The poor have we always with us.

She never disliked herself more than when she had poured the oil of flattery on the school's troubled waters.

Yet was it flattery? Wasn't it only truth? Had she not dealt with the two women justly—to say nothing about the bewildered new young serving-maid, wrapping towels round pillow-cases, or pillow-cases round towels. Oh, what did it matter?

What then did matter?

These rumours of Hitler's Nazi movement in Germany? There swam before her tired mind the memory of that summer holiday in the Black Forest, of tables outside a vine-wreathed inn, and Ernst, lean, brown and eager, in the khaki shirt and shorts worn by hundreds of young Communists—drinking her health in beer after a long strenuous walk. Ernst, who wanted peace and comradeship and a mystical unity of like-minded youth—Ernst whose mother had been a Jewess . . . Ernst, who had disappeared, and who had, some said, been beaten to death at the Dachan concentration camp. These things happened to one's friends. They were important. It was important that two years ago Sarah had attended a meeting of German teachers and professional women, serious, dogmatic, experienced—decent women, sincere in their intentions. And to-day? Where were they? Under what sad compromises were their bright hopes buried? By what specious arguments did they defend their present standards?

She thought of her own dreams for the world. In her desk lay notes, neatly clipped and arranged in coloured folders, of her talks on current affairs—The growth of world unity—The task of an international Labour organisation—The League grows up—Disarmament. Beyond her personal troubles lay the deep fatigue of one whose impersonal hopes do not march with history.

Am I doing any good here? she asked herself, seeing all that was imperfect in her school, her failures in diplomacy, her impatience with the governors, her betrayal of Lydia Holly. She ought somehow to have found a way to keep that girl at school. She ought to have saved Miss Sigglesthwaite's dignity. She ought . . .

Running a staff, she thought, was like controlling an experimental factory for high explosives. At any moment the stuff might go off from quite unexpected causes. No permanent peace was possible.

But did she want peace?

Miss Parsons' humble dream of tranquillity was not hers. She was not humble at all. She had unlimited confidence in her own ability.

Yet, if so, why was she here, coping with a matron's grievances about towels, or a governor's eccentricity over grocers' contracts? Surely her place was out in the big world fighting for those principles in which she so deeply believed?

She searched her heart. This is my school. I do what I like with my own.

Her mouth set in a thin line. She drew note-paper towards her. She returned to her interminable letter-writing—to Mrs. Rossiter about Laura's quarantine, to Mrs. Twiggs, a prospective parent, arranging an appointment, to Colonel Collier about the playing-field—twenty-three letters.

At half-past six she put her letters on the post tray, filled her case with senior history examination papers to be corrected, put on her hat and closed her office for the day.

It was a perfect July evening. The little town swam in warm liquid light. From the height of North Cliff Sarah could look down upon the uneven roofs of grey slate and red tiling, the bare forest of wireless posts, strung with a fine cobweb of aerials, the motley crowd along the esplanade, the wide stretch of the sands. The formlessness and disorder of the place attracted her. It was raw material. She wanted to make use of it—she was not afraid of hard work or responsibility or isolation, but she feared futility and failure. She feared the waste of her ability and vigour on ill-judged enterprise. Am I a fool? she asked herself. Is it worth while?

On the pale flattened sea a fishing boat, a mile or more away, trailed its widening spearhead of ripples across the surface. If I could sail in one of those, thought Sarah. Her head ached. The heavy case of papers to be corrected dragged at her arm.

She let herself into her house, where still three measles cases were accommodated in her first-floor bedrooms. She sat down to an hour's work at her papers. At eight o'clock she and the nurse ate a cold supper together. Later, she climbed up to the attic where she had slept during the measles epidemic.

She liked the attic. Its dormer window faced westward across the outskirts of the town to the fields beyond, where already a group of tents had been pitched by holiday-makers. Sometimes at night Sarah looked out and saw them glowing like convolvulus flowers lit from within, lying mouth downward on the darkening field. Once she had heard music. Sometimes laughter. These sights and sounds gave her great pleasure. Music and lantern light and laughter seemed to her proper accompaniments for youth in summer-time.

But this evening, being mid-week, the camp was deserted—no laughing boys dragged out their mattresses to air on the sun-baked turf, no girls tossed paraffin recklessly on to smoking fires. The sun had dipped below the flat horizon. From the houses pin-points of light appeared. Now on the allotment an old man called his hens. Now the revolving lamp from the lighthouse trailed its pale wand of light across the landscape. Now the lights of a car swept down the Hardrascliffe Road and disappeared. Now from the stile at its western end two figures, a boy's and a girl's, entered the campers' field.

Sarah watched them idly, her elbows on her window-sill, her pointed chin propped on her hands, the cool breeze fanning her aching head.

The boy and the girl did not cross the field directly; they kept to the shadow of the hedge, moving furtively. When they came to the point opposite to the tents, the boy went forward. Sarah could hear his low unanswered whistle. He approached a tent and, kneeling, undid the flaps and threw them open. Then he went round the enclosure, peering into all the others. No one was there. The camp was empty. He beckoned to the girl.

Sarah watched her move across towards him, slowly, as though reluctant yet drawn by an irresistible attraction.

She knew quite well what drama of youth and folly and love she was observing. Those children thought that nobody could see them.

The boy vanished inside the tent, the girl stood outside. Her dark figure was outlined against the dun grey canvas. With a queer little gesture of defiance, she pulled off her beret, and Sarah could see how she tossed the thick fair hair that hung about her shoulders and turned her head slowly, from south to north, surveying the town as though taking leave of her familiar childhood.

She waited so long that the boy came out again to her. In the growing twilight their figures remained separate, and to Sarah flashed the thought: She's going to fail him. She's going to run away at the last moment; and, without criticising the wisdom of her foreboding, she felt she could not bear it for him—if the girl should fail him now.

But the boy put out both hands, and the girl took them, and he drew her in after him to the open tent and closed the flaps behind them, and soon tent and field alike dissolved in darkness.

Sarah stood entranced, until her lulled reason reasserted itself. "What have I done?" she asked; "perhaps that's one of my girls." It was too late to run out of her house now, to follow the two and interrupt that childish and potentially tragic honeymoon. The lovers were lovers now, and no long arm of discipline, morality or wisdom could undo what they had done together.

But what astonished Sarah was not her acquiescence, nor her recollection of the brief pain that pierced her when, for an instant, she had thought that the girl was going to run away, it was the realisation that when the boy had held his hands out, her imagination had seen in the dusk hands held out to her also; her ears had heard a whispered invitation, and her dreaming mind had devised the vision of a face smiling up at her ardently from the shadows. And the face and the voice and the hands were those of her antagonist, the governor, the councillor, the father of Midge, Robert Carne of Maythorpe.

"I love him!" she cried aloud, as though struck by sudden anguish. Immediately she felt that she understood everything. All her past slid into an inevitable and discernable pattern; all her future lay before her, doomed to inevitable pain.

She knew love; she knew its aspect, its substance and its power. She knew that she faced no possible hope, no promise, no relief.

She moved from the window and switched on the light as though the bold realism of electricity might dispel that revelation. But the small white room with its sloping roof, its painted chest, its narrow virginal bed, only imprisoned her all the more closely in her knowledge.

She turned off the light and went downstairs slowly to her sitting-room. Setting out her work she began again to correct examination papers. But her hand trembled so that she could hardly hold her pencil, and every now and again she looked about her, as though to reassure herself that all this was a bad dream. But there was no escape.

She was caught, trapped in emotion, torn by fear and pity, by anger because he was her enemy, by sorrow, by desire. She had thought herself past this tumult, this disaster. She had thought that she could live safely in impersonal action, forgetful of herself, concerned only with the children and their future, with the building of a new world for them, with the fulfilment of a large impersonal hope.

But she had been dragged back to consciousness of herself. A school teacher of forty—plain, red-haired, with large bony hands and light short eyelashes, a little common. The knowledge of her physical defects scorched her. Humiliation, for all her grand ideas of noble unself-consciousness, consumed her. Because she loved and desired to be loved, she exposed herself to vanity. She became vulnerable, afraid, disarmed before a hostile world.

"Oh, no," she cried to her heart. "Oh, no, no, no!"

But the silent room, the books, the reflection of her pale distraught face in the small gilt mirror, answered—Yes.

CHAPTER IV

NYMPHS AND SHEPHERDS, COME AWAY

"I don't like it. Great girls. All ages. Naked up to the thigh. No. I'm surprised at you allowing it. I am indeed, Huggins."

Mr. Drew put his foot down.

Huggins had been a bit surprised too, though he should have known what he was in for that day when he called upon the Hubbards.

"After all," he said weakly. "It's for a good cause. The hospital's charity. Christian charity. And then it's not as if I'd known what they would wear."

"It's what they don't wear," Mr. Drew corrected him.

As an estate agent Arthur Thomas Drew did business round about Kiplington in a small way, but he did moral censorship in quite a large one. He was on the Kiplington Watch Committee, and he watched indeed. It was he who, hearing complaints about the ethical tone of the penny-in-the-slot machines along the esplanade, had instituted an ad hoc committee for their inspection. Thus it happened that a band of four men and a woman—Alderman Mrs. Beddows—one Sunday afternoon when the esplanade was closed to the public, marched solemnly from one machine to the other, dropping in their pennies, listened to the tinkle, click and whirr as the machine was set in motion, and thoughtfully examined the revolving picture sequences, which had been advertised by such seductive titles as Through Winnie's Window and What the Butler Winked At.

"All very disappointing," confessed Mrs. Beddows later. "Nothing more than one or two women in boned corsets, a fat man in a night shirt, and a couple of chamber pots. If that's the kind of thing that amuses the gentlemen, I should say they were welcome to their little pleasures, poor dear things."

Mr. Drew had not agreed. The machines were duly banished, and their critic turned his attention to the Public Libraries. In his mind a librarian's duty was mainly that of moral censor. Repeatedly he called the harassed Mr. Prizethorp's attention to volumes which he found "stinking with sex." "Public incinerator's proper place for them," he would say of all modern novels. His daughters sometimes wondered where he had acquired a knowledge of literature so extensive that he could pass such wholesale judgment on it. According to Mr. Drew Aldous Huxley was a "disgusting pervert," Virginia Woolf a "morbid degenerate," and Naomi Mitchison "not fit for a lunatic asylum." "No, I've not read it all through, but I know enough," was his favourite condemnation.

Therefore the classical carnival organised by Madame Hubbard at Councillor Huggins' suggestion, in aid of the Thirty Thousand Fund for the Kingsport Hospital, disgusted Mr. Drew. He sent his daughter home and himself remained a martyr to public duty, seated upon a narrow bench in the shilling enclosure, scolding Huggins.

Usually these two agreed. Both were Methodists; both were Puritans; each sometimes could render the other a little service. Drew had often notified the preacher of possible haulage contracts, Huggins had introduced clients requiring homes to the agent.

Therefore this doubt cast upon his moral judgment in the matter of the carnival wounded Huggins. He balanced himself, in considerable physical as well as mental discomfort, upon the wooden bench, and wished that he had brought Nellie with him. His solitary state had made him defenceless before Mr. Drew's attack.

Until now, the day had been a success. The children's sports went without accident. The weather had been exemplary. Even when the sun had fallen below the roof of the Floral Hall, it still reached the far-out tide, illuminating the waves as they broke to creamy radiance and creating an illusion of afternoon at sea, though evening darkened the Esplanade Gardens.

Teas had been served in the Floral Hall—two shillings with crab, ham or potted meat, one and six with fruit salad, a shilling plain. And even the so-called plain teas included cheesecakes, tarts, scones, spiced bread, currant tea-cakes. Experienced as Huggins was in public teas, he felt proud of this one. When the South Riding does anything, it Does It.

It was a pity that the High School disapproved of Madame Hubbard. That Miss Burton tried to stop her girls joining the classes. Well, of course. Still, she was coming to the carnival with Mrs. Beddows.

Charity was charity, and Hardrascliffe had raised fifteen hundred for the hospital at its own three-day bazaar. We must do something.

There was an interval between the dances.

"Coming for a stroll?" asked Drew.

They disentangled themselves from the benches and strolled off under the yet unlighted festoons of coloured electric bulbs, between the stalls selling ices and Kiplington Rock, and the deserted sands.

"Good few people," commented Drew.

Huggins was about to reply when his gaze was arrested by a sight of terror.

This was nothing more than a young man and woman standing beside a lemonade stall. The young woman was drinking—from a bottle, her arms raised, her head thrown back, her round creamy throat exposed and her bright blue dress straining across her maternal bust. Spellbound, Huggins watched her Adam's Apple twitch as she swallowed the gassy liquid. Then she finished, drew the back of her hand across her moistened lips, gave the empty bottle to the young man, and turning, stood staring at the councillor.

She laughed a loud, careless laugh that showed the red pit of mouth between her strong yellow teeth. She came forward, her hand thrust out. "Hallo, Alfred!" she shouted. "How's yourself? Meet the hubby."

Huggins found himself shaking hands with Reg and Bessy Aythorne.

"Ah, excuse me," he said to Drew. "I must have a word with these young people. I haven't seen them since their marriage. Mrs. Aythorne used to come to my services at Spunlington."

He thought that Drew strolled off without suspicion. After all, a lay preacher has a wide circle of acquaintances.

"Well, and how are you both?" he asked bravely enough, in his rich patronising preacher's voice.

"Not so bad."

"And how do you like our show?"

"Bit too classy for me. I like something with a bit of go in it, don't I, Reg?"

She nudged the rabbit-faced young man who was her husband.

"Tha's right."

"We wanted to see Mr. Huggins, anyway, didn't we, Reg?"

"Tha's right."

"Well. You see me. Here I am," said Huggins. Brave words, but he felt dreadful. His protruding eyes searched the Esplanade for some place of shelter. Facing Bessy among all those people, he suffered from a sense of nakedness, of indecent exposure.

At intervals along the Esplanade Gardens, the corporation had built rugged archways. Made of hollowed blocks of clay from the cliffs encrusted with small pebbles, they reached the high-water mark of local marine architecture. Clumps of purple stone crop, white arabus and pink valerian had been planted about their surface. Huggins' desperate eye lit on one such archway now. A bench had been set across it; it had been used as a sheltering place for eaters of oranges and chocolate, and as a convenient retiring house for dogs and children, but thither Huggins led his two young friends.

"Aren't you going to ask after the kid?" jeered Bessy.

"I hope she's well."

"He."

"Ah—yes. Of course. He."

"Oh, come off it! Let's get to business. Are you going to pay Stillman's interest on those damned sheds?"

"Pay the interest? Why—no. Of course not. The sheds are yours. That's your business."

"Is it? I see. Nice lot of use they are to us. We don't want 'em. Stillman can foreclose."

"Oh, but he can't. They—I, they are as it were only a loan to me."

"Well, we can't help your troubles. We aren't going to touch 'em. We don't care. The shop's not going as well as all that. We can't afford to pay for your property. I just thought I'd let you know. If you want to keep those sheds, pay your own interest, or let Stillman take 'em. We can't do it. We've got to keep your child, you know. It takes a bit of money."

"My child?"

"Spitten image of his dad, little Alf is, isn't he, Reg?"

"Tha's right."

"Alf? You've called him Alfred?"

"After his pa. Why not? It's only natural."

"But—but—this is blackmail."

"Is it? It seems sound sense to me, anyhow. Reg and I are keeping your kid for you. You're paying maintenance by setting us up in business. You can't expect us to pay your interest for you too. You'll have to fix it up yourself with Stillman. Or you can lose the sheds. Or you can take your own kid and keep it. Can't he, Reg?"

"Tha's right," said the obliging Mr. Aythorne.

"I—I—" gasped Huggins, but they had done with him. Without mercy, they laughed and went away.

Oh, God, thought Huggins. What shall I do now?

The sheds were his only security for repaying Snaith. He might pay Stillman's interest, but business had gone badly. Besides, it was sheer blackmail. Once he began, the Lord alone knew where it would all end.

He stood, racked by suspense, staring out at the care-free, moving crowd.

Drew saw and hailed him. He had been confiding his disgust at the morality of the carnival ballet to Lovell Brown. Huggins approached them, not knowing what else to do. Drew turned to the reporter.

"Well. Here's a member of the Carnival Committee. You know Councillor Huggins, I suppose?"

"Yes, rather. Been to Spunlington lately?"

Spunlington! The councillor's jaw dropped. Had Brown seen him now with Bessy? Was all his folly known?

"Well, Dollstall, then?" smiled Brown, and Huggins knew that the worst had happened.

It must be known—his connection with Spunlington where Bessy had been, with Dollstall, where she now lived. All was lost. Huggins tried to swallow. His mouth was dry. His eyes stared out from his deep pit of despair at the bright gala crowds and the floodlights illuminating the grass stage between the corporation flower-beds.

Almost he felt release from his long penance of deceit. If everything was known at least he need no longer hide a secret scandal.

"I—I don't get you," he gasped.

"Don't you remember," asked the reporter, "how I met you last at Dollstall? I was coming back half frozen from a ploughing match, and stopped for a drink at the pub there. You were on your way to preach at Spunlington?"

"Oh, yes, yes, of course. I'd forgotten."

"Whenever I catch you, you're always on your way to some good work," grinned Lovell.

The reaction was so great that Huggins almost fainted. He knew now the measure of his love for his good name. It meant everything to him—honour—friendship, the opportunity for service. And indeed he desired to serve his generation. He leaned against the low sea wall, feeling sick and dazed with relief, yet aware that his escape could not be permanent. At any time the horror might recur—so long as Bessy was in the South Riding. Why hadn't he seen that she went far away? To London? Manchester? Even Leeds would have been better.

Mr. Peckover was coming towards their group, his round face beaming.

"Well? Good-evening, Huggins. Good-evening, Drew. 'Evening, Brown. Hope you're giving us a good report?"

"I'm glad you like it, Mr. Peckover," Lovell grinned mischievously. One up for the Church of England, he was thinking.

"Oh, quite classical. Quite refined. Different from all that jazz Mrs. Hubbard seems so fond of."

It's all right. It will be all right, Huggins told himself. He was accepted, welcomed. No guilt, no fear wrote itself across his forehead. He wiped his face with a big white handkerchief.

"Hot night," said Mr. Peckover.

The Ladies' String Orchestra had replaced the brass band. They were beginning to tune up, conscientiously drawing bows across cat-gut; in a moment they would be sawing and grinding away in the full vigour of Part II of the carnival programme—"In Ancient Arcady, A Masque of Song and Dance."

The audience sought their seats again. It seemed impossible to Huggins that all this had happened during the brief interval of one night's entertainment.

"What's the next item?" asked Drew grimly. He never bought programmes if he could borrow one. Huggins produced his—a folded yellow paper. His thin spatulate thumb made a broad shadow over the fine print in the lamplight.

"The Shepherds' Quarrel," he read, "danced by Lydia and Violet, sung by the Ladies' Choir."

Through the crowd moved round the vivid blue of Bessy's dress. Above the clamour of voices he could hear Bessy's unrestrained cruel laugh. Oh, God, I should have got away! He felt trapped.

"Shepherds. Well," observed Mr. Drew, "at least they should be adequately clad."

But Daphnis and Chloe, as Madame Hubbard conceived them, were attired very differently from Mr. Naylor and his South Riding colleagues.

To the wail of strings they sprang forward into the yellow floodlights, crossing the dark green lawn. Vi Alcock fled, a slender blushing Chloe in a brief lilac tunic. She knew that Bert Holly was watching her from the crowd, and it was to him she danced, flushed with the bloom and joy of her first love-affair. Her fair hair tossed above her girlish shoulders, her arms and legs were bare. The imperfect light hid the blemishes in her beauty—her coarse red hands, her feet deformed by ill-fitting shoes, the rather common prettiness of her little face. Only her grace and passion were revealed, the golden gleam of her tossing curls, the flying drapery of her lilac tunic. After her, Lydia Holly, brown and sturdy, a frowning fierce young shepherd waving a crook, danced with serious concentration.

She too was aware of a member of the audience. Sarah Burton, cool and charming in her green summer dress, sat in the reserved seats between Joe Astell and Mrs. Beddows. She hadn't left Kiplington yet, then. She was there—Scarlet Sally, in her soft chiffon. Sarah Burton, with her hair like an autumn leaf, Sarah, who didn't want girls to learn dancing with the Hubbards—Sarah who had let her down.

Very well. Sarah should see what Lydia could do. It was Sarah whom she pursued, leaping, spurning, springing across the flower-beds, a dynamo of vitality. It was Sarah whom she ultimately caught with her crook and humbled, crouching formidably above her.

But Violet, soft, panting, defeated, prone on the grass before them all, was yielding in love to Lydia's brother.

A burst of clapping, like the patter of hail on a roof, rattled round the arena. The tune of the fiddles changed. The Ladies' Choir advancing, rather cold in white tunics, broke into the song chosen by Madame Hubbard. Its words might not be wholly "classical" but its rhythm was irresistible.

"I hate you, I loathe you— I despise and detest you— Oh, why don't you kiss me again?"

Violet and Lydia were on their feet now, miming the shepherds' quarrel. Into their act Violet threw all her newly-acquired youthful amorousness, the fear and desire and surrender learned in a camp tent west of Kiplington. Into it Lydia threw all the misery and bewilderment of her past six months—her mother's death, her exile from the school, Sarah's betrayal, the illness of her small brother and sister. She danced frustration as Violet danced fulfilment.

"I'll make her see," she swore.

And Sarah did see. She was amazed by the performance. She had thought Lydia capable of many things, but not of this wild passion and power of miming. It had not been necessary to remind her that Lydia was worth saving.

And it was not of Lydia now that she was thinking.

For Sarah was clasping and unclasping the green velvet bag on her lap and repeating to herself, "I hate you, I loathe you, I detest and despise you—" But Carne had never kissed her once. Would never kiss her. Never, never, never, never. And she must put him out of her mind, or learn indifference.

It was easier to hate than to be indifferent. She would teach herself to think only of his preposterous public policy—not of his strong hands so tenderly ministering to sick animals, not of his vigil beside his little daughter, not of the dawn that they had watched together, coming up out of the dark summer sea.

She looked at Joe Astell's stern face for reassurance. Joe, who was so clear, so definite, so determined. Joe was a good friend. Joe would teach her how not to love her enemy.

"Not," observed Drew, "what I call a nice song."

Huggins did not think it a very nice song either.

His affair with Bessy Warbuckle had never pleased him. At best it had been a furtive and shameful fumbling in the dark plantation—not love, but a restless appetite; not discovery, but a quest for something that he had never found. Yet even now, watching those dancing figures, watching the slow swaying movement of the singers, Huggins was haunted by her. Not by Bessy so much as by desire, not by love but by hunger for love, for warmth, for gaiety, for some irresponsible grace of life. It was not possible for a man like Huggins to conduct his personal life perpetually as though it were a public meeting. Nelly was no wife to him. And she wore her mouse-coloured hair imprisoned in a hideous net that was enough to put off any man.

Bessy had been nothing—a lay figure to which Huggins lent for an hour or two his homeless imagination. Yet even that brief and unsatisfactory make-believe had landed him in this complexity of trouble.

If he had money he could send her away and never hear of her again. A little rat like Aythorne would go anywhere for money. Bess had always longed for the excitements of a city. If he had money. . . .

If he had money he need not kow-tow to a man like Drew. He could have arranged the carnival according to his own taste. He could have paid the Hubbard piper and so have called the Hubbard tune. He could have censored those too suggestive words, those over-abbreviated tunics. The morals of Kiplington would have been safe in his keeping—if he had money.

If he had money he would never have got into this mess, in debt to Snaith, blackmailed by the Aythornes, too badly worried to do justice to his preaching.

If he had money, he could do anything. He could be a public benefactor like Snaith—laying foundation stones, endowing chapels, building orphanages. Goodness was easy to the rich. How much harder was it for a camel to pass through the eye of a needle than for a poor man to enter the Kingdom of Heaven?

The ballet was moving forward, the dancers dipping and twirling from the darkness into the golden light. Above the lamps the sky was dark peacock blue, pricked with stars.

Money, money. If only I had money, Huggins groaned in spirit. Oh, God! He prayed, but his eyes were caught by whirling muslins. Sweat ran down his face. He was in agony.

Gladys Hubbard, simpering, twisting her raven ringlets, minced forward into the arena and stood confident, posed between the dancers. The tune changed again.

I won't think of him, Sarah was vowing to herself. My work needs all of me. I'll get that Holly child back to school; I'll see her through her exams. I'll work with Joe for that new housing scheme. I'll get my new school. I'll look to the future—to the world outside. This pain is monstrous. It's humiliating. I'll hate and despise him.

The orchestra paused. The dancers were still. A girl's high birdlike soprano rang through the night.

"Nymphs and Shepherds, come away, come away,
Nymphs and Shepherds, come away, come away,
Come, come, come, come away!"

The light brilliant voice rose through the silence, gay and heartless, effortless as a nightingale's.

Snaith? thought Huggins. Is that the clue? Snaith showed me the way. He put a weapon into my hands. Leame Ferry Wastes? The housing scheme. The rising value of real estate there? After all, there's my life insurance. I could get hold of that. Stillman would hand over the sheds—That's Aythorne, Stillman, me—no connection now with Snaith. Safe. Subtle. . . .

Through the dusk along the row of profiles he saw Stillman's dark square face, his upturned nose. A humorous inept face for an undertaker's. Huggins wriggled cautiously out of his seat.

"In this grove let's sport and play!" sang Gladys.

The dancers sported and played, rippling and curtseying round her.

Huggins pushed his way along the back of the form and touched Stillman's shoulder.

"Nymphs and Shepherds, come away, come away!"

"Can you spare me a minute? I want a word with you."

Together they stole away on to the asphalt walk by the sea-wall.

"Friend Alexis, tune your reed, tune your reed,
For to sound across the mead?"

Above the crowds, the waning colour of the ballet, the hushed wash of the rising tide, that invitation carolled, piercing, disturbing.

"Would you like to make a bit of profit on that mortgage of yours? The sheds of Aythorne's?"

If only I had more money I'd enlarge the boarding house myself, Sarah was thinking.

"All our crowd to dance proceed. . . ." sang Gladys Hubbard.

"We'll frolic, with laughter!"

"I tell you, I know it's a certainty. I'll ask Drew. You'd take Drew's judgment?" Huggins persisted. "If I had capital of my own I'd get hold of land there. The new road will make a difference. You'll see, drainage—access."

"Till night shall end our holiday."

Two by two the dancers were leaving the arena; the fading lights lent mystery to their silent figures. They moved like shadows into deepening shade.

"Nymphs and Shepherds, come away, come away!"

More than the dancers now desired to escape, to steal away from the crowds, the lighted garden, the friends, the greetings.

"Come, come, come, come away?"

The grass was dark now and the stage was empty. To that shrill sweetness the carnival had ended.

The last dancers to leave the arena were Daphnis and Chloe. Arm in arm they stole quietly, slowly, across the darkened grass.

None of the spectators had observed the little red-eyed man who stood waiting for Lydia at the performers' entrance.

During the final song Mr. Holly had stumbled through the standing crowd, and waited, dazed and mute, to tell his daughter that he had been summoned to the Fever Hospital to be told that Gertie had had a relapse after her mastoid operation and was dying. She had died while he was in the matron's office.

Lydia listened, standing in her brief tunic against the cloakroom door. Performers brushed past her and her father, laughing, dropping coats and slippers, teasing, joking, protesting their thirst, their fatigue and their enjoyment.

Of course, she should have known that she could taste no joy without immediate retribution. She was different from other people, doomed to disappointment and remorse and pain.

Her round brown face set stolidly.

"I can't find Bert," gulped Mr. Holly.

"No. He'll have gone off somewhere."

And well she knew where he had gone, and with whom.

"Just let me get my coat, Dad. I'll come with you."

"Eh, Lydia, I heard 'em say you were fine," sobbed Mr. Holly.

"Come away, come away! Nymphs and Shepherds, come away."

Gertie is dead, thought Lydia. I left her to dance in a carnival. I was dancing when she died.

"Till night shall end our holiday,
Come, come, come, come away!"

Dry-eyed, frozen-hearted, she linked her arm in her father's and led him from the crowd.

"Good. I'll get hold of Drew at once," cried Huggins, clapping the undertaker on the shoulder. Everything was going splendidly. He was on his way to make a fortune. Snaith had taught him.

"Come, come, come, come away!" the song rang in Sarah's ears. She was inviting Mrs. Beddows back to her house to supper.

"Oh, Bert! Isn't the tide rising? Are we safe?"

Violet stood with Bert Holly between the dark cliff and the moving sea. Not far off now, it dragged at the grinding shingle, pushing a white uneven line forward towards the watching lovers.

"Come away! Come away!"

In the Quay Road the fish and chip shops did a roaring trade. Their cheerful windows poured cascades of light on to the dark pavements. Their salty smell, their crisp sound of frizzling fat and shouting voices, enlivened the street.

The news of Gert Holly's death was spreading round the town. It added a touch of pathos to the drama of the carnival. That poor little thing, dying while her sister danced. Here was appetising matter for disapproval. Lydia oughtn't to have come! Suppose she spreads the measles? Heartless, with her sister so ill!

"Nymphs and Shepherds, come away!"

Queer, to think of dying during a carnival! Beyond the bustling, glittering shops lay the darkened cliff and the soft surging sea. Like death beyond life. Like mystery beyond the reassuring and familiar details—the fillets of plaice and skate lying brown and hot on their wire grids, dripping fat; the chips swimming in vats of boiling oil; the bright polished covers of the stove, the piles of newspapers beyond the counter.

Poor Mr. Holly's had a pack of trouble. I always say they live like animals in those caravan places. The little boy's in hospital too now, isn't he? Did you say two penn-orth of fish and one of chips, love? Peas, Mrs. Marsh? To take away? How's your girl?

"Come away! Come away!"

A faint wash of tide lapped the hidden day now. The sands were covered; the cliffs were cold and silent. The lamps of the town shone bright and separate as terrestrial stars below the unbroken darkness. The lovers, the dancers, the bargainers, the planners had gone home to bed.

"Nymphs and Shepherds, come away, come away,
Nymphs and Shepherds, come away, come away,
Come, come, come, come away!"

CHAPTER V

CARNE VISITS TWO IDEAL HOMES

The journey from Maythorpe to Harrogate had become for Carne a road to Calvary.

He would try to vary it. Sometimes he drove to Kiplington, sometimes the whole twenty-five miles to Kingsport, sometimes he went by bus to York, sometimes by train, changing at Leeds. But whichever way he went the peculiar pain of approaching Harrogate tormented him.

He had sat too often in those cross-country trains staring blindly through the windows, uncertain of what new anguish would await his journey's end. Now at least he had abandoned hope that things could ever be better. Yet, after his reason ceased to believe, his heart still hoped. As the train drew near to Harrogate, his mouth dried, his throat choked with the throbbing of pulses normally un-noticed; a pain convulsed him as though he were being dragged away from his own entrails like a victim of medieval torture.

So that by the time he had reached Harrogate Station and walked across the Stray and down St. Stephen's Road to the Laurels (Private Nursing Home for Nervous and Mental Cases), he was himself in such a state of nervous and physical exhaustion that he almost felt qualified to become a patient.

To-day he reflected, I'm getting older. Since that heart attack last summer he had tired more easily. He was nervous as a kitten; he did not sleep well. The magnificent body which had never hitherto given him a moment's trouble, except when he broke a couple of ribs or a collar-bone out hunting, had begun to fail him.

Tramping across the Stray he was assailed by irritation. The well-corseted ladies in tweeds, taking their dogs for a walk, retired colonels exercising their digestions, schoolgirls in uniform, nursemaids with prams, exasperated him by being alive, free and indifferent. He hated Harrogate. A cavalcade of riders on hired hacks, galloping past with bad manners and insecure control, spattered his well-pressed suit with mud. He swore at them.

The grounds of The Laurels were surrounded by a high stone wall. In a porter's lodge an elderly janitor lisped, "Good-afternoon, Mithter Carne." The house itself had been a prosperous business-man's residence built fifty years ago in the centre of a formal urban garden, well-kept and uninviting, with asphalt paths, mown lawns, bone rockeries, and neat clipped shrubberies of variegated laurel and privet. Even on this August afternoon, when the bright sun shone after a mild thunderstorm, the garden had a still forbidding air as though order mattered here more than happiness, and gaiety were a lost art. There were patients out-of-doors, strolling along the paths or lying on the veranda under a red-striped awning, but Carne knew better than to look for Muriel there.

As ever his eyes lifted to a barred first floor window, though he knew that his wife no longer sat waiting for his arrival, beating the iron rods with fine bruised hands, cursing him piteously for his desertion.

He was shivering as he entered the dark cool hall.

Yes, matron was in her office. Yes, she would see him.

He pulled his weary body up the five shallow stairs.

The matron sat as usual in the bright office that blossomed all the year round with chintz tulips, hollyhocks and parrots. There was a bowl of roses on the central table and a work basket on the upholstered sofa. It was a pleasant friendly room. Carne hated it.

He could not hate the matron. Had he done so he would not have left Muriel in her home for half an hour. He liked her quiet efficiency, and her grey hair parted beneath her starched white cap. She fulfilled his notion of what a matron should be.

But, God, how he loathed this business!

She rose when he came in, welcoming him, saying, "I'm glad I didn't miss you. I wanted to see you."

He mumbled, "I'm sorry the cheque was delayed. After harvest . . ."

Her gesture of protest cut him short.

"It's not that. You know we trust you absolutely. We've been through too many sad times together to doubt each other, haven't we?"

Carne frowned. It had never occurred to him that he had gone through his "sad times" with any one. He had been alone, completely, always. He sat down at her invitation.

"I've been discussing Mrs. Carne's case with Dr. McClennan."

"H'm?"

She shook her head to the desperate hope in his unhappy eyes.

"Much the same—to all outward appearances. But you know, Mr. Carne, for some time now I have felt it is really not much use keeping her here. Don't misunderstand me. We're only too willing to have her. She's no trouble. Only—I'm being frank—I know that this is an expensive place, because we intend treatment here to effect cures. . . ."

"Well?"

"You know—you've known for a long time—there's nothing we can do for Mrs. Carne now except keep her warm and clean and kindly treated."

Those words, "warm and clean and kindly treated," with their suggestion of a less than animal existence, were too much for Carne. He rose and began to pace the room.

"What do you suggest?"

"Why not put her somewhere—less expensive. I know that this is a bad time for farmers. I respect your desire to do the best for her. But there are—cheaper homes—or the County Mental Hospitals."

"Oh, no!"

"But really they are good places. Quite different from the old idea of an asylum." In her crisp quiet voice she outlined improvements, the skilled attention, the food, the private bedrooms.

"I'm a county councillor. I know all that."

She watched his white stricken face. She thought, some people get used to this. He never will.

"Why can't she stay here—where she knows you?"

"I'm afraid, Mr. Carne, that she knows no one."

He stood by the window, playing with the curtain. A pretty girl ran across the lawn, stopped and looked in at him and smiled disarmingly. Then, very discreetly, she began to unbutton her linen dress. An attendant came, spoke to her, and led her away. She seemed disappointed. He turned away, shuddering.

"Why not talk to McClennan?" suggested the matron.

"I'll take your word for it."

"As a matter of fact, if you can't bear the thought of a county place—I have two or three private addresses. There's a place in Manchester."

"I might have a look at them some time."

"Why not?"

She wrote.

"Can I see her?"

"Of course. You know your way."

She was deeply sorry for him. She respected him. She thought, I hope he gets some consolation somewhere. I wouldn't mind, myself. When they brought her tea, she went upstairs to find him.

The big first floor room faced south-west and was flooded with golden light. It was bare of furniture, for there had been times when Muriel Carne did not lie as she lay now, prostrate and motionless except for the rise and fall of heavy breathing. It was no longer necessary to strap her into bed. She remained oblivious of the days and seasons. The green dawn filled her room, the dull grey mornings, the dark blue nights, the chill white of snow. She never noticed. When the nurses attended to her, she gave no response. When her husband sat by her bed, fondling her hand, repeating softly her name, "Muriel! Muriel! Little love, my poor one, my little one," she lay flaccid, unconscious, her fastidious features coarsened, her once mobile face uninhabited by intelligence.

He never dreamed of envying her nullity. He was stricken by the pain of remorse as well as sorrow. He blamed himself. He had brought her to this. My love, my little love. Forgive me. He had torn her from her home, her life, her customs. He had alienated her from all her family. He had robbed her, then, in one moment of jealous passion, had forced himself upon her. He had, very assuredly, destroyed her. There was no comfort.

Loss may be forgotten; wounded vanity heals; but even death could bring no cure for this disaster. Joy and sorrow, success and failure, were made equal by it. All pleasure had been bought for him at her expense. While he rode, dined, laughed, met friends and mastered horses, she lay there. Never again could she partake of joy. There was nothing that could ever happen, in heaven or on earth, which could erase the record of his violence. Oh, my love, my little love, forgive me.

The matron said, "Oh, Mr. Carne, they've just brought me my tea. Won't you come and join me?"

"I'm sorry. I must get to my brother's. He's expecting me."

"I won't keep you then."

But she wanted to say—at least have a drink with me before you go there. You'll need it. She had met William Carne, the architect. She knew that there was no harmony between the brothers. The efficient snobbish builder of villas for West Riding manufacturers was not the matron's idea of a man at all. As for Mavis Carne—his lean rapacious wife, trained like a greyhound for the vigorous athletics of social climbing—"she's a horror," the matron thought.

But she knew Carne's habit of going for all unpleasant business, head down, blindly obstinate, like a bull at a gate. He had to see his brother, so would get it over, marching off into the hot August afternoon to find an address vaguely indicated on Will's new note-paper as "Greenlawnes, Harrogate." It was over six months since he had visited William and Mavis and meanwhile they had moved to a district even more exclusive and expensive than the last. They had built their own house. That was excellent. It meant that they must be doing well, and so could help him without any inconvenience to themselves.

With characteristic lack of consideration they had not thought of telling Carne how to find their house. No taxi presented itself, so he trudged down the sunlit road on the hot pavements. He could walk twenty miles across the fields, but town defeated him.

He loathed the thought of asking Will for money. He had learned no graces of the mendicant's art. He only wanted a loan—for harvest wages till he could sell his wheat and for the monthly account at the Laurels. He did not want to go to the bank again. Fretton was growing difficult. Interest mounted higher. He was aware of the chancy nature of credit.

Carne tried to reassure himself, but his mind was not ingenious. It lacked the subtleties with which some varieties can reassure themselves. He could have reminded himself that William was, after all, his younger brother, that he had played with him in the big tin hip-bath beside the nursery fire, hauled him up straw stacks, taught him how to ride the donkey. He could have reminded himself that Will had always been a bit of a coward, howling when the pony had run away with him, lying when a box of cigarettes was discovered in the cave they had hollowed out of the oat-stack, whimpering as a new boy at St. Peter's—while he, Robert, had cuffed him into shape, championed and fought for him, idly magnanimous, stupid at lessons, brilliant at athletics, a natural leader in a country where muscles, courage, hot temper and slow good-humoured dignity are considered adequate requisites for leadership.

Will had done his sums and drawn his little pictures and married a smart wife and made a lot of money. That was no reason why Carne should mind sounding him for a hundred pounds to see him over harvest.

But the further he tramped the more clearly Carne knew that he did mind it. He hated the long hot walk, hated asking strangers to guide him: Can you tell me where is a house called Greenlawnes? Mr. William Carne's place? The architect? He hated facing Mavis, who always seemed to be about the place. He hated the embarrassment of explaining his position.

By walking three times in the wrong direction to avoid asking questions, Carne found it took him an hour and a half to reach Greenlawnes from The Laurels.

The house stood back from the road in a smart prosperous geometrical garden. The lawns had been mown, the hedges clipped, the begonias planted in unhesitating rows. There was a cubist bird-path, a crazy-paved sunk garden, a rubble tennis court, a grass court, a rose garden. The house was all white and chromium, and rectangular, with windows cut out of the corners "like rat-holes in a soap box," sniffed Carne.

A maid in a musical comedy uniform answered the door-bell and regarded Carne with a glacial manner which belied her gay appearance.

"No, sir, Mrs. Carne isn't in yet. No. I'm afraid not. Very likely; they have a lot of callers."

"I'll come in and wait. And I'd like a wash," sighed Carne.

The hall was black and white and scarlet. A bowl of glass fruits stood on a glass-topped table. The bathroom was green and black with fishes writhing along the green tiled wall and a bath into which one descended by marble steps. The drawing-room was off-white, with immense white sofas, and vases filled with sprays of pearly honesty, and an uncarpeted floor of pale polished silvery wood.

Well, well, thought Carne. After this a hundred or so will be nothing.

There were cigarettes in glass stands on the stone mantelpiece. There was a cocktail bar like an operation theatre in one corner. The maiden offered Carne a cocktail. He hated gin; he wanted a cup of tea or an honest whisky and soda. He wanted anonymity; he wanted death. He sat himself down in one of the vast billowing chairs and waited.

The fatigue, the heat, the emotions of the day had overwhelmed him. When his sister-in-law came clicking on high restless heels along the corridor she found him lying sprawled, his hands hanging to the floor, his head tilted backward, deeply asleep.

"Well, well," she called in her high mocking voice. "Don't let me disturb you, my dear boy."

He sprang awake with a grunt and stared at her painted malicious face, her black pencilled line of eyebrow, her white linen sheath of costume. She was straight, brittle and inhuman as a glass wand.

"Don't mind me. Tuck up again and go bye-bye by all means. I'm expecting some perfectly lousy people in in a few minutes. They'd be charmed to see you. Lazy creatures, you farmers. Have a cocktail?"

"No thanks. Where's Will? Didn't he get my note?"

He levered himself with an effort from the enveloping cushions.

"Out, poor pet. Chasing non-existent business. Well, if you won't drink, I must. I've been having a perfectly frightful afternoon. I'm done to the wide."

She busied herself with the glittering and tinkling surgical instruments of the cocktail bar. "Simply too exhausting. Duty calls, dunning—always the perfect wife, I am. Everything for poor dear Will's sake."

She settled herself with her drink upon the sofa. She looked as cool and unnatural as a gilded lily.

"Throw me a cigarette. Mantelpiece. Well, how are the dear dark elemental things of the countryside—the cows, aimless, homeless and witless, aren't they? The passionate peasants?" Carne bent over her to light her cigarette. "You're putting on weight, you know." She poked with a pointed raspberry-painted finger-nail at his waistcoat. "Tummy running loose. Fat of the land. That's country life. Poor Will's like a scarecrow. It's an 'ard world."

The "lousy people" began to arrive. They came from tennis courts and hotel lounges, from golf-links or motor rides. Their shrill, clipped voices rang in Carne's aching head. Their lean clipped figures swam before his eyes. Darling, how frightful, marvellous, putrid. So at the ninth hole . . . completely off my drive. . . . Monte Carlo—Gleneagles—Wimbledon.

Oh, hell, thought Carne. Yet he was vaguely cheered by all this evidence of prosperity. He had been himself—in another far-off life—to Cannes and Monte Carlo. He did not want to be reminded of bitter-sweet memory.

He caged himself in a corner, glowering silently. By the time his brother arrived, he had less than an hour left before his train time.

The unspoken ferocity of his mood gained him private audience in the small breakfast-room. He stood with his back to a bleak little panel in the wall which, during cold weather, was an electric fireplace, and scowled down at the lean, nervous architect who had the high perspiring forehead and querulous egotism of the hypochondriac.

"It's all very well for you, Bob," wailed Will Carne. "Open air, good country food, your own farm, no worries, plenty of exercise, regular food. You look marvellous, marvellous. Jove, I'd give a lot to feel really fit again."

Carne grunted. He was staring with contemptuous appreciation at his brother's paraphernalia of luxury.

"You don't know what it's been like, this last two years," moaned Will. "Every one scared stiff. Not a soul building. Private people worried, corporations bitten by the economy bug. Sweating your heart out for contracts you don't get. Whistling for your bills."

"This house," suggested Carne, "must have cost a penny or two."

"You're right, my dear chap. You're dead right. Had to do it, of course. Way of business. But God knows how it'll ever get paid for. Owe the bank over two thousand already, and Mavis sold her Imperial Tobacco Shares to pay for the furniture. None of our old stuff would do, of course—and it sold for a song. You've no notion how lucky you were, sticking to the land. How's Maythorpe?"

"Much the same. Castle's very bad."

"Castle? Castle? Let's see—he was shepherd, wasn't he?"

"Foreman."

"Of course. I remember. Fat chap with a vile temper. Threatened to thrash the life out of me when I left the fold-yard door open."

"The young bullocks got out."

"You know, I often think I wouldn't mind being back at Maythorpe. Peace. Fresh air. I'm not at all well these days, you know, not at all well. Nerves. Blood pressure. Indigestion. Live like a cabbage, the doctor said. Cut down work. Don't worry. Don't worry! So simple, isn't it? You know, I was just wanting to talk to you, Bob. Glad you dropped in to-day."

Carne thought of the long and arduous climb which that casual "drop" implied.

"You must be sittin' pretty—Government so hot about agriculture an' all—wheat quotas, beet subsidy—all the rest of it. When you want a little spot cash, all you've got to do is to sell a gee or something. By the way, did you get the Hunter's Cup again at Flintonbridge this year?"

"No."

"Oh—well—as I was saying. The doctors are all agreed that I must get away. We were planning Le Touquet. Or perhaps some little quiet spot in the South of France. You need sun, he said—and by God, he's right. I'm done. No relaxation. Up till all hours. When it isn't on duty in the office, it's on duty meeting the right people—bridge—drinking—Mavis has been a brick! I can't tell you the way that little woman's thrown herself into my interests. So, what I was going to say was—could you let me have fifty quid or so till Fawley's cheque comes in? Couple of ponies would do it."

William, of course, had always been the bright one, the clever boy at school, the spoiled son of the family. Robert, slower-witted, more patient, less completely preoccupied by his own desires, had again and again permitted his junior to exploit him, but until Mavis drove him that evening to the station in the new Humber Snipe (acquired, of course, for "business purposes"), he remained unaware how completely he had been defeated in the unequal contest.

When he proclaimed his lack of money, Will had immediately devised a dozen ways in which he could procure it. He could sell horses, he could sell his silver cups, he could sell some of his antique furniture. ("My dear fellow, your house is simply chock-a-block with sellable stuff. Chock-a-block.") It appeared that he was simply smothered by his great possessions. He had not begun to realise his available assets.

He settled himself down in his third-class carriage. Mavis kissed her hand to him with raspberry-coloured lips.

"Bless you," she breathed. "I knew you'd help us out. Good old Bob."

Carne recalled an anecdote of a great-uncle Jim, of whom it was said, "You may go to borrow a shilling from Jim Carne, but you always end by lending him a guinea." He decided that there was something in heredity.

CHAPTER VI

MR. MITCHELL FACES AN INQUISITION

The South Riding had turned gold for harvest. Through the pale standing corn self-binders whirred behind the nodding horses. In the rich placidity of the mellow fields the brown-armed harvesters piled sheaves into stooks behind the reaper. In the stack-yards labourers forked with rhythmic movement, tossing sheaves from the wagons to the stacks. Children rode back in the empty rattling wagons carrying 'levenses for the men, beer, cold tea, cheese and bacon cake. North of Garfield came rumours of a motor-tractor, that reaped and thrashed in one tremendous effort, but that was still a monster, a curiosity for distrustful comment.

The golden tide of corn had rippled right to the huddled brick of Yarrold Town. Those warm rose buildings piled themselves against the exquisite height of Yarrold Parish Church, a legacy of twelfth century devotion, its delicate grey stone melting into the pale quivering summer sky of nineteen-thirty-three. Corn, brick, and stone, food, housing, worship composed themselves into a gentle landscape of English rural life.

In the motor-bus, grinding along the softened tarry highway, Joe Astell rode to the Public Assistance Committee for the Cold Harbour Division of South Riding.

For him it was a journey without satisfaction. Because his heart was tender and his imagination keen, the details of individual need and suffering hurt him. He would fight the battle for humanity in terms of an extra two shillings a week, a grocery order or a sack of coals. He would attempt to soften the inquisitional harshness of men and women who enjoyed, he thought, this business of hunting down the miseries of defeat, the shameful expedients of poverty. They got their money's worth out of the joys of interference.

But Astell found no joy even in victory. The grudging ameliorations of a system which kept the defeated alive, so that they might not rise in their despair and seize for themselves and for their children those things they needed, gave him no sense of pleasure. This was no work for him—this mild solicitude for bare existence. He should be up, away, fighting to change the system, not content to render first aid to its victims. The picturesque streets of Yarrold closed in upon him. He saw not the lovely shades of the old brick walls, soft rose, warm purple, the patchwork of rough tiled roofs, the rambler roses frothing and showering round the small closed windows; he saw poverty and disease, stunted rickety children, the monotony of women's battle against dirt, cold and inconvenience. The insecurity and loneliness of old age. Deprived of those natural consolations which come alone from work found worth doing, Astell despised himself, his task, his colleagues. An immense fatigue of disillusionment devitalised him. He climbed from the bus, a sad dispirited man.

Beyond a garden wall two girls and a tall young man were playing tennis.

"Forty-fifteen!" called a girl. She stood back for her service, tossed a ball in the air. "Jack, you foul pig. Play!"

Play—they could play if they wished on this warm August morning—these boys and girls of the fortunate middle-classes. Joe thought of the grim north country term of Play, which meant the enforced idleness of unemployment.

I can't stand this much longer, he said to himself, and swung left to the building used by the Public Assistance Committee.

It was a disused Congregational Chapel, bought cheap during the War by the Yarrold Urban District Council and used for offices. To-day it was still partitioned with rough boarding and wore an air of gloomy improvisation redeemed from secularity by stained glass windows which imparted to petitioners and adjudicators alike complexions either decomposed or jaundiced, as the green and blue and yellow rays fell on their faces.

The committee was assembled when Astell crossed the passage where the applicants sat waiting and entered the room by one of its rough unpainted doors. They sat on three sides of a hollow square of tables, facing the chair where their victims would appear. Colonel Whitelaw, a youngish popular landowner, presided. Mr. Thompson, the relieving officer, a thin decent red-headed man, shuffled his papers.

He had lost over a stone since he undertook this work twelve months ago. His war record, his disability—three fingers off the left hand and he had been an engineer—and his eager honesty had won the job for him. But to-day his anxious face and troubled gesture proclaimed him as much a victim of the slump as those whose cases he examined. Astell nodded to him, aware of his harassed, kindly, rather muddled mind, of his pretty extravagant wife who had been a typist, of his debts, his unwise generosities, and his terrors.

He did not nod to Colonel Whitelaw.

He sat down in a chair near the relieving officer.

"Well—I think we're all here, aren't we? Alderman Tubbs can't come. Oh, Carne's not here yet."

"Harvest. He'll probably be late," said Peacock.

David Shirley the coal-merchant whispered to Astell, "If harvest lasted all year, we might get a bit of business done."

Carne was a notable objector and interrupter, "safe-guarding the rate-payers." Safeguarding his own skin, thought Astell.

Before each member of committee lay a small pile of papers. Each recorded a story of individual defeat. Here were the men and women who had fallen a little lower even than those on transitional benefit, the disallowed, the uninsured, the destitute. The Means Test was no new humiliation to them. Since the days of Queen Elizabeth those who had become dependent on their neighbours had to submit to inquiry and suggestion. What was new was the type of person who came to ask for outdoor relief. The middle-class worker fallen on evil times, the professional man, the ruined investment holder.

Astell was not moved by the special pity for these which distressed his colleagues. If their plight marked the failure of capitalism, so much the better—so much the sooner would end this evil anarchy with its injustice, its confusion, its waste, its class divisions. So much the sooner would come the transformation to the classless planned community. But he was not happy. His ruthless theory guided uneasily his tender heart.

The committee slipped into its usual routine.

The chairman read out a name.

Mr. Thompson, coughing nervously, stripes of blue and emerald shifting across his face, stood up and read out the applicant's particulars.

"Millicent Ethel Roper. Single woman. Sixty-one. Occupies one room in private house belonging to Esther Snagg, widow. Rent five and sixpence. Crippled with rheumatism. Does a little charring when well enough. Only living relative married sister in Barrow-in-Furness. This sister used to send her a little money, but her husband, a riveter, is now unemployed, so the gifts have stopped. No other resources."

"How badly is this woman crippled?" asked the chairman. He himself had suffered from rheumatism ever since his adventures in the mud of Passchendaele, and was inclined to be tolerant to rheumatic cases.

"She seems to vary. In the damp weather she can hardly move from her chair."

"She ought to be in an institution," said Mrs. Brass, the jeweller's wife.

"She's very insistent that she doesn't want to go there. She declares that most of the year she's self-supporting. She only needs help over her bad times."

"Had she ever any other calling?"

"Dressmaker. But her hands are too crippled now."

"Well. We'd better see her."

The relieving officer went to the door.

"Miss Roper," he called, his voice more peremptory than his intentions, for he was both sorry for her and nervous for himself.

There was a pause, and then the little creature hobbled in. She was indeed, deplorably deformed. Her head was drawn to one side by contracted muscles. Her hands were so cruelly distorted by lumps and swellings that they were more like monstrous fungi than human members. But her face with its sideways glance was undismayed. Her shrewd brown eyes swept the committee with alert intelligence.

"Come here to the table, can you, Miss Roper? And sit down, won't you?" The chairman prided himself on his easy manner.

Miss Roper sat down.

She was entirely unintimidated by this tribunal that had power over her future.

"You used to be a dressmaker?"

"Yes—I was, till I lost the right use of my hands. Look at 'em. Bundles of carrots at first you could have called them. Bundles of potatoes now, more like." She thrust out the mottled lumps.

The traditional humour of the poor angered Astell. He felt humour to be an inappropriate emotion. The Shakespearean tradition of finding the lower classes funny, whatever tragedy touched the kings and nobles, outraged his humanity. But Miss Roper was a character. She refused to conform to his sense of decency.

"How long is it since you were able to sew?" continued Colonel Whitelaw.

"Six years now—I sold my machine. A beauty. Treddle, it was."

"Then you've done office work?"

"Charring. Scrubbing wherever I could get it. Many's the time I've done your husband's shop, Mrs. Brass. And not before it needed it. You'd be surprised the amount of muck folks carry on their feet. Just like you'd never guess the muck an' sweat they get on their clothes until you start remodelling."

Miss Roper was enjoying herself. She loved talking and all audiences were welcome.

"And recently you have not been able even to do much cleaning?"

"No. Look at me hands. Look at me knees," said Miss Roper. She raised her skirt. Before the shocked gaze of the committee she exposed a grey alpaca petticoat, a pair of black wool stockings, and the blue and white striped frills of flannelette knickers which she proceeded to pull back with cheerful vigour. "Look at that. Would you like to kneel on that scrubbing a step?"

"No—no. Of course."

Hastily the chairman waved away all doubts of her disablement, horrified by the thought of further revelations.

"Don't you think," Mrs. Brass suggested—she had been irritated by allusions to her husband's place of business—"Don't you think you'd be happier in an institution? We've got those nice new buildings up in South Street. You'd have proper medical attention and no worry there."

"I dare say I should. But I do quite nicely with Mrs. Snagg. All I want is a bit of something towards my rent and a bit to live on and I can manage till I get my old age pension."

"But aren't you very lonely in that back bedroom? In South Street you'd have companions of your own age and much more comfort."

"It's not comfort you want. It's a bit of fun," said the disconcerting Miss Roper. "Lonely? Not me. Why, there's Mrs. Snagg, as nice a lady as you could wish for. Reads the tea-cups and can tell a story as good as any one in Yarrold. There's her daughter and her grandchildren popping in an' out. I keep an eye on them for her when she needs it. Then there's the whist drives. I always go when I can get some one to pay my ticket and we divide the prizes. I'm awful lucky with cards. You've no idea. And then there's my gentleman friend, Mr. Barnes, you know."

"I'm afraid—I don't." muttered the chairman.

"Not know old Ricky Barnes of Newbegin, the carrier? Why, every one knows Ricky. He goes to Cold Harbour Colony and Pandy Creek way in a covered cart with an old piebald horse. Many's the time he calls for me and I ride with him. We've been keeping company for nearly thirty years."

"Then why don't you marry him?" asked Mrs. Brass. "He's a widower, isn't he?"

"Yes, but you see, it's this way. He promised his dear wife—Mary Ellen Barnes, as nice a little woman as I ever wish to meet—he'd never marry again if she was taken from him. So he can't, can he?"

"But really"—to Mrs. Brass, to Colonel Whitelaw, to other members of the committee, it seemed preposterous that just because of a minor point of delicacy the rate-payers should have to provide for Carrier Barnes' beloved, when he possessed a good-sized cottage and a business which, if modest, was certainly adequate to support a couple.

Miss Roper fully appreciated their position.

"You see," she said disarmingly, "I don't say Ricky wouldn't help me. But I'm a Primitive and a Christian and I don't believe in ladies taking presents from their gentlemen friends. Do you now? All this modern compassionate marriage and what you read in the papers, it may suit some. But I've always paid my own rent and been self-respecting, and if you'd let me have my rent and a bag of flour, and a grocery order, and perhaps a sack of coals to see me through the winter, I should get on nicely, no trouble to any one."

"Has—has any member of committee any further questions that they would like to ask Miss Roper?"

No other members had. They were defeated.

"Then perhaps, if you'd wait outside, Miss Roper."

"Good-bye all, and cheerio, I'm sure." And out she shuffled.

The judges of society faced each other. What could they say?

"Well, dash it all," stammered the colonel, "we can hardly ask the woman to live in sin to save the rate-payers' pockets, can we?"

It was agreed, reluctantly, that they hardly could.

"I never believe," commented Mrs. Brass, "in these submissions to a Dead Hand."

The decision was recorded that Miss Roper should receive eight shillings a week and a grocery order.

The members' door opened and Carne entered.

"Sorry, Whitelaw."

He slumped down into his chair.

Astell regarded him with disapproval. It was harvest time, yet a not too prosperous farmer could attend committees to cut down the meagre grants by which society staved off the scandal of coroner's verdicts: Death from malnutrition. To Astell, Carne's presence there meant only one thing. As for himself, he was not much better. He was acquiescing in something that was all wrong.

He watched his enemy across the table.

But Carne that day took no active part in the proceedings. It seemed as though by bringing himself to the committee he had exhausted his energies. He sat with his arms folded, his eyes on the papers before him, in a dream, while his colleagues considered the case of Mrs. Timms. Her husband had just been disallowed transitional, then fallen ill, then she couldn't manage on her daughter's earnings and five shillings a week from a son in Manchester.

They had next before them an old couple on the old age pension. The husband was suffering from diabetes, and his special diet and bus fares for treatment in the hospital left them behind in their rent and without fire or lighting.

"It's warm now," said Carne. "And the days are long. You can't want as much coal or lamp oil as in winter."

"Maybe not," replied the little woman with dignity. "But my husband can't sleep if we go to bed too early. This illness makes him cold and nervous-like. You can't sit hour after hour in the dark. No one could stand it, let alone a diabetic."

"Still—"

"Carne," thought Astell, "draws his dole from the Government, his wheat quota, perhaps a grant for sugarbeet. Yet he wants a sick man to sit in the dark."

He felt the slow surge of anger like poison in his veins. As though with sympathy for the diabetic, he began to cough—furious because Carne had noticed him and looked across the room at him with kind concern. His treacherous body exposed him to the insult of his enemy's compassion. He rose and, muttering something, left the room to get a drink.

When he returned they were discussing the case of a man, wife and three dependent children. The man was a hawker by trade, but having spent his capital had now no goods to hawk. He let one room for three shillings a week. His rent was fifteen shillings, his insurance ninepence, and his light a shilling. He was granted a nine-shilling grocery order, two shillings' worth of coal and his rent. Astell fought for more money instead of the grocery order. He was defeated.

An unemployed casual worker who used to pick up odd porterage at the docks and who also had a wife and three dependent children was offered thirteen shillings and sixpence cash, and thirteen shillings and sixpence grocery orders and two shillings a week for coal. This time it was Carne who intervened. Surely the thirteen-shillings-and-sixpence cash order was excessive?

"But they must have boots, bedding, cleaning materials," broke out Astell.

"This brings their income to twenty-nine shillings. I have good men doing a full week's work for thirty shillings," said Carne gravely.

"All the more shame!" Astell began, but the chairman cried, "Order, order! The next applicant—Frederick Mitchell. I understand that you know something of this case, Astell, don't you?"

It was Mrs. Beddows who had sent him out to the Shacks to see the Mitchells. Sarah Burton had suggested to him that Mrs. Mitchell might look after the Holly baby and Lennie when term had started, in order that Lydia might get to school. Mitchell himself had confided in him. He had been shown "Bella Vista," and the walnut bureau, Peggy Mitchell, who had not yet got measles, Mrs. Mitchell, small, large-eyed, inclined to be hysterical.

But the case was not one which deeply moved him. These people with their treasured china tea-set, their respectability, their contempt for "lower classes," grated against his most darling prejudices. He had handled his visit badly. He was aware that the Mitchells regarded him as a worse inquisitor than the self-deprecating Thompson. He could hear, in his over-sensitised imagination, their comments when he had gone. "These Socialists are harder on you than the gentry. Carne, now, he is a gentleman. He does know how to treat you."

Astell disliked these families who had seen better days. . . . He did his duty. In his harsh, unsympathetic voice he retailed the details of the Mitchells' case. He knew what arguments appealed to the committee. He despised himself for displaying them.

Thompson opened the door and called:

"Mr. Mitchell."

Mitchell entered.

Everything about him signified the black-coated worker—his hair neatly sleeked with water, his well-pressed, shiny, pin-striped suit, his white collar, his jaunty yet humiliated manner.

"You were in the Diamond Insurance, Mr. Mitchell?"

These were the representatives of society—the solid family men—income-tax payers, before whom Fred Mitchell had laid the well-worn arguments for security. Have you thought of your wife's future? Your little daughter, what is she worth to you?

His familiar slogans now returned to mock him. They ran round and round his brain. He fidgeted with his tie.

The chairman repeated his question.

Mitchell started. His mouth contracted with dumb effort. He saw Astell's face, stern with dislike and forced benevolence.

He croaked out his confession: "I had a book."

He had reached the bottomless pit of humiliation. A pauper. On the rates, begging for food tickets. He remembered his office in Kingsport where he had had two clerks and a boy under him. He had been going to buy a car.

He could not speak. This was a nightmare in which his feet were chained so that he could not flee from horror.

May I put a little scheme before you?

Oh, God, how are we going to live?

A choked groan, half a sob, shook his body.

This was the worst of all. He was going to make a fool of himself.

A deep voice from one of the places to his right made him start violently.

"You know, Mitchell, it's a hell of a feeling asking for money, but it can't be as bad as for the chap I met last week who went to Harrogate to borrow a hundred quid from his younger brother."

Nothing more surprising had ever been heard at that table. If the ink-pots themselves had spoken, the committee could hardly have been more taken aback. All faces turned to Carne.

"And did he get it?" smiled Whitelaw, ready for any diversion.

"No," drawled Carne. "Before he could even ask, his brother touched him for fifty quid and he went home and sold some furniture an' lent it."

"Well, Mr. Mitchell," the chairman took up the cue, "at least we shan't try to borrow from you, at the moment. Wait for a year or two—then you may be in our shoes and we in yours."

They laughed—Fred Mitchell shakily; but the crisis was passed. He was a man among men, a human being—a pariah no longer.

He withdrew from the dreaded inquisition comforted. The temporary order for groceries which Thompson had given had been confirmed; in addition there was to be milk for Peggy, oil for the lamp and stove and a cash grant of 15/-. Little enough, God knows, but they would manage. The committee, Colonel Whitelaw had explained, had to work within strict legal limitations; they could not go beyond their powers; but Carne's little joke, the friendliness, the personal sympathy, had taken the sting of humiliation out of pauperism.

He cycled back to the Shacks in better spirits than he had known for weeks. If Peggy did not get measles, and she showed no symptoms yet, life might be tolerable.

But Astell was left staring at the ink-splashed table, chewing the bitter cud of self-contempt.

I'm no use, he told himself. I'm no use. He had set out to comfort Mitchell, but Carne had done it. Carne, who grudged pennies and shillings from the shameful pittance of the very poor, Whitelaw the suave snob, without an ounce of imagination, who had the easy popular company commander's way with privates. These men who profited by injustice, who perpetuated anarchy, who had never risked one hour's discomfort to relieve oppression, could yet by a feeble anecdote, a trick of laughter, do something that Astell, who had given health, ambition, happiness and half his life to man's service, could not do.

Mitchell, he thought with scorn, the black-coated worker. Deep had called to deep, middle-class to middle-class. So Carne had saved his vanity.

It did not occur to him that Carne would never recognise in Mitchell a member of his own class. Carne never thought of himself as belonging to any class. He was Carne of Maythorpe. Mitchell was a poor devil down on his luck.

Carne had a slow mind and little sense of humour. But the thought had touched his mind that he and this fellow were in the same boat, asking for public assistance for their private needs. But Mitchell seemed to be making the better job of it.

It was half-past one when the committee adjourned for lunch. Astell went off through the crooked street, shimmering in the hot sun, for his meal—a glass of milk and a sandwich at the baker's. Three men marched in single file beside the pavement, playing a drum and two mouth organs. "Genuine Welsh Miners" proclaimed a notice on their collecting box.

Suddenly Astell's patience failed.

I'm through, he said. I'm off. This is no place for me. These local committees. You can't fight on them. You can't alter things here. Once the laws have been passed, we only can administer them. He saw his work here as something worse than useless. Why struggle to get another Labour man on to the U.D.C.? Why lecture on "Imperialism or War" to twenty bored old women of the Co-operative Guild in Unity Hall? Futile, futile, futile. Why should he do it, when he might be back, fighting not to mitigate but to change the system? To save his life? What did his life matter?

He turned and dropped sixpence into the miners' collecting-box, despising his weak-kneed bourgeois philanthropy.

It was his lunch money.

BOOK VI

MENTAL DEFICIENCY

"Resolved—That the following Report made by Members of the Visiting Committee after their Statutory Visits be received and entered on the Minutes:—

'We have visited the Hospital to-day and found all the patients quiet and comfortable. Few complaints were raised, except the usual ones from those who ask to be sent home.

"The painting of the men's quarters is certainly overdue, and the children are still too crowded. We visited their playground and are of the opinion that it would be far better for the mental defective juveniles to be accommodated in some other quarters.

"All curative work must be handicapped by the present cramped conditions.'

November, 15th.

(Signed) A. Snaith. Emma Beddows. P. Tubbs."

Minutes of the Visiting Committee of the South Riding Mental Hospital. December, 1933.

CHAPTER I

TEMPORARY INSANITY IS ACKNOWLEDGED AT THE NAG'S HEAD

"Temporary insanity," Topper Beachall read slowly, syllable by syllable, from the evening paper. "Tem-por-ary insanity. They all say they're insane, chaps what shoots themselves. Go on, I say."

Nobody went on.

Hicks wiped his mouth; Sawdon lit his pipe; Grandpa Sellers spat into the brass shell-case beside the fireplace.

It was an October evening. Harvest was all in. The vase-shaped pikes bulged gracefully in the stack-yards, crowned by pointed thatches. The larger oblong stacks made great blocks like solid buildings. A slight ground-frost rimed the bare fields and stiffened the Michaelmas daisies in the cottage gardens. But the Nag's Head bar-parlour was snug and trim, and the tales of tragedy read by Topper Beachall seemed only to augment that intimate cosiness.

"'Father of six found hanged in scullery with braces!' I don't blame him. I know what it is to be a father. If he'd hanged some of his brats with him, you couldn't wonder. 'Actress elopes with first husband.' Now I should say she was mad. Here's a lass wed a chap an' doesn't like him an' gets shut on him an' marries another, an' then runs off wi' first again—now that is potty, if you like."

Tom Sawdon jerked the tin cap deftly off another bottle of ale. He refilled his own glass.

"How's Castle?" he asked Hicks.

"Bad. Can't speak now. Beats me why they let him go on living. If he was a horse, they'd have put him down long ago."

"Or a dog," sighed Sawdon reminiscently.

The door opened and Lily poked her head in.

She had changed. Had these men not watched her daily transformation, they would have found it hard to believe that this bowed fleshless figure, hung about with ill-fitting, tumbled clothes, was the body of pretty Lily Sawdon. Her grey watchful face retained only the ghost of that delicate mobility which had charmed them. Her voice had declined into the whining monotony of complaint.

"There's a car in the yard, Tom," she said. "They'll want petrol."

"All right. I'll go."

Lily withdrew. Tom swung up the flap of the bar counter, and swaggered, none too steadily, from the room.

"Hasn't our friend," asked Topper, with a backward jerk of his head, "had a drop too much?"

"They all go same way at Nag's Head." Grandpa Sellars pushed back a lump of coal with his heavy boot.

"Nag's Head's all right," said Hicks. "You'd take a drop if you had to live with Mrs. S. Women are all alike. I thought she was quite a niceish bit when we first came down here; but now there's no pleasing her. Fret, fret, fret. It's enough to drive any chap to drink."

"She's nobbot poorly," Grandpa suggested charitably. "She's the living spit of our poor Anne Eliza that died forty years ago of tumour—nicest little woman in South Riding—then went queer as Dick's hat band. Tumour. All tumour. She sickened fourteen year before God took her, and sent her husband and two children into their graves first—trying to drown their sorrows. Aye. It's a bad business. They all go same way at Nag's Head."

Beyond the door, Lily Sawdon crawled back to her place by the fire.

So this is what it all had come to—Tom drinking himself to death, she a scold, the customers' aware of her real trouble. This was the end of all her striving, her self-sacrifice, her martyred silence.

The winter was approaching, yet she seemed little nearer death than when she visited Dr. Stretton. And if she did not die soon, it would be too late for Tom.

The odd thing was that since she had been taking those tablets, life had not actually seemed so wretched. Possibly she had let herself go a bit. Expecting death, she had ventured to relax her life-long discipline of daintiness and good humour. She had retired into a secret world that was not all torment.

Often, for days together, she was hardly conscious of the life of the village or her neighbours. She had withdrawn into the flat-faced stucco-covered inn as into a nunnery. The hundred yards up and down the road outside the door measured her universe. Their shallow borders of turf and thorns and nettles, their rusting hedges, their lightly frosted cobwebs, represented all that she hoped to see again of natural beauty. They were enough.

The days were long, heavy with pain and weariness, but she could live drowsed from acute awareness. People passed her like shadows in a fog. She had no contact with them. If she spoke, she could not remember what she said to them. Nothing, not even pain, was very near her. But towards the evening her senses quickened. Slowly the power of the strong drug waned. She came alive then. These were the dangerous hours, lonely and vulnerable. She was exposed again to pain or ecstasy. These were times when she felt brilliantly receptive; lights grew brighter then, colours more vivid, the gay trivial music danced in her mind.

Then she would sit in her wide western window, watching the sun set over the flat broad fields. It laid bright patterns of gold on her floor and table, it caressed in final salute her chair by the fire. The long procession of the hours culminated in this ceremony. If it failed her, she grew childishly angry. She snapped at her husband, she whined, she even wept.

But after sunset came the long quiet evenings. On her good days she would sit and read or listen to the wireless. It was dangerous to sew or move about much; she might startle to life the sleeping pain. But voices came to her out of the silence, singers and jesters and actors from Broadcasting House. She acquired favourites and enemies. She loved the songs that she had known as a girl—"If I built a world for you, dear," "Melisande in the Wood," "The Indian Love Lyrics." She delighted in "Soft Lights and Sweet Music." She found certain comics funny. Mrs. Waters' daughters made her laugh, and Lily Morris she found vulgar but a real scream.

At ten o'clock Tom closed the bar and joined her. When she heard the thump of the hob-nailed boots on the brick tiled passage she would set the kettle closer upon the glowing coals and put out the pot for their final cup of tea. And with the tea she took three of her tablets, not caring if Tom caught her at it, surrendering to the heavenly comfort of the drug, enjoying even the strong bitter taste of the rough round disk laid upon her tongue before she swallowed.

Then she would let go of her short-lived sensibility and float away again into unawareness, hardly knowing how she crawled up the stairs to bed, glorying in the luxury of oblivion.

But there were still times when she woke before the dawn, clutching herself, gasping with agony. Then she could lie and hear Tom's heavy breathing and know that the men were right; he was drinking too much now. And sometimes she could hardly resist the temptation to scream out to him, to implore him to help her, to make for her the impossible, the monstrous journey to the washstand, where in a drawer lay those round white tablets, those merciful, beautiful, incomparable gifts of Dr. Stretton.

She had not yielded yet. Morning after morning she had crept, livid with pain, to her secret store, her most intolerable nightmare that she should one day find it bare. That fear pursued her far into her dreams. It hunted her down long corridors of sleep. It aroused her early in the mornings, haunted by a panic that was of the body rather than the mind—the panic that even this remedy should fail her, that she would be left at the mercy of her pain, disarmed, defenceless. And that could not be thought of save with horror.

But now she had been made aware of a new, immediate disaster. She had managed her own pain; she had found consolation, but Tom was drinking and it was she who was driving him to ruin.

She had not meant to do it; she had been so proud of herself, so proud because she had never told him. And all the time he had been bearing with her, cheerfully shouldering the whole work of the inn, building up the business, never complaining. He had even done her the supreme service of appearing to enjoy himself. He had polished brasses, tinkered with cars, served drinks, cut bread and butter, done his work and hers as well with generous gusto. And only when her lassitude, her irritability, and her dazed and drugged remoteness had bewildered him, did he seek peace in his own stores of beer and whisky.

Oh, Tom, Tom, Tom.

She had preened herself with secret vanity, as a martyr, a sacrificial priestess of wifely love. Now she was broken by humility.

Oh, my darling, my darling, what have I done to you?

The kitchen was very quiet. From the bar came occasional stampings and shoutings and muffled bursts of laughter. Two farm lads were throwing darts for a bottle of Guinness.

Temporary insanity. She had been insane to think that she could deceive him without loss.

I've got to tell him. Maybe it's too late, but I've got to tell him. Tell all. Confession.

Almighty and most merciful Father, we have erred and strayed from Thy ways like lost sheep. Almighty and most merciful love. . . .

The latch clicked. Its metallic sound had often infuriated Lily. She started at it, bracing herself for her ordeal of confession.

She set the kettle carefully; she pulled herself carefully from her chair and started to lay out cups, pot, butter, bread.

I'll make a bit of toast for him, she thought.

The men were going now. She heard the good-nights; she heard the laughter; she heard, "Now, Topper, behave thysen, lad," she heard, "Good-night, Grandpa."

She crouched before the stove, her toast on a fork, her kettle humming in the fire, her table spread. And thus Tom found her.

"Hallo? Toast, eh? Getting hungry, were you?"

He did not reproach her. He did not remind her of the many nights when not even the kettle was boiling ready for him. He sat down opposite to her in his shirt sleeves—for he had been washing up the glasses—and took the cup from her with hands that were almost steady. Seeing his cheerful pleasant face, a little puzzled, she realised more acutely than ever how she had failed him. The half-dozen sentences that she had framed deserted her. She dropped her face into her hands and began to cry.

"Why, Lily! Come, old lady. What is it, eh?"

"Oh, Tom. I've done all wrong. I've been so foolish."

"Well, we all have our bad turns. What can't be cured must be endured, you know."

But though his words were light and there was raillery in his voice, his eyes were serious. He knew that whatever this was, it was no laughing matter.

"Tom—tell me. Honest—Have I been awful lately?"

He twisted a bit.

"Well—mebbe not quite yourself."

She nodded.

"I know. I hadn't realised—I—it sounds silly, but please believe me, I didn't know how awful it must have been for you."

"That's all right."

"Tom—please—promise you'll answer truly."

"Now don't you go fretting yourself."

"No. Tom. I mean this. This is important. Please, dear."

"All right. Go ahead, Lil."

"Tom, have you guessed what's wrong with me?"

She was shivering now, and he sat up, aroused to alert attention.

"You really want me to say?"

"Yes."

"Then—I'm not sure. But I've guessed—Oh, Lil, don't think I've blamed you. I made a mistake too. I should never have bought this place. It's been lonely for you. And you not strong. At your time of life—It's been my fault from the beginning. That's why I didn't say anything. I thought, 'She'll get over it. . . .'" Then he stopped. On her face was not contrition nor shame, but bewilderment. It was her turn to stare at him.

"Why—I—Tom. I don't understand. What do you think it is?"

"Here, Lil. I told you not to fret. Whatever it is, it doesn't matter. Those white tablets—you—feel to need them, don't you?"

"Yes—but . . ."

Then suddenly she saw.

At Leeds a Mrs. Pollin, two houses down the road, had taken drugs. Her conduct, her husband's tragedy, their broken home, had been the bye-word of the neighbourhood.

"Tom—you didn't think I was like Mrs. Pollin, did you?"

He did not speak, only put out his hand, and that dumb gesture moved her out of all self-consciousness or reticence, so that she slid out of her seat and knelt there on the hearthrug, her hand in his.

"No. It's not that, Tom. Darling Tom. It's not as bad as that."

With joy she saw that she had for him now not bad but good news.

"You know that day when poor old Rex was put down?"

He nodded.

"Well, you remember I went into Kingsport?" She was glowing, eager.

"Well, I went to the doctor. I'd been having a bit of a pain—here. I thought I'd better do the thing well while I was about it. And Tom, you mustn't mind. I don't mind. Look. Look at me. I couldn't mind and look like this, now could I? Darling Tom, it's cancer. They can't operate. It's not always painful, and I may live for years still. Those tablets stop the pain when it does come on. Tom—you are not to mind."

She struck his hand with her own weak fleshless fingers.

"You're sure? He might have been mistaken."

She shook her head, biting her lip now.

"No. I've been twice since. There's no mistaking."

"Oh, Lil—why didn't you tell me?"

"I can't think now. I can't forgive myself. I thought somehow I could keep just the same. I didn't realise. . . ."

"Oh, Lil."

"I've been so bad to you. It was cruel of me. I never thought. . . . I meant to be kind, Tom. You do believe I only meant to be kind?"

He nodded, speechless.

"I love you so much. You can't think how much I love you. You've been so good to me."

"Lil—is it bad?"

"A little—sometimes."

"When you've—not spoken?"

"Sometimes it was the pain—but more often the tablets. They're wonderful. They make it all unreal, Tom. Sometimes they make you a little unreal too. That's hardly fair, is it? You're so nice to me."

"Can't we do anything? I'll go to Stretton. Don't they have treatment nowadays? All that in the paper. Radium, isn't it?"

"No; I asked. Not for my sort. If there had been, I'd have told you. Honest."

"You wouldn't have kept back—just to save telling me?"

This time she lied light-heartedly. "No. I ought to have gone earlier. But I thought it was all nerves. Tom, don't take it badly. There's nothing to fret about. We can't live for ever. Only—only."

He looked up at her with silently imploring question.

"Don't hate me too much when I'm hateful."

"Oh—Lil."

He gathered her into his arms then and sat holding her on his knee, like a child again. She felt his cheek wet against hers, but whether with her tears or his, she could not say. Even the smell of beer about him seemed homely and comforting—nothing dreadful.

It was all right now. He had been blaming himself for it, thinking that she was like Mrs. Pollin. This was what came of lying. Never again would she insult him by telling him anything but the naked truth.

That even now she had deceived him about the fatal delay in treatment did not occur to her. She had forgotten that their journey from Leeds had really sealed her fate. Because Tom shared the knowledge of her illness, she felt now redeemed and purified, as though she had told him everything. She lay back in his arms, upheld and enclosed by truth—completely happy.

She hardly knew when he carried her up to bed.

CHAPTER II

MIDGE PROVOKES HYSTERIA

The bicycle shed stood behind the High School buildings, a long dim jungle of steel and wire beneath a sloping roof. Showers dancing on corrugated iron almost deafened the members of the Anti-Sig Society huddled together in one corner with winter coats bunched round their ears and cheeks bulging with liquorice allsorts.

Above them hung a notice-board on which was pinned a sheet torn out of an exercise book bearing the peculiar inscription, "A.S.S."

Judy		6
Nancy		4+
Gwynneth	}	
Midge	}	3
Enid		2
Maud	}	
Phyllis	}	0

From time to time day-girls entered, abstracted bicycles and pedalled off into the rain, paying small attention to the conspiratorial group in the dark corner. The bicycle shed was a recognised committee-room for unofficial school societies.

"Judy's got top marks. Judy presides," said Nancy.

A plump child with limp straw-coloured hair wriggled on to the lamp shelf.

"Midge Carne has an idea," she announced.

"We ought to re-read the rules of the society."

"Why?"

"That's the right thing. Before every meeting."

"No—not the rules, the minutes."

"Well, we haven't any minutes."

"I founded the society," said Midge. "I say it's the rules. Judy can read them."

Judy lit a bicycle lamp and bent forward to bring a battered exercise book into range of its narrow delta of light. She read:

"This society shall be called the Anti-Sig Society or A.S.S.

"Its object is the abolition of the Sigglesthwaite monster from Kiplington School.

"Members are elected by a committee consisting of Midge Carne, Gwynneth Rogers, Nancy Grey and Judy Peacock.

"The society meets weekly and gives marks to the members, judged by their behaviour towards the Sig.

"Marks shall be given for the following points:

Ordinary cheek in class	1
Personal insults	2
Picking up dropped hairpins	2
Drawings—(if good)	2
If good and in a public place	3

A really splendid piece of cheek, affecting every one 10

Also whoever does it shall be called Queen A.S.S. for the term and preside at all meetings.

Top marks otherwise for the week make a president.

"This society was the idea of M.C."

"I have a really splendid idea," announced Midge.

"All right. Get up on to the president's seat."

Judy slid down; Midge climbed.

She sat on the shelf dangling her legs, looking down on to the ring of upturned faces in the lamplight.

These were Them. These were her friends. She had triumphed. In the first term of her second year she sat there, presiding over Judy and Maud and Gwynneth warm and secure in the confidence of their friendship. She was one of a Group, a Family. She belonged.

Her triumph was all the more sweet because she had nearly lost it. She had returned to Maythorpe after the Measle Term to the worst summer holidays that she had ever known. After the bright precision of Miss Burton's little house, after the discipline and companionship of school, Maythorpe seemed lost in unhappy desolation.

The neglected lawns grew tall as a watered meadow. The unpruned roses straggled across the paths and dripped from the leaning archways. Apples rotted as they fell below the orchard trees. No callers came, but as human life receded from the old house it seemed to take to itself its own non-human populace. Mice scratched and whimpered under the bedroom floors; bats hung in the attic; earwigs and spiders ran up the window curtains. When Midge tossed her tennis ball accidentally against the ivy, sparrows and starlings flew out with such shrill chatter that the whole house seemed to have come alive to scold her.

Her loneliness first bored, then terrified her. Elsie, disgruntled and dour, banged about the kitchen. Her father was out all day. Castle was worse. The harvest had not gone well. Hicks was just awful. Daddy had sold three hunters before harvest. The morning when they went away, Trix, Ladybird and the Adjutant, Midge stood on the step that led from the little tiled back-yard to the great gravelled stable-yard, and watched Hicks lead out of the stable first the big bay, then the grey flea-bitten spotted mare, the Ladybird, then her father's bright golden heavyweight, the Adjutant. Carne took the bridle reins, looked at their mouths, bent down and felt their knees. Ladybird was saddled; the other two wore their stable cloths. Hicks mounted the grey, and Carne handed him the bridle reins of the others.

"Be back about four?" asked Carne.

Hicks did not speak. Midge saw his ugly, rather comical face distorted by an odd convulsion. He nodded; he chirruped to the horses; he was off down the drive, riding one, leading two. Carne watched them go.

Midge ran down to him, torn by forebodings, urgent to ask, "Daddy, where's he gone? What's happening?"

But Carne did not seem to hear her. He strode off past the stables towards the hind's house beyond the western stack-yard without a word, his face set hard as stone.

So Midge was glad when the holidays were over.

She returned to school eager yet suspicious, sniffing its atmosphere, shying back from innovation like a suspicious and timid little animal. Her habit of suspecting the worst made her inclined to see every change as frightful. There were over fifty new girls and they were awful, slummy, common, with appalling accents. There was another boarding-house along Cliff Terrace. There was a new form, the Remove, and Midge was in it. "It's for us duds," said the irrepressible Judy. "Not at all," Midge replied. "It's for delicate girls who need special attention and don't take matric. That's why I'm in it. I had measles very badly, and Dr. Campbell says I must be careful of my heart."

But, heart or no, Midge missed the special privileges of illness. Miss Burton had withdrawn from her brief intimacy. She was preoccupied with new buildings, new girls and reorganisation. People said that the school was being a success, but what mattered to Midge was whether she could be a success inside the school. She was uncertain again, and insecure.

So something had to be done, or life would be too wretched. "The sensitive girl, aristocratic and delicate, looked with dismay upon the vulgar rabble surrounding her," she told herself. It was bad enough that Miss Carne of Maythorpe should be herded with all these tradesmen's just too frightful daughters, but if, on top of that, she was to find herself, Lord Sedgmire's granddaughter despised by her inferiors, she could not bear it.

Then, with a sudden ecstasy of creation, she invented the Anti-Sig Society.

Ragging the Sig was fun and it was easy. It was part of a popular and legitimate Kiplington fashion. It was Sporting.

There was no intention of malice in it. Mistresses, with their huge statutory powers, were fair game. They were not human beings. They did not possess the common human feelings. Their lives were mysterious. They appeared at the beginning of term and vanished at its close. From the Great Deep to the Great Deep they went, incalculable, inapproachable, unreal.

Therefore for girls to persecute them was heroic. All the risk, all the adventure, lay on the side of youth, which must brave the anger of entrenched authority. Therefore Midge, swinging her thin brown legs in the light of the bicycle lamp after second school, surveyed her audience with legitimate pride.

"Listen," she said. "You know our nature prep.?"

"'Write a study of some living creature whose habits you have observed for yourself,'" quoted Maud.

"I've got a marvellous idea. You know how she loves the stickleback. The little stickleback? Why not the Sigglesback? Who'll dare to write an essay on the Sigglesback? We've studied it, haven't we? We've observed it for ourselves?"

She watched her great idea rippling across their faces like light on water.

"The sigglesback—a bony little creature—cold-blooded—lives in the mud."

"Builds nests."

"In its hair."

The idea was catching on.

Here was creation. Here was glory.

"It prefers dirty water."

"It never mates."

Glory, glory, glory. Midge was a leader. She was popular. She was safe. Friendship encircled her. Leadership enthroned her. When had she doubted? When had she been afraid?

"It's marvellous!"

"Midge, you're priceless!"

"Shu-uh!"

The creaking door at the far end of the shed opened. The Sigglesback herself, dank hair in a fringe below her drenched felt hat, mackintosh dripping about her tall bowed figure, botany specimen tin slung from her shoulders, entered pushing her bicycle.

She found difficulty in shoving it into its place. She had been collecting leaves and bark and Mycetozoa for to-morrow's lesson. She was almost blind and half crying with exhaustion after pedalling her cycle against the blustering wind. She was a figure irresistibly comic.

The choking giggles in the corner roused her.

She raised her mild short-sighted eyes and saw Midge Carne enthroned, the ring of girls below her, the A.S.S. notice fluttering by her head.

Pushing her bicycle painfully into its place, panting with effort, she withdrew. The suppressed giggles broke into a guffaw as she shut the door.

"My dear, I could have died!"

"Midge, you were awful?

"Do you think she'll guess?"

"Whatever will she say?"

"She'll never dare do anything. She can't report us unless she shows our essays to Sally and she'll never dare do that! The Sigglesback. Long live the Sigglesback!"

"Bet you she never even sees the point at all."

It did not occur to them that their gloating voices rang clear and unmistakable through the wooden wall, and that Miss Sigglesthwaite, trudging up the path to the science room, heard every word.

She did not stop to listen. She had been educated according to a code which declared eavesdropping to be dishonourable. But though she despised these children, though they bored her inexpressibly, she could not learn complete indifference to them.

When on Thursday evening she packed the pile of nature notebooks into her basket and cycled back with them to her lodgings, she was acutely aware of hatred and contempt surrounding her.

Miss Sigglesthwaite's landlady served her with high tea. It was less trouble. She had to-night provided a smoked kipper. Because Agnes was late it seemed a peculiarly dried and bony kipper, yet its oily effulgence penetrated the air of the bed-sitting-room as though it had been the fattest and juiciest on the east coast. Before she entered the room, Agnes had a headache; she had not been there long before she felt sick as well. Edie's letter was no more cheerful than usual. Her wireless battery had run down and she had decided to economise by selling the whole thing.

She dismissed her tea uneaten, closed her window because the fire smoked when she opened it, and shut herself in with the nature notebooks.

There was no reason why she should dread them so much. She scolded her apprehensive mind and cowardly heart. After all—what were these vulgar stupid little adolescents? Why should she care whatever they did or said?

She laid the books on the crimson tablecloth; she brought out her red ink and her marking pen. She sat down stalwartly beside them. She breathed her prayer for grace, "Lord, give me patience."

She opened Gwynneth Rogers' composition upon "The Life and Habits of the Sigglesback."

Gwynneth, Maud, Nancy, Enid, Midge. Mechanically underlining words, surrounding blots with red circles, counting spelling faults, Agnes Sigglesthwaite went through the blurred uneven pages. She learned that she was dull, dirty, ugly, boring; that she had silly manners; that her hair was a bird's nest and her dress untidy.

"The sigglesback never mates; it is too bony. Also it has a most peculiar smell. It builds nests in its hair for breeding purposes. It has no voice but a kind of piping squeak when it is angry."

They were not clever children. They had small powers of invention. Their venom outran their wit.

But it was enough for Agnes. It was too much.

Oh, cruel, cruel! They want to drive me away.

Do they think I like it? Do they think I want to stay here? Do they think it's fun to put aside the important work I know I could do, and set nature essays to be mangled by their crude nasty little minds?

But they're right. They're right. That is what makes it intolerable. Because I ought not to be here. I'm no use with children. I dislike them. They bore me.

But Mother—Edie? How can I let them down? "My clever daughter, Agnes." Oh, God, what shall I do?

Wasn't it enough that I had to hate my work? Must they make me hate myself too?

Unattractive, dreary, tired. . . .

Ought I to have gone on wearing that old jumper?

But it doesn't smell. Oh, no, it doesn't smell!

Am I like that? "It has no voice—but a kind of piping squeak when it is angry."

I am Agnes Sigglesthwaite. I won a scholarship to Cambridge. Professor Hemingway said I had a distinguished mind.

She touched her withered cheek with anxious explorative fingers. She moved to the looking-glass and gazed at her thin defenceless face, the mild blue eyes, the soft small unformed chin, the pretty mouth undeveloped as a child's, the long reddened dyspeptic nose. She looked and looked. She could not believe that Agnes Sigglesthwaite, her father's darling daughter, the brilliant scholar, the beloved respected sister, had come to this.

Oh, no! she moaned. Oh, no!

The landlady turned off the lights in the basement and went to bed. The public house at the corner closed, and the men tramped home. The last train whistled, leaving the coast for Kingsport. Face downwards on the floor of her dreary room, beneath the white singing light of the incandescent gas, Agnes lay, calling upon her God who had turned His countenance from her, her father, who was dead, and her own fortitude, which had been exhausted. In her room at Maythorpe, watching the slow march of the moon, Midge lay and shuddered. God, I've been brave. I've proved myself a leader. Let them like me, God, please make me popular.

But Midge slept long before the science mistress. Agnes woke to hear her landlady on the stairs, panting up with the clattering breakfast tray. She crawled to her feet and stood as the door opened.

"Dressed already? Early this morning, aren't you?"

"Yes," murmured Agnes.

The hot tea revived her a little. But she felt so strange that she had to sit, clutching the arms of her chair as the room waltzed round her, up and down, swaying sideways, like the golden swans on a merry-go-round.

It was nine o'clock before she rose from the table. She must go to school. She must not be late for prayers. She gathered her books together.

Half-way down the stairs she remembered that she had not washed her face. That was very dirty. She climbed up again panting, but once in her room could no longer remember why she had returned.

She was late for prayers after all, so went straight through to Form Remove, where she was due to take first period. When the girls filed into the form room, marching demurely, they saw her standing vaguely beside the blackboard, white-faced, red-eyed, her hair in wild disorder.

Members of the A.S.S. glanced at each other. They winked to keep up their spirits.

"Good-morning, Miss Sigglesthwaite."

"Good-morning, girls. Sit down"—the customary formula.

They sat.

There was a pause. She looked vacantly at them.

Jennifer Howe, form prefect, who was not a member of the A.S.S., said helpfully:

"Shall I give out the notebooks for you, Miss Sigglesthwaite?"

"The notebooks. The nature notebooks."

Agnes lifted a green-covered book and looked at it. Her voice sounded thick and strange. "Yes. I have read your nature essays. I have also read notices in the cycle shed. We will have a viva-voce examination. Midge Carne!"

Midge sprang to her feet, vibrating with heroic tension.

"What does the A.S.S. stand for?"

"I—I—"

"Nancy!" pause. "Gwynneth!"

No answer.

"Come here, Midge."

Midge marched to the desk, swaggering. If she also trembled none knew it—not even herself.

"Is this your work?"

"Yes, Miss Sigglesback."

It was a slip of the tongue, a trick of nerves. Midge gulped back a snigger.

"You formed the A.S.S.?"

"Yes."

"You are its president?"

"Yes."

"You organised this—this—" a thin dirty finger trembled on the offending books. The snigger broke from control. Midge began to giggle.

"So you think it's funny, do you! To persecute some one who never did you harm? To drive me away when I have my living to make? To organise a cruel malicious attack, a—a—Because your father's a school governor you think you can do what you like. But I tell you, I tell you . . ."

The mumbling furious voice scared Midge out of all sense. Her terrified giggling rose to shrill frightened laughter.

"You laugh now! You dare to laugh at me!"

The science mistress rose from her chair and towered above the child.

"You beast! You little beast!" she hissed, and with the ruler in her hand struck twice at the child's thin sallow face.

Midge gasped.

Never in her life had any one struck her.

For a moment shock overcame her pain.

Then, as at the second blow, the sharp edge of the ruler caught and cut her delicate skin, she shrank back with a startled cry.

Miss Sigglesthwaite looked down at her handiwork and for the first time she knew what she had done. Her violence had restored her sanity. She became completely calm.

Carefully she laid down the ruler on the blotting-paper, straightening it with meticulous precision.

"Girls," she said, "get out your botany text books. Turn to page 184. Start learning the lists that you will find there. Midge, go back to your seat. Jennifer, you are in charge."

She turned to the door. Jennifer, astonished beyond question, sprang to open it. With a dignity that she had never shown before, Miss Sigglesthwaite left the room and stalked down the passage.

She went straight to Miss Burton's office and entered. She saw the head mistress seated at her desk.

"Yes? Well, Miss Sigglesthwaite, what is it?"

Sarah was none too pleased at the interruption. The time-table over her desk showed her that Miss Sigglesthwaite should be giving a natural history lesson to Form Remove.

"I wish to hand in my resignation."

"Your what?"

"My resignation. I am leaving at once. I have hit Midge Carne. I have cut her cheek open."

"Hit—Midge?"

"I wanted to kill her," observed Agnes calmly. Then, with a vague gesture. "I don't—feel—very well."

She sat down on the chair facing Sarah's desk and, with a mumbled apology, lost consciousness.

CHAPTER III

MR. HUGGINS TASTES THE MADNESS OF VICTORY

Motorists down the Pudsea Buttock road could see a notice-board on a square brick house from which faded letters peeled, proclaiming:

Alfred Ezekiel Huggins. Haulage Contractor, Carrier.

The house stood back behind a little garden, tangled with leggy chrysanthemums and Michaelmas daisies. Beyond it loomed the lichen-mottled roofs of dilapidated stables, sheds and granaries which had belonged to it when it was a farm. To the north, protruding like a pimple from the high wall of the barn, bulged Mrs. Pidney's cottage. The little Pidneys were always overflowing from their cramped quarters into the more spacious domain of Mr. Huggins, scrambling over shafts, falling off step-ladders, hiding themselves in lorries, and nearly driving Mrs. Huggins frantic.

For Mrs. Huggins was a constant sufferer in the same way in which some women are constant readers. She suffered from rheumatism, neuritis, headaches, nervous dyspepsia and the Gentlemen. One gathered from her whispered confidence to refined female friends that the Gentlemen constituted a chronic though mysterious disease, hardly to be mentioned in polite society.

Nellie Huggins would have it known that she had seen better days. Her father had been a schoolmaster and she referred to herself as belonging to the professional classes. This November afternoon she stood at her scullery sink, "just washing out a few trifles," when the Pidney children erupted over the wall. Mrs. Huggins never had a vulgar washing day. She just "washed out a few things" when she needed them, thus preserving her amateur status as it were, in domestic labour, and constantly bemoaning her maidless condition. Also, for the same reason, while she did housework she always wore a hat—perhaps influenced by the news conveyed in bound volumes of The Ladies' Realm that Edwardian hostesses lunched in theirs to proclaim their occupation's temporary nature, and to keep their wave in for the evening.

Wearing her hat now she rushed from the back door. "Well, I never! You children! You know you're not allowed here! Such a mess! Such a noise!"

She might as usefully have rebuked the wind. She watched their animated progress across the hay pile.

"I'll tell my husband when he comes in!"

It was no use.

Spurling, the man, was out. Alfred was out. The lorry sheds were empty. Mrs. Huggins was left alone to face tradesmen, telephone messages and marauding children.

She retreated into the house, removed her hat and retired into the small stuffy drawing-room.

She would not sit in her kitchen. She was a lady. She lit the lamp, poked ineffectively at the crumbling coal dust in the hearth, and drew the venetian blind. November evenings closed in early on her.

She kept ferns in a pot instead of an aspidistra, and her piano was open with music on the stand—"The Rustle of Spring," a very difficult piece, but she had once been able to play it until her hands were stiffened by rheumatism. Now she preferred hymn tunes, dabbing at the keys with vindictive fingers rather as though she were smacking them because they had displeased her.

She was thus engaged when her husband entered.

"Hallo, Nell! Tea not ready yet?"

This was so obvious that comment annoyed her.

"You're early."

"Yes. I've got some friends coming in."

"Friends?"

Her eyes dilated in horror and indignation. The slightly enlarged goitre above her collarless bodice throbbed.

"Only to talk business—after tea."

"Oh. I see. . . . You might have told me."

Huggins looked at his wife.

Her most distinctive article of attire, when she had removed her hat, was a circular hair net of dark solid mesh bound by an elastic around her head, imprisoning her polished prominent brow and mouse-coloured hair. So obvious and aggressive was this tribute to respectability that one hardly noticed her pinched delicate features, her soft upturned pink nose and china blue slightly protruding eyes. Over her tweed skirt she wore a cardigan of grey wool, held together at the throat with a cameo brooch. She was not beautiful. She did not rest Huggins' eyes. But once she had been a pretty woman. Once she had charmed her husband by her fragile and genteel femininity. Now that earlier Nellie was completely lost to him, enchained behind that hateful imprisoning net.

Again and again he had wanted to tell her how deeply he hated it; but he never could.

"I suppose," she said, "I had better light a fire in the other room, if you want to talk to your friends." The other room was a dank unused little place on the far side of the passage. It smelled of furniture polish and blackbeetles, but Nellie preferred it to the kitchen. It was not vulgar.

"Very well, my dear. If you like, I'll do that." Alfred was handier in a house than one would have thought him. He enjoyed lighting fires and laying meals. He whistled as he broke the damp green sticks, and watched the smoke curl round his balls of rolled newspaper.

"I ought to have a maid. I can't be expected to do all this work single-handed," Nellie complained for the fiftieth time when they sat down to tea.

"All right, my lass. You shall have one."

"Yes. When we're all in our graves, worn out with worry."

He glanced at her half humorously.

"Much sooner than that—if you can keep from falling off your perch for a bit longer—the Lord willing," he added piously.

The piety was sincere.

He helped her to move the pots into the kitchen and was still out there when the front door-bell skirled shrilly under the twist of an impatient hand.

She went. She found Mr. Drew and Mr. Tadman and ushered them both into the drawing-room.

"It's the girl's evening out," she explained, saving her pride.

She retired to tell her husband.

He stood in guttering candle-light in the small scullery, adjusting a clean collar and whistling to himself. The tune was unfamiliar to Nellie.

"Nymphs and Shepherds, come away, come away!"

In that uncertain light he towered formidable, big, bearded, jolly, not at all refined. The flame caught his watch chain in a noose of gold. His full red lips were pursed exultantly.

"With music! With dancing!"

He did not even know what he was whistling; he only knew that the weight which had oppressed him during the past eighteen months was about to be lifted; that he was excited, that he was gloriously confident.

A natural gambler, sensualist and adventurer, his religion had diverted his temperamental appetites, but now it was providing an outlet for them. He was gambling on faith. He trusted in the Lord.

"Well?"

Nellie Huggins had been about to make one of her astringent protests, but that glowing vigour checked her. She announced meekly, "They're here. Drew and Tadman."

"Good," said her lord and (for the moment) master, and, as he passed her on his way to the front entrance, absent-mindedly pinched her bony backside, forgetting that she was his wife, remembering only that she was a female lurking with due docility in the shadows.

He swaggered in to the drawing-room, on the top of the world.

"Hallo, Tadman. 'Evening, Drew. Got the stuff there?"

They had. Drew, the estate agent, produced a leather brief case, and from it a set of plans which Huggins recognised. He had seen something like them once in the big library of Snaith's house.

Drew had been down to the Wastes. He had seen the progress of the new Skerrow-Kiplington road. He had talked to Astell. He had attended a meeting at which the Socialist alderman had presided while three of his Labour friends from Kingsport had denounced the slums there. Housing. Housing. "We've got to make the whole Riding housing-conscious," Astell had said.

"That's a good phrase," commented Huggins. "Housing-conscious. Have you talked to Stillman?"

"Yes. He's fed up right enough. He says there's going to be difficulty collecting interest on his mortgage from those Aythornes. He told me if he'd known what sort of a slut the woman was and how she was going to neglect that little shop of theirs, he'd never have taken it on."

"He'll part, then?"

"He'll part."

"Good. Then, Tadman, you'd like to take that on, I suppose?"

The grocer grunted.

"I want to be safe," he said. "I'm a family man."

"We're all family men here."

"But what are you putting in?"

"I'll tell you. I'm so sure of this thing," declared Huggins, "I'm withdrawing my insurance policy and buying up this here."

He took his pencil and drew a ring round a plot of land east of Stillman's.

"Why don't you take up Stillman's mortgage?"

"Purely personal reasons. I tell you—I've preached in Dollstall. I've known those young people." Candour beamed from his shining eyes, his friendly face. "Why, I even helped to put 'em in touch with Stillman. I don't want to get mixed up in their affairs—see? It might look as if I'd done it all out of self-interest."

That seemed good enough. They accepted that.

"How much land is covered by the mortgage?"

"Twenty acres, freehold. And of course the sheds. I'll tell you something. If you put machinery in them, you can claim higher compensation from the council when they take the ground over," explained Drew.

"How much did you say Kingsport Corporation paid for their land east of Fleetmire Dock?"

"£240 an acre—and that needed draining too. You ought not to get twopence less than £230 here—even if it goes to arbitration."

"Well—well." Tadman hesitated, turning his money over in his pockets. "I don't pretend it isn't tempting. Twenty acres—at £240—that's £4,800."

"And dirt cheap at that," put in Huggins. "Mind you, I'm a councillor. I'm a keen housing man. I've thrashed this out with Astell. I want houses built for the poor and I want 'em cheap and I'd give my life's blood to see 'em done soon and reasonable. That's why I dare to gamble. I'm putting all my own savings into this."

"You're not on the Town Planning Committee yourself, are you?" asked Tadman.

"Yes and no. It's like this. I'm on the big Housing Committee of the Council. I'm not on the small joint sub-committee with Kingsport Corporation that's discussing this particular housing estate. That's why I'm free to act. All open and above board."

"But you trust Astell?"

"To the last farthing. Astell and Snaith—why—Snaith . . ."

But he did not explain that he felt he was acting here almost as Snaith's agent. Snaith had prompted him. Snaith had trusted him. He saw now everything quite clearly. Snaith had been testing him out when he gave him that five hundred pounds. Like the master who gave his servants sums of money, one talent, two talents, all the rest of it. He was not meant to bury it in a napkin. He had been meant to use it. And he was going to use it. He was going to make the present profit on Tadman's brilliant deal; he was going to make a nice little sum on his own bit of property. He was going to return Snaith his original loan with interest, to quit himself of all responsibility to Reg and Bessy; to send them off to London or Canada or somewhere, with a nice little nest egg, and to free himself for ever from the handicap of poverty. He would go to Snaith redeemed, strengthened, invigorated. And Snaith would say, "Well done, thou good and faithful servant. I made thee steward over a few things and thou hast become ruler over many things. Enter then into the joy of thy Lord."

It was the Lord's doing. Huggins had been a sinner. All right. He had confessed it, hadn't he? Confessed and been forgiven.

Forgiveness implies the power and opportunity to make reparation. Huggins had prayed for these. They had been granted him. He had first of all been guided to Snaith, and Snaith had helped him. Snaith had lent him £500 to pay off Bessy. He had hinted to him about the sheds on the Waste, and Huggins had been quick enough to take his hint and use it. Aythorne had bought the sheds and mortgaged them to Stillman. Then, being what he was, he and Bessy had refused to pay the interest and Stillman was displeased with his investment. Now, Snaith, still acting as the Lord's deputy, had shown Huggins how to persuade Tadman to relieve the undertaker of his mortgage, how to make a deal himself on rising land-values, how to make ten per cent. commission on Tadman's profit of four thousand pounds; how to impress Drew, who would have the remunerative handling of all the various transactions; how to do good in the South Riding while reaping a few little incidental profits for himself.

The magical accumulations of Big Business, the conjuring of profits out of the naked air, enchanted Huggins. They confirmed his faith. Faith was, after all, the redeeming virtue. He thought of Abraham offering Isaac on the altar; he thought of Moses leading the children of Israel out of Egypt; he thought of Daniel in the den of lions; he thought of his life-savings paid to the Ramington Panel Company for thirty-two acres of Leame Ferry Waste, and he knew that all acts of faith in God were justified, though they might be performed by men who had once been sinners.

The interview was at an end. Tadman's remaining doubts were satisfied. The two callers climbed into their car.

Drew pressed the self-starter. The engine had grown cold in the frosty air; three times it gurgled and was silent, then its splutters settled into an easy purr, its headlights streamed down on to the wayside path, and it moved away.

But Huggins did not go in.

He remained outside his door gazing up into the star-filled sky. The stars seemed enormous in the keen autumn air. Huggins faced them without shame or misgiving. He could stand up now before their naked challenge.

Already he was free, already victorious. Debt, dishonour, guilt and apprehension left him. They that sow in tears shall reap in joy. He that goeth on his way weeping, and beareth forth good seed, shall doubtless come again with joy and bring his sheaves with him.

He ought to go round the buildings and shut up for the night. His nailed boots struck sparks on the flinty cobbles. He rattled chains, tugged bolts, stooped down and caressed the old toothless retriever bitch who drowsed with her head hanging out of the wooden kennel.

Loving-kindness, elation and triumph warmed his soul. When the Lord turned the captivity of Sion, then were we like unto them that dream. The evening stars sang together above him. The dark sheltered village slept at his feet. He felt extraordinary tenderness towards it. Oh, rest in the Lord, troubled souls, anxious and encumbered with small afflictions. Lie down and rest, have faith. He careth for you. I waited on the Lord and He inclined unto me. His yoke is easy and His burden is light.

From the house he could hear muffled music. Nellie was back at the piano. She had resumed, as a protest against his earlier interruption, her solitary service of song.

He stole back softly and saw her, the hymn book open before her, the dried grasses and paper asters in the piano vase trembling as she struck the easy chords, her head tilted backwards.

She was singing, but she started and stopped when her husband entered the room.

"All right. Go on, lass," he said kindly.

She gave him one scornful glance, then, as though to contrast the human with the divine love, began in her reedy soprano:

"The King of love my shepherd is, His goodness faileth never. I nothing lack if I am His, And He is mine for ever."

That was a snub for Alfred. She had better friends than he. He need not think that he was her only hope. Her lacks—of a maid, of water laid on, of a private motor-car in which to be driven to Kingsport, were his fault; but the divine goodness never failed.

"Perverse and foolish oft I stray'd,"

Alfred had joined in now, his rich vibrating bass sweet as brown treacle.

"And yet in love he sought me. And on His shoulder gently laid, And home, rejoicing, brought me."

His big hand strayed along her angular shoulders. Slowly, slowly, her anger disappeared. After all, he was her husband. Perverse and foolish, perhaps, but kindly too, and a preacher, a very good preacher, which was something.

She had enjoyed the prestige of Drew's Austin saloon standing outside her front-door all the evening.

Did Alfred mean what he said about a maid? Perhaps—perhaps. . . .

The prospect of the future became less narrow. The voices of husband and wife mingled and fused.

"And so through all the length of days, Thy goodness faileth never: Good Shepherd, may I sing Thy praise Within Thy house for e-e-ver."

She plunged her head down to meet the final chord, but the buttons from his cuff had caught her hair net. She gave a little cry, but he had swept it off. Her fading mousy hair, soft as a child's, that he had once loved to touch, fell about her face.

"Oh—Alf! my net!" she protested. But she was too late.

With a gesture of ineffable triumph he disentangled the hateful object from his button and tossed it into the fire.

"There!" he said. "I've been wanting to do that for close on fifteen years! You've got pretty hair, you know."

His big bearded face went down to the soft curls, his hands caressed them. Shaken by the music, by surprise, by his once familiar gesture, she did not turn away.

Next morning Alfred Ezekiel Huggins thanked the Lord for having restored to him his lost home comforts.

CHAPTER IV

MRS. BEDDOWS PAYS A STATUTORY VISIT

From a high window in the Administration Block Mrs. Beddows looked down upon the South Riding Mental Hospital near Yarrold.

She looked with love.

What she saw was a colony of stark red buildings. Some had tall chimneys like factories; some were like nonconformist chapels with gables and small high windows; some were like warehouses. Between them lay cinder paths and asphalt yards. To the west a large kitchen garden displayed draggled greens and wintry apple-trees as offerings to beauty.

To the refined residents on the outskirts of Yarrold, these structures were an eyesore. To Mrs. Beddows they were a great achievement.

With her physical eyes she could see red brick and corrugated iron, dug soil and trodden grass; but with her imagination she saw splendours accomplished by co-operative effort—the new boilers for the dining block, in which enormous puddings, rolling oceans of soup and acres of cabbage could be cooked at need. She saw the chintz-covered chairs in the staff sitting-room, the new linen cupboards adequately stocked at last, craft rooms where hands undirected by normal intelligence could learn extraordinary cleverness of bone and muscle.

Her judgments were not æsthetic; they were social, and they informed her that this place was good. She had known homes desolated by the ugliness of one helpless, beloved, unbiddable idiot child. She had seen the agony of spirit in men and women doomed to watch the slow dwindling of reason in those they loved. She had witnessed the tragedy of Maythorpe, and her heart was sore for that irremediable defeat. In her youth every village had its familiar "Fondie," its witless youth, gentle or dangerous.

And her gratitude for the relief of these afflictions steeled her to make her statutory visits. She could look without flinching at the padded rooms where frenzied creatures tore wildly at the leather which at once protected and imprisoned them. She could pass from bed to bed where bodies lay, like houses tenantless, bereft of all but a strange physical survival. She could even face the more harrowing experience of refusing the pleas of the intermittently sane.

They came to her with trust in her honest kindliness.

"Oh, Mrs. Beddows! You know who I am. You know I am as sane as you are. Please, get me out of here. I'm not mad. I'm not mad."

There were others who had accepted their defeat. They greeted her as a familiar friend with touching dignity. She knew now the eccentricities of the patients. She was prepared to collaborate in their life-long dreams. She asked after Kate Theresa, the lively kitten now growing into a fat spoiled playful cat, the darling of the bedridden old women. She paid the requisite compliments to the farmer's wife, who tied up her hair with artificial flowers and thought that all the doctors were in love with her. She comforted Miss Tremaine, the saintly deaconess, who wept all day at the thought of Mortal Sin. She stroked the cheek of the "baby" held by Mother Maisie, who had killed her own child eighteen years ago in the basement scullery where it was born, and who ever since had crooned and hungered over a roll of towels cuddled in her arms. She played the pitiful games of make-believe, doing it for Carne's sake. Because of her friend she must, she felt, help those who shared his suffering.

But the day tired her. Standing here with Matron on the top corridor of the Administration Block—she had been brought here to see the site for the new cisterns—she sighed as she looked down into the November garden. So much sorrow seemed to lie below her. Her ankles ached with tramping the stone corridors; her heart ached with the thought of work unfinished. The matron was telling her about the children's wing. It was overcrowded. There were thirty children at least who did not need such close confinement.

"When will you give us a country home for them? There are several who are really almost normal."

"Oh, one day. Soon, I hope. Ask Alderman Snaith."

The consciousness of her three-score-years-and-ten arose and smote her. There was so much to do that she must leave undone.

She fought her lassitude, summoning her resources of valiant optimism.

"I hope you've got a nice cup of tea for me when we're through this? Any lemon buns?"

"If Mr. Tubbs hasn't eaten them all."

"Come on, then. Let's see. Just the voluntary patients' ward now, haven't we?"

"That's all. Yes—do go there. There's a Mrs. Ford of Cold Harbour who's always asking for you—a sad case—intermittent melancholia and attempted suicide. She tried to hang herself two months ago. Such a nice woman."

They descended the stairs and traversed a covered bridge into another block. Here on the third floor a wide glass-roofed gallery was surrounded by the small cubicle bedrooms of the women paying patients. It was comfortably furnished with easy-chairs, bright pictures, plants in pots and magazines on the table. Here women sat knitting, reading, writing; one played patience; at a corner table a bridge game was in progress. As Mrs. Beddows entered, she heard "Three hearts."

"Double three hearts."

The place might have been a women's club, except that by the table an attendant was showing a small girl how to knit. When the door opened the child turned her head and her face was the face of a woman of sixty-five.

From her game of patience rose a tall handsome woman. Her black dress was neat, her dark grey hair was coiled in a dozen plaits round her stately head. Dignity and authority moved with her. She walked like a queen.

"Alderman Mrs. Beddows?" she asked gravely. "You don't remember me?"

"Mrs. Ford?" Prompted by the matron Mrs. Beddows smiled. An over-brilliant pleasure lit the woman's sombre beauty. "You remember me?"

"You lived at Cold Harbour?"

"Twenty years ago. In the house by the Willows. Your boys used to come and play with mine."

"Of course. I do remember. Dick and Eddie Ford. They used to go spiking for flatlies in the mud."

"Aye, and what a mess they got their boots in. There was your Dick."

"He's in Australia."

"We called them the two Dicky birds. And Willie . . ."

"He's a widower. He lives with me now."

"And Bertie, the best of the family. He stayed on with my boys."

"He—what?"

Bertie was Emma Beddows' favourite—the boy who might have been brilliant as Chloe, if he had not coughed his life away with gas poison in a military hospital at Etaples. He had not been nineteen.

"Yes," Mrs. Ford said eagerly. "They all went to France—your boy and mine, and liked it so much they decided to stay there. Mine have come to see me two or three times, but they always go back again. And Bobbie Carne. He went too, but then, he came back. A pity he left poor Mrs. Carne behind. Do you remember her? Such a pretty creature. It didn't suit her to be left behind. He should have taken her." She sighed deeply. "You know, I'll tell you something. She couldn't stand it. She went off her head. Lovely she was—and brave, afraid of nothing—a great rider to hounds. Now she's hunted herself. They say the mad are happy. Don't believe it. I've seen—I've seen some things in my life. She'll never be better. No more use to her husband. What's a woman for if she's no use to her husband? Better be dead, I say. Better be dead."

"Yes, we know you feel like that," the matron began soothingly, but Mrs. Ford silenced her with a queenly gesture.

"Why does God do it?" she asked. "Mrs. Beddows; I've asked Him. I've talked to Him, as woman to man; I've reasoned with Him, asking Him the question. Where's justice? Where's mercy? Where's the everlasting Providence? With him alone in that house and her shut away from him? Who's to give him his tea when he comes in from a day's hunting? With her longing for him and crying out to God? Poor thing, poor thing!" She raised her hands above her head and exclaimed with astonishing emphasis and passion. "I curse God for it. I curse Him. Let Him open the earth and let hell swallow me. Let Heaven open and rebuke me. I curse God."

The other women hardly lifted their heads. They tolerated each other's eccentricities, absorbed in their own thoughts, patient and indifferent. The fury and drama of Mrs. Ford's denunciation affected them no more than another's magpie habit of kleptomania, or the gentle persistent indecency of a third.

And suddenly Mrs. Ford was silent. The tears filled her fine eyes and rolled unchecked down her smooth sallow cheeks. The matron took her and led her to her cubicle. She lay down meekly and let herself be covered.

"She'll go to sleep now and be all right to-morrow. Every few days she'll be like this," said the matron. "Her husband left Cold Harbour after her first attack. They've been living in Hardrascliffe. She comes back here every so often, though sometimes she'll be perfectly normal for months together. We can't find out why she's got Mrs. Carne so much on her mind. Curious, isn't it? Apparently she used to go up to Maythorpe Hall to do sewing for her, and took a great fancy to her. That must be a sad case."

"It is," said Emma Beddows.

"Well. It's always Mrs. Carne now that troubles her. It's Mrs. Carne that's shut away. Never herself."

"Oh, poor thing. Poor thing."

The sadness of life swirled about Emma Beddows in great engulfing waves.

"Well. I don't know. She still has her use in life, you know. She's about the best influence we have here. Gentle, unselfish, wise. Wonderful with the other patients. A rare and fine personality. We don't choose our way of service in this world," said the matron.

They were wandering now through the long corridors and across the garden towards her little room where she served tea to visitors. Emma Beddows moved slowly.

"She's beginning to feel her age," thought the matron. "I hear Maythorpe Hall's coming on to the market," she observed irrelevantly, her mind still busy with the problem of housing defective children.

"Maythorpe?" Mrs. Beddows stopped dead.

"So Dr. Flint heard from Dr. Campbell. He attends the Carne child, you know."

"Yes—but—Midge isn't ill now?"

"Well—she's upset—and no wonder."

Why hasn't he told me? What is this? Why haven't I known? Mrs. Beddows wondered.

"That accident up at school—"

"An accident?"

"Oh, nothing serious. One of the mistresses had a bad attack of hysteria. She laid open the child's cheek with a ruler. Not very good for her. She's an unstable little thing. Heredity bad, of course. We ought to have her here."

There was no malice in the matron's calm voice. She believed in the remedial work done by psychiatrists at her hospital; residence there conveyed to her no sense of stigma.

But Emma Beddows' heart turned over, and rose, cold, to her throat.

"She's not bad? It's not affected her mind?"

"The mistress?"

"Midge?"

"Not yet."

Not yet. The placid ominous threat of the specialist. She could not forget it. And she could not bear it for Carne.

Walking between the drooping cabbages, the neat raised dykes of celery, all the ordered ugliness of the asylum garden, she protested against her uneasy spirit.

What if Carne had been right? What if this was the wrong school for Midge? What if Sarah Burton's appointment had been a mistake? Carne had not wanted it. Mistresses in well-conducted schools do not cut children's cheeks open with rulers. Why hadn't she heard? Why hadn't he told her? Because it was she who had persuaded him to send Midge to Kiplington? Anguish racked her.

She followed the matron into her sitting-room and endured the greetings and excuses of Alderman Snaith and Councillor Tubbs, already installed with Dr. Flint and drinking tea.

"Come in. Come in, Mrs. Beddows. I've left you a lemon bun."

"Here's an angel cake made by one of our women. She worked in Ainsworth's confectionery place. Marvellous cook. Try it."

"What's the trouble?"

"Paranoia . . ."

"Let me see, two lumps, Mrs. Beddows?"

"Mrs. Beddows—you know Carne. We want you to persuade him to let us have Maythorpe Hall cheap."

She roused herself. The wounds to her pride and friendship smarted sharply, but she must learn the worst.

"Matron was telling me. But I don't think it would be suitable."

"Position's excellent. Air good. Grand garden, and we need a farm for the men at Minton."

"But who said Carne was going to sell? No, no more to eat, thanks."

Food would choke her. She gulped down the blessed tea. Oh, why didn't he tell me? she mourned.

"It's not official." Anthony Snaith's voice was precise and soothing. "The property really belongs to the bank that holds the mortgage. It's been losing heavily. Carne's done it well; the land's in good condition, they say, though the house is pretty bad. But it's been farmed extravagantly, and he can't keep it up. I think we could get it very reasonably."

"But does Carne want to go?"

Emma Beddows could force herself to ask just that.

"Well. In the circumstances—the choice is hardly his. He could hold on a year or two, I suppose. I don't know what his resources are—of course, this is strictly confidential."

"Ain't it a bit dilapidated—the house, I mean?" asked Tubbs.

"Yes. But we should have to make considerable alterations in any private house, and because this has been let go so badly, we should get it all the cheaper."

Tubbs sniggered.

"It's suitable enough in one way. Maythorpe's always been a bit of a madhouse. It'll be a real one now."

Oh, God, prayed Emma Beddows to that seat of incommunicable justice, you can't let this happen. It's too cruel.

But whether the cruelty was to herself or to Carne, she hardly knew.

She heard Snaith continue: "That's why I feel it would be a good idea for us to press in every legitimate way the need for a new children's home. In our visitor's report, for instance. It will strengthen our hand with the finance committee."

She wanted to go home. She wanted to go to bed, to lie with her mind drugged happily by the absorbing incongruities of a Wild West romance, to forget this world in which doom fell inexorably, and men were cruel, and even benefit for defective children was bought at the price of ruin and defeat. She felt her age pressing upon her, with her swollen ankles and smarting eyes and aching knees. But something in her, stronger than disappointment or resentment or fatigue, controlled her actions.

Her statutory visit over, she was driven by the Mental Hospital car to Yarrold station; but there, instead of catching the Kiplington train, she took a bus to Maythorpe. Jealousy, curiosity and determination to take her place as Carne's intimate friend might move her a little, quicken her breath, scald with hot tears her eyeballs, stiffen her tongue; but over-riding these ran her love, her generosity, her grief which was for him, not for herself.

The Maythorpe drive seemed unusually long that evening. She felt as though she would never reach the dark bulk of the house, piled beyond the sad chestnuts and limes and sycamores. She was too weary even for speculation when she entered the open sweep of lawn and gravel before the porch, and saw a small saloon car standing there.

Elsie opened the door.

"Is your master in?"

"Why, it's Mrs. Beddows. Yes, do come in. I'll make you a nice cup of tea. One of your own kind." Elsie liked the alderman, and, in her bustling welcome, had opened the dining-room door and thrust her in before Mrs. Beddows could ask: "And who's the visitor?"

Unannounced therefore, she entered the long shadowy room, lit at one end by fire and lamplight. So far was it from door to fireplace that the alderman could at first see only the lamp and tea-tray on a low stand between the fire and the great table; then, as they turned towards her, she observed, seated comfortably in two arm-chairs, tea-tray between them, Robert Carne and a woman. For a second her mind leapt back for twenty years and she thought "Muriel!" But the firelight caught the red gleam of the woman's curling hair, and she knew Sarah Burton.

She had dragged herself there to comfort, warm, uphold him, to offer help with Midge and counsel about finance. She saw that he had already found a confidante.

Her quick wits failed her.

"Oh," she gasped.

They rose and came forward, Sarah quickly, Carne with his slow deliberation.

"Oh, Mrs. Beddows. This is nice of you. Come to the fire."

His welcoming smile drew her forward; but some unrecognised shock withheld her.

"I came to inquire after Midge."

"Oh, she's practically all right again."

"How did you hear?" smiled Miss Burton.

"You'll have some tea?" Carne peered solemnly into the big silver pot. "This has gone a bit cold. I'll get some fresh . . ."

"Elsie's looking after me," Mrs. Beddows permitted herself that small satisfaction. She refused the low chair vacated by the head mistress and settled herself in one turned from the head of the table. "No. I always sit here, thank you. Robert knows I've no use for low chairs—don't you?"

She was establishing intimacy around her, shutting out Sarah, proving the ripe confidence of her old friendship.

"I wish you'd tell me how you got to hear about Midge," repeated Sarah, a little pucker of worry about her brows.

"I suppose it might have been Wendy?" teased Mrs. Beddows.

"But she doesn't know. No one knows, unless her form has gossiped. I tried to stop them. But of course . . ."

Girls will talk—you can't trust Judy. I suppose I was was a fool to keep it quiet.

Candour and malice warred in Emma Beddows' mind; candour won.

"As a matter of fact, I heard to-day at the Mental Hospital, through Matron who'd got it from Dr. Flint, who'd heard from Campbell."

"I thought there was such a thing as professional secrecy," said Sarah, a little bitterly.

"Not in the South Riding. And after all, you're a public institution. Ah, good, Elsie. Just how I like it."

The maid set the new teapot on the tarnished tray. Carne looked at his older visitor, then silently rose and went to the sideboard, returning with a whisky decanter.

"You'd better have a pick-me-up," he said. "Been visiting?"

"Yes."

Her gratitude for his thoughtfulness was beyond reason. She watched his fine big hands measuring out the drink—the whisky, the tea. His fingers were still well kept, but a nail was broken; there was dirt ingrained in two deep cracks, and a scratch across the knuckles. He had been working. An impulse made her want to seize those hands, caress them, weep over them, because she was so sorry for him and loved him so completely.

All she said was: "Here. I've got to catch a bus back to-night, and you'll have me up before my betters as drunk and disorderly." She gave an unsteady little laugh, then turned to Sarah. "Now, I've heard the story that's going round." She told it. "You'd better let me have your version."

"Well"—Sarah plunged into the story. She told of Miss Sigglesthwaite and of her own unfulfilled desire that the woman would resign. She told of the A.S.S. and Midge's part in it. With delicate tenderness for the father's feelings, she gave her interpretation of the lonely child's bid for popularity. Her low husky voice was appealing in its humour and vitality. It became obvious to Emma Beddows that Sarah was minimising her own efforts to set the trouble right. She was still nursing in her own house the shattered science mistress. She had visited Maythorpe that afternoon to bring home the partially restored Midge—now enjoying a pampered invalid tea upstairs in bed.

"She's really well enough to come back. I don't think there'll be any scar. It wasn't deep. But I wanted to keep her out of school for a bit. She's not going to have the luxury of martyrdom if I can stop it. I'll see that by the time she comes back to school the girls have something else to think about."

She would, too. Mrs. Beddows recognised Sarah's competence. A thought which had been playing round in the remoter senses of her mind suddenly defined itself.

"Did Dr. Campbell say that she ought not to be by herself so much?"

"Yes. I rather wanted her to come as a boarder, but I quite see there are objections—" Sarah began.

"Why don't you let her come to me?" the alderman asked. Suddenly she felt the problem simplify itself. "We've got that little top room free still, and she could go into school every day with Wendy."

She sat back and awaited battle.

It did not come.

Sarah and Carne stared at each other across the tea-table.

"Do you know," Sarah said at last. "I believe that that's a very good idea."

"You two women seem determined to manage my affairs for me," said Carne, and his sad smile embraced them with equal benevolence. At half-past six Mrs. Beddows rose and gathered up her magenta scarf and big leather bag.

"Must you go now?" Sarah rose too. "Can't I give you a lift? I practically pass your house."

Three thoughts simultaneously possessed Mrs. Beddows' mind. She had scored over the boarding of Midge; she dreaded the fatigue of the bus ride; she would, by accepting Sarah's offer, avoid leaving her alone with Carne.

She smiled: "That's very kind of you."

She had not removed her own worn sealskin jacket, so stood winding the scarf round her throat as Carne helped Sarah into her grey fur coat. There was a moment when the younger woman slid her thin arms into the sleeves and leant back for a second against Carne as he pulled the furs up and round her; when Emma Beddows, her perceptions sharpened by the day's conflict, caught the expression in Sarah's face. Good Heavens! she thought; she's in love with him.

The revelation came to her as suddenly as it had come to Sarah six months earlier. She did not think that Robert was in love with Sarah, but it struck her that he well might be attracted.

Driving home in the dark she asked abruptly:

"What d'you really make of Midge?"

"It's hard to say," Sarah was steering carefully. Her gloved hands on the wheel were steady and firm. "She may be all right and she may fly to pieces. I should say it's touch and go."

"More go than touch, if you ask me," snapped Emma, at war with jealousy and apprehension.

Perhaps just because she was conscious of malice, she dragged herself to another final effort.

"Worrying business for you—this about Miss Sigglesthwaite."

"Oh, yes. Poor thing. I feel horribly to blame—though I don't see quite how I could have helped it."

"Never mind, my dear." Emma patted kindly (though tentatively, because of the steering) the hand on the wheel. "I think you ought to know that all of us—the local people, you know, and the Higher Education Committee—are quite pleased with you. You seem to be doing a good job of work among us."

"Oh, am I?" gasped Sarah, with spontaneous and unmistakable relief. "Well—that's something. Thank you. Thank you very much."

CHAPTER V

NAT BRIMSLEY DOES NOT LIKE RABBIT PIE

Rabbit pie was the trouble. And pork.

Mrs. Brimsley could not eat pork. Her stomach, usually a docile organ, could not accommodate it. Yet when Bill Heyer, one-armed as he was, succeeded in snaring a rabbit just below the cabbage patch, pork immediately suggested itself to Mrs. Brimsley's mind, and pork and rabbit she served, very tastily, with onions and carrots and circles of hard-boiled egg in a nice crisp pie.

"What's this?" asked Nat, prying with his long nose across the tablecloth.

"Rabbit pie."

"Why aren't you taking a bit?"

"Because I can't eat the pork. I'm boiling myself an egg."

"Here." Nat pushed back his plate. "Are you trying to poison me?"

"What's the matter?"

Hal Brimsley opened his sluggish eyes, and Bill, who always ate midday dinner with his next-door neighbours, grinned expectantly.

"I know you want shut on me. Well I know you'd like to be rid of me," roared Nat. "But you've not done it yet. I know what you want. You want to drive me and Peg out so as we won't have no place to go. But you're wrong. We're coming here, and it's you who'll go—bag and baggage. So you can think on." And he lifted his plate of rabbit pie, scraped the contents carefully back into the dish, cut himself a hunk of bread and cheese, and stalked off into the November fog.

"Well," Bill's genial voice broke the awkward pause. "That's a rum 'un. I thought it was only when there was an R in the month that rabbits poisoned you."

"That's oysters. When I was cook at Lissell Grange," began Mrs. Brimsley, whose wits were quick enough, but whose emotional reactions were slow.

Then she awoke to the enormity of her son's behaviour.

"How dared he? How dared he? After all I've done for him. No one can say a better cook lives in the South Riding. I work my fingers to the bone. Stay in night after night. Never been so much as to pictures for three years. And he throws it back into my face."

"Nay, nay, Mother. In tid' pot."

"Pot or no pot. I won't be answered back."

"But look here, Mrs. Brimsley—" Bill was all for peace and reason. "It's only natural, if you come to think of it, that he should want to wed. Peg Pudsey's not a bad sort of girl. He might do worse."

"Aye; but he'll not do that. I'll have no Pudsey here. Kin to that drunken, greasy, ditch-digging beast. Beast man, they call him. Hard on the dumb beasts, poor things. We've been respectable here and respectable we'll stay. Thank you very much."

She rose and pushed back her chair.

"You can wash your own pots," she announced.

"Where i'you going, Ma?" gasped Hal.

"The pictures!"

She might have been saying "The Devil."

And to the pictures she went, catching the afternoon bus to Kiplington, a formidable woman in maroon plush hat, bear stole and cotton gloves.

She was deeply hurt. Nat was her favourite son. She felt that by courting Peg Pudsey he had betrayed her.

It wasn't fair. He wanted to rob her of her vocation, to bring another housekeeper into her domain. She felt too young for that. She could not stand aside yet.

She had been kitchen-maid at Lissell Grange when she began walking out with Nathaniel Brimsley. She was two months off eighteen when she married, a jolly laughing girl, brisk as a terrier, and capable as a head waitress at Lyons Corner House. At nineteen she was mother of Polly, the eldest of five girls, now all out in the world, married or in service. She was not fifty yet, and she was hanged if she would play second fiddle to a girl of Pudsey's. She knew, she knew what happened when brides entered the homes of their mothers-in-law.

Tightly clutching her bag she sat through the news reel, all sport and soldiers, the comic, all American slang that she could not understand, and the big romance, which brought tears to her eyes. Lovely she thought it. It filled her with vague longings.

She looked at the languishing lady on the screen and saw sinuous movements, hips slim as a whiting's, wet dark lips and lashes luxuriant as goose-grass in a hedge bottom. She thought: I'm a back number. Nobody wants me. The boys are sick of me. She remembered her square, uncompromising reflection in the polished mirror above her chest of drawers.

The star on the sofa leant back to receive her lover's passionate embrace.

Well now, that's not what I call nice, criticised Mrs. Brimsley. If I caught one of my girls carrying on like that, I know what I'd do to her.

Yet she had her memories.

She remembered that day when she threw the basket of gooseberries right into Nathaniel's face because she was so sick of its solemnity. The sequel to her rebellion had been far from solemn. When 'Thaniel (she had never called her husband Nat) was roused, he was a One. Well you knew.

No, it wasn't all fun being a widow. There were times . . .

The screen drama approached its climax. The misunderstanding between husband and wife dissolved in the catastrophe of a motor accident. The erring woman knelt by her husband's bed. "Darling! Darling! I never meant it. Come back to me. I love you!" The glycerine tears rolled down her lovely cheeks.

Mrs. Brimsley's experienced eye swept the huge flower-filled bedroom. There's not much time for that sort of thing in a real illness, she thought.

Her husband had died after three days of double pneumonia, and not thus had she wrestled with death in the crowded bedroom, the chimney smoking, the window stuffed with rags against the draught, the children crying in the yard and the unmilked cows bellowing from the paddock.

And then she had lost him.

He had been a good husband to her, old though he was. He had left her a tidy sum of money too, made during war-time when farming was farming, so that she had five hundred pounds of her own in savings bank.

The boys could stand on their own feet now. If she wanted a little house, she could take one. If she wanted to clear out and be a lady, why, she could. She could always get a day's charring, or cooking, or keep a little pastry shop.

But she did not want that. She wanted to be needed. She wanted to feel her hands full of necessary work and her services appreciated. She wanted to scold her family and sacrifice herself as she had scolded and sacrificed at Cold Harbour Colony. Anything less meant an end to active living; and she was not ready to make an end.

She left the picture theatre even more discontented than she had entered it. She had settled nothing, asserted nothing, not even enjoyed herself.

She wanted a cup of tea, though she grudged the pence spent on such extravagances. She compromised on a twopenny cup in a nasty little sweet shop, then went bargain-hunting until bus-time. Her outburst of prodigality had cost her one shilling and her bus fare. She felt wildly reckless, and displeased with herself because of that.

The white sea roke blew up the street and billowed into rolling yellow fog that had lain day long across the coast. Shop windows suffused a pale glow at intervals along the street, but Mrs. Brimsley could not tell the grocer's from the draper's without pressing her face close against the window.

At the bus stop a shivering group prophesied delay.

"I'll never be home to get their teas at this rate."

"Then they'll have to get it theirselves."

"Oh, my hubby's never got his tea since we were married. I doubt if he knows where to look for caddy."

"Good-evening, Mrs. Brimsley. What brings you here!"

She spun round and saw at her side, twinkling and irrepressible, Mr. Barnabas Holly.

She remembered, with unaccountable pleasure, how she had boxed his ears. They had met several times since then. He amused her and she enjoyed their incessant but good-humoured bickering. He was out of work now.

"I might say the same of you," she retorted.

"Well then, I'll do better than you. I'll tell you. I've been in high society. Mind you, no more than I ought to be if we all had our due. I've been taking tea with the head mistress of the High School, Miss Sarah Burton, M.A."

"You never!"

"And why not? Wasn't my girl Lydia smartest of the lot there? I've been seated on a cushioned couch with Lady Sarah, drinking tea out of a thimble and discoursing on the universities in a way more edifying than you'd imagine."

"Go on."

"'I can see where Lydia gets her imagination from,' says she. 'If all parents was as intellectual as you, Mr. Holly,' says she, 'I'd be a happier woman, that I would,' says she, passing me cake cut in bits no bigger than a tit's arse-hole, begging your pardon. I've had bad luck as you might say since my old woman died. A good mother if ever there was one. And I had to fetch Lyd away from school to look after the kiddies. And it isn't good enough."

"What are you going to do?" asked Mrs. Brimsley, as usual intrigued by any domestic problem.

"That's the question, as Shakespeare said. That is the question."

The bus rolled round the corner of the street, trailing clouds of swirling fog. The group shifted. Mr. Holly took charge.

"Now then, hand us that basket. Ups-a-daisy. Of course I'm coming with you. Think I'd let a pretty woman like you go home alone on a night like this?"

"Where's your cycle?"

"Now you're asking. Now you're asking. That's right. There's less draught here on the driver's side. I know how to choose a place in a bus, I will say. Fact is, I popped the bike. Had to get a new collar and so on to face her highness. Here, young fellow, two to Cold Harbour. Oh, got a return, have you? Well, come to think on, you would have. Single to Cold Harbour then, and make it a good 'un."

"What d'you think you're going to do at Cold Harbour?" asked the widow, stimulated and intrigued by the preposterous little man.

"See you safe and sound into your home. What d'you take me for? Miss a chance of a chat with the only woman in the South Riding who knows what to do with a rolling pin? Not likely."

The bus rocked cautiously southward, stopping to let down passengers as it went, parting the soft heavy curtains of mist before it. Two lads in the back produced a mouth organ and began to experiment wheezily with reminiscences of Jack Payne.

"D'you like going to pictures?" asked Mr. Holly, producing a poisonous-looking little pipe and rubber pouch from Woolworth's.

"Who said I'd been to pictures?" she bridled.

"No one said you'd been. I asked you if you like to go. Might take you one day, when I remember." He winked slowly at her, tugging at his pipe, his hands cupped round the match. The air of the bus by now was rank with the odour of tobacco, wet boots, wet mackintoshes, fog, and the Irish setter leaping and whimpering on its lead in the gangway.

"You and the pictures! I can see you taking me there. Losing yourself in the pub is more like your line."

"No, no. I've turned T.T. since I found my Ideel." He winked again. His arm stole round her tightly armoured waist.

"Ideel my fathers! All you care about is cupboard love. Hanging round my place to get a slice of cake."

"It's better cake than Miss Burton's, I can tell you that. I could do with a bit now, if you ask me. Come to think on, d'you know a better love than cupboard love with as good a cook as you about? At least I know your value."

"That's more than some do," she sighed. For, though she had no intention of letting Mr. Holly get fresh with her, it was pleasant to find a confidante for her grievances.

"Is it? Well, I say it would be a crime not to appreciate you." The arm round her waist gave a warm hint of a squeeze.

She took no notice. Her grievance overwhelmed her. "Then there are some pretty fine criminals about," she exploded, and suddenly the pent-up anguish of her soul overflowed in a torrent of confession.

The comfort she gained from the experience astounded her. Mrs. Brimsley was accustomed to silent men, to men who dealt daily with concrete things, who said less than they thought, expressed less than they felt, and damped down all emotion by the cold water of common sense. Her youthful vivacity had broken itself against the impregnable fortress of her husband's disapproving silence. Even her son had scraped back the offending pie into the dish instead of throwing it at his mother's face, as would have been far more likeable and natural. The Brimsleys were always boasting that there was no nonsense in them. After thirty years of them Mrs. Brimsley felt that she could do with a little nonsense.

Now Mr. Holly, whatever else he was, an idler, a prodigal, a shameless little heathen, was full of nonsense. He was a talker. What he felt, he said. He did not leave the atmosphere thick with unspoken thoughts. He said, indeed, far more than he meant, which was at least a change.

But he was genuinely interested in other people. He enjoyed news; he relished gossip. He had ideas. "I might," he frequently speculated, "have been a poet, if I'd thought on, or an actor." He was a great singer in public houses. If an egotist, he was not a cold one. He listened with judicial gravity to Mrs. Brimsley's grievance, and laughed to scorn her sorrow with most flattering attention.

"You not wanted? You on the shelf? A fine looking, bonny woman like yourself, with your light step and your light hand on a pastry board! You not wanted? Why, you're the only sort that is wanted. You're the salt of the earth, and don't I know it?" He sighed. That sheltering impersonal arm round her waist tightened.

"A fat lot of use to me that is. Stuck away in Cold Harbour with one son that wouldn't know spring chicken from a black pudding, and another that knows all right, but would rather have cocoa and jam and Peg Pudsey than boned turkey and bacon cakes and his poor old mother. As for Bill Heyer, he's as nice a chap as you could wish, but he's not human. There's something about a bachelor as neat in the house as he is that isn't natural, I say. He might as well 'a been a girl."

"That's right. It's not natural. Though maybe if he had two arms instead of one they'd be tickling to get round you."

With lady-like oblivion Mrs. Brimsley ignored altogether the arm which was already round her waist.

So preoccupied were the two on their front seat that they did not notice how the bus moved now more quickly, now slowly at foot pace, in the enveloping fog. They had even forgotten that there was a fog at all when a violent jolt suddenly threw Mrs. Brimsley right into her escort's arms, and he on to his knees beneath her, gallantly shielding her from further shock.

Two children screamed, the setter yelped, a basket of live chickens flew from the rack and landed on an old gentleman's bowler hat; the conductor called "Ups-a-daisy! Keep on smiling! Keep on shining!" But the left fore-wheel of the South Riding Motor Services Bus was in a ditch.

"Oh God! Oh God!" gasped Mrs. Brimsley.

"Tha's all right. Tha's all right," muttered Mr. Holly, his mouth full of her hair. For her hat had fallen off, and she lay draped across his head and shoulders in an attitude not unlike that known as the fireman's lift. She had lost her fur; she had lost her paper carrier of tomatoes, tea, heather-mixture knitting yarn and Zam-Buk; she had lost her nerve completely. But Mr. Holly's arms were round her, and Mr. Holly's chest, as he struggled up and levered her back on to the now sloping seat, seemed a pleasant and comfortable place on which to have hysterics. So Mrs. Brimsley, an energetic woman with courage enough to face life's real crises without faltering, abandoned herself to the luxury of this lesser occasion, and laughed and cried in unashamed abandon.

As it happened no great damage had been done. The bus had been crawling at foot pace down the road, the driver had mistaken smooth turf for smoother highway; but the ditch was not a deep one. Beyond the death of two chickens in the basket, and the complete annihilation of Mrs. Brimsley's tomatoes under Mr. Holly's trousers, no one was seriously hurt.

But the bus was firmly lodged in the ditch, and the ditch was somewhere—rather vaguely—just past Maythorpe.

"All fine and dandy, fine and dandy," sang the conductor. "No, no one's hurt. Not even the dawg here."

"What are we going to do? Oh, let me out. Help me out. Oh, how are we to get home?"

"You just sit tight. I'll get you home. We can't be so far from a telephone. I'm just going to ring up the office, and they'll send an emergency relief. It's no use getting out—unless you like to walk. We shouldn't be more than an hour at the outside. Sit tight and keep warm—unless any of you fancy a nice cold walk home."

It was the only sensible thing to do.

The angle of the bus was unusual, but not entirely uncomfortable once the passengers had rearranged themselves, and it made Mrs. Brimsley feel more natural when she found herself seated on Mr. Holly's knee drying her eyes with his new cotton handkerchief, bought in honour of Miss Burton.

At first there was desultory conversation among the travellers; they talked of the fog, the cold, of other accidents, of their probable locality, of Maythorpe and its inhabitants; but soon the youth with the mouth organ recovered his breath and spirits, and before they fairly knew what they were doing, the company had developed naturally into a sing-song choir.

Mrs. Brimsley lay back in comfort. She could feel the vibration of Mr. Holly's chest as he swelled, with an unexpectedly sweet and tuneful voice, the familiar chorus:

"Daisy, Daisy, give me your answer, do, I'm just crazy, all for the love of you!"

His arm tightened protectively round the widow's waist.

"It won't be a stylish marriage, For I can't afford a carriage . . ."

An old song. Why, they'd sung it when she and 'Thaniel were courting.

"But you'll look sweet, upon the seat, Of a bicycle built for two!"

"What is your name? Daisy?" breathed Mr. Holly.

"No. Jessy. Give over now," giggled the emotional girl, who, a few minutes ago, had been the brisk and formidable Mrs. B.

"I'm not going to give over. I haven't talked to anything as nice as you since I were a lad, and I'm not going to waste my chances."

Mr. Holly spoke with surprising firmness and authority. He did not snigger; he did not play silly tricks which alienated her; he simply held her warmly and companionably in his arms—and she liked it.

All those clever children, she thought. You can see he's a loving father.

The mouth-organist struck up The Lost Chord. Mr. Holly cleared his throat and began to sing softly. Jessy stirred in his arms.

"Go on, go on. You know it. Give us a solo," some one called.

Delicately he shifted his pleasant burden, and his true clear baritone rose into the humming heat of tobacco, petrol, dog, fowls and human stuffiness.

"Seated one day at the organ I felt weary and ill-at-ease."

That's a good song, thought Mrs. Brimsley, a song associated with chapel anniversary teas, and Sunday School, and holy pictures hanging on the walls of respectable houses. Classic, thought Mrs. Brimsley. Just because it was not a love song, because it brought into that queerly-huddled group the solemnity of Sabbath, the memory of good religious thoughts, The Lost Chord moved her. Mr. Holly's voice rose and fell, and his chest with it, and she with his chest.

She was cut off from her usual considerations of worry and respectability. Here, in this crowded bus, she was detached from past and future. She could relax her vigilance, lie back, let go her burdens of foresight and self-defence, and submit to the comforting influence of the little man who gathered breath for the dragging sweetness of "the sound of that great Amen."

The passengers clapped. Their applause confirmed Mrs. Brimsley's happiness.

"Who taught you to sing?" she asked, trying to twist her voice to fashionable tartness.

"Oh, my dad was a great singer, and I used to do tenor solos in chapel at Farrowhill. You've got a sweet voice, I bet."

"Oh no. I can't sing. But I love listening."

"Do you?"

Suddenly she remembered his idiotic song about the donkey driver, and his graceless head grinning through the hole in her stable roof. This time the memory only made her smile.

They were pressing him for other songs, and he was willing. He sang "Sweet Genevieve," and "Drink to me only," and "Londonderry Air," sung with a wailing sorrow that would have wrung tears from a far harder heart than that of Mrs. Brimsley, lying so cosily in the singer's arms.

No courting could have been more effective.

He did not woo her; he made himself the hero of the hour. He wiped from her mind the memory of his reputation as a feckless ne'er-do-weel. She remembered only his brilliant daughter, his friendly ways, his laughter, his voice which could charm the birds off the trees, his humour which could change a morning's cup of tea into a party, his ready tongue, his sympathy.

By the time that the relief bus arrived, she had remembered her five hundred pounds, her quarrel with her son, and the Council Cottages to be built, they said, on a new housing estate between Skerrow and Kiplington.

Miss Burton, Alderman Mrs. Beddows, Councillor Huggins and Alderman Astell were all racking their brains for a solution of the Holly problem. Who would look after those motherless children if Lydia went to school and college?

They need not have troubled. Lying against his heart, drunk with music and happiness, Jessy Brimsley promised to share Barney Holly's future and be a second mother to his family.

CHAPTER VI

TWO IN A HOTEL ARE TEMPORARILY INSANE

Sarah had arranged to spend her Christmas holidays in her sister's new house at Bradford-on-Avon. She had also decided to stop on her way there for a night in Manchester, to complete her neglected

Christmas shopping, and to see her late head mistress, Miss Tattersall, as she passed through on her way to the Lake District.

Sarah enjoyed Miss Tattersall and enjoyed shopping. She had a grand time pouring out to her late head mistress the story of her mistakes and triumphs. She told the full tale of Miss Sigglesthwaite (now packed off to her mother's home in a state of convalescence), of the inspector's report (admirable); of the intolerable and still unmarried Dolores (not so good); of the plans for Lydia's return (doubtful), and of the anxiety about her future career (a matter for determination). She received encouragement, reproof, criticism and sympathy. She nearly made Miss Tattersall lose her train.

It was with a sense of exhilaration that she returned to her final shopping. Confession to her friend had lifted a burden of responsibility from her shoulders. She felt hopeful and stimulated and younger by ten years, because she had been again for a short time the junior mistress, consulting the wisdom of an older colleague.

Always resilient and capable of abrupt detachment, she was able to put behind her the anxieties and disappointments of the term, and the dull pain that since last summer had underlain all her more personal thoughts. With gay gusto she flung herself into the business of buying rubber animals for her nephew, handkerchiefs for her brother-in-law, silk stockings and amber satin underclothes for her sister.

Her arms were full when she emerged into Piccadilly. It was raining, but the shops were so bright that one noticed it only in the glitter of pools along the uneven cobbles. On the wet pavement women stood selling flowers in odd-shaped curving baskets; chrysanthemums, vivid dyed crimson leaves, holly, tight little bunches of scarlet tulips and roses in buds hard as porcelain.

She stopped before a basket of red and yellow rose-buds. "Oh," she thought, "I must have some for Pattie."

Sarah had known poverty so well that caution usually controlled her spending, but that evening recklessness was in the air. Christmas was coming; holidays stretched before her; she was going to see Pattie whom she loved, therefore she loved everything—the jostling shoppers, the squatting flower girls, the posies of white and green and crimson, the freedom of spending the night alone in the second-rate hotel off Piccadilly. When she pushed her way round the revolving doors of that establishment, her cheeks were burning with bright wind-lashed colour, her eyes shone, her little green hat had been pushed to one side; her arms were full of golliwogs, crackers, boxes of preserved fruits and a great bunch of crimson roses; her red hair curled round her vivid face. Small, laughing, burdened with frivolous purchases, she struggled into the warm, half-empty lobby, and found herself face to face with Robert Carne.

He was standing with his back to the fireplace, looking over her head into nothing; there was upon his face a desolation so haggard and so hopeless that for a second she hardly recognised him. Then she stopped with an unvoluntary gasp, and a box of candy slid from her arm and smacked on to the floor beside her.

"Oh!" she gasped.

He started and saw her. For a moment he too blinked in surprised uncertainty. Then Sarah saw his face transformed by a smile which was to her the most lovely and astonishing thing that she had ever seen, and which would remain in her memory as lovely and astonishing until she died.

For he was glad to see her. He smiled with radiant welcome. It was as though his spirit returned to its blank habitation, as though she had witnessed a resurrection from the dead.

She stood before him, passive, expectant, happy. All possible journeys had led toward this end.

Then he stooped and picked up her dropped parcel and held out his hands to relieve her of the others, and both inquired simultaneously: "What are you doing here?"

It was she who explained, suddenly grown over-voluble with the singing joy which had no reason and no justification.

"I'm on my way to my sister's. Christmas shopping. Those are candied fruits and this is a golliwog. D'you think my four-year old nephew will be too old for golliwogs? Why are little boys supposed to like them, when they turn up their noses at dolls? Did you?"

He drew her towards a small glass-covered table and helped her to set down her parcels.

"Are you staying in Manchester?" he asked in his slow deep voice.

"Just for to-night. I go off to-morrow morning."

"So do I."

She had no words, yet her mouth was full of them. She showed him the handkerchiefs for her brother-in-law, asking his opinion, which he gave judiciously.

Into her witless pleasure stabbed a terror of loss. At any moment he might get up and leave her. She must hold him.

"Heavens!" she cried. "I sympathise with housewives. An afternoon's shopping is more exhausting than twenty speech days." But she did not look exhausted. She glowed and laughed beside him, bright as the holly. "I've had no tea. I've got a terrible room up on the fifth floor that looks like a scene set for a Russian tragedy. I can't face it until I've had a glass of sherry. Is there a bell anywhere? Won't you have a drink with me? Unless you're rushing away to dine somewhere?"

He beckoned to a waiter. Her heart stood still at his silence until he said: "Do you like dry, brown or medium?"

"Dry, please."

He ordered two dry sherries, and sat back in his chair, contemplating her with appreciation.

He's pleased to see me, sang her heart; he's pleased to see me.

It was all she asked then—that they should sit there together, the door revolving beside them and disgorging its procession of business men, commercial travellers, and shopping women, the fire leaping, the palms doing their drooping best to appear exotic, the waiters hurrying with their plated trays.

The sherry arrived. Sarah said: "This is mine. I ordered it—I'm always having hospitality in your house." She tossed half a crown on to the salver before he could unfold his note-case.

"Very well," he said. "But then you must dine with me—unless you have another engagement."

"None. I'd like to."

This is a dream, she told herself. I shall wake up. After all, he is a governor of the school; I have been good to Midge; he couldn't not ask me.

It appeared that they had little to say to one another.

She asked, stupidly: "How's Midge now, really, do you think?"

"Much better."

"It was a good idea, sending her to Mrs. Beddows."

"Yes. She's there now. I'm going up the day after to-morrow to bring her home for Christmas."

"That's a good woman," said Sarah, twisting the stem of her glass between her fingers, watching the firelight catch the golden sherry. She felt generous towards Mrs. Beddows because she was so happy.

It was a quarter to seven.

"Well," she said, "if I'm to wash my hands—and write a note, which I should do—I suppose I'd better go and do it. What time do we dine?"

"Seven-thirty—would that suit you? or quarter to eight."

"Seven-thirty—why not? I'm hungry."

The lift rattled up and up, bearing her to her ugly room.

It could not depress her. She found something comic and lovable in its gaping grate, lined with soot-smeared white paper, in its sofa and "easy" chair upholstered with drab-coloured rep so deeply engrained with dirt and smoke that it felt dank and smooth to touch, and in its immense whited sepulchre of a broad double bed. The sounds of Manchester reached her from the square below as she unpacked her bag, brought out her best dress of peacock taffeta, her satin slippers and her new silk stockings. Shivering more with excitement than with the chill damp room, she flung off her travel-crumpled clothes and washed and powdered her slim youthful body. She re-dressed herself without remorse in the satin under-garments she had bought for her sister; she brushed her flaming hair; she pulled on and smoothed round her the rustling taffeta. She examined her face forgivingly in the dim greenish glass, darkening her brows, reddening her lips, not even wishing this time for the beauty which was not hers. She saw a small light figure, vivid and inhuman as a paroquet, with blazing hair and dancing eyes, rising from full skirts that floated out like a rich blue and emerald shining flower.

It was still only quarter-past seven. She had learned to dress so quickly in her full hurried life that even now she could not force herself to be slow; yet she could not bear to wait in the cold grim room. Down the corridor she moved, her taffeta whispering across the wide landing, past the lift and down the stairs.

She could not go straight to the lounge where she had arranged to meet Carne. She must seek other diversion. Of course, she knew, she had a note to write.

On the first floor landing a notice with an arrow pointed to "Writing Room." She followed it, and found herself in an apartment not unlike a station waiting-room. It lacked human occupants, but there was accommodation for them. Round the walls stood desks, back to back, with dusty blotting-paper gummed to their surfaces. Inkwells in which the moisture had long since dried, crossed nibs, and half-torn envelopes.

If she had wanted to write, this equipment might have deterred her. But she wanted nothing. No words could describe, to no one could she communicate, this extraordinary rapture which had transformed the universe—because she was going to eat a third-rate dinner in a second-rate hotel, with a ruined farmer who was father to one of her least satisfactory pupils.

She could not keep still. The wide skirts of her dress swayed round her as she moved about the room, examining the elaborate but dusty stationery, and the papers on the circular table in the middle of the room.

Who, she wonder, reads The Textile Mercury? or Iron and Steel, the Autocar, the Iron and Coal Trades Review, the Electrical Times? Ah, the times are electrical, she thought, "perhaps that's what's wrong with them," and trembled, quivering with laughter at her small feeble joke, pressing her palms on the cold, smeared mahogany, because she suddenly found her eyeballs pricking with hot irrational tears.

"Five minutes to go yet," she thought, and sought other distraction, for she could not face Carne immediately on the half-hour, as though appearing punctually for school prayers.

On a shelf near the fireplace stood a row of severe little books. She went to them and read their titles—Light, she read, Protection and Vindication. She pulled out Vindication and saw that it was by Judge Rutherford of the International Bible Students' Association. She remembered seeing advertisements of his meetings years ago outside the Albert Hall. She had wondered then what they were all about. Well, any time was a good time to learn. She opened and read at random:

"Jehovah is the husband man, and Jerusalem stands for his woman. She was 'married' to Jehovah and brought forth her offspring to him. Moreover thou hast taken thy sons and thy daughters whom thou hast borne unto me, and these thou hast sacrificed unto them to be devoured. Is this of thy whoredoms a small matter?"

Too much for me altogether, she began to think flippantly, then suddenly crushed the volume between her hands and bowed her head. Oh God, she thought, I should like to bear his child.

And with that desire she felt again the hot tears rising, and thrust the book back into the shelf and turned again to face the desks, the blotting-paper, the circular table with the Electrical Times opened on it.

I shall remember this room until I die, she told herself.

She opened the door, closed it carefully behind her, and walked away slowly along the corridor.

As, when a child, she had nibbled her biscuit slowly, tasting every crumb, hoarding each grain of sweetness, so now she walked slowly along the passage, slowly to the head of the stairs, and slowly down. At every step her wide skirts rustled round her, her shoe buckles sparkled in the electric light; she was conscious of her bright incongruity in that dull, solid place.

Carne was standing in the lounge facing the staircase. His face was no longer bleak with misery. His eyes met hers, and held them with a welcoming smile as she walked down and towards him.

He had changed into a dinner jacket, and she felt that they two made a gala party in the clattering and commercial atmosphere.

All she said was: "Have I kept you waiting?"

And he, verifying his remark by a glance at his wrist-watch, said, "Exactly one minute, thirty-five seconds." And they both laughed.

They went into the dining-room; it was more cheerful than the lounge and bedrooms had suggested. Carne had reserved a table by the fire. Only three others were occupied. They had a sense of convivial privacy there, in a little alcove, with the shaded lamp and the yellow chrysanthemums and the attentive waiter.

We shall have nothing to talk about, Sarah told herself. She was mistaken. He asked her questions, mostly about places that she had visited, and she was surprised to learn how much he knew. Paris she had expected, but not Biarritz, Monte Carlo, Vienna, Baden-Baden. She found in herself an appetite to learn every episode of his history. When he mentioned Budapest, and added "the Hungarians—you can get on with them—wonderful chaps with horses"—she wanted to know when he had formed his opinions, why, how and where.

He had ordered a light hock, rather scornfully, saying that all the wines were bound to be bad there. She was no connoisseur, and she drank little, yet she felt a rare exhilaration threading her veins. Only to sit there, eating indifferent food, listening to his slow voice, watching his hands manipulate knife and fork, meant a timeless ecstasy.

He no longer treated her as though she were Midge's teacher. She was a woman and charming, and he was entertaining her. She prayed desperately that she might do nothing to jar upon him, yet her consciousness of the times when she had made other men think her attractive calmed her panic.

From far away sounds of a dance band reached them.

"Is that wireless?" she asked idly, to fill a pause in the conversation.

He asked the waiter, who replied that it was a dance band, that every fortnight there was dancing in the ballroom, tickets five shillings—half a crown to residents.

Her fingers tapped the tune on the tablecloth. He asked her, "Do you like dancing."

"I love it—but I haven't danced for over a year, I think."

"Nor I—for far more than that."

"You like it?"

He shrugged his shoulders. She felt his dark eyes regarding her sombrely. Suddenly she wanted so badly to dance with him that she nearly wept.

The waiter was serving them with fruit salad in little metal cups. She wondered—when did he dance last? With whom? She was not jealous of his wife, but she could have gladly killed the other women whom he had ever held.

She said: "Do you remember the war-time dance mania? Were you ever at the Grafton Galleries?"

A shadow crossed his face. "Once," he said. She cursed herself, guessing that she had aroused unwelcome memory. But what were you to do with a man whose entire past was raw with wounds—either to himself or to her? There was no safety. The taste of pineapple in her mouth was the Grafton Galleries. The flavour of tinned apricot was the flavour of grief.

"What about having our coffee in the lounge?" he asked.

"Why not?" It would perhaps prolong the evening. They would have coffee. They would have cigarettes. Oh, God, God, God, make him like me a little. Make him like me enough to be glad to spend the whole evening with me.

But of what use is prayer? When prayer becomes necessary, she thought ruefully, its futility is already proved.

She swept out of the dining-room before him, with all the dignity of which her small figure was capable. The saxophones and violins wailed louder. They were playing a stupid little tune called "Didn't want to say good-bye." Sarah paused, and Carne came up beside her. He too was listening. The silly persistent music beckoned them. They went on into the lounge and drank brandies with their coffee.

Conversation flagged. The bright distant places were overshadowed. The pink and white azaleas of Monte Carlo, the mountain-shadowed gardens of Aix-les-Bains, the wild seas of San Sebastian froze themselves in the memory; Muriel had been there; pain dwelt there. Sarah would not touch them.

He handed her his cigarette case, gold, plain, slender. Inside was engraved in square letters, "R. from M." and a date.

I don't care, Sarah told herself, taking a cigarette. It was a long time ago, and he got little satisfaction out of her. She has been shut away for fifteen years; there must have been others.

"What about this dancing?" he asked suddenly.

Again her heart stood still.

Suddenly she felt. I can't bear it. If I dance with him, I'm lost.

But smiling, she said, "Well, what about it? It might be quite agreeable."

"There doesn't seem much else to do—in Manchester. Unless you like those film things."

"I don't suppose there's a good film on. And I'm sure you loathe them."

They went down to dance.

The underground room was rather hot and tawdry. Couples in every stage of morning, afternoon and evening dress were dancing. They danced well and badly. The only rule was that ladies must take their hats off. A coloured limelight swept the jogging gyrating crowd.

It's not real. It's all impossible, thought Sarah. Big and black and white Carne stood before her, solid as a cliff. Into her mind flashed that vision of him in the snow on his black horse. She slid into his arms.

She was conscious of his height, his strength and her smallness. She made herself deliberately as light, as small as possible. Perhaps, she thought, if he hardly notices me he'll think I'm Muriel. Perhaps he'll forget I'm any one and only remember that he's enjoying himself.

He danced as she would have expected—well but gravely. Between the dances, they sat at a little table and he drank whiskies and sodas and she sipped lemonade. It occurred to her that unless he had a very strong head, he must be growing a little tight, but he showed no signs of it in speech or movement. Once he ordered the band to play a special tune, and her spirits rose absurdly. He wants to dance this with me, she thought. This tune is mine.

To her disappointment, it was not a tune she recognised, and again she wondered, How does he know this kind of thing? With whom has he danced?

She began to remember that, even if she had met him earlier, there would have been no hope for her; she was a blacksmith's daughter and he was a snob.

He is a snob and stupid, she told herself, thinking by reasoned criticism to cure her infatuation; but it was useless. His arm was round her. His hand held her hand. She could feel the hard uneven thumping of his heart; her body was pressed to his, interpreting by a profound foreknowledge his movements before he could make them. I know, she thought, when he's doing to dip, pause, turn; I know nothing of his mind, nothing, nothing, nothing. But I know what his body is going to do before he does it. His body was a thick impenetrable fortress. She could never learn his heart.

And suddenly this contact of her body with his, which she had desired so hungrily, became unbearable. She lost step; the invisible current between them snapped.

"Let's sit down," she said, and he led her to her seat.

It was half-past eleven. Dancing continued until midnight. Earlier she had resented that closure; now she longed for it. She forced herself to smile airily.

"Well, what about it? Eleven? I have a train to catch at eight o'clock and all those parcels to pack." She rose.

"Won't you let me get you another drink?"

Did he want her? Was he trying to keep her? The pale handsome mask of his face said nothing, yet as she looked at it she knew, He's ill, he's old, he's tired, and he's lonely. She wanted to punish him because the flame that burned her had not even touched him. She did not sit down again.

"Oh, I've drunk enough—far more than is seemly in a head mistress on holiday."

"I'd forgotten that you were a head mistress."

Her heart leapt.

"Well—if you must go—" But his voice was reluctant.

"I—Don't you think we shall both be tired?"

"Then why not just sit?" he asked. "After all, it's early."

He wants me to stay; he wants me to stay, she triumphed.

"You don't have to hurry away then, in the morning?"

"No. As a matter of fact,"—his long lashes lifted and his dark eyes frowned at her, as though it were she who had hurt him—"I've got to go round here looking for some kind of home for my wife."

It was the first time that he had ever mentioned her and the shock robbed her of breath. She thought—then he is a little drunk or he wouldn't tell me that. She said, "I'm sorry. That must be rather a grim business." She sat down again.

"It is. It's damned grim."

"Must she come to Manchester?"

"Perhaps. I may be getting a job here."

"You? A job?"

"Riding school."

"But are you going to leave Maythorpe?"

"Not if I can help it. But it's as well to have a second string to your bow. Depends what the Government do for us. And the market—and the season too. Can't tell in farming. Depends on so many things outside yourself."

The whisky had loosened his tongue. The dancing had excited him. His dark eyes blazed in his white face, and he repeatedly made a puzzling gesture. He would put his hand on the table, draw in the well-shaped but now work-stained fingers, stretch them out again, and stare at them, as though they were giving him some kind of trouble for which he could not quite account.

"Are you thinking of selling up, then?" she persisted, recalling rumours.

"The place isn't mine to sell. It belongs to the bank, and the bank's in Snaith's pocket, and he wants the farm for his lunatics." He beckoned the waiter and ordered another whisky; she sat regarding him, now quite coldly observant.

"Do you believe in curses?" he asked suddenly.

"What kind of curses?"

He held the tumbler against the light, measuring the whisky before adding the soda.

"When I ran away with my wife, her mother cursed me. Of course she was mad at the time. My wife is mad now, you know. In an asylum."

"I know."

"She is the most beautiful woman I ever saw."

"I know. I saw her portrait."

"She hasn't recognised me for over a year. Do you think Midge is like her?"

"No," lied Sarah. "She's more like you."

"Sometimes I think I'm going mad myself."

"That's natural enough. But it's morbid. I've never met any one more sane."

"Do you think so? How do you know? You don't know me."

"Oh, yes, I do. I know you quite well."

"You know me—eh? You've watched me? You see how I crack up in emergencies? How they've got me down?"

"No. No. They haven't."

"They've got me down. They'll sell Maythorpe over my head. Castle's dying. Midge is better off with Mrs. Beddows. Muriel doesn't even know me. And you would prefer not to be here with me. I'm giving you a hell of an evening."

"No," said Sarah.

"Not a hell of an evening?"

"No."

"You don't want to go and leave me?"

"No."

Then he gave her an extraordinary look—a sideways look which was quizzical, explanatory—and frivolous. That was the word—a frivolous look. He's drunk, she thought. And he takes me now for a little tart. That's the kind of man he is. That's the kind of way he thinks of women—all but his wife. I'm a little tart.

And because no man had ever treated her lightly before, her breath came in quick jerks and her palms moistened; but she sat and smiled, her will riding calm above her panicking body.

"You don't want to leave me?" he repeated.

"No," she replied.

The programme was approaching its conclusion. The lights grew dim; the orchestra wailed softly into a waltz.

"Come and dance this."

She rose. If he was drunk, he still could dance. They were locked together in perfection of physical sympathy.

The tune changed to "Auld Lang Syne."

"This is the end," he said.

"No," she repeated. "It need not be."

Again he flashed at her that look. This time she met it, and smiled fully and frankly into his eyes. His arm tightened.

"Sarah?"

"My dear?"

"Do you mean that?"

"I mean anything you like."

He stopped and almost lifted her from the crowd. The band played "God Save the King."

"Do you mean that I need not be alone to-night?"

"Yes. I mean that."

"May I come to your room?"

"Yes. It's on the fifth floor. Number 517."

"517," he repeated, looking down at her with calm appreciation.

Her mind was quite cold. He is drunk, she thought; he has forgotten who I am or who he is; he thinks I am a little tart. Well? I am Sarah Burton; I have Kiplington High School; he is a governor. This may destroy me. Even if I do not have his child, this may destroy me.

I will be his little tart; I will comfort him for one night.

"You mean that? Sarah?"

"Wait half an hour. I will have the door unlocked. No one will notice. You can come straight in."

"Five hundred and seventeen," he repeated, and she twisted from him, slipped between the couples, and was away.

This is the end; she repeated his words. She meant the end of her security as a respectable and respected professional woman; she had loved before, but never with this abandonment of pride. She would have him, drunk or sober. She would humiliate herself if necessary. She would have him though he had even forgotten her identity.

As she climbed the ten steep flights of stairs, she pressed her hands together in an agony of apprehension in case he should not come.

She undressed and lay in the broad white bed awaiting him. She had turned out the central light, and beside the bed the shaded hand-lamp illuminated only her red roses in a jug, the huge white counterpane and her still, expectant face. The ugly desolate room was lost in shadow. She smiled, thinking, This is my bridal chamber. She remembered her disgust when she had first looked at it. But it was the only room, they had said, available. She smiled, in amusement at her past disdainful self. It was a lovely room. She listened to the noises in the corridor. She heard doors bang, the lift rattle, bells ring. Slowly, too slowly, the hotel began to settle itself down for the night. By instinct rather than sight she knew when the door opened. She sat up and held out her hand.

"Come in, my dear."

He closed the door behind him. She could see in the shadow his tall figure. She heard his quick panting breath. He must have run up the stairs, avoiding the tell-tale lift.

"You're—sure?" he gasped.

"So sure, my dear," she steadied her voice with an effort, "that I know now I have never been sure of anything before in my life."

She felt rather than saw him move towards her; she caught the gleam of a dark red dressing-gown, of ivory flesh.

Suddenly he stopped.

He had taken hold of the brass rail at the foot of the bed. She heard a quivering groan. The bedstead rattled with his violent seizure. She cried, "Oh—what is it?" and raised the lamp and saw his face distorted with agony, his snarling lips drawn back from his chattering teeth, his skin a livid grey, smeared with perspiration.

She sprang from the bed and stood beside him. For an interminable period he did not speak.

"What is it? Oh, what is it?" she cried. It seemed to her that more than a physical torture racked him.

Then the attack withdrew a little and he became aware of her. He tried to smile.

"It's all right. Heart. Nothing."

"Come and lie down."

He shook his head, but she put her arm round him and between two spasms of pain got him on to the bed and covered his jerking body.

"I'm going to get you some brandy."

"No." He made a violent effort. "Nitrate of amyl. Little tin in my waistcoat pocket."

"What room? What's your number?"

But the onslaught of pain attacked him, and he could only sit, his arms stretched out, trying to stifle his groans of agony. The bed shook. Sarah thought that the whole hotel must hear those half-checked cries. Then again he spoke.

"Hundred and six. First floor. It's all right, though. I can go in a minute."

"Have you the key? In your pocket?"

She had to climb on to the bed and kneel there, fumbling about in his tumbled silk gown until she found it. Then she pulled her own wrap round her, opened the door and was off like a lapwing down the corridor. As one flies in a dream, she raced down those stairs, hardly touching the steps, swinging wildly round the banisters. Once she met a little fat man, boiled lobster red from his bath; once she thought she saw a night porter in the distance. Then she was down; she had found Room 106; she unlocked the door; she began to search furiously among his neatly folded clothes. In the waistcoat pocket of the brown tweed suit was a small tin. Nitrate of amyl.

She was off like the wind again and up the stairs. When she re-entered her room, the pain had come again. He was on his face, wrestling with the pillow.

She tugged at the little tin, breaking her nails, for it was hard to open, then finally prising it up with nail scissors. It contained small white bundles tied with cotton. She had not a notion how to use them. Despair filled her. He would die.

She came close to the bed. "How do I use these?" she asked in a loud clear voice, as though she must penetrate curtains of pain to reach him.

He stretched out an inhuman, clawlike hand and seized a bundle, crushing it between his fingers. He turned and held it against his twitching nostrils. She saw that his face had changed incredibly. The flesh seemed to have shrunk from the prominent skull and the hawk-like cartilage of the nose. He was a stranger.

She imitated him, breaking another capsule; she managed to hold him up against the pillows, because that position seemed easier for him. The strange odour of the amyl filled the room. She did not speak, kneeling half on a chair, half on the bed, to reach him.

Slowly she felt the tension relax, the agony slide from his limbs. His eyes sought her face.

"I'm fearfully sorry."

"Tell me what else I can do?"

"Nothing. It's better."

"Will it come again?"

"Don't know."

"I'm going to call a doctor."

"No. Don't leave me."

"But I must. I shan't be a minute."

"No. No. For God's sake. Amyl."

The pain was coming again. Again she fought it, holding him, and the capsules to his face. She was torn by uncertainty. Which ought she to do—stay here with him? Rouse the night porter? He might die there.

And even as she crouched above him, feeling through her nerves the tortures of his pain, her cold mind, entirely calm, considered. I could tell the hall-porter I heard him here in the passage groaning and got him into my room. No. They know he's on the first floor. I shall say he knew me—I'm his daughter's school teacher. He felt ill and came to me for advice and fainted.

She waited until she felt that she dared leave him. She was conscious of everything—the scent of whisky, amyl and tobacco, the texture of his faded but admirable silk pyjamas, his shabby handsome crimson dressing-gown, the chill of the room, the vase of roses knocked over in her struggle to get him to bed. She knew that he might die, that there might be an inquest, that her position in Yorkshire might be ruined, and it came to her mind that if a doctor could save him and she did not fetch one, she would be guilty of his murder.

But he had clutched her arm so fiercely that she could not break away until he let her. She was his prisoner completely.

She saw that when he came to her he had brought with him sponge and towels. He had been pretending to go to his bath. She smiled at the limitations of well-meant deceit, and wondered. How often has he played this game before?

The pain swelled, then subsided. He lay back limply, his head on her breast. She tried to move it gently to the pillows so that she could slip away and fetch a doctor. But he opened his eyes and smiled at her.

"It's all light. I think it's gone now. I'll be all right in a few minutes."

His voice was a whisper. All strength had left him. It seemed incredible that in so short a time such power could be annihilated.

She said, "Do you know what it is?" meaning to tell the doctor so that he could bring remedies.

"Angina. That stuff's marvellous. Campbell gave it to me. It's the only thing."

"Don't talk now."

"I'm all right. I can lie here for a few minutes if you let me, and rest. Then I can go."

"You mustn't move."

"Oh, yes." The reaction had left him weakly hilarious. He grinned up at her. "This is just like one of those what-d'you-call-its in a moral story book. I do apologise—such a trick to play."

He seemed now to be almost amused by his predicament; but she was not amused. Wrenched suddenly from the crest of expectation to the horror of suspense, she felt herself violated, outraged.

She forced her voice to lightness.

"Listen," she said. "I'm going to leave you for a moment. I shall tell them that you felt unwell, so came to me, the only person you knew in the hotel. I'm your daughter's schoolmistress."

"You don't look it," he grinned, and closed his eyes. From a half-sleep he whispered, "There's no need. No one can do anything. Let me rest."

"Shall I put off the light?"

"Please. And don't go—I might want—that stuff."

He still held her hand. With the other, she turned out the lamp and sat there, crouched on the chair beside him. She was pierced with cold, but her shocked and tormented nerves shook off her physical chill. She could see the lights from the lamps outside forming geometrical patterns across the ceiling. The noises from Piccadilly invaded the room. Far below her, workmen on shifts all night were repairing the road. Late home-going cars swept the square, the moving fingers of their headlights sliding along her wall. She moved her own fingers to Carne's wrist and felt his uneasy pulse. It seemed odd to her, jerky and unsteady, and again she wondered if she should fetch a doctor. The very fact that this might be to her disadvantage urged her.

But his hand was in hers, and she thought that he was sleeping. Perhaps rest might save him. The attack had passed. She tried to think about angina pectoris, to recall any cases of which she had ever heard.

It is my fault entirely, she told herself. I made him dance; encouraged him to drink. I let him come to me. It was all too much for him. If he dies, I have killed him. The big cotton drays began to clatter again across the cobbles. From her seat by the bed, Sarah could not see her watch. It was still quite dark. The water from the overturned jug had been dropping on to the carpet with a slow drip, drip, drip like blood. One rose had caught itself by its thorns and hung head downwards like a drop of blood against the dim white cloth.

Again she thought, This is my bridal chamber. This is my lover, and turned towards the man on the dark bed.

He moved in his sleep and groaned a little, then murmured, "My love, my love, my dear and little love."

She knew that he was thinking of his wife.

She thought—This story could not have a happy ending. It did not even have a happy beginning. I deserved this. Whether he lived or died the results were equal. He belonged to a past age; his world was in ruins. There was no hope for him—alive or dead.

Her mind raced hither and thither seeking comfort, but she found none. She had not even amused him for one evening. She had nothing, nothing, not even the joy of losing, for he had never been hers.

Then she ceased even to question, and sat still, as though she were part of the furniture, waiting for him to wake up or to die.

At last he stirred. He said quietly, "Are you awake?"

"Yes. Are you better?"

She turned the light on.

"What time is it?"

He released her hand. It was lifeless with cramp. She looked at her watch on the dressing-table and said, "Half-past five."

"Then I'd better be moving."

"Oh, please don't."

"I'm quite all right now—really. It's all over. I know this game."

He pulled himself cautiously upright on the pillows, thrust his long legs from the bed, groping for his slippers.

She found them for him, and would have put them on, humbly grateful for this small chance of service, but he pushed her gently aside.

"Oh, no. You've done too much."

She could tell that he was better—weak and still a little dazed, but himself again. He sat on the edge of the bed apologising.

"I—have no words."

"You need none. I—I wish you were not ill."

"So do I." He gave a little half laugh. "Is that my key?"

"And your amyl."

She handed him his possessions.

"Let me at least get the lift for you."

"No. I shall be all right. It's downstairs this time."

He stood up. She saw that he was a man of over fifty, ravaged by illness, shaken, weak. He tried to smooth his tossed hair, and she saw now that it was brindled with silver. He fastened his crumpled dressing-gown and looked down at her, not knowing what to say.

Then he saw the overturned vase.

"Oh—your roses!"

"I knocked them over." She turned to pick them up. She did not want to look at him any longer. Her heart was sick with grief.

"I am so sorry." He was apologising for the tumbled flowers, but she knew now that this was all he would say.

With a smile half shy, half swaggering, he took one rose and pushed it, with a trembling hand, into the buttonhole of his red dressing-gown.

"Good-bye—and thank you. I don't suppose I shall see you in the morning. I shall probably rest till noon."

"Promise to send for a doctor if you feel ill again."

"I promise."

He pressed the rose more firmly into its place as though this frivolous gesture were his final comment on a closed episode, then smiling at her, turned and with extreme care walked across the room and out of the door. She followed him and saw his tall figure move down the dim corridor. She hoped that he might turn his head before he vanished. But he moved straight forward, grasping the stair rail, and climbed slowly down, out of her sight, out of her life, she thought, for ever.

She closed the door and went back to her bed. She saw the dishevelled clothes and the hollow left in the pillow by his head. She pictured again the night as she had intended it to be, and as it had been. She looked into the future and saw no happiness for him, no comfort for herself.

Shivering with cold, with misery and with exhaustion, she crept into the bed where he had lain and found the sheets still warmed by his warm body. Drawing them closer, fitting herself into the place that he had made for her, she thought, this is the one mercy that he has shown me.

Then, warmed by his warmth, she lay, shuddering, till dawn.

BOOK VII

FINANCE

"3. That the Committee recommends the raising of the County Rate from 8s. 10d. to 12s. 6d."

Minutes of the Finance Committee. January 22, 1934.

"12. That the several resolutions on the Minutes of the Finance Committee of the 22nd January 1934 be and the same are hereby approved and confirmed."

Resolutions of the County Council of the Administrative County of York, South Riding. February 1, 1934.

CHAPTER I

MRS. BEDDOWS RECEIVES A CHRISTMAS PRESENT

Life at Willow Lodge moved through a cycle of festivities—Christmas, Easter, Whitsun and the Summer Holidays—with smaller feast-days interspersed between them, horse shows, bazaars, the Flintonbridge Point-to-Point, the High School Speech Days.

But of all these focal points the most active, persistent and inescapable was Christmas. The season began almost as soon as the little boys ran round the Kiplington streets shouting "Penny for the Old Guy" on frosty November evenings; long before notices went up in the lighted Kingsport windows, "Please Shop Early," its imminence overshadowed all other Beddows' activities; it rose slowly to its climax with the carving of the family turkey at midday dinner on Christmas Day, and subsided gradually through Boxing Day, the maids' holidays, indigestion and crumbling evergreen decorations until the old calendars could be thrown away, the garlands taken down, and the New Year had come.

The normal ardours and endurances of a Christmas season were multiplied twenty-fold for Mrs. Beddows by her own temperament and her husband's parsimony. It was true that since Willie came to live with her she had had a little money to spend upon her benefactions. But her heart was so generous, her range of acquaintance so wide and her delight in human relationships so unstaled, that she could have spent a national income without difficulty. As it was, she was put to desperate straits to accommodate her lavish tastes to her narrow fortune.

All through the year she and her family set themselves to accumulate the objects which she could bestow as gifts at Christmas. In a chest on the front landing known as the glory hole they stored the harvest of bazaars and birthdays, of raffles, bridge-drive prizes, bargain sales, and even presents which they had themselves received at former Christmases. Into the glory hole went blotters, pen-wipers, and painted vases, dessert d'oylies, table-centres and imitation fruits of wax or velvet, lampshades, knitted bed-jackets and embroidered covers for the Radio Times, all the bric-à-brac of civil exchange or time-killing occupation. The indictment of a social system lay in those drawers if they but knew it—a system which overworks eight-tenths of its female population, and gives the remaining two-tenths so little to do that they must clutter the world with useless objects. Mrs. Beddows did not see it quite like that; presents were presents; bazaars were bazaars, and Sybil was teaching the Women's Institute class raffia work and glove-making. Surely these were good things? She did not question further.

Early in the month the contents of the glory hole were brought down into the dining-room and sorted. Aunt Ursula's plant pot might do for the Rectory people; but Mr. Peckover's framed verse ("A Garden is a lovesome thing, God wot") must not be sent to Dr. Dale. All last year's donors must be this year's recipients, but once the known debts were honourably fulfilled, the real excitement of the season started. As cards, hair-tidies and markers began to arrive by every post, they were checked against the list of out-going presents, and consternation reigned in Willow Lodge if it were found that Cousin Rose, who had sent a cut-glass vase, had been rewarded only by three coat-hangers in a cretonne case. Unexpected gifts sent the family ransacking drawers and cupboards to find suitable q.p.q.'s. (Beddows' jargon for "quids pro quos.") The nearer the approach to Christmas Day itself, the lower ran the supply of possible exchanges, until finally even this year's presents were hastily repacked and despatched again hot from the post, with cards altered and brown paper readdressed.

Beside this transaction of civilities, there was the real business of benevolence to which all ready cash must be devoted—orders of beef to every Beddows ex-maid and her husband—(and since all maids at Willow Lodge left to marry, the list was formidable)—coals and blankets for ageing or invalid neighbours, toys, oranges, pennies and sweets for all the local children, and parcels of tea, cake and even whisky to dozens of often disreputable acquaintances who seemed to re-emerge in Mrs. Beddows' consciousness only at Christmas time.

Nor was this all. To Willow Lodge at every season came beggars, derelicts, victims of domestic quarrels or economic injustices, the aged, infants and invalids; but between December 15 and January 5, the pilgrims doubled in number and desperation.

On the day before Christmas Eve Mrs. Beddows had already interviewed a farm-worker whose wife was prematurely in labour, and for whom a nurse had to be found by persistent telephoning; a poultry-keeper, who had fled to Yorkshire after failures in the south, on whom the bailiffs had descended to seize incubators and hens against unpaid removal bills, an elementary school teacher in trouble about the local Christmas Tree (which the squire had suddenly refused, on hearing that the nonconformist children were to share it), and a mother who had just discovered that her schoolgirl daughter of sixteen was going to have a baby. Between the dining-room and the drawing-room Mrs. Beddows trotted, resourceful, indefatigable and domineering. She put the fear of God into the bailiff's men; she suggested that the school teacher could get a tree from Colonel Collier's plantation for the asking if she and her boy friends would provide the transport; she rang up the Kingsport rescue worker about the schoolgirl, and she returned to the parcels in the dining-room exhausted but triumphant.

"Well," she exclaimed, clearing a tangle of string and handkerchief sachets out of the arm-chair, "we may be poor, but you can't say we don't see life."

"The post's in, Mother," said Sybil.

"Oh, my goodness! And I was hoping for a nap. Your Uncle Richard's sent me The Ranch of the Crooked S. I thought I might have a look at it. Oh, by the by, has the Hollies' parcel gone yet?"

"No—it's all packed, but I had a happy thought. Why shouldn't I deliver that and the Maythorpe and Cold Harbour parcels by car when we take Midge home to-morrow? It would save postage."

"That's certainly an idea." She sat, her hands full of the newly arrived letters and packages, frowning.

"The Shacks. . . . Have you heard what's happening there?"

"Mrs. Mitchell's leaving. She's going to have another baby."

"Where's she going?"

"Her mother. She'll have her back if she separates from Mr. Mitchell."

"Oh, poor things. But for the time being I suppose it's the only thing. It seems a pity, though. I could have got her a nurse. . . ."

She turned her thoughts to the other residents at the Shacks.

"If only the new housing scheme goes through, Holly might get a job there . . . they might move into one of the new houses."

She remembered how bitterly Carne opposed the housing scheme. The complexity of life assailed her.

Without eagerness she began to open the envelopes. She was tired. The burden of life lay heavily on her shoulders. She looked across the room at Sybil, on her knees by the sofa wrapping a parcel. She thought: She should have married. How have I failed there? She was cut out to be a wife and mother. She sighed.

"Here's a card from old Dr. Menzies. Have we sent anything?"

Below it was an envelope marked "Crown Hotel, Piccadilly," and addressed to her in Carne's stiff squarish writing.

She opened that, frowning a little because Carne was not a correspondent, and she was expecting to see him next day when Midge returned to spend Christmas with her father.

"DEAR MRS. BEDDOWS," she read—"I am writing to ask another favour of you." He was almost the only man who used the long old-fashioned "f" for "s." "I wonder if it would be very inconvenient to you to keep Midge on for Christmas? I know that she is very happy at Willow Lodge, and I fear that if she came to Maythorpe I could not give her the festive season which a child ought to have. Castle is very bad and things are not too good with me at present. I have been inquiring about accommodation here for my wife but have found nothing suitable.

"Your ever grateful friend, "ROBT. CARNE."

It was the longest letter that he had ever written her.

"Things are not too good with me." Ah, well she knew it. Maythorpe mortgaged and the bank impatient, Snaith eager to buy the farm—for a mental home; Castle dying, Muriel no better. Carne had said that he would stick at Maythorpe till he was forced off; he had said that he could last another year; but she knew that he had gone to Manchester to inquire about employment at a riding school there. He's too old, her heart cried. He's too old for that.

She remembered other Christmases at Maythorpe. Once in her childhood she had attended a dance there, when Robert's grandfather was master. She remembered the great decorated kitchen, with holly hung from the rafters among the salt-rimed shrouded hams and puddings, a fiddler on the back stairs, and a feast of cake and fruit and pasties, wine and whisky. Always there had been carol-singing on the drive, the square hall blazing with lights and pennies for the children. Until this year Robert had kept up some pretension of festivity. Now no more. He had cut down the timber except round the house itself; the rooms were untenanted by guests; the glory had departed.

Her only comfort was that in his extremity he could turn to her. He trusted her.

She held his letter, her longing to help and comfort him surging over her. "Things are not too good with me." It was the nearest approach to a complaint she had ever heard him make.

"Granny," Peter broke into her reverie, "you're wanted in the kitchen. The turkey's too big for the tin."

"Let me go," Sybil began.

"No. I will."

Rousing herself, glad of the need for action, she levered her weary body from the deep chair, and hurried off.

As usual, she found twenty details requiring her attention. Sybil might manage the housekeeping with competence and order, but the final word always was her mother's. It was nearly half an hour before she returned. The afternoon was waning, and the hall was almost dark. From the dining-room came a burst of light and laughter. It seemed to her, as she opened the door, to be full of people. A clamour of voices greeted her. Midge's shrill wild laugh, Peter's cackling shout (his voice was breaking), Wendy's glad guffaw, and another voice, deep and vibrating—Carne's voice.

While her hands and tongue were busy in the kitchen, she had been thinking of him with such love and sorrow that this unexpected re-encounter shocked her almost as though she had met a ghost. She had been thinking of his lonely Christmas, picturing him in the empty dining-room, eating his dinner alone with Muriel's portrait; she had been grieving over him, wondering what she could do to help him.

And now she saw him, seated by her fire, the centre of a delighted and boisterous uproar.

She could hardly believe her eyes.

He had brought his presents—a party dress of flowered silk for Midge, a hunting crop for Peter, a bracelet for Sybil, for Wendy a scarf of painted chiffon, for Jim, a tie-pin with a fox's head, and for Willie a shagreen cigarette-box.

Midge saw her. "Granny, come in. Come in! Look what Daddy's brought me?" She danced up and down, the rosy silk fluttering like a banner. Carne turned slowly and rose to greet her. Seen between those flushed excited faces his big dark figure seemed of other, different substance. He looks ill, she thought; he looks old. She began to reckon his age and decided that he must be fifty-three. He looks sixty. Oh, my dear, my poor one, what have they done to you?

"You've not come to fetch Midge away after all?" she asked.

He shook his head. The child sprung up and down.

"Oh, Granny, do say it suits me? Does it fit? Peter, don't crush it!"

"Look at my crop, Gran."

"And look at this lovely thing." Sybil held out a round, freckled arm with the gold bangle clasped on to it. Watching Carne's grave appreciation as he looked down at her pleasure, Emma Beddows thought, not for the first time—Oh, if he were free and could have married Sybil.

She moved towards him and began to inspect the presents. At first she thought he had gone crazy with extravagance. Then she began to recognise one by one the bracelet, the scarf, the cigarette-box. These were his things and Muriel's. The former make-believe that she would return to use them was at an end.

"You'll stay for tea?"

"No. I've got to get back. Castle's bad to-night. I've promised to go round there."

"Then you'll have a drink? Get him one, Sybil."

"No, thank you very much."

"Did you ride over?"

"No. I've got Hicks with the trap. I don't want to keep the horse waiting too long."

"Then I'll come to the door with you."

On her return from the kitchen, she had forgotten to remove her apron. Passing the mirror in the hall she saw reflected her plump, sturdy, plebeian figure beside his tall one, and sighed, desiring the impossible—that she could be young and lovely and desirable, that she could comfort him in his adversity.

He said, "Is it really all right about Midge?"

"Perfect for us, but you'll miss her."

"I shall be all right."

"Look here, why don't you come and eat your dinner with us?"

"I've promised to stand by Mrs. Castle—"

"But . . ." she saw his resolution and changed the subject. "How d'you think Midge is looking?"

"Splendid. This is the place for her. I—well—I wanted to ask you something."

"What?"

She had opened the door. Its oblong was filled with the pale star-flecked radiance of the green evening sky. Hicks was leading his trap up and down the road outside the gate, its yellow lights crossing and turning beyond the dark laurel hedge. Carne leaned against the door-post. She saw fatigue in all his slow calm gestures.

"I've been talking to my solicitors this morning," he said, "and I want to ask you a tremendous favour. Don't answer now. Think it over. If anything happened to me, would you be Midge's guardian?"

"But my dear boy! I'm seventy-two—old enough to be your mother."

"I dare say. But you're young enough in some ways to be my daughter," he said, and she could hear in his voice rather than read on his face his friendly grin. "And I was nearly knocked down by a taxi in Manchester. It made me think of my latter end. If anything happened to me—the child would be rather lost. By the way, I've written to Sedgmire about Muriel."

"Oh!"

Mrs. Beddows realised what that implied.

"If I died, I expect they'd look after Muriel. They always would have done—if I'd leave her alone." He tossed his cigarette on to the path. "But Midge is a different matter. I don't want those Harrogate people to handle her."

"Quite."

"She wouldn't be any financial burden. I've kept up my insurance. Five thousand when I'm sixty or if I die before that. It's hers, of course. Only, I want to be sure I'm not putting too much on you."

"No—no. I love the child. I'd do anything. . . ."

"I know you would. That's just it. I exploit your goodness. I always have done."

She could hardly breathe. Joy, release, triumph enfolded her.

"I don't think you know how fond I am of you," she said.

"Perhaps I do."

Hicks had turned the horse again; the dog cart was approaching them, its lamps faint and small beside the great lights of the passing motor-cars. In another moment this little interlude of tenderness would be over.

"By the way," he added, "that reminds me." He fumbled in his waistcoat pocket and brought out a little box wrapped in tissue paper. "I brought a little present for you too."

"For me?"

"Yes. I want you to have it. You will know why. Good-bye. Merry Christmas to you."

He took her hand, smiled, then very gravely stooped and kissed her soft wrinkled cheek and was off, out of the gate. She heard him call to Hicks; she saw the moving lights stop still; he climbed into the cart; he shook the reins, then the hoofs were off again, trot-trotting away from her into the starlight.

She put her hand to her face and touched it gently. He had never kissed her before. She had not dreamed of it. With trembling hands she began to undo her Christmas present. The paper contained a small brown case lined with white velvet, and on the velvet lay the brooch, a spray of emeralds, diamonds and rubies, which he had bought for Muriel when Midge was born. He had slipped into the lid a little card on which he had written, "For Midge's Granny, in gratitude."

"I want you to have it," he had said. "You will know why." She knew why.

She had tried to give to Midge the protective love which her mother could not give. He had recognised her endeavour and was grateful. He had given her the brooch he bought for Muriel, and he had kissed her.

She knew now where she stood with him, and she was happy. Her jealousy and pain were taken from her. Whatever problems and griefs still lay before her—and she had no doubt that they would still be many—she realised that her long years of patient loyalty and service had at least brought this difficult and strange relationship through to triumphant confidence and love.

CHAPTER II

MR. HOLLY BRINGS HOME A CHRISTMAS PRESENT

It was Christmas Eve, and the children had been wild with excitement. No matter how much Lydia might protest that she had nothing for them, they still persisted in believing that Christmas must be Christmas. Certainly, earlier in the afternoon Miss Beddows had driven round with a piece of beef, some oranges and crackers. Lydia would prepare a dinner with these for them to-morrow. "If Daisy had only made her cocoa-nut ice now—" Bert had said.

But of what use was Christmas?

Lydia sat by the oil stove in the outer room, too tired to move. She was facing a bitterness of disappointment which destroyed her. She wanted to go to bed and to sleep and never to wake again. There was no hope in life; promises were treacherous; pleasure poisoned.

In the next room lay her sisters, Daisy, Kitty and Alice with the baby. Beside her on the bunk Lennie slept. Sometimes he ground his teeth and tossed his arms about. He had never been really well since he had measles.

Bert was spending Christmas with the Alcocks. They had accepted him now as Vi's young man. He had got free. He talked of going to lodge in Kiplington, protesting that really it would be better for his family, since Mr. Holly was now on transitional benefit, "and if old Tadman gives me a rise they'll only dock it off Dad's allowance." It sounded logical enough.

In any case, why should Bert stay there—among the squalor, the discomfort, the wretchedness of the railway coach? Lydia, groping for grievances, found justice. She was fond of her brother and could not see why his life should be spoiled as well as hers. But because she was intelligent enough to learn generosity, this did not mean that she was without resentment.

Why had she been born? she wondered, or if born, then why gifted with desires and abilities? She let her mind wander backwards through her short life. It seemed now to her that while her mother lived, she had known a period of perfect happiness. That rough ungainly figure, that sharp tongue, that vigour and impatience all presented themselves now before her memory as symbols of sheltering love and understanding. She had lost them—and lost them in such a way that her mother's death mocked devotion and outraged loyal service. Lydia had tried to be good and loving and unselfish. She remembered her mother lying on the bunk, haggard and weeping. This was what came of love.

And Gertie was dead and Lennie always ailing. The baby, dragged up anyhow, was a little rat. Lydia hated it, refusing to give tenderness to what had killed her mother. Often she hoped that it might die, and feared her hope.

Her father had moments of jollity but no sense. He exasperated her as he had exasperated her mother. He would be coming in soon, wanting some cocoa, talkative, volatile, soft.

And these would be her companions now, for ever, since the Mitchells had left the Shacks and gone away. She had not liked Nancy Mitchell. A cat, if ever there was one, shrewish, nagging; but she was company.

"Don't worry," Miss Burton had said. "It's all right, Lydia. We'll find a way. Even if you have to lose one term, I won't see you defeated. You know Alderman Astell? Well, he and three other aldermen and councillors are trying to get a new garden village built somewhere between Kingsport and Kiplington. If that happens, there'll be work for your father, and you'll be able to move into one of the new houses, and then there'll be neighbours to come in and do the cooking and look after the baby. Even before that, we may get a woman out from Maythorpe."

But there was no woman in Maythorpe willing to undertake the responsibility of the Shacks. Chrissie Beachall was more and more occupied at the Nag's Head, where Lily Sawdon was now almost completely bedridden. Mothers of young girls ripe for service disliked the idea of their daughters having to cope with the turbulent Holly children. "They're no better than gipsies. They live like pigs," said the respectable villagers.

So Lydia believed in promises no longer. She had seen too much of life, death, birth and poverty. At sixteen a forlorn cynicism quenched her once robust vitality. The charm of beauty no longer could seduce her; she had ceased to hope for any better future.

The wind whistled round the railway coach, rattling the ill-fitting tin chimney. The children had made some attempt at Christmas decorations; hedge clippings from the evergreens at Maythorpe had been stuck behind the picture of Queen Victoria's Jubilee over the bunk. A string of coloured paper streamers, made at school, hung from one side of the carriage to the other. In the sugar box which was cupboard and pantry, lay the joint, the tea, the sugar; but Lydia had piled the oranges in an old pudding basin. They looked pretty. She could see them now, in the dim yellowish glow of the oil lamp.

Before he left Bella Vista, Mr. Mitchell had given her his copy of Shakespeare's complete works. But Lydia no longer found in reading a solace for her spirit. She wanted to pass examinations; she wanted to take her matric. History, chemistry, algebra, maths and Latin. . . . She could do all these things and essays too. English was easy. She wanted problems, formulæ, long tables and categories to master. Her young mind was hungry for facts and propositions and solutions. She enjoyed its power. She knew that she was clever. But something had broken in her spirit; that resilient gaiety would elate her no longer. The Mitchells' desertion had finally defeated her.

For she was not quite sure just what had happened. Fred Mitchell was drawing public assistance. That was all right. Any one did that if they could. And Peggy had not had measles. Then somehow

Mrs. Whitfield, who was Nancy Mitchell's mother, had come down one day and seen Nancy at her work, feeding her dusty chickens, the baby crying, Peggie and Lennie playing in the pen together, and Allie and Kitty and Daisy coming home for their meal. And that had done it.

There had been a row, a monstrous row, between Fred Mitchell and his mother-in-law. It brought to an end Nancy's half-hearted labours. Mrs. Whitfield swept her and Peggy back to her home in Grimsby. Fred Mitchell was left to close the house at the Shacks, and sell the chickens; a van came for the furniture, and three days ago she had seen him off, pedalling away on his push-bike, into the unknown. She did not know whither he had gone. But during the tornado of departure Lydia had learned that her family lived like pigs, that Nancy had been disgracefully put upon, that gentle, nervous, kindly Fred was a wife-murderer worse than Crippen, because he did it slowly, and that the Shacks was a place of dirt, disease and misery. No wonder every one despised her; no wonder Sarah Burton let her down.

Miss Burton had gone, it seemed, to Manchester. From there she had sent to Lydia a lovely but maddening Christmas present—a school satchel filled with writing blocks, fountain pen, rulers, compasses, and all other equipment for her school work. It had arrived the day before Christmas Eve, and Lydia, in a burst of sullen rage, had given it to her father. "Go on. Take it. I shan't want it. I never shall go to school again. See if you can get a couple of shillings for it. Kitty must have some new shoes, and Daisy needs hers soling."

Not love, but hatred, underlay that gesture. Lydia did not sacrifice Sarah's present to her sisters. She hated her sisters and her schoolmistress, and cursed the present from Sarah as a mockery.

So Mr. Holly had gone off that afternoon to Kiplington. "Let him sell it. Let him sell it," the child swore, her head on her fists, her matted unkempt hair falling over her wrists, her elbows on the table. I hate him. I hate every one. Oh, Mother, Mother!

The door creaked and Alice stole through. "I'm thirsty, Lyd. Has Father Christmas come yet? Aren't you in bed? I want a drink of water."

"You get back to bed, or I'll give you such a hiding you won't know you've got a bottom for a week," Lydia scolded; but she dipped a mug into the bucket and Alice drank.

"When's Dad coming in?"

"I don't know."

"Is it very late?"

"Yes. Get to bed."

The clock was broken; Lennie had pulled it over. Mr. Holly had his watch with him. It might be anything between nine and midnight. Lydia shooed her young sister back to bed.

She opened the door of the railway coach and peered out into the night. It was Christmas Eve. Once she had really thought that the angels came and, singing, announced the birth of the Son of God.

As if any birth could be a matter for rejoicing! As if any night could be a holy time.

They were running extra buses that evening to Cold Harbour. One was coming now along the Maythorpe road. Its lights approaching and the rattle of its progress made Lydia feel a little less forlorn. The Shacks were not so isolated when those cheerful galleons of glass and metal, lighted and crowded, rocked past the campers' gate.

This particular bus retarded; its brakes shrieked; it stopped.

That'll be Dad, Lydia thought without enthusiasm. She turned up the wick under the warming kettle. The gate wailed as somebody opened it.

Lydia remembered other occasions when she had waited for her father. It must be memory which made her think now that she heard a woman's voice as well as a man's. She crossed to the door again. Surely there were two figures approaching along the cinder path?

She began to shiver. She was not a nervous girl, but the loneliness of the Shacks, the darkness, the misery of her vigil, had all played on her nerves.

Who was this coming?

Her father? She could hear his jolly voice—market-merry, he was. If he's drunk the money from my satchel! she thought. Then—it doesn't matter. It's all the same.

She had no faith in him.

But this was a woman's voice too and a woman's laughter, torn by the wind, scattered along the air. A wraith? A ghost? Her mother coming at Christmas to reproach her because she had danced when Gertie died?

Oh, God! sobbed Lydia, and shrank back against the wall of the railway coach, the bread knife in her hand, ready to defend herself from spectres, brigands, bogies, or the returning vengeful dead.

It was thus that Mrs. Brimsley, her hands full of Christmas parcels, her cheeks flushed with a couple of Guinnesses, her future husband's arm round her buxom waist, climbing up into the coach, encountered the girl who was to be her step-daughter.

"Hallo, Lyd," cried Mr. Holly, on the top of the world. "How's doings, lass? I've brought you a Christmas present."

Lydia and Mrs. Brimsley stared at one another. Mrs. Brimsley saw the bleak yet cluttered misery of the home, the pathos of the "decorations," the queer girl, cowering against the wall, a knife in her hand, for all the world like one of those cinema films "Attacked by the Indians." Lydia saw a plump and homely woman, middle-aged, panting a little, her hat slightly on one side. Mr. Holly saw nothing but his clever daughter and the lady who was to be his wife.

"Let me introduce you," he said gallantly, setting Mrs. B's basket of groceries on the table. "Mrs. Brimsley, Lydia. Lydia, my dear. This lady's your new mother."

He's drunk, thought Lydia. He's brought home a drunken woman. Oh, well, she's harmless, then.

Fear and shock had made her feel rather queer, but she went to the cupboard and put down a loaf with the bread knife on the table, as though she had held it there for simple reasons, instead of having armed herself against wild panic and the menacing unknown.

The woman stood holding her parcels rather helplessly, and said, in a voice that was both kind and shy, "So you're Lydia."

The girl stooped for the cocoa tin and did not turn her head.

"Yes," she said sullenly, resenting everything—most of all her own moment of unreason.

"Well, now—" began Mr. Holly; but Lennie at that moment woke and wailed.

Lydia sprang to him.

"Hush up, Dad—you've woke him. It's all right, all right, my lambie." She bent over the thin little boy. "It's all right. Lyddie's here." She knew his scares, his sudden starts of terror.

"Is this the little chap?" asked Mrs. Brimsley. She set down her parcels now and crossed to the cot. She looked at the kneeling girl and the shuddering child, still half asleep, choking with sobs, his stick-like arms round his older sister's neck.

"You woke him," Lydia said resentfully, and her sullen eyes sought for the first time the invader's face.

"I'm sorry. I hadn't realised he was in the room. I've only come in with a few presents for the children," said Mrs. Brimsley, "just until the next bus. I didn't mean to frighten him."

"It's your hat. He hates hats."

"I'll take it off."

She did. She put it down on the table and stood, her neat hair parted, her mild face bonny in lamplight.

"Maybe he'll come to me. I've reared three lads myself," said Mrs. Brimsley. "They're grown up now. Let me have a try with him."

Lydia rose slowly and stood back. She watched Mrs. Brimsley stoop to Lennie and speak to him. "Hush, Lennie, hush." Her voice was low and kind, her arms were motherly. She sat down on the bunk and lifted the flushed sleepy child, still jerking with sobs, on to her knee. The kettle boiled. Lydia rushed to it.

Mr. Holly stood balancing on his toes and heels, hands in his pockets, letting his coppers tinkle between his fingers. He was pleased as punch with himself and his experiment.

"Make a cup for your stepmother as well, Lyd."

"Stepmother! Get along with you, you haven't got me yet. Hush, little Len, did we frighten you then, my laddie? He's thin, isn't he?"

"He had measles last summer," Lydia defended him. "He was bad."

She set the cups on the table, then saw that her father had brought back her school satchel.

"Oh—wouldn't they take it?" she asked.

"I didn't try. You'll need it. Mrs. B. and I are going to splice up, my girl, as soon as we can find a house to go to."

"A house?"

"I've got a bit of money. Not much," Mrs. Brimsley said, half eagerly. She was treating Lydia like a grown-up person, explaining, propitiating.

"Oh."

Lydia had a vision of her father and Mrs. Brimsley going off to a house and leaving her to look after the children.

"So you'll be needing your school things," said her father.

"How? Who'll look after the children?"

"I shall. If you'll let me," said Mrs. Brimsley. "You'll all come to live with me, and I'll look after the little 'uns, and you can go back to school."

And, understanding though she might be in many ways, she never knew why Lydia flung down the cocoa tin, and ran out of the coach into the night, sobbing wildly, wildly, because she could not trust promises, and because she did not believe that she could have been set free.

CHAPTER III

COUNCILLOR HUGGINS PREPARES FOR AN ELECTION

From the ragged edge of the cliff the aeroplanes zoomed up into a midsummer-blue sky, catching the January sun on their silver wings. The big bomber carried a silken streamer on a long rope tied to its tail; the little fighter danced round it like a mosquito. Above the shore, above the yellow sands and blustering white-flecked sea, they dipped and roared and circled.

It was one of those January days which mock the summer.

Mr. Huggins, looking up, smiled with pleasure.

"Pretty things, eh?"

"When you don't think what they're for," growled Spurling.

He and his employer were carting pebbles from the beach below Maythorpe for the footpaths in the Esplanade Gardens, and both men were bare-armed in working overalls.

Spurling annoyed Huggins. The grizzled taciturn fellow spoke too little, but when he did open his mouth, his intention was invariably to put his employer in the wrong. After all, Huggins, not Spurling, was the councillor and lay preacher; it was his business, not his labourer's, to see hidden moral meanings, political significance, in slums or aeroplanes. He knew what Spurling meant. He had lived through air raids even if he had not, like Spurling, been to Flanders. He was not unaware of political evils—poverty, injustice, war. He spoke about them. Why, only last Sunday in South Street Wesleyan Church at Yarrold, he had begun a series of talks on "Liberty—what do we mean, and what does God mean?" And had dealt in grand generalisations with Hitler, Mussolini, Stalin and God, explaining their plans for the world with equal confidence.

He had done his duty and was, he thought, at liberty now to surrender himself to the pleasure of the wide level shore, the tossing waves, the gulls and planes blowing together about the windy sky. He had earned, he considered, the right to enjoy them all.

For in these days he had regained assurance. He had returned again to the blessed protection of the Living God and felt purified and happy. He had repented of his sins and been forgiven. Nellie was his loving wife again. Bessy and Reg had moved at last to London. The council had accepted the principle of a joint building scheme with Kingsport.

Time had left behind the old dark year of 1933; leaving Huggins a humbler but wiser man, with a more profound understanding of sinners and their route from the valley of humiliation into the green pastures of righteousness. 1934 was to be Annus Mirabilis for the South Riding.

In February the rates would go up a bit; that was essential. All the worse for those councillors who, like Carne and Gryson, stood only for cheese-paring economy. Then in March the elections would take place, and from what Huggins had seen, enough new blood would come on to the council to make the Town Planning Scheme at last a certainty. Astell had been working, speaking, canvassing, lobbying; Snaith had pushed ahead and secured his hospital fund: Miss Burton had worked up her High School governors till they were almost as discontented as she with her makeshift buildings. As for himself, he, Huggins, had sold out his life insurance and bought for £400 a nice little strip of land in Tadman's name, just below Drew's, along Leame Ferry Waste. Drew had filled the sheds there with cake-crushing machinery bought from a derelict mill near Doncaster. He and Tadman were, they said, "experimenting," and the council would have to compensate them handsomely, when they took over the old buildings.

Huggins shovelled shingle into the lorry with a blithe conscience. The wind tugged at his coat and blew sand in clouds racing along the shore to sting his face. It dragged back the spray from the tumbling waves, catching them by the hair as they reached their crest and crashed down into the shrieking shingle. The rhythm of his hard muscular labour filled him with contentment.

All that he had done, he had done honestly. Snaith had initiated him into the mysteries of Big Business. Snaith was a good man. God intended His stewards to use their wits to increase their power, so that they could build schools and suburbs, endow lectureships and fight the devil. The war planes, playing their lovely dangerous game in the fresh cold morning, had been sent up by money; money could fetch them down, could beat swords into ploughshares and make the desert blossom.

But the rates must go up. And that meant opposition. The real trouble would lie with men like Carne and Gryson. Specially Carne.

Huggins leant on his spade and paused, deep in thought.

There were, he considered, two ways of dealing with obstructionists; tie up their own interests with progress, or get them off the council. Both were possible.

He had been studying ordnance surveys with Tadman and Drew, and had realised that Carne held three small paddocks on the south of the Skerrow road, just opposite to the Wastes. He had bought them in the rich days after the war as a convenient half-way house for keeping cattle and sheep he intended to sell in Kingsport.

Huggins remembered a jest of Tadman's at their last meeting. Carne wanted to sell the fields. He was hard up. True, they were not likely to become as valuable as the Waste itself, but they were something. If he held on to them, and if the scheme went through, he might reap a profit.

Ever since then, Huggins had been thinking. He was new to the game of high finance and his ideas came slowly. But once they came, their force was overwhelming, he could endure no delay; he must act at once.

He threw the last shovelful of stones into the lorry.

"That'll do now."

He began to peel off his overalls.

"You'll drive back. I've got business in Maythorpe."

"How're you going? Up steps by Shacks?"

"No. I can get up here."

Spurling looked at the broken slopes of clay.

"I wouldn't. It's crumbling all time. Not safe."

"It's all right."

Huggins wanted to risk something. He wanted to prove his certainty. The good hand of his God was upon him, and he was unafraid.

The engine of the lorry was cold and would not start at first; the wheels churned helplessly in the sand; but Huggins put his great shoulder against the side, and it seemed to him as though in his new strength he had really lifted that weight and sent the vehicle bumping and rocking away across the sand.

He felt that he could do anything. When he turned to climb the cliff his body seemed blazing with power.

Yet the ascent was less easy than he had imagined. Footholds were treacherous. The lumps of clay broke off in his hands. To his left the rich brown earth of a landslide recalled Spurling's reminder; cracks an inch wide opened in the peeling ledges; after the next rainstorm the water would wash away those thick slices of mud.

He had to go cautiously, resting on his great stomach lest the turf-covered ledges should give way beneath him. He was a big fat man, but he was no coward, and his muscular strength was tremendous. He was enjoying himself. He had not played a daft trick like this for years, and to climb Maythorpe Cliff, even for a boy, was no small effort.

The surface of the clay had been dried by wind, but beneath, it was moist and slippery. Twice he slid downwards, tobogganning on his belly, bumping and swearing; but at last his eyes came on to the level of the edge, and he could peer over, into the blue-brown plough land.

Very odd it looked; the furrows towering like bulwarks, fringed with bristling stubble, formidable as a forest. Grunting and cursing, he got one knee over the ledge, and hauled his bulk over, blown but happy.

Well, that had been a pull, and risky too. At any moment, tons of earth were ready to fall. If he wanted a sign from God, he might consider that he had been vouchsafed one. He could go upon his mission with confidence, assured that if the Lord had not intended him to go, He could have stopped him.

He pulled handfuls of dry wicks and couch grass from a hedge bottom, and brushed himself down as well as he could, before he set off across the fields to Maythorpe, picking his teeth with a hawthorn twig and grinning, because Nellie would never believe that he had climbed Maythorpe Cliff.

The drive to the hall had not been raked for weeks; deep ruts cut into its weed-locked gravel; the gate hung loose from one hinge; a broken chimney-pot lay on the bird-flecked terrace. Huggins had thought once that the poor were blessed; he knew now that prosperity is God's reward for virtue.

He rang twice before Elsie answered. A great rawboned woman, thought Huggins critically. Well, whoever gives Carne his bit of comfort, I doubt if it's his housekeeper.

She told him that her master was up the fields. Huggins did not mind.

"It's a grand day for walking. I climbed the cliff to get here."

Elsie was not interested. She thought that men like Huggins should come to the back door.

"If I should miss him, tell your master that Huggins called. Councillor Huggins—about a county council matter."

He trudged on. It was, as he had said, a grand day for walking. The stack-yards and stables were oddly quiet. The low ivy-covered rows of loose-boxes were empty; the chalk road to the fields scarred with ruts half a foot deep. On both sides the bare winter fields stretched to the horizon.

Huggins whistled as he strode, but even so, he heard the sound of slashing and rootling in the fence before he saw anything. Peering over, he found Carne, in shirt sleeves and waistcoat, instructing a lad in the difficult craft of hedging.

For a minute or two, Huggins stood watching his fellow councillor. A strong man himself, he was a judge of physical agility. Those deft rhythmical strokes with the slasher, that sure movement of hand and knife impressed him.

"Now you have a go," said Carne, and stood back, handing his instrument to the boy, who tried to imitate him with quick nervous prods.

"No. This way. Stand easier. Loosen yourself up a bit, and don't be scared of it."

Carne was patient. He knew his job and was a kindly teacher. There were few rural crafts which he could not perform better than his men. He could thatch a straw stack, load a wagon, open out a field before harvest with a scythe, lift an eighteen stone sack of wheat and swing it across his shoulder. He was about to lose Maythorpe, not because he could not farm it, but because he had lived for years beyond his income, drawing out of the farm more than it could stand.

His hedging and ditching became a finished art; but he was not, it appeared, as fit as the preacher who watched him, for, having demonstrated to the boy what ought to be done, he leant back against a post, looking grey and drawn.

"Good-morning, Mr. Carne."

Huggins peered over the hedge and Carne started. There was neither welcome nor reproof in his voice as he replied, "Good-morning."

"Can I have a word with you?"

"Yes."

Carne gave a few further instructions to the boy, caught up his coat from the bough where it hung, then vaulted easily over the low slashed hedge. The two men fell into step, walking back to the farm. "Well?" Carne inquired.

Huggins cleared his throat. The Lord directed him.

"You're taking the chair at this 'Keep Down the Rates' meeting in Yarrold?"

"Yes. Well?"

"Don't you think it's a bit of a waste of time?"

"Why?"

"They're going up anyway. Eight and ten to twelve and six."

"Well?"

"Look here, Mr. Carne. I'll be straight with you. We're not always on the same side of the fence, but I like you. You're straight. I don't want to see you out of the council."

"Kind of you."

"Don't you think that if you always run against the tide you may be out next March?"

"That's my business."

"Maybe you don't mind? Maybe it's true that you're selling up and clearing out anyway?"

"Who told you that?"

"It's all over the Riding. Public Health Committee's after your place, isn't it?"

"Look here, Huggins. I'm a busy man, if you're not. If you've got anything to say, will you say it? I'm listening."

"Good. I'm talking then. Would you like to make a little easy money?"

"Are you a fool, or do you think I'm one?"

"Come, come. This isn't a confidence trick, you know." Huggins laughed rather nervously, but his spirit was still secure. "You've been opposing the new garden-village building scheme with Kingsport."

"I have."

"You think it'll send the rates up."

"It will."

"You can't afford higher rates."

"No one can."

"Quite so. But that's not the only reason, is it? You're not doing this just for your own sake, are you? If you could see your way round it, you would, wouldn't you? If you could use this building scheme as a way of saving Maythorpe, you wouldn't chuck it all up, would you?"

"I don't know what you mean."

"All right. All right. You will in a minute." Huggins' deep belly chuckle reverberated in the bright morning. He was looking down at the dark domain of Maythorpe, shrouded with trees, flanked by its colonies of buildings; no one would want to lose that noble property.

"You've got three paddocks up by the Skerrow road."

"I have."

"About fifty acres."

"Seventy-three."

"As much as that? All the better. You've been trying to sell them."

"Oh. D'you want 'em?"

"I wouldn't mind 'em, if I had the cash. But I'm a poor man. I've only got a tip for you—stick to them."

"Indeed? Why?"

"Stick to 'em, man, and pray God that Leame Ferry Waste's bought by the council. Don't you realise what'll happen to all that property?"

"What's all this?"

"In a few months those paddocks will be valuable building sites and you'll make enough on the sale to pay interest on your mortgage for a couple of years at least, I shouldn't wonder."

They had come to the stack-yard gate. Huggins hoped that Carne would invite him back to the house for dinner. He was hungry. He knew of the hospitality of Maythorpe. After all, he had come to do Carne a service. The least the farmer could do was to invite him to a meal.

But Carne stopped, leaning back against the gate post, his hands in his breeches' pockets, and stared insolently at the preacher.

"What's your game? Why d'you come to me like this?"

Huggins smiled.

"I want to see this housing scheme go through. I know slums. I was born in one. So was Snaith. We're out to abolish 'em. But we know your influence on the council. We don't want to fight you. We'd rather you came in with us."

Snaith's name was a talisman. It stiffened the ground under Huggins' feet.

"Come in with you on what?"

"Well, obviously land values are going up all round there. At least they will, when once the site of the new scheme is publicly known. You remember what happened at Clixon. As a matter of fact, two or three of us have an acre or two here and there round the wastes now. It's worth nothing now, but just wait a month or two."

"I see. I see." Carne nodded. "Some of you have been buying up land so that you can sell it to the council if that site is chosen?"

"That's the idea. More or less."

"And you want me to do the same?"

"Want you? I want nothing. I'm just telling you for your own good."

"And all I have to do is to call off my opposition to the town planning scheme?"

"That's as you choose. But unless the scheme goes through, you get nothing from your land."

"I see."

It was dinner-time. The men were coming down to the Hinds' House for their midday meal. They had loosened out their horses from plough and harrow and rode sideways, the hanging harness clinking. Two by two the great beasts slouched down to the pond to drink. Carne leaned back against the gate and watched them. The riders greeted him as they passed, taking their place in a procession as rigid and formal as that of a diplomatic dinner. They called "Morning, Maister," touched caps and forelocks, and he saluted each with his friendly smile.

He'll never part from all this without a fight, thought Huggins. I've got him just at the right moment. The Lord sent me.

The horses plunged into the muddy water and bent their necks. Some waded deep to their bellies, running their twitching nostrils above the rippling surface. They drank with a gurgling and sucking sound, throwing back their heads with a rattling of chain and collar. The water tossed from their velvet muzzles. The first couple lurched up from the pond, the second, the third, the fourth, the fifth. Their great hoofs clopped, their accoutrements clinked, as they rolled down to the stables.

A gaggle of geese strutted along behind them, stretching white necks, squalling belligerently, glaring at Carne and Huggins with scornful, yellow-rimmed eyes. At last Carne spoke.

"You're suggesting that I should join your gang and help you to make a fortune out of cheating the council by buying up the Wastes before you decide to build there—eh?"

That was hardly how Huggins would have put it. He began to say so, mildly. A sheep dog bounded lightly across the yard and began to caress Carne's hand.

"Do you see that horse pond?" asked Carne.

"Yes—what of it?"

"Once, when a cheating liar of a dealer came here with as dirty a proposition as yours, I chucked him in," said the farmer. "What about it?"

"I don't know what you mean."

"Don't you? Then I'll tell you. You and your Snaith and Tadman and the rest of you are a lot of swindling, gambling thieves. It's you that make local government a dirty game. And I'm not just telling you. I shall tell the council; I shall tell the papers. And if you want to turn me off the council to save your skins—just try it."

"Oh, come now, Mr. Carne," began the preacher.

But Carne had seen his shepherd across the yard, and hailed him.

"Did you say you'd got a pair of black twins already?" he shouted.

"I have. You owe me half a crown, sir. You bet I wouldn't have 'em before Easter."

"Come on, then. Let's see 'em."

And, without a further glance at the baffled preacher, farmer and shepherd went into the fold yard. The eight foot wooden doors swung behind them with a crash. Huggins was left outside, hungry, humiliated, furious.

I'll make him pay for this. Thieves? We're not thieves. The fool, the pig-headed fool! I'll ring up Snaith to-night. All right, Mr. Squire Carne of Maythorpe! Wait till the March elections. You won't have a walk-over this time. By God, you won't!

CHAPTER IV

A PROCESSION PASSES THROUGH MAYTHORPE VILLAGE

On March 6th Castle died; on March 8th he was buried. That was only right and proper, and he had a handsome funeral. What was less seemly was that on this day also the elections were held for the county council.

Hicks and Pudsey argued over this in the stable early on that dark spring dawn. They had gone there with the wagoner and third lad at five o'clock to groom the horses for the funeral procession. Four big bays in a clean-scrubbed wagon were to bear Castle's body to the churchyard.

"Well, it's my idea we should have put off funeral till to-morrow," Hicks said.

"Wouldn't do. He's a fat man. He'd stink," objected Pudsey.

"Not in his coffin. There's many wait three days and longer. What about those bodies brought up from the south by train?"

"I remember in France there was a shell hole full of dead Jerries . . ." began the wagoner. But they hushed him up. His war-time recollections were apt to turn the third lad's stomach, and they did not want any accidents.

"I'll tell you this," Hicks declared. "It was damned dirty work putting up that fellow to oppose Carne anyhow. Who is this Dollan anyway?"

"Why, he's yon chap in the bungalow along Cold Harbour Road—retired solicitor."

"We all know that. What I want to know is who is he? Why is he here? Who's been getting at him?"

"They say he's a friend of Alderman Anthony Snaith," muttered the wagoner. He was polishing the vast flank of the shire horse till it shone like mahogany. The men had fixed lanterns to the hay racks. The yellow lights left the rest of the long stable in warm velvet darkness; beyond the shadows, the other horses stirred and coughed, or kicked against the wooden partitions, rattling the ropes of their halters through iron rings.

"Come over, lass," called third lad, hissing cheerfully. This early morning vigil, this funeral, this revealing political conversation by his elders, added enormously to his sense of sophistication. He'd have something to tell them when he next went to North Wirral. You mightn't get much money at Maythorpe, but by God, you did see life—the foreman dying on Tuesday, the master fighting an election on the Thursday, and a great funeral with cold dinner in the Hall kitchen.

All over the village great yellow posters announced on walls and hoardings:

"Vote for Dollan, the Progressive Candidate. Don't let Reactionaries starve your County."

Carne had refused to put up posters. He could not believe that any of his neighbours would vote for his opponent. He had held his one meeting as usual in the village. The third lad had attended it. He thought Carne a fine chap.

"You all know me. You know you can trust me. You knew my father before me," Carne had said, with that touch of awkwardness which passes in England for sincerity. "We've been through some bad times together. We all hope for better times. But we know that there's nothing to hope from crookedness and cheating. Up till now we've kept county politics clean. We mean to keep 'em so. If you send me back I'll do my best to stop any dirty games that men may play here."

The schoolroom had been only half full. Every one knew Carne. They knew too that he was in a bad way. Maythorpe Hall bore its own evidence of poverty. Perhaps it might be as well to try some one else. This fellow Dollan was a new-comer, but he was a South Riding man all right. Retired from Kingsport. A free spender. Grand gardener too. He'd done marvels at the bungalow called "Threeways." And a Wesleyan. That was something. Most villagers of Maythorpe were also Wesleyans.

The third lad had been along to Mr. Dollan's meetings too. They were much more lively. Mr. Dollan talked grandly about local government, about the people's Rights and real Democracy. It appeared from his speeches that the landowners had ground the faces of the poor for their own advantages. The unrepaired cottages, the inadequate water supply, the disgrace of rural slums like the Shacks—(Why a disgrace? thought the third lad)—were due to the iron hand of obstruction.

"Well, it's your own fault," shouted the lively Mr. Dollan. "If you want that sort of thing, you can have it. Do you like having open drains outside your front doors and earth closets stinking under your bedroom windows? Do you like having a school that's not fit for a pigsty, and risking diphtheria and scarlet fever and typhoid for the kiddies? All right. All right. I'm not stopping you. Go ahead. Vote for your local landowners. I shall be only too pleased not to have to spend petrol in going to Flintonbridge on your business."

"What I say is, it's just like Snaith's dirty game to send a man here when he knows Carne's down on his luck."

"All the same, I wish Maister'd put up a few posters," interpolated Pudsey. "Over in't village they like a bit of paper."

"What good did paper ever do any one?"

"Nay; I know nowt about that, but I'll tell you one thing," said the beast man. "My lass Peg's walking out with Nat Brimsley. An' Mrs. Brimsley's the sort of mother-in-law would put grey whiskers on a cat. But they say she's sweet on old Holly of the Shacks, an' if new Housing Estate's built near Kingsport, he'll get a job and maybe a house there an' she'll wed him. So's my lass can have Nat, and go to Cold Harbour."

"What's that to do with it?" demanded Hicks.

"Why, just this. Carne's out to stop 'em building, isn't he? And if he stops 'em building, there's no new home for Mrs. B. She won't go to Shacks. And if she doesn't get off with Holly, our home's no place for me with Peg stuck as a mule and Nat round every night mucking up kitchen till there's no place to sit for them canoodling."

This was too long a string of cause and effect for Hicks. All that he knew was that Carne was badly treated. Snaith was a snake in the grass, and Pudsey a fool and a drunkard and his girl no better than she ought to be. Death and contention overshadowed Hicks. A dumb misery of premonition oppressed him.

The dark stable smelled of straw and dust and horses and old leather harness. The third lad was brightening the brass ornaments for the breast bands and the collars, perched on the corn bin, spitting into the brass polish. The sour smell of blacking added its pungent flavour to the atmosphere. They were good smells. Hicks, bereaved of his own hunters, desolate and anxious, found solace in the farm stables that he had once despised. But Castle's death disturbed him, reminding him of the transitory nature of all human greatness. Brief life is here our portion.

Maythorpe had stood as firm as the plains and wolds of the South Riding. Cubbing, hunting, horse shows and point-to-points had been as much part of the perennial season as seed time and harvest. And now the hunters were sold, and Castle dead, a mortgage was on the farm, and an upstart opposed Carne in his own village.

The stable door creaked. Morning had come and the other lads were busy. It was time to set down the polished leather bands, the chains, the brushes, and go home for breakfast. Pudsey must water and feed his stock; from the cow shed came the steady spin of milk into the buckets.

Cocks crew from the cart shed. Fowls roosted in the low rafters, scattering their droppings over the great newly painted wagon which was to be Castle's bier.

Hicks left the dark stable for the grey stack-yard. A chill wind nipped his face. It might be fine, but it was bloody cold still. In the dim light he saw figures moving, Shepherd, up all night with his lambs, coming out of the fold yard, his dog like a shadow leaping and cringing round him; Dolly Castle mincing from the cowshed with the fresh milk for breakfast, the second lad after her, anxious to carry her bucket for a kind word as fee; another figure, taller than the rest, Carne, wakeful and uneasy, coming to see if the wagon was ready.

They stopped in the lee of a tall threshed oat-stack.

"Well, Hicks?"

"Aye, we're about through."

"Good."

In the meagre light Carne looked older, haggard. He had taken Castle's death badly. The groom watched him.

They said down in the village that he was taking more whisky than was good for him. Wasn't it enough to make any man want to drink?

It was of Carne that Hicks was thinking as he walked behind the wagon later that morning.

The Church of Holy Trinity, Maythorpe, stood nearly a mile southward from Maythorpe Hall. The squat grey tower was Norman, but the rest of the building was an architectural medley, fruit of various periods and diverse seasons of devotion. A fringe of tall black trees encircled the grave-yard, chestnuts and sycamores and elms. To their topmost boughs still clung the ragged ruins of last year's rookery. The rooks had nested high—sign of a fine summer, and that promise of good weather had been fulfilled. They were beginning to build again high in the trees, but the year was still cold. The hedges were covered with tight reddish buds. In the undergrowth of the ditches along the road purple dead-nettle, the silver-haired rosettes of giant thistles and green foliage of hedge-parsley announced the spring, yet a harsh wind whipped the mourners as they trudged to bury Castle.

The slouching pace was set by the heavy horses. Their harness shone, their brass tinkled as they trod forward, the steady rolling gait of the plough. The wagon creaked. Its sign "Robert Carne, Maythorpe" was almost the only part of its surface not covered by greenery. Laurels and burberry, privet and holly had been laid along its outboards. The coffin itself had been piled with bright spring flowers, tulips, and daffodils from Kingsport, snowdrops and aconites from the local gardens. Behind the wagon walked Mrs. Castle and Dolly, and young Castle limping upon his crutches. Carne had wanted Hicks to drive him, but he had refused, a prickly, difficult fellow.

Behind the Castles came Carne, behind Carne his fellow labourers. Cottagers came to the doors as the slow procession passed them. From almost every house at least one man or woman joined the mourners. This big genial man whom they were burying had been widely known and liked. He could tell a story, he could thatch a straw stack, he could clip a sheep or plough a furrow with the best of them. He had been strong and solid, jolly and undefeated. He had ruled his Hinds' House as a good head master manages a school, the young lads under him drawing some sense of power and pride from that authority. His wife had kept good table. He had been a kind neighbour, a friendly drinker. And he was dead.

A passing motor-car stopped to watch the procession. The townsmen had never seen anything quite like this before. Slowly, without thinking, they removed their hats. At the Nag's Head, a ghost was standing in the doorway. Lily Sawdon, leaning on Chrissie Beachall's arm, looked with envious eyes at the laden wagon. Tom slipped out from the door and joined the groom. "Couldn't get away before," he whispered. He was in his Sunday clothes, and a black tie. Grandpa Sellars limped out from his cottage, and took his place in the rear, mumbling and grunting. He had not thought that Castle would go before him, and the triumph of survival was worth the fatigue of walking.

As the horses turned the corner of the village street up to the churchyard, the off leader reared suddenly, almost knocked over by a car that whipped round the corner without sounding its horn, a gay car, hung with vivid yellow ribbons and great placards announcing:

"Vote for Dollan. Come to-day and save your county. Don't let reaction strangle local development."

The car was a big saloon; the street was narrow; the four-horse wagon took up more than half the room. The wagoner, who was driving, knew his business. He soothed the restive leader, got the others back into the middle of the road, and the car had to pull sideways on to the narrow pathway, and stay halted as the funeral procession passed.

As he came level with Dollan's car, the groom spat viciously.

"No good. Too late. He'll get in," muttered Sawdon.

"Get in?" gasped Hicks, incredulous.

"I'm afraid so. It's got out that Snaith's going to bring a libel action against Carne. It'll ruin him. He's up to the neck in debt already. They're saying too that he's selling Maythorpe for use as a madhouse. I've heard plenty of talk."

And it was so.

"They're saying too, Dollan's lot, that this do to-day comes under corrupt practices. They could sue him for it—giving a free feast to village on election day."

After the funeral there was to be a dinner in Maythorpe kitchen. That huge stone-paved room had been used before on many more festive occasions. Lady vocalists had sung there at war-time recruiting meetings. Trenchers had twirled there at Christmas parties. Holly had hung across the bacon hooks, with scarlet berries, and girls had been kissed, playing Postman's Knock, behind the half-closed door.

Now the big trestle tables were set for eighty. Beef and ham, bacon cakes and spice bread, apple pasties and great blocks of cheese, were spread along them, and urns were already singing on the banked fires. There was beer for the lads and port wine for the ladies and a drop of whisky for the veterans like Grandpa Sellars. Carne had promised Castle to bury him handsomely, and handsomely he had done it. What if this was election day? What if the laws were fussy? The Carnes of Maythorpe had never yet run a funeral meanly, and Castle had been in their service for fifty years.

Trouble might be closing in on the farm—debts, law suits, ruin; but Carne would keep his obstinate faith with Castle, his obstinate pride, his obstinate sense of honour.

The vicar had come down to the lych gate. His white surplice fluttered above the flowers, the white narcissi, the yellow trumpeting daffodils and the scarlet tulips, as the bearers shouldered the coffin from the cart.

"I am the resurrection and the life, saith the Lord."

Dolly Castle, brazen till now, red lipped and stubborn, bent her pretty head with a stifled sob.

"We brought nothing into this world and it is certain we can carry nothing out. The Lord gave and the Lord hath taken away; blessed be the name of the Lord."

Carne followed his foreman's body through the grave-yard, into the porch, into the crowded church.

"I said, I will take heed to my ways," read the vicar, "that I offend not in my tongue. I will keep my mouth as it were with a bridle: while the ungodly is in my sight."

It was not true; Carne had not bridled his tongue; he had offended; he had taken no heed to his reckless wilful ways. He would bury his foreman with pomp and feast his neighbours; his debts were unpaid; his enemies in Kingsport were discussing warrants for libel with their lawyers.

"My heart was hot within me, and while I was thus musing the fire kindled; and at last I spake with my tongue."

He, Carne, the silent man, had spoken; the fire had kindled; he had done for himself, though he did not yet quite know it.

"Lord, let me know mine end, and the number of my days: that I may be certain how long I have to live."

The doctor at Manchester had said:

"If you go slowly, you're a youngish man, there's no knowing. You might have another attack. You might live till seventy. But I must warn you. Your heart's in a pretty poor condition. You've had two attacks. Any sudden exertion, any anxiety . . . I wouldn't promise anything."

"Hear my prayer, O Lord, and with thine ears consider my calling: hold not thy peace at my tears.

"For I am a stranger with thee: and a sojourner, as all my fathers were.

"O spare me a little, that I may recover my strength: before I go hence, and be no more seen."

That night, after counting votes in the school house, it was announced that Mr. Stanley Dollan had been elected County Councillor for Maythorpe by a majority of forty-seven votes.

CHAPTER V

THE HEAD MISTRESS INTRODUCES A GOVERNOR

On March 15th Kiplington High School was to be inspected by Miss Emily Teasdale.

Sarah had met her in London, knew and liked her. She looked forward with confidence to her visit. She was aware of the merits of her staff and pupils. Seated at her desk, preparing for Miss Teasdale, she reviewed in her mind Miss Masters' energy, the devotion of Miss Parsons, the vitality of Miss Becker, and the brisk ability of Miss Vane, Miss Sigglesthwaite's successor. She regretted bitterly that for this term Lydia was missing, but she had planned herself to coach the girl twice weekly; next term her father might be married, and then at last the star pupil could settle down to work uninterrupted.

As for the school's defects, its indifferent buildings, the abominable cloakrooms, the cramped and distant games field, Sarah hoped for as adverse a report as possible. A real denunciation from Miss Teasdale might wake up the governors a little and strengthen her own hand in her fight for bricks and mortar.

She expected the inspector at half-past eleven. Miss Teasdale was motoring herself from Kingsport.

Sarah had been teaching for the first period and her unopened correspondence still lay on her office desk. She and Dolores had had one of their weekly arguments, and Sarah still felt a little deflated and limp in consequence. If only Pip would hurry up before I go mad, she thought. It had been easy to get rid of Miss Sigglesthwaite; but Miss Jameson stuck like a limpet to her job.

With quick precision Sarah opened her letters, cutting the envelopes neatly, sorting their contents—business, receipts, bills, estimates and the rest of them—letters from parents or staff about school vacancies—personal communications. She received fewer and fewer of this third category. She had become increasingly absorbed in her professional affairs. She neglected her friends. The school, the school, the school filled her deliberate mind. "You're becoming a monomaniac," Pattie had told her.

There was one envelope addressed in a slanting scholarly hand which was familiar. Sarah unfolded the thin blue paper and read:

"26a Canning Terrace, Tunbridge Wells, March 13th, 1934.

"MY DEAR MISS BURTON,"

It was from Miss Sigglesthwaite. A wave of nausea rocked in Sarah's mind. She still felt that she had treated Miss Sigglesthwaite shabbily. She had given her rope to hang herself, longing to replace her. She had sacrificed her and secured her efficient Miss Vane, fresh from Cambridge. She had let her become the victim of bad mass-bullying, and had left unpunished the ringleader of her tormentors.

With stern self-discipline Sarah compelled herself to read the letter.

"MY DEAR MISS BURTON,

You may doubtless be wondering why you have not heard from me. I apologise for any lack of courtesy, but knowing your kind thoughts for me I waited till I had cheerful news to send.

"I can now report that my own health has already shown great improvement, and that I have found another post.

"I am now installed as daily companion to an elderly lady living here who is almost blind. I conduct her correspondence for her, read to her, and wheel her out when it is fine in a bath chair. You would be amused at her literary tastes, and so am I. I shall soon become an expert in the works of Ruby M. Ayres, Pamela Wynne and Ursula Bloom. Do you know any of these novelists? I assure you that they have opened up a new world to me. My salary is not princely, but as I can live at home, we have been able to give up our maid and my sister does the housework while I relieve her at night, by looking after our poor mother, so I think with care we shall be able to manage if we can both retain our health.

"And now, my dear Miss Burton, may I at last be allowed to thank you, not only for your extreme kindness to me after my breakdown, but for your more than generous and heartening letter which arrived last week? Please believe me that I shall never forget your patience with my shortcomings; and your sympathy when they proved at last too much for me. I realise that I should have retired earlier, but you know my circumstances, and I am more than grateful that you never uttered one word of reproach.

"I shall always watch from afar your career in the world of teaching with the warmest interest, remembering how in your youth and vigour you found generosity enough to show kindness to my stupidity and failure. I feel sure that you will go far and I shall always rejoice in your well-deserved success.

"Believe me, yours gratefully and sincerely, "AGNES SIGGLESTHWAITE."

Sarah laid the letter on her desk, and sat staring out to the sea. A fishing smack with a brown sail dipped and tossed there and sometimes disappeared. Sarah held her breath till it re-emerged, but she was not really thinking of it. She was picturing the tall lank woman pushing her employer about in a bath chair through the streets of Tunbridge Wells, her hair pins tinkling behind her to the pavement, her skirt unbuttoned, her jumper gaping above her waist belt, her mild chin quivering below her sensitive mouth. She could hear her cultured voice pronouncing with its habitual precision the declarations of love, the luxurious descriptions of feminine underwear, the conflicts of vice with virtue, so frequently encountered in her employer's favourite literature.

"So there goes the most distinguished scientist we have ever had on our staff—or ever will have," she thought, and her heart rebuked her.

The simple generosity and goodness of Agnes Sigglesthwaite were too much for her. She had become morbidly self-reproachful for her part in that affair. She had lain awake telling herself that she had sacrificed the science mistress for Midge Carne, that it was Midge whom she should have sent away, that the child was hysterical, vain, a centre of exaggerated emotion, an unhealthy influence in the school.

She forgot the weeks when she had sheltered Miss Sigglesthwaite in her own house, sitting with her at night and reading to her, pouring into her exhausted mind the optimism and resilience of her own unstaled philosophy. She forgot her unstinted efforts to beat the sickness and sorrow of the over-burdened woman. She only remembered that her kindness had been mingled with impatience, her benevolence soured by her planning mind.

"A companion to a blind lady who lives here." And it's my fault, she groaned in spirit. She put the letter in the basket marked "to be answered," and picked up the next one.

But the telephone rang, and when she lifted the receiver she heard her friend Joe Astell calling to her in his hoarse and breathless voice.

It brought some comfort to her. The knowledge of his sympathy and support had meant much to her during the past difficult weeks. She knew that he liked and respected her, and his appreciation helped her to retain a modicum of her own self-respect.

"Hallo! Oh, it's you, Joe."

"I rang up to wish you luck. This is the great morning of your inspection, isn't it?"

"Oh, how nice of you. Yes—in about half an hour she's coming."

"Well. You'll be all right. The school's all right. You're doing a grand piece of work. I just rang up to tell you so in case you might forget."

How kind of him. How kind of him. Her heart was warmed and reassured by his goodness. People were kind. People were nice.

For no reason that she could imagine, she found herself fumbling for her handkerchief. The intrusive tears that now so often pricked her eyeballs were at their inconvenient game again. The slightest thing nowadays, and she wanted to cry. Ridiculous.

She was blowing her nose when Miss Masters knocked and came in.

"Oh, I just wanted to ask you. That new anthology—The English Galaxy. Do you think one can let the lower Fifth just have a free run in it? If Miss Teasdale asks me what they're reading shall I show her that?"

"I should think so. Is this it?"

She took the volume and idly opened it. She read the first poem on the first page.

"O western wind, when wilt thou blow That the small rain down can rain? Christ, that my love were in my arms And I in my bed again!"

A pain more physical than mental wrenched her. She wanted to howl aloud in her wild wretchedness. She bowed herself low over the desk and muttered.

"Yes. I remember the book. It's good, I think," and held her breath till the young English mistress closed the door.

Then she sprang up and began to pace her room. Oh, God! she thought, what fool was it who said that work heals longing? Had she not drowned and choked and stifled herself with work? Not a detail escaped her; not an opportunity had she neglected. She had hurled herself upon Kiplington High School with energy sufficient to have saved Napoleon's retreat from Moscow. She had bullied governors, lobbied education officers, flattered parents, scolded and charmed and petted her staff and pupils.

But at a word, a name, the phrase of a waltz, a silly line of doggerel, she was up and tramping as she tramped now across her office, her hands pressing her aching breasts, her veins empoisoned, the Nessus shirt of humiliation scorching her.

Christ, that my love were in my arms!

She could not escape him.

All through the Christmas holidays she had waited at her sister's home for him to write. At first she had tortured herself because he was ill; he might be dying, and she could get no news of him. Then Astell wrote to tell her of his own most recent campaigns on behalf of the housing scheme, and his successes, and mentioned Carne as a defeated enemy. He was alive, then; but sent no word to her. Had he been shocked? Had he been embarrassed? Had he been sickened by her crude pursuit?

Night after night she agonised, in forced inaction, living through their brief hours in each other's company, picturing herself as he might see her—the images growing more cruel every hour. A schoolmistress of forty, ugly, clumsy, vulgar, not a lady, with big, reddish hands and a head too large for her small body—a blacksmith's daughter and he was a snob. An elementary schoolgirl, aggressive, sharp of tongue. She compared herself with the portrait of Muriel Sedgmire, lacerating herself with his wife's beauty.

She no longer criticised him. He might be obstructive, stubborn, stupid; his values might be anti-social, his vision narrow. But he was hers, hers, hers; and she could not touch him. She had seen him completely disarmed, helpless, unconscious, wracked by pain, beyond all control or knowledge, and she loved him the more for it.

It was herself whom now she criticised, her age, her manner, the flaws of her mind and body. Well she knew the shape of her sister's bedroom. Had she not lain there, extravagantly burning the electric light till four and five in the morning, because she could not bear to lie in darkness, watching the image of the man she loved forming and melting against the night?

She remembered every detail of their growing friendship—the first encounter at the governor's meeting, the quarrel in the snow on Maythorpe cliff, the night at Minton Riggs when the calf was born, the anxious evenings and dawns when Midge was ill. Again she held back the curtain for him and they watched the sun rising out of the sea—all the world a melting dazzle of pale primrose and silver. Again she sat in front of his fire talking about the future of Midge, when Mrs. Beddows came and found them together. Fate had compelled them to share birth and death and sickness; conspiring to force them into a rare intimacy.

Oh, why did I spoil that? Why did I spoil that? Why couldn't I leave well alone? I could have helped him. I could have been his friend. I could have comforted him. She saw herself growing old beside him, in honourable and enduring intimacy, relying upon him, as she relied upon Joe Astell, whom she could ring up for counsel at any hour, to whom she could tell almost anything.

But she had destroyed all that, and he avoided her. Terrible things had happened. He was ill; she knew that. She had made intensive inquiries about angina pectoris. She knew now the measure of his physical danger.

He was ruined. Every one said that Maythorpe could not last till harvest.

Then he had lost his seat on the council. She had heard about that. He had been wild, they said, with jealousy and malice. (She did not believe that, but she knew him to be obstinate and reckless.) He had spread rumours that Snaith and Huggins dealt in corrupt practices. Snaith had served a writ for libel against him, for a speech that he had made in his election campaign. Snaith was claiming three thousand pounds in damages. He could never pay it. He would fight, and then he would be ruined.

Oh fool, fool, fool, she cried to the ghost inhabiting her heart, can't you see they'll destroy you? Oh my dear, my love, why must you be so stubborn?

But the ghost was unresponsive; the man eluded her. She had never seen him since that night in the hotel. Midge was now boarding with the Beddows, so he no longer drove in his cart to fetch her. He had not come to the last governors' meeting. His name was on every casual lip, because of his spectacular prelude to failure; but Sarah could not even speak to him.

I have lost him, her heart cried. It is all my own fault. Oh, why, why, why?

She could find no comfort, for she had thrown away the one chance she had ever had of being his friend.

If only he were not menaced by death she could bear it better; but the thought that any hour might be his last tormented her. He will die, he will die, and I shall never see him.

Twenty times she wrote notes to him; twenty times she tore them up again.

If he would speak to me. If I could have him alone, only for five minutes. If I could see him, tell him just what I feel for him—that I am his friend, that I don't care what he thinks of me, that I don't even care if he dislikes me, so long as he knows that I stand by him, that I am here always, loving him, trusting him, caring for him.

Christ, that my love were in my arms!

The parlourmaid tapped at the door and entered. Sarah stood still, expecting Emily Teasdale.

"Mr. Carne to see you. Mr. Carne of Maythorpe."

She heard his heavy tread along the passage. She dropped into her chair. Her knees were water.

"Let him come in," she said.

He came in.

Drums banged in her head. The walls of her room contracted, swelled, contracted. Disks of blackness floated before her eyes. I'm going to faint, she thought. That would be a judgment on me. She knew that he was standing in front of her desk waiting for her to speak. With an effort that seemed to tear her heart from her body, she raised her head and faced him.

"Good-morning," she said. She could hear her voice, dry and small. "You're quite a stranger. Won't you sit down?"

With astonishment she thought: But he isn't ill! I've never seen him look better. There was more grey in his hair, but his eyes were bright, his usually dead white skin bronzed a little by exposure to wind and rain, the lines round his mouth relaxed. She had been torturing herself because he was dying and he wasn't ill at all. He had defrauded her. She remembered her wakeful nights, her suspense, her misery, and was suddenly very angry.

He sat down and smiled at her—not intimately, but with a kind of liberation, as though he too were unexpectedly relieved of something.

"Good-morning," he said formally. "I couldn't come to the last governors' meeting."

"So I understood."

"But I've just got the minutes and I see that you've managed to persuade the other governors to promise you fresh buildings if the new housing estate goes through."

"I shall need them."

"It's perfectly ridiculous."

"Don't you realise that I shall probably double my numbers?"

"Who's going to pay for them?"

"The rate-payers and the Board of Education."

"The rate-payers. Because the rates have gone up I suppose you think you can get anything?"

"Not at all. I only ask for what is reasonable. I feel I may be more likely to get it now."

"Since the elections?"

"Yes. The new county council seems quite sensible."

"Because people like me aren't there any longer?"

"Perhaps."

Her anger was fed by the flame which had consumed her since December. Lips tightly compressed, eyes bright, she faced him, small and furious, in arms against everything that he stood for. She could not believe that last time she had seen him he had tossed moaning upon her bed; she could not believe that she had lain weeping for him every night since then. She saw his solid body, his dark brown tweed suit, his bowler hat (who can feel romantic about a man who wears a bowler hat? she asked herself), the obstinate lines of his big handsome face. She thought, what a fool he is! She thought, he's just like Mussolini.

"I suppose you think that because I've been got rid of from the council I'm going to retire from all public work? You're wrong."

"I hadn't thought very much about it," she lied.

"You're very thick just now with Snaith and Astell. Perhaps you don't know that they have been organising one of the worst pieces of corruption that has been practised in the South Riding Council since it started?"

"I've heard that you've been saying so, but it isn't proved yet."

"Naturally you stick up for your friends."

"Naturally."

"You're hoping that I shall resign from the Board of Governors and leave you a free hand."

"I hadn't thought about it."

"Then I'm telling you." He leant across the desk. He too was furious now. His eyes were blazing. Their faces almost touched in their burning rage. "I shall do nothing of the kind. I intend to stay as long as I can. I shall denounce your fine friends and do my utmost to keep down your mad extravagance."

"I warn you. You're making a fool of yourself. You think you can stop progress and reason. You can't, any more than you can make the moon stand still."

"Why should you think that your ways are progressive?"

"I know what I'm doing."

"Do you?"

She read into that question all his contempt for her self-betrayal. She had flung herself at his head and now he mocked her.

She sprang up, so that even from her few inches she could look down on him.

"I can't understand why you let me have your daughter at my school if that's what you think of me," she cried, answering, not what he had said, but what her heart said. "But let me tell you it's no privilege for us to keep her. She is without exception the most tiresome, hysterical, unwholesome, worst-mannered child I've ever had to deal with, and I shall be delighted if you take her away."

Then he got up too, and his control deserted him.

"You are asking me to remove my daughter?"

"I shall be delighted."

As he grew hot, she grew cold.

They faced each other.

"You may think that as a governor you confer an inestimable privilege on the school by leaving her here. I assure you that really we can do quite well without her. And without her father upon the board."

"The matter hardly rests in your choice."

He looked so comical, blazing down at her, his great jaw out-thrust, his bowler hat in his hand, that she broke into a bubble of laughter.

"Really, I do love your notion of governoratorial behaviour. You come bounding in here like a bucolic Mussolini and expect me sit down meekly under your denunciations. And there's a lady bird crawling up your collar. If you had the slightest notion how funny you looked!"

"Damn and blast you, woman!"

She thought that he was going to strike her and smiled up at him, receptive, mocking, inviting him to lay his hands on her, when she heard the parlourmaid's shrill and childish voice announce "Miss Teasdale, m'am, to see you."

She spun round as the urbane handsome school inspector entered.

Carne's reactions were less rapid.

"Oh, Miss Teasdale, how are you?" cried Sarah, over-effusive, on the crest of a wave of hysteria yet unbroken, which never now would break. "It is nice to see you again. You found your way all right? Do come in. This is one of our governors, Mr. Carne, of Maythorpe."

She caught a glimpse of a huge dark lowering figure, Jove from the thunder cloud, heard a rumbling mutter, saw an inclination which might be a bow or a menace, and he was gone.

"One of your local problems?" smiled Emily Teasdale, who liked Sarah.

"One of my local problems," agreed Sarah, and her high light laughter rang down the passage after him.

She hoped he heard it.

CHAPTER VI

CARNE RIDES SOUTH

When Carne strode out of Sarah Burton's office, he was furious. He experienced all the physical symptoms of discordant passion. His pulses thumped in his temples, his throat was dry, his palms moist with perspiration, his breath rapid; but as he left the High School and walked rapidly down the street to his lawyer's office, he was surprised to find how soon his rage diminished.

For the fact was that part of him had really enjoyed the quarrel. He was the hot-tempered son of a hot-tempered father, and for many years he had suffered from the necessity of controlling his turbulent nature. The women with whom he had been most closely associated, his mother, whom he had loved and who had died, Muriel whom he adored and feared, Midge for whom he felt troubled solicitude, Elsie who gave notice if even mildly rebuked, were not of the type to whom a man can let himself go. One of the attractive qualities about Sarah Burton was the sense of robust self-confidence which she gave him. A real red-head, a fighter; she could look after herself. He felt at home with her and had, though he hardly knew it, gone out of his way to pick a quarrel with her as a self-prescribed tonic for his over-strained, exhausted nerves.

He had, indeed, a wretched day ahead of him. For the rest of the morning he sat closeted with Briggs, hearing exactly what kind of a fool his lawyer thought him. Within his heart he was almost growing sorry that he had ever called Snaith a thief and Huggins a cheating swindler. But since it seemed that he was beaten anyhow, he might just as well go down in a grand uproar as retire meekly from the South Riding. If he could expose this scandal before he went, he would at least leave his mark upon the county; he might not check corruption, but he would not be forgotten.

So he spent his morning with Briggs and his afternoon with his bank manager. He had decided to sacrifice Maythorpe; that was clear. The bank must take it, and if it sold the place to the Public Health Committee, that was its own business. After all, Midge was provided for; Sedgmire would pay for Muriel; Carne could go to that riding school outside Manchester.

It seemed odd to him that he was so indifferent. Perhaps when everything was lost, one cared no longer. Odd too that he could not see himself in Manchester. He did not really believe that he would ever lead out hacks for the fat wives of manufacturers, nor teach Lancashire schoolgirls how to groom their horses. Before the summer was over, he would have left the county; he would have begun a new life. But he just did not believe it.

On his way from the bank he met Mrs. Beddows, walking.

"Where are you off to?" she asked.

"Home now. I'm just fetching my horse."

"And I'm just off to the High School. Sybil's picking me up there and going to drive us home. They've had the inspector to-day."

"I know. I saw her." Carne heard himself chuckle.

"When did you see her?"

"This morning. Fine big woman."

"What were you doing up there this morning?"

He rubbed his chin with a shy boyish movement. Then he smiled at his friend.

"Having a grand blow up with Sarah Burton. My word, she's got a temper, hasn't she?"

"You mean you have. Whatever were you quarrelling over?"

"Blest if I know now. Oh, yes. The new buildings. You know, really, she asks a bit too much. She practically told me to take Midge away."

"Robert! It's not serious?"

"Not on my part."

"Can I tell her so?"

"If you want to." His curious buoyancy took possession of him. Uncharacteristically he added, "Give her my love and tell her she's a grand lass. I wouldn't miss quarrelling with her for a great deal."

But when Mrs. Beddows reached the High School, Sybil and Wendy and Midge were already waiting, Sarah closeted with Miss Teasdale, and the message, which was no more than a joke at most, went undelivered.

It was nearly six o'clock before Carne handed a shilling to the ostler and rode Black Hussar out of the inn yard.

The evening was wild with wind and clear with the lucid radiance of a stormy sunset. The big black horse pounded heavily across the cobbles and out on to the smooth cemented road. It had been raining heavily, and the polished surface was wet with showers and silvered with opalescent oil.

"Steady, boy, steady." Carne reproved his horse. "You're not in for the Grand National." He did not want him slipping and straining his back again.

He trotted briskly on to the esplanade. A heavy pall of cloud overhung the sea. Waves crashed in foam round the solid breakwaters. The gulls blew screaming about a livid sky, but to the west, over the level land, a glory of liquid gold flooded the fields.

If I'm not back soon, I shall be caught in a storm, Carne told himself, and decided to take the short cut along the cliffs.

He passed Dr. Dale, cycling home from a missionary talk; he passed Astell, taking the air after work at his printing press; he saw Huggins swaggering cheerfully from Drew's office. He buttoned his coat against the buffeting wind, and turned his horse towards the south cliff path.

On his way home he had arranged to call on Dickson. He should catch him just before his evening round with the milk. Carne had given his three tenants notice, and had been arranging with the bank that they might buy their own land on easy terms. These were the men who could make modern farming pay, smallholders, milkmen, who asked only peasants' incomes, and set all their families to work for them in the fields and buildings.

Came felt no enmity for his successors. He felt extraordinarily little enmity for any one, even for the defrauding councillors whom he fought. Though he attributed his failure to their malice, his loss of his seat on the council to their opposition, he was amazed at the lightness of his spirit.

That young doctor in Manchester had cured him of all enduring bitterness or hatred.

For Robert Carne was in his way, a religious man. He worshipped the creator of earth and heaven, the Lord of Harvest, the Ancient of Days and Seasons, who had in his beneficent providence ordained that Yorkshire should be the greatest county in England, which was the grandest country in the world, the motherland of the widest empire, the undoubted moral leader of civilisation, the mistress of the globe. He worshipped the God of order who had created farmers lords of their labourers, the county and the gentry lords over the farmers, and the King lord above all his subjects under God. He worshipped the contrast of power and humility implied in his religion, and on Sunday evenings, in the pew which was his property, sang that God had put down the mighty from their seat, and had exalted the humble and meek, with no effect upon his social principles.

He had attended funerals and memorial services; he knew that man who is born of woman cometh up and is cut down, like a flower, fleeth as it were a shadow, and never continueth in one stay. His mother had died when he was a boy; his father, a powerful and passionate man, during his son's brief honeymoon with Muriel Sedgmire.

Carne knew all about death. He had seen it on the hunting field and on the race-course, he had seen it during air-raids on the remount depôt where he had served in France. He had himself risked death a hundred times as sportsman and as soldier.

But he had never thought very much about it.

And now he knew that he lived under a threat, and quite calmly, since as a farmer he was trained to accept what was inevitable, he had come to terms with life.

Quietly and unobtrusively, on his return from Manchester, he had prepared himself for death, sitting up late at night in the small smoking-room, clipping elastic bands round rolls of paper, adding, subtracting, reckoning. His affairs were all in order.

He was tired. Never in all his life, not after the longest day's hunting, not after devastating scenes with Muriel, had he known such devitalising, such complete fatigue. His arms ached; a compression wound itself about his chest; he found himself muttering as he rode about the fields: I'm so tired. Oh, God—I'm so tired. Yet he was curiously little troubled.

A burden of responsibility had fallen from him. Always since he was a boy he had carried it. As eldest son, farmer, squire, husband, landlord, father, he had shouldered his obligations to other people.

But now he had been released. He was going to die. Somebody else must assume that burden for him. Somebody else must mend the roof of Dickson's cowshed. Somebody else must expose corruption on the council. Somebody else must restrain the High School governors from indulging in extravagant new buildings. Somebody else must buy party frocks for Midge, take her to the dentist, and decide whether she should have special drill for her round shoulders.

It would have surprised Astell, meditating upon his own valediction to the South Riding, to realise how Carne, riding home along the cliffs to Maythorpe, thought with pride and anxiety of his own work on the council. He really believed that by fighting Socialism, expenditure and pauperism he was serving his generation and his people. So long as he lived he would strive for his principles, but death meant an easy surrender of his sword to any one wise enough to take and wield it.

He feared no more. His worst moment had come and he had survived it. Sitting at his desk in the small smoking-room, using the last sheets of his handsome expensive note-paper, he had written his first and last letter to Lord Sedgmire. After that, no other ordeal was intolerable. He had met his father-in-law on two occasions. There had been the interview when he went to Shropshire to declare his love, and announce that he intended to marry Muriel. That had been a tremendous scene. Lord Sedgmire had stamped up and down the great gaunt silver gallery and finally ordered Carne out of his house for ever. Lady Sedgmire, in her winged satin chair, had cursed and wept until her companion—a trained mental nurse—had conducted her, wailing and prophesying, from the room.

Carne had not gone home then. He had settled himself down at the local inn and waited till, on the following midnight, Muriel, superfluously dramatic, had climbed from her window and come to him, bright-eyed, furious, in a mackintosh, calling, "Take me in! Take me in! I cannot bear it!" So he had taken her—there—before the wedding, and married her three days later in London by special licence.

It had been a nine days' wonder, a society elopement, a grand news story. The gossip columnists of two continents had reported how Lord Sedgmire's daughter, the beauty of three seasons, had been locked in her room by irate parents, and run away with a polo-playing farmer. There had been photographs of Muriel in her court dress, and photographs of Carne in his polo kit, Carne holding a cup won in a point-to-point, Carne, in his velvet cap, riding to covert.

He had never been surprised that Lord Sedgmire hated him. He shared his father-in-law's prejudices. He thought the publicity perfectly appalling. He never understood Muriel's obvious enjoyment of it.

Only once again did he see Lord Sedgmire. In 1918 he had returned from France to find his infant daughter a little squirming red rat in the nurse's arms, and his wife quietly raving with a persistent monotony which terrified him, and the doctors gravely diagnosing mental derangement.

He had driven his sluggish temperament then to rapid action. He had engaged nurses, sent for specialists. Everything that could be done, he had done. And when the final verdict was known, the disease named, defined and docketed, Carne had travelled down again to Shropshire, and called for the second time on his wife's family, to announce the outcome of their ill-omened marriage.

It never occurred to him to evade the interview. All his life he had ridden straight at his fences. He faced his father-in-law and told him that, as the result of childbirth, his wife had lost her mental balance, and the doctors doubted her complete recovery.

"You knew her mother went that way?" Sedgmire asked, his white eyebrows bristling ferociously.

"Muriel told me," Carne said, "after we were married."

"I suppose you blame me, eh? Want me to take her back now—damaged goods, hey?"

"I'm damned if I do, sir. But I thought I ought to tell you."

"All right, my boy. Very right and proper. If ever you've had enough of her, I'll take her back. Make proper provision for her. But on conditions, you know. On conditions. You'll have to give her up and leave her alone."

Carne's jaw had set. His stubborn smile had stiffened itself on his troubled face. He had stalked out of that house all pride and independence, vowing never to take a farthing from the Sedgmires, but to give Muriel every luxury of treatment or of comfort that money could buy.

He had kept his vow until he learned that at any moment he might cease to be able to write another cheque. Then he sat down and curtly explained the situation, declaring that as long as he lived and earned, he could keep Muriel, but if he died, there was money adequate for Midge alone.

But even now, in his new and strange tranquillity, his mind shied from the memory of that letter and of his father-in-law's unexpectedly kind reply. Something warm and genial in the old man touched a chord of sentiment in Carne's heart. He still loved lords. He still was proud to be Lord Sedgmire's son-in-law. But the whole episode was too painful for voluntary recollection.

Riding south now, between the glazed purpling furrows and the white leaping waves, he escaped as usual from memory into judgment. He cast an experienced eye across the fields. Foster's out ploughing late, he thought. That's just it with smallholders. No trade union regulations, no tribunals. You can get on when you work on your own.

Those seeds are forward. I wonder if we can persuade Naylor to get the lambs out early enough this spring.

There was a yearly battle between shepherd and farmer. Carne preferred his seeds and lambs to grow up together, nourishing each other, Naylor, his eye on the lambs alone, liked to keep them under his eye as long as possible, in the paddocks round the farm.

A wheeling flock of seagulls screamed and circled up from the cliff. The black horse started and slithered on treacly clay. The path had been kneaded to the texture of butter by the small pointed hooves of a flock of ewes. A burst of sleet blew suddenly from the sea, stinging Carne's face. He must hurry on but the path was bad, worse than he had believed it. He dared not canter on such a slippery surface. He flapped his rein and started forward into the long easy hacking trot of the riding farmer.

He was still thinking of Muriel. She haunted him as he rode south against the storm. Always until now he had reproached himself because he had married her and marriage had destroyed her. But now from his new-found assurance and pride of death, he could see the situation with greater justice. He had not pursued her; she had pursued him. From the beginning the choice, the initiative, had been hers and not his.

He loved her. He had been shaken by amazement at their first meeting, profoundly stirred by her beauty, her courage, her spirit. But it would never have occurred to him to cross the barrier which divides the county from sporting farmers. He was temperamentally conventional and emotionally docile. He would have served her in silence and lent her horses, sought for her picture in the Tatler, cherished her memory, and married a tennis-playing lawyer's daughter from Kingsport. But Muriel had willed it otherwise.

It was she who manoeuvred their more frequent meetings. It was she who got herself invited again in the spring to the South Riding. It was she who persuaded him to buy a two-guinea ticket for the Hunt Ball at Lessill Grange. It was she who led the way to the high north tower. The leads were flat there, and artificial battlements gave a castellated effect to the nineteenth-century building. The snow powdered the roof and outlined the gables. She drew away from him and leaned in her scarlet cloak against the broken parapet, her face upturned to the moon. The swing and beat of a waltz rose from the unseen ballroom. Afraid of her, afraid of himself, afraid of her fierce charm for him and of his clumsy troubled passion, he said, "It's cold up here. Hadn't we better go back to the others?" Her high disdainful voice was cold as the frost. "By all means. Go down. I should hate you to catch cold." And he, "But you? I'm all right. It's you who'll catch cold." And she, "But I'm not going down." Incredulous and stupid, he gasped, "Eh? What did you say?" She stamped her satin shoe on the white snow, and cried, "I'm not going. I don't want to go. Don't you see, you fool? I don't want to go back to them—ever?"

To this moment, riding against the twilight storm, he could feel again that tumult of his senses as he blustered, "But you must, you know. Your people will be waiting." "My people!" Her high shrill laughter flicked him. "Always thinking of my people, aren't you? Oh, my dear Robert. What an impossible snob you are."

Snob? Snob? Of course, he always thought of her people. Was it not her family which divided them? He stared at her, torn, furious, intimidated, not knowing how to take her—never knowing how to take her.

Then suddenly came the moment when she had swayed recklessly backwards, hanging out, her hands clutching the stone, over the black dizzy air. Still halting, stupid, he had stood there protesting, "That's dangerous. Come back, Miss Sedgmire." And she, laughing, jeered, "I'm not coming back. Don't you see? I'm not coming back. I don't want my people. I don't want comfort. If you want me, come and get me. Look?" And she dropped her hold and leaned back, her arms outstretched to him, so that if he had not leapt forward, always quicker to move than to speak in any crisis, and caught hold of her hands, she must have fallen, down from the tower to the paved court below.

He had never understood her. Did she mean to do it? Did she really mean to kill herself unless he caught her? For once she lay in his arms his leaping instincts spoke louder than all the cautious faltering of his mind. Later he was to learn that her recklessness had no limit. The final barrier which less abnormal people set between themselves and complete foolhardiness had been omitted from her composition. But he never knew her, never, never. In all her fears and rages, her tempestuous outraging of conventionalities, her insolent mockery, her melting tenderness, she remained a stranger to him, lovely, enchanting, perilous, incalculable.

Nothing had happened as he had expected. She had flouted the county, upsetting rectors and insulting squires. She had been charming to his poorer relations, bewildering in her bonhomie to his farm labourers; Hicks and the men and the villagers adored her; she rode like a wild cat, danced like a bacchante, and took her own wild way from Maythorpe to Mayfair, from Paris to Vienna, from

Monte Carlo to Baden-Baden. And wherever she went she dragged after her or summoned to her the farmer whom, for a thoughtless whim, she had desired to marry.

Perhaps she loved him. He would never know. They had had moments, though her rages were more frequent than her surrenders. Once she had thrown all his possessions, one after the other, out of their hotel window in Monte Carlo. Once she had maintained a terrifying silence all the way in the train from San Sebastian. She had gone there by herself, then telegraphed ordering him to join her, and when he came, lumbering across Europe, anxious and uncomfortable, she turned upon him, rated him for his incurable stupidity, and spoke no further word to him for a week.

He did not know if she had been faithful to him. She had boasted of a lover at Baden-Baden. She had once denied that Midge was his own daughter. She declared that she did not know which of the officers with whom she had played in her final escapade before his fatal last leave in the winter of 1917 might not have been the father of their child. And when it happened that the outcome had proved so tragic, when, after the child was born, she relapsed into intermittent insanity, there had been times when he had longed for proof that this was not his doing, that the one occasion when he had forced himself upon her, taking by violence what her whim refused, had not been the final cause of her destruction.

He did not know, and he would never know. She had not loved him as he understood love, had never desired to shield, to serve, to comfort; had never glowed with a rapture that lit the world with burning glory—as the pale slope of the earth burned now along the far horizon—because the beloved was near to be seen, heard, fondled.

But he had loved her. That at least she gave him, in return for the pain, the conflict, the violation of all his decent habits. She had dragged him from his familiar limitations, from farming, from sport, from comforts and conventions; she had shamed, outraged, derided, ruined and betrayed him. But she had given in return this unique experience. He had loved her. And because he was at heart quite a simple person, love for him had not meant—except for that one night of jealousy and anger—violence and domination and possession. His love had suffered long and was kind; it envied not, was not puffed up, sought not its own interest, was not easily provoked, and thought no evil. It had asked only the privilege of service—and that had been given in unusual measure. Loving Muriel Sedgmire had cost Carne all other things that he had been reared to value—and he had never even asked himself if she had been worth their loss.

Yet, just because he had never been certain of Muriel, it had amused him to flirt and quarrel with women like Sarah Burton. She was a grand girl, a sturdy, fine, vital, unfrightened creature. The thought of his illness in the hotel humiliated him. He was ashamed and disappointed. He felt that he had cut a poor figure. Even to remember what happened recalled that nightmare pain—the rending, overwhelming, unspeakable agony when he had rolled sweating and panting, incapable of control, making a complete fool of himself.

She would forgive him. He was sure of her fundamental courage and generosity. But it would be long before he would forgive himself—except, thank God, for the fact that it had happened with Sarah and not with Muriel.

He had not been surprised by her advances. He knew that women found him attractive, and he liked them. These brief and casual encounters had made the bitter tragedy of his marriage bearable. They meant nothing to him after they were over but a certain flattery, a certain gratitude, a certain memory of passing pleasure. He hoped that the women enjoyed them as much as he did.

The path grew narrower. Here the cliff had crumbled. In one case the furrows led straight into empty air, where headland and all had been washed away after a heavy rain.

The horse trod carefully. Carne had left the reins loose. He was massaging his fingers. A pain in his arms made him wonder if this was the ghost of an old pain or the herald of one that was coming on. He groped for his nitrate of amyl and remembered that he had left the tin at home in his other waistcoat. He did not want to be seized by an attack here on the cliff. He urged the horse more quickly, but still his mouth curved in a smile of preoccupation. Below him, the waves broke as they touched the landfall, reared and fountained, tossing their spray with the sleet into his face. He had little love for the unquiet water, but to his right lay the element that he had always trusted. The land stretched dark and unbroken to the sunset. A curious tawny bar of copper lay pressed between the dark clouds and ragged trees of the horizon. It reminded him of something.

He was watching it idly when a startled blackbird lurched from a wind-blown thornbush, squawking shrilly, and was off with a flurry of black feathers and golden beak. The horse, rearing sideways, brought his feet down together on to an overhanging ledge of turf. Beneath that sudden blow the earth broke and crumbled. Carne's mind was on the sunset, and the confusion of its colour with some pleasant recollection. Before he could draw his reins, it was too late. Recognising Sarah's brave oriflamme of hair, remembering her gallantry, comforted and flattered by her kindness, he turned to see the white waves roaring upwards beneath him, and saw no more for ever.

BOOK VIII

HOUSING AND TOWN PLANNING

"The Clerk submitted the Draft Preliminary Statements, Schedules A. & B. in connection with the Kingsport (Southern and Eastern Districts) Town Planning Scheme which had been received from the Kingsport Corporation and South Riding Joint Committee, and the Committee considered the observations of the County Surveyor on the Schedules.

"Resolved—That the Committee consider the Kingsport (Southern and Eastern Districts) Town Planning Scheme—Schedule B.—should if possible be incorporated in the South Riding Rural Planning Scheme, and that the Clerk be instructed to take the necessary steps for inclusion of the scheme in the draft to be submitted to the County Council."

Minutes of the Housing and Town Planning Committee of the South Riding County Council. April, 1934.

CHAPTER I

ASTELL AND SNAITH PLAN A NEW JERUSALEM

The daffodil sheathes bent in the harsh bleak wind. Beneath the shrubbery the soil was brindled with frail sooty-faced snowdrops and green-frilled golden aconites. Jonquils and narcissi pierced with their upthrusting spears the unmown grass; but showed no flowers. Snaith strolled round his garden, a froth of cats at his feet.

Now he scolded a tabby for the hideous vice of bulb-eating; now he stooped and touched a rich purple tuft of primula on the rockery; now he stood contemplating the hard black buds on the half-hollow ash-tree.

He did not love the spring. He felt himself alien and outcast among all this building of nests, this mating of birds and animals. The wild white-flowered dead nettle, with its sweet honeyed lip, the clinging goose grass and gross squatting dock were inimical to him. He saw the fierce needles of fine green corn, the young savage lambs knocking and thrusting at their mothers, the swelling reddish buds on the hawthorn hedge, combine in the monstrous battle for rebirth, and it angered him that so fragile a creature as a wren, a mouse or daffodil should renew its lusty life while he moved through the earth without desire of increase.

He was aware that sometimes, in his plans for the happiness of the South Riding, he was moved by a secret desire to press down, to raze, to subjugate the spring. He would bind it with cement and concrete, crush it with engines, scoop out great wounds from the fecund earth, and set there race-tracks and roads and villas. He would drive away the rustling, purring, mating creatures that lurked in the banks and hedges. All this chaos of natural life should respond to his dominating will. It should. It should.

But, of course, he knew his spitefulness to be folly. Nature and life and the spring would break through all his barriers. Desire must fulfil itself even in a garden village. Why else must his enterprises provide walnut suites (8s. 6d. a week easy payment terms), constant hot water, sheds for perambulators? Oh, nature would get back on him all right, and from his barren bitterness he must cry to these clerks and artisans and little shopgirls, Love, Mate, Beget, Increase. Here, behind this green door, is the birth control clinic, behind that blue one, a mothers' and babies' club. In the Polytechnic you can learn cookery. He would plant a garden for the nursery school, where brown-limbed children would roll like living flowers, in their sun suits of blue and yellow and vermilion. My girl's got a scholarship to the High School! What's the matter with little Tommy, please, Nurse Johnson? Have you seen Mrs. Walker's twins? Down the twilit, lamplit pavements girls would hurry beneath melting turquoise evenings to buy pink petticoats of artificial silk to wear at dances in Unity Hall. Love, locked out with the moles and mice and hedge-sparrows, comes home at night by corporation tram. It was not possible, it was not possible, to shut out the spring.

Very well; he must abet it. In his own reasonable cautious way, he would say to life: Fulfil your own nature. He would say to man: Increase and multiply. Oh, all ye creatures of the Lord, bless ye the Lord, praise Him and magnify Him for ever.

Yet though his mind accepted this, his body ached with a nervous fatigue and discontent. He was sick to death of intellectual consolations and reasonable arguments. He hungered for the great crises of passion, the yielding to violent emotion, the surrender of choice that was denied him. He was a man rent by inward conflict.

He looked up to see a bus from Kiplington stop at his gate, and Astell's lean ungainly form slouch loose-limbed up his drive like a sick greyhound.

Snaith came forward to greet him.

"It was good of you to come," he said. "I hope it wasn't a trouble."

"On the contrary," Astell replied, coughing harshly, "it suited me very well."

The colleagues stood, formidable and controlled masters of law and effort, against the turbulent chaos of the spring.

"Come in. Come and have tea. It's a bit cold here."

They went into a small room on the ground floor, Snaith's drawing-room, all ivory and green and honey coloured, a delicious room. An immense white cyclamen laid back its snowy ears and snarled with crimson lips from the broad window-sill. A fountain of mimosa splashed from a porcelain jar. The cold landscape was framed in glowing green silk curtains, shot with firelight.

Astell saw neither the elegance of the Adams fireplace nor the perfection of the flowers. He unwound his scarf and came to the point.

"Have you decided?"

"Yes."

An amber-coloured cat leapt on to Snaith's chair and settled there. It added frivolity to the conversation.

"Is Carne going on with his idiotic case?"

The housekeeper entered with a glittering tea-tray.

"Do sit down. He says so. Do you like Indian or China tea?"

"He hasn't a leg to stand on."

"No."

"It'll ruin him."

"Possibly." Snaith chose Indian tea from a silver caddy, and warmed the shining pot.

"What damages are you asking?"

"Ten thousand. Do you prefer cream or lemon?"

"Oh—anything—Has he got ten thousand pounds?"

Few could perform better than Snaith the priestly rite of tea-making, but it was hard to conduct the ritual in the face of Astell's almost contemptuous indifference. He would see no distinction between Snaith's Earl Grey mixture and the brown treacly stuff from the urns at Unity Hall.

"How true is it—this about Stillman raising a mortgage and selling it to Tadman? I suppose there's nothing in it?"

Astell gobbled the small puffed scones with appetite rather than appreciation.

"Oh, that's quite true."

"True?"

Astell gaped with amazement, swallowed a crumb, and choked.

"Perfectly true. It started because I lent old Huggins five hundred pounds—"

"But that's what Carne said!"

"Quite. Carne made several perfectly true statements."

"But. . . ."

"With this money Huggins acquired, in the name of a chap called Aythorne, the sheds on Leame Ferry Waste."

Astell stared.

"Aythorne let Stillman the undertaker acquire a mortgage, in order that he might buy a shop in Dollstall."

"But—but why did Huggins . . ."

"Because he had reasons for marrying off a girl to Mr. Aythorne."

"Oh!"

"Huggins, who is not on the Joint Committee with Kingsport, but who is on Town Planning, thought he was sure we were going to build on the Leame Ferry Waste site. Therefore he persuaded Tadman and Drew to come in with him, to buy off Stillman, to get hold of the rest of the site, to put machinery in the sheds so that they could claim damages, and to advertise valuable building property, in order that the council would be forced, when they wanted it, to pay through the nose."

"And you knew this?"

"At first I only guessed a little. Lately I have made it my business to find out everything I wanted to know."

"But this is all just what Carne said."

"Yes."

"Then—then—Carne's got his case."

"Oh, no."

Snaith picked up another slice of wafery bread and butter, folded it with precision, and smiled at the bewildered socialist.

"Oh, no," he repeated, "because the Joint Council is, on my persuasion, not going to recommend Leame Ferry Waste."

"Not—going—to—"

"No. No. I think we shall find that Schedule B—you remember the land on Schedule B?—is the more convenient."

"You mean south of the new road—the old point-to-point course?"

"Yes."

"But that's out of the question. Surely. The high land value—good agricultural land—"

"Not so high as the Waste now that Drew's advertised a 'valuable building site.'"

"It's so far from Kingsport—we shall have that fearful Clixton business again—the men unable to pay their fares to work—and taking them out of the sums needed for food."

"Not if the Kingsport Electricity Association runs that new light railway we discussed, with cheap workmen's tickets."

"That's one of your shows, isn't it?"

"It happens to be so."

"I see. It'll be rather a good thing for you, won't it?"

"I hope so."

There was this at least about Snaith, thought Astell he was no hypocrite. He did not pretend to be a philanthropist when in truth he was raking in profits. Snaith continued, bland and genial.

"We shall bring forward Schedule B as the recommendation from the joint committee. I have the Kingsport people in my hands now, I think. I have promised to straighten out that mess with the new maternity home. They're very keen on it."

"Quite."

Astell's sardonic humour greeted Snaith's frankness. He recognised this bargaining, intriguing, compromising world. So long as he worked with Snaith, he must play his game.

"The rates will go up again a little," Snaith continued, balancing a lump of sugar on the slice of lemon floating in his cup—a water-lily on a leaf, he thought fancifully, applauding his own taste for metaphors. Chinese, he considered it. "But that won't matter so much. These new people will stand it. The garden city will bring to the South Riding a quite different type of rate-payer. These tenants in our council houses belong to a new generation—the age of the easy purchase system, of wireless and electricity and Austin Sevens. They want good motor roads, because they dream one day of driving their own cars. They want libraries and schools and clinics and cheap secondary education. They attend lectures in town's women's guilds and women's institutes about 'The Rates and how we spend them.' They have a quite new kind of communal sense. Don't you agree with me?"

"Yes," murmured Astell, and suddenly was aware of the immense relief of liberation, because he was reaching the end of all this casuistry and bargaining. He was tired of compromise.

He had seen what it could achieve, a better hospital here, a more generous benefit rate there, the eyes of one or two councillors opened to reality. Because he had worked with Snaith in the garden village scheme, instead of exposing his selfish and predatory methods, slums would be pulled down, a certain number of families would move out into the red-roofed, neatly-ordered council houses. There would be gardens for them, with fruit and vegetables, and broad green plots for children to play in; there would be hospitals and schools and libraries. Fewer mothers would die in childbirth, fewer babies would sicken in airless basement bedrooms, fewer housewives would collapse into lethargy, defeated by the unending battle against dirt and inconvenience.

Perhaps it was worth while, but this was not what Astell wanted. He had not struggled and sacrificed health and prosperity and ambition in order that a few Kingsport shopgirls might gratify their snobbish ambition of decorating their houses with leather suites, and dream of possessing a Morris Cowley.

Nor was he one of those men who enjoy fighting over detail. There were such, and he knew and admired them. His great friend in South Africa had been a man like that, who constituted himself the gadfly of the Chamber of Mines, harrying them first over a point of workman's compensation, then over the interest on the deferred pay system, then over the rates for piecework underground. But these were not Astell's ideas of a good fight. While on the county council he had compromised with capitalism in order to achieve certain concrete results. Now he was sick of it. Now he would get free.

I'm going away, he gloated. I'm getting free.

He beamed at Snaith through his round glasses.

"Good," he said. "I wish you luck with it. And, by the way, you mention secondary education. Don't forget the new buildings for the High School. I think we ought to move it inland a bit, and make a big boarding-block for the whole Skerrow-Kiplington area."

"I'm not likely to forget with you here to bully me," smiled Snaith.

"But I shan't be here. That's just it."

"Shan't be here?"

"No. I'm retiring from the council and clearing out."

"Your health?" There was genuine kindness and anxiety in the quick inquiry. "It's worse?"

"No. Better. That's just it. I'm going back to Glasgow. Got an organising job on the Clyde."

"My dear fellow! You can't do it. It'll kill you in a couple of years."

"Will it? And does that much matter?"

"But—but we can't spare you."

The little alderman was really troubled.

Yet it was not so much for Astell that he was grieved, as for himself. Here he was up against it again, up against that uncalculating generosity and rashness which plunged into action, which identified itself with an impersonal aim. And it troubled him.

"You can spare me very well," smiled Astell. "After all, you hardly know what I am and who I'm like. You've only seen a sick man. While I was here, I more or less kept truce. But you just wait a little."

"Shall we see you preaching revolution?"

"I hope so."

"And turning us all upside down, and destroying instead of creating?"

"No—in order to create. Look here, Snaith, you and I have worked pretty well together, but we're in opposite camps really. You want entirely different things from what I do."

"Do I? How do you know? How do you know what I want?"

Astell smiled. He was a free man. He was happy. He spoke from the exalted height of his own renunciation of security. He said, "I know what I want, you see. And whatever you want, it's not the same as this. I want a great co-operative commonwealth of free peoples, all over the world. Without distinction of sex, race or creed. I want to see them controlling their own lives, what they do and how they do it. That means control of things, of raw materials, transport and industry. It means real economic as well as political democracy. It means social equality. It means spiritual freedom. And that isn't going to come by working as I've worked here. Oh, I know that all this is useful—so far as it goes. But it's not changing men's values. It's not destroying their destroyers."

"You mean, it still leaves evil-minded individualists like me to be able to reap a little profit?"

"Yes. I do."

"And you would destroy me?"

"Neck and crop."

"You won't, you know. You'll only destroy yourself. The English don't take easily to revolution."

"Do you think any revolution's been easy? All revolutions are bloody and barbarous. But so is life bloody and barbarous in present circumstances. As for me, I've tried acting the invalid and taking a cushy job, and I don't like it."

"I see." Snaith sighed, envious of a passion that was beyond caution, of a faith that could over-ride the scepticism that ate into his own desires like acid. "You're like the old Spanish knights who greeted each other with the wish, 'May God deny thee peace and give thee glory.' That's it, isn't it?"

"Oh, I don't know," squirmed Astell uncomfortably. He had no taste for metaphors and proverbs. He saw the fun of the fight before him, the smoke-filled halls, the older grey men with union badges in their buttonholes, the piles of fingered, soiled press cuttings in the offices. He was going back to work—back to life. He was happy, yet it never occurred to him that Snaith was envying him with a tormenting and bitter envy.

Snaith's manservant came in with the evening paper.

"Sad thing this about Mr. Carne," he said.

"What sad thing?"

Christie spread the paper on the lacquered table. Snaith read slowly the big black letters of the headline: "Fatality feared to well-known Yorkshire Sportsman." And underneath: "Cliff Fall of Mr. Carne."

"What is it?" asked Astell.

"Look at this."

Astell came and stood behind him. Together they read.

"It is feared that Mr. Robert Carne, the well-known Yorkshire sportsman and gentleman farmer, who for thirteen years was member of the South Riding County Council for the division of Maythorpe, has met with a fatal accident. Last night he left the Crown Inn Stables at Kiplington at about 6 p.m. to ride home to his residence at Maythorpe Hall. On his way, he had arranged to call at Spring Farm for a business interview with his tenant, Mr. Eli Dickson. As he did not appear, Mr. Dickson visited Maythorpe Hall and learned from the servants that Mr. Carne had not arrived. It was supposed that business had detained him in Kiplington, but early this morning Mr. T. Beachall of Maythorpe, while gathering drift wood along the Maythorpe sands, at low tide, noticed a new and substantial fall of earth from the cliff, and on it, partially buried, the body of a horse. He quickly summoned help from Maythorpe village; the carcass was disinterred, and recognised as the famous Black Hussar, for many years winner of the Hunt Cup at the South Riding agricultural shows; Mr. Carne was riding this animal when he left the Crown Inn. His riding crop and hat were also found, but so far there has been discovered no trace of his body, which, it is thought, may have been washed out to sea. The path along the cliff had been newly broken and there is no doubt that while riding home yesterday evening, Mr. Carne found the earth breaking under him and was thrown from his mount in the act of falling. The coastal erosion along the south cliffs has long been a cause of anxiety to the local authorities. . . ."

"Suicide?" asked Astell.

"I doubt it," Snaith replied.

There was a great deal more in the paper. About the Carnes of Maythorpe and their beneficent activities in the county; about Carne's marriage to the Honourable Muriel Sedgmire ("now for some years an invalid"), about his war service, about his sporting and athletic prowess, about Midge ("now a pupil at the Kiplington High School for Girls, of which her father was a governor"), about the currents of the tide and the improbability of Mr. Carne's survival after such a fall, even if the tide had not been high that evening.

"Could he be alive still?" asked Astell. "Could this be staged?"

"I hardly think so."

"A getaway? He was in a fearful jam."

"Yes; he was. But he wasn't the sort to run away."

Snaith did not want to think so. He did not want to think of his opponent as less noble and obstinate than he had believed him.

He was shocked. This was something unforeseen and violent, something that disconcerted him, upsetting calculations.

Astell was less distressed. To him Carne had been a nuisance and an obstructionist. He had never forgotten that incident of the Public Assistance Committee, when the farmer had proved abler at comfort than himself. He could not pretend to feel any deep emotion. Carne was merely one enemy to his cause the less.

"Will this affect your plans—Schedule B, for instance?" he asked Snaith.

"No. Why should it?"

The little vice-chairman of the council seemed distracted, staring now at the paper, now at the dancing flames. Astell left soon. He had given his notice of withdrawal; he had agreed, as his last service to the council, to accept and work for Schedule B. He caught his bus in order to take a meeting at the Co-operative Women's Guild at Dolstall.

But Snaith could not so easily evade the thought of Carne's accident. Directly Astell had left, he set in motion the obsequious instruments of his active life. He seized the telephone and rang up the police, the bank, the lawyers. He became master of the facts of the situation. He learned of Carne's financial failures, of his swollen expenses, of his recent efforts to set his house in order. He learned that already the insurance company was a little dubious. He tapped his pencil against his teeth and pondered, inexplicably distressed and yet somehow gratified by his discoveries.

He did not know quite what emotion moved him. He left the telephone, put on his overcoat, and went out into the garden. Away to the west the final tattered banners of a vivid sunset paled the sky. A ploughman, topping the rise, stood silhouetted for a moment against it, a grave traditional figure. On Snaith's lawn his ancient ash creaked in the nagging wind. Old, thin, decaying; it had better come down, thought Snaith.

The Carnes of Maythorpe, he thought, were like that tree,—rooted deep in the earth; they understood that; their leaves and branches were lifted high and all men saw them, a conspicuous growth, proud, decorative. What they could not see, what they had never learned to recognise, were the winds that blew—from all the ends of the world, Canada, Argentine, Denmark, New Zealand, Russia. They had thought that if they attended to Maythorpe, they would survive. But the wind and the rain and the storms from west to east, taxes and tariffs and subsides and quotas, beef from the Argentine, wool from Australia, economic nationalism, fashions and crazes—all those imponderable influences of which their slow, strong, rigid minds took no heed—these would destroy them. If Carne were dead, or if he were in flight, what difference did that make? He was defeated. The tree must be cut down.

Yet there was no triumph in Snaith's heart as he stood with his hand on that half-hollowed trunk. Carne had lived; he had been rooted deep in the soil; he had loved and hated and begotten and feared and dared. He had never shrunk back from life; he had done everything that struck his limited imagination as worth doing. When he fell into a blind passion for his peer's daughter, he had married her. When his country went to war, he put on uniform. When his hounds hunted, he rode after them. He never held himself back as Snaith had done. His violent, immense, instinctive growth had brought him sorrow, but he had known colour, increase and passion. He had lived.

And I? thought Snaith. Between Carne who lived by instinct and Astell who lived by an idea, he felt that he was nothing—a stream of water, cold, metallic, barren, without colour or form, moving along its self-chosen channel till the sand sucked it up and it disappeared. Unfecund, flavourless, formless—a direction—a flow—a nothing. Here lieth one whose life was lived as water. It has evaporated; it no longer exists.

Then with a twist of vanity he lifted himself above his self-disgust.

After all, water has power, he thought. It does not only reflect pictures, it turns wheels, it irrigates valleys, it drives dynamos. Snaith thought of his houses, his works, his railways. Even now on the far bank of the Leame the ragged lights began to twinkle, first one, and then another; the trains roared up to Kingsport; the ships moved silently along the river. This was his world. He had largely helped to build it.

All that Astell could do was to stir a few more Clydesiders to sedition. All that Carne had done was to leave a wife who was mad and a daughter of tainted stock, a ruined farm and a dark romantic memory.

But I—thought Snaith. When he died the entire face of the South Riding would have changed, because he once had lived there.

I shall do better than any of them, he told himself.

At Willow Lodge Alderman Mrs. Beddows held to her heart a sobbing quivering child, comforting her own sorrow by giving comfort.

Along the widening strip of earth-clogged sand, Hicks groped with his lantern, seeking for his master. Heyer and Sawdon followed him.

Up in her attic bedroom Sarah Burton crouched on her bed, dry-eyed, shocked by incredulous dismay and grief and horror.

She could hear her shrill wounding anger, telling Carne to take his daughter elsewhere. She could feel her shameless pursuit, her uncontrolled repulsion. She did not know if he had killed himself, as some were saying, or had fallen by accident, or if, perhaps, his illness had come upon him. But she could feel in her own body the wild sickening lurch as the horse stumbled, the rush through the cold air, the furious shock of the icy water. And she could not bear it.

It is my fault; she lacerated herself with her reproaches. I could have helped him. If I had thought of his need more than my pride. But now there is no comfort. Grief passes and life closes over loss; but for this, there is no remedy. He is dead and now I can never comfort him.

Oh, no, I cannot bear it. I cannot bear it. There will be no end for ever to this pain.

CHAPTER II

THREE REVELLERS HAVE A NIGHT OUT

The cymbals clashed and were still; the violins held their last faint piercing note, then faded; the saxophone wailed to silence. Only the drums rattled their implacable thunder as eight hundred and seventy-six hearts quickened their beat, eight hundred and seventy-six pairs of lungs drew in their breath and held it, and the fifth Cingalese cyclist slowly reared himself upright from the shoulders of number four, who was already perched upon the shoulders of number three, who stood straddled from those of one and two as they swooped abreast round the stage on their glittering bicycles.

It was the fourth turn before the interval during the second house at the Kingsport Empire on the Saturday evening after the gigantic victory of the Kingsport Rangers over the West Riding Wanderers, and the city was en fête. There were well over a thousand people at the little Empire, but some were asleep, some in the bar, some already so much exalted by beer and noise and victory that they were incapable of further heightening of excitement as the human column swung circling, the head of number five hidden behind dark crimson drapery. After that glorious contest in the mud on the ground between Skerrow Road and St. Swithin's place, after that last goal shot just before the whistle blew, even the sight of men risking their lives lacked flavour.

The air was thick with the sweet sickly pervasions of beer, rank tobacco, oranges, hot packed humanity and some perfumed disinfectant that the attendants, like amazons slaughtering invisible foes, sprayed haughtily down the gangways during the intervals. During the act of the Dillar Dancing Belles, streamers, balloons and paper balls had been flung from the stage into the auditorium, so that performers and audience were linked together by a broken net of scarlet, green and yellow. Balloons hung like bubbles between the stalls and circle. Every now and then an enterprising spectator made a grab for one, winning shouts of applause or boos of derision, which distracted attention from the hard-working artistes. Several youths in the gallery had brought the rattles and toy trumpets with which they had encouraged the football players, and with these they now saluted the actors in this other drama. Three men, leaning over the parapet of the upper circle, wore paper caps bearing the favours of the Kingsport team, and as a sign of applause cheered on every turn as it appeared by the View Hallo trumpeted down a toy bugle.

A shipowner's wife from London, who had taken a box to amuse her artist friend, swept with her glasses the blurred mist of the auditorium. "We may not be highly refined here in the north," she observed, "but you must admit we do enjoy ourselves."

The five Cingalese cyclists swept circling off the stage; the crimson curtains fell together. The illuminated panels pricked out the figure 8, and the orchestra blared its raucous comment.

The curtains reopened to disclose a Jewish comedienne, fat, restless, vital, her bold eyes snapping, her harsh merry voice almost irresistible. If it had been quite so, she would have been delighting London or New York instead of Kingsport.

"Watch those three," the London lady instructed her friend. "Too sweet, the little man with the trumpet. Not a care in the world. I adore him."

"Up for the match, I suppose," said the friend intelligently. "Look, the poor fellow with the rattle has only one arm."

The comedienne wagged her plump buttocks at the stalls, leering over her shoulder. She made a joke which was not very funny but extremely coarse. The lady in the box beamed with proprietary delight.

"Robust, isn't it? The real thing this. Several hundred cubic feet of sheer enjoyment. I doubt if you would find a tougher audience in England—seamen drinking their pay, touts, tarts and tote-operators. The air positively stiff with S.A., B.O. and all other fashionable human qualities. Oh, do listen to the little man with the trumpet!"

For behind the comedienne galloped a team of chorus girls, with bells across their brassières and plumed tails streaming behind. They curvetted, trotted, reared and pranced, driven by a young man dressed as a coachman, while the Jewess sang:

"Who wouldn't change a ten-bob stall for a not too loose loose box?"

An equestrian joke which enchanted the London party by directing attention to their own position.

The little man in the circle gave the Hark For'ard, and the Empire was well away on a chase for that rare quarry, the corporate emotion of mass delight.

"He's too delicious," screamed the lady, her eyes wet with tears of laughter.

Hicks conscientiously played the fool, but a dull ache constricted his throat and oppressed his chest.

There was no reason why the sight of the chorus girls dancing like ponies should remind him of the four stiff legs of Black Hussar sticking through the mud like the legs of an upturned table. There was no reason why, when he shouted and laughed and applauded, his heart should feel wild with pain. Three weeks had passed since his first sight of that catastrophe. Police and lawyers had questioned him. Mrs. Beddows had been kind to him. Mr. Briggs had told him to stay on and look after things about the stables and garden until the sale. Tom Sawdon had suggested to him that when it was all over he might come down to the Nag's Head and run in partnership on his savings. Everything was all right for Hicks—"Hicks will be all right"—as Jim Beddows informed his wife.

And he was all right. Had he not driven over with Tom and Bob to a grand football match? Had he not had a fish supper followed by drinks at the York Rose Hotel, and was he not now having a high old time at the Empire? And attracting the attention of half the house by his abandonment of gusto?

If only we could have buried him like a Christian; Hicks was thinking. He gave Castle a slap-up funeral, didn't he? He never let any of us want for nothing—neither man nor horse.

Horses. Those girls don't know nothing about horses. I'd like to see 'em look at a really decent horse. Now Burlington Bertie—that was a grand animal, by Albert the Good out of Sweet Sophia. Knocked himself to pieces in that box on the line between Derby and Manchester. Left alone he was. Always hated trains. Glorious stallion for stud. Now Carne would never have let a thing like that happen.

Carne had let Black Hussar break his back on Maythorpe Cliff.

Come off it! That was an accident. The cliff crumbled.

There was that little skewbald thoroughbred Carne bought for the missus. Showy mare. Regular devil she was; but neat on her feet. And Mrs. Carne could do anything with her. A real circus horse. Ride her upstairs if she liked. Had done. That's a fact. That time they were off to the meet and Mrs. Carne was ready first for a wonder, already down on the drive and waiting. Only times she wasn't hours late was for hunting. Carne was up in his dressing-room. Couldn't tie his stock. One thing he never could do. Always lost his temper. Called out of the window, Come and give me a hand! But she was in the saddle and cried, Damned if I do. Always free in the tongue for a lady. And he called, Oh, come up. Be a sport. Sport, she screamed. Lot of sport we shall get. You've kept me waiting half an hour already. Nonsense, he said, for he had a temper too. No wonder, when you think of the old man. Don't exaggerate, Muriel. I've only been five minutes, but I may be half an hour if you don't come and help me. Ordering me to dismount like a servant! she cried. I never ordered you. Don't dismount then. I'll come without the damn thing, he cried, and she said, I'm not going to ride with you looking like a fool, and turned the skewbald's head, and gave her a smack with her crop, and rode her in, straight through the front door and down the hall and up the big front stairs, slithering and plucking she climbed, but keeping straight on at it and into Carne's dressing-room, and there she faced him.

Hicks had raced up behind, fearing the worst, and found Carne in his shirt sleeves, his stock round his ear, gaping at Muriel, who sat still as a statue on the shivering mare. And then, what with surprise or fear or sheer bad manners, the little animal planted her four feet stiffly down together and began to make water, a great streaming torrent, there on to Carne's grand crimson carpet, soaking down to the drawing-room ceiling, so that the patch was there to this day. And the missus screamed with laughter like she did sometimes, and Carne lifted her clean out of the saddle and stood holding her, her arms round his neck and her hat off, and she limp with laughing, and he said to Hicks. Take that disgusting brute away, and carried his wife through to her bedroom and slammed the door. It took Hicks half an hour to get the mare downstairs, but the Carnes never set off on that day's hunting.

The Jewish comedienne and her ponies pranced away. A strong man replaced them, who bent bars of iron and lifted pianos, and hung upside down from a trapeze with a rod suspended from his mouth on to which more and yet more weights were slung.

A strong man, not only strong but agile, his muscles flexible as elastic and tough as steel. Heyer, whose shoulder had been aching all day since he stood on the damp football ground, thought of his own maimed body. As Hicks was bereaved of Carne, of horses, of the old values and loyalties which composed his world, Heyer was bereaved of more than his physical capacity. He too had lost a way of life, a set of values.

He knew that war was evil. With the British Legion he had passed resolutions about profiting from death and all the rest of it. But as he watched Sacho the Strong flex his huge muscles, and shouted applause at his spectacular feats, his mind was back in the worst experience of the war, the mud of Passchendaele. His feet again groped for the duck-boards through the foetid water. He was carrying rations up to the front-line trenches; the pack ground into his shoulder, the foul ooze seeped through puttees and boots. The fear of falling into that filth tormented him. Yet as he sat in his plush tip-up seat, leaning over the parapet into the boiling cauldron of the Kingsport Empire, he envied that younger self. He suffered from a sick nostalgia for the young Bob Heyer who had been Scotty's friend, who had two good arms, who could himself play football instead of watching it, who could box, swim, dig, and was one of the best all-round athletes in the company. It was Scotty who had gone down into the mud, and for whose body they had groped in the stench and ordure of a flooded crater. Nothing in all his life had been so horrible as that . . . yet until he got his blighty he had known good times again. Boxing at the base; the ring in the tent at Amiens. The acid sweaty smell of men crowded together in woollen uniforms, the arc lights, the referee. The sing songs in that estaminet near Abbeville. The relief from responsibility, the good fellowship, the pride of manhood and living that grew up there in France under the menace of death. He hungered for it. He knew that all other years must be lifeless and dull compared with those. He would continue to farm. He had his friends, Tom and Geordie. He would spend his evenings when he could in the Nag's Head. But something more than his arm had been left behind in France. He would walk now maimed and bereaved till death.

The strong man was followed by a famous Whistling Comedian.

"Oh, I adore him! Watch our three musketeers in the circle now. This'll be popular."

It was. The three in the circle all applauded furiously as the familiar little phrase, whistled off stage, grew louder, and the comedian strolled forward, peeling off his gloves, removing and folding his coat.

Tom Sawdon applauded. But he wished that the whistler had not chosen this special tune. He was one of Lily's favourite broadcast entertainers. She had sat so often, her head a little on one side, her thin fingers raised, her lips pursed in sympathy. Now, listen—you! she had commanded. Isn't he fine? Isn't he grand?

Lily was now in hospital. After unthinkable weeks, Tom had induced them to take her. She was kept under drugs now. She did not know him that afternoon when he had visited her. She was already dead, so far as he was concerned.

"Just a little story," began the comedian, "about a Scotsman who came down to Yorkshire and said . . ."

"Ha, ha, ha!" roared the three in the circle.

"Just listen to them!" cooed the lady in the box.

She could not see the ghosts marching through their minds as they laughed and listened. There was that grey pony from Texas, Huckleberry, that Carne tried to hunt when hounds met at Yarrold. Only time I ever saw a horse bolt with him. Gave one look at the hounds, got his tail between his legs, and was off like the wind.

That time we got that lift in a mule-wagon, along the Rouen Road, and the driver half-boiled and the mules took fright and we ran right into a staff car and the mule put his head in at the window and old Turnip Face thought he was having D.T.s. . . .

That time the colonel and I came home unexpected, and the big house was shut and we went to Lily's, and she made up a bed for the colonel in our front room and roasted us a chicken.

All their dreams for the future, all their memories of the past, swarmed round them, wounding them, mocking them, as the comedian replaced his gloves, whistling pensively, and strolled again off the stage.

It was their memories that they applauded.

"What about a drink?" asked Bob.

They made for the bar.

"Now," explained the lady, "we all go and squash up in a perfectly revolting bar, packed with pimps, ladies from the dock and God knows what, and drink frightful beer, out of the most disgusting glasses, and it's all too he-mannish and Hemingway for words."

The atmosphere of the Empire bar was certainly robust and pungent. Two cynical barmaids, one elderly, hennaed and fatigued on aching bunions (she had three sons to keep), one young, skinny and avid, slapped down the glasses on to the beer-ringed counter as fast as they could fill them. The drinks ordered were as various as the company. Sherries, ports, beers, whiskies, stouts and even such exotic luxuries as crême de menthe and cherry brandies for the ladies who sat in the wicker chairs, exposing fat calves in light mud-splashed stockings bulging up from tight high-heeled patent shoes. One, drinking gin and ginger, boasted a little green toque ornamented with black osprey. A great port wine mark half covered one side of her face. She had been married three times. Pearls dripped from her bosom.

The more rustic Hicks looked at her and her friends. "Tarts," he observed.

"Not a bit," Sawdon, more sophisticated, told him. "Old clo' dealers, and fish and chip shopmen's wives having a night out."

It was a night out. The Empire sold the noises of happy uproar with its tickets. True, no single face in all the company there was lit by real gaiety. True, that behind the toasts, the jokes and cat-calls, thoughts of death, sickness, unemployment and loss tugged, nagging, at their minds. The laughter was not loud enough, the jokes were inadequately brutal, the good fellowship too ephemeral, to drown that consciousness. Yet on the whole these Yorkshire men and women were having a good time. They had paid for it and bought it; they enjoyed it. It was something as definite and tangible as the counter, the palms and the marble topped tables. Eee, I did have a good time at the Empire last night. I did an' all.

They did, and all.

Young Lovell Brown was sharing the enjoyment. He was showing off with the splendid self-assurance following three whiskies to a little platinum blonde with startled blue eyes. Perhaps she was really startled by Brown's stories, perhaps the mascara on her eyelashes made her eyes water unless she opened them very wide.

"My dear girl," he was saying, "it stands to reason. Absolutely. There's a fellow in debt—thousands—jolted off council—wife mad—mortgage on farm—little girl to keep—dotes on her. What would you do?"

"I'd like another mint," said the blonde sensibly.

"Crême de menthe, miss, and look nippy," commanded Lovell.

If they'd invent a lorry I could drive with my feet, thought Heyer, we might get on.

Lily liked crême de menthe, thought Sawdon.

Hicks moved nearer to Lovell Brown, his face glowering deeper crimson. So this was what the—were saying, was it?

"A man like Carne of Maythorpe," continued Lovell, enchanted by admiration of his own deductive powers, "doesn't ride far along a cliff path after heavy rains without knowing what he's in for. He doesn't take out a life insurance and let it lapse, then suddenly pay all up a few weeks before he's supposed to be killed—for nothing. Does he?"

"When does the show start, ducky?" asked the girl.

But Lovell was well away.

"No. Let them find the body, I say. If there is a body."

"Just say them there words again," commanded Hicks quietly.

"I beg your pardon." Lovell swung round.

"What you was saying—about Mr. Carne."

"Oh, Carne? You interested in the case?"

"Yes. I am."

"Good. So am I. In on it for the Chronicle. Press, you know. Personally, I don't think there's really much doubt about it. The insurance company'll be a fool if it pays up. There's been too much hanky panky about here lately all together."

"Has there?"

"All that business about the Town Planning Scheme. Carne accuses Snaith and others of corruption. Snaith brings a libel suit. Carne loses his seat. Can't stand up to it. Stages a getaway."

"You mean he never did fall over that cliff?"

"That's what I mean, my friend."

"That he broke a good horse's back to save his face, eh?"

"That's it. Right first time."

The bell announcing the second half of the programme whirred over the door; the big commissionaire in blue and silver paused by the bar; couples began to squeeze their way past to the tortuous stone passage, but a few found greater hope of entertainment in the sight of the little red-faced groom dancing up and down in rage before the young reporter.

Tom Sawdon and Bob Heyer both drinking quietly in a corner, noticed nothing. Their first notification of the quarrel came from a fierce—"Take that, then!" A girl's scream and shout, and the resounding smack of a fist on flesh, from the crowd at the far end of the bar.

"Go it! Atta boy! Now then! Now then!"

The big commissionaire pushed round the door. Sawdon and Heyer sprang to their feet in time to see young Lovell, who was a pretty useful boxer, catch a neat punch on the side of the groom's jaw, and send him staggering against the wall of onlookers.

"Now then. What's all this?" asked the commissionaire.

"I haven't the slightest idea," drawled Lovell, pulling down his cuff and feeling on top of the world. Hicks, vituperative and unappeased, raged against the restraining hands which held him.

"He didn't like what this gentleman said about Carne of Maythorpe," volunteered the lady with the osprey.

"Carne? What Carne? Who's Carne?"

"Gent what chuckened hisself ower cliff," explained her friend.

"And what is Carne to you?" inquired Lovell haughtily, hoping that his blonde was suitably impressed.

"He's been groom at Maythorpe for forty years or more," explained Sawdon. "You should keep a civil tongue in your head about your betters—Mr. Carne was a fine chap, and all us from Maythorpe liked him."

"He'd never have broken a horse's back—never," gasped Hicks.

"I see." Lovell was beginning not to feel quite so clever.

"He's gotta take it back, the dirty little tike, or I'll knock his bleedin' head off."

"You won't. He's a boxer," sighed Heyer. "All right, Geordie. You come along of us."

"The young feller didn't mean no harm."

"Live and let live, I say."

"I can tell you this—your Carnes and your Snaiths and your Colliers. Blasted capitalists, all of 'em, grinding the faces of the poor."

But on the whole the company was with Hicks—including Lovell. For the young reporter was, though often silly, a generous romantic boy, and he appreciated loyalty; he felt that perhaps he had gone a little too far; he had libelled a man who perhaps was really dead.

"After all," explained Sawdon, with the paternal benevolence practised by sergeants towards inexperienced subalterns, "you couldn't know that. You were only airing your theories—like. You weren't in a position to know the facts."

"That's right," said the lady with the osprey.

"All right, old chap," said Lovell handsomely. "I take it back. Didn't know I was speaking of a friend of yours."

After all, he had knocked the little fellow down. He was the better man. He could afford to be generous.

"You apologise?" growled Hicks.

Seeing that now the room was completely on his own side, Lovell smiled with patronising superiority.

"All right. I apologise."

"You don't think he did it on purpose?"

"You tell me he didn't."

"All right. He's apologised. Come on, Geordie." Heyer and Sawdon led him out.

"That's right. Come along, Crystal," said the lordly Lovell.

"Marvellous. A real scrap thrown in. You can't say I haven't done you proud," said the London lady. "Do you want to go back for the second half, or shall we go home for a little drink now?"

Out in the side street into which the exit door opened, the little groom broke from his friends' solicitous clutch, collapsed on to a municipal dust bin, and hiding his face in his hands, abandoned himself to grief. Beer, humiliation, excitement and misery had become too much for him. He sobbed with the unself-conscious surrender of a child.

His one consolation lay in his repeated inquiry, "He took it back, didn't he?"

"That's right," Heyer soothed him. "You made him take it back."

"Carne never done it."

"That's right. He was just a young fellow, talking off the top."

"I made him take it back, didn't I?"

Seeking their car, the occupants of the box saw the three figures grouped together in the dark cobbled lane. The light from one yellow lamp cut into the dark blue shadows. The chimney pots humped a jagged silhouette above them against the moon. Their lugubrious attitude struck the visitors as irresistibly grotesque.

"The three musketeers," observed the lady. "Dead tight. Aren't they just too adorable!" She passed them with her company, catching her fur cloak round her shoulders to shut out the chill April air. They did not see her.

For each, a world had ended; locked in their private misery, united in common desolation, they did not notice their charming admirer who stood, balanced on high heels on the cobbles, holding her sables with a white jewelled hand. They did not notice her until she addressed them.

"Thank you so very much," she said in her high fluting voice. "You just made our evening for us. Too kind."

They turned to see her step into her car.

CHAPTER III

COUNCILLOR HUGGINS VINDICATES MORALITY

The Housing and Town Planning Committee of the County Council was in session. It had before it the two schemes—Schedules A and B submitted by the joint committee which, together with members of Kingsport Corporation, had discussed the preliminary problem of rehousing dwellers from the Kingsport slums in one of the rural areas of the South Riding. It was certain that a new garden village would be built. The defeat of the former obstructionists on the council, Carne, Gryson, Whitelaw and their friends, had ensured that. Snaith was vice-chairman of the newly-elected council, and chairman of the Housing and Town Planning Committee. And Snaith was one of the most ardent advocates of housing reform.

Lovell Brown, hanging about the corridors, an imposing bruise over his left eye where Hicks had struck him, encountered Alderman Mrs. Beddows, hurrying to her room. Her room was the little office which, with its own cloakroom, had been set aside for the use of lady members of the council.

"May I have a word with you?" he asked.

"Well, you know I fine every man a guinea for my Nurses' Hostel fund if they come trespassing into my private premises," she said. She was making an effort, forcing her vitality and humour to override the sorrow and desolation of her heart.

She's looking her age now, thought Lovell.

"Will sixpence do?" he chaffed. "Press, you know."

"Come in, then."

"What's going to happen about the new garden village?"

"I'm not on Town Planning. Ask Alderman Snaith."

"Which site do you favour, Mrs. Beddows?"

"My people want Leame Ferry Waste on the whole; but they aren't unreasonable. They'll put up with whatever's best for the Riding. It doesn't affect us much."

"And do you think Mr. Snaith knows what's best for the Riding?"

She paused. She had sat down at the square table with its green baize cover, and was sorting pens in a little tray.

"I'll tell you what Snaith knows," she said, "and you can put this in your paper. He knows that we—all of us, aldermen, councillors, chairmen of committees, we come and go; but the permanent officials stay on. The experts—Mr. Smithers, Mr. Wytten, Mr. Prizethorp and all the rest of them—they are the people who really matter, and in the end they mostly get their own way."

"Isn't that what you call bureaucracy, Mrs. Beddows?"

"I don't know what you call it. It seems to me common sense. Those men spend their lives on the job of local government, and have little to gain from any particular vote."

"Well—if you say so. . . . There's one other thing, Mrs. Beddows. What about this Maythorpe mystery? Do you think Mr. Carne was drowned?"

A change came over her face. The young reporter remembered stories of her rather comical friendship with the missing farmer. He knew that she was looking after the child. He began to wish he had not asked the question.

"You mean do I think that Mr. Carne staged an accident in order to run away from his responsibilities?"

"Well, you know what people are saying."

She stood up. Her squat square body had never assumed greater dignity.

"I'll tell you not only what I think, but what I know. Robert Carne may sometimes have been obstinate and sometimes unwise. But in all the years I knew him I never once saw him do a dishonourable thing. Nor did any one else. He never ran away from danger; he never shirked responsibility. He was one of the most honest and courageous people I ever knew."

"I didn't mean . . ."

"Mean? You only meant that you had listened to silly sensational stories. Like a lot of other people you'd like to think that a fine man was really no better than his neighbours. You'd like to be able to prove a nasty story. It's an excuse when you feel you haven't behaved any too well yourself, now, isn't it?"

Her face was red with indignation. The young man, abashed and discomforted, wished himself a thousand miles away; and what would have happened next is difficult to say, if at that moment the Town Planning Committee had not adjourned, and its members come clumping down the stone corridor past the open door of Mrs. Beddows' office. Delighted of an excuse to escape, Lovell muttered an apology, ran out and button-holed the chairman. Snaith as usual was walking by himself, neat, self-contained, uncommunicative.

"Have you any news for me, Mr. Snaith?"

"News? You'd better ask our clerk."

"Have you chosen a site?"

"Certainly."

"A or B?"

"B."

"Good. Splendid. Unanimous?"

"No. No. . . . Hardly unanimous. But adequate. Well, Mrs. Beddows, and how are you?"

Lovell Brown, turning away with his unexhilarating news that a garden village was to be built on this site rather than that, missed what would have interested him far more—the strange contortion of the woman alderman's face as she looked at Snaith without answering and then quietly shut her door against him.

She was not his political opponent; she did not disapprove of his business technique; she did not, like some of his detractors, shrink from his curiously dry and metallic personality. But she was still too raw from the shock of Carne's death to face his antagonist with equanimity. She did not believe that Snaith had treated Carne badly. She didn't even believe that Snaith had started the rumour about Carne's having faked his accident. She simply could not bring herself yet to speak to the man who had defeated Robert, and who still lived and triumphed now that Carne was dead.

The old lady's getting a bit deaf, was Snaith's first thought. Then he realised that the snub had been deliberate, and he shrugged his shoulders and went along to the little room which bore the card on its door.

"Vice-chairman."

He sat down at the desk and rested his head on his hands. This was his room; he had fought for it and won it. He held it as a pledge that one day, when old General Tarkington had retired, he would stand in his place; he would be chairman of the County Council; he would, to all practical purposes, rule the South Riding.

He could do it; his clear mind grasped detail; his concentrated will altered opinions. He could see the district he loved both as it was and as it should be. By an effort of the imagination he shifted his desires from his own inadequate self to this part of England. From Hardra's Head to the Leame he would set his mark upon Yorkshire. He might, in himself, be nothing, unloved, unfulfilled, unhappy; but he would identify himself with the happy and triumphant development of his county. I am the South Riding; L'état, c'est moi, he told himself.

He had the field to himself now; Astell was retiring, Carne was dead. There was no other man on the council with power enough to thwart him. He sat in the cold April sunlight that flickered among the chestnut trees outside his office window, and he shivered, tasting the acrid flavour of unshared victory.

The door flew open.

"And now, Mr. Snaith—" he heard.

He looked up to see Councillor Alfred Ezekiel Huggins scowling down at him.

"Oh, Huggins . . ."

The big preacher was wearing a carnation in his buttonhole. He had paid threepence for it in Kingsport market that morning. He had decked himself for the result of the Town Planning

Committee as for a bridal feast. He came anticipating the triumph of his well-laid schemes. He had seen them thrown heedlessly to the winds.

"And now, Mr. Snaith, perhaps you'll be good enough to explain yourself."

"Explain myself?"

"What does this mean about Schedule B?"

Wearily Snaith drew the plans towards him.

"I thought you understood. We have decided to abandon the Leame Ferry Waste site and build south of the Skerrow road, north of Garfield."

"So I heard. That's clear enough. I heard you were rigging the committee, but what I want to know is, what about the Waste? What about those sheds?"

"Sheds?"

"You can't have forgotten. Those sheds we bought last year. You and I. You really. You made out the cheque yourself to Reg Aythorne. Five hundred pounds."

"Oh, yes, to Mr. Reginald Aythorne. By the way, how is Mrs. Aythorne?"

There was no mistaking the demure sideways smile. Huggins opened his mouth to roar and then controlled himself.

"All right, I believe. They've moved south."

"Ah. Very gratifying. That must be a great relief to you."

"I don't know what you mean and I don't care. What I want to know is, what's going to happen to the Wastes? You can't just get away from it like that . . ."

"Like what? What are the Wastes to me?"

"Look here, Mr. Snaith, I'm not one of your clever business friends. I'm a simple sort of chap without much education, and you know it. I want this in A.B.C. language, please, and no funny business. I want to know what you're going to do and what you expect me to do. We can't go on working in the dark like this. We should tread on each others' toes. Here it is as I see it."

"Do tell me. And sit down, won't you?"

Huggins sat.

"As I see it. Here we are going to build a new housing estate. You call up Astell and me and tell us that your money's on Leame Ferry Waste, so to speak. You call me up a second time when I'm in a tight place . . ."

"Excuse me, you called on me."

"Same thing. And you put me on to a good thing in land values. You lend me five hundred pounds and we invest it in them sheds on the Waste for security. Good. All right. But now you go to the Kingsport Corporation, and you sit on a joint committee, and you come back and tell us you don't want Leame Ferry Waste after all. Oh, no. It's no use to you, that isn't. You want us to build south of the New Road. Where your new railway's going. Well and good, well and good. But what about the sheds, eh? What about our little investment, eh?"

"I've never pressed you for repayment, have I?"

"Pressed me? Repayment?"

"That five hundred pounds. That little loan—because your daughter's husband was in debt?"

"Good God, man, you don't think we'd let it stop there? When we'd got a good tip? Why, Drew's put in two thousand and Tadman another thousand, and Stillman wouldn't part with the mortgage from Aythorne's shed, and I've sold my life insurance to buy the forty acres below Tadman's lot!"

"Oh, that's the truth of the affair, is it?"

"Of course it is. Did you think we were all too slow to take your tip?"

Then Huggins saw that Snaith's light eyes shone with disquieting brilliance.

"You don't mean—you didn't—" he stammered. "Surely you knew we should . . ."

"Conspire to defraud the county council?" suggested Snaith. "No. I can't say that conclusion was uppermost in my mind. So it was you, Huggins, was it, who gave away your little plan to Carne by inviting him to join you. Why, I should like to know?"

"To stop him spoiling it all," Huggins explained eagerly, sure here at least that he was on safe ground. "If he came in with us, he wouldn't fight us on the council. That's the way to get a man, you know. Make it worth his while to be on your side."

"But what if you can't? In this case, you see, it didn't quite come off, did it? He demanded an inquiry into land purchase and libelled me."

"That can't hurt you much since he's dead," said Huggins brutally.

"No. Perhaps not. But I dislike imputations of corruption."

"Well, it was you that put us on to it. It was your idea. You said. . ."

"Nothing at all about a conspiracy to force up land prices, I think. Really, you are even more stupid than I imagined. Didn't you realise that this kind of thing can't be done in the dark? Real estate can't change hands and no one be any the wiser. There is such a thing as conveyancing; then there have to be leases and documents. I should have thought that a child in arms would know enough to steer clear of that kind of folly."

"Every one does it."

"Every one? Not in the South Riding. Nor in many other county councils, I think. Oh, I realise it has been done by certain members of town corporations, but sooner or later it usually comes out. And not very prettily, either."

But Huggins had had enough of Snaith's school-masterish superiority. He lent across the desk dark and menacing.

"Then why the hell did you put me on to it? What did you invest your five hundred for? Don't tell me it was charity!"

"I shouldn't dream of being so stupid as to call it charity."

"I suppose you meant to have a gamble, and then got scared by Carne, and went doubling back."

"To have a gamble. Yes. But not quite in the way you mean."

"Then will you please tell me what you do mean. Because I give it up."

"My dear Huggins, has it never occurred to you that there are more ways than one of gambling? Some people prefer horses, some cards; others go in for the stock exchange. Now I prefer to lose money on human nature. I pride myself on knowing it, and I like to back my fancy. Now there were several ways I could have spent that five hundred pounds—bought another motor-car, though I already have one, invited a number of people whom I dislike to share meals, which would give me indigestion, in my house which I prefer to have to myself. Travelled to America, which I have no desire to revisit. Added another wing to my house—which is already large enough. But no. On the whole I decided to expend it upon my hobby. That would give me more pleasure. So I handed it over to you, to see what you would make of it. After all, I had admirable Biblical precedent. Would you spend it on your family, your women, your social reputation—or would you put it into a napkin and bury it in the earth? Apparently you used it, very properly, to buy off Bessy Warbuckle's blackmail, and then, fascinated by the ease of the game, tried to turn speculator. But it's no good, you know. It doesn't suit your naturally open, simple and sentimental nature."

"You mean—you just lent me that money to see how I'd act?"

"Certainly, and allow me to assure you that it was worth it."

Slowly Huggins rose. He towered over the little alderman.

"You did this to amuse yourself, did you? For fun, eh? You've not just made a fool of me. You've made me sin. For fun. Not for gain, not to get yourself out of a scrape, not to beat an enemy. Just for fun. Gambling with human nature—for your hobby. Because you're rich and clever and know a thing or two we poor chaps don't, eh?"

Huggins was a preacher. Eloquence and moral indignation were his forte. His training and experience came now to his aid. He never paused for words.

"All right. I'm not complaining. I shall take my medicine, don't you fret, and face my colleagues and tell them we've been fooled and we shall have to stand the racket. But just understand this, please. I'm a sinner. I confess it. And I've caused others to sin. And I shall bear whatever just penalty God exacts of me. But you, you, you!" The great raw-beef fist shot out. "You, who gamble with human souls for your amusement—who tempt others to fall into traps that don't happen to threaten you.

You, who go creeping and crawling along the earth on your belly like the snake you are, seeking what Christian's soul you can send to perdition, with your little loan here, and your little job there, and your hints and your tips and your insinuations, pushing others over the brink of hell and holding back yourself! Always on the right side of the law while you hurl others to destruction. You—you—you!"

Words at last failed him. Striding round the desk he took the little alderman by the shoulders, lifted him clean out of his chair, and shook him—shook him till his eyes protruded, his lips turned blue, and his teeth rattled and finally stuck sideways on their loosened plate half-way out of his mouth in an extraordinary independent grin. Then he dropped him, like a broken doll, into his seat and stood contemplating his handiwork.

Snaith slid forward, only half conscious, incapable of movement.

Huggins fell to his knees.

"Oh, God," he prayed, "behold us sinners. Look down upon us in Thy everlasting mercy. Thou knowest our inmost thoughts, whatever they be, righteous or unholy. Do judgment, Oh, God, according to Thine infinite pity. Oh, Lord, I have been Thy servant. Let me never be confounded. Amen. Amen."

He rose. He strode out of the office and down the ringing stone corridor.

He knew that he was a ruined man. He would retire from the council. He had thrown away his savings. His reputation was at any man's mercy.

But he breathed great draughts of air into his lungs. Triumph exalted him. He had told Snaith what he thought of him. He was triumphantly free. He had spoken his heart before God in admonition.

He was due to give an address at the Davis Street Methodist Church at half-past five. He kept his appointment. He took as his text: "The sixth chapter of the Epistle of St. Paul to the Ephesians, tenth verse: Finally, my brethren, be strong in the Lord and in the power of His might. Put on the whole armour of God that ye may be able to stand against the wiles of the devil. For we wrestle not against flesh and blood, but against principalities, against powers, against the rulers of the darkness of this world, against spiritual wickedness in high places."

It was the sermon of his life.

Anthony Snaith, whom he thus accused of spiritual wickedness and identified with the powers of darkness, took longer to recover. He rose stiffly, pulled out his teeth and found the plate cracked, put them in again regretfully and began to straighten his hair.

He was trembling violently. Since his oppressed and bullied boyhood he had retained a horror of physical violence. What Huggins had done to him had affected him more profoundly than in its immediate consequences.

There was a carafe with water and a tumbler balanced upon it on the side table. Snaith groped his way towards this, gulped down a long drink of the tepid and dusty fluid, and felt rather better. He sat down and tried to come to terms with himself. His pulses were leaping, his head ached, his whole body trembled in an ague.

Yet his collapse was wholly corporeal. Already his quick mind was analysing the experience, already his thin lips twitched to a doubtful smile.

For Huggins was wrong. Snaith did not wish men to do evil. He was only torn between two principles of desire. Sometimes he wished to frustrate and thwart men's natures, so that they might all be as he was, impotent of passion. In that desire lay negation and lethargy and death.

But sometimes he wished them to fulfil their natures. He remembered very well his desire for Huggins. That five hundred pounds had been the price of life, of vitality, of fulfilment. Tempestuous, lustful, violent, whatever the preacher was by nature, that he should be. Poverty should not frustrate him. Fear should not hold him back.

And he had run true to type. On the whole, that was very satisfactory. Even this ridiculous business of buying up the Wastes had a crude liveliness and initiative about it. Snaith could imagine those earnest Kiplington tradesmen cherishing their dreams of enrichment in their crochet-decorated parlours. Well, well, well. Not entirely wasted money.

Not entirely wasted because even his bruised body and aching head reminded him that he had not, after all, that day been quite without experience of passion. He had been literally swept off his feet by an orgasm of fury. He had been, as they say, shaken well out of himself. And there was an odd masochistic pleasure to be found in this contact with energy, even though the energy itself were hostile—a sort of vicarious satisfaction, a novel response to unfamiliar stimuli.

He retied his tie in front of the little mirror, observing with critical attention the pale secret face reflected back at him.

It had done him no harm, and it would do Huggins good. Huggins would be a wiser, more honest man for that day's work. For after the storm, Snaith reflected, came the whirlwind, and after the whirlwind (seeing that he was as good a Methodist as Huggins and knew his Bible), after the whirlwind, he thought, the still small voice.

CHAPTER IV

MIDGE DECIDES TO GO HOME

Tom Sawdon was cleaning the petrol pumps in the Nag's Head yard when the Cold Harbour bus stopped and a stranger alighted and stood looking up and down the level road. He was a tall slouching old fellow with a tweed deer-stalker cap and long grey moustaches that blew in the brisk May wind.

"Hi, you!" he shouted. "Which way to Maythorpe Hall?"

"Straight along and it's on your right. Big stone gateposts among trees, with eagles on them."

"How far?"

"Matter of a mile and a half to the gate. Half a mile up the drive."

"Humph! Puff!" The old man had a chortling, irritable cough. "They told me the buses passed the gate."

"So they do if you stay in them long enough. You got out too soon, sir."

"Fellow shouted 'Maythorpe'!"

"That's right. This is Maythorpe village."

"What time's the next bus?"

"About half-past five."

"Damnation!"

A lively old fellow, a gentleman, Tom decided. Also a possible fare. He wrang out his cloth.

"Any taxis round here?"

"I have one, sir."

"You have, have you? How much d'you charge to drive me to the Hall—and back?"

"Five shillings fare, sir. But I charge for waiting."

He wished he dared trust Hicks to drive the car yet; but Geordie, though willing, was a slow learner. He had been too long with horses to acquire rapidly the mechanical sense desirable in chauffeurs.

The old chap was chuffing and hemming. Finally he decided to take the car. Tom pulled on his coat and shouted to Hicks. Odd that though Lily had been in hospital for nearly four months, and dead for nearly three weeks, he still looked for her as he passed by the kitchen window.

The Sunbeam was running well. Tom knew how to drive her. Steel and wire wore better than flesh and blood; they were more easily repaired.

Smoothly they swooped round the illogical turnings of the road; they swung into the drive of Maythorpe Hall. The hedges were bare as broomsticks. A cock pheasant whirred clucking from the thick bramble-bound undergrowth; trailing its splendid tail like a comet, it sailed overhead.

"Preserve game here?" asked the passenger.

"They say the late Mr. Carne was a grand shot."

The drive needed weeding; hedge parsley and dead nettle frilled its deep ditches; fallen trees drew acute angles among the vertical lines of beech, ash and birch. Suddenly the road turned and widened; Tom brought the Sunbeam round with a sweep in front of the pillared porch.

The old man climbed out stiffly. He saw the crumbling steps, the gaping blank oblongs of window, the flowering currant bush that dropped its bright pink blossoms like bunches of exotic grapes on to the lichen-covered tiles.

"Is this the place?" he asked.

"Yes, sir."

"Looks empty."

"They left the maid as caretaker, I think, sir."

The stranger mounted the steps; a squatting toad flopped down from one of the cracks and stared up at him, bright jewel-eyed.

"Cheerful," muttered the old man.

He put out his hand and tugged at an iron knob beside the door. It pulled outward, screeching hideously. Far away a bell tinkled through empty passages.

There was no reply.

He pulled again.

"Humph, humph," he grumbled.

"It's not the slightest use," said a clear high voice above their heads, "pulling that bell, because they can't hear you upstairs, and the front door won't open."

At the sound, the old man started back, and both he and Tom saw, hanging over the stone balustrade above the porch, outlined against the white racing clouds of the turquoise sky, a child's thin face and slender shoulders. Her straight hair fell in elf-locks beside her cheeks; her wide brown eyes were scornful.

"What the devil!" gasped the old man.

"Hallo, Sawdon," said the girl. "If it's a reporter you've brought, you can take him away again. If it's an agent, it's no use, 'cause the lawyers are settling everything and we're probably sold already to the county council. And if it's some one who wants Mrs. Beddows she's upstairs and this door's jammed. You have to get in through the drawing-room window."

"And who the devil are you?" roared the old man.

"Miss Carne of Maythorpe," replied the girl, with hauteur. "Who the devil are you?"

He started, staring at her, but pulled himself together.

"That's my business. I want to see Mrs. Beddows."

"Is she expecting you?"

"She wrote to me."

"All right. I'll come down and let you in."

With a whisk of brown tunic and grubby white blouse, she was gone. The old man stood rubbing his nose with his finger. He turned to Tom.

"Do you know that young woman?"

"Oh yes, sir."

"Is that true? She's Miss Carne?"

"That's right. Every one round here knows her."

"What sort of child is she?"

"All right, sir. A bit wild."

Tom thought he heard a kind of wintry chuckle; but Midge had reappeared round the corner of the house.

"I've told granny. She said you were to come in. This way."

She led him round the south face of the Hall. To their left was a flowering wilderness, sheltered by old brick walls on which fruit trees straddled. There had been lawns here, and beds and borders. Now daffodils waved among the unmown grass and primulas grew below the tangle of unpruned roses. Over a weed-grown rockery splashed white arabus and tiny saxifrage.

A French window opened on to the broad flagged path.

"This way. This was the drawing-room," said Midge proudly.

She led him into the empty sun-washed shell of a room. Painted cupids flaked petals of gilt and pink from the ceiling; the candelabra had been torn from the elegant panelled walls. In one corner lay a broken harp, its strings coiling out from its ruined frame.

The old man gave a sort of gasp as though he recognised something.

Midge led him though the door into the dark hall. Its dim rich illumination came through the drawing-room and the stained glass of the front door; it danced on a delicate golden sea of dust. Piles of packing cases, bundles and picture frames obstructed all free passage. The old man stood blinking, like a grand yet mangy eagle among the debris.

He was watching Mrs. Beddows descend the stairs. Her round face was red with exertion. She wore a white apron, none too clean; but the brooch Carne gave her sparkled and glowed at her throat.

"I am Mrs. Beddows," she said in her cordial Yorkshire voice. "Did you want to see me?"

"Yes. I did."

"Who are you, please?"

"My name's Sedgmire."

She did not at first catch it.

He handed her a card. She had to pull down the pince-nez pinned to her dress and stare at it, puckering her face. Midge stood gaping, the colour ebbing and flowing under her transparent skin.

"Lord Sedgmire?" faltered Mrs. Beddows, frowning.

"Grandfather!" screamed Midge.

"That remains to be seen," growled the old man. "I want to talk to you." He turned to Mrs. Beddows.

"Of course. Come into the dining-room. This is Midge Carne."

"So I see. So I see. And you're her guardian. I got your letter."

"I didn't expect you here."

"I thought I'd better come and see for myself, eh?"

They went into the dining-room. It still bore its air of shabby grandeur. The crimson curtains had gone, but the big oak table, where twenty guests could sit without any crowding, lay with a bloom of dust on its polished surface. The silver cups had gone, but the arm-chairs still stood on the thread-bare carpet before the fire. The painted terra cotta walls showed darker squares where the family portraits had hung; but from above the mantelpiece there still looked down with wonder and pride and scorn, as though she had preserved those emotions through twenty-five years since she last saw her father, the wild strange loveliness of Muriel Carne.

"Ah," breathed the old man, and stood still, facing it.

"A good likeness?" he inquired at length.

"Yes. Robert had it done five years after their marriage."

He looked at it, nodding his head several times, then glanced from the portrait to Midge. The resemblance was unmistakable.

"Wouldn't you like some tea? How did you get here?" asked Mrs. Beddows nervously, rubbing her plump, work-soiled hands.

"Bus to Maythorpe. Had to take a taxi. Oh, there's a man outside."

"Midge, go to Elsie and tell her to get us some tea, will you?"

"The man's Sawdon," said Midge.

"Well. Give him some too. He's a great friend of ours," explained Mrs. Beddows. "Poor fellow. Just lost his wife. We all like him. Go along, Midge. Your grandfather wants to talk to me."

The child made a grimace, but she obeyed. One obeyed Mrs. Beddows.

Yet somehow she felt that she had been defrauded.

All her life she had dreamed that some day the Sedgmires would appear and bear her off to her rightful place and splendour, to a castle, to parks, to rose gardens, peacocks and titles. But since darling Daddy's death the vision had been infinitely more compelling. There was no question now of Mummy's return. Maythorpe was lost—lost in some strange way before Daddy's death. Midge was a prisoner in the dull security of Willow Lodge. She had not even gone back to school for the summer term. These excursions to Maythorpe, upon which she had insisted, to help Granny Beddows pack and sort the things, had been her one excitement—they cast the sole glow of drama on the monotonous days.

And now here suddenly Lord Sedgmire had arrived. And glory had not blinded her. He was an old man who looked like a gamekeeper, in Tom Sawdon's hired car. And when he saw her, he sent her to the kitchen.

Instead of going immediately to Elsie and asking for the tea, she rushed upstairs to her old room and flung herself weeping on the floor.

Down in the dining-room Lord Sedgmire laid his tweed cap cautiously on the dusty table.

"Do sit down," said Mrs. Beddows.

He did so, with creaking joints, and stared at her.

"You're an alderman?"

"Yes. A county alderman."

"Bless my soul. Can't keep pace with these new-fangled ideas. Women in my time . . ." his barked dry utterances faded. "My—er—son-in-law left you guardian to this child."

"Yes. But of course all the legal business is held up. The body hasn't been found. We can't get probate."

"So I understand. Most unfortunate. Think the fellow's dead?"

She turned aside for a second, then, with an obvious effort, answered, "Yes."

"Humph. Suicide, I suppose. Got himself in a bloody mess, insured his life and killed himself. Hummph." He pursed his lips with frowning speculation. "No near relatives?"

"There's a younger brother. An architect at Harrogate. Nothing wrong with him, but not much use, and the wife's no good. Not for a child. All fish and finger-bowls and no common sense."

"Which you have, eh?"

She answered his challenge, her brave head lifted, the white bib of her apron rising and falling to her quick breath.

"Robert Carne trusted me."

"You knew him well?"

"Ever since Muriel's illness."

"Ah."

It was the old man's turn to fight emotion.

"I understand that now there's trouble with the insurance company," he said dryly. "They're not satisfied. Prefer to know he's dead before they pay up, eh?"

"That'll make no difference to my husband and me. We're not paupers."

"What I can't see is why you should do this, Mrs. Beddows. I've made a few inquiries. I know they think well about you here. You've got nothing to gain. The girl's a handful, I can see, and delicate, I understand. You're not a young woman. What d'you get out of this?"

"You never knew your son-in-law, did you, Lord Sedgmire?" asked Emma Beddows.

Her blood was up. She could fight now—not only Carne's father-in-law, but all his enemies. She had fought lawyers and bank managers and the insurance company. She had fought her husband who had objected to her assuming responsibility for Midge. She had fought her own fatigue and disinclination for fighting. Suddenly, since Carne's accident, she had known herself to be an old woman and tired. The thought of coping with Midge, her tempers and her moods, secretly appalled her. But Robert had trusted her. That was her glory. She would never let him down.

"You never knew Robert Carne much, did you?" she repeated.

"Can't say I did. Can't say I wanted to."

The old man gave his dry chuckling cough.

"When a common farmer takes advantage of your daughter in the hunting field, follows her home, rushes her off her feet, carries her back to his place, drives her into an asylum and then chucks himself over a cliff to leave the mess he's made for other people to cope with—you're not exactly inclined to make friends with him."

"So that's what you think."

"What would you think, madam?"

"I'll tell you not what I think, but what I know," said Emma Beddows. "Your son-in-law was the finest man I ever met. He loved your daughter. And she loved him, don't doubt it. He wasn't just what you call a common farmer. The Carnes owned Maythorpe for five hundred years. It was one of the show places in the South Riding. When I was a child we all looked up to the Carnes like gods. They mightn't have a title, but they were gentry; they took the burdens of gentry on them. Their name was a power. Robert Carne was the best looking of the lot; he'd been well educated. Isn't St. Peter's, York, a good old school for you? He was a sportsman. There wasn't a girl—farmer or county class—in the Riding wouldn't have had him."

"He oughtn't to have married my daughter, Mrs. Beddows."

It was a cry from the heart, but it did not touch her.

"You mean your daughter should not have married him. There's no taint in the Carne blood—man or woman. You know—oh, forgive me—but you know, Lord Sedgmire, where, if anywhere, there was bad heredity."

"I never asked him to mix up with it," said the old man proudly. "I forbade the marriage."

"Yes, by blustering and swearing and driving Muriel till she was set on it."

"She?"

"Did she run away to Carne, or did Carne carry her off?"

"He hung round in the village."

"Of course. Do you think he could have run away and left her, so unhappy, and you shutting her up? He wasn't that sort."

"He's run away now, hasn't he?"

"Oh, we don't know. We don't know. We shall never know," she wailed. The façade of her fighting courage almost cracked. She made a terrific effort. "Listen," she said. "Never mind how or why they did it. Let's take it they were young and loved each other. But the moment they were married, I can tell you this. Robert set himself to do his best for her. At first it was change she wanted and foreign travel. Baden-Baden, Monte Carlo, Vienna."

"Yes," he nodded, almost absent-mindedly. "Her mother was like that."

"Hunting all winter. Fishing sometimes in Norway. Well. He could afford it those days. He had the house done up; he entertained, or he took her away when there was no hunting or sport here. He and his fathers had been first-rate farmers, and the farm's a good one. He spent more than he should have done, but they could manage. Then the War came. He joined up. They put him in charge of a remount depôt. He knew everything there was to know about horses. First, he was in England, then in France. She couldn't go abroad so easily. She stayed on here and hunted. She kept open house for the young officers. She entertained. They used to play poker here at nights. One heard stories. Then she took to going up to London. Some sort of war work, she said. We never knew what. I say she missed Carne. He always steadied her. Then he came on leave in 1917 and found her in London with a lot of officers. I believe there was a scene. She enjoyed scenes, you know. Not like a Yorkshire woman. Then the child was to come. She was back here with the groom and servants. She was rather queer. But she wouldn't go away. He came on leave again and was worried to death. It was then he asked me to look after her. Believe me, she had every attention. But when the child came we could tell at once that something was badly wrong. We sent for Carne. He got leave somehow. He did everything. Got specialists from London, nurses, treatments. He told us to spare no expense. I came over here and did what I could. He had to go back. It was—awful. I never knew a man more torn. Never think, never think, Lord Sedgmire, he didn't love her."

"Well?"

"Well, since then, everything has been done for her. It's not been a good time for farmers since the War, and Carne had already spent too much of his capital. The old foreman who looked after the place during the War was a good man on the land, but not so good at business. Carne came back. The doctors ordered Muriel to nursing homes. He sent her here, there, anywhere that they thought held the ghost of a hope for her. He drained the farm of every pound he could get from it. He cut down every expense."

"I understand that he was able to hunt and all the rest of it."

"He schooled and sold hunters. It was one of his most profitable lines. He had a name for them."

"Humph."

"If you don't believe it, come with me. I'll show you something."

She rose and he followed her.

"As things got worse," she said, "he started to sell property. A bit of timber here, a pasture there. Then he got a mortgage on the farm. I suppose you know it all belongs to the bank now? Then he began to sell his own possessions, the silver cups, the family portraits."

"Portraits?"

"Yes, you know. Even farmers have faces, and the Carnes were handsome. They had a Lawrence and a Raeburn, and some others by not such well-known artists. I don't know much about pictures, but I do know a bit of good furniture when I see it. You came through the drawing-room? You saw it was empty? I suppose you thought we've got rid of the furniture since—the—the accident? You're wrong. Carne did that. There were some gilt chairs and a bureau belonging to his great-grandmother. He sold them." She led him into the hall. "Do you see those ledges? They were covered with china. Old blue Minton, double dinner service, and Spode, very valuable. He got rid of those too. This was the smoke-room. There was oak panelling—four hundred years old. That went to America. He had a collection of old fowling pieces in the gun-room. Some museum took those. Come upstairs."

Up the stairs they went, the shallow uncarpeted steps creaking beneath them. She opened a door from the bare boarded passage.

"I want you to see that your daughter didn't come here into hardship."

She entered the whispering shadowed room. He paused on the threshold, blinking, but she went forward and pulled aside the soft green taffeta curtains with a rattle of rings along the thick brass pole. First through the south window and then the east, all the green May landscape to the Leame and to the sea lay spread before them, framed in the faded silk.

"Look," she said. "This was the room he furnished for her. It's not been touched till now. Look—here's the bathroom. Here's his dressing-room. He bought this suite for her. Look at the wardrobe. Here are all her clothes. Velvet, fur, satin. Do you call this hardship? Look at the linen, fine as cobwebs. And thirty pairs of shoes. Tell me, Lord Sedgmire, could you have done much better for her?"

"Oh, God," said the old man.

"In a way, I don't blame you. She was the only child, wasn't she? It must have been hard. But you see—what about Robert? Mind you, I think he was a fool. He'd have done better if he'd not tried to give her everything that she thought she wanted. But it's difficult to refuse when you're in love. Before she was ill, she always could get round him. He felt he owed her so much because in marrying him she'd cut herself off from all her family; and after she was ill, he felt he couldn't do enough for her because it was all his fault."

"His fault?"

"He thought that by making her have a child, he'd sent her out of her mind. It wasn't true. I don't believe for a minute it was true."

"What do you mean?"

"Well, the doctors were never sure it was the child. And if it was. . ."

"You mentioned something about a lot of young officers. And that it was the talk of the place."

She said nothing.

"Mrs. Beddows."

She faced him, her lips compressed.

"Did you mean anything by that?"

"You're her father."

"So I know her inheritance. Is this child Carne's?"

"He claimed it."

"Is it like him?"

"Not in any way. But that's nothing. He claimed Midge. He doted on her. He'd have done anything for her except sacrifice Muriel. He always accused himself of having forced a child on her."

"I see. And you. What do you think?"

"I think we shall never know."

"I see."

He sighed heavily, standing gaunt and old in the faded finery of his daughter's room. Suddenly Mrs. Beddows felt sorry for him. Her antagonism abated. He was an old man, and he was, she believed, fundamentally both honest and decent.

He turned to her.

"You want to keep this child? I shall, of course, see that you don't suffer financially. We too," he half smiled, mimicking her. "We're not too well off—land values, you know—but we're not paupers."

"I told you we could manage," she said sullenly.

"Of course. But you must see that it would be impossible for me to let you. There's another thing. Do you really want to keep the child? I quite see I can't force you to give her up. My son-in-law left you her guardian. He obviously thought you would be good to her. But I came here with an idea in my head."

He sighed again. All this was exhausting and saddening.

"What was that?"

A sudden fear caught at Emma Beddows' heart. He wanted Midge.

Now that she saw that she might lose the child, she knew she wanted her. Not that she found her lovable; she was too much like Muriel who had ruined Robert. But she was the pledge of Robert's trust and love, the one thing left that she might hold of him.

"My nephew and his wife live with me now, since my wife died. He really manages the estate for me. They have one child, a girl, a little younger than Midge. It's lonely at our place. Not many neighbours. My great-niece is delicate. We haven't sent her to school. She has governesses. Then perhaps Paris or Vevey. One of those finishing places. Then a season or two. It would do her good to have companionship."

Emma Beddows thought. She thought of the High School. Sarah was good for the child in one way. But then there would be all the talk. Kiplington was full of gossip. Had Carne run away? Had he committed suicide? Was it an accident? She had not dared to let Midge go back to school yet.

"I think," she said slowly, "it depends upon Midge herself. She's old enough now to know what she wants. She's sixteen. Small for her age. Delicate. Backward. But she has something in her."

And even as she spoke, she knew that already she had lost the child. Midge would never make a professional woman, or the sensible wife of a lawyer or auctioneer. Mrs. Beddows knew her insatiable taste for grandeur. She might be elegant; she might even make a successful social hostess. She would never fit into the plain provincial society of Kiplington.

Emma had lost her last link with Carne. Midge would go to Shropshire. Maythorpe would be sold to the county council. It would become an institution. I shall never visit it, Mrs. Beddows thought. I will not go on this committee. She was an old woman, and yet she would survive the young, the strong, the beautiful.

"Granny!"

The girl's shrill voice rang up the stairs. Midge had come to an end of her weeping, washed her face, and gone to Elsie full of plans and graces. She knew quite well what she desired to do.

"Granny! The tea's made."

"All right. We're coming."

She gave one look at the old man. They did not speak. They went downstairs together to the dining-room.

Midge was seated by the chipped japanned tea-tray. The spout of the brown pot was broken, but she had found an old silver cream jug, and the china was Crown Derby.

"I thought you were never coming. Aren't you thirsty? Grandfather, do you take cream? Sugar?"

"You seem to have established your claim to me all right, young woman. What do you suppose I came here for, eh?"

"Why, to take me home to Shropshire, of course," said Midge.

CHAPTER V

THE HOLLIES GO PICNICKING

Across the fields in the fresh bright May morning, the Holly children went to picnic, Lydia, Daisy, Alice, Kitty and Len. Len was very small. They had to carry him sometimes. But he had protested with screams against being left behind.

They had planned to walk to the Leame foreshore from Cold Harbour. Early that morning the Cold Harbour lorry, which Geordie Hicks was to drive and Sawdon owned, called round at the Shacks on its way from taking milk to Kiplington Station, and brought the children to Mrs. Brimsley's cottage. She had given them milk and bread and butter and furnished them with a large two-handled basket. "Put Lennie on it if he gets tired," she said, "and I'll tell you something. Don't dare to look inside till you touch the water. That's what my mother used to say. 'Now if you begin to eat before you've seen sea, you get stomach-ache.' You get along now, and then you'll get back again."

It was the first Saturday of the summer term. Miracles had happened. Lydia was at school again. All the complexity of the situation which had kept officials wakeful, sent teachers scouring the country, and driven aldermen grey-headed, had been solved by the charm of Barnabas Holly's voice and the maternal instincts of Mrs. Brimsley.

Already she had the baby with her at Cold Harbour. She and Holly on Sundays went by bus to look at the little bungalows near Minston. They were going to take one. She had her bit of capital. He would get a job on the new Housing Estate there; the small children could go to Minston School; Lydia could still cycle out to Kiplington, and in winter or bad weather go by bus.

It might be thought that Mrs. Brimsley got nothing out of this deal, but the fact was that she was getting what she wanted—a man to court her, a baby to hold in her arms, a family to need her. Already the baby turned to her with fat bubble-blowing smiles; already Lennie held out thin little arms to her; already Alice and Kitty brought to her their woes and triumphs, holes in their shoes, tales of their teacher, cuts and bruises.

The only person whom she had not yet won was Lydia—Lydia who had everything to gain from her father's marriage.

Lydia's brown face was set and sullen now as she trudged in her torn tight velveteen frock, with her little brother. The tawny wicks on the banks scratched their bare legs; their broken sandshoes trod nimbly on hard baked furrows.

"Now, you leave that basket alone, Dais," Lydia commanded sharply. "If you start peering, you'll start eating, and then there'll be nothing left for our dinners."

"There's boiled eggs an' oranges an' cheese cake. I saw," Kitty gloated.

"Greedy guzzler."

"Greedy yourself!"

"Oh, stop it. Both of you!"

The huge shallow sky cupped over the wide green landscape. White clouds like the ghosts of mountains moved across it. Down in the flat fields the children could see nothing but the fierce bluish green of the young spring corn, or the brownish grass and stubble. There were growing lambs on the grass, now rough and venturesome, with blunt black faces and curly foreheads like little hornless bulls. They pretended to be ferocious and Alice and Kitty pretended to be frightened.

"I've found a dandelion," shouted Alice.

"S'not. Colt's foot," Daisy snubbed her.

"Colt's foot? Miss Clever! Dolt's foot, bolt's foot, goat's foot."

"Miss Clever yourself. We had it in nature object lesson. Sucks."

"I don't care. I knew all the time. Sucks yourself!"

Like a great building, towering above the dykes, a ship moved up to Kingsport. It seemed to be gliding silently along the next field.

"Oh!" cried Kitty. "What is it?"

"A ship."

"A ship? In the field?"

"It's not in the field. It's on the river."

"On the river, really?"

"Yes."

"But I can't see the river. Where is it? When are we going to get to the river?"

Indeed it seemed as if they could never reach it. Each time they scrambled up the side of a bank, they could see from the top a gleam of silver; they could see the scattered houses standing two by two in sturdy partnership, over the wide Dutch colony. They could see the windmills and the spire of

Cold Harbour church and its clustering trees. The good expensive roads were raised on banks above the marshy land. The wide drains lay like canals, slicing the fields. Sometimes beyond the bank lay a drain and the children had to walk a mile or more seeking a bridge.

"I'm getting tired of this picnic," sighed Kitty. "There's a blister on my heel."

"Let's look. It's nothing."

"I'm getting hungry. When can we have some food?"

"When we get to the Leame," Lydia insisted.

She did not like her stepmother. She was jealous. With black and bitter resentment she thought her father vile to marry again. Yet she would, all the more because of her hostility, keep her promises made to Mrs. Brimsley.

She tramped along, Lennie pick-a-back across her strong young shoulders. Mrs. Brimsley had sent them on a picnic. Very well. On a picnic they would go. She would owe her nothing willingly, not even the small debt of disobedience.

It was hard, it was maddening, that Mrs. Brimsley should be the one to whom she owed her return to Kiplington High School. Oh, she would pay her back; she would pay her back. This much at least Lydia had decided.

But how he could! How he could kiss her, mess about with her, put his arm round her on the bus, sleep with her—after mother had died, after he had killed mother—that was what Lydia could not understand.

She could not bear it.

Lydia did not want to hate her father. She knew that he was proud of her. People liked him. The little man had a gay and jolly way with him. Miss Burton had said, 'You know, Lydia, you are much more like your father than you'll acknowledge.' Sarah hadn't seen mother moaning on the bunk, her hair round her face, crying that she was done for. Sarah hadn't seen mother moaning among the nettles. That was what father had done. That was what men did.

Oh God, I hope he does it to Mrs. Brimsley.

Daisy was saying something.

"Now you run a bit, Lennie, along this nice grass. What, Dais?"

"Oh, you're too dreamy. Too grand to hear us now. I was saying I suppose they'll put me into service. I'm damned if I go."

"You know you mustn't say damned. What would you like to do?"

"Fly to Australia. Like Amy Johnson," said Daisy unexpectedly, spitting out of her mouth a roll of well-chewed grass.

"I'm going to get married," answered Alice.

"Well, Amy Johnson married, didn't she?"

"I shan't. I shan't ever marry. Ooh, ups-a-daisy!" Lydia lifted Len up the steep piled bank. The highest dam they had yet encountered rose before them. "You take the basket, Dais."

"You'll be an old maid. Like your precious Miss Burton."

"She's not an old maid."

"Well. She's not married. And she's getting on, isn't she?"

"Dad says she's a nice piece. Why does he call her a nice piece?"

The dam was covered with tall silvery grasses. It was steep and slippery. Lydia pushed Lennie to the ledge above her head, then returned for the basket.

"Oooh," said Lennie. "It's big."

"What's big?"

Lydia hauled up the basket, then scrambled herself to the top of the bank and looked.

She stood, shading her eyes, the wind whipping her bare legs, her arms, her hair, and she looked across the salt marsh and the Leame to Lincolnshire.

It was here at last, the river that she knew so well from a distance, and yet had never till now approached.

A fleeting gleam of silver, the lights on a ship, a word from an old gossip—she knew the Leame all right.

But here it was at last, spread wide before her.

Immediately below the bank stretched the grey-green carpet of salt-marsh. Sea-samphire and sea-aster grew there, and the coarse puffing sea-meadow grass; here and there lay pools blinking up into the vivid blue of the sky; an overflow stream rounded into a pond, and beyond the pond lay more marsh, and beyond the marsh another, lower bank, the last rampart of the county, and beyond the bank the bold silver sweep of the Leame itself.

It was high tide. From Lincolnshire to Yorkshire the Leame filled its banks. Its waters, five miles wide, lapped against the little rivulets and indentations, sucking and gurgling. A tramp steamer went chugging out to sea, sending ripples to beat against the mud. A motor yacht, light as a bird, swished down the smooth wide water.

"Oh!" cried Lydia, and though she had always known the sea, grew aware of a new and strange exhilaration, as though she had been released from a captivity.

"Come on!" the children shouted.

They took hands, the little boy and the basket held between them, and down they slid, down to the salt marsh and across it, skipping over hummocks, slooshing in and out of water holes, racing toward the furthermost embankment, and even beyond that protruded a ledge of mud and grasses, of shiny velvet turf and bristling reeds. And there they halted, with nothing at last between them and the Lincolnshire coast but the sparkling water.

Far, far away the dim hills rose behind little houses, dolls'-sized buildings—a town, some factories, a water tower.

"Ooh. Is that Cleethorpes? I do want to see Cleethorpes!" Alice cried.

"Well, now we're here," said the more prosaic Daisy, "can't say I think much to it, now we are here. Where's basket?"

Lydia could withhold from them no longer the meal their prospective stepmother had provided.

They unpacked the basket and saw that Mrs. Brimsley had done them proud. Nothing that Mrs. Holly had provided had ever equalled this. Hard-boiled eggs, ham cake, cheese cakes and buns and oranges, and even a bottle of milk and a mug for Lennie. There was salt for the eggs in a screw of paper.

They'll think this is all. They'll forget mother, thought Lydia. They don't know Mrs. Brimsley's a rich widow and can afford it. She had a vague notion that if her mother had been a widow, too, she could have afforded a grand picnic like this.

"Look, my name's on," cried Alice. "ALICE. Written on my egg."

"Here's Lennie's. We've all got it," said Daisy.

And, sure enough, they had; written on every egg was a printed name. The biggest and brownest egg was Lydia's.

She means to get round me, the girl thought, viciously breaking the amber shell against a stone. But she could not hold her resentment. There was something in the way the picnic basket had been arranged, in the green paper serviettes wrapped round the cake and buns, in the oranges, and in the bottle of milk, so carefully wrapped and labelled "For Lennie. One dose of cow's medicine." She knew that Mrs. Brimsley was not only kind. She had humour. She and Dad together, they made a pair, they did.

Her mother? Well, her mother was something different. But this Mrs. Brimsley could look after the children. She would release Lydia of a burden. She would be kind to them. She had the superfluous energy which mother had lost, in her battle against poverty and dirt and nature. Mrs. Brimsley would be more fortunate. Her own days for child-bearing were over. She would give to her new family the good-humoured indulgence of a granny.

Mother wanted me to get on. She wanted me to win scholarships, Lydia thought.

The salt stuck to the glazed bluish surface of the hard-boiled white of Mrs. Brimsley's egg.

Perhaps after all it's not treachery—not—not forgetting mother to let Mrs. Brimsley help us.

I can always pay her back when I've been through college.

She held the warm brown shell of the egg in her hand.

When lunch was eaten, the children went off exploring. The tide had begun to recede. It was unveiling the long stretches of purple mud, where the men would sometimes come and spike for flatlies. Sweet-tasting fish, these, delicate as trout, the cottagers declared, but bony, so hard to eat in lamplit kitchens.

The children idled along towards the sea-coast. Eastward the land curved in a curling lip. As they went, they discovered treasures, flotsam from the tides, an old leather glove, a basket, lobster pots, a rusted frying-pan.

"Where does it all come from?"

"Up the coast. There's a current washes it down."

"Oh, might that be our frying pan?"

"There's a pineapple tin. Bet it's what Bert brought us on Lennie's birthday."

"Is there a pineapple in it?"

"Course not—silly!"

"There's summat here. Come here, Lyd! Old clothes, like."

"No, sacking maybe."

"No. It's got a boot on. It's a—" and suddenly Alice screamed and rushed to bury her white scared face in Lydia's velvet frock. And Lydia, peering above the frightened child, saw also what was lying half submerged in the mud, one arm floating limply along the water, its head mercifully buried in clay and weed.

"Come away, come on, Len. Come away!"

They turned then, and hurried, stumbling along the waterside, up and over the bank, across the salt marsh. They dropped Mrs. Brimsley's basket; they ran away, away from that monstrosity mourned by wheeling sea birds that circled and screamed above it. Panting, running, sobbing, their picnic ruined, the Holly children ran.

CHAPTER VI

MRS. BEDDOWS SENDS SARAH ABOUT HER BUSINESS

"What if you did quarrel?" asked Mrs. Beddows. "What if you didn't like him? That's no reason for insulting his dead body."

"Oh, no. It's not that!" Sarah cried.

"He was one of your governors. He's having a public funeral. The coroner said it was death by misadventure. It's only decent to go."

They sat in Sarah's sitting-room. Mrs. Beddows had called to tell Sarah that she must attend the funeral. As her final service to Carne she was arranging that he at least should have a worthy funeral.

Sarah crouched in the window-sill, looking out to sea.

It was here that she had watched the dawn with Robert, that night when Midge was ill.

She said:

"I don't want to. I dislike funerals. I hate this public display about death. I don't intend to go."

She shut her mouth obstinately.

She looked ill; she looked haggard; she looked her full forty years. Her navy blue dress was unbecoming and hung in ugly angular lines round her thin body. The flaming brightness was fading from her rich hair. There were shrewish petulant lines round her tired mouth.

Mrs. Beddows was not at her best, either. The news of finding the body and the inquest had distressed her. She had been crying, the difficult rending tears of age; they made her head ache, they hurt her heart; and now they were threatening to harass her again.

She looked at Sarah Burton who had proved so unexpectedly difficult and she sighed with sudden defeat.

"I can't possibly get away then," Sarah persisted, with hurried and uncharacteristic insincerity. "If I make a precedent I shall spend all my time attending funerals. . . ."

"Oh—stop!" cried Mrs. Beddows, her patience ended. "For goodness' sake don't go, then. But don't talk to me like that. Don't you see I can't stand it? I've had about enough."

"I'm sorry."

There was a pause. The two women sat silent. Mrs. Beddows licked her lips and made an effort. She spoke at last in an altered voice.

"I really came partly to talk about Midge. You know Lord Sedgmire came over a fortnight ago. We had a talk. He wants to take Midge to live with them in Shropshire."

Again that queer hostile silence from Sarah struck her. This is too much, she thought. Haven't I had enough to face? It's too much.

"So I've got to give notice, I suppose, of her leaving here."

"I thought you were her guardian."

"Yes. But I've got to do what I think best for the child. I don't think it's good for her here. There's too much talk. I've sent her away now to Whitby with Sybil for a week till the funeral and all are over. She wants to go to the Sedgmires."

"I see. She would. Of course."

"I went down to see them in Shropshire last week. I like the niece. She's a fine woman, I should say. It's a glorious old place. After all, that's Midge's real atmosphere. She belongs."

"She was always a little snob."

"Oh—Miss Burton! Why must you be so—" the alderman paused. "You used to like him once. When Midge was ill. Surely—"

"Surely. I liked him once."

"Then why can't you behave decently? You know I loved him. You know he was my friend—more like a son to me. Can't you keep back your prejudices at least—until he's in his grave?—keep a civil tongue in your head. Do you think it's fun? Do you think it's easy for any of us to face it? You only quarrelled with him about politics and so on. But we who loved him—we shall have to stand there and hear those words, and see the flowers, and listen to the rector talking about death being swallowed up in victory, not knowing—not knowing, whether perhaps he failed in the end."

"You mean—you think he killed himself?"

"Oh, how can we tell? It wasn't like him. But all that about making his will, and the insurance, and his dealings with the bank, and coming to me—Why did he fix up everything so if he didn't know—if he hadn't planned. . . ."

"Do you think suicide a sin, then?"

"Perhaps not exactly a sin. But it was so unlike him. He never shirked anything. No matter how unpleasant. And he wasn't the sort to look so much ahead either. It worried me when he gave me this." She touched the brooch at her throat. "It was Muriel's. It worried me when he asked me to be the guardian. Why did he do it just then—if he hadn't known? That's what I've asked myself day and night. Why did he do it?"

"Because," said Sarah quietly, "he knew he was very ill."

"Ill? Robert Carne? Nonsense. He never had a day's illness in his life."

"Oh, yes, he had. He had at least two. And he suspected that the third would kill him."

"What do you mean?"

"He had angina pectoris. Two attacks. And the second was a bad one."

"Angina—How did you know?"

"I happened to be there once, when he had an attack."

"When? Why didn't you say anything? Why didn't he tell us? When was this?"

"Just before Christmas."

"Just before—why—it was before Christmas he began to make all his arrangements."

"Yes. I know that."

"You mean he had this attack and immediately after—"

"Yes."

"But why—why didn't you tell me? Why didn't he?"

"Because it might have been a little awkward."

"Awkward? For him?"

"And for me."

"I don't understand."

"It is awkward now. But I am going to tell you. I am sick of deception and concealment. I am sick of guarding my reputation. I thought I wanted to go on teaching here. I don't. I want to go away. I want to give up teaching. I think I want to die," said Sarah.

"I don't understand. What is all this?" asked the alderman.

"It may not have occurred to you," Sarah said in her dull lifeless voice. "But I was in love with Carne. Oh, he wasn't with me. Not at all. Though I think he liked me. We got to know one another when Midge was ill. But we'd met before, of course. In curious circumstances. I flatter myself that I didn't betray my feelings—at first. Then at the beginning of the Christmas holidays I went to Manchester, to see Miss Tattersall, who was passing through there, and to do some shopping before I went down to my sister. I'd taken a room at the Crown Hotel—You knew it?" For she had seen Mrs. Beddows start.

"No—but—" Emma remembered that this was where Carne's letter came from. She nodded. "Go on."

"When I reached the hotel before dinner, I found Robert Carne there too."

"Ah!"

"Yes. He did not know I should be there, of course. What followed was entirely my own doing. I invited him to have a drink with me. Then he could hardly avoid asking me to dinner. He was lonely, he was miserable, he was troubled. He had spent the day looking at mental homes that might do for his wife, if he had to sell Maythorpe and work in a riding school. He had not found one that he liked. After dinner, we danced. He had drunk—a good deal. I took care that he did. Do you understand? I wanted him to be drunk. Because if he was drunk he might forget for an hour that he did not love me. I made him dance. I am quite a good dancer. Then we had some more drinks. Do you understand? Then I asked him to come to my room."

"Oh, God!"

Mrs. Beddows covered her face with her hands. After a moment she said:

"Do you want to go on?"

"Yes, please," said Sarah. "He came, of course. In the circumstances, it was inevitable. But the dancing, the exertion, and then running up five flights of stairs to my room was too much for him. He had an attack immediately. He was very ill. I thought he was going to die. He had nitrate of amyl in his room. I got it for him. By morning he was better. He went down to his own room. I left the hotel and went home to my sister. I do not know what he did next day, but from that time he must have known that life might end at any moment."

"Oh," Emma Beddows hardly breathed the word. "Oh, I see. I see."

She was looking straight before her and seeing, not Sarah, but Carne as he stood in her doorway, giving her the brooch which had been Muriel's. Her hand went up to it. She fingered the stones, then suddenly withdrew it and cried, "He was your lover!"

"No. No. He was not. He—he was ill too soon. I meant him to be." Sarah stood up. "I tell you here and now that I would have given all I have for one night—one hour. Even knowing that I should be only a passing fancy. I should have gone away. I should have left Yorkshire. I should not have cared what happened to me afterwards. But he did not—he did not—you must believe that."

"Oh, I believe it."

Sarah came over to the alderman and stood looking down at her.

"And believe this. It was all my doing. Never for a moment would he have dreamed of it. We had been together many times. He had had ample opportunity. Until that night I do not think it ever even entered his head that I was a woman. And even then—he never so much as kissed me."

Sarah went back to her window seat. She knelt, looking out to sea. The light was fading. Her little eastward room was almost dark. After a pause she continued.

"So you see. You know everything now—what sort of person I am, and how unfit to keep school here. You are a governor and an alderman. You can deal as you think fit with the situation. But I will send in my resignation at once."

Then the strength went out of her, and she could speak no more. She leant back with her eyes closed against the deep embrasure. She wanted only to sit quite still and say nothing.

Mrs. Beddows was quiet too until she asked, "Why did you tell me this?"

"I believe you loved him. I have never been able to give him anything. I thought that you might at least know the truth about him. He was a sick man. He knew he must die. He tried to make preparations for that. He did not kill himself."

"And you think—I shall expect you to resign now?"

"Of course. I am what is known as an immoral woman. Not only that, but your friend, Robert Carne, disliked me. Don't men hate women who throw themselves at their heads? I tell you. I took the initiative; I made him want to come. In a moment of impulse and desire, he might have taken me. But when all that happened was this frightful attack, of course he loathed me."

"Why do you think that?"

"We never met again till the day he died. He never wrote. Why should he? He avoided the governors' meetings—everything. Then suddenly—on the day of the inspection it was—he came to call to scold me about my action over the new buildings. We had a frightful quarrel. We were quarrelling when Miss Teasdale arrived. He rushed out, and she asked me, 'Is that one of your local problems?' Problems? My God. So you see, I have lost everything, even his good opinion of me. And it is my own fault completely. No blame to him. Oh, no, no blame to him."

"Wait a minute," Mrs. Beddows said strangely. "What time was it when he called on you?"

"In the morning—about—Miss Teasdale came at half-past eleven—Why?

"What difference can it make? Oh, let me go. End this interview. I cannot bear much more. Haven't I given you what you want? Haven't I torn my heart from my body to give you back your idea of Carne—my Carne?"

"I'm just remembering. It was the afternoon I saw him," Mrs. Beddows said. "Why, yes. And he gave me a message for you."

"A message? For me?"

"Yes. I never thought it was important. In one way it wasn't. Just a light word. He said, 'Give her my love. Tell her she's a grand lass. I wouldn't miss quarrelling with her for a great deal.'"

"He said that? And you never told me?"

"It went out of my mind. I thought it half a joke. I never thought it might be important to you. I'm very, very sorry."

From her pit of misery, Sarah stared fiercely at the alderman.

"You're telling the truth? You're not fooling me? Not fobbing up something to comfort me with?"

"Why should I?"

"Oh, I don't know. People do."

"But I know he liked and admired you. He told me once that he wished Midge had half your courage and generosity."

"Ah—but he altered his mind when I behaved—like a bitch in heat, like a cat on the roof—"

"Hush. Be quiet. I won't have you say such things. It's ugly and horrid and false and doesn't help. He didn't. He admired you."

"Why did he never speak, then? Why did he leave me alone, thinking he hated and despised me? It was cruel, cruel. One word—only one word—just to show. . . ."

"Oh, can't you see? He wasn't the kind to talk. He never spoke a word, unless he was in a temper, when silence would do. Just like his father there. Then I expect he was a little embarrassed too for being ill with you. Ashamed."

"Ashamed?"

"Those men who are so proud of their bodies. He was—"

"Why—yes—"

"I expect he didn't know what to say, so he said nothing. He hadn't much imagination, you know. He didn't think much of what other people might be feeling, or what effect he might have made on them. He often hurt me too, without meaning it, just by not seeing. Being rather blind. Only with Muriel he used to be so sensitive. He'd force himself to imagine what she felt, and usually I think he tortured himself imagining that she'd take things even harder than she did. So don't you worry. Nobody despised you. And you mustn't despise yourself—any more."

But Sarah had gone back to her seat and she bowed herself in the darkened window, and, for the first time since she heard the news of Carne's accident, was lost in weeping.

After a little while she felt a gentle experienced hand stroking her fallen head and a tired kind voice that spoke in a weary monotone.

"So you mustn't think of resigning, because you are needed here. I don't say you've behaved well. I don't think you did. You were foolish and reckless and very, very wrong, and it's this kind of thing that leads to so much misery. But I'm not one to condemn you. Because for years I've thought far more of Carne than was good for me—or Jim. Mind you, I don't say I loved him the way you did. More as a son. I'm an old woman. But when you're seventy you don't always feel old. I know I don't. There are times when you find yourself thinking of yourself as a girl. 'Now the girl went downstairs.' 'Now the girl put her hat on.' And then you look in the glass and there's a stiff heavy lump of an elderly person facing you, your face all wrinkles and the life gone out of your limbs. But you can still feel young. And if I'd been your age—and thought I could comfort him—though it's always wrong and leads to misery, I've sometimes wondered . . ."

"But I loved him and hurt him. I hurt him. It was because of me he rode so recklessly. . . ."

"You flatter yourself, my girl. He had plenty to worry about without you."

"Oh, it's no use hiding it. I made him ill. I roused him, to satisfy my desire. If only I'd never spoken, kept still, held back. I cannot bear this pain."

"And who are you to think you could get through life without pain? Did you expect never to be ashamed of yourself? Of course this hurts you. And it will go on hurting. You needn't believe much what they say about time healing. I've had seventy years and more of time and there are plenty of things in my life still won't bear thinking of. You've just got to get along as best you can with all your shames and sorrows and humiliations. Maybe in the end it's those things are most use to you. They'll make you a better teacher, anyway."

"I shan't teach any more."

"Oh, yes, you will. You can't take all your experience and education and training if you go and throw it all up just when you might be of some service? I call that cowardice. Not playing fair either."

"But what use? I? Now?"

"Now listen to me, my dear. I don't know much about your past life. You may have done many wrong things in it for all I know. You may have been loose in your morals, as they say all young people are nowadays. That's not my business. I don't know and I don't want to. But I tell you what is my business, and that's the kind of woman you are and the teacher you will be. Up till lately you've always been pretty successful, haven't you? Scholarships, honours, promotions. You're good-looking in a queer sort of way. You're attractive. You're young for your age, and strong, and confident. And you did your work well—up to a point, I think. You were good with the bright ones, Lydia Holly and Biddy Peckover, and the scholarship girls. You took pains with Midge—for other reasons. But what about the stupid and dull and ineffective? The rather dreamy sort of defeated women? You hadn't much use for the defeated, had you? Not much patience with failure. Well, now at last you know what it is to be defeated. Now you know what it is to feel ashamed."

Sarah hardly listened.

"If only I could tell him I didn't mean it. If only I could explain. I was only angry. When I said I didn't want Midge at school, it was because I loved him so unbearably. I told him to take her away, you know."

"And now she's going away. I'm sending her."

"So I can't even take that back. I can do nothing."

"And did you expect to get through life with no word spoken you couldn't take back, with no failure you couldn't turn to triumph? Oh, my dear—you haven't begun to live yet."

"But if this is living, I cannot bear it. I cannot bear myself. Whatever you tell me, I can't stay here. I can't do it. Don't you understand? I cannot bear this body that he did not desire. I wanted his child, don't you see? I never wanted a child before, but I wanted his child."

"I dare say. And now want must be your master. As it has been to many women. As it will be to many of the girls that you'll be teaching. It's no use only having a creed for the successful. Robert wanted what he couldn't have. He wanted Muriel not to have had the child and lost her reason. He wanted himself not to have forced it on her. Rightly or wrongly, he thought he had sent her mad. He never thought of her without pain or shame. Now you know something of what he felt. Now you can understand him and those who feel like him. Now perhaps you are fit to teach a little."

"But how can I teach here, when the things I know are right are all the things which he resisted? I cannot work for the world that Robert wanted; I cannot work for the world he did not want. My triumphs would be only defeats for him. My success would only be bought at his expense."

"Still thinking of triumphs? How do you know that you won't fail?"

"You're right. I don't know. I only know that I cannot bear this pain. There's no hope. No remedy."

"Yes. I understand that. And when there's no hope and no remedy, then you can begin to learn and to teach what you've learned. The strongest things in life are without triumph. The costliest things you buy are those for which you can't even pay yourself. It's only when you're in debt and a pauper, when you have nothing, not even the pride of sorrow, that you begin to understand a little."

Sarah lifted her ravaged face.

"I expect I shall begin to hate you in a few days, because of all the things I have told you. I never meant to expose myself like this. But tell me, tell me, why should I love him like this? I'm not a green girl. I'm not inexperienced. I didn't even like him. He was everything I dislike most—reactionary, unimaginative, selfish, arrogant, prejudiced. Yet—he has filled the world for me. I can see nothing else now. Oh, why?"

"You've got him wrong. He may have been all that you say he was, but he was much more. He was courageous and kind and honest. He was, in dealing with people, the gentlest man I ever knew. He knew all about loving. He let a woman destroy his whole life, yet he never blamed her. To the end he worshipped—yes—and respected Muriel—and was grateful for all she'd given him. He never ran away from failure; he never whined, never deceived himself, never blamed other people when things went wrong. In the end—it's not politics nor opinions—it's those fundamental things that count—the things of the spirit."

"In the end? In what end? In no end I've ever heard of."

"Perhaps not. Perhaps in an end too far away for us to dream of. So you see,—you've got to stay and work here, Sarah Burton. Because you belong to the South Riding, and he loved it. Maybe his ideas were wrong and his ways old-fashioned. Maybe all that we do here isn't very splendid. As I see it, when you come to the bottom, all this local government, it's just working together—us ordinary people, against the troubles that afflict all of us—poverty, ignorance, sickness, isolation—madness. And you can help us. You who belong here, and who were clever, and went out into the world to gain your education—"

"And came back to lose it here," Sarah smiled wearily.

"Very well then. To lose it. And start again."

"But—I've done so badly. I hate myself so—"

"Well, quite a few of us have to get through life without too good an opinion of ourselves and yet we manage. You'll learn even that, you know, one day."

The telephone rang, cutting into the quiet darkness. Outside the window only the faint bar of the afterglow lay along the eastward horizon above the silent sea.

Sarah rose and moved clumsily across the room. Mrs. Beddows heard her fumbling blindly for the receiver.

"Yes? Hallo? This is Miss Burton."

All tone had left her dead weary voice. "All right. Very well. I may be a little late, I have a governor with me. Tell them I'm coming."

"What's that?"

"Only a staff meeting. I'd forgotten."

"You must go."

"Yes."

"And you'll come to the funeral to-morrow."

"Yes."

"And you'll stay on and work here."

"I don't know. I must think."

"You will stay. I don't think you're a coward either. Well. Ugh! my knees. They're stiff if I sit long. I'll leave you. Have you any whisky in the house?"

"Why? I—yes—I'll see—"

"No hurry. Take a strong one before you face that meeting. I don't hold with it. But there are times. Good-bye, my dear—and brave—girl. God bless and comfort you—and thank you."

"Oh—for what?" breathed Sarah.

The little woman paused at the door. She was buttoning her coat round her. Her weather-beaten face was broken with grief and tenderness.

"For loving my dear boy—and wanting to comfort him," whispered Mrs. Beddows, and went off into the darkening town.

Sarah went to her staff meeting. She heard nothing. She made mechanical replies. She congratulated the women on Miss Teasdale's favourable report. Nothing that any one said made any impression on her.

When it was over she took her little car and drove out, under a small horned moon, to Maythorpe.

The gate was still off its hinges, the drive lay open. She drove down below the budding limes and sycamores.

The house lay bare and blank in the faint moonlight. She climbed from her car and sat on the cold stone step, trying to feel near the man whom she had tried to hate, believing that he despised her, and who had not despised her, and whom she could not help but love.

All her life she would love him, and all through her life she would fight against him. His ways were not her ways, his values were not her values. She had followed her reason, until her passion crossed it, and now she sought, beyond reason and beyond passion, some further meeting-place.

She had lost her faith in herself and her opinions. She was certain of nothing. The solid earth beneath her feet had melted, and she had fallen into a gulf of grief and shame. Take what you want, she had cried in arrogance. Take it and pay for it.

She knew now that the costliest things are not the ones for which those who take can pay. Carne had paid. He would continue to pay—for all she bought now, for all impersonal triumph, for all that she might achieve in the South Riding. She would remain his debtor.

She knelt on his threshold, her arms round the crumbling pillar, her cheek on the cold stone.

"Oh, my love, my love," she cried to the unresponding darkness.

Bushes stirred. A bat fluttered silently. Far away in the pit beyond Minton Riggs a fox was barking.

I cannot touch you, she thought. I cannot reach you. There is no comfort or thanks now that I can bring you. All my life I can do nothing but destroy where you have builded and build where you destroyed. Forgive me. Forgive me. I have nothing for you—nothing, nothing, nothing.

But even as she cried out that there was nothing, beating her hand against the pillar which soon itself would stand no longer there, she became aware that perhaps there was something. It was no visible or audible presence, no ghost of the man she had loved, no reassurance that in his darkest hour he had indeed turned to her and found comfort in the thought of her. It was no more than the faintest fading of her isolation.

Something had happened. Quite simply she knew that she was not entirely alone, not arrayed against him; for he was within her. She had become part of him and he of her, because she loved him. He had entered into her as part of the composition of her nature, so that they no longer stood in hostile camps. She could no longer hate herself, for that would be hating him too. He would not hate her for what she was doing, even if she stayed and fought against all that he had stood for.

This sense had nothing to do with what he felt for her, for that was little; nothing with what she felt for him, for that was, perhaps, too much. It was as though, each of them having known love so intensely even though not for each other, they had entered into some element greater than themselves, and, being part of it, existed eternally within it, and, being thus transformed, become part of each other.

It was not a sense of comfort—of pain, rather—but these were the intense creative pangs of birth, not death. Her rational, decisive, rather crude personality seemed to enlarge itself, with desperate travail of the imagination, until it could comprehend also his slow rectitude, his courage in resignation, his simplicity of belief.

For she knew now not only her failure but his sorrow. She entered at last into part of his experience, and understanding him, felt isolated no longer. She could endure what lay before her because he had endured and she had loved him.

She rose slowly, and began to move forward, groping silently round the dark eyeless house, bidding farewell to it, not for herself, but for him. She, who would help to destroy it, as she had helped to destroy all that Maythorpe stood for, she blessed the cold stone, touched the black scentless ivy.

She crossed the empty yard, and stood by the stable windows. She put her hand on the mounting block, and felt the hollow step worn by his foot and those of his forefathers.

Every creature was asleep; each stall was empty. The house was a shell of memory. Only the ducks had been left upon the horse-pond. They were awake and stirring.

Sarah could hear their soft and drowsy gabble and the liquid sound of their rootling for insects in the mud.

Then she saw them, white as swans in the moonlight, swimming away across the dark smooth water.

EPILOGUE AT A SILVER JUBILEE

The aeroplane ran lightly across the turf, drawing dark wheelmarks along the sheen of dew. Then it danced, brushing the daisies, cleared the low hawthorn-sprinkled hedge, and was away up into the clear sweet air.

It was half-past six on the morning of May 6th, 1935, the day of the Silver Jubilee. The aeroplane carried a pilot and three passengers—Lovell Brown, engaged to write a descriptive article on the South Riding decorations, a staff photographer from the Kingsport Chronicle, and Sarah Burton. She alone was there for her own entertainment. Hearing, the previous week, of Lovell Brown's intended flight, she had pleaded with his editor for the fourth seat in the aeroplane, and he, who thought well of her and valued her friendship, had been willing to gratify her curiosity.

For Sarah had only flown earlier by Imperial Airways across the channel. She had never before this been in a small open monoplane, looking down on to the familiar country.

They swept north first, up the coast to Hardrascliffe. On the wolds the small dark villages dotted the green landscape. Over each the plane swooped low, so that the photographer might make pictures of the garlanded streets, the bannered steeples, the white marquees and tents in the open fields, prepared for Jubilee teas.

It was a green and white carpet, green pastures, gardens and plantations, white tents, white daisies, and white hawthorn hedges. Long morning shadows striped the living green.

Sarah carried a letter in her handbag. She had received it the previous Saturday, read and re-read it, and knew it now almost by heart. She was thinking of it as she bounced and swayed over the South Riding. It was from her friend Joe Astell.

"MY DEAR SARAH," he had written,—"No, I do not propose to come and join your Jubilee ballyhoo. Except for unavoidable circumstances I should have been travelling to London for Sunday's demonstration against it. Don't you know me better? I had enough of being a good citizen when I was on your county council. I'm a militant again, thank God, quit of the shame of compromise.

"Of course I see your point. One could regard it as an opportunity for a general beano, a moment of sunlight between storms. Or even, as you say, a demonstration of national unity—of common fortune. But my dear silly girl, this mass hysteria and empty shouting do not represent that classless commonwealth of equals which I want, and which you say you want. Don't delude yourself.

"They've chalked on a wall opposite my office—'Flags to-day, gas-masks to-morrow.' Well, Sarah, is that so much off the point? Anyway, I can't rejoice here. We have miles of docks with grass growing between the truck lines. Men I used to know as the finest workmen in the world, skilled artisans, riveters, engineers, are rotting on the dole. Oh, no, they don't starve; but they suffer from heart disease, T.B. and, worst of all, perhaps, hopelessness. And the tragic sickening fact is that their only chance of re-employment lies in this arms race. They can return to life only by preparing for death. It's a mad farce, and I don't like myself any better for enjoying the incidents of the battle. Of course I do enjoy them. I've loved the fight, though my heart sickens for the defeated, and I don't like the flavour of the future.

"You'll have to work for a revolution, Sarah. I know you don't want it, and it's a bloody, brutal prospect. But we can't build anything permanent on these foundations.

"At least I fear so. Though sometimes I hope you may be right. You're a grand girl, Sarah, but, in spite of all your civics, classes and so on, I don't think you're a politician. Your mind is too vague. You see ends, but not means.

"Does all this sound dispirited? I'm not, I promise you that. The fact is I'm mortally afraid of growing reconciled and complacent in my old age, and you were right about one thing. I haven't stuck this job for the two years I promised myself. I'm laid up again after a hæmorrhage. The open-air speaking in the by-election did it, I suppose. Still, we got our man in, and it was a bonny fight. I'm going up to the Trade Union Sanitorium at Pitlochry, as soon as there's a bed. I don't suppose they'll allow me to come back here again.

"Personally I find I mind extraordinarily little. If I hadn't had a shot at it, I should have been eternally ashamed. But now I'm tired, and glad enough to give over. I'm only sorry I stayed so long among the flesh pots of Kiplington.

"Maybe that's why I can't get too indignant even about your Jubilee. I can only feel glad that you'll get your buildings out of it. I shall think of you, Sarah, stalking about your corridors in that palace of glass and chromium. I shall imagine you trying to look six feet high and ferociously determined, whereas I believe you're at heart a bit of a sentimentalist and gentle as a dove. Still, if you can go on scolding silliness, laughing at sentimentality, debunking all the cant and humbug, wrestling with parents and governors, you'll make a thundering good job of that school. I know it. And I shall be glad it was partly through my work that you have a decent place to work in. I believe in bricks and mortar. Whatever else I may have failed to do—and that's a lot—at least I left behind in the South Riding a better battlefield for so brave a fighter. Don't let your work be spoiled by bogies. I don't know how, but I have a feeling that even if another war should come, and gas choke your girls and bombs shatter your classrooms, something will have changed, something be made better by the good work you did there. That's as near to mysticism as I ever get—the belief that good work is never wasted.

"Go in and win, my dear.

"Your friend and comrade, "JOE ASTELL."

They were flying above the cliffs now. The blue sea danced and sparkled, glittering. Little dark fishing smacks cluttered its joyous surface.

This is the edge of England, Sarah thought. The bulwark that no longer fortifies. The plane floated easily, now above land, now above water.

Above the Huggins' yard in Pudsea Buttock a huge Union Jack flapped grandly, but to the passengers in the plane it showed no more than a solitary dot of colour. Lovell was too high up to see and to describe the ingenuity of the loyal villagers who had chalked their flagstones red and white and blue.

Farther south the new road from Skerrow to Kiplington lay like a polished sword across the country. North grew the pale and dusty rushes of the Waste, its undergrowth unchecked, its bogs undrained. The grass with reeds and rushes was there, true enough, but the desert did not yet, because of men's complicated motives and self-interests, blossom as the rose. But south of the road, signs of the birth of the garden village were already manifest. The streets had been marked out; piles of rose-red bricks lay heaped in the green paddocks; soon enough the houses that Snaith had dreamed of, with their electric stoves and gardens and porches for prams, would rise there, and be lived in, and be thought of as "home" by children who knew no other.

"And he carried me away in the spirit to a high mountain," thought Sarah, who had read through the Jubilee service to the girls, explaining and interpreting after her own heretical fashion. "And showed me that great city, the holy Jerusalem, descending out of heaven from God." Far to the right gleamed the slate roofs of that great city Kingsport, its satellite villages sprinkled along the silver Leame. Hardly from heaven, Sarah thought, but of the earth, earthly. Greed, ambition and stupidity have made it, an honest homely desire for a livelihood, passion and anguish and perplexity. It has been built by Mr. Holly with his roving eye and frivolous temperament, by Huggins, with his passion for righteousness at war with his appetites, by Snaith, subtle as a serpent, yet serving his generation, by Topper Beachall, who is little more than a kindly stupid animal.

"And the nations of them that are saved shall walk in the light of it."

Oh, saved? thought Sarah. Who is saved? What is salvation?

And the thought of war threatening this placid country sickened her. She was shaken by foreboding, and weakened by old sorrow.

They had crossed the road; they had photographed Minton village. The red roofs of Yarrold clustered round its moth-grey abbey. Before them now spread the dimpled plain of Cold Harbour Colony. To their left lay Maythorpe.

The plane dipped. The photographer wanted a picture of the ancient church and the maypole, its ribbons fluttering, on the green outside it. As the pilot brought his machine down close to the earth, they swooped right over the empty shell that had once been Maythorpe Hall. Already the work of demolition was in progress. The roof had gone, the inner walls lay bare, and looking down Sarah saw, for the first and last time, the room that had been Muriel's. In the ravaged garden lay the tubs of cement the girders of steel, the scaffolding, waiting for the erection of the new institute for mentally defective children.

Then her heart failed her. She had thought herself cured. Time, work, necessity, courage she had summoned as the allies of forgetfulness. But they had failed her. She knew, she remembered, and she was assailed by suffering.

What did they matter now, the grand new buildings for which she had struggled, the foundation of her great girls' public school? Her work, her ambition and her reputation?

Whatever she did, her success must be his failure. All this transformation of the country, these new villages, this school of glass and chromium and cement, all these were witnesses to his defeat.

He had tried to hold the South Riding in its old likeness, to preserve tradition, to dam the tide of change. And she had helped to ruin him.

I do not want to go on living, Sarah thought. She hated her body which had not allured him, her mind, which must betray him till she died.

The plane was floating above the banks of the Leame now; the tide was out; long shelves of mud lay exposed, soft purplish brown, tussocked with reeds and pocked with silver pools.

This was where the children had found his body.

Her perverse mind filled itself with pictures of that beloved body tossed in the water, whirled in currents, driven slowly round the point of the cliff to that low shore where they had found it.

I cannot bear it, she repeated to herself. I do not want to live.

She had been for some months aware that the battle for serenity is a long one. Victory is not won overnight. Anguish, pushed to the back of the mind during the daylight, returns overwhelming in the darkness.

She suffered not only sorrow; she suffered shame. If he had loved me, even for an hour, she sometimes thought, this would not have been unendurable.

She wanted to get away from the South Riding, and not only from the South Riding, from herself. As long as she lived she would carry Carne's image with her, the image of a defeated man, whom she had helped to destroy, and, in that treachery, had betrayed herself.

The camera-man was shouting to the pilot. He wanted to photograph the flags festooning the little quay of Cold Harbour itself, the flat-bottomed boats in the harbour, the toy-like wharf.

The pilot turned swiftly, perhaps too swiftly, for the wind here was uncertain, and in that second, the machine had stalled, and Sarah realised that they were dropping sideways, swift as a stone, down to the glancing water.

She knew then that her desire to die was false. She did not want it. She had work to do. What held her was not love, nor fear, nor hope of happiness, nor any lofty purpose of achievement. It was the small and nagging knowledge that if she were not present to bully architects, the new school buildings would not fulfil her dreams.

The earth was coming up now with smooth silence. A wall of mud and water rose perpendicular against her right ear, then span dizzily, circling moonwise towards her.

This was how death came, then, the water leaping upwards, the sky receding, the mind steady and vivid, and all life in one instant offering its riches.

She turned and smiled at the appalled young face of Lovell Brown, tilted towards her. But even as she smiled at death, unwilling but unafraid, the pilot recaptured control of his machine, the engine roared, the falling wing straightened a little, the nose lifted, the aeroplane steadied, straightened, and might indeed have lifted, had not the tip of a wing hit a taller hummock of grass, and quite slowly, elegantly, the whole affair somersaulted over, scattering its occupants bruised, breathless, shaken, but otherwise little injured, in the mud.

Sarah, who had seen the wall of earth climb, approach, recede, then vault over her head with dazzling velocity, received a bang above her left eyebrow, and plunged into darkness, to awake with her mouth full of mud, her body sprawling along a narrow pool.

The Cold Harbour villagers, who had perceived the eccentric conduct of the aeroplane, rushed to the rescue, much relieved to find four muddied fliers staggering to their feet. The only serious casualty was the machine. Even the photographs, their owner hoped, might be uninjured.

The urgent business was the return to Kingsport. The lorry had left. One Cold Harbour resident, keeper of a small store, owned a motor-bicycle with a side car. He agreed to take Lovell Brown and the camera-man back to their office in order that the afternoon edition might have its photographs. Sarah rang up Tom Sawdon and asked him if he could bring his car to drive her home.

So it happened that the head mistress of Kiplington High School, her red hair plastered with mud, a cut on her cheek, a fine black eye developing, drove through the Jubilee morning with Tom Sawdon. She was bruised and shaken; her head ached, and her left side seemed all stiff and twisted. But she was elated with a senseless exaltation.

She had been shaken out of sorrow. She had looked into the clear face of death and known her lover. She would fear no longer—not even Carne's sad ghost. She would live out her time and finish the task before her, because she knew that even the burden of living was not endless. Comforted by death, she faced the future.

All the way to Kiplington she listened to Sawdon's gossip, hearing more of Cold Harbour and Maythorpe and those who lived there, than she had learned during her years in the South Riding.

She had time to bathe, breakfast and change into gala clothes, before she joined her girls on the asphalt square behind the school for the procession to the esplanade where the Jubilee Service was to be broadcast. News of her exploit had rustled through the town, and as she appeared, her battered face striped with court-plaster, a lump like a prize-fighter's disfiguring her left eyebrow, the girls, formed up already in procession, broke into spontaneous cheers.

She pretended wrath, but was secretly pleased. She knew that she had done the right thing again. By surviving an air crash on Jubilee morning she had lived up to that legend of audacious unconventionality in which the girls delighted. Popularity might be a bubble, but it was a bubble which kept alive prestige, not only for herself but for all that she tried to stand for. It was the charm by which she drew the girls after her idea of the good life.

She raised her hand.

"There is nothing in the least clever," she said cuttingly, "in having accidents. The clever thing is to avoid them. However, it is natural that you should enjoy my making a fool of myself—the customary attitude to authority." They cheered again. She waited, a strangled smile twisting her lip. Then she said, "About this service. I've discussed it with you quite enough. Perhaps too much. But there is one thing I forgot to mention. You'll be singing that strangely moving hymn written by Cecil Spring Rice, 'I vow to thee, my country.' There's a couplet in it I've been thinking about this morning:

'The love that asks no questions, the love that stands the test, That lays upon the altar the dearest and the best. . . .'

Don't take that literally. Don't let me catch any of you at any time loving anything without asking questions. Question everything—even what I'm saying now. Especially, perhaps, what I say. Question every one in authority, and see that you get sensible answers to your questions. Then, if the answers are sensible, obey the orders without protest. Question your government's policy, question the arms race, question the Kingsport slums, and the economies over feeding school children, and the rule that makes women have to renounce their jobs on marriage, and why the derelict areas still are derelict. This is a great country, and we are proud of it, and it means much that is most lovable. But questioning does not mean the end of loving, and loving does not mean the abnegation of intelligence. Vow as much love to your country as you like; serve to the death if that is necessary. . . ." She was thinking of Joe Astell, killing himself by over-work in the Clydeside, dying for his country more surely than thousands of those who to-day waved flags and cheered for royalty. "But, I implore you, do not forget to question. Lead on, girls."

They marched before her, a little subdued, these schoolgirls in their brown tunics, Lydia, Nancy, Jennifer, Gwynneth, the citizens of the future, she thought, with a grimace for all inadequacy, hers as well as theirs.

Lydia was going to college in the autumn. She had passed her matriculation, she was sure of a major county scholarship; she would probably win the Snaith Bursary for distinction in mathematics. The Holly family was safely settled in one of the new bungalows near the Skerrow road. Yet something was lost, Sarah knew. Some spring of confidence, some ease of temper, had been stolen for ever by premature adversity from that big, heavy, sullen, gifted girl who had encountered too early the irony and bitterness of fate.

Still, she was saved from complete disappointment. If we have done nothing else, thought Sarah, falling into line in the procession behind the girls, we have saved Lydia Holly.

But we shall do more, she thought, as she followed them to the esplanade, her eyes blurred by the dizziness of headache, but her mind alert with the activity following shock. She was still a little exalted, lifted out of herself by the excitements of that morning.

The Esplanade Gardens were thick with the crowd assembled for the United Service. The white surplices of clergy and choir boys fluttered. Uniforms glittered; the massed ranks of school children outlined a hollow square. Before the bandstand stood the Mayor of Kiplington, surrounded by the members of the corporation, the county council and other officials. Loud-speakers had been erected along the garden; through them emerged the bland informal voice of Commander Stephen King-Hall describing the scene as he saw it from St. Paul's Cathedral.

The Reverend Milward Peckover, nervous and excited, stood awaiting his cue, coming all the way from London. He was dazed by the miracle; but Dr. Dale beside him looked capable of sustaining responsibility for all the modern world of science on his broad shoulders. In the crowd Alfred Ezekiel Huggins, no longer councillor (his financial failures had deprived him of office), but still glowing with patriotic fervour, cleared his throat, and squeezed his wife's arm.

Sarah took her place and looked at her neighbours. The low roar outside St. Paul's reached them, accompanied by the scream of the sea against the pebbles and the cry of swooping gulls. But it was not of the King and Queen that Sarah was thinking. Her mind, like her eyes, rested on the people near her—the colonists of Cold Harbour who had run out to help her earlier that morning, heedless of the possible danger from a burning plane, Bob Heyer, crippled, disappointed but unconquerable, taking his disability as a kind of sport; George Hicks and Tom Sawdon, drawn together by bereavement, yet making the Nag's Head a place of social gaiety; Grandpa Sellars, very old and gentle, looking forward to his treat that day at the Old People's Tea.

They were not very fine nor very intelligent. Their interests were narrow, their understanding dull; yet they were her people, and now she knew she loved them.

She saw the bright bold eyes of Madame Hubbard; Madame was fearfully and wonderfully arrayed in purple satin. That night she was to produce a cabaret show in the Floral Hall as part of the festivities.

Sarah still banned the Hubbard tuition for her pupils, but though she opposed, she admired, she even envied. She was aware of the debt owed by the South Riding to that rich vitality and undaunted spirit.

There stood Bert Holly beside his girl Vi Alcock. Tadman's was closed; they had the day together. Sarah remembered that scene in the twilit field and wondered, without bitterness, how many such scenes ended in happy courtship and successful marriage, instead of the tragedies which are always prophesied.

Suddenly from the loud-speakers crashed the National Anthem, and the townspeople and bandsmen, school children and corporation, took it up, a trifle belatedly but with spirit, and in time to pass on to the familiar "All people that on earth do dwell." They were singing with the whole kingdom, perhaps the empire. They were banned in the unity of mass emotion.

Sarah could not remain immune. Question everything, she had urged, and was guarded against acceptance. This morning service was not even for her the pinnacle of the day. That afternoon Sir Ronald Tarkington was to lay the foundation of the new High School buildings as part of the ceremonial of a Jubilee dedicated, by instruction of the Prince of Wales, to youth.

"Oh Lord, open Thou our lips." "And our mouth shall show forth Thy praise."

Kiplington, with London, Manchester, Edinburgh, Liverpool, and a thousand scattered hamlets, responded, chanting:

"O God, make speed to save us, O Lord, make haste to help us."

Only if we help ourselves, thought Sarah, wary and critical. And even then?

She recalled her earlier certainties. Take what you want, said God: take it and pay for it. She remembered Mrs. Beddows' caveat: Yes, but who pays? And suddenly she felt that she had found the answer. We all pay, she thought; we all take; we are members one of another. We cannot escape this partnership. This is what it means—to belong to a community; this is what it means, to be a people.

And now she was reconciled to failure, glad of sorrow. She was one with the people round her, who had suffered shame, illness, bereavement, grief and fear. She belonged to them. Those things which were done for them—that battle against poverty, madness, sickness and old age, the battle which Mrs. Beddows had called local government,—was fought for her as well. She was not outside it.

What she had taken from life, they all had paid for. What she had still to give, was not her gift alone. She was in debt, to life and to these people; and she knew that she could repay no loan unaided.

"Have I not commanded thee?" came the grave voice through the loud-speaker. "Be strong and of a good courage; be not afraid, neither be thou dismayed."

Oh, but she was afraid, afraid of failure, of weariness, of the lassitude which comes of hope defeated. How could she endure the years when the ecstasy never happened, the great moment never arrived?

"And the city had no need of the sun, neither of the moon to shine in it."

Oh, but I need the sun, moon and stars; I need glory, thought Sarah.

She saw in front of her the young faces of the children, round, fresh and eager, unscarred by experience. She saw the lined faces of the women, their swollen hands reddened by work, the wedding rings embedded deep in the rheumatic flesh. She saw the bent shoulders of the men. She knew that these, the companions of her pilgrimage, faced life without the consolations of triumph, the stimulus of success. Their sturdy endurance in obscurity made her ashamed.

"And the nations of them that are saved shall walk in the light of it: and the kings of the earth do bring their glory and honour with it."

Well, what if the glory never came then? If the honour was hidden?

Sarah thought of Mrs. Holly, dying in the railway coach, reluctant, because her death must mean failure for her daughter. She thought of Mr. Huggins, bawdy and pious, spreading scandal and enthusiasm—"a bit like David the Psalmist, when you come to think of it," Mrs. Beddows had said of him; of Anthony Snaith, sad, subtle, frustrated, but working off his neurosis in the service of his locality, Sir Anthony Snaith, perhaps he would be, in the Jubilee Honours; she thought with love and gratitude of Joe Astell; she dared at last to think of Robert Carne.

No; there was little glory; yet she had learned a little. Take what you want, she had said in her crude assurance. She understood better now the real terms of that spiritual bargain. She knew who took and who paid; she was less sure of what she wanted, what they all wanted.

The service had passed over her dreaming head. The loud-speaker had croaked and failed a little. It was Mr. Peckover who took up the prayer, when the dim archiepiscopal voice a hundred miles away faded to silence.

"Almighty God," he intoned bravely and clearly, "the fountain of all wisdom, who knowest our necessities before we ask and our unworthiness in asking; we beseech thee to have compassion upon our infirmities, and those things which for our unworthiness we dare not and for our blindness we cannot ask, vouchsafe to give us, for the worthiness of Thy Son, Jesus Christ our Lord."

On that humility, upon that nescience, perhaps the more lasting wisdom and certainty might be founded. Humbled, healed, softened, Sarah raised her eyes and looked upon her fellows.

They were no more beautiful, noble or intelligent than they had been before, but in the official group of local authorities, she saw the red wrinkled face of Alderman Mrs. Beddows, and Mrs. Beddows caught her glance, looked at her, shook her head, and smiled. In Mrs. Beddows' smile was encouragement, gentle reproof, and a half-teasing affectionate admiration. Sarah, smiling back, felt all her new-found understanding of and love for the South Riding gathered up in her feeling for that small sturdy figure. She knew at last that she had found what she had been seeking. She saw that gaiety, that kindliness, that valour of the spirit, beckoning her on from a serene old age.

Manufactured by Amazon.ca
Bolton, ON

26977763R00215